ACCLAIM FOR SUSAN WILSON'S EXCEPTIONAL NOVELS

THE FORTUNE TELLER'S DAUGHTER

"A compelling blend of romance, intrigue, and passion . . . a rich story, filled with likable, interesting characters who leap off the page."

—*New York Times* bestselling author Kristin Hannah

"A beguiling bit of storytelling."

—*Publishers Weekly*

"A poignant drama. Susan Wilson builds characters that are deeply layered and quite compelling."

—*Romantic Times*

CAMEO LAKE

"As in her previous work, *Hawke's Cove,* Wilson uses a clear grasp of family and marital dynamics to bring us a touching story of people dealing with real problems in a very human way."

—*Library Journal*

"Wilson's tale is a sensitive scrutiny of one woman's struggle to discover what she wants in life."

—*Booklist*

"A deep and compelling read."

—*Romantic Times*

"This is a beautiful love story full of strong emotion; of tragic endings and beginnings; of healing and forgiveness. It touches something deep inside of us all. A great novel, Ms. Wilson."

—*Old Book Barn Gazette*

"*Cameo Lake* is a moving, unforgettable tale of the many facets of love. Delving deeply into the complexities of the heart, this powerful story of endings and beginnings, healing and forgiveness will strike a chord for all readers and resonate in their hearts. Susan Wilson is a superb storyteller, deftly weaving all the story's elements into a vibrant, richly patterned tapestry. . . . I highly recommend *Cameo Lake*. It's a book you will remember long after the last page is turned."

—AOL's Romance Fiction Forum

HAWKE'S COVE

"From the pen of Susan Wilson comes a gem of a story that can't fail to touch all who read it. . . . Wilson writes with compassion as she tells these stories separated by time and brought together by a common thread. Romantic and tender, *Hawke's Cove* will appeal to a wide variety of readers [who] will cry, be joyful, and be surprised at this story that proves love is timeless."

—*Under the Covers Reviews*

"Sentimental and sweet, Wilson's tale proves her an empathetic storyteller whose plain-spoken Yankee characters have strong appeal."

—*Publishers Weekly*

"Susan Wilson weaves two stories into one with the touch of a master magician. . . . The characters are all warm and their motives feel genuine."

—*Midwest Book Review*

"Wilson's writing is like filigreed platinum; delicately spun and priceless. *Hawke's Cove* is a poignant, evocative love story."

—*BookPage*

"The lessons about choices and never-forgotten love are haunting."

—*Library Journal*

Also by Susan Wilson

The Fortune Teller's Daughter
Cameo Lake
Hawke's Cove

SUSAN WILSON

A novel

BEAUTY

POCKET BOOKS
New York London Toronto Sydney Singapore

POCKET BOOKS, a division of Simon & Schuster, Inc.
1230 Avenue of the Americas, New York, NY 10020

Previously published as a trade paperback in 1997 by Scribner
Published by arrangement with Crown Publishing Group

ISBN: 0-7434-6053-7

First Pocket Books printing July 2003

10 9 8 7 6 5 4 3 2 1

POCKET and colophon are registered trademarks of Simon & Schuster, Inc.

For information regarding special discounts for bulk purchases, please contact Simon & Schuster Special Sales at 1-800-456-6798 or business@simonandschuster.com

Cover art by Robert Hunt

Printed in the U.S.A.

Dedicated with love to my family

Author's Note

I know that the legend of Beauty and the Beast is possible. Like the fairy tale, this true story has a lovely heroine and an ugly hero. Unlike the fairy tale, it isn't Beauty who needs to discover the man inside the Beast, but the Beast himself. Being a true story, there are no physical transmutations, only intellectual ones; the only magic mirror that of the soul in love.

Harris Bellefleur

Love looks not with the eyes, but with the mind,
And therefore is winged Cupid painted blind.

WILLIAM SHAKESPEARE,
A MIDSUMMER NIGHT'S DREAM,
ACT I, SCENE I

There is many a monster who wears the form of a man; it is better of the two to have the heart of a man and the form of a monster.

MME. LEPRINCE DE BEAUMONT,
BEAUTY AND THE BEAST

Beauty

Prologue

CROMPTONS HAVE ALWAYS BEEN PATRONS OF MILLERS. For centuries in England, and since 1635 in New England, the aristocratic Crompton family has sat for formal portraits painted by Miller artists. It is said that the only reason we found our way to America was because the Cromptons, though strict Puritans, desired to keep the tradition and imported the Miller family.

I've seen many of the portraits: long-nosed, high-browed, blue-eyed faces looking out over starched ruffs or lacy jabots; fashions of their times revealing more about the era than the sitter. Personal interests hinted at: the first Neville Crompton standing, one hand on the head of a greyhound; his great-grandson sitting, one hand on a globe, as their fortunes began to encompass shipping and worldwide commerce.

My ancestors were good at what they did. Their works are important enough in antique art circles to warrant hanging in small museums in this country and England. One, a portrait of Neville Crompton, even hangs in the Yale Center for British Art in New Haven.

Yes, Cromptons have always been patrons of Millers.

One

My father held out the letter in a hand that shook a little with the tremor he'd had since my mother died, the sheaf of paper quivering like a breeze-rattled leaf.

I wiped the paint from my hand on my rainbow-streaked jeans and took the thick vellum. I scanned the typed letter, two paragraphs, brief and to the point.

"What do you think, Alix?"

"I thought the Crompton line had died out."

"No, this must be the son of the man my father painted." My father shrugged. "Too bad he's decided to follow the tradition. He's out of luck."

"Why?"

"Alix, you know I'm no portraitist."

I did know. The bold talent, which flourished over the course of four hundred years, had been diluted and grown weak until it was only by force of family legend that any of us called art our livelihood. A good commercial artist, my father was not gifted, though he made a good living. I was too honest with my father to disagree with him. Although he could do a credible job, there would never be anything remarkable about his painting. "So what are you going to do? Break with tradition?"

My father took back the letter, squeezing it along the fold. "You go. You're the real artist in the family."

"No, I couldn't, Dad. It's your commission, and besides, he wants Alexander Miller."

"He's written to Alexander, but he'd be far more pleased with the work of Alix."

I remembered then the first time my father had seen my work. Not the art projects of an adolescent, but my first real attempt at disciplined art, a portrait of my mother. I'd worked on the charcoal sketch in secret, slipping into the art classroom after school, not letting anyone see it. Drawing my mother's youthful face from memory, trying not to show her recent pain and withdrawal in the picture. It was an optimistic picture, a pretense she'd never left us.

He'd held the small picture out at arm's length. It trembled slightly, making me aware for the first time that his hands would always shake. A curtain fell across his gray eyes and his face became unreadable as he studied the sketch. Picking at the dry skin of my lips, I waited for his verdict. He set it down and slowly shook his head from side to side. Oh God, I thought, he hates it. Then his eyes cleared and he held me close.

"You take the commission," my father repeated.

"You know I dislike portraiture."

" 'Dislike' doesn't count." He stuffed the letter back into the tissue-lined envelope and tossed it into a pile of mail. "He's offering good money."

My father rarely yelled when I was a child, but his words often struck their mark, drawing me back in line, and now his words were more than clear. Since my layoff the previous fall from the private girls' school where I'd taught Art Appreciation, my father had financially supported me in my attempt at making a go of being a full-time artist. It was a trade-off: I attended to his household needs and he paid my rent.

"A working artist doesn't always work for his own muse."

I wanted nothing more than to go home. But my paints were open and the canvas stretched and the light in the small studio I shared with my father is best at that time of day. I touched one finger to the envelope. "I'll go for you. But I think you're wrong—surely you can do a portrait."

He hunched over the kitchen table, pressing his hands down. "Go back to work, Alix. Your paints are getting dry."

"So who is this guy?" Mark slipped his wool sweater over bare skin.

"A rich patron, just like a modern Medici, supporting the arts." I stuffed my hair into a scrunchie and ran some water into the kettle. "Believe me, I'm not crazy about doing this, but my father can't." I didn't want to go over the same ground with Mark. Once over with my father was enough.

"How long will you stay there?"

"I'm hoping he'll let me take a few Polaroids and come back here to work on it. I'll have to spend a little time interviewing him so that I know him well enough to paint a decent portrait. I simply can't paint someone I don't know."

"Is that why you've never painted me?"

"Who says I haven't?" I countered, pulling down mugs from the shelf. "You were the rooster in the piece I just sold. Didn't you recognize your eyes?"

He smirked and I could see his withdrawal into poutiness, which had little to do with my remark and much to do with my not being around and available. A thirty-something photojournalist, Mark was talented enough to earn a living at it in our small New Hampshire town by freelancing for city newspapers. He was passionate only about his work, and it was often when his artistic star was low in the sky that he would come around and make noises about permanency. Sometimes I was almost suckered into thinking that maybe my determination to be successful in my art could peacefully coexist with husband and children. Then I would come to my senses. What woman could flourish as a painter as long as there were the constant demands of other people's needs?

I set his mug in front of him and kissed the top of his head. "I won't be long."

He didn't answer, instead flipped through an old *New York Times Magazine,* squeezing the pages at their corners as he turned them, leaving them creased.

The day I left was one of those crystal days in midwinter, the air so cold it hurts to breathe. The sky was an empty jewel-blue. The car, mercifully, turned over on the first try, and I threw the Sentra into reverse. Iced gravel spun out from under the tires as I backed out of my driveway. I spotted Mark's truck coming toward me and we stopped side by side on the deserted country road.

"Don't be gone long, Alix."

"It's a job, Mark. I'll be gone as long as it takes."

"You are a painfully slow painter."

"Only when I'm creating. This is replication of what is there. A man's face."

"Where will you be staying? Maybe I'll come up." The words came out of white puffs darting from between his lips.

"You can't. I'm staying at his house."

"Do you have to?"

"Mark, let's just leave it alone. I'll be home as soon as I can." I suppressed my impatience enough to throw him a kiss, but he made no move to catch it.

Leland Crompton lived at the northernmost tip of the state, beyond the reaches of the national park in the White Mountains. From my southern town it was a drive up the highway for a couple of hours and another hour or so on secondary roads.

"They lived in Boston when my father painted Walter Crompton," my father said, studying the map through his half-glasses. "Beacon Hill." I'd stopped by his house on my way out of town.

"Long way from Beacon Hill, this Riseborough." I took the sheet of paper and folded it, tucking it into my purse. "I'll find it."

With typical, less endearing than annoying, parental cautions, my father urged me to fill up the tank twice and check my tires.

For once I held my tongue and bit back the retort "I'm thirty-six years old, Dad!" I didn't even think to say, "Then *you* go." Instead I gave him a hug. "I'll be fine, don't give me a thought." I was more mellow than usual that morning. We walked out to my car together; he leaned on my arm as we came across the snowy lawn as if afraid of slipping. When I hugged him good-bye, he felt warm to me and a tiny alarm bell jangled. "Are you okay, Dad?"

"Fine, Alix. Just tired."

Before I backed out I sat and watched as he made his slow way back to the front porch. When had he grown so feeble? Overnight he'd gone from vigorous middle age to old. I was glad then that I'd held my tongue.

The stinging sunlight sparkled off the latest snowfall, and traffic was heavy before Waterville, my halfway mark. I allowed myself one quick lunch stop and checked the hand-drawn map Leland Crompton had sent with his retainer. What had seemed relatively clear before now seemed threaded with erratic blue pen.

Now, off the highway, down a switchback road etched into the cleavage of a pair of mountains, I pulled the Sentra off the road to study my map in the waning light. Sunset comes earlier in these regions where the mountains obscure the light by late afternoon. Clouds had come in, urging their way over the tops of the mountains, lowering to meet the rising mists filtering between the pines, and I clicked on the overhead light. Then I got out of the car and took a handful of clean white snow to wash the headlights. I stretched and breathed in the cold mountain air. A light breeze stroked back my hair and I pulled my collar closer. It was suddenly fully dark and the deep blue of it touched me. There were no artificial lights here beyond my headlights. Could I ever imitate this exact shade of blue-black without masking the density or losing the depth? Could I paint the portrait of a stranger? I shivered and climbed back into my car. Illuminated by my headlights, the lumps of snow along the edge of the road looked like pearls.

Another half-hour of right turns and left forks and suddenly I caught sight of lampglow in the distance. A massive iron gate stood open, a wrought-iron rose tooled on it. In the light of my high beams, I could make out iron thorns. Compulsively I checked the directions crumpled in my hand. Yes, this was my landmark. I turned the Sentra into the mile-long drive and wound my way up the hillside between even rows of pines.

The drive circled in front of an imposing fieldstone house with hipped roof. I could see a wing striking out away from the main house, its symmetrical match on the other side. A massive central chimney sent a fine mist of wood smoke to the sky. Twelve mullioned windows looked out over the front, but only two downstairs windows showed any light.

Suddenly the front door opened and an older woman darted out, her hands fluttering as she half-galloped over to the car. "Willie will get your things, never mind that, come in, come in." Her barrage after so many hours of silent thought seemed an assault. "You needn't—" She stopped in mid-sentence. "I'm sorry, I thought you were the painter fellow. What do you want?"

"I *am* the painter fellow."

Three distinct lines formed over her nose. She stepped back from the car and let me out. "Willie will bring your car around to the garage." She pronounced "garage" in the English way, a curious affectation in an otherwise ordinary New Hampshire accent.

Like an automaton, I handed my keys to Willie, a stooped middle-aged man who spoke not at all but bobbed his head and would not look at me.

As I slammed the trunk lid down I chanced to look up and thought I saw a curtain move in an unlit upstairs window.

Walking ahead of me, Mrs. Greaves led me into the house. "Well, well, well, you ain't what we expected." She snatched my left hand, darting at it like a pigeon on breadcrumbs. Her hand was soft, the thousand lines in it smooth as lines on paper. "Who are you?"

"I'm Alix Miller. When my father couldn't come I did." A little heat of embarrassment licked at my face. "I'm here to paint Mr. Crompton's portrait." I tugged to release my hand, but her grip was firm.

"Why didn't you tell us you were coming instead?" She strengthened her hold.

"I don't think I thought it really mattered." And I wondered why it should have. "I'm a Miller and an artist."

"You're very pretty." Mrs. Greaves dropped my hand. "Not married?"

Surprised by her non sequitur, I merely shook my head.

I followed Mrs. Greaves up a long flight of stairs to my room. A mahogany banister ran in a slow curve up the stairs to the gallery. I trailed my fingers on it, marveling at the warmth and smoothness of its unbroken length. I could not find a join anywhere along it, as though the whole thing had been coaxed out of one great length of wood.

All along the gallery portraits hung. A little beat of excitement lurched in my heart at the sight of my own ancestors' work. I wanted to stop to examine them, but Mrs. Greaves's quickstep along the gallery and down another corridor allowed no dallying.

"Dinner is at eight," Mrs. Greaves said, opening the

door to my room. I stepped in and she closed the door, pulling hard against the swollen jamb.

By some magic, my bags and canvases and paint box were already in the room. The room was large—a pair of long windows filled one wall, a double bed with a blue coverlet stood foursquare on the left, and a double dresser with a narrow rippled mirror stood opposite. Two good engravings were the only decoration. An Aubusson carpet in deep blues and maroons was bordered by a hardwood floor. The walls were the faintest blue. A very masculine room, it had the faint odor of cedar. From somewhere in the house I could hear classical music, then it stopped and I heard nothing more.

I had more than an hour and spent it unpacking and washing up. Dinner at eight. I had brought only one dress and hoped that if dinner at eight was de rigueur here that my host would not mind seeing it on me for a few nights running.

I brushed on blush and stared into my own hazel eyes, recognizing the nervous tension in my smeary attempt at eyeliner. If he was anything like his house, my host would be imposing. I had tried not to imagine Leland Crompton at all. How old he was, forty or sixty, pleasant or taciturn, I had no idea, and my anger at my father for putting me in this position fermented. Had the house been in Boston, or a modest garrison colonial in Newburyport, it might have been easier, but this English country house surrounded by miles of desolate mountains had an ominous quality about it, unrelieved by the cool Mrs. Greaves and the silent Willie.

I was ready when at seven-thirty there was a tap on my door and Mrs. Greaves came in. "Mr. Crompton begs your pardon, but he is not feeling well and will not be able to join you at dinner."

A surge of relief belied a bass note of disappointment, but perhaps it would be easier to meet my patron in the light of day.

A wash of moonlight spread across my room, bathing everything in a silvered half-light. It woke me and I rose to draw the curtains closed. For a moment I looked out of the mullioned window, the bulk of the surrounding mountains a dark backdrop against the milky light illuminating the courtyard below me. Something moved. The pallid moonlight was swept with a shadow, then empty again. I could not tell if it had been animal or human or just my imagination.

Two

"Mr. Crompton won't be down today, but asks that you make yourself comfortable. The house is yours to use, and there are some fine walks if you've a mind to hike." Mrs. Greaves had finished clearing my breakfast dishes. I had half-expected her to forbid me some portion of the house.

"If he's not well, I can come some other time." I set my coffee cup back into its saucer, a schoolgirl's hope of early release waiting to be tapped.

Mrs. Greaves sighed. "No, he wants you to stay."

Visions of an invalid floated through my imagination, my setting up my canvas in a dimly lit sickroom, some old geezer in a wheelchair scowling back at me, his lower body covered by a dull-colored afghan, just the tips of his leather-soled slippers peeking out. Shaking off the image, I nodded at Mrs. Greaves. "Of course I'll stay."

The landscape in the bright morning light was magnificent and I itched to make some preliminary sketches. I take ideas from nature and convert them to shapes and colors and textures, which sometimes others find attractive. A mountain may be only hinted at in the finished work, but its essence, its soul, is there. So I took a small notebook, bundled up against the cold, and let myself out the back door. A bank of garage doors faced me and I peeked in to see my car sandwiched between a station wagon and a sports car completely shrouded in canvas. I dug my mittens out of the glove compartment of my car and set off.

I noticed tracks in the snow, large footprints and beside them the tracks of a dog, the pairs of prints interweaving as the dog had crossed and recrossed the man's path through the formal garden as it terraced downward toward the woods. They branched away and were lost beneath the pines, where the snow had toppled off the warming branches. I plodded on, watching for blaze marks laid out along the way.

Higher and higher I climbed, my breath moistening the scarf around my face. Despite the cold I grew warm and unzipped my jacket, letting the fresh, cold air cool me. I pulled off my hat and shook out my hair. The cathedral pines whispered above me, bending gently to warn one another of this intruder in their midst. I reached a promontory, which thrust out from between the pines and extended out over a view of the valley that now lay beneath my feet. Wind-dusted rocks offered a decent dry seat and I took out my pad and began to sketch.

I drew until my fingers were numb and my seat frozen. The light had already begun to change and I realized I had been gone for hours. I grew a little nervous when I couldn't see any blazes on the trees nearby and I wondered how long I had traveled without noticing any. Worse still, my footprints in the snow had been covered as the rising wind had blown snow off the pines. "Well, this is a fine mess," I quoted to myself, and headed downhill in the resolute belief that downhill would eventually lead to a road. By now I was cold and hungry and feeling very stupid. How long would I have to be gone before someone sent help?

The annoyance I felt quickly transmuted into genuine fear when I could find no blazes and every trail dead-ended in brush or rocky outcroppings looming above me in malevolent bulk. Dusk was closing in with winter suddenness and I knew that even if I found the marked trail, the light blue blazes would soon be invisible in the color-robbing gray of twilight. I started running, the calf-deep snow pulling on my muscles, holding me down like seawater. All the stories I had ever heard of lost hikers popped into my head like rabid prairie dogs, and I fought against panic.

I tripped over a buried root and pitched headlong down the steep slope, unable to prevent myself from tumbling for yards before coming to a halt against the rough bark of a fir tree. Stunned, I lay panting and didn't hear anyone approach until a gloved hand reached down to me.

"Are you all right?" a deep voice asked me. "Are you hurt?" So resonant was this voice it seemed as if I were being spoken to by an echo.

"No, yes, no, I'm all right I think." I took the proffered hand and was hauled to my feet to look into the most grotesque face I had ever seen. Mere bad looks or horrible accident had not shaped this face. Deformity had done this. A heavy brow rose up over deep-set eyes.

The cheeks were of unequal shape, giving the face a twisted, asymmetrical look above a prominent jaw. The hatless head was large, like a paper bag children have stuffed and drawn a face upon. His nose was large and hooked and his ears, beneath a thick mop of graying brown hair, were like saucers. It was almost as if the craggy outcroppings had suddenly transmogrified into a man. My instinctive revulsion showed, and he dropped my hand.

"The house is straight ahead, beyond that spruce, no more than a hundred yards." He turned and walked away with an ungainly gait. A large mongrel burst out of the woods and came to heel beside the man.

Ashamed at my rudeness, I called after him, "Thank you!"

He waved a hand without turning around, as if he had not expected anything different from me.

Once in the kitchen, Mrs. Greaves fluttered her hands and chided me for my foolishness, unwilling, evidently, to believe that I was a seasoned hiker. "I just lost track of time." I patted my pockets. "Damn."

"What?"

"I've lost my notebook."

"So you've nothing to show for your foolishness?"

"I suppose not."

"Mr. Lee says he'll be down for dinner. You go have a hot bath and dress now. I'll send up tea."

"Mr. Lee?"

"I've known Mr. Crompton since he was a boy. Since he turned fourteen I've called him Mr. Lee." Mrs. Greaves set a tea tray on the counter.

"What's he like?"

She moved to the sink and began running hot water.

Her face was reflected back in the darkened window; I could see the furrowing of her brow as she wrestled with her answer. "What does he look like or what is he like?"

"The latter. I'll see soon enough what he looks like." I thought back to the encounter in the woods, a little hunch forming.

"Mr. Lee is a nice man. I think it's safe to say that. Not given to anger. Quietlike."

"What does he do for a living, or for fun? I like to know my subjects before I paint them, not from only their lips, but from those around them."

"He writes. You know, novels and such. Stories. Good ones. I think he does that for fun as much as for profit. Between you and me, he need never earn a penny of his own in his lifetime." She shrugged a little, as if to minimize what she had said, and set the kettle on the stove. "Run and get your bath."

I paused along the gallery to study the portraits, taking childish pleasure in seeing the artists' names on the tiny brass plaques. Alfred Miller, 1723; Ezekial in 1752; a second Ezekial in 1767. The eighteenth-century Cromptons all sat, the colors in their clothes still lovely in shades of blue and cream and brown. I liked Ezekial's work. He gave a little more depth to the painting than most of his contemporaries, the roots of Dutch painting evident in his style. The first portrait was of an eighteenth-century Crompton family—father, mother, and three boys, ages about three through seven. The second, of the same family fifteen years later, wives and grandchildren at the feet of the patriarch. I tried to sort them out from the first portrait, but the numbers were wrong, one of the boys was gone.

* * *

The long refectory table was set at either end, two places separated by the candles, whose yellow flames wavered as I walked by. My host was not yet there and I felt awkward about sitting, but did not know where else to go. Instead I stood by the long window and looked out into the night. Floodlights illuminated the terrace, brushed clean of snow. Ironwork benches flanked the perimeter, and again I saw the rose worked into the filigree. I could hear a chiming clock strike eight. I wandered around the formal room, admiring the antique china displayed in a breakfront and the small landscape hanging beside it. As I turned away from the painting, my eye fell on my notebook, set beside my plate. I touched its cover and opened it. The felt-tip marker had gotten wet and the sketch of the valley had bled, making a flannel patchwork of it.

"I think it's still a nice picture," Leland Crompton said as he came into the room.

"Thank you, but it was only a rough draft for concept." I had guessed that my patron was the man I had encountered in the woods and so managed to cover my shock at seeing him again.

He limped into the room and stood at my seat, pulling it out for me. I sat and he went to his own. "Mrs. Greaves is a very fine cook. I hope you'll enjoy your stay with us."

I lay my napkin across my lap and sipped my water, all the while wondering if I had offended him earlier.

"Thank you for rescuing me this afternoon."

"You were nearly here."

"I feel rather foolish. . . ."

He cut me off, not impolitely. "It happens."

I did not know which he meant, my being lost or my rudeness.

The candles were thick and obscured my view of him. Mrs. Greaves brought in the soup course, dimming the lights with the rheostat as she left the room.

We made the small talk that two strangers are given to when forced together. Nice weather, cold for this time of year, how was the drive up. All the time my mind teased itself with the question, How am I ever going to paint this man? How am I ever going to stare at him long enough to replicate that face? Why does he want me to do this? Soup cleared, the main course was brought in and we struggled through the second course of conversational ploys. How long had I been painting, what school? I realized he was doing the questioning and cast about for a question of my own.

"Mrs. Greaves tells me you are a writer."

"Yes."

"Novels?"

"Yes. And short stories."

I had not opened any conduits with that gambit. "Mr. Crompton, I need to get to know you a little if I'm to paint you.

"Yes, I suppose that's true."

He was silent for a time, busy with the remains of his dinner. Then, finally, he folded his napkin and rose. "Ms. Miller, will you please excuse me." He held up one large hand to keep me in my seat. "Please, stay for dessert and coffee. The television is in the room third door on the right from here. Make yourself entirely at home." He moved awkwardly away from the table and walked out of the dining room with an obvious self-consciousness, utterly aware of my eyes on him.

* * *

Alone again at breakfast the next morning, I made up my mind to leave. This was a useless exercise and I had work at home to finish before my show in March. If he wasn't going to sit for me, was only going to leave me to cool my heels in this lovely house with the wonderful meals, well, forget it. I ripped the ruined sketch out of my notebook and threw it in the wastepaper basket. The sky had clouded up overnight. If I got an early start I could be home before it began to snow in earnest.

Just at that moment of decision, Mrs. Greaves came into the dining room. "Mr. Crompton will see you in the solarium." That was it, then, my window of opportunity closed. When I didn't move she snatched at my breakfast dishes. "Go on."

The south-facing solarium extended into the formal garden and I imagined that in summer it was like being out of doors. The surrounding mountains were bluish above the snow, pine trees and bare deciduous branches making a mosaic against the sky. A bird feeder hung in the near foreground, filled now with flickering chickadees. The light, even on this overcast day, was wonderful.

"Will this do as a studio?"

"Absolutely . . . it's perfect." I walked around the space, holding out my hands to see where the shadows might lie. I couldn't have built a better studio.

"I had it added on a couple of years ago. It really doesn't fit the architecture, but I love it."

He was looking out over the garden, his hands on his narrow hips. From the back, except for the slight hunching of his shoulders, he could have been normal.

* * *

My canvases and paint box had been brought down and I fussed with the easel, struggling as usual to get the stripped wing nut positioned just so in order to keep the easel standing. He watched me for a minute, then fished an elastic band out of a ceramic pencil holder and in a moment had jury-rigged the easel into a more or less secure stance. I set a rectangle of stretched canvas on the easel and lowered the brace to hold it. We stood side by side for a moment, both looking at the blank canvas, a snowy lawn as yet undiscovered by dogs and children. I was struck then with sudden doubts that I could do the job. As if aware of my thoughts, Lee moved away from me.

"Where do you want me?" he asked, and then hunched himself over to the corner I pointed to, sitting in one chair, then another as I directed.

"This will take some time," I cautioned. "From beginning sketch to detail, this could mean some very long hours."

"I'm aware of that."

"I could take some photos and paint from them. Then you needn't spend all day sitting."

"No. This is the way it has always been done. This is the tradition between our families, isn't it?"

"Yes, I suppose it is. I hadn't thought of it that way. Tradition."

"Like Tevye, we have our traditions that make life bearable." He hooked his heels into the rungs of the bar stool he sat on. "Now, how should I sit? As you can see, I have no bad side."

I smiled at his wry remark, feeling a little pang of relief that he had acknowledged my difficulty.

I tried to pose him verbally, barking directions like some demented furniture mover. "Up-to-the-left-no-down-a-little . . ." In Life Art class, models posed for us. Smooth-skinned, wraith-thin, or muscular, completely at ease sitting nearly nude for strangers, the check at the end of the session no doubt making up for these theater majors' vestigial modesty. With casual fingertips, we'd move the various models through poses of our own desire, touching them into shape as if they were clay, not flesh. Faced now with this imperfect and shy man, I could not bear to touch the misshapen face, though my words could not contrive the most genuine pose. When my instructions became ridiculous at last, I set down my pencil and swallowed my hesitation. I saw the squeamishness in his eyes, and like an animal unused to being touched, he flinched reflexively against the feel of my fingers on his chin. Except that it was misshapen, it felt like any chin, vaguely rough, as if his razor were old.

I looked down as I pressed his large, gnarly hands together on his knees. I was surprised at their feel, warm and smooth, the large knuckles belying the softness of the skin on the back of his hands. There is such intimacy in touching someone's hands, shaping them or guiding them. I wanted very much to turn them over, to feel the palms, to get a sense of his labors. But I didn't.

"Now, Mr. Crompton, you must try to look relaxed, like you have your portrait done every week." I stepped back to my easel, pencil poised.

He laughed. The sound boomed from his barrel chest, startling me into laughter. "Lee. Please. If we're to spend hours in each other's company, I prefer you call me Lee, if I may call you Alix."

"Okay. And remember, if you want to stop at any time, just get up. I'm a cruel artist and forget my subjects are alive."

After a few minutes of silent work he cleared his throat in a stagy manner. "Alix, you must overlook my bad manners yesterday. I'm not used to society and it takes me some time to regain the social graces."

"You've nothing to apologize for," I answered, knowing that it was I who should be apologizing. But I couldn't bring myself to speak of our encounter in the woods, was too cowardly to say why I had reacted so abominably. Instead I countered, "I should apologize for not warning you my father couldn't be here."

"No matter. A Miller paints a Crompton in any event."

"Tradition."

As a sip of wine after abstinence warms the heart and sends a message of relaxation to the body, I was suddenly at ease. Lee's friendliness this morning soothed away the strain of new acquaintance. Both of us shy, we had somehow moved past the first barrier.

Over the next few days, our sessions settled into a routine. I'd breakfast alone, then join him in the solarium by eight. He had a marvelous stereo system and the four morning hours of work were accompanied by a wide range of music, from Respighi to Neil Young. He was a patient sitter and had an unlimited ability to remain still. The light was best in the morning and we kept to only those hours before lunch. After lunch he'd retire to his own work and I was left on my own till dinner. Much of the time I spent sketching versions of the slowly developing portrait.

It had been a long time since I'd drawn from life. So much of my work was pure imagination that it took some time to harness the necessary discipline. I was so often taken with painting the beautiful, or representing emotion or thought with visually exciting color or shape, that to render on canvas a true representation of someone whose exterior is so grotesque was a challenge. There have been artists who have made the normal grotesque. I was attempting to make the grotesque normal.

Three

"YOU HAVEN'T SEEN THE WHOLE HOUSE, HAVE YOU?" Lee asked one morning as he handed me a mug of coffee. As we took a ten-minute break I watched him discreetly as he walked around the room stretching this way and that to loosen joints stiffened by two hours of motionless sitting. I had passed from visitor to artist and observed everything about him with an anatomist's eye.

I'd been there for four days and had seen only these few rooms downstairs and my bedroom. "I'd love a tour." I sipped the coffee and added a half-teaspoon of sugar.

"Good, after lunch I'll show you around."

"It won't interfere with your work?"

"My work is just at that stage when the characters are being completely willful and I can't make them work. Exactly the time to take an afternoon off." He climbed back on the stool and fell easily into his pose.

He'd never mentioned his writing before and his speaking of it now pleased me in some little way.

We toured the house after lunch. Lee was patient, letting me admire the great many works of art he had displayed on the walls and in various niches. "Much of this belonged to my parents and grandparents. I've added only a little in the past few years."

"Do you go to the auctions?"

"No. I have a man who knows my taste and sends me descriptions." He touched a painting into line.

We came to the library, a lovely dark green room with walls of books and an old-fashioned sliding ladder to reach the ceiling-high shelves. The deep green carpet absorbed our footsteps; instantly our voices dropped to hushed library tones. I ran a finger along the spines of the many hardcovers filling the bookshelves, smiling at common interests and authors. John Gardner's *Grendel, Freddy's Book,* and *Nickel Mountain* were prominent among the fiction.

"Are your books here? The ones you've written, I mean."

"I write under a pseudonym," he said, and handed me a hardcover copy of a mystery novel. *Another Fine Mess,* A Tyler Bent Mystery by Harris Bellefleur.

"You! You're my favorite, I've read all of this series!" I was laughing and hugging the book to me. "Why ever did you kill off Molly Tripp?"

"She was becoming a nag," he retorted and that bell-like laugh sounded up from his chest. I handed him back the book, but he shook his head, resembling in the muted light of the library the head of some great beast. "I killed off Molly, not because she was a nag—that was a flip remark—but because all of Tyler Bent's partners end up dead. If I had spared her, why who knows, maybe they would have had to sleep together. Tyler is a man doomed to be alone."

Again, I handed the book back to him, but he pressed it back into my hands. "Please, keep the book. I'd like you to have it, unless you already do?"

"No, I don't have my own copy." I opened it. "May I ask for an autograph?"

He seemed oddly pleased. "I never get to do this."

Slowly it dawned on me how isolated Lee Crompton was.

"Let me think of something suitable and give it back to you before you leave."

We wandered up the stairs to the gallery, where I was able to tell him a little about the painters of his ancestors. "Ezekial was better than Alfred, he had a clearer touch with expressions. Alfred was a little heavy-handed." I pointed to the second Ezekial painting. "Who's missing in this one? One of the three boys isn't there, but I can't tell which one."

"Roger, the middle son. He died shortly before his twenty-third birthday."

"How sad," I murmured. "How?"

"Disease." He paused. "It has been suggested that he had the same disease I have. Acromegaly."

I looked at him, his profile massive in the late afternoon sun. "Have there been many cases in your family?"

"One per century documented. I'm the twentieth-century man. There won't be any others."

"Yes, genetic counseling is really a modern miracle," I said without thought.

He looked at me with something of a rueful smile playing about his mouth. "That doesn't enter into it for me."

The tour seemed to end at that moment and Lee excused himself to write some letters. I stood for a long time before the eighteenth-century Cromptons and wondered at a disease that would leave its mark upon a family in such an insidious way. In the centuries before ours such anomalies were sometimes called punishment, or the work of the devil. I knew a little about the disorder, a pituitary tumor that caused abnormal growth in the head, hands, feet, and thorax. But how a man of twenty-three might die of it I couldn't figure.

When the phone rang that afternoon I realized that I had not heard any phones ringing during the week I'd been at Riseborough, which had made the house seem all the more peaceful. That the phone was for me was a jolt, and I was immediately concerned. I hadn't called my father since coming to Riseborough, and now the flicker of concern I had felt when I left him sparked again, mingled this time with general guilt.

But it was Mark. "When do you plan to come home, Alix?" He was on the cordless phone and his voice was tinny, a vague hum surrounding his words. "You remember I've got a dinner on Saturday and you promised to come with me."

"Mark, I'm not finished, not nearly," I protested, and immediately began to get angry. As usual, his needs and desires were immediate and pressing.

"Alix, you've been there since last Saturday. Surely you get the weekend off. You can go back."

It would do no good to remind him that his creative life had kept him away from several important occasions in my life.

"Look, it's not like you're up there because you want

to be," he said. "Weren't you just going to take a couple of Polaroids and come home?"

"It's working out just fine doing it from life," I admitted to him and, I realized, to myself. "I'm enjoying it."

But in the end I promised to come home on Saturday and attend the newspaper awards dinner. Though complaining all the while about having to wear black tie, he pressed me enough that I was certain he expected to receive an award. It would be a big moment for him, and of course I should be there. I tried not to think of my March opening. I knew he wouldn't attend. Despite knowing the date for months, he'd planned a backpacking trek with some buddies that same weekend.

I hung up the phone and leaned against the kitchen doorjamb. "Damn him," I muttered, and smiled at Mrs. Greaves.

"Boyfriend?"

The term seemed dated. "Sort of. I don't know what he is." I helped myself to a cup of coffee from the Mr. Coffee. Sliding onto a stool, I leaned both elbows on the counter. "Tell me about Lee. What was he like as a boy?"

"Why?"

"I don't know, just curious about him."

Mrs. Greaves poured herself a cup and looked at the clock. Sighing, she nodded. "He was a little hellion."

This was so far from what I expected her to say that I choked.

"I mean he was a determined, sometimes not very nice boy. Oh, he was good enough as a child, but adolescence burned in him like fire. One scrape after another. Very full of himself and with a God's-gift-to-women attitude, which I sometimes think was his downfall."

Once again she looked at the clock, then at me. Something in her attitude had softened, and she motioned for me to follow. "He hasn't always been like he is now. I'll show you."

She had a suite of rooms off the kitchen. On every surface were photos: family groups, individuals, pets. I realized then that there were no photos anywhere else in the house, only the paintings. She took a small photo in a cheap metal frame from her nightstand. "This is Lee at fifteen."

An adolescent boy looked out from the picture. Too unformed yet to be called handsome, it was a nice face, just on the edge of solidifying into manhood, the fair down on the upper lip still safe from the razor. I was caught by the dark blue eyes, much like those of an idealized cherub in a Renaissance painting, but it was the charming smile that lit the boy's face that held my attention, and I could see that despite the horrific changes the disease had made in Lee's face, it hadn't touched his smile.

"That would be his second year at Groton. Here"—she handed me a second picture—"this is fifteen years later. You can see the beginnings of the disease."

A candid shot, taken at some unexpected moment, with Lee not looking at the camera but away. The boy in the first picture had changed, changed beyond growing from a boy to a man. His hand, resting against one cheek, was outsized, the swollen knuckles obvious in the close shot. Though his features had not enlarged grotesquely yet, his face was softer, less defined, and his ears and nose were already large. His eyes were no longer willful but locked in private thought and I knew before she said it that this was the last photo taken of Lee Crompton.

"We came to live here a year or so after that picture. It was the family's summer home, and Lee has made it his home since then. We've been here nearly ten years."

"Where are his parents?"

"Divorced years ago, when Lee was at Groton. His father died some years after your grandfather painted him; she's still alive, living in Boston. She doesn't come." Mrs. Greaves took the picture out of my hands, looking at it before placing it beside another. "He grew into a nice man, didn't he?"

Her words surprised me, then I understood what she meant. "Yes, he is a very nice man."

She wiped her hands down the length of her white twill apron and left me standing there. A sudden chill wafted from a slightly open window.

At dinner I told Lee that I would have to spend the weekend in Boston. I explained about Mark's dinner and the possibility of his receiving an award.

"You must be very proud of him," he said, not looking up at me.

I stared a long while into my soup dish. "I am."

"You don't sound convincing."

I looked through the candelabra at him. "Don't I?"

"No. Why?"

"Sometimes I think it would be easier to be unconnected."

"How can you say that?"

"This relationship sometimes takes its toll on my art. He resents the time I spend on my work."

"He's said that?"

"Not exactly, but sometimes Mark gives me the impression that he believes that his work is more important than mine because mine is, I don't know, somehow less tangible than his. I've never reported on street people in Nashua and my abstracts don't often sell." I caught myself. Why was I telling Lee this?

"He was probably raised to believe that a man's work is always more important than a woman's. So many men have been lost to their own self-importance that way."

"Lee, are you a feminist?" I teased.

"Alone here, with only the company of a strong-willed housekeeper and a weak-minded gardener, yes. I am an advocate for women's rights, for social reform, for many causes I can touch only through my own wealth."

I set down my spoon and Lee rang for the second course. "I'm thinking I should probably leave Friday." I knew Mark wanted me home Friday, but I hesitated. "Though maybe I should head back earlier. I hate to sound trite, but I haven't a thing to wear to this dinner."

"I have hundreds of catalogs. Why not look through them, and if you find something it can be delivered almost in no time."

After dinner we settled into the television room and against the background of some shlocky Sunday night movie, we thumbed through stacks of catalogs.

"How about this?"

"Too young."

"Or this?"

"Too old."

"You'd look great in this."

"Too risqué! What about this?"

"Not risqué enough. You want to be dynamite, don't you?"

And so it went until he found exactly the right dress. "Perfect."

"Perfect."

* * *

"Bad-dog, come back here!" Lee bellowed after the ugly mongrel who accompanied him on his walks. "Damn it, Bad-dog, leave it!"

The rangy mutt pulled his nose out of the carrion lying in the snow-covered road and loped back to Lee. "Good Bad-dog." Lee bent to whack the beast on his springy ribs.

"Good bad dog? Isn't that a trifle oxymoronic?"

"He was mostly bad dog when he arrived here. His real name is Ralph, but Bad-dog has always suited him better."

The dusty afternoon sky threatened more snow, a pinky aureole surrounded the sun as it lowered. We'd been walking since lunch, a long, wandering walk while Lee pointed out favorite places and birdlife. The snow-laden air was warmer than it had been and didn't send us back to the house for a long time. Our progress was slow, convenient logs offered us frequent resting places. Although he was solicitous of me, I knew that the effort to carry around his own weighty limbs tired Lee, and I was happy to pace myself to him. The fresh air brought color to his cheeks, tinging his ears pink.

"Oh, look"—I pointed down the slope beyond the guardrail—"a pond. It looks like someone's shoveled it."

"Wiggy's Pond, best skating around." He stepped forward. "Do you skate?"

"Not very well." I moved ahead of him, sliding a little down the tree-crowded slope. "Look, there are kids skating, let's watch." But when I turned, he was gone.

I scrambled back up the hill and caught up to him. "Hey, wait up!"

He slowed, but did not stop. When I finally drew beside him, he was apologetic. "I'm sorry, it's just that I don't like to be seen by children. They often get frightened."

"Those weren't small children, Lee, they were teenagers."

"They're worse, they don't run away."

By the time we got back to the house it was much colder and Mrs. Greaves had hot chocolate ready for us. Leaving wet boots and gloves in the kitchen, we dropped jackets in the hallway and settled in front of the fire in the library, stretching out our stockinged feet to soak in the warmth.

"I didn't mean to be curt back there." Lee eased his bulky frame against the couch. "When I first began to show signs of the disease it wasn't so obvious. I moved about in the world without much difficulty. But as I grew . . . and grew and grew . . . it became more and more difficult. People were curious, but mostly kind. I wasn't treated as my ancestors in acromegaly were once treated, as freak show displays.

"One day I was walking down Boylston Street. My eye was caught by the display in a toy store window and I wasn't looking where I was going. I ran right into a mother and her little girl. The child looked up and took one look at me and began crying. Despite my apologies, the mother raised her hackles and said, 'How dare you be out on the streets to frighten little children!'

"And I couldn't answer. She was right, I had no right to do that. So I retreated."

"You never leave here, do you?"

"No. I can't. I invented handsome, debonair Tyler Bent to live my life for me. Alix, if you had ever seen the fear in that child's eyes, you could do no less." He smiled at me, a lopsided smile that yet had a charm to it. "But, thankfully, you can only imagine it, you will never experience it."

"How could anyone have been that ignorant or cruel?"

"Every time someone sees me for the first time, I see that same look. It is instinctive and unavoidable."

I remembered again my own reaction and I was ashamed.

Four

A BRILLIANT JANUARY SUN TOUCHED THE PANES OF glass in the solarium windows and the warmth filtered into the room. I stood in a tee shirt mixing paints with a palette knife. Lee came in and set down the coffee pot.

"Come give me your opinion," I said.

"Of what?"

"Background color. I would almost paint in the windows and the garden beyond, but I think that the overall effect would be too cluttered."

"Do whatever you think will work. I can't offer an opinion." He edged away from the canvas without looking at it, stopping to pour two mugs of coffee. He carefully measured a half-teaspoon of sugar into mine.

"Lee, you haven't looked at this. Not once."

He climbed on the stool and hung his head a little. "Alix, I'm confident that your work is wonderful, but I will not look at it. That's not meant as an insult to your abilities, but a problem of mine."

"Then why am I doing this?"

"Because it has always been done. Because it will go into storage and some descendant from a different branch of the family will discover it someday and know that Millers still painted Cromptons in the last decade of the twentieth century."

"That's not quite good enough."

"You're right. The truth is, I thought that it was a pity to break the tradition just because I refuse to have it hung. Very simple. But I don't want to see it."

I stood for a long time, unable, it seemed, to touch the brush to the canvas.

"Have I upset you?"

"No. Well, yes. You've sort of skewed my focus. I have been doing this with your approval in mind, and now, if you aren't going to hang it, it becomes unimportant and I could draw a stick figure with blue eyes and call it *Portrait of Lee Crompton.*"

"That would do. Maybe I would hang that."

"Lee, don't be self-denigrating, it's not attractive." I had lost my concentration utterly and began closing up paint tubes with angry, jerky motions. "Let's not work today. Like your characters, if the paint won't go on in the right places, I can't make it."

"I'm sorry, Alix." He slipped off the stool and stepped toward me.

With a hasty jerk, I pulled the sheeting over the untouched portrait. "No need to apologize. It's your portrait to do with as you want. I'm just the hired artist, you're the patron."

I had squeezed paint all over my hands and I went

into the tiny lavatory in the hallway to wash. I noticed that there was no mirror in it, and I realized then that except in my own rooms and Mrs. Greaves's there were no mirrors anywhere in the house.

Half an hour later a light knock at my bedroom door startled me. "Alix? May I come in?"

Having spent the last half-hour going over my angry words and trying to gird up my courage to go apologize, I felt my heart begin to pound. "Lee?"

The door opened and Lee came in, pushing it wide as he did. "Do you want to go skating?"

"What about the children?"

"It's a schoolday. There won't be anybody around till after two."

"I don't have any skates." But I was reaching for my sweater.

"I've got a garage full of cast-off skates from dozens of Cromptons. I'm sure we've a pair to fit you." Thirty minutes later we were in the station wagon heading for Wiggy's Pond.

The pond was cleanly shoveled, the white contrails of skaters' blades etched into its surface. Looking straight down I could see the grass frozen in perfect arrangement. Closer to shore the grass burst through the ice in frozen bouquets. Bubbles appeared like evil eyes. Farther out the ice darkened and I could no longer see through it.

Lee knelt in the snow to pull the lacings tight on my skates. My foot in his huge hands seemed as tiny as Cinderella's. His own skates were immense black things with wicked-looking blades. I wobbled onto the ice, taking an exploratory stride before pushing away from shore. Tongue firmly balanced at the corner of my mouth, I completed eight or ten pokey little strides before crashing. A whoosh of skate blades circled around me and Lee hoisted me to my feet. "Like this," he said, and pushed off, gliding around the pond in a graceful arc, great long strides, a quick reverse and a slow glide. I stood frankly open-mouthed. This great clumsy giant could skate like a dancer. The ice freed him from the constraints of gravity. Awkwardness melted away and grace was revealed. My fingertips throbbed to take pencil in hand and record this. He danced around me, pleased with my reaction, executing figures, racing off and back. He came to a sudden stop in front of me, the scrim of ice shooting away from the blade of his skate.

He'd shrugged off his jacket and stood now in a dark blue Norwegian sweater and a cranberry-colored down vest. Warm from his exertions, he'd thrown off his hat and gloves. Thick hair curled about his ears, he pushed it back from his massive brow and cocked his head, looking strangely impish for such an ugly man. After a heartbeat of a pause he held out one hand. "Will you skate with me?"

I put my hand in his. "Like this," he said, and pushed off. Together we sailed out over the pond as the January sunlight struck sparks off the ice. He turned me and slid an arm behind my back; side by side, like contra-danseurs, we glided back and across the ice. We dashed in and out of the shadows of trees that surrounded the pond. Now like waltzers, we faced one another and my strides were mirror images of his. His right arm lightly touched my back, with his left he held my hand. Every few strides, my face brushed up against the slick cloth of his vest. He kept his strokes short to accommodate the difference in our heights.

One two three, one two three, we danced over the silver-gray surface. Gracefully toeing the ice, Lee let me slide by him and turned me into a twirl. For one brief instant I forgot he was not an ordinary man. In the next, I was newly startled by his visage, and in the third moment, I knew that more and more I would forget how he looked and think of him only as Lee. He let go of my hand and bowed, his long arms sweeping the ice. "Thank you, Miss Miller."

"My pleasure, Mr. Crompton," I answered, attempting a curtsy.

Mrs. Greaves had left us a cold lunch, which we warmed with nips of sherry in our coffee. It was Thursday, her half-day off. "She'll have left us something to heat in the microwave," Lee assured me.

"I can cook, she needn't have done that," I protested.

"It's our routine, Thursdays and Saturdays she's off, and every other weekend. She drove a hard bargain coming up to live in this backwater. My mother has never quite forgiven me for stealing her."

"She's very fond of you."

"It would be trite to say that I think of her as a mother, but the truth is, she's been a good friend in some difficult circumstances."

I remembered then what Mrs. Greaves had said about Lee's mother, that she never came up. "If I ask a personal question, please feel free to tell me I'm out of line."

He nodded. "Ask away."

"Do you have friends who come and visit? Tell me you aren't alone here all the time."

"I have two or three friends who come who were at school with me. But, like everyone, they have busy lives and it has become harder and harder for them to get up here. We stay in touch over the phone now mostly. Why do you ask?"

I shrugged. "I don't know. Really." I poured another touch of sherry into my glass. "I suppose that I'm rebelling against the idea of someone so nice being a recluse."

He didn't say anything, simply rubbed a massive hand over his face as if to erase what was there. "Alix, a true recluse wouldn't be in touch with the world as I am. I'm connected through the phone, fax, computer. I can see it, even if I won't let it see me. Accept that"—he held my eye with his—"please."

"I'm sorry, I've absolutely no right to say anything." I looked away from him, releasing us from the topic.

"I have to get to work. I've played hooky long enough."

The sunlight in the solarium was still bright and I cozied up on the floral couch to sketch. What Lee didn't know was that I was making sketch after sketch of him. Late at night as I sat up in bed, listening to the wind rattle the windows, I took my pencil and pad and drew him from memory. He would never let me photograph him, so I took the day's memories and committed them to paper. Lee pitching snowballs to Bad-dog; sitting on a log gesturing toward some bird in flight; dozing in front of the TV. His hand, long and gnarled, resting on Bad-dog's silky head.

Bad-dog came in and sat beside me, one eye cocked hopefully on the leash hanging on the doorknob. I sketched our morning on the ice, thinking how like a diary my sketchbook had become. Vignettes of a very surprising week. Bad-dog suddenly got to his feet and muttered a little in the instant before I heard the back doorbell.

It was the UPS man with my dress. I raced upstairs and opened the bag. Lee was right, it was dynamite. Short, black, velvet, it had a deep square neckline and a fitted bodice gently flaring as it reached my hips, a dancing dress.

"Is there a pizza place anywhere nearby?" I asked, joining Lee in the kitchen.

"Tony's, in Riseborough proper. It used to be very good when I was a kid. Why?"

"I just thought instead of mucking about heating things, we could get a pizza and some beer." I took the phone book from the shelf. "I'll buy. What kind do you want?"

"They don't deliver."

"I'll go get it."

"Alix, Riseborough is ten convoluted miles away. I can't hope to give you directions."

"So come with me." I saw the reflexive beetling of his brow. "You stay in the car and I'll go in."

"All right." Suddenly he grinned. "It's been a very long time since I've had pizza. Lived on the stuff for years as a kid, but Mrs. Greaves won't let anything remotely take-out into the house."

"Then we'd better burn the box!"

That incredible deep laugh sounded again, driving Bad-dog to his feet. "Bundle up, we'll take my car."

Underneath the canvas cover lay a 1968 MG. Bright red and pristine, the two-seater sat like a toy beside the Chevy wagon. Lee rubbed a gloved hand along the door. "My high school graduation gift. Can you believe it, such a waste on a boy. I never worked for it, barely appreciated it. Only through the grace of God did I never rack it up, though I had enough opportunities."

"It's beautiful. What's the word . . . mint. Mint condition."

"Willie is the curator for this museum piece. He spends half his time with it. His greatest pleasure is when I let him drive it to the gates." Lee pressed a button and the garage door raised itself. "Hop in."

I eased myself into the cockpit of the passenger seat and fished around for the seatbelt. The top was down, and I was grateful for the blanket Lee pressed around me.

Willie's care was evident in the immediate turnover of the engine, no hesitation, no sputtering. Lee slid the car out of the garage, and in a smooth arcing motion we were out on the long drive and flying between the trees. I felt as if I were skating again, so smooth was the feeling beneath me, so cold the wind whistling over my head.

Riseborough is one of those quintessential New England towns, a lovely big common bordered by white-fronted stores and brick banks. Oak trees planted a century or more ago give the grassy common character, as do the trees arcing over the wires along Main Street. Here and there stumps of the victims of blizzards and disease poke up, put to use now as kiosks and found-mitten holders.

A blue neon beer sign announced Tony's Pizza. Lee pulled over to the opposite side of the street. "I'll just spin around the block while you go in."

He dug into his back pocket, but I stopped him. "I said I'd treat!" I got out of the car and darted across the empty street. Tony's was a slice of every American pizza place. The odor was exactly the same as the place in my town. Strong cheese, tomato sauce, and beer. The wood floor was gritty with tracked-in snow and there were rings on the counter from wet bottles of beer and cans of Coke. "Miller," I said, and laughed when the guy behind the counter lifted a Miller beer from the cooler. "No, no, pizza for Miller!" The men around the bar hooted. "I'll buy you a Miller." "Wouldn't mind getting my hands around that Miller." "Need some help with that?"

I shook my head, aware of the flirting and not offended. "Thanks anyway, but I've got a date."

One of the men got a little more aggressive and stood up. "Yeah, but I bet I'm more of a man. Ditch him and come with me."

I held the pizza out in front of me and glared at him. He was shortish, middle forties, a little paunchy, with the look of a man who was probably considered a prize in his youth but had gone downhill and didn't realize it. "Sir, my date's easily twice the man you are." I shoved my way past and escaped through the door.

The MG was nowhere in sight, so I ducked into the pharmacy next door. I picked up some pantyhose and shampoo and poked my head out again. There he was, once again across the street in the darkness of the unlit green. One last stop at the package store to buy the beer and we were quickly out of town. "I like Riseborough. It's a real small town and hasn't been discovered by the chi-chi set yet."

"I suspect because there's nothing up here to attract them. Too far to commute to Boston or even Nashua comfortably. No college, no ski resort. There is a small artists' collective, but nothing really active. People are born here, and either live here and die here or leave and never return."

"You weren't born here." I felt the warmth of the pizza against my jeans.

"No, but it has proven ideal for me. Being limited in my social life, the scenery has its compensations." He came to a stop sign.

"Don't you get restless?"

"Of course. Sometimes I take drives at night and go for miles, all night sometimes. I go to Vermont, or down to Boston and just absorb all the sights. I sit in dark parking lots in malls and watch families and couples. It's fodder for my pen. That helps the restlessness. Especially if I accidentally encounter someone. My resolve becomes renewed."

"Resolve to stay out of sight?"

"Yes."

"Then it must have taken a great deal of courage to invite me to come and paint you."

"You may recall, it was your father I invited." He chuckled and I blushed a little.

"When was the last time you met someone new?"

He shifted, his big hand bumping my knee. "A couple of years ago."

"Tell me about it." The shadows from the overhanging trees darkened the tiny open cockpit even as the lights from farmhouses flashed across our faces.

"As you can imagine, anyone with a big house on a remote road in the mountains becomes an object of curiosity. Most of the town elite, if I may use the term, know who I am and"—he gestured with a hand—"what I am. The local Episcopal priest comes and is comfortable with me. The town clerk sends me absentee ballots and we talk on the phone. My dentist, obviously, and my physician are friends. But, on occasion, I am forced to go out. I'd been having trouble with my eyes. One of the manifestations of acromegaly is rapid onset of blindness, so I rushed to the ophthalmologist. Even as scared as I was, I was very careful to make a late appointment and to explain that I have certain anomalies that might be disturbing. No problem, Dr. Lewis knew all about me. Well, he neglected to tell his office secretary. Alix, you should have seen her face. You'd think I was Frankenstein's monster." His laugh began to rumble.

"Lee, that's awful. What kind of adult would act like that? Weren't you hurt?"

"I've long since gotten over being hurt by ignorant reactions. But it isn't fun and not worth the freedom of being at large in the world. No, my freedom is cerebral, my night drives satisfactory after a fashion."

He turned into the driveway.

"But would you rather it were otherwise?"

"Would I rather be normal?" The question hung there, and I felt very small.

We zapped the pizza back into life in the microwave and settled in front of the fire Lee made. I found a Sade disc and put it in the CD player. Lee raised his bottle. "To half-finished paintings and pizza."

"To half-finished novels and little MGs."

Sade's music lent a sense of poignancy to our little meal. I couldn't put my finger on it for a while, then knew. If this were any other man, we'd be dancing the will-he-or-won't-he-try-to-sleep-with-me-tonight minuet. If he were any other man, I might want him to. I hid behind the beer bottle as I wrestled with my inner shame. I was no better than that mother in Boston or the ophthalmologist's secretary. I could be his friend but I did not want him to touch me as a man.

"When will you go?" His deep voice startled me.

"I was thinking that I should go tomorrow. I need to do some things at home."

"Ah."

"But, if I may, I'd like to stay till Saturday morning." I rushed my words, feeling in some private place that I owed him something. "We can work Saturday for an hour or so and then I won't have lost too much time." I fought back the sense that I was betraying Mark by choosing another work morning over his request to come home Friday.

Lee smiled, and again the charm beat into submission the deformity. "I'd like that. When will you be back?"

"Monday. I'll leave first thing and be up here by lunch." I reached for another slice of pizza. "Is there anything I can bring back? Books or CDs or Chinese food?"

Lee shook his great head. "This may be an outpost, but I lack very little. Just bring yourself back, okay?"

"I promise." And again I felt the poignancy edge into my heart.

Five

The new dress hung on a padded hanger, lurking behind the closet door like some taunting luxury. I touched the soft fabric of the sleeve and stroked it between my fingers. I caught sight of myself in the rippled mirror, hair roughly poked into a scrunchie, baggy blue jeans, and paint-streaked tee shirt. I thought, Why not? and began to strip.

After a long shower and half an hour's fussing with my hair to twist it into a vaguely sophisticated style, I slipped on the dress. The image that looked back at me in the mirror now was of another woman. I nodded to myself, pleased with the results. The short dress revealed flattering lines, emphasizing the curve of my hips. The square neckline showed off my shoulders, hinting at décolletage. I slipped on the black pantyhose I'd bought at the pharmacy the other night and felt that quantum transformation from ordinary to sexy.

Then I looked myself in the eye. "What *are* you

doing, Alix?" What if he thought I was coming on to him? Would he assume something I never meant? Or worse, what if he thought I was teasing him? Could I be unwittingly cruel to a man I certainly liked but never in the way for which I was dressing? I beat the panic back. I was a woman who enjoyed dressing up. Who could fault me for that? Surely he would know better.

I heard the hall clock chime the hour and knew he'd be in the living room with wine poured. Our habits, only a week old, were formed. A little unsteady on my heels, a great deal of long leg showing, I came down the stairs, one hand gliding along the seamless banister.

Lee held out my glass of wine and raised his glass. "You look stunning. Your friend Mark will certainly approve."

"Thank you. I'm sure Mark will like it, but I wore it because I thought you should have a chance to see what you picked out." I took a quick sip of the chardonnay and cursed myself for behaving like a flirt.

"You need a piece of jewelry. A pendant of some sort. No, silver. Silver beads." He looked into his glass, his massive brow knit in some private thought, then raised his head. "Shall we?" He stood aside as I preceded him into the dining room. I noticed immediately that my place had been set to his left instead of at the opposite end of the long table where I had sat all the other evenings, looking at him through the obscuring prisms of the candelabra.

After a few minutes, I stopped worrying that he'd misunderstand my innocent intention in wearing the dress. He got me to speak of my work, my recent goals for myself and my art. I confessed I was not a portrait painter, but an experimenter, using combinations of materials and shapes and forms to express concept and emotion. "I use broken shards and fabric, or varying thicknesses of paper. Color, lots of color. I try to capture the real colors in the world. The night I came here, I kept thinking I needed to capture the color of the night."

He was a good listener, prompting me, asking leading questions to keep me going. "What if, when you finish something, you don't like it? What do you do?"

"Sometimes I cut it up and cannibalize it. Sometimes I just scrape at the canvas and then gesso it over and use it for practice."

"What themes are you working with now?" He poured another bit of wine for me, his hand so large it covered the label. I liked his question, it was the question of an artist.

"Animals. I'm using the features of barnyard animals to represent human characteristics."

"How?"

I thought back to Mark's complaint that I'd never painted him. "Well, cockiness as a rooster's coxcomb. Or small-mindedness in the eye of a chicken." I laughed behind my wine glass. "Of course, an awful lot of what I do is my own private joke."

"You pick interesting human attributes, nothing trite like hate or love." He studied his wine glass, withdrawing for a moment into private thought.

As he guided me into my car the next morning Lee leaned forward and for a split second I thought he was going to kiss me. Instead he handed me the copy of his book. I opened it up to the flyleaf to read the inscription, "To Alix, with best wishes, Harris Bellefleur." I smiled but was oddly disappointed.

Then he said, "Bring back slides. I'd like to see your work."

A flush of pleasure mingled with the alarm prickling my neck. "I will. I'd love to show you my work."

He stood back and raised one massive hand in farewell. I tooted the horn and arced down the drive. As I passed through the rose-adorned gate I smiled; the coming weekend was just an interruption in a period of very good work.

My apartment smelled a little funky as I opened the door. Despite the cold, I threw open the windows. The fresh January air barreled in and fluttered the various notes and cartoons magnet-stuck to the fridge. A new note caught my eye: "Welcome home! I'll be by early for a reunion." Almost as soon as I had finished reading the note Mark burst into the room. "Hey, it's cold in here," he said, and began shutting up the windows.

"It smells, leave them open for a minute." I raised the kitchen window again.

Mark reached from behind me and pinned me against the counter, sliding his hands over my breasts. "Hey, I missed you. Did you miss me?" Turning me around, he kissed me, edging his tongue into my mouth. Within seconds we were in the bedroom, his anxious fingers tugging at my clothes. The sheets were chilled, but we soon warmed them. Afterward I lay spooned behind him, one hand on his firm hip. As he dozed, I rose up a little to study his face. Mark's shaggy good looks had always attracted me, long before we'd become lovers. Fair, usually unkempt, his hair was now clubbed back into a ponytail; frilly ends had pulled out from the elastic and framed his face. His hand lay on the pillow, a hand I had drawn many times, long and narrow. I knew the feel of it on my skin and between my hands, I knew that at the base of each finger were hard calluses from woodcutting all winter.

I eased myself back on my pillow, pulling the blanket up to my chin, struggling a little to get it from Mark. I sighed, touching on a melancholy whose source eluded me.

The phone rang. When Mark failed to react, I leapt out of bed and dashed into the kitchen, wrapping a flannel shirt over my nakedness.

"Alix?"

"Lee?"

"I just wanted to make sure you got home all right."

I held the phone close. "Yes, just fine. Got here about an hour ago."

"Good. Well then, see you Monday."

"I'll be there."

"Listen, Alix?"

"Yeah?"

"Knock 'em dead tonight."

I laughed.

"Good-bye."

"Lee? Thanks for calling."

"Who was that?" Mark stood in his shorts, arms crossed over his chest against the cold air still blowing in.

"Lee. Lee Crompton." I buttoned my shirt and pushed past him to get my jeans.

Cautioning me not to be late picking him up, Mark galloped down the stairs and out, his pickup truck leaving a new rut in the sun-softened mud. Pressing my forehead against the cold pane, I stared out at the departing truck and tried to touch the unhappiness within me, tried to give it a name. As if I were some gallery visitor without a guidebook, I wandered about my place, the second story of an old farmhouse, the land around it long since given over to subdivision. I looked at the sum of my exposed life hanging on the walls and stacked behind the couch. Every available space on the walls was covered by my work or by the works of others, including my father's and his father's. Studio photos of generations of Millers loitered in the narrow hallway to my bedroom. Their silver-tinged faces peered back at me as I lingered there. I stepped closer, hunting for resemblances. Were those dead-ahead eyes brown or green beneath the ram's horn eyebrows? Edward Miller, my father's grandfather, sat with an insouciant slouch, surrounded on either side by his coterie. For a short time around 1880 he was famous and followed. His hand, drooping elegantly as his elbow rested on the chairback, was ringless. I held up my own and examined it. Like Edward's mine was ringless, too, and I smiled to think in my veins passed the blood of such a man, whose own hand painted Lee's great-great-grandfather. I'd seen the portrait, a dour old man, his clipper ship fleet represented by a tiny painting in the portrait.

Tradition, Millers paint Cromptons, keeping food on Miller tables and paint in Miller paint boxes. Our two families were inextricably linked, yet knew each other not at all. We wandered through different circles, coming together only once a generation, like some kind of rite.

I looked at my great-grandfather again, trying to read the thought behind the steely eyes. Had you already painted Neville Crompton, or was that in your future?

It came to me then, the reason for my melancholy. I was the last. The last Miller to paint a Crompton. And the portrait I labored over would never be seen.

Six

A PERSISTENT BANGING ON THE FRONT DOOR PENEtrated my blow-dryer deafness and I ran to open it, wondering why Mark didn't just let himself in, then remembered that I was to pick him up. A uniformed courier stood there, clipboard in one hand. "Alix Miller?"

"Yes?" My heart beat oddly, a little frightened.

He held out the clipboard. "Sign here."

I scraped a nearly inkless pen over the multipart form, which he pulled apart with a professional snap and handed me the canary copy. He then swung a manila-colored envelope out from under his other arm and handed it to me. Closing the door, I studied the form, the carbon-weak signature of the sender indecipherable. Like a child, I squeezed the padded envelope, feeling the object within. I tugged at the pull tab and shook out a rectangular box. A piece of paper fluttered out behind it, little bits of packing material clinging to it like lint.

Dear Alix,

I want you to have the enclosed for your dinner tonight. I found them in a dresser in the attic some years ago and was told they were my grandmother's. As I mean no presumption, I hope that you will keep them.

I opened the green velvet jeweler's box. Silver beads lay against satin, their polished surfaces warming in the light. I held them up, admiring the perfectly formed drops as they graduated to a large central bead, beautifully filigreed. Looking closer I could see tiny roses etched into the pattern. I unclasped the old-fashioned box clasp and held the necklace to my throat.

Reflected in the hall mirror, I could see that Lee had been right, the silver beads were perfect with the black dress. I touched the filigreed bead. He meant no presumption, but what should I assume? I couldn't accept a gift like this, I shouldn't—a family heirloom, an expensive piece of jewelry. In the same mental breath I loved how they looked. Okay, I thought, just for tonight. No permanent gift. No matter what he said, a gift like this comes with strings. Long, sticky emotional ones I wasn't prepared to be entangled in.

The morning seemed so long ago. We'd only worked for a couple of hours. Lee had been unable to sit still, complaining of tingling in his hands, something the disease manifests now and again, he'd explained. With Mrs. Greaves out, I'd made us a lunch of grilled cheese while Lee shared *New Yorker* cartoons with me. We'd laughed over them and I burned the sandwiches.

I touched the beads at my throat, a talisman. "Don't do this to me," I said.

* * *

The dinner in Boston was predictably boring, speeches laden with inside jokes among the photojournalist coterie. I smiled, laughed, and sipped white wine behind a mask of good humor. My mind crept back to Riseborough, even as my fingers touched the silver beads. My left-hand neighbor commented on them.

"Thank you, yes, a friend gave them to me."

At that moment, Mark chose to swing his attention away from the journalist on his right. "Who?"

A pernicious wave of flush rose up my neck to my face, as if I had something to hide. "Lee Crompton."

Mark's fingers closed over mine as they lay on the white tablecloth. "He's the guy who called you this afternoon. Who is he?" Mark was fighting to keep his voice mildly curious.

"Mark, he's the man I've been painting all week. Remember?" I shot off the answer in a tone designed to imply impatience with his not knowing this.

At that moment the awards program began and Mark let go of my hand. But as the master of ceremonies began to announce the first category, Mark leaned over. "We need to talk about this. Later."

"There's nothing to talk over," I hissed.

"Not now, don't talk to me now."

I began to pray that he'd win an award in the vain hope he'd forget about arguing. I was tired and had no strength to defend something that needed no defending. We'd planned to spend the night at the Copley Plaza, and a night in a hotel room with a man angry at me was not a pleasant thought.

God heard my prayers, or perhaps Mark's, because he was brought onstage for a prize in a best photo category. It was for his photo of the owners of a local barn holding each other after a horrible fire had destroyed their stock and their dreams. Taken from a distance, the two embracing forms against the backdrop of the burned-down barn was a touching picture and one of my favorites. I had even stolen the emotional theme for one of the unfinished projects slated for my March show.

At any rate, Mark and several of the other prize-winners grouped together and declared open season on Boston. We roved from club to club, reggae, blues, rap, finally coming to rest at the hotel in the early hours. I lugged Mark's inebriated form into the elevator and then out, fishing through his pockets for the key.

"Easy, old pal." I bent under his weight. "Let's make it to the bed!" I extricated the plaque from his hand and set it on the writing desk.

"Hey, Alix," he called out from the blankets.

"What?"

"Do I need to be jealous? Of Crompton, I mean."

"No. Now go to sleep."

"Good." In seconds he was out, one foot on the floor to prevent the room from spinning around.

I sat on the end of the other bed and stared at myself in the mirror. Slowly I unclasped the beads and took them off, holding them in my hands for a long time before I put them away.

Seven

"I really wanted to go to the Museum of Fine Arts." I knew my voice was edging on petulance.

"Okay." Mark's capitulation would have a hook: "Then you've got to treat me real nice." He held open the covers.

"Don't I always?" Shucking off my leggings and baggy sweater, I climbed in to lie next to him. "Didn't I already bring you coffee?"

He rubbed his face against my bare shoulder. "You forgot the rolls."

"Bastard," I cried, and pummeled him until we wrestled ourselves into laughter. Last night's drinking had no effect on him this morning and he was quick and rough. In fifteen minutes I was in the shower. "Make me another cup of coffee," I called as I toweled my hair.

He thwacked my bare bottom as I walked by, jolting my good humor with a little annoyance at this old and irritating trick. I sipped the new coffee and cringed; as usual he'd put in too much sugar.

We separated at the museum; I headed off to the newest exhibit in the Gund wing, he off to his own interests. I wasn't taken with the exhibit and in a sudden flash decided to seek out portraits, hoping to find some inspiration among the old order. Finding a bench, I sat down and communed with the several portraits before me. What made them art as opposed to private record? Not every portraitist became famous or hung in a museum, so few of my ancestors had. My painting of Lee had progressed to the point where I could begin detailing it, adding the spark of life to the sketch. Any portrait can be a representation of the outside of a person; a good one speaks of the inner man. I wanted very much to reveal the soul that I had begun to know that lay beneath Lee's horrible exterior.

I examined cheeks and hands and postures and colors in the portraits before me. Finally I decided that my father was right, it was the life in the eyes that made the difference. A really good painter told something about the sitter in the expression. Cunning, mischievous, brilliant, sweet-tempered, or dour.

It shouldn't be so difficult, then, I thought, to paint Lee. With his massive features, deep facial lines, and mobile expressions, I should be able to capture the man behind the distortion with ease. If he would let me—but as soon as he sat, it was as if he became a lifeless statue. A gargoyle. I had not even begun to attempt his face. For the entire time we'd been at it, I'd only created the outline of his form, stroking in cautious hints of the shape of his face. It was only in the little pencil sketches that I had captured him. Those showed life and interest and a human being. From those I could do a creditable portrait. And again I felt that jolt of sadness that my efforts were for nothing. I reasoned with myself, as I sat there in front of a Sargent, that it was his money, his choice what to do with the finished painting. It was never going to be my personal masterpiece, no portrait would be. So what did I care if he stored it for all eternity under a burlap cover in the attic of the Riseborough house? No, that wasn't my problem. That he wouldn't even look at it was.

I shook off my reverie and looked at my watch; within our agreed-upon time frame I had fifteen minutes left for the gift shop. I wandered around the museum store almost as if it were another room in the exhibit. Tiny reproductions of masterpieces adorned book covers and coasters. Instructional toys and silly objects, jewelry and posters crowded the space, filling the visual sense with overstimulation and the spendthrift sense with excitation. I could withstand most of it, until my eye fell on a copper wind chime fashioned with a rose as the central clapper, the five chiming pipes like thorny stems. I could see it hanging in the solarium, could imagine its melodious sound airborne even as my hand touched the display. Delicate tones sprang out, not tinkling but bell-like in their quality.

"Fifty percent off," the saleswoman said as if talking to someone else, then turning to face me. "It really is pretty."

Mark joined me at the cash register. "What'd you buy?"

I showed him and he screwed up his face. "Why? You don't have any place to hang that."

"It's not for me."

Most of the time Mark is amazingly uncurious. At other times he displays a ferreting quality most annoying. "Who?"

"Lee."

"Why?"

"I don't know. It just seems perfect for his house."

Mark was silent all the way to the car. I unlocked it and climbed in, he stood outside. The biting city cold ruffled his fair hair and he shoved his hands into his pockets.

"Come on, it's unlocked," I said, shoving the key into the ignition. "Mark?"

"You go. I'm going to stay in town for another day."

"Don't be ridiculous."

"Ridiculous?" He leaned into the car. "No more ridiculous than buying an expensive gimcrack for a rich patron." With that he slammed the Sentra's passenger door and stalked off.

I felt sick. Leaning my forehead against the steering wheel, I fought tears, not the first I'd felt in recent months. I knew he expected me to leap out of the car and follow him down the street, I knew that he'd close down on me until I declared my error, until I manipulated his forgiveness. I raised my head, tears hardened into stone. I watched his back in the mirror as he strode away, hands shoved in his pockets and head down in his characteristic walk.

"I don't need this bullshit," I said aloud, and turned the ignition key. How dare he make assumptions about me. How dare he sully an impulsive and innocent act with implications. I passed the street I might have turned down to go around the block and head him off. I kept going. I negotiated the light Sunday traffic up Route 9, merging onto 95, all the time driving on automatic pilot while my active attention chewed on Mark's sulk.

It wasn't as if he'd ever said let's get married, or let's live together, or suggested any other permanent arrangement. Then I could understand his periodic bouts of demanding my complete attention. Mark said he was a man on the move, the future could mean Los Angeles or New York or even Europe. That had suited me. Equally, my own declaration, early in our acquaintance, that I could never roam far as long as my father was alive had effectively set the framework of our relationship.

In many ways we were poles apart, yet, like magnets, we could not resist each other. I was rooted, he ready to sever ties; I cared deeply for my father, he could not understand filial attachment and the flashes of jealousy in his petty remarks drove splinters into my heart. He was not above forcing me to choose, and his silence was so much deeper than my father's.

Our art was the thing that had brought us together, and often the thing that set us apart. As a photographer, his stimulus was from the outside, what he saw he reacted to. As a painter, my muse was internal, what I thought and felt brought out to the canvas. I respected his work, he criticized mine in the name of being helpful.

This late in the day on a Sunday in January, the traffic north was minimal and I cruised along, WGBH blaring a Beethoven quartet, the counterplay between the violins, viola, and cello voicing the drama in my heart until the last twisting rise to the tonic chord, which seemed written expressly for my state of mind.

Mark and I had met at a group show in which we both had pieces. I had an abstract in acrylic called *Old*

Man with Rake and I watched him examining it, watching for the expression that would encourage me to approach and introduce myself, or, depending, keep my back to him and never speak. I was at the stage in my career when even slight disapproval touched me personally. Attending my own shows bordered on neurotic. For days I would deny I was even going to attend, then worry about what to wear. I practiced witty conversation and defenses for my work. I watched Mark, then walked off.

Driven away from my own work, I set about studying others', coming to rest in front of a dramatic black and white photo of a Peruvian mother and child. Mark was suddenly at my side, studying the same picture, one hand rubbing his short beard, up and down, using just his fingertips under his chin in a manner which would become so familiar to me. "So, what do you think of this one?"

"I like it. It's a marvelous study." I stepped back a little, putting an inch more distance between us. "Who is he? The photographer, I mean?"

"Mark Kramer."

"I don't know his work."

"I'm somewhat familiar with it," he whispered in a gallery voice.

At that moment a woman breezed through, an older man in tow. "Mark, sweetie, I want you to meet Donald Stone." She darted for Mark's hand and pulled him away from me with an icy glance over her shoulder, garnished by a red-lipped smile. Mark threw me a grin even as he was hauled off to do the ingratiating gallery jive.

He found me later, holed up in the gallery cafe.

"Why did you do that?" I asked.

"Do what?"

"Pretend you weren't the photographer."

"For the same reason you pretended you weren't the artist who painted *Old Man with Rake."*

Flushed, I stammered, "But you didn't like it, and I told you I liked the mother and child."

"I do so like your work."

That was the first great lie he told me. Now he no longer took the trouble to lie, he no longer seemed to care about my feelings, and his truthfulness was hard-edged. "Grow up, Alix," he told me the last time I got angry at his criticism of my work. "Get used to it if you want to make it in the art world."

I signaled for my exit.

Eight

Although it seemed an eternity had passed since I'd last slept in my own home, I was agitated and afraid that my phone would ring and that I would have to deal with Mark, deal with the reality of him rather than the creature of my imaginary arguments. So deep was my anger that I wanted no possibility of contact with him and thus decided to spend the night with my father. I'd stop home only long enough to throw more clothing in a bag and water my plants. I won only imaginary fights, when every word was orchestrated and my points were heard and scored. When it came to reality, Mark seemed never to stick to the script. My best shots were deflected and used against me. Tired, upset, I had no strength to engage the battle tonight.

My answering machine was flashing like mad. Choosing to ignore it, I emptied my underwear drawer into a tote bag and hunted for the watering can. That done, I shrugged on my coat and flung the bag over my shoulder. The insistent red light caught my eye and I relented. I was being pessimistic, maybe Mark had left a conciliatory message and I was being stubborn.

It was my father: "Alix, call me as soon as you get in," the message ran and his voice seemed tentative, a thread of anxiety woven into the nine short words.

With conflicting disappointment and relief that Mark hadn't called, I shut the machine off and dashed down the stairs.

"Dad, what's up?" I called from the kitchen as I let myself in the back door. A slight smell of yesterday's soup lingered and dishes were piled in the sink. My booted foot crunched on broken glass as I walked through the room. I called again, "I'm home, Dad." I bent to pick up the glass, then heard him call me.

I found him in the living room, sitting bolt upright in his favorite chair, his breathing labored and a film of sweat glazing his forehead. "Alix." He smiled, pain erasing the smile instantly. "I think I'm in a little fix here." His fingers clutched at the arms of the chair.

I called 911, and the next few hours were a complete blur. It seemed to me, after the fact, that the ambulance was there instantly. Time lost its power for me, hours seemed seconds. I was suddenly in the small emergency room of the local hospital and a cup of coffee was thrust into my hand. I couldn't tell the nursing staff from the doctors, no one wore whites like on TV, everyone wore stethoscopes around their necks and Nikes on their feet. I focused on giving information. I racked my brain for details of Dad's history. Why didn't I know his medications? Did he take anything? Had he been having problems before this? Allergies? I shivered, an icy breeze slipping in as the pneumatic doors swung open again.

Then I waited. Year-old *Smithsonians* entertained me while the staff monitored my father, waited for blood-gas tests, made him comfortable. While my eyes read the words, my mind made decisions: I'll monitor his eating better; I'll spend more time with him; I'll maybe even move back home. I sighed involuntarily with that thought.

"Alice Miller?"

I didn't correct her. "Yes?"

Birkenstocks on her feet and baggy sweater over leggings, the doctor led me into a tiny room, the sole furnishing two plastic chairs. "It's not his heart," she began.

A heat wave of relief stung me, quickly doused by her next words: "I want to keep him here and run some tests. I think that we may be dealing with"—she caught herself, aware suddenly of the need to be gentle—"something else."

"What?" I was in no frame of mind for prevarication.

"I think your father may have cancer."

"How can you say that? Why?" I was on my feet, denial spilling from my mouth. "That's not possible. Not again."

"Please, Alice."

"Alix, it's Alix. Please tell me why you think that."

It was too much, too much to take in at once, but over the next few days I learned a great deal about how this evil lies in wait until it can rear its ugly head and steal our loved ones without a by-your-leave.

My mother had died of it when I was fifteen, and the question that spun through my mind now was, why had he lived so long without her only to die of it, too?

Pancreatic cancer. A tumor lying dormant and painless suddenly comes alive and all living becomes dying.

Into subordination go all other concerns when faced with death. When Mark finally called me on Tuesday, I had no strength to care that we'd fought, and he had the grace not to mention it.

"I'm sorry about your dad," he said, but quickly turned the brief conversation toward his own news. Once again his star was on the rise, the *Boston Globe* had offered a good assignment.

"Great, call me when you get back," was all I could manage to say. Mark Kramer was at the wrong end of the telescope and getting farther away from my reality.

I'd called Lee on Monday, speaking only with Mrs. Greaves, explaining my problem with a sense that someone else was speaking. She murmured, "Poor lass," which sent the first tears rolling. "If there's anything I can do," she said, as had so many others whom I had called with the news.

"No. Thank you, though. If there is, I'll call," I promised her, as I had promised ten others, determined not to call anyone for help, but to shoulder this burden myself and be the brave little trouper I had been when my mother died.

Once the pain had come under control and all the tests had been administered, only one decision needed to be made.

"We'll start an aggressive campaign of chemo and radiation, in Boston, of course. We can maybe eke out another six months that way." Dr. Mulcahey reached for his Rolodex. "I'll put you in touch with a top oncologist at Dana Farber."

"Wait, no." I sat on the edge of the Naugahyde visitor's chair. "We don't want to do it that way. That's not living, Dr. Mulcahey."

Dr. Mulcahey threw himself back in his chair, which protested with a squeak. "Alix, it's your father's decision, but I don't think he should give up."

"I don't call it giving up. But you know he saw my mother struggle to fight it, only to finally lose the battle. Every day a skirmish in hell with chemo or radiation or pain. No, Dr. Mulcahey, he knows exactly what he wants and I support him in it."

Dr. Mulcahey shot forward, his chair squealing louder. "Treatments have improved since your mother's illness. Twenty years ago much of what she endured was still experimental."

"Have they eliminated the side effects from chemo?"

"Of course not all." His impatience was beginning to show.

"Is the cure no longer worse than the disease? Have they been able to make the quality of a life in cure as sweet as a clean death?"

"There will be times of remission, when the drugs begin to conquer the cancer, and aren't those few weeks or months infinitely better than letting it run its course uncontrolled?"

"It cannot be controlled, only held back like the Dutch dike. With pain control, and surrounded by people he loves, we can make his last months sweet and uncomplicated." I paced the room now, walking in and out of the patches of sunlight barring the floor through the venetian blinds.

"You are talking about your father's death, Alix."

I stopped, the sunlight and shadows laying bars across my body. "Haven't you been?"

"It may take a year. Are you committed to waiting a year for death, or working for a year to give him life?"

"You bastard, it's what he wants!" I cried out. "It's

what he wants. My mother was a young woman, it made sense to fight. But Dad's seventy-three. He doesn't want to do it. I won't make him do it."

"All right, all right"—Dr. Mulcahey threw up his hands in a stage gesture—"then please contact Hospice. Do that much for him anyway."

"We already have." I was outraged, as if giving my father death with dignity was some sort of filial selfishness. It occurred to me then that in these litigious times Mulcahey was worried that someday I would come back to him and accuse him of not trying to save my father. "I will, Doctor, in no way hold you accountable for our decision."

He looked up at me with rheumy blue eyes peering over the horn-rimmed frames of his half-glasses. To save him denial, I left.

Nine

Hospice helped me set Dad up at home. They taught me how to administer the morphine; how much would ease the pain and how much would make him sleep. The living room had been made over into a bed-sitting room, the paraphernalia of illness neatly laid out on the antique breakfront. When he felt better we played games, chess, checkers, and the like. Some days he preferred just to watch television and we spent hours letting Sally Jessy Raphaël and her ilk entertain us with the pathetic of the world. The sunlight played upon the screen, fading it to gray, and he dozed as the guests told their tales like bards of old, entertaining the bored princes. He lay in his recliner, fingers clutching intermittently at the arms. He was withering. The flesh of his forearms raddled now, a million silky lines cascading downward when he raised his hands. I watched his life's juices being sucked away by this invisible tyrant, while all around us were results of his life's work, vital images pulsing with energy. I took to changing the paintings and line drawings so that he could see them all before he went. "Before I go, I want to see . . . before I go." It was as if he were waiting for a flight.

One afternoon he woke with a start. "Alix, go work. You musn't waste light like this."

"No, there will be plenty of light another day."

"Alix, go. You can hear me if I call. Go paint a nice picture for your show."

He'd forgotten that I'd withdrawn my participation from the March show. It was the middle of February and I hadn't touched brush to canvas since that last Saturday at Riseborough. But I had been sketching—sketching my father as he lay there, asleep or awake, comfortable and in discomfort. I was recording it on thick white paper in my notebook. Someday, I knew, it would be translated into a piece of work dedicated to him. I recorded the wasting away, the deepening lines as his face hollowed out. I penciled in the expression of resignation and the grim-lipped fight against despair.

"Alix, go paint. I would really like to know you're working. I hate unfinished projects and the studio is cluttered with yours."

When I began another sally of protest he held up one hand. "For God's sake, child, give me some time alone!"

"Oh, Dad"—I leaned over and kissed him—"of course I'll leave you alone."

I took him at his word and went home to my apartment, which had grown cold and dusty without me. All the plants were dead. My answering machine light was bleating. I'd left the message where to call on the tape, but evidently someone had left a message here anyway.

"Alix, I didn't want to disturb you, but I thought I'd call and see how you were. It's Tuesday, February second, about six-thirty. Give me a call if you want to talk." Lee's voice was soft and resonant over the speaker, full of concern, and suddenly I wanted nothing more than to talk with him. I felt a jolt of something I could only call homesickness. Mantra-like, I kept thinking I want to go home, I want to go home. I wanted to be out of this nightmare and in a safe harbor. Lee's voice brought me back to a brief time when his home had been a haven of quiet and work for me. I hadn't needed it then, now I longed for it.

My calendar was still on January. I lifted the page and looked at February. Valentine's Day had passed unnoticed and it was now the 17th. He'd called almost three weeks ago and probably thought I didn't want to talk to him.

I twisted the thermostat to 70° and set the kettle on the stove. Coffee made, I punched Lee's number and listened to the ring.

"Hello?"

"Lee?"

"Alix, how are you?" His voice was so sweet that I was unnerved and tears began to flow as they had not in weeks. He kept repeating my name, but I couldn't speak. All of it waited to burst forth, but all I could do was cry. As I sobbed Lee kept up a soothing litany. "Alix, it's okay, let it out. Let it out, let it out. You've been holding on but it's okay to let go."

Finally I reached that plateau where tears and weeping are silly. "Oh, Lee, I'm so embarrassed. You must think I'm a jerk. Calling you just to bawl."

There was a slight pause, a little throat-clearing second. "Alix, I'm touched that you did. I just wish"—he paused again, and I sensed instantly his next brave words—"I wish that I was there."

"Come!" I lurched to my feet. "Please come tonight!"

He didn't say anything, and I could feel his indecision. "Are you sure?"

"Please. I'm at my father's all the time with no one else. Take one of your night drives and come visit me."

"It wasn't my imagination then, was it?"

"What?"

"That we're friends?"

"Yes." I pressed my back against the doorjamb and slid to the floor. "Yes, we are, and on the basis of that friendship, will you come help me sit with my dying father?"

"Dad"—I touched his shoulder—"someone is coming to visit tonight."

"Who?" More and more he disliked having people come to see him.

"Lee Crompton." I took the blanket from him and helped him to his feet. "My patron. My friend."

We shuffled down the hall together. "I can't see anybody," he said before he went into the bathroom. "I can't have anybody see me like this."

I smiled a little. "Lee is different, Dad. He'll understand that."

He shook his head before shutting the bathroom door.

The house had begun to take on the odor of illness and I was painfully aware of it. I set about baking apple pies to mask the punky smell emanating from the living room. Lee would arrive around seven-thirty, and I had stopped at the grocery store for dinner. Dad was still eating at the table, so I'd planned a roast beef dinner for us. That Dad scarcely managed soup most of the time was irrelevant.

I had just pulled the pies out of the oven when the phone rang. It was Mark, and in the instant that I recognized his voice I realized that the ringing phone had made me fear that it was Lee canceling. My relief that it was Mark instead came through in my voice and he commented on it.

"You sound chipper tonight."

"Well enough. Are you coming by?" Mark had come two or three times in the beginning, but his excuses not to stop by and visit my father had been at the ready recently.

"Actually, no. I'm going to New York tomorrow and I thought maybe you could break away for a little while and we could, well, have a little time together."

"Mark, I can't." I knew that he meant a little time together in bed.

"Alix, you can't lock yourself in that house forever."

"It won't be nearly that long."

"Right, well, okay. But, you know, I'm going to be gone for at least a week." After a beat he added, "Alix, this could be the one. The career booster."

I know he wanted me to ask him all about it, to turn the key that would start him on his career monologue. Ordinarily I would have, but I had a roast to put in and a sick father. I cut him off. "Mark, listen, have a great time and good luck with the assignment. You can tell me all about it when you get back."

"Maybe, maybe I will, Alix. Or maybe I just won't come back. You never know."

"Mark, is that a threat?" A side effect of my father's

illness was my own directness, a loss of finesse. There was silence and I filled it. "I don't need your ego, Mark Kramer. I have enough to deal with, so either be my friend or leave me alone."

"Who was that?" Dad asked.

"Mark."

"Will he be coming by?" My father liked Mark, liked his work. He was circumspect about the peculiar relationship we maintained; only occasionally did he hint that it should be more permanent.

"No. He's on his way to New York."

"Still pursuing the big one, eh?"

I smiled. "Something like that."

The doorbell rang at six-thirty. Despite his being an hour early, I knew it was Lee, no one ever came to the front door who wasn't a stranger. I was acutely aware of the messy pile of wood on the porch and the tatty little rug in the entrance hall. Wishing I'd had time to change, I stroked my hair back and jerked open the heavy oak door.

Time had softened my memory of him and the reality was a little unnerving. He was larger than I remembered him, and I saw the monster before I saw the man. Then suddenly he was Lee, my skating companion and model, and I pushed into submission the involuntary reaction to his looks and concentrated on the kindness of his being there.

I brought him into the living room, where Dad was in his recliner, the IV drip slowly easing the evening's pain. "Dad, this is Lee Crompton."

The drug slurred his speech and fogged his mind, but old social skills carried the day and he extended the hand not engaged to the drip. "Mr. Crompton, my daughter tells me a great deal about you. She's enjoying her stay with you. No, I mean . . ."

"Yes, I enjoyed her stay with me very much." He glanced at me and smiled. "She's also told me quite a bit about you."

The opening gambit made, I slipped away to make us drinks. When I came back laughter greeted me, rolling chuckles from my father's throat, Lee's vibrant roar surrounding it. Somehow I knew I was the butt of their joke.

"What gives, guys?"

With one voice they protested, "Nothing!"

Dad sipped his orange juice and Lee and I had a glass of wine; conversation rolled along gently until Dad fell asleep as he often did after his medication.

"This is a great house, Alix. When was it built, about 1800?"

"Actually, 1783. It's been in the family since the Civil War, when Edward Miller purchased it. He had designs on being a gentleman farmer, so he bought this farmhouse way out in the country surrounded by woods and pastures and set about raising horses and children."

"Isn't he the one who painted my father's great-grandfather, the whiskery old fellow in the blue tunic?"

"That would be about the time, anyway." I sliced off another fragment of cheese and munched it. "Of course, subsequent Millers added and reduced the house to their personal likings and the fashions of the times. Our own improvements have been new PVC pipes and a rather expensive septic system. And, as you can see, we are no longer way out in the country. Not like you."

He finished his wine and set the glass down on a napkin.

"Would you like a tour?"

"I'd love one."

We wandered through the house, lingering here and there as Lee's eye fell upon some antique or piece of art. He seemed so much bigger in the low-ceilinged house; I kept warning him to duck as we passed through two-hundred-year-old doorways with their unforgiving lintels. So much of what Millers put into this house remained. Now that most of the rooms were unlived in, it had the feeling of a museum exhibit. When I lived here the rooms were often winter cold, but my early memories were only of the warmth of the sun coming through the tiny multi-paned window. I was sleeping in my old room now, near the back and overlooking the lower meadow. A childhood room, it bore remnants of teenage fascinations, which my father had never cleaned out. My high school pennant still clung bravely to the wall beside my streaky mirror, where I had spent so much time experimenting with preteen styles.

A photo of my mother in a cheap dime-store frame sat on the nightstand. I'd found it in a drawer and taken it out, propping it against the lamp when the cardboard foot wouldn't hold it. She looked so young, maybe only eighteen or twenty. She wore pedal pushers and a white Peter Pan blouse. In the black and white photo, her long hair might have been auburn or plain brown. She straddled her bike and her eyes were alight with some joke forever a mystery. I had studied that picture, over and over again, trying to hunt down the clue that her life would be over before she was forty-five.

"You look like her." Lee stood at the foot of my narrow bed, his back to the mirror.

I looked at the picture again, picking it up. "I've never seen the resemblance."

"She was lovely."

"She wasn't when she died."

I set the picture down carelessly and it slipped, rattling the glass.

The kitchen ell had been modernized in my grandfather's day, and restored to its oldest form in my father's. This had always been my favorite room, and its soapstone sink and real butcher block offset the dishwasher and microwave. A farm table instead of countertops served as the work area, and an enamel-topped sideboard provided a perfect piecrust-making surface. I stopped to check the roast and light the fire under the potatoes and carrots.

"So where's your studio?"

I'd forgotten I'd told Lee I worked at my father's house. "The studio is through the back door. Would you like to see it?"

In the tradition of New England farmhouses, ours was "Big House—Little House—Back House—Barn." Our studio was in the back house segment, the barn long gone. A short breezeway connected it, open on one side and heaped now with wood. The studio was freezing. The only source of heat, the woodstove, was now dormant. My several abandoned works stood out as the overhead lights came on. Sheets covered the easels and stack of canvases. Dad's work on his drawing table lay under a sheet of thick polypropylene.

"May I?" Lee touched the corner of the sheeting covering my work.

I got that little chill I always do when someone wants to look at my unfinished pieces, but nodded.

He lifted the cover from a small painting, a landscape with bits of real grass and stone worked into the thick oil paint. The predominant colors were blue, red, and yellow. Off to one side was a face, a little like the angels carved on eighteenth-century headstones; round, slightly cherubic, it hovered out of context with the rest of the painting. I hadn't decided whether to leave it in or paint it out.

I puttered around while Lee looked at all my work. Something like staring at the ceiling while the gynecologist roots around, I can't watch anybody examine my unfinished work. The cold in the room began to numb my feet in their thin Keds, and I motioned that I was leaving. "Stay longer if you want to." I went back to the kitchen and poked the carrots with a wicked-looking fork.

"Alix." Lee came back into the kitchen and held his hands near the oven. "Alix, they're great."

"What?"

"What do you think I mean? Your paintings, of course," he chided. "I want to buy the cherub painting."

"I like that, the cherub. I hadn't thought of it that way, but you don't have to buy anything. Please don't feel obliged."

"Alix, I'll feel deprived if I can't have that painting." His shaggy eyebrows rose and fell. "You do sell your work, don't you?"

"I'd be lying if I said I only paint for private expression. Of course you may have it"—I raised the wicked-looking fork—"but as a gift. Don't you even think of buying it. Just tell all your friends what a marvelous painter you've discovered and recommend me."

"I can't . . ."

"I accepted your beads. Quid pro quo, Mr. Crompton." And we laughed.

* * *

Dad sat at his accustomed place at the head of the table in the dining room. Outside the wind had picked up and it sang through the overhead wires, haunting in its almost melodious whistle. Except for my forgetting the rolls in the oven, the meal turned out well. I hadn't really cooked for a long time and was pleased with the result. My often elusive appetite surfaced, the red meat tasting so good after weeks of soups and quick meals. Lee, used to professional cooking in his house, was kindly complimentary. I looked at my father and saw that he'd touched nothing on his plate. "Dad, come on, eat something," I chided. "No dessert if you don't."

He didn't answer and I could see the fog of morphine like an aura around him. His fuzzy gray hair stuck up at all angles from lying on it all the time. His sweater was buttoned wrong, and when he looked at me he looked puzzled.

"Dad, eat something."

"I don't want to," he retorted.

"Just a little," I cajoled, frightened a little at his outburst.

"No."

"Dad." I was angry now, embarrassed that he would be such a child in front of company. I opened my mouth again, but Lee stopped me.

"Alix, leave him alone."

"Lee, he has to eat."

"No, not right now. Let him be."

The tip of my fork rattled against my plate. Abruptly I stood and began gathering dirty dishes. "Why don't you go into the living room and I'll put on the coffee."

I stood in the kitchen, leaning against the soapstone

sink and staring at my own reflection in the night-darkened window. I shook my head to clear it of the scene and went back to the dining room to finish cleaning up. Dishes clattered together as I carelessly piled them one on top of the other. I filled the sink and dropped them in; cauliflowers of soap foam splashed over the edge, dripping down and under my feet. I forgot to plug in the coffee maker and made jagged cuts in the pie.

"Alix, are you all right?" Lee leaned against the doorjamb, his head grazing the lintel.

"No. I'm tired and cranky," I answered, and felt a lump in my throat that would easily become self-pity if I let it. "I'm so tired, Lee. He doesn't sleep at night and wants company. It's got to be like being a new mother. Every morning at four o'clock he wakes me up and we sit up rehashing old problems and reliving old pain until he falls asleep again around six and I'm left awake."

"Go to bed, Alix. I'll take care of him tonight. I don't think it matters who sits with him, as long as he has somebody here."

"But there are medications and . . ."

"I'll take care of it."

"I can't ask you to do that, Lee. I'm just grateful you came to visit."

"I came to help. Let me."

I was too tired to debate the issue. The tantalizing idea of a night's uninterrupted sleep was too appealing. "Okay, but don't do the dishes. I have all day tomorrow to do them."

"No, I'll stay with him." Lee plugged in the coffee maker. "Go to bed, sweetie."

I yawned, nodding. As I moved out of the room I turned back. "Lee?"

He turned around, his great head canted to one side.

"I'm really glad you're here." From across the room we faced each other and when I looked into his eyes I saw for the first time, in their perfect china blue, the eyes of the boy in the picture. Two things had not been lost to the disease.

Ten

BUNDLED UP IN THERMALS AND A FLANNEL SHIRT, I crawled into my bed in the heat-deprived back bedroom and fell into an instant and deep sleep. Sometime during the night I was wakened. I started to climb out of bed, then lay back—Lee's deep voice pierced the night and I knew he was with my father. I closed my eyes again and knew nothing more.

There is a kind of miracle in waking naturally. Eyes open, the miasma of weariness is gone. There is no soul crying out for more sleep. Thus I awoke, the sunlight beaming in through the paned window to lie upon my bed in oblong patterns, illuminating the patchwork like some stained-glass window across my lap. With amused horror I saw that it was after ten o'clock. I bolted out of bed and slipped down the backstairs to the kitchen. A pot of coffee lingered on the burner, my mug waiting for me on the clean table. A note rested against the sugar bowl.

Alix,

Your father passed a fairly comfortable night, I think. I have given him his medication this morning (8 a.m.) and he's eaten a little. I have to go now, but please call me and call on me.

Lee

P.S. I took the painting. I hope that's all right.

L

I bucked a wave of disappointment. I heard the television go on in the living room and went to bid my father good morning.

"Hey, sleepyhead," he greeted me, holding open his arms in a way he hadn't for a long time. I knelt into his embrace and tried not to notice the scent of illness about him. "I like that friend of yours, he's a pretty good card player."

"Does that mean you beat him?"

"Yeah, but he gave me a run for my money."

That evening I called Lee. As usual Mrs. Greaves answered, but wouldn't put him on the line. "He's upstairs with a migraine. He's prone to them, you know."

"Part of his disease?" I was compelled to ask.

"I guess so. Anyway, he'll be sorry he missed your call."

"Tell him thank you, Mrs. Greaves. Tell him I'm sorry I slept so long that I missed him. Tell him"—I was scrambling now—"tell him I really loved having him here and that soon we'll get back to working on his portrait."

There was a heartbeat of pause before Mrs. Greaves spoke. "Alix, don't encourage him. Don't set him up for disappointment."

I felt myself go scarlet. "Mrs. Greaves, that is the farthest thing from my mind. Please just give him my message." I hung up, trembling from the unprovoked assault on my intentions.

I wondered then how much of her influence had kept Lee a virtual prisoner in that house.

That afternoon Robin Gates came into our lives. As naturally as a long-time habit, she banged on the back door and let herself in. She plunged in, taking charge without offending, offering encouragement when we would give up, occasionally spending the night when she saw the raw exhaustion creep up on me again. We were lucky enough to receive a morphine pump so that Dad could administer his own dose as he needed it. She played interminable hands of three-handed cribbage and never once lost her temper when Dad became aggressive or whiny. Or even when I became aggressive or whiny.

About my age, she was a widow, had been for two years. Her husband, Daniel, had died of the same cancer my father had. Hospice had saved her life, she liked to say, and so she donated her time as a volunteer, helping others crawl through the same tunnel she'd gone through.

"It's not supposed to be easy. Every emotion you have will come into play. The best I can offer you is that at the end you will go on with your life. Your mourning is now. You have a gift in that you know what's going to happen and you can say all those things you think you need to now, before it's too late. And hold back those things you should." Robin added coffee to her perpetual cup. "And you need to work. Your dad talks all the time about how great an artist you are. Paint something for him."

"It's cold in the studio."

"Build a fire, Alix. Warm yourself."

The stove was full of ash, so first I cleaned it out, then I performed the ritualistic fire-lighting task that had so often been prelude to my work. Bunch up newspaper, crumpling up current events with ads for white sales across the land. With my red hatchet I struck splinters of kindling from old shingles, mingling them with angled ends of two-by-fours gathered from work sites. The flame caught. I fed the incipient fire choice bits of wood, and satisfied at last that it would survive, I loaded the Tempwood stove with two oak logs and set the lid down.

I stood in front of the empty easel, the absence of my landscape with angel conspicuous. Lee had taken the choice from me, whether to keep the angel or paint her away. A stretched canvas sat on the workbench and I took it up, setting it in place of the missing painting. Studying my tubes of color, I waited to warm up. The afternoon sun suffused the room with lemony light and the impression of heat. The studio has three sides of windows and four great skylights, which can open in the summer. The light is unfettered by shadow anywhere and now I stood in the midst of its power and my hand went to the canvas, nearly blinding in its whiteness. I pressed my fingers to it, closing my eyes and imagining what might go there, entering willingly the dream that allowed me to create. Then I reached for my brush.

"Alix, phone call!" Robin called from the kitchen door, shattering my concentration and bringing me out of the dream.

Clearing my head with a physical shake, I set the brush down and grabbed a rag to wipe my hands. Mark's first question was, "Who was that?"

"Robin. She's here from Hospice."

"Nice voice."

"She's wonderful."

"So how are things?" Mark never mentioned my father by name anymore.

"Why don't you come for dinner and we'll tell you."

"I can't, Alix. I'm actually still in New York. I just thought we could talk a little." His voice is Mark's barometer, revealing emotion when his words do not.

"Sure." I wished I'd closed up my paints, but settled down on the wide-board floor to listen to him. My preoccupations had so removed him from my circle of concern that a flash of guilt jolted me. Beyond our recent troubles, I knew that we cared for each other. He needed to have me listen. "How is the assignment going?"

"Good." Again his voice revealed his inner concern.

"Tell me about it."

For half an hour he filled me in on his assignment, a photo essay on AIDS babies in a hospital in Manhattan. He'd spent the week shooting photos of these children, their parents, foster parents, the staff who care for them. "They wanted my perspective as a small-town writer seeing this firsthand for the first time. It's so horrible, Alix. You have no idea."

"Your pictures will show it to me."

"I don't think I can do it."

"Why?" I sat up.

"Because I can't put what I've seen on paper."

"You've just told me about it. Write it just that way, and the rest will come."

"Alix, they put in my arms a tiny infant. That baby,

weak and sick, looked up at me and made eye contact. I held out my finger, and it took it."

"That's sweet, Mark," I murmured, trying to picture him actually holding a child.

"Then, today, they told me he'd died." I heard his voice break and I felt my own tears rise.

"Mark, come home."

"No. I can't. I have to finish it. I just wanted to talk to you about it. I'll do it." His voice had cleared and I could sense his control was back. "If you have help now, why don't you come to New York for the weekend?"

"I can't, Mark. Robin is only here for a little while each day. Besides, I can't leave him now. He's failing fast."

"Okay."

"Mark, it's a little like being with the AIDS babies—there is only a short time to make him happy and comfortable. And that is the only thing I can do right now. Don't ask me to forfeit even a day of it. It would ultimately be a day I would regret."

"You'd regret being with me?"

"Not being with you, but being away from him. Certainly you can understand that?" I was standing now, and the always dormant anger that Mark seemed so capable of provoking in me lately began to awaken.

"Of course I do," he answered, with only a fraction of hesitation. "I'll be home in another week. I'll come by."

"I need you, Mark. I could use your support."

"And I could use yours."

It was no good, the dream state I had worked in was shattered, so I covered up my canvas and banked the fire. Robin had left and Dad was quiet in a morphine daze. I thumped around the kitchen for a while, sorting out misplaced dishes from Robin's efforts. My mind traveled over the past week, rambling between the effect Robin's presence had had on us already and my conversation with Mark. I wondered, too, why Lee hadn't returned my call and a sudden rise of concern made me drop the dish towel and head for the phone.

Once again Mrs. Greaves answered, but this time Lee was there.

"Lee, are you okay?"

"Yes, why?"

"Your migraine. I hadn't heard back from you, so I got worried."

"How did you know . . ." He paused. "Ah, I think I understand."

"You never got my message, did you?"

"Nope."

"She's very protective of you."

"I know." I could tell by his voice that Mrs. Greaves had not left the room. I assumed Lee was using the phone in the kitchen. "Is your dad all right?"

I told him about Robin and the morphine pump and how quickly, even in a week's time, he had begun to fail. "He can't get out of bed now and Visiting Nurses come in twice a day. Otherwise I tend to him, and I've begun to wish that I'd taken up nursing as my Aunt Mildred always advocated when I mentioned art school. It would have served me well now."

"You're doing just fine. I watched you with him, and I know it isn't easy, being parent to a parent, but you're doing it. Do you want me to come down?"

"Lee, I can't keep asking you to break your schedule. Of course I want you here, but it isn't fair of me to ask it of you."

snappy, irreverent, political, and aesthetic conversations of old were gone and in their place loomed domestic concerns. Flashes of old interests sometimes showed, little blazes of heat lightning, telling me that all this was temporary for them, that someday they would return and engage the outside world again.

Robin was a nice contrast to my other domesticated friends. Her two daughters were past the stages of infancy and early childhood and Robin was independent enough not to need to speak of them in terms of defining her own life.

"To age and all its privileges." I raised my glass of Chianti.

"Like what?"

"Like not being carded." I struggled to find another privilege.

"I bet you're still carded some places."

"That's not exactly true." But I was pleased with the compliment. "And you certainly don't look a day over twenty-eight."

We continued on in that vein for a long time, our association being so one-dimensional we had a hard time seeking out other topics. We only knew each other through this episode in my life. "Episode," that's what Robin called it. It was like television. Tune in next week and see if Alix Miller's dad has died and she's gotten on with her life.

But after a glass and a half of Chianti we began to mellow into that freestyle familiarity between women.

"So what's with you and Mark? Your dad seems to think your not marrying Mark has something to do with him."

"Oh God, no. First of all, even if he asked me, I'm

not sure I would do it, and I certainly haven't remained an old maid because of Dad." Yet when I spoke those words I wondered at the tinny sound my lack of conviction gave them. Is that what I really wanted, for Mark to ask me to marry him?

"Why call yourself an old maid? Aren't we past that yet? It's the nineties, after all."

"Right. Well, you know how it is. If you haven't been married or divorced by thirty-five, you're either gay or ugly."

"And?"

"Neither. Just not ready to do the domestic bit."

"Artistic temperament?"

"Maybe. Artists are sublimely selfish people. We need privacy and space. I can't imagine myself putting away my paints to go fix dinner or run to a PTA meeting."

"Maybe you just haven't met the right man."

"You have pizza on your chin."

I took a bite of my own, less because I wanted it than I needed to think about what she said.

"So tell me about Lee."

The moment she said his name I realized I'd been thinking about him.

Robin lifted a gooey piece of pizza, catching the string of mozzarella on her tongue and reeling it in.

"You know about him," I hedged.

"Not really. You're very quiet about him. I know more about Mr. Mark than I do this mysterious night visitor."

I pushed the melted cheese back onto my slice of pizza, remembering then that night in Riseborough and our impromptu pizza party in front of the fire. I looked up to meet Robin's brown eyes. "I think he may be my best friend."

"Funny thing to say about a guy."

"He's very special. He's, well, different."

"Nice different?"

I smiled. "Physically different."

Robin's dark eyebrows shot up under her bangs. "How? Is he gay?"

"He has acromegaly. Do you know what that is?"

"Gigantism? Abnormal growth, right?" She bit into a second slice.

"Right."

"So he's not handsome."

I choked on my wine, sending myself into a coughing fit. Control regained, I answered, "No. Rather like a drunk Thomas Hart Benton had drawn him. But he's not horrible," I found myself going on. "He's so wonderful that it's easy to forget he's not easy to look at. I mean, it would be logical that his soul would be as ugly as his face, but it's not. It's like he's trapped in this monstrous body."

"Like the Beast in the story."

I set down my slice of pizza and wiped my hands, surprised at a moistness in my eyes, which was not forced there by my choking. "Yes. Exactly. And like the Beast, he lives reclusively, afraid of other people."

"But not you."

"No. Not me."

"You must be Beauty."

Twelve

I CAME TO DREAD FOUR O'CLOCK IN THE MORNING. The Nightingales said it was the hour of death. I don't think they, or whichever one of them it was, meant to upset me, rather that I should begin to expect the end soon. I'd wake, listen, and wait. Straining, I would listen for Dad's stertorous breathing and relax again to fall asleep. If I didn't hear anything, I would creep down the stairs like a child and come to stand beside his bed. I'd watch his labored breaths, my own breaths urging his on.

It was late March and the date of my show had long gone by. I noted its passing with regret, and a little bout of self-pity. Robin caught me arranging what would have been my five exhibition pieces. "Nice stuff."

"Thanks." I flushed a little, taken aback by her praise. "Someday I'll bore you with my portfolio."

"I wish I could do something like this, something meaningful."

"Oh Robin, how can you say something like that? What you do takes more nerve and talent than my meager work here. What you do is so sublimely meaningful. And so lacking in the self-absorption that drives my kind of work."

"Giving the world a great painting can never be selfish," she protested, but I don't think she understood what I meant.

I wanted to explain to her, but at that moment Mark walked into the studio.

I hadn't seen him in a few weeks, not since before he'd gone to New York to do the article on the AIDS babies. As usual, he looked good and I could see a slight rise in Robin's eyebrows. I hastily made introductions and Robin left us alone in the cold studio.

"Will you go in to see Dad?" I asked Mark after a little while.

He looked up from cleaning his camera lens and didn't answer. I could see the reluctance in his hooded eyes. Finally he capped the lens and sighed. "Yeah, I will. Maybe later."

"He'll be happy to see you."

"He barely knows me."

"Mark, I don't believe you!" I heard shrillness in my voice and I stopped. "Look, it's no big deal. Do it or don't. Don't agonize."

"I said later. I mean it." He stood up and came over to where I was leaning against the chopping block. He put his arms around me and slowly rocked me in time with the soft music filtering into the kitchen from the living room. Slowly he lowered his face to mine and kissed me. Meeting the resistance of my hard mouth, he said, "Don't set up walls, Alix."

"I'm not. This is my reality right now, and you need to be involved in it if you care about me."

"I care." Again his mouth covered mine and this time I gave in. "Let's take a little break, you need some diversion and Robin's here. No excuses, get your keys and let's go for a ride."

I would have declined, I would have fought to stay put, but I knew that he was right, a break would do me good. "All right, but just for an hour."

My apartment is less than a mile from Dad's house, so we decided to walk. The fresh March air was still chill from winter's relentless possession; our breath came out in filmy puffs, and I remembered as a child pretending to smoke, my parallel fingers mimicking my mother's cigarette fingers. By the time we got to my place we were chilled by the cold and hot for each other. It had been a long time since the hotel in Boston and my desire had long been beaten back by the siege engines of grief and exhaustion. Heedless of the stagnant cold air of the closed-up apartment, we flung ourselves together like yin and yang.

For a moment all the tension and stress melted out of me and I floated above it all, empty of all emotion, hovering in that touch-made illusion of peace.

We cuddled together under the body-warmed blankets and soaked in the last rays of afterglow. Finally Mark shifted and sat up, pulling me against his chest. "Alix, I was right."

"About what?"

"They offered me a job, staff photographer."

"The *Times*?" I pulled away from him, but he held me back against him.

"None other. The thing is, Alix, it means living

there." His hand stroked my bare arm. "I'll be traveling all over the world, but I'll be based in New York."

This was the point where he was supposed to say, "And I want you to come with me," and the point where I was supposed to say yes. Forget that I hate New York and forget that I wasn't at all sure I loved Mark enough to make that sacrifice. I was at that stage of womanhood where settling down was seriously overdue.

I wanted to scream, "But what about us?" Except that a small, undefined as yet, part of me was wild with the relief that the spectre of permanency in our relationship had now withdrawn. Equally I wondered at his callousness. Had he really seen our relationship as so casual, so insignificant, that I was very nearly the last to know about his move, or had I moved so far away from him in my own recent troubles that I hadn't heard him? As always, nothing was simple where Mark was concerned.

I hugged him and managed to rise above the thousand conflicting emotions fighting for eminence. "I'm happy for you, Mark. It's what you've been working so hard to do."

"I start right away." He shifted a little. "The thing is, Alix, I'm leaving today."

"You've already got a place to live?" I was drowning in a mixture of relief and abandonment.

"I'm sharing with a couple of guys until I find my own place. We're all on the road, so it should work out. No one will be around enough to get on each other's nerves."

"So this is really a good-bye," I said finally, unable to look him in the face for fear he'd be constrained to say something he didn't feel.

"No, no, of course not. I know that once"—he

caught himself a little—"once you can, you'll come to see me, and I'll be back as often as I can."

"I'm going to take a shower." I slipped away from his touch and into the icy bathroom.

Running the water as hot as I could stand it, I stood under the stream and shook. The water began to cool as the tank ran out and I slammed the faucet off. Steam filled the tiny bathroom and I cleared a porthole of mirror with the end of my towel. There was my face, pale, darkened only by the circles under my eyes. My hair tumbled down from the towel, and in the harsh fluorescent light I saw a possible streak of silver in the light brown. Not much longer, I promised myself, and realized for the first time the relief I would have when it was all over. I wanted it to be over. I wanted to get on with my life.

Bundling on my flannel robe, I rewrapped my hair and came out into the living room, where Mark lounged, my sketchbook in his lap.

"I'll go make coffee."

I had just put the fire under the kettle when I heard laughter and Mark sidled into the kitchen, my sketchbook in his hands. "Alix, I can't believe you let me be jealous of this!" Hooting with laughter, he handed me the book, its thick pages turned to a sketch of Lee. Underneath I had written, "Lee and Bad-dog in the Library." It was one of the better sketches of Lee, in the sense that it looked like him, a study intended to develop what would go into the portrait. Of course, it was a picture of an ugly man.

"God, to think I was worried."

It was only simple ignorance, but his attitude appalled me. "You bastard," I said, shutting off the burner.

"Hey, Alix, don't get mad. You weren't playing fair

with me making me think this guy was a rival." He was still laughing but the raw anger on my face penetrated. "Alix, I'm sorry. I know I was just stupid."

"At one time you might have been stupid to think Lee Crompton was a rival, but certainly not because of what he looks like."

"Alix, take it easy, I was kidding. I'm sure he's a great guy. You just should have told me."

I was beyond anger now. This man was about to leave me behind, and yet had the ego to speak to me of rivals for his attention.

We walked back to my father's in silence. The air had gotten drier and our breath no longer preceded us.

Thirteen

I WOKE ABRUPTLY, FULLY AWAKE AND ALERT. HAD I heard my name or had I dreamt it? Four o'clock. Already the spring dawn was weakening the absolute dark of the night. The cold in the unheated room was winter-deep, and I pulled on a heavy sweater as I went downstairs. As I reached the fifth step, warmth touched me and I could hear the faithful old furnace roaring in the basement. I tugged my hair out from under the sweater and stole toward the lamplight of the living room.

In the past few days he had begun the descent into death. Most of my time had been spent simply sitting next to him; he was rarely awake, as the expenditure of energy he needed to live exhausted him. An IV against the inevitable dehydration, and a catheter discreetly leading out from under the bedsheet to a bottle on the floor, were the lines that held him to this world. The Nightingales came twice a day to bathe him and rub soft lotion into his papery skin against the threat of bedsores. He'd become so delicate that even a wrinkle in the sheet could destroy his skin. Even if we were helpless against what was destroying him internally, we could keep his external body comfortable.

Robin sat forward in her chair, leaning over my father but not touching him. She heard my steps and turned with a smile. "Come to him, Alix. It's time." She stood up and embraced me, then left the room. I heard the front door close gently and the start of her engine.

I knelt beside my father's bed. I could hear Dad's breath, raspy in the stillness. The death rattle. In the mild lamplight, his face was gray and whiskery, no longer the face I knew, but the face of a stranger lingering on a foreign shore. The oxygen tubes glistened in the light, yet he labored for breath in the body's own instinctive struggle.

"Don't fight it, Dad. It's okay to go. I love you." I stroked his forehead with one hand, the other clutched his hand. "I love you, Dad."

My father struggled against letting go. The raspy moist breathing increased, irregular, painful to hear. He made sounds, but no words.

I remembered then Robin's talk of helping her dying husband over the bridge to death. I let go of Dad's hands and held my own up to be taken. "Take my hand, Dad. Let me take you there, let me take you halfway. We'll go to the bridge together. When we get there, when we get to the middle, I'll turn around and come back. But you must go on ahead. Mom's there. She'll be on the other side. Come with me, Dad, it's time to go."

Beneath the closed eyelids I could see movement, as if he were watching something.

"It's not a long walk, Dad. There's no pain on the other side. Let me take you."

A flower blooming against all odds, Dad's hand rose from the blanket. The tremor suddenly gone, he placed it in my hand and his fingers closed over mine.

My face wet with unvoiced tears, I laid my cheek against his chest and waited.

Fourteen

Early on Dad and I had planned his funeral. "No use denying it needs to be done"—he'd been a little sharp with me—"and I'd like to have some say. Now, no primitive rituals. No calling hours, no open casket, none of that stuff."

"How about a New Orleans jazz band?" I scruffed a charcoal shading onto the sketch I was making of him.

"That's good. I kind of like that idea. They really know how to send a person off!"

We'd gone with a simple Service of Commitment at graveside. So many of his friends and scattered relatives had responded to our request to come visit him while he was able that we did not feel the need to go further with the ceremonial aspect of his death. They had seen him to say good-bye while it counted. Thus only a handful of us stood out on that mud-rich March afternoon, the air full of imagined spring. The Hospice people, our faithful VNA nurses, one or two friends who were closer than most, and dear Robin made up the majority of the group. Mark had called with his condolences, but had not offered to come.

"Do you want me to come?" Lee had asked, and I knew it was something he would do if I said yes.

"Lee, you don't need to come, I have plenty of support here now. But I would like to come up and finish the portrait as soon as possible. I need to get away from here."

I smiled at the sudden relief in his voice. "By all means, come as soon as you can. Everything is waiting for you. Just come."

"Okay. I have one or two things to take care of here and I'll be there."

"Alix?"

"I'm here," I said.

"Are you really okay?"

His sweet concern sent a trilling of emotion through me. "Lee, what would I have ever done without you?"

It was harder than I had thought it would be. The brief service seemed so abrupt after the prolonged waiting for death. The brown casket perched on the metal bars seemed so sad, impossible that it contained the shell of the man who had been my father. For a moment I regretted not having the archaic open-casket ritual, the primitive need to see the deceased one last time. I shook off the regret, the man who had died with my hand holding his bore no resemblance to the man who had shown me how to put life in the eyes of a painting with a simple stroke. No, eventually I would remember him as he had been, not as he died. Not too tall, a little portly in his middle years. I would remember his laughter, not the emaciated wraith he'd been at the end.

As I lay my bouquet of roses on top of the casket at the end of the service I saw Robin. I smiled at her and was suddenly struck by the fact that she too was soon to be out of my life. I couldn't bear that, and the first tears of the day stung my eyes.

"Stop that right now." Robin handed me a wad of Kleenex. "I'm fixed tight in your life, my friend. You know that the friends of adversity are friends forever. Besides, I want you to be my witness when John and I get married next year." And in that fashion, Robin announced her engagement to the man she'd mentioned with increasing frequency over cups of coffee. A moment later John Betters joined us and offered his condolences in a soft and sincere voice.

Afterward a few people came back to the house. By the time the sandwiches were all gone, the false spring afternoon had given way to snow clouds. The last to go, Robin and John stopped me in the hallway. "We're going out for Chinese. . . ."

"No, you two go on ahead, I think I'll just open a can of soup. I really don't feel like going out," I said, convincing them easily. I hated the idea of being alone, but their apparent need for time together was obvious to me and I smiled as they dashed down the porch steps, promises of an eggroll called back at me. As they drove off, the first flakes of the late season snow began.

The heavy front door closed me in, and I was alone. I puttered about, lining up the many cards that had arrived, sticking my fingers into the arrangements that people had sent in lieu of making a donation to the American Cancer Society. I stood for a moment in the doorway of the living room but did not go in.

I ran a broom down the gritty front hall and shook

out the tatty little rug. I stood there on the front porch with the brown and green rug in my hand and snapped it again and again, the bits of sand flinging back and stinging my face. Suddenly the old fabric tore in my hands and I viciously wrenched it in two, flinging the halves out into the yard. Heedless of the cold, I watched in fascination as the falling snow covered the two pieces of rug, burying them.

In fifteen minutes I was in my car and on the highway.

It had stopped snowing by the time I reached Waterville and the road was clear, so I sped up. My mind was utterly numb, the past three months had succeeded in preventing me from feeling anything right now. I fiddled with the radio and finally shut it off, jamming in a tape and forgetting to switch the mode button. Thus I drove on in silence, occasional tears running into the corners of my mouth, which I wiped away as if they were someone else's.

It was past ten o'clock when I took the exit to Riseborough. It had begun to snow again, the storm following me north. Depending on vague memory to find Lee's turnoff, I ended up in Riseborough proper and struggled to remember how to get there from the green. The convoluted country roads and the total absence of street signs confused me utterly and I had to backtrack to the green. The only lights still on that Wednesday night were those in the pizza place. I parked in front and dashed in, slipping a little on the snowy pavement.

"Do you have a pay phone?"

"There's one at the corner." The man behind the counter was the same as that other night, but this time the place was deserted and he was alone. "Don't go out, use mine." He lifted a black rotary dial phone onto the counter. "Local call, right?"

"Thank you, yes." I struggled to get my trembling fingers into the holes of the dial.

Mrs. Greaves answered with a slightly alarmed tone and I realized that she had probably been asleep. "Mrs. Greaves, it's Alix Miller. I'm so sorry to wake you, but I'm in Riseborough and I'm lost!" I saw the guy behind the counter smirk a little.

Before she could say anything, Lee's voice came on the extension. "Alix, are you all right? Where are you?"

"Tony's Pizza." I smiled at the guy. "I'm sorry, Lee. I took you at your word and just ran off."

"I'll be right there," Lee said, brooking no suggestion that he simply give me directions. I laid the receiver back in its cradle and Tony, as I thought of him, put it back under the counter and then placed a slice of pizza in front of me.

"You can't loiter here." He went back to reading his magazine and I studied the melted cheese atop the slice.

Twenty minutes later I saw the headlights of a car and I went to the glass-front door to see Lee's station wagon pull up beside my Sentra. I burst from the restaurant to the car with more apologies, quickly stifled.

"Leave your car here. We'll come get it tomorrow."

I unlocked the trunk of my car so that Lee could lift my hastily packed bag. The bag from the museum store, long forgotten in the trunk of the car, poked out from under the spare tire where it had lodged. I reached in and hauled it out.

"Hop in." He shut the door for me, and got in.

"I'm sorry to do this to you," I began again. "I probably dragged you out of bed. . . ."

"I did say 'just come.' " Lee laughed, and the sound

shattered the embarrassment that had enclosed me.

The snow burst around the wagon in sudden obscuring squalls. Lee drove on, concentrating now on the road. As we eased out onto the winding road that led to Lee's gate, a deer leapt out in front of the car. Momentarily dazzled by the car's high beams, it froze. Lee touched the brake and we slid a little, fishtailing on the empty road. Lee's arm was flung across my chest in an instinctive protective thrust. The deer broke and ran.

A few minutes later we were home, shaking the snow off our boots and creeping through the darkened kitchen. In the library Lee poured us both a little sherry. We sat facing each other in front of the cold fireplace. I sipped the sweet liquor and felt its loosening attributes relax me.

"Was it so very awful, Alix?"

"The service?"

"Yes, the service, that and it all being over. You've been absolutely focused for three months, and suddenly it was finished. Like a competition when you prepare for months for a minute's shot at glory. I suspect that's what made you run away."

"There I was, all alone. All the visitors gone, the flowers already beginning to wilt, and that goddamn hospital bed still in the middle of the living room. What was it doing there? Why were the oxygen tanks and piles of johnnies still there?" My voice began to pitch higher and I was almost sick to my stomach. "I didn't understand. Dad was dead, and everything was still there. Robin is introducing her fiancé and everyone was pretending it was all back to normal. Even me. We all were acting as if he'd just gone out for a walk."

Lee hitched to the front of his chair and leaned his elbows on his knees.

"It was so fucking quiet. Then I tore the rug by accident. I hated that rug, the little one by the front door. The one Dad bought Mom and she hated it too but never told him."

All the built-up tension and anger and grief overtook me then and I shook as if with palsy, but the tears would not come to relieve the pain.

Lee stretched out his hands. "What can I do? What can I do to make it better?"

"Just hold me."

We faced each other. I met his kind blue eyes and read the reluctance in them. I knew what I was asking. I knew it was so very difficult for him. Except on that day when he'd held me in his arms as we skated over the ice, Lee had never touched me, had shied away from being touched.

"I need to be held, I need you to hold me."

"Alix, I . . ." His mobile and ugly face contorted with a private anguish.

"Please."

He stood and opened his arms. I went into their safe harbor and welcomed the weight of his arms around me, tenderly holding me close in acknowledgment of my fragility. His wool sweater scratched my cheek, then absorbed the flood of tears, which, at his touch, were released like poison from a wound. His cheek rubbed against my hair and he murmured to me as if to a child. Slowly his arms strengthened, closer and closer he held me, and my own arms went around him until we held each other.

As naturally as weeping, I raised my lips to his, and for one instant they were gently met. At once he let go of me.

Fifteen

Early morning sun warmed the solarium. My easel and paints were exactly as I had left them back in January, thinking then that I was only going away for the weekend. A sheet covered the portrait, and now, alone in the room, I flipped it back and scowled. It was all wrong. I had painted the still faceless form of a man, yet even the posture was not Lee at all but some contrived image. Anyone who knew him would never think a good thing of this painting. I stirred up a jar of gesso and began painting the whole thing out. Big fat strokes of white obliterated the stranger I had painted.

Lee came in, coffee tray in hand. I had the eerie feeling that no time had elapsed, that I had never gone away. I had expected some tension between us, the awkwardness of last night's scene playing itself out in my head overnight, but if he felt awkward, Lee gave no hint of it. When I looked at him, pouring out the mugs of coffee and measuring out my half-teaspoon of sugar, a curious feeling of relief flooded me, as if I'd come home from a long unhappy journey. Whatever else, we were still friends.

"I'm starting all over." I took the mug from him and pointed to the white canvas. "It wasn't any good."

"Really?"

"I once told you that I needed to know my subjects before I could paint them. Well, I know you now. What I paint this time will really be you."

"Frightening thought," he jibed, as he went to the stool and sat down.

I shook my head. "No, no more posed pictures."

"How else can you paint a portrait?"

"Just get comfortable and talk with me. I'll handle the details."

"I know what I've missed about you."

"What?"

"Your reticence."

I heaved a wadded paper towel at his head.

The morning sessions went too quickly. I knew what I wanted to do, and the paint went on easily, my hand moving instinctively to stroke the colors into place. I deliberately began to slow down, afraid that once done, the planned-for future, the "after it's over" time of new life would have to be invented. My life could not stay the same, yet I did not see the road I wanted on my life map.

"You're looking pensive." Lee came in, lighting the lamp next to me, as it had grown dark.

"Do I?"

"What's the matter?"

I shrugged. "I don't know. Maybe I've just had too much to think about, too many upheavals. I'm feeling a little at a crossroads, and I don't know what to do next. I should decide what to do about my father's house and whether or not to stay where I am. I need to find a job. But I haven't got the strength to face any of these problems."

"So give it time. Maybe in a month you'll know what you want to do." He stood up and rested his hand on the back of my neck. I leaned a little against it. "There's no hurry, Alix. No need to make any choices right now." He dropped his hand and moved to the stereo.

"The other thing is that I know I haven't come to terms with Mark's going to New York. I'm still feeling like a decision was made for me that I had no voice in. On the other hand, I wouldn't have wanted to make that choice out of some misguided fear of being alone." I thought of our last time together. "Truthfully, Mark wasn't always all that wonderful to be around, he can be very ugly."

"Like me?"

I wouldn't let him get away with it. "No, Lee. Not like you." I took the CD from his hand. "You are the most beautiful person I know. Beautiful where it counts"—I pressed one hand over his heart—"right here."

He turned away as always, but not before I felt a crack in the wall around my heart. Just out of sight, I knew my path was near.

I hung up Bad-dog's leash in the mudroom and kicked off my boots.

"Alix?"

"Right here!" I called to Lee.

"Look what I found." He met me in the hallway

and we went into the solarium. He handed me two photos.

"Are these your parents?" The photos were of portraits, one of a middle-aged man and the other of an exquisite woman, shown full-length, her sable coat draped dramatically around her.

"Yes, these are the paintings your grandfather did. I was a little boy then, but I remember him. Don't look for any family resemblance, it's long gone."

"Your mother is beautiful." The portrait showed a fine-boned woman, a woman whose beauty had deepened with the passage of time. Probably forty in the painting, she held her head with a tilt to her chin that implied a certain satisfaction with life. A slight smile teased on her lips and I was pleased with my grandfather's work. "Is it like her?"

"Very."

"Mrs. Greaves tells me you don't see her much."

"Ever." He noted my silent curiosity. "We speak on the phone once a week. She just has never been able to come to terms with me."

"Your own mother?"

"Not very maternal, is it?"

"I can't imagine it. She's lost something very valuable."

He shrugged. "My Boston Brahmin mother had one child, probably against her wishes, one who turned out somewhat rebellious, and, in the end, quite unpresentable."

"Surely she loves you?"

He stood contemplating the photo, then said, "In her own selfish way, perhaps."

I touched his shoulder, a comradely touch, and for once he didn't shrug me off.

"So how's our portrait coming?" His abrupt change of conversation startled me out of my thoughts.

"Take a look and see for yourself."

"Someday."

"Someday it will be green with mold in some damp cellar."

"No, I intend to send it to my mother as a gift."

"I thought you were going to store it for some future discovery."

"I'll let my mother do that."

I was shaken a little by his words. I didn't know what to say, so said the obvious. "It's nearly done."

He set the two photos down on the work table near my paint box. Slowly he raised his face and smiled at me. "Go slow, okay?"

"I am."

Sixteen

THE ALMOST SPRINGLIKE AIR OF THE DAY BEFORE chilled dramatically and we were plunged back into winter as a second March snowstorm blew in from Canada. It seemed to me as though Riseborough was always in the grips of winter, and I couldn't begin to imagine the stark oaks on the town green in full leaf.

Bad-dog whined and paced and finally we shrugged ourselves into our coats and took him out. The big mutt cavorted around the fresh snow, burying his brown nose in it and tossing it into the air. Lee tossed snowballs for him, and we laughed as the puzzled dog looked all around for the disappearing balls. The storm had subsided by late afternoon, reduced to fat moist flakes that would not survive the next intimation of spring. A palette of grays moved swiftly overhead; charcoal gray and seal gray clouds blew along, the arctic wind freezing them into shape and sending them to the sea. Above them the pale gray sky and below a few white wisps clung to the mountaintops. I pulled a pencil and small notebook out of my parka pocket. We paused for a little while at Wiggy's Pond so that I could sketch.

Announced by the crunch of their footsteps breaking through the snow-covered grass, two young boys burst through the tree line, a toboggan skimming along behind them. Reflexively, Lee turned his face away, pulling his hood close. They quickly passed us and disappeared into the woods. Bad-dog trotted off behind them.

"Hey, Bad-dog, come back!" I called.

Lee shook his head, the hood slipping off. "Forget it, he's an incorrigible boy-follower. He'll come home when they do."

My fingers were frozen and I stuffed the pencil and notebook back into my kangaroo pocket. Lee's hand suddenly dipped into my pocket, pulling out the book. He held it up in the fading sunlight, and nodding, said, "Nice, very nice. You've got a light touch with landscape. Will you paint me another one someday?"

My mittenless fingers touched his as I took back the book. I could feel a warmth in my cheeks; the sweet sense of pleasure in his approbation was almost overshadowed by that of his easy familiarity in taking the book from my pocket.

There was a filmy barrier between us. Every day that passed and I painted his portrait and spent hours with him I felt this film bulge with pressure. Someday, I knew, this film, this barrier, would be penetrated and there would be a perfect understanding between us.

"That damn dog," Lee muttered as he shut the mudroom door against the frigid air. "I've never known him to not come home."

"Maybe the boys thought he was a stray and took him home."

Lee shook his head. "He's got a license and a name tag, no excuse."

"Lee, maybe they took off his collar. You know little boys. 'Hey Mom, look what followed me home.' "

Lee smiled his crooked grin and tugged at my loose braid. "Right." I loved the feel of his hand on my hair.

It was a Thursday, and we helped ourselves to left-over stew as we balanced on the bar stools against the island counter. The tall kitchen windows looked out over the back garden, and as we ate it began to snow again, the hard little flakes sparkling in the flood-lights. Just as we finished loading the dishwasher Mrs. Greaves came in.

"Town's all a flutter tonight, Mr. Lee," she said as she shook the snow from her kerchief. "Two young boys've gone missing."

I dropped a fork and it hit the floor with a bounce.

Lee bent to pick it up. "For how long?"

Mrs. Greaves shrugged. "They aren't sure. The kids had a half-day of school today, teacher workshop days or something. You ask me, they're out all too often."

"Mrs. Greaves, how long do they think the boys have been gone?"

"Could be from noon onward. They've got the search teams all forming down on the green right now."

"Mrs. Greaves, we saw two boys this afternoon, near Wiggy's." I shut the dishwasher and looked at Lee. "Who are the boys?"

"Tommy Lewis and Travis something. About twelve years old."

"Travis Michalik. His father is my attorney." Lee

turned to me. "Alix, what about the boys you saw today?"

"About twelve would be my guess."

"What were they wearing?"

I thought back—one had waved at me, the one who'd worn blue. "A dark blue jacket and the other one, a brownish down vest and an oatmeal-colored sweater underneath. I could see snow pants on both of them, not jeans."

"Hats?"

"I suppose. Don't all little boys wear hats?" I was a little puzzled at this intense questioning.

"Boots?"

"Yes, and gloves."

"Good, if they're lost, maybe they're fairly well protected."

"They were pulling a toboggan."

"Ah"—Lee rubbed his chin—"dressed for sledding. Probably headed for one of the clearings."

Then I recognized it—it was Harris Bellefleur working. Lee reached for the phone.

"The police pretty much figured out the same thing we have," Lee said, hanging up. "But knowing they were near Wiggy's might help narrow the field down. They've got about fifty searchers."

"Will they let us know if they find them?"

"I hope so." Lee stared out into the floodlit backyard. "I should have looked at them, Alix. Maybe then they would have run home instead of going on. After all, the woods are full of monsters."

"Lee, that's absurd."

"It's happened before."

"And I should have called out to the boys, asked where they were going."

"At least you looked at them, and you've got an artist's eye. The detail on the boys' clothing identified them immediately to the police."

"I'm glad of that."

He stood for a long time leaning against the kitchen window; only the periodic tapping of his fingers against the molding revealed his inner agitation. The snow dazzled like silver confetti in the floodlights, hard and cold. The wind swirled it into eddies that skipped along the brick walkway. Beyond, out of reach of the floodlights, yet luminous in its bulk, lay the mountainside.

"Every year or so someone dies on that hill." He shifted his weight, the crookedness of his shoulders becoming more pronounced.

"Lee, I'm sure they'll be all right. It hasn't been all that long." Even as I said them, the words seemed ludicrous, platitudes from bad television.

"Eight hours is a long time, Alix. Exposure is a hell of a way to die."

"What can we do?"

Lee turned away from the window. "I can search through the trails above here. There are a lot of connecting routes between here and Wiggy's, and if they were looking for new toboggan runs, they might have ventured too far and ended up over this way. If Baddog's with them, he'll hear me a long ways off. I just have to whistle and listen."

"My very first day here I got lost in those woods. By the grace of God I tumbled out of them and landed, as I recall, at your feet."

"I remember." He placed one great hand on my shoulder.

I touched his hand and gripped his wrist. "I'm going

with you. No one should go out alone on that mountain."

He didn't argue, only increased the pressure on my shoulder slightly before pulling away.

The needle-like snow beat on us, clinging to eyelashes and scarves, burning the skin with cold. We carried heavy flashlights and in his backpack Lee carried a thermos of hot coffee, dry mittens, socks, and a wool blanket. I carried a second wool blanket in my backpack with sandwiches. Mrs. Greaves had packed this winter picnic with disapproval evident in her tight lips. "You'll catch your death and to what end? Let the officials do their job."

"Mrs. Greaves, that's not very neighborly of you," Lee chided gently.

"Police will find them." She jammed the sandwiches into my backpack, nearly taking me off my feet in doing so. "Miss Miller needn't go with you, she should stay here with me."

"Mrs. Greaves, I couldn't sit still. Really, this is what I want to do."

"Uh huh." There was something so skeptical in her eyes that I turned away. It was as if she doubted my intentions.

After we were out for about an hour, I knew that Lee was right, exposure would be a hell of a way to die. I tried not to think of the two boys, huddled together, the snow settling over their cold bodies. And where was Bad-dog? We whistled until our lips grew chapped.

The new snow wasn't deep, but pockets of old snow, preserved beneath the canopy of pines, caught us at the knees, sucking us down and filling our boots. Despite the high-tech L.L. Bean clothing I wore, I was soon cold to the bone. The wind spun the treetops, its cold exhalations stinging our faces, blowing the needle-hard snow into our eyes and mouths. We both wore woolen scarves looped across our lower faces, but the driven snow eagerly worked its way into the folds and against our skin, where it instantly melted into a cold wash.

We worked our way east to west, then back, doglegging up the southern face of the mountain. Lee directed our progress with a compass and fluorescent paint. It would not do to lose us, too.

I stumbled, catching my foot against a hidden root. I hit the snow hard with an audible *whoof.* Lee was by me in an instant, lifting me from the snow and brushing it from the front of me. Only his eyes were visible between his hat and the scarf.

"I'm okay, Lee." I let him help me to my feet.

"I think we should stop here."

"What?"

"I mean to rest for a few minutes. It's nearly midnight."

He pulled the scarf down and I remembered then my reaction to him the last time he had pulled me from the snow. But now it was not revulsion that shuddered through me.

"Lee . . ." I wanted to say what I felt, but there was something in his form, hunched over the thermos as he poured out the coffee, that twisted my sentence into something banal. "Thanks for picking me up once again."

"Never too often." He chuckled.

The little warmth I had enjoyed while moving dissipated, and I began shivering.

"Here, take one of the blankets." Lee reached for my discarded backpack.

"No, we'll need it dry when we find the boys."

I could tell by his silence that he had begun to doubt.

"We will find them, won't we?" I sounded like a child struggling to maintain a belief in the tooth fairy.

"I don't know, Alix. But I have to keep trying." The steam from the coffee he held in his hands rose, giving his monstrous face an ethereal and primitive look in the yellow torchlight.

"Do you know these boys well?"

"No. I know Jerry Michalik, the one boy's father. Decent chap. Always speaks of his son when he comes to the house. A hockey player, good student. His best pal is the other boy, Tommy. His parents run the bed-and-breakfast on the main road into Riseborough. They're both in sixth grade. Both honor roll students." Lee sighed then, and downed the last of his coffee.

"How do you know all this?"

"I read. The *Riseborough Sentinel* is a weekly paper devoted to telling neighbors about one another. I know more through that and my three or four loose connections in this town than I bet most people know about their neighbors in any city. And let us never forget the incredible information highway that is Mrs. Greaves."

I laughed, but felt sad. It wasn't the same. Not the same as potluck suppers and attendance at church, not the same kind of intimacy that bonds a person to their town or their neighborhood or even their family. He knew of them, yet he had not let those boys look at him as he'd sat there that afternoon enjoying the same last effort of winter as they were.

"Do you want me to take you home?"

"No!" I recapped the thermos. "I'm in this as long as it takes."

"Okay."

Suddenly I needed a simple hug. Just that kind of human contact that would confirm our resolve. I hesitated, though, a fraction too long and he shrugged on his backpack and consulted the compass. "This way," he directed, and I followed.

Mercifully the wind died down just after midnight. The still air was bitter cold, but suddenly we could hear the echo of our calls, and in the stillness our footsteps crunched in the hard old snow, underscoring the silence between our shouts. We climbed higher and higher into the wooded mountainside, the undergrowth thickening and the rocks beginning to jut out. The moon edged its way from behind the broken clouds and silvered our path.

"Lee, I can't believe that they could have come this far. It would have been dark two hours after we saw them, and they would have been lost long before they got this high."

"Maybe. But there's a clearing near the summit; if they made straight for that they might have actually gotten there in time to do some tobogganing. I think they might have gotten lost coming back down." Lee put his hands around his mouth and called, "Travis! Tommy!"

Our ears strained to hear the sound of young voices calling, or a dog barking. Nothing.

"After this pass we'll head west only. If I'm correct in assuming they did get to the summit, they'll have come back down initially on that side." He sounded breathless, his voice, raw from shouting, was gravelly.

"Lee, don't you think you'd better stop for a few minutes?" He was pushing himself, I knew it. Our sedate walks had often tired him, his awkward shape forcing him to work harder than another man might.

"No," he answered a little sharply, then stopped. "I'm sorry, I don't mean to be short with you. You've been great all night. I am a little tired, but, Alix, I don't dare stop. It's getting so late that any lost time could mean the difference."

"Lee, maybe they've been found. I don't think you should kill yourself."

"It doesn't matter. We keep at it, I keep at it, at least till dawn."

"Why, Lee?"

"Because . . ." He stopped, some truth captured before it slipped out.

"Lee? Why is it so important you find them?"

He came to a full stop then, the moonlight throwing his long shadow over me, his face reduced to only his eyes looking back at me with a sorrowful fullness. "Alix, once I was a man who had the same desires as any other to have children. Yet I never will, so the children of this little town . . ." He stopped, then went on. "Because I live life vicariously, I feel these boys are mine."

"But you won't even let them see you."

"No, I won't. But I read about their schoolboy victories and their Halloween parties and their acceptances to Harvard or their marriages to out-of-towners. I watch their growing up from my house on the hill and I know them. They don't need to know anything about me. That isn't important."

He turned back to the path and called, his hoarse voice barely carrying. I came up behind him and laid one hand on his arm, then shouted the boys' names as loud as I could. My echo reverberated back into my ears, mocking the timbre of boys' voices.

* * *

"Listen!" Lee hissed, bending a little to catch the sound. A crashing sound, undergrowth being buffeted, and suddenly Bad-dog burst through a stand of brush, tail wagging, long ears flapping with some doggy joy at finding his master standing there. Lee pulled off his mitten and thwacked the big dog on his side, then ran his hand down the silky reddish fur. "He's warm, his topcoat. He's been lying down on something—or someone—warm." Lee pulled his mitten back on and began retracing Bad-dog's footprints. The dog had scuffed through the snow, and in the light of the flashlights the parallel lines of his track were easy to follow.

Within minutes we found the toboggan, upended but not broken. We called more frantically. Now our greatest fear was that they had been injured, yet there was no sign of them near the sled.

"Most likely they deserted it when they realized they were lost," I conjectured.

"I don't think so. That's an expensive toboggan. Knowing young boys, they probably wouldn't dare leave it, more afraid of being yelled at than of being lost. I don't think they're far. We need to head downhill, bearing west."

I was slightly mystified. Then I remembered, this was Harris Bellefleur. Smiling to myself, I stepped into his footprints.

"Tommy! Travis!" Our voices wreathed the night with puffs of frozen exhalation. Then, like a miracle—no, more like a wish unexpectedly granted—voices answering ours.

"Here! Over here!" Just above and to the west, their sweet boy voices chimed through the dense undergrowth and we crashed through it, no longer mincing around the difficult thickets. The ancient tangle of puckerbrush and thorny whips of vines seemed to fight back, but Lee plowed on ahead.

There, huddled together beneath barricaded evergreen branches, were the two boys. Bad-dog immediately burrowed back in with them, turning back to face his master, his silly dog eyes delighted with his find.

"Are you okay?" Lee knelt in the snow in front of them, and I saw that he'd pulled his hat low and his woolen scarf tight around his face. Only his eyes showed and then only when the light from my flashlight touched him.

"We're so cold." One boy's voice shook more from emotion, I think, than shivering. They were beyond shivering. In the harsh beam of the flashlight they were blue with cold.

Lee quickly removed his gloves and touched their faces. I did the same and was alarmed by the depth of the cold. It was almost like touching the dead.

"I can't feel anything," the boy with the blue coat said.

Lee unzipped his coat and then began removing the boy's boots. He looked at me and I bent to do the same with the second boy.

"Travis, put your feet here," Lee said, and pulled the boy's feet under his sweater and against his bare skin. He winced with the cold, then laughed. "It's like shoving an icicle down my shirt!"

The boy laughed a little, but the tears of pain still glinted in the flashlight's glare.

In the meantime I had done the same with the second boy, who had to be Tommy. Feet secure against my body, I began rubbing his hands. They were so cold that my own seemed to burn with the touch of them.

"Get the blankets, Alix."

I wrapped the boys in the two woolen blankets and fished out the dry socks.

"Better?"

The boys nodded simultaneously.

"Okay, everyone onto the sled." After hefting first Tommy and then Travis onto the toboggan, Lee carefully tucked the blankets back around them, a shadow play of tucking little children into bed.

He picked up the rope and tugged. We were on a fairly level piece of ground and the toboggan stuck a little. He shifted it, then pulled again. I knew then that his strength was going. He'd exerted himself far beyond his reserves. I stood beside him and grasped the rope in my own frozen fingers. Together we pulled and the sled broke free.

"How did you know he was Travis?" I whispered as we hauled the toboggan.

"He's wearing a Blue Devils' jacket. Hockey player. Tommy didn't make the team." He leaned closer and whispered, "Not a very good skater."

"You really do know them, don't you?"

"Yes."

I laughed and tried not to think of the pain in my feet.

The first light of dawn grayed the sky as we descended the mountain. Rather than moving westward in the hopes of meeting more of the search party, we simply descended, following our own fluorescent blaze marks. It took forever, as we struggled to follow paths clear enough to pass the toboggan through. The boys fell asleep on the sled, Tommy's head pressed against Travis's back, Travis asleep bolt upright. Their sleeping bodies seemed so much heavier than their awake ones.

I moved like a sleepwalker. One foot in front of the other. The pain between my shoulder blades from the drag of the sled was like a knife between them. We stopped talking, our last reserves of strength needed just to move. I dreamt of my warm bed in the blue room even as I trudged through the heavy wet snow.

Downhill should have been easier, but eventually the weight of the toboggan forced itself against us and we fought to keep it in control. As the dawn clarified our surroundings, I looked at my companion and was alarmed at the grayness of his face. The scarf had slipped away and exhaustion had deepened the cragginess of his features. He seemed hewn from the very rocks we negotiated around.

"Lee, we need to stop for a few minutes."

"Alix, are you all right? I didn't mean to make this a marathon for you."

"Lee, I'm fine. I just think a short rest would do us both good." I looked back at our cargo. "They'll sleep."

He nodded and dropped the rope. He yawned and seemed to notice for the first time that it was nearly full light. "Beautiful, isn't it?"

"You've done a wonderful thing here tonight, Lee."

"So have you." He raised his arms and stretched. "Thank God we found them."

"You found them, Lee. I just came along, Tonto to your Lone Ranger."

He turned then, and for one fleeting instant I thought he was going to put his arm around me, but he only touched my shoulder. "Alix, I couldn't have done it without you. You were my mainstay, and you probably don't even know at what point I would have given up if you weren't here."

I didn't know what to say, so joked, "Well, Kemo sabe, shall we finish this trek and go get some breakfast?"

I could see the house. With full dawn the wind had picked up a little, yet was, it seemed, a little warmer.

"Why don't you go on ahead, Alix. Call the police and let them know we have the boys."

I let go of the rope and plunged down the slope, Bad-dog gamboling beside me in canine enthusiasm for the latest move in this all-night game. The back door opened even before I reached it. Mrs. Greaves, bundled in her overcoat, darted out, Willie just behind her. "Where is he? Is he all right?"

"Yes, we've got them, Mrs. Greaves, we found them." I was breathless suddenly and felt the tingling of exhaustion in my eyes. "Please, call the police." She stayed where she was, staring past me and toward the path to the trails. I pushed past her and went to the phone. Almost before Lee reached the yard, I heard the wail of the ambulance and the cacophony of emergency sirens. The dawn silence carried their sound to us from miles away. I went back out to help carry in the boys.

"Alix"—Lee was still muffled behind his woolen scarf—"will you talk with the authorities? I can't." He laid Travis at the other end of the couch from where I'd put Tommy. Tucking in a new warm blanket, he turned back to me. "Alix, do this for me."

I reached up impulsively to remove his scarf, but he dodged my hand. "Alix, please."

"All right." I saw the blue flashing lights of the police car against the wall and turned to look out the window. When I turned back Lee was gone.

Seventeen

SOMEONE PUT A CUP OF HOT COFFEE IN MY HANDS. I clenched it, and allowed someone else to slip my coat off. A man, maybe an emergency medical technician, tugged off my boots a little too energetically, making the coffee slop a little down my sweater. He apologized and we laughed.

Others hovered around the boys, both of whom were now very talkative. Their parents had arrived hard on the heels of the authorities and the living room was filled with loud voices, weeping mingled with laughter. Bad-dog was made much of and took advantage of the commotion to jump on the couch and snuggle back down with his buddies.

To my befuddled mind it was as if being drunk at a party—I heard voices but could not distinguish words. Then I was lifted from the vortex of exhaustion by a caffeine-induced second wind so strong it was as if I had slept all night. I was embraced by a variety of people, all of whom began to clamor for Lee. I made his apologies, citing his exhaustion as cause for his sudden disappearance. My own tiredness began to creep back up on me, and it was with relief that I noticed suddenly they were gone and only the state police sergeant and Lee's doctor remained with me. I answered Sergeant Duchesne's questions for a few minutes and then was alone with Lee's friend and physician, Dr. Fielding.

"Have you seen him?" I sat in one of the Queen Anne chairs beside the fireplace. Dr. Fielding squatted next to me, my feet in his hands.

"He's pretty wiped out, but I think he'll be all right. It was a monumental feat for him to attempt, but it won't have done him any harm." Dr. Fielding had known Lee for years, and I felt enormous relief at his diagnosis.

He ran a light finger up the sole of my foot, and when I twitched he smiled and let go of my foot. "And how are you?"

"I'm okay. I think I'm warm, finally." I rubbed my face. "Just enormously tired. Any frostbite?"

"No. You're very lucky. It was damned cold last night."

"Tell me about it." I laughed. "And the boys?"

"Surprisingly healthy, but I think Tommy may lose a toe. That dog was the difference between that and a whole different ending to this story."

"Good old Bad-dog." I reached out and stroked the object of our praise, who obligingly leaned his muzzle on the chair arm. My moment of second wind evaporated and my head spun with exhaustion.

I felt Dr. Fielding pull me to my feet. "To bed, Alix Miller. You did a heroic thing tonight."

"No, I was just Tonto." I took his hand in mine and

held it, forcing him to look me in the eye. "Is he really all right, Doctor?"

"If he hasn't taken a chill, and I don't think he has, he'll be fine." Dr. Fielding squeezed my hand. "You're fond of him, aren't you?"

I nodded.

"Try to talk him into accepting some credit for this, would you?"

I smiled and nodded again, too tired to answer with words.

I slept the sleep of the dead. Dreamless until waking, then filled with icy images and distortions of what we had gone through. I saw ledges in my dreams, and falling, I startled myself awake. The afternoon light struck the mirror over the sink in the bathroom, catching my eye as I lay under the blue coverlet and keeping me from going back to sleep. I climbed out of bed and stood for a long time in the shower, soaking up the heat from the water. I had forgotten to turn on the fan, and the small guest bathroom was filled with steam. I took my hair dryer and made a clear circle in the mirror. The face that looked back at me, framed as it was by the foggy moisture on the mirror, was untouched by the night's experience. There was nothing there that said I'd somehow joined the ranks of heroes. I didn't feel heroic, only happy. Happy. I hurried to get dressed.

Lee wasn't downstairs. Mrs. Greaves hadn't seen him yet. I ate the savory soup that she made for me, listening all the while for Lee's step. I wandered into the solarium where the last of the March afternoon's light had turned gray and thrown everything into dusky relief. Under the artificial light of the overhead fixture, I examined the portrait. I was pleased with it.

I was hungry again and could smell the roast Mrs. Greaves was making for dinner. "No sign of him yet?" I asked her as I helped myself to a carrot.

"Nope. Still asleep. He's worn out, Miss Miller. He shouldn't have done it. It'll kill him."

"Mrs. Greaves"—I put a hand on her shoulder—"Dr. Fielding says he'll be fine. He's not delicate, he's a healthy man."

She shook her head in disagreement, but said nothing further.

At six o'clock the phone began ringing. As if by some tacit agreement the media had let us sleep off our adventure; they were now ravenous to get the story. Every ten minutes the phone would ring and Mrs. Greaves would answer it in her deadpan way, "Crompton residence. No, he is still unavailable. Yes, I'll tell him. Good-bye." The phone would strike the cradle with a plastic clatter.

By dinnertime I was worried about Lee. I crept up the stairs to his door and listened. The old house had solid wood doors and no sound leaked through despite my straining ears. I kept thinking of Mrs. Greaves's skepticism and felt that lump of doubt grow in my chest. What if Dr. Fielding was wrong? I tapped on the door. Then opened it wide enough for the light from the hallway to lay itself over his bed, revealing the sleeping form there. I could hear his breathing, a little raspy but not labored. His foot beneath the covers twitched and suddenly I felt awkward and intrusive. Embarrassed, I backed away and shut the door.

* * *

"Alix, will you speak with this person please?"

It was thus that I began relating the tale to the media. Dissatisfied with Lee's elusiveness, they turned to the sidekick. "When he found them they were huddled together under a bower of evergreens they'd bent down to form a shelter. . . . They were alert and very cold. The dog? I don't know. Big, brown, and as mixed a breed as can be. We had warm socks and hot coffee. . . . About six hours, and another four to get back down. Mr. Crompton led. He's very tired. No, he's not ill. Recluse? He's a writer." I ended the interview, unsure of how much Lee would want revealed about himself. I decided less was best. They all wanted to talk with him directly and I kept promising that he would call.

I was nearly as tired by nine o'clock as I had been at dawn and retreated to my room, leaving Mrs. Greaves to unplug all the phones. As I drifted back to sleep I thought I heard Lee stirring but was caught so firmly in the net of sleep that I could not move.

With that peculiar fickleness of weather, the next day saw the first earnest salute of spring. I could hear the trickling of the snow melting from the roof as it dripped over the slate and down through the drainpipes. Steam rose from the stones in the driveway, glistening wet in the bright sunshine. I hurried downstairs, pleased beyond reason to find Lee at the breakfast table, his reading glasses perched on his nose and his newspaper spread out before him, already marked with coffee cup rings and crumbs.

"Anything about the rescue in there?" I asked, holding myself back from leaping over and throwing my arms around him.

"This is *The New York Times*. We didn't quite make it for this edition."

"I could swear I spoke with every reporter in the country yesterday."

Lee laughed a little and folded the paper away. "Thanks for fielding all the calls, Alix. I just couldn't have done it. I'll return calls today."

I looked up at him in surprise.

"What? Why the quizzical look?" he asked.

"I don't know. I guess I assumed you didn't want to talk to them."

"Talk, no pictures. I don't have to meet anyone."

"They won't be satisfied."

"No?"

"You forget, my friend Mark is a photojournalist. He lives with the motto 'Pictures say a thousand words.' "

"Mark. Right."

I felt a little warmth in my cheeks, as if I'd brought up a bad subject. "Well, I'm sure if you just . . ."

"Alix, I've been interviewed a dozen times as Harris Bellefleur; there's never a need for photos. Not without permission."

Lee disappeared for an hour while he returned the calls and I worked on the portrait. When he finally joined me in the solarium he looked a little sheepish. "Well, your friend is right. I guess reclusive authors aren't photo-op material, reclusive heroes are. Damn reporter from the *Register* badgered me until I agreed he could come and take a picture."

"Lee, you surprise me."

"Actually, it's blatant subterfuge. When he comes, he gets to take one of you and our wonder dog there."

"Oh, I get it. You're suddenly called away."

"Precisely."

He sat down and I studied the man and the portrait, refining some of the strokes. My mind was swirling like the snow of the day before, thinking of the lengths to which Lee would go to avoid being seen. Experienced enough to know that refusal would mean open season on him, he became passive-aggressive. I smiled behind the canvas, faintly amused.

The phone rang again and he snapped it up. I was so intent on my work I didn't listen until his voice went up a decibel and grew gravelly. "Mrs. Lewis, I do certainly appreciate that you're grateful, but really, no recognition is necessary. Many people were out there, anyone could have found them. I don't think the boys need to come here. No, please, they needn't meet me. That they are alive and well is reward enough." Lee glanced over at me and I could read the panic in his eyes.

"Yes, I'll think it over. But really, it's not necessary." Lee placed the handset down softly. "They want the boys to thank us in person. Both sets of parents think it's necessary."

"Lee, let them. They need to express their gratitude."

He hauled himself out of his chair. "Alix, no."

"And give me one good reason why not."

"Don't be obtuse, Alix." He pointed at his face. "You know why. I won't be a fairy tale hero. The monster may perform a good deed, but the curse is never lifted."

"Are you afraid of pity?"

He stopped pacing and looked at me, so used to my scrutiny now he no longer tried to avoid it. "Do you pity me?"

"Sometimes," I answered. "But not because of what you look like. Because of what it's done to you."

Breathless seconds passed between us. I could not take back my words, yet something in me gloried in my honesty. I had stepped over a barrier and into a new dimension in this strange relationship. He didn't answer me, but his mobile face belied his composure. Finally he simply left the room. I squeezed my eyes shut and wished I had said nothing. As I covered the portrait the content blue eyes seemed a mockery of the soul of the man.

Bad-dog and I had our fifteen minutes of fame. We dutifully greeted photographers and TV camera crews, had our pictures taken, told the story over and over again. Each time Mr. Crompton was unavoidably delayed, out of town, or ill. So sorry, please understand. Fortunately for us a successful rescue that doesn't involve heavy machinery or unhappy endings loses media attention quickly, and by the end of the following week we were left alone. I knew one of the photographers and we exchanged news about Mark. He'd met him at the airport, heading out for Somalia. I had wondered why I hadn't heard from him, although my guilty conscience had provoked me to leave three messages on his answering machine. I was afraid he'd be annoyed if I didn't tell him about my own newsworthy moment.

The town hungered for a celebration. The finding of the two lost boys had energized the community into a passion of fellow-feeling and finally it settled upon a thanksgiving service that Sunday at the Roman Catholic church where both were altar boys. First the Lewises, then the Michaliks, then the parish priest called to prevail upon the town's only legitimate hero to attend. Resolute, no, stubborn, Lee Crompton refused to be recognized. And never said why. Finally Father Vaughn, Lee's own Episcopal priest, came to call.

Unannounced, Father Vaughn showed up at the back door, bussed Mrs. Greaves on the cheek, and introduced himself to me. Tall, painfully thin, he looked almost a caricature of a rector with his white collar and tweed jacket.

"So, is our shy hero about?"

"He's in the library on the phone. Why don't we capture him in his den?" I didn't need to lead the way. Father Vaughn was well acquainted with the layout of the house, but I went with him anyway.

"You recently lost your father, didn't you?" he asked me as we went down the long hall to the library.

I was nonplussed. "Yes, last month."

My tone revealed my puzzlement and he placed a gentle hand on my shoulder. "Lee told me. I'm very sorry."

I felt a rush of delight that Lee had spoken of me to someone. "Lee was wonderful for me during the worst times." I paused before the library door. "I don't know what I would have done without him." I put a hand on his tweedy arm. "Convince him, if you can, to accept this honor. Will you?"

"That's what I'm here for." The priest patted my hand, not in a gratuitous or mechanical manner, but in an honest human gesture.

I left him at the door and went to help Mrs. Greaves.

Lee seemed to have chosen to ignore what I had said to him. He behaved as if nothing had passed between us. I itched to apologize, or to provoke some kind of dialogue to clear the air, but instead he gave me worse than no opportunity, he pretended nothing had happened. Maybe, I began to think, I took my own words too seriously. Maybe I had only thought it.

When half an hour had passed, Mrs. Greaves handed me a tea tray and I went back down the hallway to the library. I tapped on the door and went in. Lee and Father Vaughn were silent, the air thick with disagreement. I set the tray down and looked at Lee. "You won't do it, will you?"

"Do you know me so well you can read my mind now?"

"No, your face."

"You're right. Lee is being reluctant." Father Vaughn threw up his long thin hands. "I can't convince him, Alix. And we have to respect that. He doesn't want to be seen."

"Afraid he'll frighten the very children he risked his life to save." Lee shot me a look to kill but I was committed now. "Lee, what can we say to you that will convince you you're wrong?"

Stretching himself against the crookedness in his spine, Lee seemed to fill the room. His deep voice cracked from within the barrel chest. "Damn it, Alix. I have chosen a path and I am not veering from it. Drop it!"

I looked up at him, fighting the tears his anger coaxed out of me. "All right, Lee. Okay. If that is what you truly want, we can't make you."

Suddenly his shoulders drooped into their customary tilt. "Alix, I'm sorry." He looked at Father Vaughn, who had stood as well. "Hank, I'm sorry. I just can't." He looked back at me and I saw the flash of a frightened animal, then his expression resolved back into his usual face, the crags and ledges softened by a smile. "You go, Alix. You found them. You stuck it out and warmed them and hauled them down the hill. You go for both of us."

I knew then that he was truly imprisoned.

The granite church was packed. The parish priest, Father McClellan, met me in the parish hall and escorted me into the sanctuary to sit in the front pew with the boys and their families. The entire rescue effort was represented, and as I looked from side to side I recognized one of the emergency people, and there were police troopers, some in uniform, one or two in mufti I remembered vaguely. Dr. Fielding tapped my shoulder and I smiled back at him. The bulletin listed the fifty-odd searchers with Lee's and my name set off by clever printing. Special recognition was given Bad-dog as well. The day before, a huge meaty bone from the butcher's had been ceremoniously delivered by Tommy and Travis.

The processional hymn began, the organist pumping out a familiar tune, but the words seemed different. It was a beautiful service. I kept thinking it was an anti-funeral—all thanksgiving and praise. Father McClellan's homily was joyous and reflected on the acts of humans being the acts of God. What might have been a raised fist asking God why was instead raised hands praising His mercy.

Suddenly the service was over and I was embraced by strangers. I ached for Lee to be there. People surrounded me as the tangible hero, someone to see and touch. I tried to offer Lee's excuses, but they went unheeded, as those I spoke to were more set on telling me how they felt about the rescue themselves than in hearing my fabrication. And for that I was grateful. Worse than not being there, Lee wouldn't be truthful about why he wasn't. So I became the lone guest of honor, the artist heroine from out of town, while the real hero lived only three miles away and was nearly as much a stranger to them as I.

A buffet in the parish hall followed with requisite speeches from the first selectman and then shy speeches from Travis and Tommy. I was made to join them on the dais and together they presented me with a bouquet of roses.

I left as soon as I could. Sitting in my car, I undid my coat, warmed in the spring air less by the rising temperature as by the warmth of spirit shown me.

It hurt to think that Lee had, by his own massive self-consciousness, been denied this kind of love.

Eighteen

Mrs. Greaves laid two Peek Frean cookies on a plate and set the tiny silver coffee carafe on the tray with the cup and saucer. I wiped my hands on a paper towel and laid my brushes down on another. "I'll take that in to him," I offered.

"No, he doesn't like to be disturbed while he works." She tipped hot coffee into the carafe.

"I won't bother him, I promise." And I lifted the tray away from her. If she'd made a grab for it I wouldn't have been surprised. Mrs. Greaves's tolerance of me was beginning to show wear as I stayed on. Right now her stiff lower jaw spoke volumes.

I went slowly up the stairs to the bedroom Lee used as a writing room. I'd never been in it before. The door was ajar and I pushed it open with my foot. It swung open gently, the well-oiled hinges making no sound. Intending to set the tray down and slip away, keeping my promise, I came quietly into the room where the only sound was the persistent hum of the computer.

Lee hunched over the keyboard; elbows stuck out, he typed with two fingers and a thumb. Even from a distance, I could see the cursor fly across the grayish background as Harris Bellefleur gave life to Tyler Bent. Suddenly he stopped and leaned forward a little and muttered, "Tyler, you idiot, you can't do that!" With a few thumps, he'd obliterated the offending lines and forged ahead.

I began to feel like a voyeur, so I set the tray down and backed away. As I turned toward the door, I saw the painting I'd given him, framed now in an expensive rosewood frame. The late afternoon sunlight touched the greens and blues, creating a natural light for the awakening of the colors, as if a little piece of the pasture had been sliced away and framed. But above it all floated the little face, and in sudden recognition I knew it was a Death's Head. That's what that was, not Cupid or the muse it might have represented. I'd prophetically painted in Death over my landscape. I must have made a sound because he turned and saw me.

"Alix, what's the matter?"

"Nothing, I was just bringing your coffee, I didn't mean to interrupt, please"—I paused for breath—"excuse me."

"No, wait, stay. This is getting away from me, and that's when I need to stop."

"I've interrupted your dream."

"My what?"

I laughed a little. "I always call the state of concentration I try to achieve when I paint the dream state. When all else is held away and free thought guides the hand."

"Gardner."

I raised an eyebrow.

"John Gardner always said that to really write, one must allow the dream to happen."

"Well, I didn't mean to wake you, and Mrs. Greaves will have my head."

"To hell with her. Just let me get the next line on the screen and we'll talk." He turned back to the keyboard.

My eye was carried back to the painting. I was touched with unreasoning happiness that he'd hung it in here, that he'd wanted something from me. The little face smiled and the sense that it was a Death's Head passed.

"I think of it as my muse."

"You read minds now?"

"Occasionally." He laughed. "Your expression is quite revealing."

"For a moment I thought it was a Death's Head."

He stopped laughing and shook his head. "No, Alix. It was never that. It shows radiant hope."

I sat in the only other chair in the sparsely furnished room. It seemed as though, even with me in the room, he was able to return to some kind of concentration as he rolled on with the work. His longish brown hair curled gently over his ears and over his collar, and every now and then he'd run a hand through it, tugging at it as if holding on to an idea, then striking the keys to catch up.

It seemed impossible that I had not always known Lee Crompton. Our ancestors had known one another—perhaps some genetic memory broke down that filmy barrier of strangerhood. Though there were many details I didn't know, I just knew the essence of him, this man who had become my friend during a crisis in my life. I was not surprised by the wash of tenderness I felt just then, staring at his broad back as he worked. In three short months, he had filled a void in my life I hadn't known existed. I drew close behind him. He wore no aftershave, but the scent of his soap was pleasant and I stood closer.

The cipher my future had seemed filled suddenly, and I knew in that moment the path I wanted.

"One more sentence," he said, feeling me behind him.

"Take your time," I said, and waited.

"Done." He sat straighter and flexed from side to side.

I put my hands on his shoulders and rubbed, pressing away the tension with my thumbs.

"Don't, Alix."

I slipped my arms around his neck and kissed his cheek.

He shot up from the chair as if I had slapped him.

"Why do you flinch every time I touch you?"

"You mustn't."

"Why not? What are you saying?"

"Don't toy with me, Alix. I may be ugly, but I'm still a man. Just because I look like this doesn't mean I don't have the same desires as any other man."

"I know that." I backed up toward the door. I could feel my skin grow hot with shame. "Lee, I am not toying with you. Don't you think I care for you? Don't you care for me?" I started out of the room.

"Come back. I'm sorry. I'm being stupid." As suddenly as his flash of anger had happened, he conquered it and was apologetic. "Look, when I first showed symptoms of this disease I was going with a woman. The radiation therapy to shrink the tumor had a rather unfortunate side effect. My relationship with this woman was tenuous at best, and losing my desire was not a great advantage to it. So I discontinued the treatments, never dreaming just how, well, just how it would turn out. I eventually went back to treatment. In many ways, it was a blessing not to have any physical desire, as I was so obviously no longer desirable. But, Alix"—and here he touched my hand, clenching it in his—"ever since the day we skated together, I've realized that the impotence that shielded me is gone. When you wore your new dress for me, for my approval, I wanted you so badly I hurt. But I will not risk your friendship."

I remembered back to the first nights we spent together and my fear that he would play those will-we-won't-we games and that I would have to be unintentionally cruel, as there would be no way to reject him without offense. Now I looked full into his face and saw there, not a misshapen stranger, but my dearest friend.

I reached up and touched his face, and this time he didn't shrug me off. I pressed my lips against his and we kissed. I could feel him resist, and I held on. "It's all right, Lee. Let it happen."

He gathered my face between his gnarly hands and lowered his face to mine. Slowly I felt the awakening of desire, the moist flame of passion ignite as his kiss grew more ardent.

"Oh, excuse me!" Mrs. Greaves appeared suddenly at the open door, driving us apart like guilty teenagers. "I just wanted to ask what time you want dinner."

"The usual time, Mrs. Greaves," Lee got out finally.

"She knew we were up to no good," I whispered when she was gone.

"Were we?"

"Yes."

But, like the dream state, the spell was broken.

Nineteen

I WAITED FOR HIM IN MY ROOM, BUT HE NEVER CAME. Finally, just before eight, I gave up and went downstairs. He wasn't waiting for me in the library or anywhere else. A little throb of anxiety beat in my veins and I went to the kitchen to find Mrs. Greaves.

"He's gone out." Her face was completely bland, but her hands viciously scrubbed at a pot.

"Where?"

"I don't ask his business." She held the pot up to the light and scowled at it, picking at an invisible speck of scum on the inside.

"Mrs. Greaves . . ." I stepped a little closer.

"Alix, don't go wrecking his life with promises you won't keep."

"Mrs. Greaves, you've no business . . ."

"I have. He's been my worry for a long time. I don't want to see him hurt."

"Why do you think I would hurt him?" I felt my fists close against the accusation.

"Everyone hurts him eventually."

"I'm not everyone, Mrs. Greaves."

"I won't let you do it to him." She hosed hot water into the pot; a thin spray struck me in the face.

"Don't you interfere." Anger now flared. How dare this woman speak to me as though I were a malicious child? "You leave us alone."

"Us? How quick you are to link yourself with him. Sure, I know your type. All you see is his money. You can look past anything for that."

So stunned was I by her accusation that I was momentarily struck speechless. I shook my head to clear it, thinking I couldn't have heard her correctly. "What? What are you saying?"

"You'll play on his loneliness for his money. I've seen it before."

The adrenaline-spiked rage twisted my hands into fists and I shook all over. "Is that what he thinks?"

"Naturally." She slammed the pot down into the dish drain. "I'll put your dinner on a tray."

"Don't bother," I said, and went to get my coat.

The open bay revealed the empty place where the MG was kept. Long night drives. Sometimes he just took long drives. I whistled for Bad-dog and struck out for the moonlit pathway. I walked for a long time, striding along now familiar trails, ducking branches, sensing them more than seeing them as I plowed along with my head down. Eventually I came to the pond, now shimmering in the light breeze like rumpled silk. An eternity ago he and I had skated together, our hands touching, my cheek against his chest. He had rediscovered his desire then, and I had been oblivious to it. Neither of us had been oblivious four hours ago, we had both felt real passion—nothing would ever belie that.

I sat on the skater's log and held my head in my hands. How had this happened? I was a lover of beauty. My few lovers had all been handsome, especially Mark, whose smooth features were near classically beautiful. Their bodies, each of them, had been slim and strong, runners' bodies. Lee's barrel-chested torso was at complete odds with his narrow hips. Yet he skated like Boitano; hands palm downward, he sketched a circle, his skates razoring a thin single line. Gently, with courage I had not understood then, he'd taken my hand and danced me across the January ice. I sat up and looked out across the pond, and was satisfied that I knew how this remarkable love had come to be.

A duck quacked as Bad-dog flushed it. I called the dog back to heel and turned toward the house.

The entire house was dark and I thought momentarily that Mrs. Greaves had locked me out. Just in case, I fished around in my parka pocket and found my keys, a bright silver back door key recently added to the chain. I felt like a chatelaine, the keys chattering in my hand. I thought of the wind chime, its sweet melody now filling the air in the solarium when we opened a window. The morning after my return to Riseborough, I'd brought the box down to breakfast and set it before him. "A little gift for my host," I'd said. He'd held it aloft, touching the thorny brass stems individually with a delicate touch of his gnarled forefinger, then flicked them into music. "This is so beautiful," he'd said, and I was pleased when he didn't tell me, "You shouldn't have." Gracious at receiving as well as giving, Lee immediately hung the chimes exactly where I had envisioned them.

Coming around the corner, I could see that the garage bay was still empty.

After midnight, and I still couldn't sleep. Worry about his safety almost superseded my deeper anguish that he could possibly believe what Mrs. Greaves said. I fretted that she had his complete confidence and I imagined that her influence was stronger than I knew it to be. I shook off these thoughts repeatedly as the night wore on, yet each time they came back more powerful as I grew more tired. Where was he, why had he run away when the night had so much promise? Defeated by these mental battles, I got up and pulled a sweatshirt over my nightgown. Creeping down the stairs, I went to the solarium and uncovered the portrait.

Casually seated, ankle on knee, his notebook in his lap and his concentration on the work there, the portrait revealed to me the man I knew. I had chosen to paint him in jeans, his navy blue lamb's wool sweater and plaid flannel shirt beneath it, the collar loose, one corner sticking out from under the sweater. It was a characteristic pose, relaxed and unself-conscious. I squeezed out some paint and found my finest brush.

A sharp note of birdsong woke me to the realization that daylight now flooded into the solarium, making the artificial lights redundant. I moved to turn them off, turning the easel just enough to take on the yellow light of new day. From soft gray to pink to blue, the sky lightened, leaving the last bright star of night hanging in momentary suspension before it, too, faded. I looked out the windows and saw Willie arrive, his old father dropping him off. Bad-dog ran past the window, barking at the flock of chickadees feeding on the Yankee Droll feeder. I went back to the portrait. With a pang of sorrow, I realized it was finished.

Twenty

There was nothing left, then, but to pack and go. I took a quick shower and emptied the dresser drawers into my bag. It was only a little past eight, though it felt like midday. I was hungry and tired and deeply sad. Something had been spoiled and I had been the spoiler. I walked past the portrait gallery without stopping.

With my hand running for the last time down the smooth banister, I walked down the stairs. As the morning light streamed in from the long front windows, I could see clearly the seam I had thought not there.

The front door opened and Lee walked in, bringing with him the scent of cool spring dawn. I stood motionless on the stairs, relief banging against my chest as he closed the door behind him and looked up at me with a mixture of emotions written on his face.

"Are you all right?" I came down the stairs slowly,

clinging to the banister in an effort to prevent myself from rushing toward him, yet with each step I moved faster until I was nearly there. He held up a staying hand and backed away as I reached the last step.

"I'm fine. I'm sorry if I left you to your own devices, but I needed some time."

"It's okay, Lee, I understand."

"No, I don't think you do."

"So tell me."

"Last night was a mistake."

My emotions jangling, I moved past him toward the solarium. Beneath the shadow of the shrouded painting I cleaned up my scattered brushes and tubes of paint, wiping them with a rag and setting each into the wooden box, heedless of color or size. I took down the painting and set it on the floor, leaning it against a table. I struggled to release the wing nuts of the easel, finally taking my X-Acto knife and slicing the rubber band, letting the easel crash to the floor with a satisfying sound of wood hitting slate.

"You're leaving."

"It's finished." I held back tears. This man had seen enough of my tears, but of their own volition my words came. "But I don't have to. Lee, I don't have to go at all."

"No, Alix, I think it's best."

"I see." I picked up the easel and the wooden box, then stopped. "Lee, why is it best if I go?"

"Alix, it would be wrong for you to stay. No good can come of it. Only hurt." His blue eyes glistened with anguish.

"Lee, I love you." I set the boxes down and took a step closer, but he retreated. "Don't turn away from me."

"That's not possible."

"Oh, it wasn't love at first sight, I'll admit that, but I

have grown to love you as deeply as my life. Lee, don't push me away."

"How can you say such a thing?" His voice rose and the deep resonance was like a roar. "How can you think you could love something like me?"

"Never some *thing,* someone. Someone who maybe loves me."

"No, Alix! It would be so wrong, I would be ruining your life. I can't give you what you need. A woman like you needs society and children and I won't have either."

"I only need you."

"Alix, this is no fairy tale. You will never release me from this genetic spell. I will never turn into a handsome prince, not even with the magic of your kiss."

"Beauty loved her Beast as he was. I love you as you are."

"It isn't possible. You have mistaken friendship for love; your fondness, as dear as it is to me, for passion."

"No, Lee, you're wrong. Am I wrong to think that maybe you love me?"

Barely a whisper, he answered, "No." Then swung away from me. "Go home, Alix. Go live in New York with Mark."

"Lee, it's you I love, not Mark. It was never Mark."

"You don't love me." He looked down. "You have just imagined me. You have some romantic notion that you can overlook my repulsiveness." He held up one hand. "Please, Alix, don't say anything else."

The incipient tears had dried into angry hurt. I snatched up my boxes again and headed toward the door. "Mrs. Greaves says I'm after you for your money."

It took a split second too long for him to reply and I knew then that Mrs. Greaves was telling the truth.

"My God, Lee, I never took you for a fool. How

could you think that about me? I thought we were friends."

"I don't think that. Of course not. But, Alix, you have to understand, what other motive could anyone have for wanting me?"

I was thunderstruck. The man who wrote the wonderful mysteries about the masterful Tyler Bent was completely undermined emotionally by his own face.

"Who hurt you so badly you won't trust me? Who did this to you? Who hurt you so badly you won't allow yourself to believe you are loved?"

I dropped the boxes again and grabbed up the portrait. "Look at this, Lee Crompton, look and see who it is that I have fallen in love with." I stripped the cover off the picture, but Lee wouldn't turn to look at it. "When was the last time you looked at yourself?"

"Go away, Alix. Please."

My chest felt on fire with the pain of restrained tears. I closed my eyes and sighed. "All right. I'll leave. But I'm taking the portrait. It's mine. Your mother will never miss it.

I banged out of the solarium with my boxes and the canvas, pushing past Mrs. Greaves, who appeared in the hallway. Willie had already put my bag in my car and there was nothing left to do but drive away. As I passed through the gates with the roses twisted in the iron, I chanced to see the silver back door key dangling from my key chain. I touched it, with half a mind to pull it off the chain and heave it into the dirty snow, but left it, a tiny silver memory of what real love had felt like.

Twenty-one

On the day I left Riseborough I got home at about noon and had gone right to my own long-deserted apartment, desiring only the oblivion of sleep and some solitude to allow the events of the past few weeks to heal in me. The red light of my answering machine was flashing and in a passion of hope that Lee had called, I hit the Play button. A stream of calls spewed forth and I dutifully recorded all the names and numbers of people calling to offer condolences, to check on me, to sell me cable TV. My father's attorney's secretary had called about probating Dad's will.

The next few weeks were cluttered with all the ritualistic head-bobbings of lawyers and insurance agents as we worked our way through Dad's estate. It seemed as though Dad had been well insured and, as his only beneficiary, I suddenly found that I was, if not wealthy, certainly comfortably well-off. Handled prudently, his estate would allow me to work full-time at my art. It was as if he had always planned that I should be financially free to pursue my dream even while he badgered me about supporting myself.

I returned Lee's retainer. I wrote a short note, carefully composing each sentence to be honest without pleading. I asked him to please call me, that what I had said was from my heart and that I missed him. I lay the short piece of paper on my work table and left it for three days before I could reread it and finally put it in the mail. He will never believe me, I kept thinking. I felt more and more like some teenager, unsure about frightening off the object of my desire with uncautious words. Yet my heart persevered in wanting him.

I heard nothing from him. A card from Hospice came, a donation had been made in Dad's memory by an anonymous donor in the exact amount I had returned to Lee. The shrouded portrait sat in a corner of the studio, its back facing me. The anonymous designation on the card made Lee seem farther away than ever.

I waited until a Thursday night and paced around the telephone on the desk as if it were a time bomb. "Just do it," I said aloud and punched his number. Four rings and the answering machine kicked in. Mrs. Greaves's recorded voice enjoining me to leave a message at the tone. I hung up. Then called back, leaving a short message to have Mr. Crompton please call me. I pulled back from saying it was urgent, but in truth it was. Everything in my life hinged now on Lee Crompton.

I began to wonder if Lee had been right, that proximity had produced this unnatural passion in me. Each day I tested this sore theory; each day a rolling sense of loss answered, a loss that paralleled my grief. I mourned the loss of Lee as deeply as I mourned my father's death. It was difficult to separate the two. Both had filled my life and then vanished. But my father I had nursed to the end, had said my farewells and bidden Godspeed. Lee had been cut from me by his own hand.

Behind me the air conditioner revved. The phone rang and I let the answering machine take the call, too enervated by the July heat wave to get up and answer it. Robin's voice came on and I leapt up, banging my knee on the table and spilling a little of my coffee. "Robin! Wait!"—I punched the Off button—"Robin, hi!"

We nattered on for a few minutes, filling each other in on inconsequential details of our very different lives. Finally she got to the point. "Alix, John and I are moving the date up. We're getting married over Labor Day weekend."

She went on, "You know we're both too old and experienced to play bride and groom, so we've decided to simply do a civil ceremony and have a nice dinner somewhere. The important thing is, can you still be our witness?"

"Robin, of course I will. And I'll take the girls for you when you go on your honeymoon," I offered.

Robin demurred, her mother and John's were nearby and happy to have the two, Sarah and Caitlin. "Besides, his mother has to get used to these kids being part of her life now. What better way?"

"Well, you know I'm happy to if something doesn't work out." Actually, I was relieved that the little girls wouldn't be my responsibility.

"So how are you?"

"I'm okay," I said after a moment's hesitation. I'd gotten pretty good at dodging that question, put to me so often after Dad's death. A cheerful "I'm doing just fine, thanks for asking" wouldn't fly with Robin, who knew the other half of my sorrow.

"Still no communication?"

"No."

"But you've tried?"

"Over and over. Sometimes I think that he wasn't appalled so much by my schoolgirl declarations as he simply didn't love me."

"But?"

"But then I remember the look in his eyes and know that I wasn't mistaken. His face is incredibly expressive for all its deformity, or maybe because of it. He seems to absolutely lack the ability to mask his emotions. They are larger than life on his face. I cling to that, Robin, I cling to the memory of his eyes, and that's my lifeline and maybe the whole reason I can't seem to get on with my life."

That next Saturday Robin and I were in the mall hunting for dresses for the wedding when we passed a Barnes & Noble bookstore. There, prominently displayed in the faux bay window, was the latest Harris Bellefleur book, *Legacy for a Dancer,* A Tyler Bent Mystery. I caught Robin's elbow and pointed. "That's him."

"Tyler Bent?"

"No, Harris Bellefleur, Lee's nom de plume."

We went in and I picked up a copy from the display stack, turning immediately to the back cover to read the author blurb: "Harris Bellefleur has written several novels and short stories. He lives in New Hampshire." That was it, a terse little bit without photo. I riffled back to the front, stopping at the dedication page. "My God," I said and handed the book to Robin.

"To A. M., who for one brief moment made me feel like Tyler Bent," she read aloud.

"Keep trying to contact him, Alix. That's a message in a bottle if ever I saw one."

"One he wrote a long time ago, Robin. I wonder if he still feels that way."

Robin and John got married on the Saturday before Labor Day in a beautifully intimate ceremony with just six of us there to share it with them. We all knew one another, so the party was lively and a little undignified by the time they drove off to the Cape for a short honeymoon.

Robin touched my cheek with hers. "Go find him, Alix. Don't let him get away."

"I won't." But even to me the words rang false.

The air was silky, washing over me like gentle water as I lay on the dock. Somewhere a bullfrog bellowed. I opened my eyes and focused again on my book. The lowering sun sent streams of reddish light across the lake, tinting the trees of the little islets dotting the middle of the lake. Soon enough it would be too cold to sit out without a sweater, much less in shorts; soon enough the leaves would draw thousands of tourists and this deep breath between seasons would be exhaled.

I placed a bookmark between my pages and sifted through my bag for the mail I'd picked up on my way to the lake. I was thumbing through an art catalog when I read about a museum show to be held in January. At the bottom of the article was an invitation to submit work. I circled it with my felt-tip marker and added the name of the Percy Art Museum to the growing list of shows I was entering. So far I'd been rejected by the several I had already applied to, but, as Dad always said, keep trying. I'd been to the Percy Art Museum, a small but very well-endowed museum in northwestern Massachusetts. I had met the director and made a note of his name beside the circled address.

The bullfrog called again.

I let myself in the back door of the house. I'd long since given up my farmhouse apartment and had settled into Dad's house. My house. Dumping my bag and mail on the kitchen table, I hunted through the cupboards for an easy meal, my flip-flops making soft thwacks against the soles of my feet as I trotted around. I was anxious to sort through my slides to find the pieces I would submit to the Percy show. Ten minutes later, I was out on the lawn with a grilled cheese sandwich and my slides.

With a little switching here and there, I pulled two from other submissions and decided that those would go to the Percy. Then I thought better of it. I got up and went into the studio, where my most recent work hung, things I'd finished while Dad was sick, a couple I'd completed since returning home. Four framed pieces hung from the center posts in the studio, a series in egg tempera. My two landscapes soaked in the warm yellow and pink of the setting sun as they lay propped against easels. The portrait of Lee was the only thing still behind a sheet, the white rectangle orphaned against Dad's work table.

My influences and my interests were so different from the paintings captured on slides. To submit some of the older pieces was not a real indicator of my current work. Mark had always done my slides for me, and now I had work and no photographer.

Although Mark and I still spoke occasionally on the phone, we had quickly settled into an amicable distance. I couldn't ask him to shoot my slides anymore. I thought of him only infrequently and, although I tested the notion several times, I never regretted not pressing him toward a commitment. It was true what I had said to Lee, Mark wasn't the love of my life.

It wasn't until nearly Thanksgiving that I heard I'd been accepted to exhibit at the Percy Art Museum group show in January. Unbelievably, they had accepted all five pieces I submitted. The museum would host a reception on the first day of the exhibit and had sent me a box of logo'd invitations with my name listed among the other dozen exhibitors. There I was, between Darlene Lewis and Max Moeller, in lovely sans serif type, blue on blue.

I pulled out my address book and considered the roster of names there. People who'd been patrons, or classmates or fellow teachers; others who'd been briefly chums by association in some group or other; others I'd forgotten about. My more recent entries were in turquoise ink. I replaced the cover of the box and left the task to future contemplation.

Robin invited me to Thanksgiving. I knew my offering of pies and wine couldn't come close to expressing the appreciation and affection I felt for this woman who had mothered and sistered and befriended me. We made a happy party, the in-laws and various cousins, children, and one stodgy Italian grandmother in black widow's weeds and elastic stockings. Others Robin had nurtured showed up for various activities of the day, dinner or dessert or football. John's quiet demeanor was loosened vastly and he entertained us all with jokes and tall stories.

Threaded throughout this public display I saw the looks he and Robin shared with each other. Subtle touches, raised eyebrows, pleasure and annoyance, amusement and exasperation. They were already developing communication techniques that would become ingrained over the years until they were capable of speechless eloquence with each other. Such love, I thought, is a miracle. It can't happen that often.

As I went to bed that night I felt as empty as if I had fasted all day.

Two days before I had called Lee. Mrs. Greaves had answered. Although I had expected her to, I almost lost my nerve. "Is he there?" I asked with the dread certainty that he wasn't there for me.

"Leave him alone, Miss Miller. He's doing just fine without you. He doesn't need your kind of upset."

I was so startled by her candor that I couldn't speak, and before I could react the phone responded with a hum of disconnection.

It was clear to me then. He really didn't want anything to do with me. I felt suddenly as if the walls of a sand pit were crumbling around me. If I scrambled up one side, it collapsed, taking with it all the other sides.

Twenty-two

It snowed while we hung our show. Twelve of us, disparate artists with disparate work, had the museum to ourselves except for the docent who hovered around us, guarding permanent works from contagion. Our common cause made comrades of us, six men and six women; we each took the time to look at one another's work and offer compliments, wholly truthful at the moment. We helped each other fit wires to hooks and oh so carefully set down distracted little sculptures with sharp parts. There would be a dinner for us that night; the show would open at noon the next day. Giving my five pieces a last look, loving how they looked against the soft white wall with the perfect lighting, I put on my jacket and walked out with several of the others.

The two sculptors in the group had fallen upon the snow as a new medium and were instantly creating pieces, showing off a little. Pretty soon snowballs flew through the air between the two sculptures and the younger of us took up battle lines. Half an hour later, soaked and cold, we trundled off to our respective lodgings, warmed enough to one another to look forward to the dinner that night.

Late that night, a little inebriated, I found myself necking with one of the sculptors. Long-banked sensations flared in me and it was with great reluctance I finally pulled away. "I can't, Joel," I said.

"Not here." Joel Reichert was a good-looking young man, probably younger than I. We were sitting in his car, a mistake, my father would have told me.

"No, I mean, I can't take this any further."

"I have protection." His innocent assumption was almost endearing.

"Look, Joel, I'm just getting over an emotional entanglement. I'm a little fragile right now."

To his credit, Joel sat up and simply brushed my hair away from my mouth. "Okay, so how about a nightcap?"

"Yeah, that would be great."

When he dropped me off at my bed-and-breakfast, Joel kissed me gently on the cheek. "See you tomorrow."

"Thanks." I opened the door but before I shut it, I ducked my head back in. "Hey, Joel?"

"Yeah?"

"If I was ready, I would sleep with you in a minute."

He laughed and pulled away from the curb.

The museum was filled with visitors. A soft sibilance of muted voices like lapping waves on a lakeshore beach swelled and receded room to room. I spotted Joel, the docent had him surrounded by guests and he was speaking about his two very different sculptures. Catching his eye, I winked and he smiled around his explanation of material usage and meaning. I stood and listened for a while, growing nervous, knowing that my turn to speak was coming later that afternoon. The Percy requires that the artist not only hang the work, but also explain it in detail.

I drifted back to my display, studying each one as if I hadn't painted it. What would I say? What could I say that would tell a stranger what they meant to me?

The floor beneath my feet was gritty with the sand from the pathways. A slow-moving custodian came into the nearly deserted room, his long white dust mop floating ahead of him, side to side, gathering up all the grit and trapping it. The mop made a little snick sound at each turn. On the highly polished floor, he looked as if he were skating.

"Ms. Miller?" A second docent came up behind me. "We're running a little late, can we ask you to hold your talk until four-thirty?"

"Of course. I'll be the last then, won't I?"

"I'm afraid so. Will this be a problem for your guests?"

"I don't expect any guests. I only sent out a few invitations, I'm afraid. It's a long way to come for most of my friends."

"Oh yes, you're from out of state, I'd forgotten."

"I'm happy to go last."

He performed a little motion that might have been a bow.

I checked my watch. Only two-thirty. I could go back to the bed-and-breakfast, but I felt too fidgety to rest. A nervous energy that had grown all day infected me and I decided just to go for a walk.

The sidewalks in the small town were full of frost heaves and I walked with my head down to avoid tripping, going around gnarled tree roots thrust up between broken slabs of cement like clenched fingers.

Nature will out, I thought. I thought, too, of the invitations I'd sent, suppressing a little disappointment that no one had made it. I had sent only six, four to folks who might have made it and one to Robin and John, who would have come but Sarah had come down with the chicken pox.

The last I had sent to Lee. I scrawled a note inside it: "I send you this not expecting you to come, but hoping you'll let me know how you are. I remain your loving friend, Alix." Before I could think better of it, I posted it, the Percy Art Museum return address at the corner of the envelope.

Chilled, I realized that I'd been walking around for over an hour and a half. Picking up my pace, I headed back to the museum. The reception was well under way as I passed through the main foyer. Tables of wine and cheese and fruit stuck out at perpendicular angles around a floor sculpture by the sculptor I hadn't necked with. I bumped into Joel and complimented him on his talk.

"I think I sold one of them," he whispered, indicating a stout older man now bending over the floor sculpture. "Talked me down on the price, but, hell, man's got to eat."

"That's great. Hope you can make it two for two."

"You too, I'll come listen and maybe I'll even buy one."

"I didn't bring any for sale, Joel. These are from my personal collection."

"Baloney, every artist will sell. Or aren't you hungry enough?"

"Nope. Not enough." I laughed.

I hate that moment when I begin talking to a group and I am aware of every word I'm saying, as if the monitor is off and I can't think before I speak. A hollow sound coming out of my mouth and a voice in my head saying, Oh my God, I can't believe I'm saying this. Then there is that sweet moment when the subject overrides the nerves and I'm launched. A fair-size group surrounded me as I stood with my back to my work. The docent introduced me, spouting my curriculum vitae from memory. Then he fired questions at me, game as any interrogator from the Spanish Inquisition. I fielded them fairly well—medium, technique, and so on.

"The four here"—I indicated the four small rectangles with a sweeping gesture—"are of my father, Alexander Miller. He was a well-known commercial artist who died in March of pancreatic cancer." I was satisfied at the slight inhalation of breath each listener made. "I painted these from sketches I made of him during his illness. As you can see, he experienced a rapid decline, which I've chosen to emphasize by muting the colors until here"—I pointed to the last of the quartet—"where I use no color at all except this small patch of red floating above. If you take them as a series, you'll note that the patch of red has migrated from him to above him." The group did not make a sound. "I like to think of these pictures as my good-bye to him. He taught me more about art than any of my instructors here or even in Paris. He showed me how to make eyes with life in them when I was a little girl." I paused, my own recollection of distant happiness making my listeners visibly uncomfortable, like a bare patch of skin showing in the winter.

Clearing his throat, the docent squared himself and pointed to the fifth painting. "And this one?"

"This is oil on canvas."

"Please, tell us about it."

I hesitated, suddenly shy again in front of these strangers, the semicircle solidifying into a motionless frieze of faces. I felt as if I'd taken something very private and shown it to strangers. As intimate as my paintings of my father were, this one had a different pain attached to it.

"Ms. Miller"—the docent held his hands together, raising the knuckles to his mouth—"any comment?"

"No"—I turned my back to the picture—"not really." I touched the silver beads at my neck with nervous fingers.

Dropping his hands, the docent asked, "Does anyone have any questions for Ms. Miller?" and stepped back into the semicircle of people. Their faces regained individuality as they moved, restless now with the tour.

"Yes, I do." A middle-aged man with a fuzzy white beard stepped away from the group. "Why did you choose to paint your subject in this way?"

"How do you mean?"

"Using the technique you did."

I looked back at the portrait, at Lee in his jeans and sweater, his ungainly form eased by the soft brushstrokes of the Impressionist school, the whole portrait done in blues and greens and yellows.

From the center of the painting, his eyes, their blue deeper than any of the other blues, looked at me, visibly accusing, "How could you put me on display?"

The man shoved his hands into his trench coat pockets, flapping the sides of the coat as he waited for my answer.

"I wanted to show his . . ." I stopped then. "I painted this picture using the Impressionist school to"—what was I trying to say?—"my intent was to create something evocative of the quiet morning at home."

"No, no. Why did you distort the face?"

"I didn't."

After polite reexamination of my pieces, they all drifted away. A few stopped to offer comments, but I could hear nothing except the sound of blood rushing in my ears.

Twenty-three

The museum cleared out rapidly, the artists gathering their friends and families, air-kissing one another in brief hugs. "See you next week," we all said as each made his or her way back to their lives. Joel stopped me as I came back from the ladies' room. "Can we have dinner next Saturday?"

I studied the parquet floor beneath my feet and shrugged. "We'll see."

"Just dinner, Alix, no strings. We'll complain about unappreciative galleries." He pecked my cheek and was gone.

One by one the rooms were closed. I could hear the loud voices of the cleaning people, startling after the muted atmosphere of the open museum. I took the guard's chair by the gallery archway, setting it in front of my work. I sat down and straightened my wool skirt over my lap. Clearing my mind, I tried to look at my paintings with new eyes. I had been so cavalier about my memorial to my father, though he might not have felt so. I had treated his death as a subject, not associated with me at all. Still, the quartet was my homage to him, as much as the portrait of my mother had been.

The lights were turned down in the next room. I would need to leave in a moment.

I made myself look at Lee's portrait. Not accusing me now, his eyes had sweetened. A rush of the deepest loneliness washed over me. Joel's kind flirting had opened up a wound I had never let heal. I looked again at the portrait and wondered for the thousandth time, when would I give up and get on with my life? What I needed was a simple human touch and I'd rejected it, clinging to a lost dream.

I heard someone behind me and I stood to leave.

"Alix?"

Lee came out of the shadows and stepped into the harsh yellow spotlight of the track lighting. Every craggy element of his face was illuminated. He came toward me, his hands raised slightly from his sides.

"Lee, you came." My hand covered my mouth. My first impulse was to run to him, but I hung back, afraid.

We stood apart, both of us terrified.

"Lee, you came." I was so afraid that any unrehearsed words would send him away that I could only repeat those words. The reality of him, after so long, struck me into numbness, yet for the first time his face did not come as a shock, no fresh surprise at the depth of his outer ugliness. Instead I saw in his eyes the unspoken, clear telegraph of human need.

"Alix, I've been a fool. . . ."

"Oh, I've missed you so." I moved toward him.

"Alix, stop—look at me." He held up one hand. "If you think you can still love me despite everything, despite my stubbornness, despite what I am, then can you give me a second chance?"

There was less than three yards of hardwood floor between us. I looked at his shadow stretching across it toward me. Months had gone by since I'd last seen him, months of regret and ache and longing for him. Months when he hadn't answered my messages. Those three yards were either chasm or bridge. I raised my eyes and looked at him. "I spent weeks studying your face, your posture, your hands. I listened to you and you listened to me. We shared the hardest days of my life and you supported me. We found those lost boys together. If I don't know how I feel about you after all that, then I know nothing. If I don't love you now, then I'm an empty soul incapable of loving anyone."

He could say nothing else as I came across the slick hardwood floor and into his arms. He folded them around me and held me so close I could hear his heartbeat beneath his soft wool overcoat. "Oh, Lee Crompton, I was so afraid I'd never see you again."

As we clung together under the yellow spotlight, I breathed in his familiar soapy scent and listened to his story. "The day you left I was crazy to go, to jump in my car and follow you. I never doubted you thought you loved me, but I was convinced that you couldn't possibly have really fallen in love with me. I told myself it wasn't fair to encourage you, and perhaps it still isn't. Love is a physical thing. To imagine your smooth face touching mine . . ."

He touched my face now as he spoke. "I've cried twice in my adult life. Once, when I was told the damage done by discontinuing the treatments was irreversible and would only get worse. The second time was the day I let you go."

"Why didn't you call me? Why didn't you answer my messages?"

"I didn't know about your calls. At least not until recently. Mrs. Greaves never relayed your messages to me."

"I wondered if she was capable of that." I remembered her bitter words to me when I'd called the last time.

"She caved in when she saw the card from the museum."

Only one question lingered in the back of my mind, and I decided that I had to ask it or suffer the doubts. "Why didn't you ever call?"

"I was afraid to, afraid that I was right and afraid that you would tell me you realized you were wrong, that you didn't love me. I fully expected you to give me that 'let's be friends' line and I couldn't face that. I had fallen in love with you."

"But now you're here. Now you know that I have never stopped loving you."

Behind us, one by one, the room lights went off until we were standing beneath the last bank of recessed light. Lee pulled away and stroked my hair. "Let's take a look at your work."

I flushed. "Lee, I hung your portrait."

"I know. It's time I saw it." He took my hand and stepped closer to the wall. He studied the series of my father first, nodding and squeezing my hand. "It couldn't have been easy to do, but this is a wonderful monument to Alexander. I'm certain he'd like it."

All my doubts fled in the face of his understanding.

He'd known my father only at the end, yet knew him enough to ameliorate the nagging little guilt I'd felt on and off—and knew me well enough to know that I had felt that way.

As he moved in front of his own image, I felt his hand tighten over mine. I was dry-mouthed, afraid then that he would disappear again, afraid he would see my work as mockery.

For a long time he studied the portrait, his usually mobile face rock still. He released my hand and his own went to his chin, touching it as if to bring what he saw into his own sense of self, a face he hadn't seen but only touched for years.

I tormented myself in fifteen seconds with a lifetime of reproach. I loved him and had painted a portrait of the man I loved, but could he see that? What had possessed me to bring this so very private portrait to such a public forum? Because it was a good painting. Everything I knew about painting from life had jelled in this portrait. Light, color, animation, depth of feeling. I had painted it in a state of growing love and the result was art.

Still looking at the portrait, he slowly lowered his hand and reached out for me. "I'm worse than a fool, Alix. I could have kept us both out of such unhappiness if I'd just looked at this portrait when you tried to show it to me."

"You just needed to trust me."

"I do, Alix. I just needed to trust myself."

I had nothing else to say, so put my arms around his middle and hugged him, shaking with the joy of his being there with me. "I love you, Lee. I have for a long time."

He rested his chin on my head, rocking me back and

forth gently, then he whispered, "Alix, I won't keep you secluded with me like some fairy tale princess."

"It doesn't matter to me. I love just being with you."

"But it does matter to me. You see, I've only just made the intellectual leap that it's my problem that has kept me locked up for ten years, no one else's." He shifted away from me, holding me at arm's length and bending a little to hold my eyes. "Help me, Alix. Your love will bring me back to the land of the living."

"You've taken the first step, Lee. You're here."

"Actually, I took the first step this morning. I did something I haven't done in ten years." As he held me close again he told me of how he'd stood in front of the mirror in the guest bathroom, staring into the sink for ten minutes before he could bring himself to look up, and when he did he saw the face of a stranger. The forgotten crags and depressions were blended with new etchings around his eyes, deeper furrows as he drew his bushy eyebrows down into a frown. Testing to see if this face was his own, Lee raised his brow and smiled. The monster in the mirror smiled back. "So this is the face she loved. Amazing. Ugly, yes, but maybe not repulsive."

The guard came in, dimming the last light so that the room was the color of shadow. We walked out together, his huge hand easily covering mine. As we passed beneath the last undimmed light we looked at each other. If anyone as ugly as Lee Crompton could be transformed into beauty, it had happened before my eyes.

Twenty-four

From the first we knew that marriage was what we most wanted. It seemed as though every moment in between was a lost opportunity to be joined together. I think that there was an element of the Puritan ethic in our anxiety. We wanted this so much we were both afraid it would disappear.

Not for me the outward trappings of a wedding, the gown and the veil, bridesmaids all in a row. By the very foundation on which our love was built, I knew that such a wedding would be a mockery. Lee protested that he'd do anything I wanted, invite the town if I chose, but I shook my head and said no. What I wanted was him, and if we hadn't needed witnesses by law, I would have forgone any ceremony whatever. Except that I wanted Robin to come, and Mrs. Greaves would be there, of course, and his mother.

Mrs. Greaves had been a reluctant convert to our cause. I hadn't quite forgiven her for intimating that my only interest in Lee was monetary; early on his explanation for his hesitation in answering this charge was his complete disbelief in its being launched. "I can't believe for a moment that she really meant it. I think she was grasping at straws, trying to protect her adopted chick."

"Well, I didn't believe it, either, until you didn't deny it."

"Alix, I was a man in torment. I wasn't responsible for my actions." He drew me close and rested his head on mine, easing away the last of this painful memory. "Go yell at her," he said, and pushed me toward the swinging door between the dining room and the kitchen.

In the end we both wept, Mrs. Greaves and I, hugging each other close and swearing an end to animosities.

"I've never seen him so happy," she said, twisting her dishcloth into a band. "You've been good for him and I was a meddling fool to misjudge you."

It was almost too easy, but I think she wanted to believe the best of me now that I was a permanent resident in the house at Riseborough. I put aside my anger then, knowing that in her way she loved him as much as I, and wouldn't I have been as fiercely protective of him?

March carried too many bad memories for me, so we waited impatiently for April to be married. Father Vaughn officiated; Robin came to stand up for me. Dr. Fielding acted as best man and second witness. We had spent the last month teaching Bad-dog how to be ring bearer and were amazed at how well he carried it off, proudly sitting beside Lee's mother until called, then quietly waiting as Lee slipped the ring off his collar.

Julia Crompton looked barely older than the portrait

my grandfather had painted of her so long ago. Tall and elegant, her mostly brown hair swept up in a flattering twist, she epitomized the Boston society maven. Close to seventy-five, she still moved like a young woman, a graceful roll to her walk as if the books were still balanced on her head. Except for astounding blue eyes, she and Lee did not resemble each other in any way.

She had greeted me with reserve, but then, I expected nothing less. When I touched her cheek with my lips in an overexuberant expression of greeting, I could feel her shock. Lee said afterward it had been a long time since anyone had touched Julia Crompton.

With my truce with Mrs. Greaves and Lee's reunion with his mother, some closure with what was past had been made. What lay ahead of us was all fresh and pure, a new canvas upon which to paint brightness and abstract representations of life; shapes and colors that stood for our incredible passion for each other. As Lee slid that thin gold band on my left hand, I felt joined to him beyond the merely symbolic, I felt as though nothing could ever come between us. Words, his métier, were unnecessary, and even if we never spoke another word to each other, we would each still understand the other's deepest needs. We needed only touch.

But even when there is perfect love between people it seems as though barriers eventually begin to erect themselves. It is almost as if life cannot exist without challenge. Do we really thrive on facing challenges, making decisions that affect our very souls? Lee and I knew each other well. We knew that, come what may, we intended to live forever in each other's company. We were both too old to view such love as our right; too experienced to know that love is easy. Although, sometimes, we'd relive the exact moment we each first knew that our friendship was deeper than most, we both knew that actually making this love affair happen was a near miss. Often Lee would simply touch me, a hand on my neck, a touch against my shoulder, as if to confirm that I was really there. I would lean against him, snuggle my head into his shoulder and breathe in his scent. I felt a physical attraction to him I cannot explain. "I'll never tell you you're handsome, but you have a certain *je ne sais quoi* I find powerfully attractive," I told him time and again. He'd laugh and shake his great head. "Only an artist of the modern school could say something like that."

But the inevitable barriers began to grow. Not barriers to one another, but barriers to our private selves. Lee found himself unable to write. At first he denied it. Pretended that he was between books, then he began to pretend to write. Finally, after I took a call from his publisher asking where the next overdue Tyler Bent book was, I realized that my Harris Bellefleur was blocked.

"Look, I just write for fun. If if becomes a job, then I can't do it."

"When was the last time you wrote?"

"Yesterday."

"And?"

"Unadulterated crap. Alix, I can't make two words tie together that don't sound like sophomoric slop. I'm too damned happy!"

"No excuse."

That was how our discussion of his Block, capital B, began. Then he began to get annoyed at me for reminding him. Finally, to keep peace, I stopped asking and watched as he took Bad-dog out for his millionth walk.

What made it all difficult was that I was in a major artistic wave. I couldn't stop creating. All the happiness that prevented my husband from writing incited me to paint. I had canvases scattered all over the solarium, which I had unabashedly converted to my studio.

"Temporarily, until we can get the garage space done over," I promised. But the wonderful glassed-in space was so perfect, and reminded me so much of the happy hours we had spent there during the winter I first knew Lee, that I never pestered about hiring the workmen to do the job. Winter melted away and spring was triumphant and summer began with such promise.

And then my own barrier to perfect happiness began to erect itself. I wanted to get pregnant.

I should have known that my reluctance to settle down and have children at a reasonable age was simply due to not having the right man. And now I had the right man and he was terrified of having children.

"Alix, please, I've told you from the beginning that I would never have children, that I intend to be the end of the line for this anomaly." His voice was still gentle, but the tension of the argument showed in his cheeks.

"I know, Lee, but there is no need for any child to suffer the deformity you have. If, and you know that there is only a slim chance a child of ours would actually carry the defect, if he did, then surgery or radiation would be a cure."

"You would subject a child to that?"

"Lee, by the time a child would show symptoms, he would be in adolescence."

"Great. Do you know what being an adolescent boy with a growth problem is like? Can you put yourself in that child's place when suddenly his body begins to distort itself and makes him feel like an old man?"

"But it would never get to that point. We'd know if that child actually had the defect immediately, even before he was born, so we could prepare for that time."

"Oh, Alix. Do you think that, even if we could conceive a child, that I would allow any fetus to develop that carried this miserable gene?" Now his voice was raised, and I couldn't believe what I was hearing.

I went back to my canvas, and he went back to his study to pretend to write.

At first it wasn't that important to me to pursue the argument. The urge to have a baby came and went, inspired by various events, getting a friend's new baby pictures in the mail or a christening at church. But as the time rolled by and I faced first my thirty-seventh birthday, and then my thirty-eighth, I became obsessed.

Obsession, for good or ill, is unreasoning. I had been obsessed by Lee, and now I was clearly obsessed by this desire to have his child. The fact that he wouldn't even discuss it gave it an almost mystical quality. There was a female mystery out there, which I was being prevented from experiencing. Forget that my husband was a genetic anomaly whose entire adulthood had been warped by his disease. I wanted a baby. It became irrelevant to me that Lee was part of this decision. I understood why a woman would choose to be a single parent. I felt great sisterhood with those women who could not conceive. I could not conceive, either. I wish that I could have answered the simple question, What chance was there that our child would carry the gene? Our public library was connected with the Boston Public Library through computer communications and I scoured the indices for the literature. I should have insisted we get genetic counseling, but I developed an unreasoning fear that the counselors would say no.

I was torn between just allowing it to happen and the fear that Lee would indeed carry out his threat that he would never let me carry a defective fetus. Of course, I knew that such a decision was mine, but how could I make him so unhappy as to knowingly bring into this world a child with his defect? I loved him too much to make this horrific possibility real. As strong as our love was, to put this between us would damage our union beyond imagining.

Twenty-five

I SUBVERTED MY LONGING FOR A CHILD INTO A frenzy of work. Avoiding the urge to express my hormonal angst into soft round shapes and gravid imagery, I stroked hard angular shapes on the canvas. Dark colors crept in; blue and black and maroon dominated the field. Heaping gouache into tremulous piles, I etched triangles and lines through them, grazing to the color beneath, revealing latent impulses. Concentric circles shadowed in yellow thrust out from triangulated corners.

The work exhausted me. I was too tired to make love. I think that I could have eventually given up my obsession. Except that I became pregnant.

Against all odds and proving to a skeptical world that it does sometimes only take once, I got pregnant when we made love one time without protection. Caught up in a moment of passion sparked by a wine-induced wrestling match on the hearth rug, things had gotten pretty far along when Lee brought himself up short.

"I think it's safe," I whispered, unwilling to let the exquisite moment dissipate with change of venue and that unromantic insertion of diaphragm. So, like those millions of parents practicing the rhythm method, we got caught.

In the last year of my fourth decade, I was already a little sketchy with periods, so it was several weeks before I made the intellectual leap that our little match on the hearth rug was bearing fruit. Oh, but how to tell Lee what we'd done? I lay awake at night and rehearsed what I would say. Surely he wouldn't be angry. Lee was slow to anger, but neither would he laugh. As I lay with my hand against my still flat belly, imagining what it would soon be like, I knew that the most difficult discussions of our life would be taking place. In my worst imaginings, I wondered if it would drive a stake through our love. I delayed telling him, putting off the anticipated debate from weakness.

I etched a tiny bit more of the midnight blue away from the undercoat of yellow in the curling circle flaring away from the triangle. Wiping the flakes from the X-Acto knife on my flannel shirt, I stood back to examine the work for any sign of improvement.

"Looks like something vaguely familiar." Lee came up behind me and pulled me against his chest. "I know, it looks like . . ." He started to chuckle, then stopped. "Alix, it looks like a uterus and fallopian tubes."

"Stop! It does not. That's not it at all," I countered. Lee held me closer; his arms crossed over my chest, he began to rock me slightly. I looked at the painting again and could see that he was right. What I had thought of as perhaps an homage to Picasso's bull was indeed a pretty neat rendering of a woman's reproductive organs. "Damn, it was supposed to be a bull, a masculine image."

"It's very feminine." His hands gently touched my breasts, which were already sensitive. Equally as gentle, he slid his hands to my waist, then to my abdomen. "As feminine as you are."

I turned to face him. He took my face in his gnarly hands and kissed me sweetly on the lips. "Alix, are you pregnant?"

My first reaction was a smile, then I bit it back, lowering my face as I answered, "Yes."

He let go of me then and walked toward the painting. He spent a moment looking at it, gathering his response to me very carefully. He knew that however he reacted to this unwanted news would set the stage for every other discussion of it. I could read in the set of his shoulders the difficulty of it for him. I wanted to make it easier for him, I wanted to blurt out that it wasn't my fault, that I didn't do it deliberately. But he needed to believe that of me before I said it.

Beast

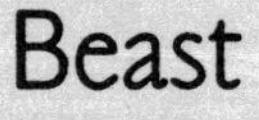

Twenty-six

I did believe it of her. I knew that Alix would never defy me in something so important. Oh, defy is such an authoritative word. I could never be that with her. She meant the world to me. She was my world.

I knew that she wanted a child because she loved me and her world was built on the normal outgrowth of that kind of love. Her parents were in love and had her; her friends loved their spouses and had children. Truthfully, the moment I realized that she was pregnant, that the subtle fullness to her breasts wasn't her usual premenstrual swelling, that the infinitesimal widening of her waist was of profound importance, I was speechless with joy. For thirty seconds I felt the incredible rush of male pride that I had achieved the basic human raison d'être. In the next thirty seconds I remembered what I was, and that this being, this collection of cells, could very likely be as frightening to the world as I am.

I faced my wife and saw that I could utterly destroy her joy in this achievement with a careless word. I could not take away her happiness any more than I could have killed her. I don't remember stepping toward her, I only remember our coming together, clinging to each other and whispering, "It will be all right. It will be all right."

Ours would be a February baby. It seemed right that our child would be born in winter. It seemed as though all significant events in our life together had been landscaped in snow.

Alix struggled to zip up her parka. There was something charming about her roly-poly struggle, and I offered to help to no avail.

"I can't believe it! I need to wear your other jacket."

I helped her into my massive down parka.

"Now I look like the Abominable Snowman," she lamented.

"Never abominable, always charming, sort of like Frosty." I patted the object of her frustration, now hidden beneath my coat.

Every day we went out and walked, ignoring the heat of summer and the cold of winter. Determined to remain fit during pregnancy, Alix was militant about this daily exercise. Even so, as she grew she began to slow down, until I was the faster walker. Now in the last of the second trimester, she was often out of breath and flushed from even a little exertion. We had worried about her blood pressure throughout the pregnancy. Clearly the doctor's warnings of complete bed rest were soon to be heeded.

So many changes come to a pair when they are expecting. None of my experience with this is new to anyone, but the exacting focus on the unborn amazed me. I would find Alix sitting rock still, listening to some internal thump or pluck, absolutely entranced, a drying paintbrush in one hand, the other seeking out the elusive movement.

In the first trimester we needed to come to terms with what might be there. As an "elderly primipara," our obstetrician's less than complimentary official description of Alix at age thirty-nine, the amniocentesis was part of the deal. Even if we had no genetic cause for concern, he would have advised it. But it wasn't mandatory to know all the results.

Riseborough is a tiny place. Boasting only the most rudimentary of institutions, elementary school, church, pizza joint, and library, it was miles from the nearest hospital and thus only attracted a pair of family practitioners to take care of most medical needs. They referred to downstate groups for specialization, and in the last two decades, had made a thriving business in knowing where to send patients with more than the treatable illnesses or well-care they kept to themselves. Dr. Trenton wouldn't begin to consider taking Alix on. Even if she had been a second- or third-time mother at her age, her skyrocketing blood pressure was enough of a deterrent to him to immediately recommend a group in Nashua.

"You're a high-risk mom," he'd said, writing the name of the group practice on a prescription pad and sliding it toward her. "You've got to keep the blood pressure under control or you'll be in for significant trouble. This group will help you."

He must have read the disappointment in her face, as I did when she reprised how she felt when he said she'd have to commute for her monthly checkups. "I'll be there to take care of the baby afterward. That's really the fun part, anyway."

"I just hate the idea of being so far from home when I have the baby." Alix dabbed a bit of paint on the latest canvas.

I knew what she meant. There had been a slim chance I would venture to the hospital while she was there if I could slip in and out at night. But to commute to Nashua, realistically it meant spending time in that town. She knew me well enough to know that I could never do that.

"Alix, Dr. Trenton is concerned about you. That's the important thing. Have you always had high blood pressure?"

"No, never. It's so strange. He told me some women just have this problem. Usually it comes with swollen ankles." She glanced down at her bare feet, ankles as slim as ever. This was still early on, and to the casual eye there was nothing different about her. "Will you still love me when I look like a cream puff?"

"Alix, please look at who you're talking to." I hugged her to me and then broached the question she had cleverly obfuscated with the talk about blood pressure. "What about the amnio? When do you have it done?"

I knew well enough that it had to be early, before sixteen weeks, so that if anomalies were detected the next awful question could be asked in time to be answered with a decision, rather than by default.

"They'll set it up for me when I have my first visit with the group in Nashua." She slipped away from me and went back to her painting.

* * *

I tried to write. Tyler Bent was clearly in trouble and Harris Bellefleur couldn't drag him back from wherever it was he'd gone. It occurred to me to try to create a new character, that just maybe Tyler was tapped out. Empty of plot or focus, maybe I needed to try my hand at another genre. I could always come up with another nom de plume and leave Harris's name sacrosanct to the detective buffs. It was no good. Detective plot or no, nothing came to mind. I stared at the few sentences I'd pounded onto the screen and gave up. My concentration was gone. Only thoughts of the unborn child filled my head. I was so afraid of the amniocentesis I shook when I thought of it. I was so afraid of finding out I was right, and then what anguish lurked around the corner for Alix and me.

When her medical group in Nashua declared driving alone from Riseborough out of the question, we hit upon a solution that, in its simplicity, made it seem ridiculous we hadn't thought of it earlier. We would move to her father's house until the baby was born. The old farmhouse was a forty-minute drive to the hospital where the doctors had their offices. Each month we'd head down and spend the night there, often inviting Robin and her husband to dinner. Mrs. Greaves would send us with enough provisions so that we needn't stop for anything, thus maintaining the integrity of my reclusiveness. I know that I'd promised Alix I wouldn't keep her a prisoner, but I had failed miserably to release myself. Except for friends like Robin and her husband, my circle of face-to-face acquaintances hadn't enlarged much from my pre-Alix days.

As we walked slowly out on that early December afternoon, the murky sky threatening snow for only the second time that fall, we talked about when we should make the move.

"I want to be here for Christmas." Alix shoved her hands into the pockets of my parka.

"You wouldn't want to be back in your childhood home, hanging your stocking by your own chimney?"

She slapped at me playfully. "No. We have our own nascent traditions here now and, besides, this is where our baby will have his or her first Christmas. I want my pregnant Christmas pictures taken in this house."

His or her. Alix had refused to be told what sex this child was. And had neglected to request what further tests might be done to determine if our child carried my genetic defect.

Twenty-seven

I LOOK BACK NOW AND TREMBLE AT THE MISTAKES I made. If only I had insisted, if only I had insisted that she take another test. No, if only I had insisted that we go to her father's house instead of letting her talk me into staying in Riseborough until she completed just one painting more. Or if I had insisted that she abort this fetus right at the start. Would I have lost her as thoroughly as I have if I had insisted on anything?

She didn't have further tests, and I was too cowardly to fight about it. The threat of her rising blood pressure made me hold my tongue, and instead I fell to believing that if there was something wrong with the child, it would be naturally aborted. When it evidently thrived, I threw my emotional anchor out on the belief that God would never send us anything we couldn't handle.

We did know that the child wasn't a Down Syndrome child; Alix had apparently allowed that possibility more importance than the potential for giving birth to an intelligent but deformed monster.

"Lee, if this baby were a Down's, I would still have it."

"At least we know we don't have that issue to contend with."

"No, but I would feel exactly the same if I had allowed genetic testing. And that's why I didn't. I would still have this child, with or without your blessing. It's my body and my child. It would kill me not to have your full support, but I wouldn't change a thing."

"Alix, we'll never know how we would have handled it. You've taken that chance from us."

"Lee, I don't mind you being angry at me. I deserve it, but I couldn't face arguing for the life of our child against you. You aren't rational about it."

Her face had taken on the rosy color that forecast her rising blood pressure and I stopped before I said something that might have physically hurt her. Instead I caved in and embraced her and felt her warm, relieved tears against my hand. How could I insist she be any other way?

I am tempted to relate every detail of our months of waiting. The watching and waiting and the soft details of expectancy. How her friends sent along tiny things that seemed doll-like to me, lost in my massive hands, hands I could not imagine holding the being in which would be so dressed; or how we each brought a new set of names to the dinner table each night to be added to a list pinned to the refrigerator door. Molly and Todd, Oliver and Margaret, Frick and Frack. We had silly names and sweet names. We agreed on the middle names, those of either her mother or father, but were reluctant to decide too quickly on the first name of our only child. I could tell how I would wake in the middle of the night in dread, the emotions of some evaporated dream still thick around my heart.

I have taken too long to tell the end of our story. Alix would have told it herself, far more eloquently than I, the professional writer, can, but Alix is gone.

We had delayed over and over the move to her father's house. Even when her prenatal visits became more frequent, we managed to have reasons to return to Riseborough after a day or two at the house. She never said it, but I think that she never quite reconciled herself to her father's absence from that place. The empty house was crowded with memories and she had a hard time working there. During the last of her pregnancy she had managed to work at home propped in bed. She was still working on a soft milky abstract with dashes of primary colors scattered throughout, her present to the unborn child.

"Dr. Fitch says I have to move down this week. I'm already two centimeters dilated, which means things are hopping."

I felt an internal twanging at finally hearing those highly anticipated words. "Why don't we just stay here now? I'll run home and bring back everything we need tomorrow."

When I was ready to leave, Alix climbed into the car. "No arguments. You know you'll never be able to find everything I need, and I'm mean enough to send you back. This way you'll only have to make one trip."

"But what if you go into labor?"

"It could be a week to two weeks. Being a little dilated doesn't mean delivery is imminent."

I had to believe her, because she'd been through the birthing classes. Mercifully she hadn't insisted I go.

"Besides, I have about ten minutes' worth of work left on the landscape and we can hang it before the baby arrives."

On the way back to Riseborough she'd been quiet, listening to the internal quarks that spoke to her. Suddenly she reached out and took my hand. "When you look into the face of your child you'll know pure love, love that will come to you without prejudice. We learned to love one another as all couples do, but this child will love you simply for being its father. Not because of, or in spite of, what you look like."

When we arrived home it was dark and a heavy cloud cover had descended over the tops of the mountains. Walking from the garage to the back door, I looked up and a first inkling of fear hit me. I should have insisted she stay behind.

In my mind the force of the storm that blew up that night and the sudden cruelty of Alix's labor are inextricably linked. Almost as soon as the first cries of the wind through the surrounding pine trees awakened me, Alix's first pains began.

It was the worst kind of storm—icy rain pelted by fierce winds, glazing everything it touched. The trees bent under the weight, soldiers fallen into postures of obeisance. I called for help. The dispatcher took all my information and called the emergency medical technicians while I was still on the phone. Somehow I was connected with one of them and I began to give them all Alix's history. I pressed them to hurry—already her blood pressure was rising with each contraction.

Alix was trembling with mixed excitement and fear. She tried to calm me by sending me to find all the lamps and candles against the inevitable moment of blackout. All my wires were underground, but the main lines were vulnerable half a mile away. It was midnight. Surrounded by our lamps and candles, we waited for help, our hands clasped together, our eyes on the Seth Thomas clock. Twenty minutes passed and another contraction began. Another twenty minutes, and another.

Suddenly the lights faded, surged, and then went out. It had been so expected, and yet we reacted with the laughter of surprise. Even before I could light a candle another contraction started and Alix grabbed my hand. "Just get me through this," she said, and buried her nails into the flesh of my thumb. When I got the lamp lit I looked into her face and read the pain there. The contraction had subsided, but her face was contorted with another kind of pain. In a panic I ran to the sleet-covered window and pressed my face against it to see if I could see the red flashing lights of the ambulance. The candle in my hand only gave me back my face in the window.

Eventually I heard a banging on the front door heralding the on-foot arrival of a pair of EMTs. Loaded down with tool boxes of equipment, they charged up the stairs and into the bedroom where Alix struggled. "Dad, you stand over there," one of them commanded, and I was so taken aback at the order that I went where directed. Eerie shadows played against the white wall above the headboard, elongated bobbing shapes mimicking the fierce activity on the bed.

"Oh, shit, lady, don't do this to me!"

"What's wrong?" I lunged toward the dark shapes. "Alix!"

In the movies they make the father leave the room when these things happen. But these two let me stay, kindly letting me hold the body of my wife while they freed the child from her treacherous womb. It was truly the first time I had ever forgotten myself and did not worry about what anyone thought of me.

Twenty-eight

I WANTED DESPERATELY TO KEEP IT A HAPPY ENDING. I really wanted the fairy tale to persist. But life mimics art poorly. There is never anything purely one way or another about it. The joy I felt in being loved, in being married, was tainted by my own fears; what was tragedy is ameliorated by the happiness I have found in fatherhood.

For nearly a month after her birth, I kept my daughter away from me. She had cost me my wife, the only person I ever expected to love me. I was like those old tales of aloof fathers and stranger children. She lived in the nursery, her nice little nanny there to be mother and father to her. Mrs. Greaves was barely speaking to me, torn between her genuine grief for Alix and her outright anger at me for being so cold.

Then I found the landscape that Alix had finished that evening before the storm. It had been her gift to this child, whom she had loved from her first moment of conception. The child she had loved so much she refused to know whether or not she would carry my defect; the child whose existence she defended against me; the child she had left me to care for. I picked up the canvas and went to the nursery. The nanny was in her sitting room and did not stir as I pushed open the door to the baby's room.

Alix was quite right when she told me that this child would love me for simply being her father. What I did not expect was the extreme power of my love for her. If she hadn't stirred at the very moment I crept into the darkened room, a tiny fist waving in the air like a miniature protest against injustices yet to be experienced, I might have crept right back out and not had that moment of epiphany. But that little shell-like fist waved at me and demanded that I at least see this interloper.

Helpless against the urge, I bent and lifted this bundle out of her cradle and held her away from me so that I could see for myself she was beautiful. I was not done with grieving, but the tears that ran that day were mixed bitter and sweet. My daughter looked at me with Alix's eyes and did not flinch.

Whatever may become of her, whether she grows into a lovely woman or suffers my fate, Alexandra Miller Crompton will always have one who loves her.

Epilogue

I CANNOT SAY THAT MY STORY IS AT AN END. THERE IS too much living in raising a child to ever think that. But Harris Bellefleur is part of a past that I now put to rest. Once I hid behind his name, my reclusiveness protected by Harris's fictional persona.

In telling our story I have broken the spell of my writer's block. In laboring to write as Harris Bellefleur, I stifled the exuberant happiness I had enjoyed, however briefly. Even as I began to tell her story, I knew that in some way Alix had taken Harris with her. When we first met I'd told her that Tyler Bent was a man doomed to be alone. After Alix died, I recalled that prediction and applied it to myself. But when I held my daughter in my arms I knew that I was wrong. I knew that Leland Crompton would never be alone again.

The Beast in the tale was released from the spell because he convinced Beauty he was worth loving. With that same magic Alix released me to be who I really am; she convinced me that I was worth being loved.

LELAND CROMPTON
RISEBOROUGH, N.H.
1995

Turn the page for a preview of
Summer Harbor. . . .

Chapter One

At the foot of the porch steps, the metal FOR SALE sign clattered in the breeze off the water. A discreet sign, with letters overarching a stylized lighthouse, all done in blue and white, advertising the local agency that handled important real estate: “Seacoast Properties, Ltd.”

“Limited to what?” Will asked.

“Limited to the wealthy.”

“Like Pop and Nana?”

“Only in the old days of yacht club cotillions and madras shorts. Today’s wealthy, the ones who survived the downturn, they put Pop’s money in the chump-change category.”

“Chump enough to send me to Cornell.”

“This house is sending you to Cornell.” Kiley immediately regretted her sharpness. She hadn’t meant to snap at him, but the impact of seeing the house, so eerily unchanged from her memory of it, was like grit against polished wood.

Kiley bent over to snag a drifting piece of paper from where it had become tangled in a rosa rugosa bush. Nowadays, the owners of these shingle-style summer-houses had landscape architects swarming over the small yards to install “native” plantings and cottage gardens. Her father had stuck in a hedge of old-fashioned privet, a couple of spiky yuccas, a scattering of lace-cap hydrangeas, rosa rugosa bordering the cement path to the front door, and let the yellowish grass do as it pleased. “This is a summer place, if I wanted a fussy garden, I’d stay home in Southton,” he’d said. It would probably be a selling point—not much to tear up, and the rosa rugosas were native.

It was frustrating, how every little action prompted a memory. A piece of litter extracted the echo of an offhand remark from her father. Even the key in her hand prompted a vivid memory of it hanging on the hook by the back door, the seashell key chain exactly as memory served. In her eighteen-year moratorium from Hawke's Cove, the house had remained inviolate in her thoughts, pristine and untouchable, and today verified her chosen memories.

Kiley had never forbidden herself memory. Sometimes, in the early morning hours when the infant Will suckled on her breast, refusing to go back to sleep, or when a Don Henley song would come on the radio, which so clearly brought back the feel of sand beneath her feet, Kiley relished the companionship of her two best friends, even if they were only embodied in selective memory.

It was out of a great need to keep this place and the good memories in the vault of sanctity that she had refused ever to come back. Nothing remains the same once reality has overridden the imaginary. How could she keep separate the cherished youth of summers in Hawke's Cove, with the tragic end to those days, if she were to actually set foot where it had all happened?

It had come as a mild shock that her parents wanted to sell the Hawke's Cove house. Her grandfather had purchased it for a song in 1933, and it had been the summer focal point of the Harris family ever since. Kiley had paid little heed to her parents' frequent conversations about the place's disposition; she always assumed that, ultimately, it would come to her. The idea of actually selling it out of the family hurt her in a place she had long kept apart from her adult self. Intellectually, Kiley knew that the place was beyond her parents, as her mother lost skirmish after skirmish with brittle bones and her father struggled for air against the emphysema slowly choking him. Childishly, she had pushed forward the hope that her parents would neglect to really do anything at all about the house, and that at some magical and ill-defined point, she would find herself suddenly able to go back to it.

When her parents abruptly announced that they had decided that the house would be sold, and the proceeds would fund Will's education, the irony was not lost on Kiley. By his very existence, Will had cost her Hawke's Cove. Now Hawke's Cove would pay for his absence. Before her parents' offer to pay for Cornell, Kiley had expected that Will would stay closer to home and go to a state college where she could afford his tuition. The sheer distance between Southton, Massachusetts, and Cornell in New York State made Kiley weak with knowing she'd see her son only rarely once he left for school in the fall. Unbearably proud that he had been accepted at Cornell, and unbearably sad about letting him go, Kiley covered her maternal angst with busyness. She focused on the minutiae of preparing for college, and pushed away the distant day in September when he would leave her behind. Maybe it was easier for parents with spouses and other children. But Will, he was her world.

Now her parents had said they wanted her to go and inventory the place, ready it for sale, as if they could order her to break her moratorium against being in Hawke's Cove with the task.

"Mother, why don't you just have the agency hire someone to pack it up, or, better yet, just sell it with the contents?"

"Kiley, I will not have strangers stealing from me."

Lydia Bowman Harris, now in her seventies, was obsessive about theft. Their Southton home had all kinds of burglar deterrents, which on average were accidentally set off once a week by her father's slowness in getting the right buttons disarmed. It was kind of a family joke.

"I can't just up and take off for Hawke's Cove. I don't know when I can get free, and certainly not for long enough to get the job done."

"You have vacation time."

"Yes, and I was planning on going to Cameo Lake with Will. It's our last—"

Her father stood up, then took a moment to pull in sufficient breath to add weight to his words. "Kiley, we buried the past, got on with our lives. There's nothing there which is going to change anything, or revive anything, or matter much anymore. We need you to do this for us. We don't ask much of you, but this, we're asking." Merriwell Harris walked with slow dignity out of the parlor.

"Don't mind him, Kiley." Lydia Harris waved a still-elegant hand in the air in dismissal of her husband's remarks. "He's not happy about having to give up the place. It was in his family for seventy years."

"Then don't."

"Why should we hang on to the place when there's no one to use it? You won't go."

"Mother, you know the memories would choke me."

"Kiley Anne Harris, for eighteen years you've done well, made a good life for you and the boy. I know we were uncompromising in the beginning, but what's done is done. I don't think that any of us would wish things had been different." Meaning that Will had not been born.

"No. Of course not. But I can only keep focused on the good things if I can keep the past out of sight."

"It was your own doing. Until you face that, you'll never grow up."

Lydia's sharpness only set Kiley's back up. No, she would *not* cross that little bridge over the wetlands that separated Hawke's Cove from Great Harbor. In some ways, she was the opposite of that old guy who took tickets at the theater when she and the boys were kids. Joe Green, it was said, could not leave Hawke's Cove, even to bring home his own boy's body for burial. They said it had cost him his wife.

She, on the other hand, couldn't return. As long as Kiley remained on this side of the bridge, she could choose idealized memories that were harmless.

At night, sometimes, she would wake from dreams of water. Complicated dreams that left her sad. For a short while Kiley had gone to a counselor, a recommendation from a nursing school classmate. All the counselor could tell her was that she needed to get a hobby; she was too concerned with serious matters. She hadn't told him anything of the past, only of her present: school, working full time, raising a toddler single-handedly. The rift with her parents over Will's existence.

"You need a break, Kiley. Find some time for yourself. Go to the shore."

Kiley stopped seeing him after that.

The dreams were cyclical and her journal noted that they most often appeared when not she, but Will, faced a life change. When he was being toilet trained, or trying out for youth soccer; when she went out with someone for more than two consecutive dates. Even as he entered high school. Periods when she worried more about him. About how she was raising him.

In her dreams Kiley never saw Mack or Grainger, but the constant of water in these dreams always woke in her the sensation that she'd been with them. Hawke's Cove, a place surrounded on three sides by the sea, providing years of summers together on the beach and in the water.

The sailboat that they lovingly made seaworthy. And, of course, the insoluble association of water and the way things had ended between them.

Kiley could imagine no circumstance that would induce her to abandon her eighteen-year prohibition against going back to Hawke's Cove. It was her self-punishment. She would forever deny herself the thing she most wanted in the belief that she deserved no less.

And that belief had held up, until Will and two of his pals got caught with marijuana.

The second most dreaded phone call in a parent's life: "Come down to the station." Kiley felt detached, as if she did this every day of her life. She brushed her teeth and combed her hair, pulled on a clean sweatshirt over her pajama top and sweatpants over the bottoms. Normally she'd never go out in such an outfit, but this seemed all right under these circumstances. No one would know her. She found her car keys and remembered to set the house alarm. She drove slowly the few miles to the police station, the radio off, as if music would be inappropriate. All the way there, she spoke aloud to herself. "At least he's not dead." If anyone had asked, she would have been unable to pinpoint her emotions. Part relief it wasn't worse, part anger. Certainly the shame would emerge, the hunt for a one-line acknowledgment of parental mortification to hand to those people who studied the police blotter and would casually ask about the situation, masking their curiosity with concern. It was almost like déjà vu. So clearly, Kiley remembered the raised eyebrows as she appeared in the market with her blooming belly. The "How are you feeling dear?" code for "What a shame, the Harris girl knocked up, and no father."

As the parent of a teenage boy in a moderately well-to-do town, there was a certain expectation that this might happen. Perhaps this was an initiation rite. "Come join those of us whose children have destroyed our credibility. You bring the coffee and we can share our disappointments." A twelve-step program for failed parents. Hadn't she played with him, taken him sledding and to minature golf? Hadn't she made him sit at the table to do his homework, even when he'd preferred to do it slouched across his bed? Hadn't she made him dinner every single night of his life? But she had left him in the care of babysitters while she pursued her certification as a physician's assistant. She had declined membership in the PTA because she didn't have time in the evening to go to meetings that weren't part of her education. Suddenly Kiley couldn't remember laughing with him.

The parking lot was empty of civilian cars, the station house door wide open in the late June night. Kiley rested her forehead on the steering wheel, her thoughts swirling. She took a deep breath and drew on her professional reserve.

That Will was exceedingly lucky not to have had the stuff on his person, and that the arresting officer had chosen to charge only one of the three boys, was almost no consolation. Will's action, whether the first and only time as he claimed, or one of many never discovered, meant that somewhere, somehow, she'd deluded herself into thinking she'd successfully raised this boy by herself. That all the long talks they'd had, all the rules she'd imposed, were laughable. In one night, he had proved that she was not the paragon of single motherhood she had occasionally thought herself, now that he was about to be launched into independent adulthood.

What had seemed, nineteen years ago, to be the hardest decision she would ever face in her life, had paled in comparison to the daily diet of hard decisions that rearing this boy had fostered. Even now, those interminable nights of wakeful debate while lying in her dorm room bed, could startle her with a clarity of memory. As if those circling thoughts had been physical, as physical as Will's first kick in utero or the labor pains of his birth. Those pains she had forgotten: not so the pangs of struggling to tell her parents she was, at eighteen and almost through her first semester of Smith College, pregnant. She deliberately told them after the sixteen week mark; deliberately and resolutely never told them who had fathered the child.

The drive home from the police station, deep into the predawn darkness, theirs the only car on the winding country route, was in a silence so extraordinary Kiley felt as if she could touch it. Will stared out the passenger window. His form filled the small space with coltish length, accentuated by the baggy jeans. There was so much Kiley wanted to say: you could lose your place at Cornell, you are risking your life, what in God's name were you thinking? But she kept silent, afraid that she would be unable to stop once she got started, and the last thing she wanted was to become the shrieking banshee of his expectations. Often enough he'd accused her of "screaming" at him when she had reprimanded him in a deliberately level voice. This time the potential for her voice to rise into a penetrating howl was so strong she would not let herself even speak. She simply told Will to go to bed; they'd talk in the morning.

A trace of gray appeared beneath the edge of her shade. Kiley watched the darkness with open eyes, unable to sleep. In that first notion of dawn, her bedroom door opened and Will stepped in.

"Are you awake, Mom?"

She heard his snuffling and sat up. At once her big, bright and independent boy was in her arms, crying out his shame and regret and pleading for her forgiveness. She rocked him, resting his head on her shoulder, wondering how he could feel so much like the little boy who once cried with the same heartsick intensity when he'd broken her favorite antique vase.

The last few months had been a tug of war between them as never before. His natural demand for independence and her equally natural desire to remain part of his life had warred mightily. Was she powerless to keep him from repeating his mistake? Despite his tears and apology, how could she really trust him not to do the same thing if peer pressure and opportunity offered?

Kiley was shocked at how damaged her trust in him was. In her predawn imagination she saw him selling his blood to support his habit, then closed her eyes against the lurid image. It was only pot, and only once—or so he said. The fact she doubted him pained her, and Kiley knew that this loss of trust between them might only be healed by separating Will from the source of his temptation, in particular, those friends of his. They weren't kids she'd known since Will had been in grade school. These were kids from one of the other towns that made up the regional school district. She barely knew their names, much less who their parents were or how much supervision they got.

What Will needed was a safe place. They both needed an interim resting place where they could mend this rent in the fabric of their relationship before he was launched on his final lap to adulthood.

Hawke's Cove had always been her place of refuge. When schoolwork, or arguments with her parents, or spats with girlfriends made Southton oppressive, she would think of Hawke's Cove, of the predictable routine of beach and reading on the porch, of the scent of damp air and hot sand. The peace that comes with being in the place you are the most happy. The friendship of Mack and Grainger.

"Will, I think maybe we should go to Hawke's Cove."

Will sat up and pulled away from her, his eyes glittering with spent tears in the strengthening light of day. "I thought you wouldn't go."

"I don't want to, but I think that we need the time away."

Will pulled away from her arms, a rapid flat-palmed rub of his eyes wiping away the small boy who'd just been there. His jaw flexed. "You know I won't do it again, I promise. Swear to God."

Kiley took the corner of the sheet and wiped her own tears from the corners of her eyes. "So you're promising to keep away from D.C. and Mike? All summer?"

There was exactly enough hesitation in Will's answer. "It wasn't their fault. I mean, it was my choice, I did it. No one put a gun to my head."

"You bought it?"

"No. I just smoked it."

"If I take the car away from you, you can't work. You're too old to ground, and I don't want to spend the last summer we're together worrying every night that, deliberately or not, you're in the wrong company."

"Don't you trust me?"

Kiley's eyes drifted to the light bordering the edges of the drawn shade. Over the years, parenting had taught her to temper her words. She knew how harsh words, even justifiably provoked, could be soul-breaking to young ears. Reprimands were always based on anger at behavior, not him. Never ad hominem, always a little retractable. Until now, when there were no words for how betrayed she felt by his behavior. By him. He had done the one thing they had discussed and agreed on time and again. If he could fail her so easily in this, would mere words repair the damage? Talk, as her mother often said, is cheap.

"No, Will. Frankly, I don't."

Will stood up and gathered his dignity around him. "I really am sorry, Mom. I know that I screwed up. It was a mistake in judgment but, whether you believe me or not, it won't happen again. It was stupid."

"So why did you do it?"

"I can't tell you."

Echoes of her own words nineteen years before. *I can't tell you.* She understood that there were times when it was enough to admit error, if not reason.

"I understand why you might not believe that I won't ever do it again, but taking me away won't give me the chance to show you that you can trust me." Will's voice had taken on his most reasonable tone, the voice he used to convince her to give him permission to do something against her better judgment. Like let him attend that party at Lori's.

"Going away will give us both a little distance from this incident, Will. We need that." Kiley hoped he didn't see that she was convincing herself with her words.

"So, if we go, how long do we stay?" Will's tone verged on curious as he capitulated.

"I'm not sure. A couple of weeks, three maybe." Kiley threw back the bedclothes and sat on the edge of the bed. Sleep was out of the question. "I have a month coming to me and July is a good time to go. The doctor is taking his vacation then, too, so things will be slow at the office." Kiley found her slippers and pulled on her housecoat. "Let's have breakfast."

Will shook his head. "Not for me. I'm going back to bed."

"We aren't done talking about this, you know."

Will stood in the doorway and shrugged a silent "Whatever," and Kiley knew that she'd made the right decision. He thought that his tears and apologies were enough. In that still childlike, solipsistic world he inhabited, Will believed that he had smoothed things over. That she was his mother and, therefore, she must forgive him. Kiley remembered how that felt. If only tears and remorse could smooth away the mistakes of youth. This indiscretion would not affect the rest of his life in the way hers had, neither would it go away.

"Tell me something." Will remained in the doorway, his hands pressed against the doorjamb.

Kiley pulled the belt of her housecoat tighter around her waist. "What?"

"What is it about Hawke's Cove that scares you so much?"

"Stuff."

"Like my father?" One last arrow fired.

Kiley knotted the belt, not looking up at Will. "Your father was the love of my life."

That was all she would ever say. That his father was someone who was kind, and handsome, and clever, whom she loved, and was now gone.

The truth was, she didn't know who his father was. Long ago she had loved two boys equally, only to find that that wasn't possible. In love, there can never be three. The uncanny part was that every now and then Will betrayed some characteristic of the one, and then of the other, as if the two had joined together to create this child; that her love had somehow caused the impossible to happen, and Will was part of all three of them.

The old summer place was so like she remembered it that for an instant upon opening the double front door, Kiley half expected Mortie the cocker spaniel to greet her. Mortie had been her dog as a child, a golden tan color which had faded as he aged, peacefully dying in his sleep right there in the corner beside the hearth in the summer of her seventeenth year. Kiley glanced at the corner, almost surprised that there was no dog bed still there. Stifling the temptation to abandon unpacking in order to tour the house as a memory museum, Kiley called to Will to start unloading the suitcases from the car.

Kiley's parents hadn't been back to the place since her mother's first fall. A shattered hip and the diagnosis of advanced osteoporosis had ended their summer pilgrimage to Hawke's Cove, despite the encouragement of Lydia's physical therapist to keep doing what she had always done. Any thought of going was compromised as Merriwell's lungs began to lose their battle against his lifetime of smoking. So, the Harris house had stood empty last summer for the first time in nearly seventy summers. No Harris had lounged on the front porch, morning coffee in hand, surveying the magnificent seascape that, no matter how often it was viewed, never failed to amaze. A three-generation continuum had been broken, aided by her refusal to come back.

Now there was Will, representing the fourth generation at Hawke's Cove, standing on the broad verandah, staring out across the short yard to the intense blue of the summer ocean. His ball cap was twisted around backward, his baggy jeans exposed his boxers, and his face was glowing with that first view of the cove which lent its name to the town. Will hitched up his jeans and turned to face his mother. "No one ever said it was this beautiful."

"It's even more beautiful during storms. The sea becomes this gray-green color and the whitecaps are like cream. You can't see across to Great Harbor, because the sky and the sea become the same color. When I was a girl we'd sit out here to watch the storms come and go, like our own private show." She let Will imagine she meant herself and her parents. But it was Mack and Grainger with whom she'd sit, enraptured by the dramatic sky, jumping and grasping hands at each bolt of lightning spearing from the black clouds into the roiling sea, like Neptune's tridents.

"Do you think we'll get any thunderstorms while we're here?"

"This is New England seacoast, so anything's possible."

Kiley grasped the handle of her suitcase and climbed up the steep and narrow stairs to the second floor. She breathed in the slightly musty salt-and-wood smell of a long-closed summerhouse. The scent acted like a door to the memories of other summer arrivals, made tangible by the same awkward weight of the overpacked suitcases, and the familiar sound of her sandals on wood floors. She half tasted the homemade chowder always left for them by the woman who used to open the house when she was a girl.

The wash of homesickness brought sharp tears to her eyes.

"Mom, are you all right?" Will's voice betrayed his surprise at his mother's quiet weeping.

"I never realized how much I missed it." Kiley laughed at herself and brushed away the tears. "Oh, I feel so foolish." But was it the foolishness of sentimentality, or the foolishness of having stayed away for so long?

NEVER BEFORE

At Rafael's first movement Elizabeth had stepped back, genuinely frightened and, at the same time, nearly dizzy with a dangerous excitement.

"D-d-don't come any closer," she stammered as he slowly walked up to her.

"Oh, but I will," he threatened softly, as his hands reached out to close around her bare white shoulders. "I intend to come a great deal closer, English. Just as close as I possibly can."

His mouth was warm and demanding as it took hers and Elizabeth made one small, involuntary attempt to escape. Feeling her resistance Rafael's hands tightened, pulling her against his tall, hard body. He kissed her a long time, a long endless time, during which Elizabeth learned irrevocably that there are kisses and then there are kisses. She melted into him, her soft, young breasts crushed against his chest—and then his mouth hardened into passion, and alarmingly she felt his lips forcing hers apart and his tongue urgently searching her sweet mouth. . . .

Other Avon Books by
Shirlee Busbee

GYPSY LADY
LADY VIXEN

Shirlee Busbee

AVON
PUBLISHERS OF BARD, CAMELOT, DISCUS AND FLARE BOOKS

WHILE PASSION SLEEPS is an original publication of Avon Books. This work has never before appeared in book form.

AVON BOOKS
A division of
The Hearst Corporation
959 Eighth Avenue
New York, New York 10019

Published by arrangement with the author
Library of Congress Catalog Card Number: 82-90558
ISBN: 0-380-82297-0

First Avon Printing, April, 1983

Printed in the U. S. A.

WFH 10 9 8 7 6 5 4 3 2 1

DEDICATION

There are four people in particular to whom I want to dedicate this book:

LINDA REASONOVER, who nagged, worried, paced the floor, encouraged, and continually bolstered my sagging ego.

My husband, HOWARD, who was just as supportive as ever and who worked so hard with me on the book. Honey, I couldn't have done it without you!

My father, JAMES G. EGAN, who spent so many hours attempting to clarify my confusing sentence structure, dangling clauses in particular!

And finally the last person, but probably the most important one of all, my dear mother, HELEN W. EGAN, from whom I inherited my great love of reading.

White Passion Sleeps

PROLOGUE

THE TALE BEGINS. . . .

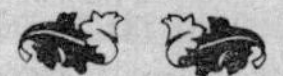

Ill news is wing'd with fate,
and flies apace.

—JOHN DRYDEN,
"Threnodia Augustalis"

"Are you going to say something to her today?" Melissa Selby asked her husband of less than a year.

Lord Selby, his blue eyes staring indifferently out at the frosty winter landscape so typical of England in February, answered in a bored tone, "My dear Melissa, as the entire reason we left London and traveled in the dead of winter to Maidstone was to speak with my daughter, I hardly think I shall delay my conversation with her for very long." He looked across the long, impersonally elegant room in which they sat sipping afternoon tea and smiled cynically. "Believe me, my dear, I want this settled just as much as you do."

Satisfied with his answer, Melissa stirred her tea in its fine china cup and asked idly, "Do you think she'll prove troublesome?"

Lord Selby chuckled sardonically at that and remarked, "Not if she is wise. Elizabeth has always been a very biddable girl, and when I explain the unpleasant alternatives to her, I'm quite positive she will look upon your choice with more than a little favor. He *will* offer for her?"

Melissa looked thoughtful. "He should. After all, you will make a generous settlement on her... and he does have rather pressing gambling debts, I understand."

"Won't his father cover those? I thought you said that he was from a wealthy family?"

"Well, yes, but apparently this trip to England was to make him stand on his own feet, something he hasn't done very well. I think he will be more than happy to marry Elizabeth and take her to America if you hint at the size of the fortune that will become hers when she marries." Her voice took on an uncertain note, as it always did when she mentioned his long-dead first wife. "It is a shame that your daughter is the very picture of her mother, although I suppose Elizabeth could be considered appealing in an insipid sort of way."

Lord Selby sent his new wife a derisive look, conscious of how much she resented Elizabeth and her dead mother. "Yes, she does resemble Anne at the same age, but you have nothing to fear—my infatuation with Anne died within two months of our marriage." His voice reflective, he murmured slowly, "I should have seduced the chit—she was only a squire's daughter—instead of being so young and foolish as to *marry* her! How very stupid of me!"

Melissa nodded her head in complete agreement with *that* statement and said briskly, "Well, then, it is all settled! Shall I send a note to him today?"

"Hmmm, why not? The sooner they meet, the sooner we shall know if he is attracted enough to make an offer for her." A frown creasing his forehead, Lord Selby added, "It may not come about, you know—he and Charles Longstreet are reported to be lovers, and if Mr. Ridgeway's taste runs in that direction, he may not want a wife at all."

An expression of distaste crossed Melissa's sallow features. "How disgusting! But I think we have nothing to fear. I have heard several times that another reason for Mr. Ridgeway's trip here to England is to find a wife. And I would think that a young, malleable creature like Elizabeth will be exactly what he would like. She won't make demands upon him, and he can continue to live his life just as he pleases." Scornfully she ended, "It'll be years before the silly chit realizes that her husband has no use for her in the marriage bed... not that it should make any difference to her one way or another."

When the stiffly formal servant informed the "silly chit" that her father wanted her in the library, Elizabeth made her way to that room with an odd sense of foreboding. Not quite seventeen, as blond and pretty as she was kind, Elizabeth always dreaded her father's visits, and she had almost been thankful for the years she had spent away from his country estate in a very strict boarding school for young ladies. At least *there* she was spared his caustic remarks and sarcastic sallies. It had gotten worse since his marriage the previous year to Melissa. Their infrequent visits filled her with dread—her father was coldly indifferent and Melissa made no attempt to hide her dislike of his only child.

Entering the library, she was relieved to find only her father present—it was so much more difficult when he and Melissa took turns baiting her. Determined not to let him intimidate her more than he usually did, Elizabeth lifted her small, rounded chin and said politely, "Good afternoon, Father. Did you have a pleasant trip from London?"

Lord Selby looked her up and down and decided that she really did resemble Anne at the same age... perhaps a bit prettier, he conceded reluctantly, eyeing the full, soft mouth and the large violet eyes. He said dryly, "You are aware that it is winter? That the roads are either muddy bogs or slick with ice, and that even the best coaches are bound to be freezing despite warmed bricks and such?"

Flushing as much from his tone as from the content of the words, Elizabeth nodded.

Seeing her flush and the small nod, he finished bitingly, "Then you also realize what a stupid question that was!"

Elizabeth remained silent. *Nothing* she did found any approval with him.

An expression of boredom settling over his features, Lord Selby said flatly, "Sit down, Elizabeth. I have something of importance to tell you."

Her mouth suddenly dry and her heart beginning to beat a little faster, she did as she was told, taking a seat in one of the chairs near his desk.

Lord Selby stood behind the desk, his clothing a symphony of blue and gray, from the expertly tailored blue frock coat to the gray moleskin trousers that showed off his manly figure. His eyes on her face, he stated bluntly, "Melissa and I have decided that it is time to take care of your future. She has chosen a nice young man who she thinks will suit you admirably. He will probably be arriving to look you over in a few days."

Her face white, Elizabeth stared back at him and couldn't control the instinctive protest that rose to her lips. "But—but... I am not even seventeen yet! I-I-I had hoped that I would be allowed one season in which to—"

"Find a husband?" her father inquired sarcastically.

Elizabeth's eyes flashed at that, and rashly she replied, "Perhaps not! I do not know if I want to wed. At least not right away. My entire life is in front of me, why should I be rushed into marriage this way?"

Almost gently, although his eyes were hard, Lord Selby said, "Let me explain a few things to you, my child. You are not an *un*intelligent girl, despite some of your obviously stupid comments, and I think you can understand what I have to say."

Elizabeth glanced away and bit her lip to keep from saying something she knew he would cause her to regret. Without even being aware of it, the fingers of one hand tightly balled up the material of her fine lavender wool gown.

Indifferent to her reaction, Lord Selby asked coolly, "Now then, if I may have your attention?" And when Elizabeth's gaze was fixed painfully on his face, he continued, "Quite frankly, Elizabeth, you are a reminder of a marriage I should never have made. Every time I look at you I see Anne, and to tell you the truth, I find it a bore. Even more so now that you are no longer in school and will be continually underfoot whenever Melissa and I are in residence." His face taking on a sardonic cast, he continued, "Melissa does not like you, as you know. She finds your presence dreadfully inconvenient. And now that there is the possibility that she may be breeding, it has become imperative that we tidy up all the reminders of my first disastrous marriage. You do understand?"

Elizabeth understood very well. Melissa had never made any attempt to hide her dislike, and now that she was possibly carrying Lord Selby's child, she would be even more jealous and spiteful. Certainly she would not care for any comparisons being made between her child and Anne's, nor would she want *any* shadows from the past to interfere with *her* marriage!

Woodenly, hiding the hurt and dismay that she felt, Elizabeth answered, "I see."

Lord Selby smiled as if she had made a clever observation. "I rather thought you would! Now then, the young man we have in mind is from America. He comes from a good family and is considered to be handsome." His voice suddenly very derisive, he added, "I can almost guarantee that he will not abuse you physically, nor make too many demands upon your body."

Elizabeth blushed hotly and wished the floor would swallow her up at such plain speaking. She was a well-bred young woman, but she still had some inkling of what her father was referring to, and she found it intensely embarrassing, as would any gently reared young lady of 1836.

Forcing herself to act unflustered, she said in a low tone, "But suppose we don't suit? Suppose I-I-I don't like him?"

"But you *shall*, my dear, especially when I point out the alternatives." His voice hard, he continued, "We have this time chosen a nice young man. Refuse him, and the next man we choose might not be so pleasant. Would you like being married to the Duke of Landsdown?"

As the Duke of Landsdown was notorious for his bestiality as well as his ugly, aged body, it was no wonder that Elizabeth shrank against her chair and blanched.

Lord Selby noted her unconscious reaction indifferently and went on smoothly, "I see that my point is taken. You *will* like Nathan Ridgeway! I intend to do the proper thing and settle a sizeable fortune on you, so do not fear that I am turning you penniless from my door...at least not yet. But refuse Mr. Ridgeway, and whatever paternal interest I have in you may vanish."

Staring at Elizabeth's rigid form and the white, stony face, he stated bluntly, "We do not want you here. I have given you all the creature comforts since your birth, but now I want you out of my life. You will have a fortune and a kind husband, and if you are wise, you will take that and be content. The alternatives are not very pleasant. Even if I continued to let you live on my bounty, it is highly improbable that you would be happy with the life you would have to lead, for you would always be an outsider to the family Melissa and I intend to have. Your presence would simply be suffered, and if your intrusion into our lives grew too annoying for Melissa and myself, I'm quite positive that another, though less suitable marriage could be arranged—one you might not like as well as marriage to Mr. Ridgeway. And if you have some insane idea of making your way alone in the world, think hard, Elizabeth, of what the future would hold for you." Brutally he finished, "Marry this young man and take yourself out of our lives."

Elizabeth glanced up at him, unable to hide the rebellion she suddenly felt, but years of rigid training made it impossible for her to defy him.

Lord Selby was aware of her turmoil, but confident of her acquiescence. He almost purred, "But of course, the decision is all yours, my child."

PART ONE

THE CHILD BRIDE

February 1836

We do not what we ought
  What we ought not, we do
And lean upon the thought
  That chance will bring us through

MATTHEW ARNOLD,
"Empedocles on Etna"

CHAPTER ONE

The wedding was over. Upstairs in the large, rather gloomy room she had known all her life, the very new Mrs. Nathan Ridgeway, née Elizabeth Selby, gazed in apprehensive wonder at the wide, intricate gold band around her slim finger. She was married! Married to a man she barely knew! A man who would in a frighteningly short time take her from England and everything she had ever known.

America was such a long way from Maidstone, England, she thought with a sudden shiver. A long way from the gentle rolling valleys and woodlands of Kent. But that was what she wanted, wasn't it? To make a new life for herself—a life full of warmth and love? To be, at last, loved and cared for? To be more than an unwelcome reminder of a match her father had decided was unworthy of his proud title and great wealth.

Her mouth vulnerable, a shadow in the lovely violet eyes, Elizabeth stared at herself in the cheval glass, wishing as she had so often in the past that her mother had lived, that Anne had not died giving birth to her. There were so many questions she needed answered, so many things she needed to know about being a wife . . . and there was no one to whom she could turn. Certainly not her father nor Melissa! She took a deep breath. No, she certainly couldn't ask Melissa, well aware Melissa considered Lord Selby's first marriage a dreadful misalliance.

But her marriage would be different, Elizabeth thought with a spurt of vehemence, her small hands closing into tight little fists. Nathan loved her! And, well, she would *make* herself love him. Already she respected him, and, given time, she was sure the mysterious exquisite emotions she had read about in the few novels that came her way would overtake her and sweep her into a wonderful world of passion and tenderness. She and Nathan would find love together. They *would* love each other forever!

Her thoughts gave her little peace, and with a brave attempt to stifle the fears and doubts that were again surfacing, she concentrated grimly on the simple task of undoing the several tiny pearl buttons on the slim-fitting cuff of her wedding dress. It was a gorgeous gown of heavy, milk-white satin, and, in a gauzy veil studded with hundreds of seed pearls, her silvery curls barely gleaming through its folds, she had looked like an ethereal creature from another world as she had walked slowly down the aisle of the family chapel not more than an hour ago.

Guiltily aware that she was deliberately wasting time and putting off the moment when she would have to join the guests downstairs, she worked faster at the buttons. She should have rung for a servant, but, knowing how rushed they all were with the elaborate preparations, she hadn't wanted to take any of them away from their tasks. Now she wished she had—unfastening the back of the gown was going to be difficult, and if her stepmother Melissa came and found her still not changed...

Sighing, her young, finely molded features rather pensive, she eventually was able to unfasten the gown and disrobe, laying aside without regret the beautiful, extravagant wedding gown. The gown meant little to her—it, like the entire wedding, had been planned for its propriety. Everything must be just so for the wedding of Lord Selby's only child.

And Elizabeth *was* a child, a lonely, lovely child, raised by servants, knowing little of her father except that he occasionally filled the huge rooms of Three Elms with his aristocratic friends and periodically trotted her out for inspection and comment. What she knew of life and the world beyond Maidstone was gleaned from books. Books were her only solace, in books she could lose herself and dream away the long empty hours.

Naturally she had gone to a fitting seminary for

young ladies, but, painfully shy, uncertain in her relationships, she had made only one friend.

Stella Valdez was everything that Elizabeth, or "Beth" as Stella called her affectionately, was not. Tall and dark, with laughing black eyes, forthright, two years older than Elizabeth and full of confidence, Stella was everything that Elizabeth longed to be. Having a family that adored her and being extremely warm-hearted herself, Stella had efficiently taken the small, pale girl under her wing. And through all the bewildering time at Mrs. Finche's Seminary for Young Ladies, Stella had shielded the quieter, gentler Elizabeth from the occasional spitefulness of some of the other girls. But then Stella had left, joining her family in the Mexican province of Coahuila, and from then on Elizabeth had simply endured her time at the seminary until her course was completed and she possessed the attributes necessary for a young lady.

But she was still shy and uncertain, despite her determination to be like her friend and idol, Stella. She wanted to have people love her—someone *special* to love her!

Again, what she knew of love was based on the smuggled novels that she and Stella had read by candlelight in their tiny room at the seminary. She dreamed, as did many young girls, of romance and excitement, of a tall, black-haired, dangerous stranger who would enter her life and, with the suddenness of a thunderbolt, sweep her away with him to a place where they would live happily ever after.

Had Anne, too, dreamed of a life of love? she wondered with a lurch of her stomach. Had her mother thought her love for the young and handsome Lord Selby would overcome all the disapproval their marriage had caused?—a marriage that was certainly *not* all his family and friends would have expected of him!

Again Elizabeth felt a chill. Would *her* husband, her husband who was so different from her dreams, have second thoughts? Would he too perhaps decide he had married unwisely and prefer to forget the existence of a wife? Would he desert her in America?

She bit her lip, wishing suddenly that she had not

let her father and Melissa force her into this marriage. Now that the deed was done, Elizabeth was having very definite second thoughts, wondering if she had been wise to base a marriage only on respect, wondering if somehow she shouldn't have rebelled against her father's wishes.

Nathan Ridgeway was certainly a handsome young man. And as Melissa, her dark eyes glittering coldly, had mentioned more than once, he was a wealthy young man, a well connected young man, despite his American roots.

And so, like many another young girl faced with a hostile stepmother, a father who evinced little interest in her and who actively wanted her out of his life, and a handsome, kind suitor pressing for acceptance of his proposal, Elizabeth had capitulated, smothering all her doubts, dreams, and reservations. What else was left open to her?

In England of 1836, William IV, "Silly Billy," was on the throne; his niece Victoria, barely seventeen and the heiress apparent, was being groomed for the royal duties that one day would be hers. Women were still almost totally under the dominance and control of the men in the family. A woman's role was plain—wife and mother. Anything else was unthinkable for a young lady in Elizabeth's position. Certainly she was not equipped to support herself—an education at Mrs. Finche's exclusive seminary was all she possessed. Unfortunately, Mrs. Finche's had been more concerned with social graces than academic accomplishments, and while Elizabeth had a smattering of geography and languages and could read and write very well, she had few other skills to offer a prospective employer. And the only respectable employment available to her was that of either governess or companion.

Governessing was out, she knew. Her age was against her, and while she herself thought little of her appearance, common sense told her that she looked nothing like a governess—and never would! Not with innocently clear eyes of violet fringed with long, dark, gold-tipped lashes, a straight little nose, a full, generous mouth with a hint of passion in its sultry curve, and hair...how to describe that hair, a sunbeam caught in moonlight? Perhaps—certainly it was masses of shining silvery ash that had a decided tendency to curl in soft tendrils about her face.

Standing in front of a full-length mirror, Elizabeth surveyed herself dispassionately. No, she would never be taken for a governess, not with her features and slender body—the body not yet fully formed, the high pointed breasts still only a delicate promise, the hips still boyishly slim—and yet, despite her lack of height, for she was a small girl, there was the unmistakable hint that someday, when her body attained its adult ripeness, she would be an incredibly lovely woman possessed of a face and body that would cause more than one man to stare after her in admiration and sensual speculation.

But just now, with her face still that of a barely-aware-of-the-world child and the small body slim to the point of thinness, Elizabeth saw nothing that could have encouraged a man like Nathan Ridgeway to plead so earnestly for her hand. But he had and she had accepted—the heavy gold band on her slender finger was proof of that!

The door suddenly opened and Melissa, in a sumptuous gown of soft sage satin with brocade flowers of the same color, swept into the room. Impatiently she glanced at the slender figure clad in the unnecessary corset and a lawn chemise standing near the mirror.

"My word, Elizabeth, haven't you changed yet? You have guests waiting below! Guests—and a new husband, I might add! Where is Mary? Didn't you ring for her?"

Elizabeth remained mute under Melissa's onslaught, knowing her stepmother didn't really expect an answer, nor would she have listened to an explanation.

Crossing the room, Melissa pulled irritably on the bellrope. "Really, you are going to have to stop this mooning about. You are a married woman now!"

Determined not to arouse Melissa further, Elizabeth smiled gently and said softly, "I don't feel any different, Stepmother. I feel just as I did before the wedding. Do just mere words change one?"

"What a ridiculous question!" Melissa snapped. "Of course they do! You are now Mrs. Ridgeway, no longer only the daughter of Lord Selby. Tonight you leave for Portsmouth, and after that for America! The words of the wedding ceremony are what made it possible! How silly of you to wonder if *mere* words can change you!"

Before Melissa could continue with what was fast becoming a vitriolic castigation, a somewhat harassed-looking serving woman scurried into the room.

Dropping a frightened curtsy in Melissa's direction, the woman, Mary Eames, said nervously, "You rang, madame?"

Melissa, her thin lips pursed into a line of displeasure, answered sharply, "Help your mistress to dress, and be quick about it! She's been up here dawdling long enough." Then, ignoring the other two occupants, Melissa gave her dark curls a complacent pat and, after twitching her voluminous skirt in place unnecessarily, approached the door. "I'll expect you downstairs in twenty minutes, Elizabeth. See that you are there! And Mary, if she is not, you will answer to me!"

Elizabeth exchanged glances with the servant, but neither uttered a sound. Instead, Mary hurried over to a carved mahogany wardrobe where a beautiful icy-blue taffeta gown hung in readiness for her mistress.

Deftly Mary slipped the gown over Elizabeth's fair head and expertly arranged the full skirt of the dress. It took only a moment to finish up the fastenings, and after straightening the frothy blond lace that filled the low-cut bodice, Mary turned her attention to Elizabeth's hair.

Mindful of Melissa's wrath if her mistress was not downstairs in the alloted time, Mary wasted little time in arranging the long, heavy, flaxen, nearly silver strands of hair in a Grecian knot worn high in the back, the front hair then being parted and coaxed into soft curls at the temple.

Handing Elizabeth a pair of long white gloves and a fan of carved ivory from India, Mary urged her to the door. Giving Elizabeth an encouraging smile, she said, "If you'll permit me to make a personal remark, miss—that is, madame—you made a perfectly lovely bride, and all of us belowstairs want to wish you and Mr. Ridgeway the very best."

Elizabeth felt a warm rush, wondering if her own shyness had kept her from a warmer relationship with her father's servants—until now they had always seemed so aloof and unapproachable. But the moment was gone, and it was too late to repine on the past. A brave, wavering smile on her soft rosy mouth, her slim shoulders held very straight, she slowly walked to the curving grand staircase that led downstairs. She would never return to these rooms again—she was going to her future! For just a moment she closed her eyes, offering a desperate little prayer that she had made the right decision in accepting Nathan Ridgeway's proposal.

Downstairs in the main ballroom, decorated for the occasion with huge silver tubs of white carnations and white gladiolus, there were others who were also wondering if Lord Selby's decision to accept Mr. Ridgeway's suit had been in the best interests of his only child. As the Dowager Duchess of Chatham whispered to her close crony, the kindhearted Lady Alstair, "After all, what does one really know of this young man, beyond his beautiful manners? I certainly wouldn't want to marry a child of mine to one I knew so little about. And the child is so young! I would have thought Melissa would grant her at least *one* season before marrying her off in this hurly-burly manner." Rolling her eyes expressively, she continued, "Of course, it must be mortifying to have such a young stepdaughter—and such a *lovely* one at that! I suppose one can't really blame Melissa for engineering the match. As for Selby's countenance of it, everyone knows he regretted his first marriage and has ignored the child. If only Elizabeth had been a boy..." There was a brief moment of silence as both ladies considered how different Elizabeth's life would have been if she had indeed been the son her father wanted. The duchess then continued, "I do feel so sorry for the child. Raised by servants and spending most of her time in that seminary. Selby has much to answer for in his treatment of her. Imagine, ignoring your own child! The poor little thing has had virtually no family life—just servants and schoolmistresses. No one to *really* care about her!"

"Disgraceful!" Lady Alstair murmured, her ready sympathy aroused. "Even if he *was* ashamed of her mother's antecedents, which were respectable, if unexceptional, there was no reason to treat his own child so cavalierly!"

"I agree, my dear! But you know Selby—a colder, prouder man I have never met." Leaning closer to her friend, the dowager duchess breathed, "Look at his marriage to Melissa. She is twenty-eight, long past her first blush of youth, and certainly one would have to call her attractive rather than pretty. But because of her birth, because of being the daughter of a duke, Selby decided she was a suitable bride. He wants that heir, you know."

Eyeing Melissa as she stood conversing with several London acquaintances at the far end of the imposing room, Lady Alstair inquired, "Do you think she is breeding?"

"More than likely—and all the more reason for her to marry off little Elizabeth to an American. Melissa will not want *her* children to share any of Selby's wealth with a half sister! I certainly hope that Selby has done right by the child."

Nathan Ridgeway, watching Elizabeth come slowly down the stairs, was extremely curious about the same thing. He had no intention of seeing Elizabeth done out of a fortune simply because her father had married a greedy, selfish woman. Smiling easily at Elizabeth, Nathan walked across the room to greet her.

"How beautiful you look, my love. Truly, I am the luckiest of men today," he said in a low tone, his eyes concealing his speculation as they roamed over her face.

Some of Elizabeth's doubts fled as she looked into his fine features. Nathan Ridgeway was definitely a pleasant-looking young man, possessing wide, thickly lashed gray eyes, a handsomely male nose, and a full well-shaped mouth. Only the most critical and discerning person would have noticed that the eyes were apt to slide away from one's gaze and that the chin had a hint of weakness. His face was fair, although not quite as fair as Elizabeth's silvery curls, and he stood a few inches under six feet, a slim, delicately boned man, his muttonchop whiskers making him appear older than his actual twenty-six years.

Giving him a shy smile—for Elizabeth was still very much in awe of her new husband—she stared down at her square-toed satin slippers that peeped from beneath the voluminous taffeta skirt and murmured, "I hope I haven't kept you waiting too long?"

Nathan clasped her hand gently in his and, bending his head closer to hers, said softly, "I could never wait too long for you, my sweet."

Her troubled heart expanding like a flower under the sun at his words, a rush of something near to love for him swept through her. She *had* made the right decision, and, given time, one day she would be able to return Nathan's love with an emotion to match what he felt for her.

They made a pretty pair as they stood there together, Nathan a head or so taller than Elizabeth, both young, both slim, and both almost startling in their fairness. More than one matron was misty-eyed as she gazed at them. Their entire future was in front of them, and what a marvelous future it would be: Elizabeth, at present Lord Selby's only child, was in line for an enormous fortune; Nathan, the youngest son of a wealthy plantation owner in Natchez, had already been given, as a wedding gift from his father, hundreds of fertile acres near the banks of the Mississippi River in Louisiana. A magnificent house on the bluff that constituted "Upper Natchez" was currently under construction for them. As for the wedding presents from the guests, the couple would lack for nothing—crystal, silver, china, linen, exquisite trifles, and numerous expensive odds and ends had been pouring in for days.

"Congratulations, Ridgeway," grated a harsh voice behind the young couple, interrupting their absorption in each other.

Elizabeth slowly turned to look in the direction of the voice, noting vaguely the way Nathan suddenly dropped her hand as if it burned him and the way his whole body seemed to freeze as he pivoted to stare at the swarthy, burly man who had spoken.

Stiffly, Nathan replied, "Thank you, Longstreet. I didn't expect to see you here."

"Oh?" the other inquired lightly. "You thought I would miss the wedding of one of my dearest and best-*loved* friends?"

Aware of a sudden, odd constraint in the air and puzzled by a note in Longstreet's voice that she couldn't quite place, she glanced from one to the other. Her first impression of Mr. Longstreet was not favorable. He frightened her just a little with his icy, icy blue eyes and heavy, almost ugly features. Striving to break the uncomfortable silence that had fallen, Elizabeth asked softly, "Will you introduce me, Mr. Rid—I mean Nathan? I don't believe I've ever heard you mention Mr. Longstreet before."

"Not mentioned me?" Longstreet said with a sharp bark of harsh laughter. "How odd! Not more than six weeks ago in London he swore undying . . . ah . . . *friendship* for me."

"Lower your voice, you fool! Everyone is staring," Nathan muttered, his gray eyes suddenly wary. Catching Elizabeth's startled gaze, he shot her an agonized look. "Excuse us a few moments, my dear? Longstreet is not quite himself."

Not waiting for her assent, Nathan grasped the other man's arm and briskly escorted him into the gardens. More than a little bewildered by the exchange, Elizabeth stared after them, curious as to how her husband had come to have such an odd friend. Why, Mr. Longstreet, she thought to herself, had acted almost jealous. . . .

That queer little idea brought to mind one of her greatest misgivings: She knew so little about Nathan Ridgeway, other than that he came of a respectable family and that her father had given his permission for Nathan to approach her with an offer of marriage. Thinking back on the past few months, she admitted that her courtship had been a very tepid affair. Almost completely innocent about relationships between men and women, she wasn't quite positive how she knew that—it was just that she sensed strongly that something was missing between her and Nathan. Certainly their courtship had not been the rapturous whirlwind she had read about in those romances, nor did Nathan resemble the black-haired, vibrant hero she dreamed about. Almost regretfully she reminded herself that Nathan's courting had been correct, and she firmly pushed away the wish that he had been more eager, more inclined to steal a kiss or a forbidden embrace. It was very vulgar and not very nice of her to continue to think such thoughts, she scolded herself. Young ladies of her station and breeding did not pine over such common and unnecessary things as kisses and stolen embraces!

Elizabeth had learned little about her married duties from Melissa, only that she was "to obey her husband and endure quietly and with a ladylike demeanor while he satisfied his base temptations." Certainly *that* did not sound very exciting, nor did it resemble the thrilling emotions that moved her favorite heroine! But then, her heroine was *in love,* not merely marrying for the sake of expediency.

Annoyed at herself for bemoaning her fate and for wishing for something she couldn't even name, she glanced shyly around the room, hoping to catch a friendly eye. In this she was more than successful, as the Dowager Duchess of Chatham and Lady Alstair, having noticed her abandonment by Nathan, swept up to her, and Elizabeth found herself warmly clasped first to the duchess's massive puce-satin-covered bosom and then engulfed in an embrace by Lady Alstair.

"My dearest, *dearest* child!" exclaimed the duchess, an encouraging smile on the plump, merry features. "You made a lovely, lovely bride. I am so happy for you and positively delighted to see you so successfully launched in life."

"Oh, yes, dear Elizabeth, you are very fortunate," chimed in Lady Alstair, her faded blue eyes kind as they surveyed Elizabeth's fragile loveliness. "Mr. Ridgeway is a most exemplary young man, and you are to be congratulated upon your marriage. I wish you *very* happy, my dear."

Flustered and slightly taken aback to find herself the object of such unexpected attention and kindly interest by two of the most formidable matrons in the room, Elizabeth could only smile uncertainly and stammer, "Why—why, th-thank y-you!"

Both elderly ladies beamed at her as if she had just said something extremely clever. Conversation would have languished then, if Lord Selby himself, looking particularly splendid in a tight-fitting tailored coat of claret kerseymere, his cool aristocratic handsomeness intensified by the high white satin stock about his throat, hadn't strolled over just as Elizabeth finished speaking.

"Deserted by the bridegroom already, Elizabeth?" he inquired dryly, his eyes flickering over to the open door where Nathan and Charles Longstreet could be seen in deep conversation.

Tongue-tied as usual in her father's presence, Elizabeth shot him a doubtful look. He so seldom paid her any heed that she wasn't quite certain whether he was really interested or merely commenting on an obvious fact. It appeared, this time at least, that he was more than a little interested, for as he watched Nathan a frown began to crease his forehead.

"Well, we can't have that!" he said after a moment's pause. "Excuse us, ladies, I intend to reunite my daughter with her husband. Come along, Elizabeth. Nathan should be ashamed of himself, neglecting you so soon." And, taking Elizabeth gently by the arm, he started firmly across the room.

It was an odd sensation for Elizabeth, walking by his side, his strong hand loosely clasping her arm. It was the first time she could ever remember her father touching her, and she wondered that it should come at a time when she was no longer under his control. Peeping up at his coldly chiseled features, she marveled that this aloof man was her father. Even approaching forty years of age, Jasper Selby was still an incredibly handsome man—tall, above six feet, and with an athletic build. It was not surprising that Anne had fallen in love with him some eighteen years before. His hair was golden brown, that shade of light hair that never seems to fade, only growing fairer with the passage of time as the silver strands replace the golden ones. The face itself was enhanced rather than diminished by the slight grooves of dissipation in his lean cheeks and the attractive creases that radiated out from piercing blue eyes.

Unconsciously Elizabeth sighed. All her life she had wanted desperately to love him, but his very nature made it impossible. How can one love a person who is never there? Love a father who has made it plain he wishes nothing to do with a daughter? At least, she reminded herself guiltily, he hadn't completely abandoned her and thrown her out into the gutter. For *that* she would try to like him and try even harder not to resent his lack of affection for her.

Selby heard the small sound she made and glanced down at her. "Something wrong, Elizabeth?"

Startled that he had even noticed, she said quickly, "Oh, no, Father, everything is wonderful."

"Well, then, let us hope that it remains so," he replied in a bored tone, effectively banishing any further chance of conversation.

Nathan happened to glance up just as they approached. With an almost panic-stricken look, he hurriedly muttered something to his companion. Longstreet instantly turned to greet them, saying with an edge, "Ah, Lord Selby, you are to be congratulated on your daughter's marriage. She certainly made a lovely bride, and I'm sure"—shooting an enigmatic smile at Nathan—"that young Nate here will make an exemplary husband."

"How very, very clever of you to notice," Lord Selby returned sardonically. "But then, you know Nathan rather well, don't you?"

His eyes like hard pebbles, Longstreet bowed. "Yes, I do. Have you any objections, my lord?"

"None, provided your . . . ah . . . friendship does not interfere with my daughter's marriage. I'm certain you understand my meaning."

It appeared that both of the other gentlemen did, but Elizabeth was completely bewildered as she looked from

Nathan's stricken white face to Longstreet's darkening one.

"Are you threatening me, Selby?" Longstreet growled.

Selby's eyebrows rose. "I beg your pardon, sir! And how very absurd of you to take exception to my words. Now, Longstreet, do calm yourself. I merely meant that I will allow no scandal to touch my daughter. Your friendship with Nathan is of no interest to me, provided you are discreet. Have I made myself clear?" he inquired in a soft, deadly voice.

Again, Longstreet bowed. "Perfectly, my lord. And I believe your views on the subject are a bit moot. Nathan and his bride leave shortly, and I think it would be impossible for even myself to create a scandal in that short time."

His eyes hooded, Lord Selby nodded. "Of course. I merely thought it wise to make certain that you understood the situation."

"Of that you can rest assured!" Longstreet murmured sarcastically.

Nathan had remained silent during the curious exchange, his eyes not meeting Elizabeth's as she stood by her father's side. Baffled and deeply mystified by the entire exchange, she stirred restlessly, wishing her father had not chosen to take such an unwarranted interest in Nathan's friendship with Longstreet. It was obvious that Nathan was very embarrassed by the whole thing, and her gentle heart went out to him. How uncomfortable he looked, she thought sympathetically.

Moved by an oddly protective feeling, she released her father's arm and determinedly crossed to stand by her husband, her small hand entwining tightly around Nathan's. It was as if she were giving him encouragement, and, smiling gently at Longstreet and her father, she said quietly, "Nathan and I appreciate your concern, but your fears are misplaced, Father, in thinking that Mr. Longstreet's friendship will cause us any difficulties. Nathan would not have a friendship with anyone who was not a gentleman."

To say who was the most astonished by her words would be difficult. Certainly Elizabeth herself was astonished that she could speak so bravely to her father, and her father was taken aback that a daughter he freely stigmatized as a foolish chit would express herself so confidently. Nathan too was caught off guard, but he quickly recovered himself, murmuring with relief, "Well, now that we all understand the situation, I propose the subject be dropped. After all, this is our wedding day."

Lord Selby gave him a faintly contemptuous smile. "Just so, and you would do well to remember it." Then, glancing over at Longstreet, he commented, "I suggest we absent ourselves, Longstreet, as the newlyweds obviously wish to be alone."

Longstreet hesitated a moment, as if he would say more, but then Lord Selby prodded him further by drawling, "Longstreet, dear fellow, I know you are saddened by the thought of Nathan's approaching departure, but really, all things must come to an end. Come along now and let the children be."

After that, Longstreet had no choice in the matter, and with ill-concealed grace he followed Lord Selby across the crowded ballroom floor. With their departure an awkward silence fell between Elizabeth and Nathan. Still slightly amazed that she had so boldly spoken out in front of three gentlemen, Elizabeth queried uncertainly, "Should I not have spoken, Mr. Rid—I mean Nathan? I didn't mean to intrude, but Father and Mr. Longstreet were having such an odd conversation—and you looked so miserable that I felt I had to do *something!*"

Nathan sent her a grateful look and, squeezing her hand, he muttered, "No. No, I'm just delighted the entire incident is behind us."

Her eyes troubled, she stared up at his faintly harassed features. "Nathan, is there something I should know? I mean, is Mr. Longstreet not a very nice man?"

His mouth tightened and he said with sudden and unaccustomed venom, "No, Mr. Longstreet is not a very nice man! I wish to God I had never met him!"

Puzzled as much by the harshness of his tone as by

what he said, Elizabeth asked, "Then why are you friends with him?"

He flashed her a strangely pathetic look and murmured agitatedly, "Because I am a fool, and I *cannot help* myself!"

CHAPTER TWO

Nathan would say no more. But from that point on, Elizabeth sensed there was something decidedly not quite right, and as the day passed she grew more and more uneasy. All the uncertainties she had experienced earlier in her bedroom resurfaced and she spent a miserable time, a happy smile pasted on her mouth as she received one congratulation after another, all the while wondering about the strange conversation and Nathan's odd words.

Her husband was as uneasy as she, that much she could tell, and he was equally unhappy. *But why?* she speculated to herself. *And what part does Mr. Longstreet play?*

Finally the whole ostentatious affair was over and the last guest had departed. Her valises and trunks were being loaded onto the coach that would take them to the train station, Nathan's baggage having been strapped on earlier. Their departure from Three Elms would be within the hour, and Elizabeth found herself, despite all her reservations, glad to leave the coldly elegant house in which she had been raised. She would probably never see it again, and that thought brought no remorse. She had been unhappy there and wished to put all the empty lonely memories behind her. Yet there was no denying it gave her an uneasy feeling in the pit of her stomach to know that when she walked out through those huge, brass-hinged double doors she would be severing whatever ties she had with her father, Three Elms, and England. She would be alone except for Nathan, and Nathan was virtually a stranger to her.

Elizabeth was staring out at the gardens in the falling twilight, realizing suddenly that she would miss her favorite rose-covered swing seat, where she had so often spent hours and hours lost in the excitement and romance of a novel by Jane Austen or Sir Walter Scott, when one of the servants informed her that she was wanted in her father's library. Slightly mystified, she quickly found her way to that book-lined, leather-smelling room.

Her father was seated languidly behind a tambour desk in the Sheraton style, Nathan nearby in a high-backed red leather chair. It was quiet in the room except for the soft ticking of a marquetry clock on the gray marble mantel. The soft glow of gaslight bathed the room, giving it an intimate air.

Nathan rose quickly to his feet when she entered and solicitously saw that she was seated in the twin of his chair near the corner of the desk. From the quick look that she had at his face, she could see that he was under a terrible strain. When he said nothing and kept his eyes averted from hers, she looked questioningly to her father.

Lord Selby smiled rather grimly. "Your husband has just suffered a reversal, and he is more than a little disappointed. I must confess that it is partly my fault. It seems that while your husband is satisfied with the amount I have settled upon you, he does not like the fact that I have set it up in a trust to be administered by a bank in Natchez."

"I'm afraid I don't quite understand," Elizabeth confessed bewilderedly.

"It is very simple, my dear," Nathan said in a mortified tone of voice. "Your father is a very *untrusting* gentleman. He has decided that I am not sufficiently competent to handle your money."

Selby gave an unpleasant laugh. "You, my young cockerel, are not competent to handle your own affairs, and certainly not Elizabeth's!"

Humiliated and showing it, Nathan surged to his feet. His fists clenched at his sides, he said impetuously, "Sir! I do not have to stay here and be insulted this way!"

"No, you don't, do you? But you *will!* Now sit down,

Ridgeway, and I shall explain it to my daughter. Hopefully she has brains enough to understand what I am saying."

Elizabeth flushed and stared at her hands folded in her lap. At this moment she almost hated her father—yes, *hated* him for the way he was treating Nathan and for the way in which he belittled her intelligence. There was silence in the room for a moment, and then with an exaggerated sigh Lord Selby murmured, "If I may have your attention, please."

Elizabeth's head jerked up at that, and, hiding her emotions behind a smooth, innocent mask, she stared back at him. Her eyes serene, she said steadily, "You have our attention now, Father. And I can assure you, I will understand every word you say. At Mrs. Finche's they *did* teach us English."

Lord Selby's eyes narrowed, and for a moment Elizabeth thought he would say more, but apparently he had grown tired of baiting them, for he said patronizingly, "I won't mention the amount of money involved because it would mean little to you. Sufficient to say, it is a fortune and should keep you in the elegancies to which you are accustomed for the remainder of your life... keep you, whatever children you may have, and your husband if that need be. But as Nathan is a fairly wealthy young man himself, that will not be necessary—" Throwing Nathan a derisive look, he finished dryly, "I hope."

Nathan's face whitened and he choked out, "How kind of you, sir!"

Ignoring his son-in-law, he glanced at his daughter and continued, "I have arranged that until you are thirty years of age, the banking firm of Tyler and Deering in Natchez will oversee your fortune. They are to pay all bills and approve all but the most trifling expenses. You will be given an allowance which should cover the various fripperies you may wish to buy yourself. But everything must be approved by them. That includes even your dressmakers' bills. When you are thirty, if in their opinion it is proper to do so, Nathan shall then have the trust turned over to him to administer as he sees fit, and," he finished cynically, "by that time I trust he will have outgrown some of his more expensive habits."

If Lord Selby had wanted to humiliate and belittle his son-in-law he couldn't have chosen a better way. It was one of the most galling things he could have done to the young man, and Elizabeth recognized it instantly. Suddenly feeling very tired, she said quietly, "Is that all, Father? If it is, I believe it is time that Nathan and I were on our way, don't you? I rather think you have accomplished what you set out to do."

It was Nathan's turn to look puzzled. Puzzled and a little surprised that the normally shy and retiring Elizabeth could speak so coolly, and to her father at that. It surprised Elizabeth also, but she had discovered a deep burning anger at her father, and with it came the courage to cross verbal swords with him. Her eyes slightly defiant, she waited for him to reply.

Lord Selby smiled, not a very nice smile, and murmured, "So, the little mouse has turned into a scratching kitten. Perhaps marriage is good for you."

With an action completely foreign to her, Elizabeth inclined her head haughtily and rose from her seat. "Thank you, Father. Nathan and I both appreciate your compliments on our marriage, and I wish we had more time to spend with you, but I believe the carriage is waiting for us. Excuse us, please?"

It was a regal leavetaking, and Elizabeth's unaccustomed rage lasted until long after Three Elms had disappeared in the distance. By the time they reached the train station, she was shaking, as much from the uncertainty of the future as the effects of behaving in such a bold and uncharacteristic manner. She was mortified to think that she had been so brazen as to speak for her husband, and somewhat fearfully she asked him, "Are you angry with me, Nathan, for saying what I did to my father? I didn't mean to speak out of turn, but I was so *very* angry."

Nathan gave a tired sigh. Gently patting her hand, he said wearily, "No, my dear, I don't mind at all. I am, if the truth be known, rather grateful that you said what you did. But at the moment I would rather not talk about it. Forget about it for now, my dear, and tomorrow or the next day we will discuss it."

It wasn't what she wanted to hear, but it satisfied her and, like the obedient child she usually was, she did just that. Besides, this would be the beginning of an entirely new venture for her, and she made up her mind in that instant that she was going to enjoy it... *no matter what!*

Entering the elegant first-class compartment that had been reserved for their journey to Portsmouth, Elizabeth discovered with pleasure the sturdy figure of Mary Eames unpacking her night clothing. Her face reflecting her pleasure, she asked with curiosity, "Mary, what are you doing here?"

"Well, I'll tell you, miss... er... madame, at the moment I'm not even sure myself! I've been in such a bustle and hustle since this afternoon that I don't know my head from my heels," Mary replied with a twinkle in her kind blue eyes. "It was only then that it occurred to your husband that you had no maid with you. He said it would be better if you had someone you knew to serve you rather than to hire a complete stranger."

A tremulous smile breaking across her face, Elizabeth said happily, "Oh, how truly kind of him! I was dreading the thought of having absolutely no one that I knew around me." And as Mary Eames had always been one of her favorite servants, she said impetuously, "Well, he couldn't have chosen someone that would please me better."

"Now that's a nice thing to hear, miss!" Mary replied with a wide grin, her blue eyes resting affectionately on the young, finely boned creature staring back at her. "I'm most happy to be here. And I can't tell you how excited I am to be able to serve you on this trip."

Struck by a sudden thought, Elizabeth inquired anxiously, "You will be coming to America with me, won't you? You don't have to go back to Maidstone, do you?"

A rather pleased and gratified smile spread over the plain face. "Why, miss, if you want me to, I certainly will! Mr. Ridgeway said we should leave it up to you, but he did ask me if I had any objections to leaving

England and making my home in America. Fancy him knowing that you might ask me to come with you!"

A warm burst of affection for her husband's unexpected intuition flashed through Elizabeth, and mentally she echoed Mary's sentiments. How clever of Nathan and how very kind of him to guess her feelings of strangeness and to realize how very, very welcome Mary's presence would be in Natchez.

The train trip on "The Planet" was uneventful—Elizabeth sleeping soundly and alone in the comfort of their first-class compartment, Nathan finding his way to the gentlemen's smoking room and apparently remaining there until they reached Portsmouth. At Portsmouth they were quickly transferred to the handsome hotel where they would stay for the next two days before boarding the ship that would take them to America. And it was there that Elizabeth's uncertainties returned to haunt her.

It was nothing that Nathan did, rather it was what he *didn't* do! She hadn't thought a great deal about it when she had slept in lonely comfort in their compartment on the train, but when she discovered that Nathan had booked suites at the hotel for both of them—her chaste state was almost certainly to continue—she not unnaturally grew puzzled. Though the facts of the marriage bed were somewhat mysterious to her, she wasn't so naïve not to realize that it was rather strange for a bridegroom to avoid sleeping with his bride. Unfortunately, she was too shy and embarrassed to question her husband about it, and those same reasons kept her from confiding in Mary. Maybe, she told herself wistfully, he was waiting until they were on the ship and finally on their way to America.

Except for his avoidance of the marriage bed during those days in Portsmouth, Nathan was everything a young bride could ask for, as he uncomplainingly escorted her about the bustling seaport town, pointing out sites of interest—such as Southsea Castle, built by Henry VIII and later taken by the Parliamentary forces in 1642 and partly dismantled, as well as the crumbling ruins of Porchester Castle, once a Norman fortress. He spoiled her outrageously, buying her little trinkets, bottles of expensive perfumes and powders, and several pieces of fine jewelry. She was flattered and delighted with the gifts, but at night, tucked up in virginal splendor in her bed, she would have gladly foregone them all to have Nathan pull her into his arms and teach her what physical love was all about.

It wasn't until the afternoon before they sailed on the evening tide that she discovered the probable reason for Nathan's tardiness in denying himself conjugal rights. She was seated alone at her table in the tearoom of the hotel enjoying a deliciously brewed cup of Earl Grey, while Nathan was busy seeing to the last-minute preparations for their journey, when one of the men sitting at a table behind her said something that caught her attention.

"I saw Charles Longstreet earlier today."

"That pederast! I thought he was mincing about London. I wonder what brings him to Portsmouth, of all places?"

"I rather think it is *who* rather than *what!* I just saw him and that American fellow Ridgeway together, and even a blind man could tell that Longstreet was enamored of the young man." The man gave an unkind laugh and added, "And that Ridgeway was spurning his advances...perhaps I should say spurning his *further* advances."

Elizabeth's face went white and, with a hand that shook, she set down her cup of tea. What in Heaven's name were they implying? One incredulous thought after another jostled frantically about in her head and none of them made any sense. She only knew that there was something about the conversation that she should understand, but it eluded her...perhaps because she willed it to?

Uneasy and apprehensive for no apparent reason, she was unable to remain seated at the table one second longer. Was it that she feared she would hear something that would bring understanding to her? She didn't wait to find out. Instead, like a startled fawn, she hurried to her room, unwilling to think about what she had heard. Once safely in her room, the words so carelessly spoken came back to haunt her and to make her wish she were a more sophisticated young woman.

Her eyes bright with almost feverish intensity, she stared out the window of the hotel at the wide expanse of the cold blue ocean. In just a few hours she would be boarding the ship that would take her from England. Was she going to let a bit of what was surely malicious gossip destroy her marriage and her future? For a second, the picture of Three Elms flashed through her mind, and the memory of Melissa's dislike as well as her father's cold indifference returned. No! She could not return there! Her future was with Nathan. Nathan who loved her and who cared for her. She must believe that, and she must dismiss the ugly conversation from her mind.

Nathan entered the room just then, his smile warm and endearing. "Well, my love, are you ready for the long journey to America? I know you will find the journey somewhat boring, but when we reach New Orleans I know you shall feel it was well worth it."

Taking a closer look at her, he noticed instantly the signs of agitation that she hadn't yet been able to hide, and, his face immediately concerned, he asked seriously, "Is something wrong, my dear?"

At the note of kindness in his voice, her heart contracted painfully. Those men were wicked, wicked creatures spreading ugly, vicious half-truths, she told herself vehemently. And then, because she was, after all, an unworldly, naïve, and bewildered child, she suddenly broke into nearly hysterical tears and threw herself into Nathan's arms.

Genuinely alarmed and astounded by Elizabeth's obvious and unexplained distress, Nathan's arms tightened instinctively around her slim body. "My love, my love, hush," he murmured softly into the bright golden-ash waves that tickled his chin. "What has disturbed you? Is it that you are unhappy leaving your home? Please don't be—I will make you happy, I promise I shall." Almost grimly, he added, "No matter what!"

Mortified that she had given away so ignominiously, Elizabeth vainly tried to stifle the sobs that were racking her body. Looking at Nathan's troubled features with tear-drowned violet eyes, Elizabeth asked with pathetic wistfulness, "Do you love me, Nathan? *Truly* love me?"

She felt him stiffen and, unable to understand her own motives, her hands clutched at his shoulders. "Tell me the truth, I beg of you! *Do you love me?"*

His eyes searching hers, Nathan gently pushed back a wayward lock of hair that had fallen onto her forehead. "Beth, what is it, my dear? You know that I love you. I wouldn't have married you if I didn't love you more than any woman in the world." His voice husky, he went on emotionally, "You are my hope for the future. And if I find that I can't... I can't... with you, then I am truly damned."

"Can't what, Nathan?" Elizabeth whispered tightly, the soft mouth beginning to tremble.

Nathan pulled her closer into his arms, the expression on his face tormented. In a voice barely audible he muttered, "Happiness, if I can't find happiness with you, then I deserve whatever the future may bring me."

For a long moment he gazed down into her face, and then slowly his head lowered and he kissed her deeply, his mouth warm and reassuring on hers. Elizabeth eagerly returned his embrace, deliberately forcing herself to be satisfied with Nathan's avowals for their future happiness. She did believe him. She had no reason not to, and so with a soft sigh she melted into him.

Nathan's arms seemed to tighten more excitedly about her slender form, his mouth moving tantalizingly across hers. It was a gentle kiss and Elizabeth was sorry when it ended. But too soon, Nathan lifted his head and glanced down at her. His face kind, he asked quietly, "Feeling better now? No more worries about whether I love you or not?"

A tremulous smile beginning to peep from the violet eyes and convinced he loved *her,* she returned shyly, "Oh, yes. I mean no!" He laughed at her indecision and she said quickly, "Oh, you know what I mean!"

"I do indeed, my dear!" Reaching out for one of Elizabeth's hands, he carried it to his mouth and gently kissed it. "Trust me, my love. Everything will be just fine. *Trust me!"*

CHAPTER THREE

In spite of the reassuring conversation with Nathan, Elizabeth found the journey across the dark-blue Atlantic to New Orleans a bewildering time. As he had done at the hotel in Portsmouth, Nathan had reserved separate accommodations for them on the *Belle Maria*, and night after night Elizabeth slept alone, as virginal as the day she had left her mother's womb.

It was a subject she could not bring herself to discuss with Nathan. But the question hovered on her lips a dozen times a day. *Why? Why doesn't he seek my bed?*

She knew little about marriage, but she knew that theirs was progressing at an odd rate. Nathan was kind to her, solicitously watching over her and attempting to keep her entertained on the long uneventful journey. Yet the closeness she had thought would come did not, neither a physical one nor a mental one. Nathan appeared to dote on her, but still she never really felt as if she knew him any better than she had on the day she accepted his offer of marriage. He was polite, he was kind, and he was concerned—he was *not* a lover!

It was Elizabeth's gentle nature to blame herself for the lack of consummation, and it simply never occurred to her that the fault lay with Nathan. She blamed herself bitterly for her continued state of virginity.

If only, she thought disconsolately, she were more beautiful, more womanly, instead of a thin stick of a child! If only she knew more of the world, of the ways to please a man. She was certain it was her own inadequacies that kept her husband from her. Upon occasion she was tempted to discuss the matter with Mary, but shyness held her back. It was too embarrassing a confession to be blurted out to one's maid.

Finally she gathered enough courage to bring up the subject with Nathan. She couldn't even get the words out, but Nathan guessed and, his face wearing a strained smile, he muttered, "Ah...er...yes, of course, I know it must seem strange to you, my dear, but I thought perhaps it would be best if we waited. New Orleans is a lovely, lovely city, and I thought it would be more enjoyable for us if we waited until we reached there to...um...begin our honeymoon."

Again reassured, and thinking how very considerate he was of her, Elizabeth was able to look forward to reaching their destination. But her worry about the lack of Nathan's ardor did not diminish. It plagued and troubled her, and no matter how often she chastised herself for being a forward piece and probably very vulgar and common too, she couldn't help but wish Nathan wasn't *quite* so forbearing and thoughtful of her.

The problem was compounded by the fact that, like any extremely romantic young girl of seventeen, she dreamed. Dreamed wild exotic dreams that on waking would bring a flush to her cheeks. Too often at night, as she lay listening to the waves breaking against the ship, her mind drifted aimlessly and she lost herself in daydreams and sleeping dreams that sometimes frightened and alarmed her. She was a married woman, if not a wife in the true sense of the word, and she should not still be dreaming of a tall, black-haired devil. But she was. It seemed every night he came to her. She never saw his face completely, it was always shadowed or in profile, but she knew it as well as she knew her own, and it haunted her. The dreams were all vaguely terrifying, and in the morning she could never quite recall what had happened, but she remembered she had been filled with terror, that there had been danger, even pain. What she did remember most clearly was a hard mouth on hers and strange, frighteningly exquisite emotions that were evoked by hard, ungentle hands on her body.

There was no one she could talk to about these oddly lifelike dreams, and she was deeply embarrassed that she could recall the man's kisses but not his face or what happened. More than once she started to confide in Mary, but her innate shyness or the fear of being ridiculed held her back. Yet there was something so very precious about these dreams that she wasn't certain she wanted to share them with anyone, even someone as undemanding and kind as Mary Eames. Instead, Elizabeth treasured them and almost looked forward to the night, the dreams...and the man!

Despite all the fears and uncertainties besetting her, Elizabeth was enthralled by New Orleans. The intricate iron-worked balconies of the houses in the Vieux Carré, the incredible array of items to be found in the French Market as well as in the numerous shops and stores, and the theaters and the various amusements to be found in that beguiling, charming city spreading on the banks of the Mississippi River all filled her with pleasure.

Strangely enough, when Nathan again reserved separate suites for them and, somewhat red in the face, suggested another delay before they indulged in the "delights of marriage" (his choice of words), Elizabeth was not surprised. She was gradually accepting the idea that for some as yet unexplained reason theirs was a different marriage from most, and that when Nathan felt the time was exactly right she would discover the...er...delights of marriage. She didn't chafe so much against the delay, for she was beginning to wonder if "it" was so awful that Nathan was sparing her the evil moment.

Still, she wondered about the intimacies of the marriage bed, and on their second night in New Orleans she somewhat timidly brought up the subject. They were both preparing to retire after a pleasant day of exploring the city, and, dreading her large, lonely bed, Elizabeth had been unable to prevent herself from asking Nathan to at least enter her bedchamber and explain, if he would, why they could not even share the same bed—they didn't have to *do* anything, if he didn't want to.

It was an awkward moment. Elizabeth again filled with mortification at her forwardness, and Nathan's fair skin turned bright red in obvious embarrassment. They stood staring mutely at each other, Elizabeth incredibly appealing in a soft clinging peignoir of lavender silk and Nathan very handsome and boyish in a robe of red-and-black brocade. For several seconds they remained thus, and then Nathan seemed to shake himself, and with a nervous smile he said, "My dearest child, of course I will enter your bedchamber! I merely wanted to give you privacy if you wished it and..." He hesitated, swallowed with apparent difficulty, and finished, "And if you want me to share your bed, I see no reason to postpone the moment."

That Nathan was as nervous or even more nervous than herself was glaringly evident, and Elizabeth's own fears expanded to a point where she very nearly beseeched him to pretend she had never said a thing. It was a silent couple who entered that bedchamber, and an increasingly apprehensive Elizabeth who laid aside her lavender peignoir and, clad only in the delicate matching gown that clung almost lovingly to her slender curves, settled herself into bed. With huge, nearly purple eyes, she watched as Nathan, with interminable slowness, shed his robe and stood before her wearing only his linen nightshirt. He quickly blew out the candle, and in the darkness Elizabeth heard the sounds of further clothing being removed. Her heart beating in her throat, she waited with a dry mouth for her husband to join her.

Nathan's entrance into her bed was somewhat gingerly, and after slipping under the satin coverlet, he lay stiffly by her side for several more moments. Then, his own agitation and nervousness nearly tangible, he slowly reached for Elizabeth.

Tentatively he pulled her next to him, and with butterflylike pressure began to touch her. His lips were warm and kind, but instinctively Elizabeth sensed that there was no passion in him. In the time that followed, that feeling grew. How she knew it she wasn't sure, she just knew that Nathan's uncertain and hesitant caresses were halfhearted, as if he wanted to please her, wanted to be passionate—but *could not!* He fumbled for some time with her small breasts, his hands moving with increasing agitation over them and his mouth pressing harder against her lips. Elizabeth tried to respond, but Nathan's inept and reluctant touches, instead of arousing passion, caused her to become even more uncertain and frightened, unable to take any enjoyment from the strange but not unpleasant sensations his touch on her body aroused. As the moments passed and Elizabeth lay next to him in bewilderment and embarrassment, not quite certain what should happen next, what she should do or what he would do, Nathan's caresses grew almost frantic, and Elizabeth had the oddest feeling that he was in the grip of some sort of angry frustration, his body pressed hard against hers. And with gentle accommodation, hers gave no resistance, but that seemed not to satisfy him. If anything it seemed to upset him further, for his movements became more and more frantic, his hips thrusting wildly against hers, the warmth of his body seeping through her nightgown, his hands pulling her tightly to him.

Nathan seemed to become aware of the nightgown for the first time then, and with a muttered comment he bunched it up around her neck, his touch on her naked flesh startling her and filling her with agonizing shyness. But nothing changed. He continued his strange, frantic caresses until Elizabeth wondered if this was what Melissa had meant by letting her husband satisfy his base emotions, as it was certainly very embarrassing having his hands on her breasts and hips. And Nathan didn't seem to be enjoying it very much either!

After several more minutes of the same activities, with an anguished sigh Nathan rested his damp forehead against Elizabeth's cheek and said in a muffled voice, "Perhaps I can do better tomorrow night, love. I think that I am just tired from our journey. Do not think too badly of me, my dear, that you are not a wife tonight in the fullest sense of the word. I love you, and more than anything I want to make you happy. Believe that, my dearest Elizabeth."

Her heart was moved by his distress, and she did not realize the significance of the fact that while Nathan lay next to her, there had been no pulsating, rigid male member to make its presence felt. She kissed him with clumsy tenderness above the eye. Shyly she said, "I don't mind, Nathan. It is pleasant just to have you here next to me. I have not liked sleeping in all these strange places all by myself."

Nathan's arms tightened convulsively around her and, pulling her tightly to his side, he said softly, "You are so good and kind to me, Elizabeth. There are not many brides who would be as understanding. Perhaps tomorrow night I will be able to... Well, tomorrow night we will see what happens. For the present let us both sleep." His lips gently caressed her cheek and he added, "I must confess, too, that it is very pleasant having you with me."

His words satisfied Elizabeth, though leaving her slightly puzzled. What was it he hadn't been able to do? But for the moment she was happy, certain that she and Nathan had taken the first step toward the closeness and companionship that she hungered for.

They spent the next day leisurely strolling throughout New Orleans. Nathan was a bit reserved at first, but upon seeing that Elizabeth truly had no recriminations about the previous evening, he soon relaxed and was his usual concerned, gentle self. Unfortunately it appeared that the day had not resolved whatever had been bothering him the night before, because the night was a repetition of the previous one.

There was a slight difference, though—Elizabeth was not quite as embarrassed or shy. At least she now had some idea what to expect, and when Nathan's hand touched her breast, she did not stiffen in surprise. She even made a clumsy, uncertain attempt to return her husband's caresses, her lips soft and warm beneath his and her small hands lightly and with trembling boldness touching his shoulders and back. But nothing seemed to do any good, and after several moments of his same fumbling attempts, Nathan tore himself away from her with a groan and said in a tone so low she could barely hear him, "Elizabeth, it is useless. I thought that with you, I could... I could... It appears that Longstreet was right—I am... I am... not capable of bedding a woman! Good God, what am I to do?"

Elizabeth felt her entire body freeze and, sitting up in bed, she asked slowly, "Nathan, what do you mean? What does Longstreet have to do with us?"

His voice bleak, Nathan muttered, "Everything and nothing. I should have told you all before we married—given you the chance to cry off! But I was so sure, so very certain, that I could put my relationship with Longstreet behind me. So sure that with your goodness and gentleness that I could be like any other man. That my past excursions into the dark side of passion were something I could forget." Bitterly he finished, "It appears that I was damnably wrong."

Elizabeth sat like a small icy statue in the middle of the bed, her thoughts tumbling and scattering like ash before a blast of winter wind. There was so much that Nathan was saying that didn't make any sense, but she suddenly remembered with a clutch of unnamed fear that peculiar conversation she had overheard at Portsmouth. What had that man said? Something about that "Longstreet was enamored of the young man." Frightened and not knowing why, she asked tensely, "Do you want to tell me about it now? Would it help you to talk with me? I would try to help you, Nathan."

He turned to her and, taking one of her icy little hands in his, he said tiredly, "I do not think it is something that talking will solve. But, yes, I will tell you about it, my dear . . . and afterwards if you wish to leave me, I will understand."

The last thing in the world that Elizabeth wanted was to leave her husband. Even if she did not love him, she was very fond of him and deeply grateful to him. He could confess that he was the greatest murderer on earth and she would not leave him, simply because he had always been kind and concerned for her—something no one else ever had been in all her short life. She thought a fleeting moment of the cold austerity of Three Elms, of her sarcastic, domineering stepmother and of her indifferent father, and she shuddered. Nathan would have to harm her physically to make her ever wish to return there.

Still, when he wept and haltingly confessed of his intimate involvement with men, with Charles Longstreet in particular, she was repelled and horrified. That two men could be lovers was almost beyond her understanding. Not even quite certain of what went on between a man and a woman in the privacy of their bedroom, the idea of two men doing those same things was nearly incomprehensible. And Nathan's further confession that he appeared to be incapable of making love to a woman, that he was in fact impotent with females, only added to her hurt confusion and bewilderment.

Most of what Nathan explained to Elizabeth that night made no real sense, but if she had been older, more experienced, more aware of what marriage and passion were all about, she might have made a different decision. As it was, filled with misplaced youthful confidence, she was certain that, given time and their own wish to make things normal, they would succeed. There was much of what Nathan told her that disgusted and appalled her even if the full import did not sink in; nevertheless, when she balanced his kindness to her against the welcome she would receive should she decide to return to Three Elms, Nathan with his shameful confession was far more appealing than England and her stepmother's wrath at the failure of such a short marriage.

She couldn't hide from Nathan the feeling of betrayal his words instilled in her breast, nor could she deny that deep inside she was angry that he had risked her future as well as his own. But Elizabeth had been taught to accept with equanimity if not pleasure the ills that often came into one's life, and she was above all things more inclined to accept what came her way than to battle against an unkind fate.

Her decision to remain with her husband was not an easy one, nor was it arrived at overnight. It had been a shock, what Nathan had told her, and for several days their relationship was strained and uneasy. They attempted to act as if everything was normal, continuing their exploration of New Orleans and dining in several of the many restaurants to be found there, but always the memory of what had been said that night hung over them like an ominous cloud. There were no more attempts to consummate their marriage, Elizabeth finding that she now dreaded the thought of Nathan's caresses where once she had longed for them.

It was something she was certain in time she would overcome, and she tried not to dwell on it more than necessary. They *both* must strive together to make their marriage a success, and while she was still slightly numbed by what had happened, she was looking toward the future optimistically. Time, she thought confidently, time would resolve their problems, and in a few years from now they would look back on this period of life and smile at their foolishness.

Nathan was greatly relieved at Elizabeth's decision *not* to leave him, and he too agreed, perhaps a little too readily, that for the present they would allow the consummation to wait. Ashamed by his own inability to function as he should, he was perfectly willing to put the incident behind him and, like Elizabeth, to hope that in time it would simply go away and they would live normally.

They were still a bit wary in each other's presence, and yet in another way their problem had brought them closer together. Nathan felt further indebted to Elizabeth simply because she had chosen to stand by him, and Elizabeth found it in her gentle heart to view his affliction with compassion.

It was decided that they were not to remain many more days in New Orleans, and Elizabeth wasn't certain whether the idea pleased her or depressed her. In a way she would be thankful when at last they would arrive in Natchez and she and Nathan could truly begin to work at making their marriage a success. But on the other hand, she made up her mind to enjoy however many more days they would be here to the fullest. She was *not* going to brood. Time would solve everything.

The French Market, off Decatur Street near the banks of the Mississippi River, seemed to make the greatest impression on Elizabeth during her excursions with Nathan. Never having been allowed to take a hand with the domestic details of Three Elms, she found the noisy marketplace was a whole new world. On one particular warm muggy morning, and accompanied only by Mary, Elizabeth, with a wide-eyed expression of amazement on her face, watched with keen interest the everchanging kaleidoscope of movement and color, while her ears were assaulted by an incredible variety of sounds.

A dozen different languages were being shouted on every side—French, Spanish, English, Negroes crying out in their French patois and the "gombo," and various Indian dialects rising and falling in the warm air. Vivid parrots in small wooden cages screamed almost continually; monkeys offered by itinerant vendors jabbered incessantly; geese, chickens, and ducks added their clucks and gobbles; and over all there was occasionaly the clear carrying song of tiny yellow canaries.

Indian squaws, wrapped in bright, gaudily designed blankets, had rows of baskets, pottery, and gaily colored beads for sale. An old Negro woman wearing a blue calico dress dispensed cups of freshly made coffee from a little street stand, chanting, *"Café noir!"* and *"Café au lait!"* as she did so. Farther down, a fat Choctaw Indian squaw sat stoically at the curb offering gumbo filé, and other herbs and roots. A tall Negress, her skin gleaming like ebony, draped in a starched white apron, her head wrapped in a garish *tignon*, sold cakes and molasses. Along an arcade of heavy pillars, Elizabeth and Mary inspected fish with gray-blue bodies glistening in the sun, wriggling crawfish, crabs with clicking claws, and heaps of fresh brown eggs, wrapped in silvery green moss. Next came the fruit-and-vegetable section, and both women were astonished by the variety to be found—strawberries, bananas, prickly pineapples, luscious Japanese plums, okra, corn, thin-skinned onions, and strange exotic vegetables that Elizabeth had never seen before, all lying side by side in tempting haphazard rows. Flower dealers seemed to be everywhere, and here and there were stalls offering cheap jewelry and singing mockingbirds. In astonishment and curiosity, Elizabeth stared at a trussed-up alligator offered for sale. Whatever, she thought, would one do with it?

The market was alive with color and movement as elegant Creole ladies in vivid silks and laces, escorted by their husbands, wandered throughout, and young Creole gentlemen, their dark handsomeness intensified by their pristine, snowy white linen shirts and gaily embroidered waistcoats, strolled with languid grace through the shifting, constantly moving mass. A comely quadroon strode proudly by, trailed by a single servant, while a huge woman with numerous keys dangling from her belt and attended by a cadaverous black slave haggled loudly with a small, coffee-tinted freeman of color over his wares.

Bemused, feeling as if she had stumbled into some exotic place found usually only in imagination, Elizabeth slowly made her way through the various sections, unaware of the fact that she herself possessed the ability to spark more than one gentleman's imagination. She was dressed this morning in a gown of soft rose silk that emphasized the tiny waist and fell in graceful folds to her flat-heeled slippers. Carrying a parasol of India muslin embroidered with a beautiful featherstitched border, her small hands clothed in rose-colored gloves, she presented a delicate and entrancing appearance. Between the parasol and the Cabriolet bonnet of white silk gauze straw she was wearing, it was extremely hard to see her face, but that didn't stop several gentlemen from making discreet maneuvers to attempt to do just that. The reward was worth the effort—breathtakingly lovely violet eyes stared innocently out from an enchanting face framed by several unruly silvery curls.

Completely oblivious of the languishing glances sent her way by many an eager young Creole gentleman, Elizabeth was examining a rather finely wrought cameo brooch when a startling familiar voice rang out.

"Beth! Beth Selby, is that you, honey?"

At the sound of that dear voice, Elizabeth whirled around, the soft coral mouth curving into a genuinely happy smile. "Stella! Oh, do tell me I am not dreaming this! How simply grand to see you, but what ever are you doing here?" she cried with pleasure, the violet eyes sparkling vividly.

"I might ask you the same! I couldn't believe my eyes when I saw you just now," Stella returned, as she swept up to where Elizabeth stood.

Stella hadn't changed very much, Elizabeth observed affectionately as she stared at her friend from the days of Mrs. Finche's Seminary for Young Ladies. Tall, with a commanding presence and dark eyes that danced from under finely arched eyebrows, Stella Valdez was just as Elizabeth remembered. It was true she was no longer dressed in the dreadful school uniform, but the warm smile on the generous mouth was the same and the husky voice with its slight, slow drawl was dearly familiar. Silently they openly assessed each other, Elizabeth still in awe of Stella's vibrant personality. That vibrancy showed in the fashionably styled bonnet of jonquil yellow silk that sat rakishly on the thick, shining black hair and in the vividness of the turquoise-and-yellow-figured gown she wore. It was an eye-catching combination, but then Stella had always liked color and had detested a fashion that insisted only pale, insipid shades be worn, Elizabeth thought with a smile.

Stella was a handsome young woman rather than a pretty one—her mouth was a trifle too wide, her nose bordered on the masculine, and she had a surprisingly square jawline. But she possessed something far more enduring than a chocolate-box beauty—a loyal and caring nature and a strong sense of friendship as well as a spirited, outgoing personality. Stella was also inclined toward intuitiveness and, as the two of them stood talking, eagerly exchanging anecdotes, she noted the faint shadows in the violet-blue eyes and the slight hint of reserve when Elizabeth spoke of her marriage and her husband.

Realizing that the French Market area was no place to hold the private conversation she wished, Stella deftly dismissed Mary and whisked Elizabeth away to an elegant house on Esplanade Avenue where she was visiting relatives. Some minutes later they were seated in a charming flagstone courtyard, a fountain gurgling merrily in the center and a Negro servant quietly serving them freshly dripped strong black coffee in delicate china cups.

The servant departed and Stella allowed Elizabeth time to swallow a few sips of the chicory-flavored brew before she asked casually, "My dear, are you truly happy? I do not mean to pry, but, when I remember my own honeymoon just a year ago, you do not radiate the happiness I would expect."

"Oh, Stell! Trust you to put your finger on the very problem!" Elizabeth exclaimed ruefully. "You always did know when something was preying on my mind."

Her dark eyes kind and encouraging, Stella prompted, "Well, then, honey, tell me about it."

"I can't! It isn't that I don't want to," Elizabeth confessed helplessly.

Regarding the troubled young features across from her, Stella said thoughtfully, "Sometimes the first few months are difficult, I understand. Especially if you didn't know each other very well before you married." Smiling, she added, "I've known Juan Rodriguez all my life, and I've known for almost that long that I wanted to marry him. That might be why during our first months of marriage we had so few adjustments to make. Perhaps as you get to know your Nathan better you'll find him not so much of a stranger."

Blinking back a sudden surprising rush of tears to her eyes, Elizabeth said with a sad little catch in her throat, "My marriage is nothing like I expected. Nathan and I can't..." She stopped abruptly, very embarrassed and genuinely not wishing to spill her troubles to the first friendly ear—even if the friendly ear belonged to her dear Stella!

But Stella gave her no time to have second thoughts and prompted gently, "You and Nathan can't what, honey? Don't you think you ought to really tell me the truth? Now, suppose you just relax back in that chair and drink your coffee and tell Madre Stella all about it, hmmm?"

Elizabeth hesitated, wanting to pour out the entire story and yet desperately wishing not to betray Nathan. Stella, she was certain, would understand, but would Nathan, if he ever discovered she had discussed such an intimate detail of their marriage? She rather thought not, and, knowing how she would feel if he were to talk about it with someone else, she decided it would be best *not* to unburden her problems to Stella.

Stella was a difficult person to fob off with lame excuses, and it was only when Elizabeth almost desperately mentioned the trust her father had set up and how mortified Nathan had been that Stella's probing stopped. "So that's it!" Stella said triumphantly. "You silly little goose! That's nothing to be worried about! Your father was probably only protecting your interests, and, while I'm certain that your husband was displeased by it, what man wouldn't be? I'm positive that in time his resentment will fade and neither of you will give it any thought." An unwelcome idea suddenly occurred to Stella and she asked anxiously, "Nathan does not hold it against you, does he? I mean, he is not ugly to you about it?"

"Oh, no!" Elizabeth exclaimed in honest astonishment. "He is all that is kind to me. Nathan has never even mentioned it to me."

"Well then, my dear, *you* stop worrying and settle down and enjoy being married."

After that the conversation became desultory until Elizabeth said gaily, "But enough of that nonsense! Tell me, how long are you to be here in New Orleans?"

Stella pulled a face. "Unfortunately we leave day after tomorrow for Santa Fe. But don't look so sad, my dear, I intend to spend as much time as possible with you until we do leave. If only we had met earlier or we had known the other was going to be here—just think of the cozy chats we could have had!"

"Oh, no! To think we will have such a short time together!" Elizabeth cried with real regret.

"We have all this afternoon, as well as tomorrow. And remember . . . at least we are on the same continent! I am certain we can arrange to meet now and then either in Natchez or Santa Fe." A twinkle in her eye, Stella added, "I would much prefer it to be Natchez. I have heard it is a wickedly exciting city—especially 'Under the Hill.'"

"You probably know more about it than I do. Nathan doesn't speak of it very often, and I haven't been able to discover much myself. Don't you like Santa Fe?" Elizabeth asked curiously.

"Of course I do! But Santa Fe is little better than a frontier town—Comanches still raid on our doorstep, and the only excitement is in the spring when the caravans of traders arrive. We do have a great many attractions, but I am sure that they cannot compare with Natchez."

"I see," Elizabeth said slowly, privately thinking it would be far more thrilling to be in a frontier town than a cosmopolitan city like Natchez.

"No, you don't, honey," Stella contradicted gently. "You are still as romantic and full of dreams as you were at Mrs. Finche's. I can see that you think the frontier would be an adventure beyond belief. Believe me, it isn't! And the first time you came face to face with a war party of Comanches, you would wish you had never left the safety of the civilized world. I am used to it, despite those three years in England. I grew up out there and I know it—but you, you, my sweet, make it into a dream world."

Guiltily Elizabeth acknowledged it, and the conversation wandered onto other subjects. It was the most pleasurable afternoon Elizabeth had spent in weeks, and both women were so busy bringing the other up to date that neither noticed the lengthening shadows. Elizabeth didn't have a great deal to say about herself, but Stella certainly did! And so she rattled happily on, unaware that her stories of life in the old Spanish province of Nuevo Méjico, or New Mexico as it was now called, fired up Elizabeth's vivid romantic imagination and instilled in her a burning desire to one day see for herself this wild untamed land. Some of the terrifying stories of raiding Comanches struck an oddly responsive chord within Elizabeth, almost as if she herself had actually lived through such an experience, and she was for a brief moment reminded of those strange lifelike dreams that had plagued her on the journey to New Orleans.

It was only when Stella's husband Juan strolled out into the courtyard that the reminiscences were stemmed. Under the cover of the introductions, Elizabeth quietly summed him up, and she could see exactly how the slim, quiet, reserved Spaniard would appeal to the more vivacious Stella.

Unlike Stella, who was only half Spanish herself, Juan was pure Castilian Spanish, from the thick dark hair to the formal bow he gave Elizabeth. He was not much taller than his wife, nor at first glance did he appear an unusually handsome man. It was only when one happened to look into the lustrous black eyes and caught the flicker of amusement that danced there, or noticed the handsome curve of his mouth and the aquiline shape of his nose, that his very real attractiveness was apparent. There was an easy warm familiarity between him and his wife, and Elizabeth was left in little doubt that here were a man and woman who were deeply in love. It pleased her and intensified her sudden wish that she and Nathan could share the same kind of relationship.

Juan knew all about Stella's schoolgirl friendship with Elizabeth Selby, and he greeted her warmly and with sincere pleasure. At first Elizabeth was slightly in awe of this polished, courteous stranger, but under Juan's subtle charm she found herself relaxing, and in a very few minutes she was chatting away with him as if he were an old acquaintance. The conversation was general until Juan asked with more than mere politeness, "Is it possible for you and your husband to dine with us this evening? I realize that it is an impromptu invitation, but our time here is so short, and I know Stella will want to spend practically every waking moment with you until we leave." A twinkle in the black eyes, he added, "And I myself have no objection to having another lovely lady to grace my table."

Stella eagerly chimed in with her own invitation, and it was only after Elizabeth had consented to send a note back to the hotel to inquire if Nathan would be agreeable that Stella clapped her hands over her mouth and said with dismay, "The Costa soiree is this evening, have you forgotten?"

Smilingly, Juan shook his head. "No, *querida,* I have not forgotten, but a note of explanation to our hostess will, I am sure, elicit an invitation for the Ridgeways to attend with us."

"Oh, no!" Elizabeth murmured, "I could not force myself on strangers that way. It would be horridly impolite."

"Nonsense!" Stella contradicted. "Margarita Costa

would like nothing better than to meet an old friend of mine. She is not the least haughty. In fact, she is the most amiable person I know of—she is too lazy to be otherwise! Her husband is exactly the same, and they would never forgive us if we did not see that they knew you were here. Come now, do say you will dine with us and attend the ball afterward. *Do!*"

"But won't the people you are staying with mind?" Elizabeth hedged.

Juan laughed. "Hardly. My uncle and aunt are out of the city until tomorrow, and the house is ours to do with as we like tonight. And even if they were here, they would be delighted to finally meet Stella's 'Beth.' Your fame has preceded you, you know."

What else could she do but accept? And so with little more persuasion she wrote a brief note to Nathan, informing him of the invitation to dine and that they were to attend a soiree later in the evening. With the same servant that was to deliver Elizabeth's missive to Nathan, Stella sent off her note to Doña Margarita. Not a half hour later, the servant returned with the two replies—Doña Margarita eagerly demanding that Stella definitely bring along her guests, and Nathan's regretful reply that he had already made other plans for the evening but had no objection to Elizabeth spending the evening with her friends. The thought of attending a soiree without him almost caused her to refuse, but Stella would have none of it.

"Don't be ridiculous, honey! Juan will enjoy escorting both of us, and there will be no impropriety attached. Now then, do not argue with me, because you know how angry it makes me!" Stella finished with a teasing threat in her voice.

And that, Elizabeth thought with amusement, was that!

CHAPTER FOUR

At Stella's insistence, Elizabeth did not even return to her hotel that evening. Another note was quickly dispatched to the hotel and in a short while Mary Eames appeared at the house on Esplanade Avenue with the clothing and various articles that were needed.

Dinner was more than pleasant, the rich spicy food of the Creole household tantalizing Elizabeth's palate. The main course, chicken *duxelles*—boned chicken breasts in a cream sauce with slivered toasted almonds—was the most delicious thing that Elizabeth had ever tasted, and she savored every bite. Dessert was a meltingly delicious orange *crème brulée* and light crepes filled with strawberry preserves that left her feeling as if she had just partaken of a meal prepared for the gods.

Replete and completely relaxed, all sense of reserve banished by Stella's vivacious warmth and Juan's quiet, unobtrusive charm, Elizabeth was almost eagerly looking forward to what would be her first soiree.

"Your first soiree!" Stella had exclaimed earlier when Elizabeth had confessed it before dinner, as they had sat in the main salon sipping a very dry sherry. "Well then, honey, we must hope that it is an evening that you will long remember. I'm certain that there are going to be several young men who remember *you!*" she had finished laughingly. "You look like an angel."

It was true. Mary Eames, instantly approving of the Rodriguezes and thinking it was time that her mistress made some friends of her own, had excelled herself in preparing Elizabeth for the ball tonight.

Wearing an extremely fashionable gown of shot silk, the prismatic rose color interspersed with shades of bright lilac, Elizabeth did indeed resemble an angel. An earthly angel, perhaps, for there was something very *un*spiritual about the soft white shoulders above the rose lilac gown and the promising thrust of her small bosom rising temptingly from the lace-trimmed, low-cut bodice. Her slender waist was intensified by the clever fitting of the gown, and the sway of voluminous skirts whenever she moved was downright provocative. The silver-blond hair had been parted on the forehead and turned up behind, the ends forming a cluster of curls, revealing Elizabeth's slender neck and delicate shell-pink ears. Not quite satisfied with the effect, Mary had placed a band of woven gold thread set with small amethysts on the bright hair, and it was the crowning touch to the already flattering coiffure. But the maid had needed no skills at all to bring a sparkle to those incredible violet eyes, nor had she needed to darken the slender arching golden-brown brows or the thick gold-tipped lashes. Elizabeth definitely had little use for any but the lightest cosmetics tonight. Her cheeks were already blooming with a rosy blush and the full mouth needed no rouge to impart a ruby glow. She was almost scintillating with excitement, the wide eyes nearly purple with anticipation, the silken-snowy skin gleaming like warm alabaster.

Like many another New Orleans family, guided by the lantern light of a servant they walked the few blocks to the Costa house. Elizabeth reveled in the soft, warm June night, her nostrils entranced by the faint scent of jasmine in the air.

"Hmmm. This is lovely," she said. "Is it like this all the time?"

"Unfortunately, no," Juan replied with a smile. "Too soon it will be the malaria season and most of the Creoles will desert the city for their country plantations. There are incessant rains in winter, but still there is something magical about New Orleans that makes one love her in spite of her faults."

"Do you come here often?"

"Not as often as I would like!" Stella murmured with a teasing note in her voice.

Juan shot her a quizzical glance. "You do not like Santa Fe?"

"You know that isn't true! It's just that I wish we could visit New Orleans more often," she confessed.

"Mmmm, I shall see what I can do about it," he said with mock thoughtfulness.

"Don't be silly!" Stella protested. "I know, and so do you, that there is too much to be done on the rancho for us to be away too long or too often. I am just thankful that you decided personally to come to New Orleans this year to see your business agent."

Her eyes round with amazement, Elizabeth breathed, "You came all the way from Santa Fe just to see a business agent?"

"Not exactly," Juan explained seriously. "I felt that Stella should get away from Santa Fe for a while, and while I trust my agent implicitly, I feel it always wise to let the people that are working for me know that I *do* take an interest in what they are doing. A periodic visit to New Orleans assures me that my man of business is honest and competent."

"I see," Elizabeth said doubtfully, and Juan laughed, pinching her gently under the chin. "No, you don't, but don't you worry that lovely head of yours about it. Leave business to your husband and, like my darling Stella, concern yourself only with the spending of the money he earns."

At his words an indignant sound came from Stella and her dark eyes flashed with vexation. Smiling and apparently uncaring that they were on a public street, Juan put his arm around his wife and, pulling her to him, kissed her lightly on the temple. His voice teasing, he murmured, "How simple it is to arouse that temper of yours, *querida*. And you are so beautiful when you are angry that I cannot resist the temptation to tease you. Forgive me? You know that the rancho would not be quite so peaceful if it were not for your hand behind mine."

Stella gave him an exasperated loving smile, her good humor instantly restored, and in quiet companionship the three finished their walk to the Costa house.

The Costa home was lit with gas chandeliers in every room, and the floor matting put down for summer was crisp and cool-looking beneath their feet. Elizabeth found herself enchanted by the quiet and refined elegance of the interior of the house. It all spoke of long-established wealth—the dominating marble fireplace of the main parlor with its elaborately draped mantelpiece and the huge mirror framed in gold leaf hanging above it, as well as the imposing dimensions of the room, gave evidence of this. The furniture was of rosewood—delicate, comfortable pieces upholstered in silks and tapestries—on the walls were oil paintings of the various Costa ancestors, and in one corner was an extremely handsome *étagère* filled with beautiful china and bric-a-brac, revealing that this was a home in addition to being an elegant mansion.

For the soiree, the folding doors dividing the two parlors had been thrown open to make a grand salon, but what fascinated Elizabeth was the way the Costas had turned part of their courtyard off the grand salon into a ballroom. Walls had been set up, a canvas ceiling stretched, and flooring put down, all of which had then been painted and decorated so that it resembled part of the house. It had been so cleverly done that at first she hadn't even realized it, but Stella had pointed it out, explaining that this was common in New Orleans whenever the guest list proved too great for the confines of the house.

Margarita Costa, a plump, black-eyed beauty with the Creole's creamy skin, was as amiable as Stella had said. Upon being introduced to Elizabeth she had warmly embraced her, exclaiming, "Ah, *petite*, at last I meet Stella's English *amie!* How happy I am that you are here. But tell me, where is your husband? Did he not come, too?"

It was an awkward moment, but Stella and Juan quickly stepped into the uncomfortable silence that followed Margarita's very natural question. To a Creole woman her husband and family were everything, and despite the reasonable explanations, it was plain that Margarita did not approve of a husband's desertion so soon after the wedding. But the moment passed and Elizabeth rapidly recovered her earlier poise and excitement as she was introduced to more and more people. Even to herself it seemed there were quite a few young, dark-eyed gentlemen who begged for an introduction, and Stella's amused "See, you goose, I told you the gentlemen would think you an angel" confirmed the fact that she was definitely the belle of the ball.

It was a heady sensation, for a shy, uncertain young girl making her first appearance at a society function. She was never without a partner for any of the various dances, and it seemed there was always an eager gentleman at her elbow offering lemonade or champagne or some other form of refreshment. Her cheeks flushed with pleasure and the wide eyes shining like violet stars, she eventually found her way to Stella's side, adamantly refusing the pleading offers of several gentlemen for the waltz that was forming. To Stella's amusement, with surprising *savoir faire* Elizabeth gently dismissed her most persistent followers, stating that she no longer wished to dance... at least at the moment.

Watching the last dejected young man stride across the ballroom floor, Stella teased, "You have broken his heart, *querida!* And I wonder how many duels you have inspired this evening. Young Etienne Dupré looked positively livid when you decided to share that last quadrille with Léon Marchand."

"Oh, no, Stella! They wouldn't fight a duel over something like that... would they?" Elizabeth asked with real distress.

Stella laughed. "My dear, a Creole will fight a duel over the size of the Mississippi River, or just for the sheer enjoyment of it. Pay them no heed."

For some minutes they stood talking, Elizabeth actually glad to escape from the rather overpowering masculine attention she had been receiving all evening. It was a pleasant interlude, for now she had a moment to catch her breath and to relax for the first time since they had arrived. She found it extremely pleasurable to be the recipient of so many compliments and to have several handsome gentlemen vying for her hand, but she had also found it somewhat of a strain. Unused to the gallantry and quick passions of the Creoles, she was more than happy to gain a brief respite from some of her more tenacious admirers.

She and Stella talked quietly as they stood near one end of the specially erected ballroom, Stella pointing out this person or that and explaining some of the more amusing superstitions of the Creoles: If a housewife dropped a fork, a lady caller was coming; if she dropped a knife, it would be a man. Also, if one slept with the moonlight on his face, he would go mad, and the howling of a dog or the chirping of a cricket were both thought to foretell a death. Elizabeth smiled at such absurdities, though she thought them very endearing.

Oblivious of her own startling fairness among so many dark beauties, Elizabeth stared with increasing admiration at the graceful manners and exquisite loveliness of the Creole women. Wistfully watching one vivacious dark-haired beauty, she unashamedly longed to be rid of her silvery-blond curls and violet eyes and to have instead liquid black eyes and hair like polished ebony.

She was jerked from her absorption in the constantly shifting scene by Stella's sudden bone-splintering grip on her arm. Glancing with alarm at her friend, Elizabeth observed that Stella was staring with fierce concentration across the room.

Her eyes unblinking on some object on the other side of the ballroom, Stella exclaimed, "*¡Válgame, Dios!* I wonder what *he* is doing here."

"Who?" Elizabeth asked helplessly, slightly alarmed by Stella's tense manner.

"Rafael Eustaquio Rey de Santana y Hawkins, that's who!" Her lips quirking in an odd smile, Stella added, "More commonly known as Rafael Santana... or Renegade Santana, depending upon whom you are talking to."

Not quite certain why this individual should have such a disturbing effect upon Stella, Elizabeth unobtrusively peered across the wide expanse of floor, looking for the object of Stella's comments. Seeing nothing unusual in the group of laughing men near the open door that led to the courtyard, she was about to turn back to Stella when her inquiring gaze was caught and held by the bold and arrogant stare of a tall man leaning negligently against the wall near the door.

He was dressed in black—a black velvet coat that stretched snugly across the broad shoulders and back, skin-hugging pantaloons that almost indecently displayed the long length of his well-muscled legs. Easily the tallest man in the room, he was perhaps half a head taller than any of the slimmer, shorter Creoles who thronged about him. He appeared indifferent to the men nearby, and Elizabeth had the strange conviction that he would be indifferent to many things. She shivered. His hair was black, so black that the gaslight chandeliers caught blue shadows in its thickness, and his skin was dark—a golden-bronze shade darker than that of any man in the room, his snowy-white shirt intensifying the darkness. His face was lean, possessing an oddly barbaric handsomeness—thick black eyebrows curved with an almost wicked slant over deepset eyes; a strong, proudly aquiline nose jutted arrogantly above a full-lipped mouth that bespoke both passion and cruelty. Again Elizabeth shivered, frightened and not knowing why. No man had ever stared at her the way this man did, his eyes openly stripping her gown from her body, his mouth curving in a mocking smile as she blushed furiously under his deliberate look of appraisal.

Quickly averting her eyes, Elizabeth stared determinedly at her satin slippers. She would not look at him again. She would not! Instead she blurted out to Stella, "I wish he would stop staring so! It is very unnerving and not at all polite."

Stella laughed grimly. "Being polite is not a manner of much importance to Rafael. He is the rudest, most arrogant and infuriating man I have ever known! And unfortunately I have known him a long time—what is more, he is a relative of sorts of Juan's."

Elizabeth swallowed painfully. A slight note of constraint in her voice, she asked, "He...he won't want an introduction, will he?"

"Knowing Rafael and seeing the way he is eating you with his eyes, I rather suspect he will, and as I don't want to see you devoured in front of me, I think it would be wise if we said good night to the Costas and went home."

Disappointed and relieved at the same time, Elizabeth had just turned to walk from the room when Stella muttered warningly under her breath, "He is coming this way."

Casting a brief, almost fearful glance over her shoulder, Elizabeth saw that it was true. Rafael Santana no longer leaned against the doorway. Instead, with all the lordly grace of a predatory animal he was stalking arrogantly across the room, his destination obvious, and Elizabeth felt her throat tighten uncomfortably and her heart begin to pound with a queer excitement.

Knowing it was useless to try to escape, Stella stopped what would have been cowardly flight and, with an exasperated smile, waited for Rafael Santana to reach them.

His eyes twinkling with cold amusement, well aware that they had been leaving to avoid him, Rafael walked languidly up to the two women. Gracefully, yet at the same time somehow conveying mockery, he bowed.

"Ah, Stella, *amiga,* how pleasant to meet you here," he said lightly, his voice a warm, deep rough velvet, the slight hint of something other than a Spanish accent obvious.

Stella, always forthright, wasted little time in polite banter. "Is it?" she returned with false sweetness. Not expecting an answer, she plunged on with "What brings you to New Orleans? I thought you were very busy with Mr. Houston's grand new Republic of Texas."

Rafael smiled grimly. "But I am. Houston wants Texas to become one of the United States of America and he has sent several envoys to help lead that cause. I happen to be one of them."

"You?"

He gave a low laugh at her open skepticism. "Yes,

little Stella, me. You forget that there are several very respectable members in my family. One of them happens to be an influential man in this fair city. He and I share some common ancestors a few generations back, and he is by way of being a . . . ah . . . cousin of mine. He is also acquainted rather well with President Jackson, and Houston thought it might be a good idea if I could convince my cousin that the addition of Texas to the Union would be beneficial to all concerned."

"And have you?" Stella asked curiously.

Rafael returned a noncommittal answer and somewhat obviously changed the subject. "Is Juan with you? I have not seen him as yet."

"Have you *looked* for him?" Stella answered tartly. "Or have you been too busy making all the young women in the room blush and run for the protection of their mothers?"

A teasing smile curved his mouth. "Perhaps a little of both. I knew you were in New Orleans, but I didn't know positively that you would be attending the soiree."

Despite the polite conversation and even though he had not as yet looked directly at her, Elizabeth, standing mutely at Stella's side with downcast eyes, sensed that he was as conscious of her as she was of him. She could almost feel his intense awareness of her, and she had the odd conviction that he was deliberately willing her to look at him. It was a queer silent battle between them, and stubbornly, not wanting to even allow him a victory over such a small thing, she kept her eyes averted. *Beast!* she thought to herself as the murmur of their voices drifted about her, and with a coquetry foreign to her, she smiled blindingly at a young gentleman hovering nearby.

It was a mistake. Uncannily guessing what she was about, Rafael suddenly and abruptly said to Stella, "Introduce us, please. You are very beautiful, but it is your friend who presently holds my attention."

Astonished by such behavior, Elizabeth's eyes flew to his, and that was a mistake, because once her gaze met his she found she could not look away from the coldest eyes she had ever seen in her life. They were like flecks of silvery gray obsidian and just as hard. There was no emotion in those thick-lashed eyes that held hers, just a frightening emptiness that chilled her.

Stella broke the uncomfortable silence that had fallen by saying with more than a touch of annoyance, "I should have known! Very well, then—Elizabeth Ridgeway, may I present Rafael Santana to you? He is a rogue and a devil, and I would heartily recommend that you have nothing to do with him."

A quickly suppressed gleam of displeasure lit the gray eyes briefly. "Thank you. Your kind words have aroused her interest far more swiftly than I could hope for," he commented dryly, and Elizabeth, who was the gentlest creature in nature, felt a strong desire to slap his handsome face. But Stella only shrugged. "It would do you little good, for I think it only fair to warn you that she is not only an English lord's daughter, but also married and very much in love with her husband."

His gray eyes fixed with sudden intensity upon Elizabeth's face, he said slowly, "Now, somehow I rather doubt that. And besides, when has marriage ever stopped me?"

Stella nearly stamped her foot with vexation. "Will you *stop* it? You are deliberately being aggravating. I have given you the introduction, and now I would appreciate it if you would go find a well and drown yourself!"

At that, Rafael laughed out loud with apparent amusement—amusement, however, that was not reflected in the cold silver-gray eyes. "I would love to please you, but unfortunately, life is too fascinating for me at the moment to contemplate such a thing. Perhaps next time we meet I shall try to follow your wishes, but right now, I want very much to waltz with the little one with a face like an angel."

And with that, not giving her a chance to accept or refuse him, he reached for Elizabeth and deftly swept her out onto the ballroom floor. Stunned and just a little breathless, for several turns around the room Elizabeth kept her eyes pinned to the diamond stickpin that rested in the pristine folds of his cravat. She was extremely aware of the warm hand at her waist, the warm hand that was surely tighter than need be, and of the fact that he was perhaps holding her closer than custom approved, and she wished she possessed the courage to reprimand him for the deliberate liberties he was taking. As the moments passed, she became more and more conscious of him—of the faint odor of brandy and tobacco that emanated from him, of the sleek muscles in the powerful body that so effortlessly propelled her around the room, and most of all just of *him*. She could feel his breath gently stirring the curls on her head and the firmness and heat of the hand that held hers, and the emotions that were suddenly stirring in her blood made her slightly giddy.

"Are we to dance in total silence, *querida?*" he finally asked. "I admire your silken hair a great deal, but I would much rather admire your eyes... and mouth."

She glanced up and once again was lost in those empty gray eyes, only they weren't empty this time—now some undefinable emotion flickered in their depths, and Elizabeth tore her gaze away, her heart thudding with thick, painful strokes. "Don't look at me that way," she said agitatedly. "It isn't polite."

He gave a strangely bitter laugh and murmured, "I am never polite, so don't expect it of me. And don't play the innocent with me, either—you know what is going through my mind as well as I do."

Not so oddly, she did know what he was thinking, and her cheeks went crimson with embarrassment. His eyes said plainly enough that he would like to kiss her, that he would kiss her if they were alone, and that if she wasn't careful, he was going to see that they were alone. Suddenly frightened of what he might do, she said breathlessly, "Please, please take me back to Stella, I don't want to dance with you anymore."

"Why, because I am too blunt? Or is it because of the husband you are supposed to be so very much in love with?" he snapped.

"B-b-both, I think," she stammered untruthfully, knowing that she hadn't thought of her husband since she had entered the Costa house, and that any memory of Nathan or her marriage had vanished the instant her eyes had met Rafael Santana's across the room.

"Liar," he said coolly. "You don't look like a woman in love, you look like a sleeping virgin waiting to be awakened."

"That's not true!" Elizabeth denied swiftly. "I do love my husband very much, and I don't think this is a conversation that does either of us much credit." With quaint dignity she said, "I think it best we change the subject."

"I'm sure you do, English, but I am finding it far too amusing to wish for it to come to an end."

Discovering that this man aroused a temper she hadn't known she possessed and unable to help herself, Elizabeth asked vexedly, "Are you this way with everyone? No wonder Stella said you were rude!"

Again Rafael smiled, and it was not a nice smile. His eyes shuttered and empty once more, he drawled, "Didn't you know I spend all my time trying to live up to the reputation that has been bestowed upon me?" He laughed that bitter laugh and added, "People would think that I was not myself if I did not commandeer the most beautiful woman in the room and proceed to make outrageous love to her. It is like putting on a performance, *querida*—they expect it and I try to please them."

Elizabeth's eyes searched his face. Slowly she said, "I think that might be partly true . . . but you must have done something originally to deserve your reputation."

"Oh, I did, English, I did. I was born!"

"Don't be ridiculous! *That* wouldn't make people think ill of you."

"No?" he mocked. "Not even if I tell you my grandmother was a Comanche half-breed who lived with an American trapper? And that their daughter, my mother, dared to marry into a *gachupín* family of long standing?"

"I don't see what that has to do with it. You can't help who your parents were. I think you place too much emphasis upon it," Elizabeth replied primly.

"Ah, English, how little you know of people . . .

especially of my Spanish grandfather, Don Felipe. He has never quite forgiven me for being born, particularly since my father's second marriage has produced no sons, only daughters."

"And because of that," she guessed intuitively, "you punish him."

"Why not?" he inquired with a quirked eyebrow.

"Well, because it isn't very nice," Elizabeth said earnestly. "You shouldn't be so—so unforgiving."

He laughed out loud at that. "But I am, *chica*. I am as unforgiving a man as you can find... and Stella has already warned you that I am not very nice!"

Elizabeth didn't like being laughed at, particularly when she had been serious in attempting to help him. Her violet eyes flashing with unexpected temper, she snapped stiffly, "Yes, I can certainly see that! You also enjoy being a boor and being just as rude as you can be! You may be very certain, Mr. Santana, that in the future I shall take care to avoid you."

"Are you challenging me, English?" he demanded softly, his head lowering closer to hers, and she had the most positive feeling that he was going to kiss her.

Her heart thudding in her breast, Elizabeth leaned as far away from him as he would allow. "No, no, of course not!" she muttered, then adding with a flash of temper, "And I wish you wouldn't call me 'English'! My name is Mrs. Ridgeway, and you would do well to remember it."

He didn't like that, she could tell from the tightening of his mouth, but as the waltz was ending, he only shrugged and a few seconds later deposited her near Stella. Mockingly he remarked, "*Muchas gracias, Mrs.* Ridgeway! And Stella, *amiga,* you can stop fretting, I have returned your lamb—unharmed!"

"But only because it suited you!" Stella replied dryly. "And perhaps," she added slyly, "because your *wife* is here?"

At the word "wife" Elizabeth felt her heart plunge to her dainty feet, but she wasn't exactly sure why the news that he had a wife should have that effect on her. She was a married woman herself and she shouldn't be having romantic notions about another man, but she discovered that she disliked intensely the thought of his having a wife. *Stop being such a witless fool,* she told herself silently, *what does it matter if he is married? In a week or two you'll be in Natchez and will probably never see him again.* Rafael did not answer Stella's obvious challenge, but only smiled infuriatingly and stalked away. Watching him as he crossed the room, Elizabeth commanded her rebellious heart: *Forget* Rafael Santana!

During the little time that they remained, Elizabeth tried desperately to do just that. But regrettably, it seemed that Rafael Santana's sardonic features had been printed indelibly on her brain, and if she let her concentration slip for the briefest second, his dark mocking face was there before her. Fortunately though, she did not have to endure his disturbing presence for very long. Stella let one more waltz elapse before she said, "I really do think we should be leaving now. If you will find a servant to bring us our cloaks, I shall attempt to find my wayward husband."

Glad to leave, longing to be alone to examine the bewildering emotions that had been stirred by one admittedly not very gallant man, Elizabeth departed from the ballroom with an eager step. She found a servant with little trouble and a moment later was shown into a small room where the guests' outer garments had been placed. The servant hesitated, and Elizabeth, guessing she had more tasks to do, dismissed her with a smile. "Thank you. I can find our cloaks and things. You may go now."

The black face softened with a smile, and with a quick curtsy the servant was gone. Elizabeth turned away and began to look for her cloak and Stella's. She found her own immediately, but it took her a few seconds longer to find Stella's India cachemire shawl. She had just discovered it beneath several other garments when a slight sound made her glance up.

Seeing Rafael Santana lounging with careless grace against the closed door, she froze. That door had been open a moment ago, and it must have been the sound of it closing that had made her look up. Forcing herself to act calmly, she demanded with her most haughty air, "What do you think you are doing? Open that door *immediately!*"

He regarded her steadily, those smoky gray eyes moving slowly over her face. There was no trace of mockery in his voice when he said abruptly, "I wish to see you again. Will you meet me?"

Elizabeth swallowed. What he was asking was unthinkable, and even she, as young and naïve as she was, knew that. A married woman did not make an arrangement to meet a man other than her husband. Deliberately misunderstanding him, she said nervously, "I shall be staying with Stella until some time tomorrow—I don't think that she would object if you came to call."

Dryly he murmured, "*Querida,* I do not want to see you under Stella's watchful eye. I want to see you alone, and you damn well know it! Now tell me where we can meet privately."

"Why?" she asked breathlessly, fencing for time, wanting someone to come and open that door and disrupt this meeting between them, and yet at the same time terrified that someone would do just that.

"I think you know why," he stated bluntly, almost angrily pushing himself away from the door.

At his first movement Elizabeth stepped back, clutching Stella's shawl to her breast as if it would offer her some protection against the tall man who loomed in front of her. She was genuinely frightened and at the same time nearly dizzy with a dangerous excitement. "D-d-don't come any closer," she stammered as he slowly walked up to her.

"Oh, but I will," he threatened softly, as his hands reached out to close around her slender white shoulders. "I intend to come a great deal closer, English. Just as close as I possibly can."

Mesmerized, her eyes clinging to the pitiless gray ones above her, she watched helplessly as he bent his head, and then, unable to help herself, she shut her eyes, blotting out the sight of that harsh face.

His mouth was warm and demanding as it took hers, and Elizabeth made one small, involuntary attempt to escape. Feeling her resistance, Rafael's hands tightened, pulling her next to his tall, hard length, deepening his kiss. He kissed her a long time, an endless time, during which Elizabeth learned irrevocably that there are kisses and then there are kisses. Later she was to remember shamefully that he never forced her after those few first seconds in his arms.

His hands slipped to her waist, bringing her even closer, closer it seemed than when she and Nathan had been in bed that night, and she was suddenly aware that this was what she had wanted all evening. Rafael had wanted it too, it seemed, for as she melted into him, her soft young breasts crushed against his chest, his mouth hardened into passion, and alarmingly she felt his lips forcing hers apart and his tongue urgently searching her mouth.

No one had kissed her like that before, and helplessly she gave a tiny moan at the unexpected pleasurable ache that suddenly hit her loins as Rafael's mouth continued its hungry assault on her lips. Giddy, plunging into a new world of physical sensations, she didn't stop him when he lowered his head to gently kiss the soft flesh that rose above the silken gown, nor did she stop him when his hand cupped her breast and his thumb brushed rhythmically across her nipple. His mouth founds hers again, his tongue urgently seeking the inner softness, and what little sanity Elizabeth had, vanished. This was what she had wanted for too long—someone to want *her!*—and at the moment she was oblivious of everything—Nathan, marriage vows, their surroundings, everything but this tall, dark, dangerous man who held her in his arms and whose mouth was teaching hers passion and desire.

It was Rafael who eventually tore himself away from her. Lost in her own world of dreamy sensuality, Elizabeth stared at him in bewilderment as he abruptly stepped back from her. The violet eyes, dark with virgin passion, clung to his face, and Rafael's mouth twisted. Breathing heavily, he said thickly, "I think you now know *why* I want to see you alone!"

Cold, icy sanity returned in that second to Elizabeth, and, mortified at her own actions and unwilling to even think about his, she whirled around and with her back to him choked out, "I think you have forgotten that we are both married... and not to each other."

There was a muttered curse from Rafael, and then with ungentle fingers he spun her around to face him. "For the love of God! What has that to do with us? You do not love that husband of yours... and don't lie to me that you do! My wife was chosen for me by my grandfather, and she has as much love for me as I have for her. So tell me, who do we hurt by wanting each other?"

Stubbornly she whispered, "It isn't right!"

"Right?" Rafael grated. "What has right to do with it? English, I want you and a moment ago you wanted me. I don't intend to be denied simply because you don't think it's right!"

He was very attractive as he stood there across from her. His hair was ruffled, falling rebelliously onto his forehead, and his silvery gray eyes were alive and filled with more expression than she had ever seen so far, but his face was angry, the heavy black brows scowling and the full mouth taut with suppressed emotion. Incredibly, she longed to throw herself into his arms and smooth away the anger. But one time in his arms had taught her that he exercised a frightening power over her, and she grimly resisted that mad temptation. Instead, staring at him steadily, she asked, "Do you expect me to believe you have suddenly fallen in love with me?"

All life left those gray eyes and they were once more empty and icy. "Love you?" he snarled. "No, English, I do not love you—I do not love anyone! But I do want you, and I have discovered that wanting usually works as well as loving."

Stricken and not even certain what she would have done if he had said he loved her, Elizabeth's eyes dropped. "Go away," she said in a soft shaken voice. "I don't ever want to see you again. You are a dangerous man, Mr. Santana, and I think it best that you find your wife and tell *her* that you want her."

A curiously bleak slant to his mouth, he retorted

tightly, "If I did, she would run screaming for her priest. You see, Consuela only *endures* the marriage bed—she does not enjoy it, nor does she make any attempt to hide the fact that she finds me abhorrent." He gave a wry smile and added, "That Comanche blood, you know. Consuela does not feel it is worthy of her noble birth." The smile left his face and with an oddly vulnerable motion his hand rubbed his neck, and in a different tone of voice, almost with a note of confusion, he said seriously, "English, I do not do this with every woman, despite what you may have heard. You are very beautiful and I am—"

Whatever else he might have said was lost, for at that moment the door was suddenly flung open so violently that it banged like a cannon against the wall. A woman, her Spanish black eyes gleaming with ill-concealed malice, stood on the threshold. She took a brief comprehensive glance and began shrieking, "*¡Aja!* I knew it! *¡Ay de mí!* That I should be so shamed!"

Rafael, his face nearly white with fury, leaped across the room and dragged the screaming woman inside. Ignoring her almost maniacal struggles to free herself, Rafael effortlessly held her prisoner. His voice a whiplash of sound, he snarled, "Stop it, Consuela, before you make a scene that even you will regret!"

"*Ay! Ay!* Tell me why you are here with *this* woman!" she demanded hotly, her dark eyes stabbing across the room in Elizabeth's direction.

"If I do so, will you stop your screaming?" he asked resignedly.

Sullenly she shook her head *yes*, twitching herself free of his loosened grip. Drawing herself up with haughty pride, she looked contemptuously at Elizabeth, who had stood frozen in the center of the room. "You are a poor, pale little thing, aren't you?" she said sneeringly. "So pale and like milk-water that you must stoop to entrapping other women's husbands!"

"That's not true!" Elizabeth gasped, her bottom lip quivering with despair. It only needed this to make a perfectly enjoyable evening absolutely ghastly. She had been wrong to let Rafael kiss her, but she certainly hadn't entrapped him. Beseechingly her eyes flew to his.

He sent her a strangely comforting look and in an icy voice said to Consuela, "Leave her out of this, señora! She has done nothing, and if you must vent your anger, vent it on me. She is innocent, and I do not want her slandered by your evil tongue."

Consuela sniffed, obviously not liking what he said, but also not inclined to argue the point. "Bah! What do I care what you do—but I will not have you shame me! If you wish to have your little *putas*, do so, but keep them away from me!"

"Consuela, say one more word against her, and I will slit that long, white throat you are so proud of," Rafael murmured with deadly softness.

"Ha! I rather expected you to threaten me—what else could I expect from a barbarian like you? It is despicable that I, with the most noble blood of Spain flowing in my veins, should be so humbled and so degraded to have a husband like you!"

Silently watching the two of them, Elizabeth had the feeling that Consuela frequently threw that statement at Rafael's head, and she pitied him. He caught the look of pity in her eyes and a muscle bunched in his jaw.

"Don't," he said quietly. "Don't *ever* look at me like that again."

Instantly Elizabeth dropped her gaze, appalled by the rage that had so swiftly lit those gray eyes. He would hate pity, she realized with a pang. Hate it and anyone who offered it.

"What in the world is going on in here?" Stella demanded from the doorway. "I have been waiting for ages for you, Elizabeth. Didn't the servant find our things?"

"N-no. I did. They are right here," Elizabeth answered feebly, wondering how much Stella had overheard and what conjecture she put on the three of them here in the room.

"Oh, hello, Doña Consuela. Did you enjoy the soiree?" Stella murmured politely.

Consuela shot her a look of pure venom, and as she was not a particularly beautiful woman, with a prominent nose and a mouth both thin and ungenerous, it made her appear almost ugly. "I might have known she would be a friend of yours!" Consuela said disagreeably. "It seems there is no one in this benighted land who is not common and vulgar, and without any morals at all."

"Now, what do you mean by that?" Stella asked smoothly, her dark eyes narrowing with quick temper.

"As if you didn't know!" Consuela shot back nastily. "You probably encouraged her, hoping I would be humiliated."

Stella smiled sweetly. "Oh no, señora, you do that often enough all by yourself—you certainly don't need any help from me! And I would thank you to leave Beth out of any argument you may have with me or your husband."

"If this were Spain," Consuela began angrily—but Rafael's furious *"Basta ya!"* stopped her from saying anything further.

Glancing exasperatedly at Stella, he said, "Stella, *amiga,* will you take the little one away?" With difficulty he added, "I am sorry this had to happen."

Her sallow skin mottled with rage, Consuela burst out, "You apologize to them! What about me? Am I, may God have mercy on me, not your wife? It is *I* who deserve an apology from everyone in this room! I demand it!"

His mouth taut with equal rage, Rafael snapped icily, "Leave it, Consuela! Don't make this any more unpleasant than it already is."

"Ay! Ay! I should have expected that from you. You will allow me to be insulted in this fashion and then you will do nothing to alleviate my shame, my pain. You are truly a savage, Rafael. A dirty, thieving Comanche savage like your grandmother!"

"Stop it, Consuela," he said quietly. "Stop it before you lose your temper."

"And if I don't, what will you do—kill me? You would like to do that, wouldn't you?" she spat out viciously. "I wonder why you have not hired some of your filthy, *estúpido* savages before now to rid you of a wife like myself!"

The gray eyes nearly black with fury, Rafael's hand snaked out and fastened with dangerous strength around Consuela's wrist. "I might just do that," he bit out cruelly. "I'm surprised that I hadn't thought of it before now!" Then, as if unable to bear the sight of her any longer, her threw her wrist violently away from him and flung out of the room.

CHAPTER FIVE

Elizabeth was never certain what happened next, for her jumbled thoughts didn't untangle themselves until at least an hour later when, wearing a soft nightgown, the silvery hair in two long braids resting on her breasts, she sat on the bed in the house on Esplanade Avenue sipping hot chocolate. Stella was with her, also partaking of a cup of chocolate as she lounged on the corner of Elizabeth's bed.

"Do you want to talk about it?" Stella asked quietly.

Elizabeth gave her a wan smile. "There isn't really anything to talk about. Mr. Santana followed me into the cloakroom and his wife found us there, and you know the rest."

Not looking at Elizabeth, Stella questioned carefully, "Did Consuela have a reason to fly into a rage?"

A guilty expression on her face, Elizabeth admitted, "I suppose so. Mr. Santana did kiss me, but how she could know that I don't know." Her eyes troubled, she added softly, "It was wrong, I know, but I've never met anyone like him before, Stella. I couldn't have stopped him, and the simply horrid thing is that I didn't *want* to stop him!" She gave a sad little sigh. "I must be a wanton woman—why else would I allow a perfect stranger such intimacy?"

"I rather doubt that *you* allowed Rafael Santana to do anything!" Stella returned dryly. "Knowing Rafael, honey, you didn't stand a chance if he had made up his mind to kiss you. I'm sorry that he took such a liberty, and especially sorry that Consuela had to cause an ugly scene. By tomorrow Consuela will be screeching out the story to everyone who will listen, and unfortunately, there are more than a few who *will* listen! I'm certain, too, knowing what a witch she is, that quite a few embellishments will be added to the story. I just hope that your husband doesn't decide to challenge Rafael to a silly duel. *That* would put a cap on the whole sordid affair!"

Elizabeth's lower lip began to tremble, and she knew that in another second she was going to be weeping like a child. Vainly trying to hide her growing distress, she swallowed painfully and murmured unhappily, "Oh, Stella, everything is such a wretched tangle! I don't want to be the subject of gossip, nor do I want Nathan to fight a duel over me! And I would give just about anything if Mr. Santana had *not* followed me! But more than that, I wish that Nathan had been there with me, and that he and I had the sort of easy relationship you and Juan share."

Stella sent her an affectionate smile. "Now, honey, don't carry on so. You and Nathan will do just fine. Time is all that you need to make a happy marriage. Why, I'll wager that in a few months you'll look back on this conversation and wonder how you could have been such a ninny. And as for Consuela, let's just hope that somehow Rafael can convince her not to create a full-blown scandal. If anyone can, it'll be Rafael." Stella hesitated and then went on in a slightly worried tone of voice. "I just wish that Juan and I were not leaving day after tomorrow. With us gone there'll be no one *except* Rafael to countermand what I'm sure will be Consuela's vicious lies. What we certainly don't want is for her to make so much scandal that it follows you to Natchez!"

Appalled, Elizabeth stammered, "B-but why would she do that? She hates Rafael, even I could tell that! Why would she slander me and expose the fact that her husband finds other women more appealing than herself? If I found Nathan in a compromising situation, I definitely wouldn't want it to be broth for all the scandalmongers!"

"Nor would most women. But then, you would have to understand Consuela Valadez de Santana," Stella returned dryly. She would have stopped there, but Elizabeth said in a small voice, "Please go on—I would like to know how he could have married such a woman. How could he love her?"

Stella's mouth twisted wryly. "That, my pet, is most of the problem. Rafael and Consuela's marriage was arranged for them. You see, despite the Comanche half-breed grandmother, Rafael's family is very wealthy and aristocratic. It is a long story, but basically this is what happened. Rafael and his mother, Doña Faith, were captured by the Comanches when Rafael was about two years old."

Elizabeth's cry of distress caused Stella to stop and look at her. "Honey, don't be so shocked—the Comanches always take captives, and women and children are stolen regularly. No one knows how many white captives the Comanches have, and it is the one thing on the frontier that every woman dreads. Few if any are ever heard of again, but occasionally, as in the case of Rafael's mother, word does come back." Stella frowned as she tried to remember the sequence of events. "I've heard the tale from my mother often enough, but I can never recall how long afterward a Comanche half-breed came into San Antonio and told of Doña Faith's death. I think it was about two years later, and he said that she had died the previous year. At any rate, she was dead, but he had seen the boy, Rafael, and said that the child had been adopted by a Comanche family and was thriving."

Her eyes wide and wondering, Elizabeth asked, "Didn't anyone try to find him? They didn't just leave him there, did they?"

Stella made a face. "Beth, it's so difficult to explain—there are so many bands of Comanches and they move about constantly. The distances are so great, some areas not even yet explored by white men, and it is almost impossible to meet with them . . . under friendly circumstances. It's as if the captives disappear off the face of the earth—some are traded to other bands and tribes and some simply die. The Santanas were lucky to even know that Doña Faith was actually dead. Sometimes years pass before anyone knows for certain the fate of a captive." Her voice gloomy, she added, "Sometimes never."

"And what happened then? Once they knew Doña Faith was dead and Rafael still alive, what did they do then?" Beth wanted to know.

"Nothing. I think, and so do a lot of other people, that Don Felipe was perfectly happy with the situation. Certainly he wasted little time in arranging a very suitable second marriage for Don Miguel, Rafael's father. That marriage, I might add, produced only girls, much to Don Felipe's disgust."

"And?" Elizabeth prompted impatiently, wanting to hear of Rafael.

"And, I guess, when it became apparent that there was going to be no male heir, Don Felipe began to think about the grandson stolen by the Comanches. I don't know how he did it—everyone thinks it was through that same half-breed, who was in and out of San Antonio all the time—but Don Felipe finally had Rafael tracked down and identified, and then had him captured by his men. It was risky and dangerous, but Don Felipe was set on it—his Spanish pride wanted that male heir, and even one with Comanche blood in his veins and raised by the Comanches would be acceptable."

Her voice full of sympathy for the young Rafael, Elizabeth asked softly, "And Rafael? How did he feel? Was he happy to be reunited with his family?"

Reluctantly Stella confessed, "Rafael was, from what anyone will say about what happened, little better than an animal, and it took them almost three years of literally 'taming' him on the family rancho before Don Felipe felt it was safe to send him to Spain for further education and training. It was while he was in Spain that his grandfather arranged the marriage with Consuela's family. Both Consuela and Rafael were forced to bow to family pressure—unfortunately for them! I've often wondered," Stella mused, "what pressure could have been put on Rafael to make him agree to the marriage. The only thing that comes to mind is that his grandfather threatened some sort of retribution against the Comanches—perhaps Don Felipe specifically named Rafael's Comanche family. It must have been drastic to make him marry Consuela."

Frowning, Elizabeth asked, "How do you know so much about Rafael's family? I wouldn't think that what you're telling me would be common knowledge."

Stella grinned. "Now, that's where you're wrong. *Everyone* in San Antonio knows about Rafael Santana! When his mother was captured by the Comanches it couldn't be hidden, nor when Rafael was stolen back—although no one knew about *that* until almost a year later—not even his father was privy to Don Felipe's actions! For one reason or another Rafael has always been the subject of gossip—even before he was born!"

"But why?" Elizabeth inquired with puzzlement.

Her grin fading and in a more serious tone of voice, Stella replied, "You see, Don Felipe has never forgiven his son for marrying the daughter of a half-breed Comanche and an American trapper. Everyone knew how strongly Don Felipe objected to the marriage, and I guess, again from what my mother says, that the marriage caused the town to buzz for weeks. Don Felipe apparently didn't precisely forbid the marriage, but he did everything he could to stop it short of outright force. And since then, everything that has happened to Rafael or anything he does only adds to the gossip."

Somewhat earnestly Elizabeth said, "It must be very hard for him to know that no matter what he does people will be talking about him."

"Ha! Not Renegade Santana! He doesn't give a damn what people say! Why, the first thing he did when he returned from Spain was disappear with the Comanches for a year! Then, with all the wealth and power of the Santana family behind him, what did he do but strike out with old Abel Hawkins, his maternal grandfather, and trap wild horses until Abe died a couple of years ago." Stella gave an odd little smile. "For that I almost admire him. Everything he owns, except what he inherited from Abe, he earned, and to Don Felipe's fury he refuses to live the life Don Felipe thinks is suitable for his heir." Stella's smile grew wider. "When Rafael joined the Texans in rebelling against Mexico, everyone thought the old man was going to die of sheer rage!" Stella's smile faded and she added seriously, "Rafael's joining with the Texans came as a surprise to a lot of people—Texans included, though there are quite a few of them who are very happy he threw his lot in with them, Sam Houston among them."

Toying with the hem of her blanket, Elizabeth asked with studied indifference, "And Consuela, how does she fit into his life?"

Stella grimaced. "She doesn't! They have lived apart for years. The marriage was already over when they arrived from Spain four years ago, and it's only gotten worse since then. Rafael avoids her, and with good reason—she is detestable!"

Elizabeth frowned. "But if that is the case, how is it that she is here in New Orleans with him?"

"Ah, she is here... but not *with* him! And I'll wager that Don Felipe is behind it." At Elizabeth's questioning look she added, "He wants a great-grandson, and how can he get one if Consuela and Rafael are never together?"

Elizabeth blushed and said with difficulty, "Doesn't it bother Rafael to upset his grandfather?"

"He thrives on it! Certainly he enjoys watching his grandfather turn purple with rage when word of his latest transgression filters back. There is such bitter hatred between those two that I often wonder how it will end. If Rafael were not Don Felipe's only male heir, I would fear for his life."

"His grandfather would not kill him! I can't believe that, Stella. Surely you are exaggerating?"

"You don't know Don Felipe, and if Don Miguel were to father another son on his second wife, Rafael's life wouldn't be worth a burnt candle. Sometimes I wonder who hates him the most—his wife or his grandfather."

"Is that why Consuela would spread lies about me? To hurt him?"

A considering expression on her face, Stella said slowly, "Partly. And partly to discredit you in Rafael's eyes, I think."

"Discredit me?" Elizabeth exclaimed. "Why would she do that? Especially if she doesn't want him anyway?"

"Ah, therein lies the secret. You see, she doesn't want Rafael herself, nor does she make any secret of the fact that she cannot bear for him to touch her. Which is why she often condones the various women who share his bed—and that is also common knowledge. Sometimes I could strangle Rafael for deliberately flaunting his carryings-on. But you see, while Consuela doesn't want Rafael for herself, he *is* her husband, and she doesn't want him to have any sort of lasting relationship with another woman. A *puta* or a whoring wife she can stomach, but someone who might *mean* something to Rafael she wouldn't put up with. And honey, I hate to tell you this, but while Rafael is notorious around women, I must confess you are the first innocent I have ever seen him trifle with. Usually his affairs are with older married women who know precisely what they are letting themselves in for. Normally, he doesn't display interest in someone as young and obviously naïve as yourself." Frowning, Stella admitted slowly, "And that's what worries me. If Consuela thinks you are different, that more than just a physical desire is motivating Rafael, then she'll do her damnedest to not only destroy *you*, but any interest Rafael may have. Now, do you see why I'm worried?"

Elizabeth nodded her head, her eyes wide and just a little fearful. In a shaken voice she murmured, "Oh, how I wish I had never gone to that soiree—but most of all I wish you weren't leaving! What ever am I to do, Stella?"

"Come now!" Stella said bracingly. "I have probably overemphasized the situation and you have nothing to fear. Rafael will more than likely soothe Consuela's suspicions, and if we are fortunate, what happened tonight between you and Rafael will go no farther. And if the very worst happens, just hold onto the thought that shortly you and Nathan will be leaving New Orleans and any scandal behind you. Truthfully, I don't honestly think she can create much of a scandal on what little she discovered tonight. Remember, all she really knows is that you and Rafael were alone in the cloakroom for a few minutes—and while she has a vicious tongue, there is only so much she can say about it."

"I hope so," Elizabeth said gloomily. "What a horrid

ending to my first soiree. I don't think I'll ever be able to attend another without remembering this one."

"Don't be so dramatic, honey," Stella chided. "A year from now all this will be behind you. Now go to sleep and don't think about it. Think only good thoughts, and think of how you were enjoying yourself *before* Rafael brought himself to our notice."

"You're right," Elizabeth admitted a little shamefacedly. "I am, I know, turning this into a high tragedy, and I shall stop it immediately."

"Good! Now sleep well, Beth, and I'll see you in the morning."

Waking shortly after ten o'clock to a bright, sunny morning, Elizabeth took time dressing, and consequently it was well after eleven before she descended the stairs in search of Stella. Finding her way to the room where they had dined the evening before, she was met there by a servant who informed her that Señor and Señora Rodriguez were out at the moment but that Doña Stella would return shortly. In the meantime would Mrs. Ridgeway like some hot chocolate and some fresh croissants? Mrs. Ridgeway definitely would!

So it was that Stella found Elizabeth happily munching away on the flakiest pastry she had ever eaten in her life, when she returned about a half-hour later.

"My, you're up earlier than I expected. I thought you would sleep until afternoon. Have the servants seen to everything you wanted?"

"Oh, yes. And why should you think *I* would sleep till noon when you obviously have been up for some time?" Elizabeth returned with a smile.

"Ah, but I had business, you see," Stella said mysteriously, the brown eyes twinkling with amusement.

Guessing instantly what kind of business, Elizabeth's smile faded and she asked anxiously, "Business about last night?"

"Yes. And do stop worrying. I called upon Margarita Costa this morning on the pretext that I had lost a glove last night, and in the process she and I had quite a little gossip about Consuela. I don't think you have much to worry about there! Consuela apparently didn't say anything last night, and if she were going to, then would have been the time to do it. Margarita was full of compliments concerning you, which she certainly wouldn't have been if Consuela had started any rumors." Looking very pleased with herself, Stella added, "I also managed to convey, ever so politely, you understand, that for some unknown reason Consuela Santana took one of her noted dislikes to you, and that Margarita should ignore any tales Consuela might spread. Margarita has no love for Consuela either! So, even though Juan and I leave tomorrow, Margarita will help to weaken any poison Consuela might spout."

"Oh, Stella, you are *so* good to me. I shall miss you very much. How dreadful that we should have such a brief meeting—I wish you were just beginning your visit instead of ending it!"

Stella's face softened. "I know, pet, I know. It does seem unfair, doesn't it? But don't worry. Juan and I will be coming back in a few years and besides, who knows—someday, you may come to Santa Fe!"

With that thought in mind, it was almost with happiness that Elizabeth bid her friend farewell the next day. Nathan was at her side, having canceled an appointment with the tailor for the express purpose of meeting the Rodriguezes. Stella did not find him exactly impressive, but she could see that Nathan had a fondness for his young bride, and it gave her hope that all would be well with Beth.

Riding back to their hotel, Nathan apologized again for not being able to meet the Rodriguezes earlier. "I am sorry that I could not come for dinner and the soiree the other night, my dear. I do hope you forgive me! If only you had let me know earlier I could have made other arrangements."

"Oh, that's all right, Nathan. I didn't mind, really. But it would have been much nicer if you could have been there," Elizabeth replied honestly, still unable to think of that disastrous soiree without a guilty quiver and just a little fear.

His gray eyes kind as they rested on her face, Nathan murmured lightly, "Perhaps it was better I wasn't with you. You and your friend...er...Stella must have had plenty of time to gossip and giggle, and you did not need a husband hovering in the background."

Elizabeth returned a determinedly cheerful comment, finding herself reluctant to discuss further her visit with Stella or what had transpired. And Nathan, surprisingly perceptive, gathered as much and politely changed the subject. They had a delightful luncheon together in a quaint little restaurant that he had discovered and then strolled back toward their hotel. Glancing at his watch, Nathan said with surprise, "My word, it is gone two o'clock and I am to meet a fellow at two-thirty about a racehorse that interests me. I know you must think me a very casual sort of husband, but would you mind very much if I left you to your own devices the remainder of the afternoon—and," he added with a guilty countenance, "most of the evening?"

Almost glad to have several hours of her own, Elizabeth agreed easily enough. "No, you go on, Nathan. I may go for a carriage ride about the city later with Mary, but other than that I think I shall enjoy resting a few hours in my room. Will you be very late?"

"I don't really know. Apparently this horse is on a stud farm some distance from the city, so we may eat dinner at an inn along the way. I expect I'll be back sometime before midnight, though. Do you want me to wake you?"

"No. I'll see you in the morning, then," Elizabeth replied quietly.

Nathan escorted her to the hotel and a very few minutes later departed. Feeling inexplicably glad to see him leave, Elizabeth had discarded her charming straw bonnet and was relaxing in her hotel suite, leafing through a copy of *Godey's Ladies Book,* when she was interrupted by a private servant in a black-and-gold uniform. At first she only listened politely to his message, but her eyes widened when she heard of Consuela Santana's invitation for a meeting that very afternoon.

Now, why? Elizabeth thought, perplexed. Why does she want to see me? Should I go? Or should I ignore it? She bit her lip nervously, staring blindly after the servant's departing figure. Perhaps it would be best, she finally decided.

The address where they were to meet was unfamiliar to Elizabeth, but as she was a stranger to New Orleans it didn't concern her. She left a note for Nathan, stating briefly that she had been invited out to visit with a lady she had met at the soiree she had attended with Stella. She told Mary the same thing and then, determined to convince Consuela Santana that there was nothing between herself and Rafael, she had the doorman of the hotel obtain a carriage for her.

If the driver of the carriage was surprised that an obvious lady like his passenger wanted to be taken to the ramparts of the city, where the gentlemen of New Orleans kept their quadroon mistresses, his face did not betray it. Who knew the whims of the fancy? Still, when they pulled up before a charming little white-washed cottage surrounded by a picket fence, he hesitated. "Um, ma'am, would you like me to wait for you?"

Elizabeth, reassured by the well-kept appearance of the cottage and overall air of respectability of the area, sent him a confident smile. "Oh, no, that won't be necessary." She added with beguiling charm, "You see, I don't know how long I shall be, but I am certain the lady I am visiting can arrange some sort of transportation for me when I leave. Thank you very much, though."

Shrugging his shoulders, he prodded his lazy bay gelding onward. Elizabeth watched him go with a sudden qualm. Perhaps she should have him wait. Consuela might *not* be as obliging as she assumed. But then, straightening her slim shoulders to nearly military erectness, she approached the door almost aggressively.

Her knock on the door was answered by an unsmiling Spanish woman of uncertain age, and with a slight nervousness Elizabeth allowed herself to be escorted into a small drawing room. The entire cottage was not large, but it was tastefully furnished and, though on a reduced scale, everything bespoke money—money elegantly spent.

A fine woolen carpet lay on the floor and gilt mirrors adorned the walls. Small, delicate, satinwood tables were scattered here and there, and two balloon-backed chairs, upholstered in a soft shade of pink, contrasted attractively with the Duncan Phyfe sofa of deep rose velvet. It was the woman seated comfortably on the sofa that reminded Elizabeth sharply that this was not just a polite visit.

Her fingers tightening unconsciously around her reticule of Moroccan leather, Elizabeth said politely, "Good afternoon, señora. It was kind of you to invite me to meet you."

Consuela, her dark eyes never leaving Elizabeth's small face, returned an appropriate comment indicating that Elizabeth was to seat herself in one of the chairs opposite the sofa. Elizabeth's courage, never very great, was rapidly disappearing. There was something so very intimidating about the still figure, dressed in a gown of dark ruby cashmere trimmed with touches of black lace, that Elizabeth felt as if she were facing the Inquisition. Consuela's black hair was parted in the center and pulled back smoothly into a chignon that lay on her neck. She wore little jewelry except for fine pearl earrings in her ears and several rings of obvious value on her fingers.

The black eyes veiled, for several unnerving seconds Consuela stared at Elizabeth before saying finally, "It was good of you to come, señora. I believe we have a great deal to talk about, but before we begin, may I offer you some refreshment?"

Elizabeth's first inclination was to refuse, but, thinking it might offend the other woman, she agreed almost effusively. "Oh, yes! That would be very nice!"

Consuela reached for a small silver bell nearby on one of the satinwood tables, and from the promptness with which the servant, Manuela, appeared, Elizabeth had the impression the woman had been waiting just outside the room for the summons. She returned almost immediately with an ornate silver tray, making it apparent that Consuela had gone to a great deal of trouble for her guest. There was English tea freshly brewed in a porcelain pot and small cakes dusted with sugar, as well as a carafe of *sangría* for Consuela.

Glancing unsmilingly at Elizabeth, she remarked,

"I assumed that being English you would welcome tea, but if you prefer you may share my *sangría.*"

Consuela seemed in no hurry to open the conversation, and Elizabeth had nervously finished one cup of tea and was halfway through a second before she realized that the beverage had been brewed far too strongly and had a bitter taste. Nonetheless she sipped it thankfully—at least it gave her something to do while Consuela made what could only be called indifferent conversation.

Growing more and more bewildered as the time passed and Consuela made no reference to her husband, Elizabeth finally managed to bring up the subject herself. Bracing herself and gathering her courage before it failed, the violet eyes steadily meeting the dark ones of the Spanish woman, Elizabeth said quietly, "Señora, I do not mean to be impolite, but I do not believe that you arranged this meeting for us to discuss the amenities to be found in New Orleans." An unencouraging silence met her words, and flustered by Consuela's lack of response she hesitated before valiantly plunging on. "I think we have skirted the thought uppermost in both of our minds long enough—your husband." Earnestly she said, "Please, señora, believe me when I say that nothing happened between us. Please, *please* believe me when I say that *nothing* occurred to—to shame you or to bring dishonor on any of us!"

Beyond a slight stiffening, Consuela did not betray any reaction to Elizabeth's sincere little speech. The haughty face impassive, she replied levelly, "You are right. It is time that we spoke of the reason for this meeting. But before we do, more tea?"

Impatiently Elizabeth declined, and feeling suddenly lightheaded, she swayed slightly in her chair. "No, thank you. I'm afraid that something I ate must have disagreed with me, and more tea will only compound the error."

"Perhaps," Consuela returned with the barest suggestion of a smile. "But then again, the condition may worsen."

Staring hazily at the other woman, Elizabeth shook her head as Consuela's form seemed to blur and become two shapes. "What, what...do...you mean?" she got out thickly, her tongue feeling as if it were covered in cotton wool.

"Merely that the tea you have been drinking is laced with belladonna. And that in a moment you will discover *exactly* why I arranged this meeting." The words were said with such satisfied malice that Elizabeth, fighting to quell a wild surge of giddiness, was filled with terror. "Why?" she managed to croak.

Consuela's thin, black eyebrows rose. "Why, señora? Very simply because I do not want Rafael to have dreams of you." Almost conversationally she went on, "He has had many women in the past and they did not bother me. I do not care how many whores he takes to his bed, but I will not have him cherishing another woman's image in his heart."

"Oh, but he doesn't!"

"Perhaps not," Consuela went on ruthlessly. "But I intend to make certain. I have given it much thought, and there are many things about an incident that both you and my husband wish to make light of that has lain heavily on my mind." Her eyes blazing now with anger, she spat furiously, "Never has Rafael bargained with me! Never! And yet in order to buy my silence, in order that I should not cause you scandal, he has agreed to accompany me to Spain—something he has flatly refused to do for years, despite my pleas. And I wonder—I wonder why? And do you know what I decided, you pale little thing?" Consuela gave an ugly laugh. "I decided that he wishes to protect you. You have touched a part of him that no one ever has—not even I, his wife! For that reason I cannot ignore you the way I have his other women. Because of that I must do something to tarnish you, to make you mean nothing more than all the others he has known."

"Oh, señora, you are wrong!" Elizabeth burst out in a shocked tone of voice. "We only met that one night and then only briefly—I mean nothing to him, nothing! You must believe me!"

"Bah! So you would say, but I think differently. And I intend to do something about it."

Whether it was the drug making her so listless or

her own inability to cope with such single-minded viciousness, Elizabeth was never certain. At any rate, with a numbing sense of inevitability, she asked dully, "Aren't you frightened of what I may do when I leave here? What my husband may do?"

Consuela smiled and somehow that was more terrifying than anything she had said or done so far. "You will say nothing—and even if you were foolish enough to do so, who would believe you? Believe that someone like myself would be bothered by an insipid, absurd little creature like you? Besides, I have taken precautions," she retorted complacently. "Your husband was the easiest to manage. I assumed that like most young men he is only interested in horses and gambling, and I was right—as the fact that he was so easily lured away to view a horse attests. I merely had to mention to a distant relative of mine, who knows nothing of what I plan, that I thought I had heard that Señor Ridgeway was interested in purchasing such an animal. That they would meet in the small society of New Orleans was just a matter of time. But I even helped that to occur by discovering where your husband found his amusements and seeing to it that my relative found himself there at the same time. He is a foolish young man, much like your husband," Consuela said contemptuously. "And by now he will have forgotten that it was I who first mentioned Señor Ridgeway's name, and that it was I who suggested that he might find it pleasant to visit the particular coffeehouse that your husband has been frequenting."

Her conceit and enjoyment of her own cleverness goaded Consuela to boast further, "As for my servant that brought the message? Piffle! He will say nothing—not if he values his skin...and those of his relatives in Spain!" Consuela smiled again, a very pleased, catlike smile. "You see, I have left nothing unplanned. My servants know the dangers of betraying me. As for the final member of my little plot, he is a very poor, and I should add, very greedy, illegitimate cousin from Spain, and he knows that if he were to breathe even just one word, that my generosity to him would cease. Besides," she added with obvious satisfaction, "Lorenzo will enjoy doing this for me, if only to spite my husband. So you see, even if you were foolish enough to speak of this, how would you prove it? Who would believe you? You are a stranger here, a stranger stopping for a visit, while I am connected to some of the most illustrious families in New Orleans. Your friend Estella Rodriguez might believe you, but she is miles from here by now. I have thought of everything, of that you can be sure."

Repelled, her eyes wide with fascinated horror, Elizabeth got out, "What do you intend to do with me?"

"Merely see to it that Rafael arrives here in time to find you naked in Lorenzo's embrace. Of course, I have left precisely *what* Lorenzo does with you up to him. You may even find his lovemaking enjoyable—according to him most women do."

"You're vile!" Elizabeth spat thickly. "You won't get away with it. I'll scream and fight and Rafael will know that I am not willing."

Consuela looked at her pityingly. "You are in no condition to fight anyone, and as for screaming, I imagine Lorenzo can manage to keep you quiet long enough for Rafael to see for himself the slut that you will appear. If you scream and protest afterward, it will look as if you are trying to excuse yourself."

With sickening clarity Elizabeth knew Consuela was right. She was incapable of resisting anyone at the moment; the belladonna effectively weighted her body with lead. But she could try, and clumsily she attempted to lurch to her feet. It was a futile gesture that only pointed out how very correct Consuela's reading of the situation was. Mortified and frightened, Elizabeth fell back against the pink cushions of the chair.

"You see?" Consuela taunted. "You are incapable of fighting anyone. Everything will go just as I planned."

Before Consuela could say more, a well-dressed young man entered the room, walking across the floor with all the grace and arrogance of a conquistador. His dark, clever face and thin, smiling mouth revealed the same hint of cruelty that had lurked in his Spanish ancestors. The black eyes avidly surveyed Elizabeth's shrinking form, and in a heavily accented voice Lorenzo Mendoza murmured, "By the Virgin! Consuela, this I would do for you for nothing, if I did not need the money. She is lovely! I should thank you for providing me with an afternoon's sport. Such fairness! I shall take great pleasure in bedding your friend."

Consuela's face showed her distaste for the subject, but she returned indifferently, "I care little what you do with her. Just make certain that when Rafael arrives here, he finds you in a compromising situation." She rose from her seat, adding, "I must depart now, I will leave you to prepare the scene. Do not take too long, though, because just as soon as I return to the house I shall start the argument with Rafael, telling him what a fool is he to believe in a pair of English eyes, and that I have proof that this *gringa* bitch is nothing but a common adulteress. I do not think he will waste much time getting here."

"Do not worry—the only problem may be that Rafael will arrive *after* I have had my pleasure! She is much too lovely for me to resist for very long, so don't *you* waste any time telling him where he can find us."

"Faugh! Your low blood is showing—you are a disgusting animal, Lorenzo!" Consuela muttered as she walked regally to the door.

"True, *mi prima,* but this is precisely why you chose me! Others might have caviled at such villainy," Lorenzo returned smoothly, the black eyes narrowing slightly and the thin nostrils flaring in obvious anger.

Consuela sent him a calculating glance. "Do not take umbrage with me, Lorenzo! We both know of your appetite for women—willing or *un*willing—and we both know that you would do *any*thing for money."

He gave a twisted smile. "You know me too well, Consuela, but remember, even a tame rat will turn if the cheese offered is rotten! So do not comment on my actions—I do what you yourself would do if our positions were reversed. Do not play off your grand airs on me. I am unimpressed."

Consuela's face turned an ugly shade of plum, her dark eyes flashing with fury. "Very well," she snapped. "We understand each other. Now I must be off—I do not want Rafael to have left the house before I arrive." And then she swept out of the room, leaving Elizabeth staring with wide, frightened eyes at the slender Lorenzo.

Slowly Lorenzo pivoted to face Elizabeth, the black eyes stripping her even as she strained back against the cushions. "Ah, my pet, do not worry," he said soothingly as he approached her. "With you, I shall be very gentle and you will enjoy me—I shall see to it."

"No! Please, señor, do not do this to me! Please!" Elizabeth pleaded, a bubble of hysteria rising in her throat. "Please, no. I beg of you, do not dishonor me."

A smile of anticipation curved his mouth. "I am sorry, but even if you resist me, I shall have you. You are too beautiful for me not to want." And with that he reached out and effortlessly swung her up into his arms.

He was a finely boned young man, his slenderness hiding the strength of a jaguar, as Elizabeth discovered when she fought to escape. The drugging hampered her, but even so, Lorenzo still would have won the fight between them. His arms tightened with frightening pressure around her. "Be still or I shall hurt you," he muttered sharply, as swiftly he carried her out of the room and toward the back of the small house.

The fear of what would happen gave Elizabeth the will and the desperation to fight with all her slender resources; her hands beat helplessly against his chest and shoulders. But the belladonna eventually defeated her, as Lorenzo's form divided into two distinct shapes, and the giddiness she had experienced earlier attacked her once more. Her thoughts were confused and she suddenly found herself babbling wild, unintelligible sentences. She knew what was happening and yet it seemed like a fantasy—a nightmarish fantasy, but a fantasy nonetheless.

Ignoring her twisting body and wildly flailing arms, as well as her disjointed words, Lorenzo carried Elizabeth easily to a bedchamber at the rear of the house. Unceremoniously he dumped her on the wide, mosquito-net-draped bed and with ruthless intensity began to strip the clothes from her body. It took time, but all too soon Elizabeth lay there naked, sprawled like a rag doll, her mind wandering, all semblance of coherent thought having vanished. The silvery hair was spread out like a silken banner against the ruby coverlet and the ivory skin gleamed in the faint gloom of the room, as she tossed and turned feverishly on the bed.

Watching her movements, Lorenzo's body hardened with desire and hungrily his gaze skimmed over her, aroused further by the small perfectly formed breasts and their pale rose nipples, before his eyes fastened with increasing sensual excitement upon the curly golden V between her legs. His breath caught in his throat at the beauty of her, the slender waist and gently rounded hips, and hastily he shed his clothes, all thought of Consuela's plan and Rafael's expected appearance fading from his mind.

Elizabeth was dimly aware of being lifted from the bed and the coverlet being thrust back before she was once again placed on the bed. She could feel the soft sensuousness of the satin sheets, and once her cheeks brushed the lacy trim of the pillow case. But she had no time to dwell on their richness or take pleasure in the softness of the bed, because Lorenzo's hard, hot body was instantly pressed against hers.

Her thoughts were no longer logical, and somewhere along the way the events of the afternoon had faded and she was involved in a particularly exciting dream—a dream where Rafael was at her side and his hands were caressing her body and his mouth searching hers. It was so much more satisfying and thrilling than the stolen embrace in the cloakroom because they were both naked and all thought of her husband and his wife had disappeared—there were only the two of them, Rafael and herself, and there were no dividers or barriers between them.

Lorenzo was enchanted at her responses, his body on fire and hungry to lose itself in the slender, silken warmth of her. Yet that very desire held him back, as he deliberately prolonged the agonizing sweetness, delaying the exquisite moment. By all the saints, she was lovely, he thought again, his eyes drinking in the flushed features, the dilated eyes and soft trembling mouth, before sliding almost obsessively down to the small breasts, the nipples erect and begging for his mouth, the slender hips moving sensuously under his hands, and the delicately formed legs that tapered to incredibly tiny ankles. He felt his body filling with such passion that even he was surprised.

Elizabeth was lost, lost in a haze of emotions that swirled and tumbled through her brain. She wanted more than these increasingly urgent kisses and movements of his hands, she wanted with every fiber for him to make her a woman, to experience passion to the fullest—and huskily she moaned, "Please, *please* take me. Now, *now!*"

Lorenzo felt his body leap with burning excitement at her words, and swiftly he moved to cover her, his hips fitting knowledgeably between her white-satin thighs. Eagerly she pushed herself up against him and then . . . and then . . . *nothing!*

She cried out in anguish when a rush of cool air across her body told her better than words that Rafael had left her with frightening abruptness, almost as if he had been torn from her, and bewilderedly she stared as Ra-f-f- No! That wasn't Rafael rising from the floor with a hate-twisted face, it was a stranger to her—while Rafael stood towering above the smaller man, his fists clenched and his features tight and furious!

Dazedly, not understanding, she watched and listened as Lorenzo said sneeringly, "Forgive me, *amigo,* I did not know she was your woman. You should have told me, but even more I think you should keep better care of her. It is not often one of your women prefers me to you, and you will understand why I could not refuse her invitation."

Rafael's jaw went rigid and he snarled softly, "Do not, Lorenzo, do not push me too far."

"Bah! She is only a woman—I will share her with you, if you like."

"Get out!" Rafael snapped harshly, the gray eyes a stormy black as they bore into the naked man before him. "Get out, before I forget myself and still your venomous tongue once and for all."

Lorenzo gave a shrug and with nonchalant insolence began slowly to dress. "She is very good, *amigo,* in bed. She especially enjoys her nipples being—" He was never able to finish that deliberately taunting sentence, for

Rafael could no longer control the rage within him and lunged at the other man.

It was an ugly fight. There was already hatred between them and Rafael with Consuela's jeering words still blazing in his brain was like a madman. He had not believed her when Consuela had shouted, "You fool! You think she is so pure and virtuous! Ha! At this moment she is at a house on the ramparts with Lorenzo. I can give you the address and you can see for yourself just what sort of *puta* she actually is. Go! Go there, you will see that I am right! Lorenzo has been boasting how very easy she was to bed." He had not believed her, had not wanted to believe her. Yet some devil had driven him to come here, to make him enter the house and walk silently to the bedroom at the rear of the house, and—and he would never forget Elizabeth's "Now, *now!*" She was indeed the slut that Consuela claimed, and he was aware of a ridiculous sense of deep betrayal and outrage. To discover that Lorenzo was the other man only added fuel to the fire, and remembering her sanctimonious words of the other night when she had so seemingly sincerely refused to meet him again, his fury exploded and viciously his fists pounded and battered Lorenzo about the room.

Chairs flew and were tossed aside as they fought like the two furious men they were, a small table being smashed as Lorenzo reeled into it after suffering a steel-packed blow from Rafael's right fist. Recovering with catlike swiftness, Lorenzo leaped aside as Rafael plunged after him, and quickly he pulled a knife from amongst his clothing.

Abruptly Rafael halted, his blue-black hair falling onto his forehead, his eyes narrowing to frightening slits. "A knife, *amigo?*" he asked with deceptive quietness. "Is this, then, to be a fight to the death?"

Lorenzo laughed nervously. "I would prefer it not be, but I will not allow you to kill me with your hands, either. Allow me to leave here, Rafael. Not even for her do I wish to die, delightful though she is," he lied.

Suddenly sickened by the entire affair, Rafael's shoulders slumped and he turned away, but in that instant Lorenzo lunged at him, the knife trailing a silver arch in the darkness of the shuttered room.

Elizabeth, watching wide-eyed and helpless, saw Lorenzo's leap and screamed, giving Rafael the second's warning that saved his life. Hearing her scream, Rafael instinctively swung away and around and half met Lorenzo's lunge. Their bodies locked together and they reeled back and forth as Rafael's hand crushed Lorenzo's fingers. Viciously Lorenzo fought back, twisting and coiling like a snake in the fangs of a wolf, trying desperately to escape the iron hold on his wrist. The knife swayed between them, a blade of death that could end the battle for either. Once, Lorenzo was able to slowly, agonizingly bring it near Rafael's strong brown throat, but with silent deadly strength Rafael turned it away and toward Lorenzo. His gray eyes bright and relentless, inexorably Rafael forced the knife gradually in Lorenzo's direction. For a moment longer they were locked together, and then suddenly Lorenzo's strength gave out and the knife plunged into his groin.

Shrieking as much from pain as fear, Lorenzo fell to the floor, his hands automatically reaching to staunch the flow of blood that spread with alarming speed. "You *bastardo!* You might have killed me," he growled with a ragged breath as he surveyed the damage.

"You won't die of that wound, and it's a pity it wasn't a few more inches to the right—then no woman would have to worry about you again," Rafael said emotionlessly.

Lorenzo cursed and somewhat painfully struggled to his feet. "You will forgive me if at the moment I do not feel like continuing this conversation? I must go and find a doctor to treat my wound."

Contemptuously Rafael watched him stumble into his remaining clothing and limp with obvious pain from the room. There was silence after Lorenzo left, and then slowly Rafael turned to look at Elizabeth, still half-drugged on the bed.

She was indeed beautiful, he thought coldly with one part of his brain, taking in the tumbled, silvery fair hair that cascaded to her waist and the perfect breasts that peeked impudently through the strands of hair.

She was half-sitting, half-lying on the bed, the violet eyes still heavy from the belladonna, but to Rafael they appeared drugged with passion. And staring at the naked, gleaming ivory skin, unwillingly he felt passion sweep his body—passion entwined with anger and a feeling of bitter betrayal! She *was* the *slut* Consuela had said—a slut who had looked like an angel and who had aroused the birth of some undefinable emotion within him, a slut who proved again that all women are liars, cheats and whores at heart!

Not aware that she did it, Elizabeth lifted her arms to him, wanting him to come to her, for it to be like it was before this terrible and confusing confrontation had occurred, and Rafael's lips thinned in disgust. Having just had one man, she now wanted another. Whore! A whore with the face and charms of an angel.

Disillusionment numbing his brain, he started to walk away from her, to leave this room before he did something violent and ugly to her. But Elizabeth called softly to him, "Don't leave me." And suddenly he didn't care anymore—she was a slut, so... well, why not take what she offered, why not use that lily-white body that had awakened new and strange emotions within him?

It was a cold, calculated thought, a Comanche thought. He wanted to punish her, to give her pain, to make certain, as he knew he would, that she remembered *this* afternoon from all the others she had spent or would spend with various lovers. And yet when he reached out and touched her something happened between them, something he hadn't expected.

He wanted to punish her, it was true, and yet inexplicably entwined with that thought was an odd tenderness he could not control. Instead of taking her brutally and coldly, he found himself wanting more, much more, the moment his hard hands reached for her and dragged her ruthlessly up next to him.

Compulsively his lips sought hers in a savage, plundering rape of her mouth, and Elizabeth gave a soft moan of distress and pain. Instantly, unable to help himself and strangely unwilling to harm her, his lips gentled, and with an angry, yearning tenderness he began to kiss her again, this time his tongue sweetly and intoxicatingly inflaming Elizabeth's already aroused sensuality.

The drug blurring her inhibitions, helplessly Elizabeth gave herself up to his mouth and ardently caressing hands, her arms wrapping hungrily around his neck, her naked body arching up invitingly against his. Innocently, only half aware of what she was doing, she offered her slender young body to him, her mouth opening irresistibly for his frankly sensual exploration, her hips moving sinuously against him.

With a soft growl of pleasure, Rafael forgot everything but the lovely, warm flesh under his hands. His mouth never leaving her body, sliding from shoulder to breast, he ripped off his clothes with urgent movements. A sigh of satisfaction drifted in the air when at last his tall, nude body joined hers on the bed. Gathering her fiercely into his arms, his mouth tasted and teased her breasts until the nipples were throbbing and tight with anticipation.

Elizabeth's small ivory body fitted exquisitely into the hard muscle and bone of his dark form, and passionately Rafael's hands traveled over her silken skin, touching, caressing, arousing until she felt liquid fire flowing in her veins. A yearning, seeking ache like she had never before experienced seemed to grow between her thighs, and Rafael's probing fingers only increased it, driving her half mad with a longing for something more, and she moaned with pleasure and frustration.

Hearing the small sounds she made, Rafael's desire became so intense and urgent that it was almost more than he could bear. Slowly, savoring the moment and yet hotly eager for it, he slipped between her thighs and thrust himself inside her.

Unaware of her virgin state, thinking he was with a woman who knew what she was about, he did not take the care or prolong his lovemaking as he might have done otherwise, and, though she was aroused to a sobbing acquiescence, Elizabeth felt a sharp, burning pain as that first plunge tore through the delicate membranes. She stiffened and instinctively sought to escape from him, her hands pushing in sudden fear against his hard, warm chest.

Rafael felt the slight obstruction and the instant change in the body that had been lying so pliant and eager beneath him, and for one incredulous second he wondered if he had made a dreadful mistake. But then the impossibility of it occurred to him and, thinking it was only a bit of coyness, a teasing on her part, his mouth fastened with determination on hers and deliberately he forced a response from her. His hands slid under her slender hips and pulled her roughly closer to him and then he began to move again, hungrily, urgently wanting the release that was only bare seconds away.

The first shock of pain lessening and his lips firmly and compellingly on hers, Elizabeth felt her earlier state of feverish arousal returning. His hands at her hips, holding her tightly to him, were both physically exciting and erotic, and she discovered an overwhelming need to press herself even closer, to eagerly meet the thrust of his body. Incredibly she began to feel a wild surge of exquisite sensations as his body continued to move upon hers, and frenziedly she twisted under him, her fingers unconsciously raking his back.

Rafael was not gentle with her, nor was he particularly brutal, but he was an angry, disillusioned man taking what he thought was a woman who had often known the ways of men. And because he was both angry and filled with a strange, bitter hurt at finding her with Lorenzo, he wasn't the tantalizing, seductive lover he could be upon occasion. He simply possessed her body and released all of his pent-up fury and passion into it.

Elizabeth didn't know the difference. She was too entangled in the fiery pleasures that were surging through her body as Rafael continued to drive himself deep within her to be aware of anything but the sensations he was creating. And then, just as the spiraling, intensely pleasurable ache between her thighs became nearly unbearable, he shuddered and it was over, his body sliding off hers.

Dazed, she stared up at his dark, angry face. Her arms tightened unconsciously about his neck and, still hungry for something only guessed at, she murmured, "Please, *please . . .*"

For a long moment Rafael looked into the achingly lovely features, the wide violet eyes framed by the heavy gold-tipped lashes, the full, inviting ruby mouth and furiously he felt his body stir with desire again. It enraged him almost beyond reason. Promiscuous bitch! he thought savagely. Bitch with the face of an angel! And yet he desired her—*por Dios,* how he desired her!

Furious with himself, Rafael wound his hand hurtfully in the mass of silvery curls and, twisting her face closer to his, he snarled, "No! I do not share my women, English. You are Lorenzo's and you obviously find it boring to have just one man in your bed. I have no intention of having a woman that is not *mine,* and mine *alone!"*

Her eyes locked on his, she asked huskily, "And would I be the *only* woman in your bed?"

He gave a twisted smile. "Perhaps. I think you are lovely enough to keep my interest from wandering to another." Then his smile faded and he shook his head. "No, English, it would not do. If I were to possess you again I would make you my mistress, willing or not, and sooner or later, I think, you would betray me, if I were insane enough to do such a thing. Besides," he finished with a thread of amusement in his voice, "you would not like the places I would take you."

For some inexplicable reason she was driven to argue with him. "How do you know—unless you take me with you?"

He shook his head. "That horse won't run, *querida.* I'll not let you goad me into doing something both of us would regret. Stay here where you belong."

Driven by some perverse devil that wouldn't let her terminate the conversation, she murmured almost defiantly, "And if I don't?"

His gray eyes narrowed and a slightly cruel smile curved the full mouth. "Crossing swords with me, English? If you were foolish enough to run counter to my advice, you would regret it, I can promise you that! Stay here where you are safe, *niña,* but rest assured that if I ever meet you again, and in similar circumstances, I shall treat you as you deserve."

With a catlike grace he left the bed and, not looking

at Elizabeth, he swiftly dressed. Fully clothed once more, he walked over to the bed and glanced at her as she lay in the tangled sheets.

Elizabeth knew he would leave her in a moment, knew he was on the point of walking out of her life, and yet, regardless of her marriage, she wanted frantically to make him stay...or take her with him. The violet eyes were bright with unshed tears and the soft mouth was tremulous as she stared up at him, wanting somehow to keep him with her, to make time stop.

There was a brief silence between them, Rafael's eyes unmoving on her features, almost as if he were memorizing them, and then with a low groan of frustration he dragged her head up to him and kissed her with a rough sort of tenderness.

"*Adios*, English," he muttered thickly, and, suddenly releasing her, spun on his heel and walked away. He didn't glance back, didn't see the bloodstained sheets that told of virginity lost and that might have made him question the lies he had been told. Sickened and disgusted, as much with himself for being momentarily blinded by a pair of wide violet eyes and an enchanting mouth, as with the others involved, he walked deliberately out of the room, the gray eyes cold and empty.

With a queer pain in her heart Elizabeth watched him go, one small tear trickling down her cheek. Unhappily she fell back against the pillows, staring blindly into space. She must have fallen into a fitful doze, for she didn't fully awaken until a hand at her shoulder shook her gently. Groggily she stared up at the woman's face above her and memory came flooding back as she recognized Consuela's maid.

Elizabeth sat up abruptly, feeling a slight pain between her legs, and, horrified, she glanced down at the bloodstained sheets as more and more memories she didn't want to face came rushing back. There is no describing the emotions that Elizabeth experienced as the full import of what had transpired flashed across her brain, but horror, fright and pain were all there as well as rage and a queer regret.

Shattered by what had happened, listlessly, like a child that has had too much to bear too soon, she allowed herself to be sponged off and dressed by the silent, oddly gentle maid. And then, barely aware of what was happening around her, she was placed in a carriage and taken back to the hotel she had set out from, what now seemed like eons ago. Resembling a small, pinched-face statue, she eventually found herself in the hotel suite that she and Nathan had reserved.

Bewilderedly she glanced around the room, her gaze locking on the note on the mantel she had left propped for Nathan, what seemed like years ago. Slowly she approached it and just as slowly ripped it into shreds. No one, her tired brain said, no one would believe her. She didn't believe it herself, except that the faint pain between her thighs told her it had happened—that Rafael Santana had taken her virginity and hadn't even known it. And somehow, that made everything so much worse....

Still moving in a trancelike daze, she wandered into her bedchamber, smiling mechanically as Mary looked up from the embroidering she was doing while waiting for her mistress to return.

Mary smiled, saying calmly, "Did you have a nice visit with your friends?"

A hysterical little laugh burst from Elizabeth and she answered feverishly, "Oh, yes. It was delightful. We had tea, you know." She was babbling, but anything was better than the truth.

Mary looked at her sharply for a moment before saying placidly, "Well, that's nice. It will be good for you to meet a few of your own companions."

Everything was suddenly more than she could bear, and in a voice clogged with pain and suppressed tears, Elizabeth said raggedly, "Would you mind leaving me, Mary? I would like very much to be alone."

Startled, but being a well-trained servant, Mary gathered up her things and departed instantly, wondering what could have made her little mistress look so forlorn... and abused.

For a long, long time, Elizabeth lay on her bed. She thought of many things during those hours that passed so very slowly—Consuela, Lorenzo, and most of all of Rafael Santana's careless taking of her. She blamed him and in another way she didn't. He had believed her Lorenzo's lover and there was no way he could have known she was a virgin, and yet...

Her eyes were dry, and despite the ache of tears behind them, she never did cry as she lay there alone with her painful thoughts. She couldn't—she was beyond tears. Instead she tried to think of some way in which some sense of this afternoon could be made, but she found no solution. If Stella had still been here in New Orleans, she could have told her what had happened, but she shrank from telling anyone else. And again the thought went through her brain—*who* would believe her? Even now *she* had trouble believing it. And, thinking of the scandal, the curious looks and the disbelief that would greet her words, she knew she would say nothing, that Consuela had won. That beastly woman had accomplished what she had set out to do—and at a great cost to Elizabeth.

What was she to tell Nathan? she wondered dully. He didn't deserve a soiled wife... a wife used by another man.

Her head pounding like a drum, she tossed on the bed. She would have to tell him, and if she did, would he then challenge her despoilers? Oh, my God, he could be killed! With a low moan she turned her face into the pillows. And it was then that the most frightening thought of all occurred—she could have Rafael's child. Oh, God, *no!*

In the end she decided painfully that Nathan had to be told some of the truth. There was no way she could avoid it, and, suffering from the shocks she had sustained during this disastrous afternoon, she could see no other path open to her. She feared most that Nathan would challenge the two men involved to a duel—her own dishonor paling in the face of the possibility that either Nathan or Rafael might die because of what had happened. Of Lorenzo's fate she was indifferent. Consuela, she realized bleakly, would escape with little more than curious looks. It was so unjust that Elizabeth quailed at the thought and knew in that instant that while she would tell her husband the bare facts of what happened, she would never allow the names of the people involved to be torn from her. It was the only way she could think of to avoid a duel. She couldn't bear it, if Consuela's plotting caused the death of either her husband or Rafael.

She heard Nathan come in not many minutes later, and then before her courage failed her or before she could change her mind, she left her bedchamber and walked slowly toward Nathan's set of rooms.

It was only then that it occurred to her that her husband might very well cast her out into the streets, or that he might not believe her...or even blame her. She stopped for a moment, shaking with terror. But she *had* to tell him—it was his right to know. It took her several more seconds to gather her deserting courage and face the full implications of the step she was about to take. It would be so much easier, she thought weakly, to say nothing. But I cannot live with this lie, she decided at last. She would tell him, and if he cast her out into the streets then it was no more than she deserved. Perhaps, she *was* a slut, she thought sickly.

Standing before Nathan's door, she took a deep breath and quickly knocked before she had time to think further. At his answer she slowly opened the door and entered the room.

PART TWO

DESTINY'S JOURNEY

January 1840

Ah love! could you and I with Him conspire
To grasp this Sorry Scheme of Things entire,
Would not we shatter it to bits—and then
Remold it nearer to the Heart's Desire!

—EDWARD FITZGERALD,
The Rubáiyát of Omar Khayyam,
Stanza 99

CHAPTER SIX

January of 1840 started out as a dreary, wet, unpleasant month. Seated in her cozy office at the rear of the house, Elizabeth stared out at the fine drizzle of rain that had been falling all morning. Rain would delay the spring planting, she thought glumly. Through her surprisingly shrewd management, Briarwood had survived the "Panic of 1837" and the three years of ensuing depression virtually unscathed, and she wanted no setbacks.

The plantation had become her entire life. The handsome white-columned house and the broad, fertile acres were her reason for living, her reason for driving herself. Every waking moment was spent lavishing thought and care on the plantation, and through her steely determination, the fallow acres had been turned into tall rows of sugarcane and corn and fields of oats, wheat, and barley.

It had not been an easy four years for Elizabeth. Outwardly she and Nathan had a very pleasant marriage, and no one, seeing their comfortable manner with one another, would ever guess that Elizabeth now slept alone and that Nathan was impotent. If he still had an occasional male lover, he was inordinately discreet about it. Sometimes Elizabeth suspected he did, knowing that he did frequent Silver Street in "Natchez under the hill."

They had persisted in attempts to consummate their marriage, but Nathan had continued to find himself incapable of doing so. Elizabeth suffered with it for as long as she could and then, after too many repetitions of the nights in New Orleans, gently but firmly banished him from her bed. That had been some two years ago. She tried hard not to feel that Nathan had cheated her, but sometimes as she lay alone in her bed and thought of the nights of pain and embarrassment they had spent while Nathan tried again and again to prove himself a man, she could not ignore the tide of unhappiness that swept over her.

It had been overwhelmingly difficult for her to confess the events of that ghastly afternoon in New Orleans, but she had forced herself to explain to her husband that another man had taken what was rightfully his. Nathan's reaction had been one of horror that she had been so mistreated, and she found herself in her husband's arms as he comforted her and attempted to soothe her, to lessen her terrible feeling of shame and to stem the tears that had fallen at last.

And it was only when she had gained some semblance of composure, when the sobs had become only heartbreaking hiccups, that Nathan had mentioned the one thing she feared most.

Watching her closely, he had said with an effort, "Elizabeth, my dear, you *must* tell me the names of these wretched people. I mean to challenge them, to kill them for what they have done to you. As for that wicked, wicked woman, whoever she may be, I can only wish for her an agonizing death. Please tell me their names—I cannot let *your* honor go unavenged. My own," he had finished with an unhappy twisted smile, "is completely in tatters—with you, my dearest, I have no honor."

Dully, she had murmured, "If you do care for me, as you say you do, Nathan, then I implore you to let it be." And knowing intuitively there was only one way to stop him, she added, "Will you make me suffer the shame and the scandal a duel will bring? Do you want it bruited about that your wife was known in the most intimate way imaginable by another man? Please, I beg of you, do not force me to endure *that* too."

It had been a telling argument, and staring down into her tear-drowned violet eyes, Nathan had known then that he would do exactly as Elizabeth wanted. He wanted nothing to distress her further, and so reluctantly he allowed himself to be swayed.

Fortunately Elizabeth's fear of a child had not been

realized, and once that was confirmed she never consciously thought of what had happened in New Orleans... except once. It had happened about a year after she and Nathan had arrived in Natchez, and Elizabeth was never quite certain if the man in question had been Rafael or someone else entirely. At any rate, she had received a jolt of queer excitement and dismay when one of the more formidable matrons of Natchez had sailed up to her that spring of 1837 and asked in an arched tone if the tall, dark stranger had called upon her. At Elizabeth's blank expression the woman had looked even more arch and murmured, "He seemed most insistent about seeing you—described you most thoroughly, and I of course *assumed* from his manner that he was some acquaintance of yours. But then, with the gentlemen one never knows, does one?" The woman had sighed theatrically and added, "I understand your reserve, my dear—I certainly wouldn't want *my* husband to know that a man like that, so handsome and devastatingly attractive, was interested in me!" The subject was dropped, but for several days thereafter Elizabeth was on edge wondering with a mixture of hope and fear if indeed Rafael had come to Natchez looking for her. It appeared not, and eventually she dismissed the incident, telling herself that Mrs. Mayberry must have been mistaken about the gentleman and whom he wished to see. And in time Elizabeth was able to push everything connected with New Orleans and Rafael Santana out of her conscious mind. That time and those events were locked away with her youth, her dreams, and her longing for love.

Oddly enough, she and Nathan, after the first incredibly difficult months, both gained a certain amount of satisfaction from their strange marriage. Nathan, his fears and secrets open between them, found his conscience considerably lightened, and Elizabeth gained growing room and freedom such as she had never known.

Outwardly the scars of that afternoon and the nights of Nathan's impotent fumblings had faded and to a certain extent healed, but instead of following the usual pursuits of a young, beloved bride, she had thrown herself into turning the raw and newly built Briarwood into a home that was the talk of Natchez. And she did it—the sumptuous furnishings, the spacious rooms all were the envy of half the wives in Natchez, and the surrounding grounds rivaled those of Brown's Gardens, Andrew Brown's plantation built near "Natchez under the hill."

Hard work in those early days at Briarwood was the only thing that kept Elizabeth from giving into self-pity. That and books. She devoured them. Oh, not the romances of her youth, but books that were peculiar for a young lady—books on farming practices, breeding genetics, and, for pleasure, the rare books that came her way concerning the early Spanish conquests and explorers of the New World. Cortez, Ponce de León, Pizarro, and even the fabulous stories of Cabeza de Vaca and his incredible eight-year journey through the uncharted wastes of what was now the Republic of Texas and the northern provinces of Mexico—she read them all. Why these men fascinated her she did not care to speculate, but perhaps it was because they had all displayed the same ruthless intensity of that silvery-eyed devil—Rafael Santana!

From the practical books she learned a great deal of farming and breeding—knowledge she put to good use; from the others she satisfied a yearning for adventure.

There was little resemblance between a young woman who now called herself "Beth" in January of 1840 and the shy Elizabeth who had gone so miserably to her husband that night in 1836. The events of that afternoon had done more than just take her virginity—they had stripped away her innocence and left in its place a shell. A shell *no* man was ever going to shatter!

She had changed physically, too, her body ripening into the beauty that had been just a promise that night. Slim still, but a slimness that did nothing to hide the small, full, upthrusting bosom, or the narrowness of the tiny waist or the slender shapeliness of her hips. Her face had matured, too, revealing the exquisite loveliness that had been there all along. She had gained a certain amount of confidence, too, with her successes with Briarwood.

No one had been more surprised than Beth at the

excellent results of her ideas concerning Briarwood. She had discovered in herself a love of the land and an uncanny ability to foresee certain economic trends. She was, she thought with an enchanting little gurgle of laughter, simply a clever farmer at heart.

But now, on this dreary morning of January, she felt a sense of dissatisfaction, a dissatisfaction that had been growing for several months. The passionate desire to prove all those haughty cotton kings wrong was gone, the challenge of taking the raw land and making it productive was gone, the pleasure of turning Briarwood house into a showplace was gone.

Will this be my entire life? she wondered wistfully. To continue to gamble with the elements of nature, to face skepticism and patronizing amusement at her attempts to try new ideas in an area where old ways died hard, and to turn a blind eye to the pitying looks of other wives whose husbands were the leaders of society? She shook her head slowly. No, that wasn't how she envisioned her future.

Certainly she had no longer dreamed of love and romance, but there was driving hunger for something more than the life in which she found herself. What she longed for she couldn't even name, she just knew that she wanted something more than to continue to live out her remaining years in this half-alive fashion. She craved excitement and new horizons, new challenges, even danger. Anything was preferable to this humdrum existence.

For a moment her glance slid to Stella's letter lying on the walnut desk, and she pulled a face. *That* was probably why she was so moody this morning. Stella was full of the hacienda and the news of the birth of her second child four months ago; Beth decided she was probably envious of Stella's happiness. Thinking of that second child, a girl named for herself, she felt a pang deep in her heart—she would never have a child—and momentarily a sudden resentment of Nathan clogged the back of her throat.

But that feeling departed soon enough, for in many ways she was grateful to Nathan—he *was* kind to her and he encouraged her to attempt things she would not have dared by herself; he infused her with courage during those times when she wondered if perhaps she had blundered and made a wrong decision.

Suddenly angry with herself for indulging in this oddly maudlin mood, she deliberately shoved Stella's letter into one of the drawers of her desk. There! Out of sight, out of mind, she told herself grimly. But the yearning the letter aroused—the longing to see Stella and the new baby—would not be banished, and the thought occurred to her that there was really no reason why she *shouldn't* see her friend and...and to travel the old Spanish route through San Antonio, down to Durango in Mexico, then head north up toward Santa Fe!

Certainly there was money enough. *Her* money was sitting safely in the bank—it had been Nathan's ample fortune they gambled with, the cautious bankers willing to pay for many things, but not the experiments with crops that Beth had tried. For a moment a satisfied smile curved her rosy mouth, remembering the looks on Mr. Tyler's and Mr. Deering's faces when she had deposited the money Briarwood had received last fall for her corn crop—the crop she had insisted upon growing in spite of their condescending advice to the contrary. Oh, yes, she had enjoyed that small triumph.

The smile faded, though, and a look of intense concentration came into the wide violet eyes. Why shouldn't she go to Santa Fe?

There was now a competent overseer at Briarwood, she had the money, and there was no pressing reason for her to remain in Natchez. The more she contemplated it, the more the idea appealed to her. To see Stella and the baby Elizabeth, and to view those wide awe-inspiring prairies. Perhaps even to see a wild, romantic-looking Comanche? The thought gave her a shiver of delicious excitement, and guiltily she admitted that in many ways she was still dreaming of adventure. How Stella would scold, she thought with a wry twist of her lips. But still...

A smart rap on the door interrupted her reflections, and she glanced over to see Nathan, who looked exceptionally dapper, entering the room. He gave her a warm smile and murmured, "Not disturbing you, am I, my dear?"

Elizabeth smiled back. "No, I wasn't doing anything in particular." And, noticing the superbly fitting claret frock coat and the slimly cut trousers of fawn moleskin, she added, "You look very handsome this morning. Are you going out?"

"Well, yes, I rather thought that I would take the brougham into town and spend the day at the Mansion House. It's so boring when it rains. At least at Mansion House there'll be others looking for a way to spend some time until evening. Then I suspect a few of us will 'go down the line.'"

Elizabeth shot him an old-fashioned look. "Silver Street again, Nathan?" she inquired dryly.

He flushed, his fair skin turning a bright pink hue. Almost defensively, he began, "Now, Beth. You know that I..."

"Never mind, Nathan," Beth replied, unwilling to discuss a subject they both found embarrassing.

Nathan hadn't changed a great deal in four years. Though he was approaching thirty, the only signs of passing time in his youthful countenance were a faint sagging of the jowl line and the slightest hint that perhaps his waistcoats fit more snugly than they had a few years back. He still wore his muttonchop whiskers and his fair hair fell in a graceful sweep across his forehead. Gray eyes abashed, he murmured, "If you don't want me to go, Beth, I'll stay the day with you."

Knowing he would if she asked because he honestly *did* try to please her, she shook her head. "No. Go ahead and enjoy yourself."

Hesitating, he finally asked, "What do you plan to do today?"

"I don't know," Beth answered truthfully. "You're right about it being boring when it rains." And without conscious thought she suddenly blurted out, "Would you mind if I went on a trip, Nathan?"

Alarmed, he crossed to her side and took her hand in his. "Are you unhappy, my dear? Have I done something to distress you? I know my... my... activities have been a trial to you, but I didn't think it worried you anymore. If there is something that I can do . . . or . . . or . . ."

"Nathan, don't! It has nothing to do with *that!*" Beth answered hastily, knowing how easily he could work himself up into an orgy of guilt and unhappiness. Her eyes searching his, she said slowly, "I would like to go visit Stella. It's been years since I've seen her. And now there is the baby Elizabeth. Oh, Nathan, *do* say you won't mind!"

"Visit Stella Rodriguez?" he asked incredulously. "Why, she lives in Santa Fe!" he finished in a voice that made it sound as if Santa Fe were situated on a distant planet.

Elizabeth smiled. "Nathan, Santa Fe isn't *that* far away, you know. It is on the same continent."

"Well, I know that!" he retorted somewhat huffily. "But it's out in the middle of God knows where! It's so uncivilized! I know Stella is your friend and that you miss her, but how can you even begin to think of going there? No, it's absolutely out of the question!"

Her eyes holding his, she murmured quietly, "Nathan, I want to go. And unless you have some very good reasons to the contrary, I intend to go."

"I see. *My* wishes make no difference to you, I take it," Nathan snapped, one hand agitatedly toying with the heavy gold watch chain that hung from his waistcoat pocket.

"You know that isn't true, Nathan," Beth replied lightly, amusement peeping in her eyes. "I shan't be gone more than six months or so, and it would mean so much to me."

"Six months! You're going to go off and desert Briarwood for six months! You actually want to leave Natchez and *willingly* spend *months* out in the middle of some God-forsaken place that is inhabited only by wild savages, poisonous reptiles, and buffalo? I cannot believe it! Beth, tell me you're not serious!"

"Unfortunately I am. I suppose you would like it better if I were going to England, though."

"England! Why yes, let's go there, my love! Now, I'm sure you would enjoy that. Why—why—we could visit your father and stepmother and their child," Nate enthused happily. "We could even cross the Channel to France. I know you would enjoy Paris, Beth."

Remembering the last time she had seen her father, Beth's soft mouth tightened. "Nathan, you're deluding yourself. I have no desire to visit Three Elms, and the thought of seeing Melissa's son is of no interest to me. Someday, perhaps, we may visit Paris, but this year it is to Santa Fe that I want to go." Why she was being so stubborn about an idea that had just occurred to her she didn't know. But the more Nathan protested, the firmer became her resolve. And it was so unlike him to deny her anything that she was puzzled. What in the world did it matter to him if she wanted to brave the rigors of travel in the wild, untamed Southwest? If she was willing to cope with the lack of amenities in Santa Fe, why should he cavil? After all, he would be comfortably ensconced here in Natchez, spending his days imbibing Mansion House's famous mint juleps and his nights gambling and indulging in his particular vice along Silver Street.

But there she misjudged him, for after several more minutes of earnest argument between them, he seated himself in a chair near her desk and said unhappily, "You are determined to go, my dear? Nothing I can say will change your mind?"

"Oh, Nate, don't look so downcast," Beth teased him gently. "I shall take Mary and several other servants to insure adequate protection, and everything will be just fine. You'll see."

"Perhaps it won't be too bad," he finally said gloomily. "When did you plan for us to leave? We can't just pack up and leave at a moment's notice, you know."

Astonished, Elizabeth stared at his depressingly resigned countenance. "Us? We?" she repeated stupidly. "You're going with me?"

Looking slightly affronted, Nathan replied testily, "Well, of course I am! You don't imagine I would let you go unescorted out into the wilderness, do you? Why, *any*thing might happen! I couldn't sleep a wink not knowing where you were or if you were safe. What kind of a monster do you think I am, Beth? I simply wouldn't enjoy myself at all while you were gone."

She was touched. Beth's eyes were misty as she stared at his face. "Oh, Nathan, it really isn't necessary. If I take a half a dozen or so of the male servants and Mary and a serving girl or two go with me and... and if we join up with a caravan, we should be safe. And once I'm at Stella's everything will be just fine."

"Yes, that might be true, but getting to and from dear Stella's may be the problem. I don't mind confessing to you that I am not a particularly brave man. And the thought of crossing the plains and all the unknown dangers that entails I find rather unnerving, but I couldn't rest easy unless I were with you. Besides," he added simply, "I would miss you!"

"Oh, Nathan, dear! Are you certain you want to go with me?"

"Of course I don't want to go! Why do you think I just spent the last hour or so trying to get you to change your mind?" Nathan muttered pettishly. "But if you insist upon haring off into an unexplored wasteland, then I must go with you." His face wearing the expression of a martyr, he inquired, "When do you plan on leaving? I will need at least a week to prepare myself." Then, recalling the magnificent new cream-colored coat, lined with velvet, that his tailor was currently designing for him, he amended, "No. I would need two weeks. Hobbins won't have that coat done for another ten days. I must have it before we leave."

Beth smiled to herself. Nathan was ridiculously vain about his clothes, and she wondered with amusement how he would cope on the long, dry, dusty journey down into Mexico before swinging up towards Santa Fe. But somehow, she decided fondly, despite all his posturings and little foibles, he would indeed cope!

The next days passed in a whirl of activity for Beth, the hours flying by, meshed into one continuous haze of frantic packing and anticipation. Beth wrote instantly to Stella apprising her of their approximate arrival; as she sealed the letter she sent up a fervent little prayer that the letter would reach its destination before she did!

The overseer of Briarwood was given a detailed account of what was to be done in their absence, and

Nathan's velvet-lined jacket was finished on time. The servants who were to accompany them were chosen and readied; accommodations on the steamboat that would take them to New Orleans were obtained; reservations were made for a hotel in New Orleans; and their place on a packet leaving from that city to Galveston Island in the Republic of Texas was secured.

Everything was ready, Beth thought happily as she undressed for bed some three weeks later. Tomorrow she would start the first phase of the long, dangerous journey to Santa Fe, and she was nearly sick with excitement. Tomorrow couldn't come soon enough, she decided drowsily after tossing for what seemed hours. Tomorrow the adventure begins.

The next morning, however, things began to go wrong. In her haste to double-check the last-minute packing Mary Eames stumbled over one of the valises, left by a careless servant at the top of the huge, sweeping staircase; she somersaulted wildly down the many steps, breaking her leg in the process.

Beth, agitated and distressed by the accident, considered postponing the trip until Mary's leg had mended, but once the doctor arrived and set the leg, Mary convinced her that it was absurd for everything to be undone because of her clumsiness.

Grimacing at herself as she lay comfortably propped by pillows, her leg plastered and resting on several more fluffy down pillows, and hovered over by two wide-eyed young Negresses, Mary said sensibly, "Don't be silly! Everything is arranged. All the reservations, all the packing, *everything!* It is my own fault that I'm not going to be able to go with you. And I see no reason for you to undo all your plans just for me. Go ahead and leave. I shall be perfectly all right, and after all, what could you do to make things any different?"

Torn between the desire to leave as planned and an equally strong desire to remain at Mary's side, Beth dithered for another few minutes. Then, finally making up her mind, she asked anxiously, "You really won't mind if we go on without you?"

"Of course not, child! Charity was going along to help me with your clothes, and she is trained so beautifully that I feel confident she can act as your maid. Press into service one of the other girls, if you like, to assist her, but *please*, do not delay your journey because of me."

Knowing Mary was right, Beth wasted little more time, and the entire entourage—ten husky, eager young male slaves, two giggling Negresses, Nathan's two servants, two wagons, and the coach containing Nathan and Beth—pulled away from Briarwood's oak-lined driveway three hours after the time originally planned for their departure. Beth's face was bright with excitement and the violet eyes were blazing with the spirit of adventure as the carriage pulled away. Beth didn't look back either. At last, she was going West—West to Stella, West to meet her dreams!

CHAPTER SEVEN

They stayed only one night in New Orleans, and the morning of the last Monday of January found Beth waking to the gentle hush of the waves against the packet taking them to Galveston. She was glad they hadn't remained long in New Orleans—tired from the riverboat trip from Natchez and sleepless with excitement at the prospect of boarding the ship for Galveston, she'd had no time to dwell on the events that had occurred the last time she had visited New Orleans—no time to recall a pair of mocking gray eyes, or to wonder if Rafael Santana remembered the girl he had taken so carelessly in a small house on the ramparts.

Charity proved a very able maid, deftly helping her mistress dress in a lace-trimmed, white linen spencer and a very full skirt of green-printed muslin over a light and cool crinoline. A leghorn straw bonnet edged with green velvet and short white gloves laced with green silk cord completed the picture. It was an exceedingly pretty picture, too, that Beth made, with her violet eyes sparkling and the silvery-blond hair arranged in long ringlets on either side of her face.

Unaware of her own startling beauty, eagerly Beth stepped outside her room and crossed the deck to stand near the railing, and watch the almost turquoise waters of the Gulf of Mexico. She was well and truly going to Santa Fe, she thought with growing pleasure. And determinedly she quelled the desire to pinch herself to see if she was really standing here on the deck of the ship.

"Good morning, my dear," Nathan said suddenly to her right, jolting her just a bit.

"Oh, Nathan! What a start you gave me!" she exclaimed.

"Sorry, Beth, I thought you heard me coming," Nathan replied absently, his eyes slightly puffy from a late night at the gaming table below decks.

Guessing what he had been up to, Beth asked resignedly, "Did you lose very much last night?"

Nathan pulled a face. "Enough. But nothing to worry over, my dear." He hesitated a moment, then said almost reluctantly, "I wonder . . . would you mind if a young gentleman joined us at our table for breakfast?"

Beth stiffened, and incredulously she stared at her husband.

Nathan instantly realized the train of her thoughts and burst out anxiously, "Now, don't look like that, Beth! You don't think that I would bring a young man that I . . ." He broke off, horrified that she thought him capable of subjecting her to a meeting with one of his amours. Stiffly, he said, "Sebastian Savage is a young gentleman from New Orleans who happens to be traveling to San Antonio. I met him last night, and as we are both traveling to San Antonio, I thought it only polite to have him join us. If you object I shall have to make an excuse. Though," Nathan muttered worriedly, "*what* I shall tell him to explain my sudden reversal, I have *no* idea!"

Instantly contrite, Beth said quickly, "No. No, that won't be necessary. And Nathan . . . I apologize. I should have known you would not do such a thing."

His eyes troubled, Nathan murmured, "Beth, I know it has not been easy for you. But please believe me, my dear, you will never have to worry that I would deliberately harm you any more than I have already."

Gently she patted his arm. "I'm sorry I jumped to conclusions, Nathan. Let us not talk of it further—I shall look forward to meeting Mr. Savage."

Easily diverted, Nathan said eagerly, "You will like him, I am sure. He is a young man, not much older than yourself, I think, and very merry and lively. I think you will find his company extremely amusing and pleasant."

Beth smiled. "Perhaps. But tell me what business

takes him to San Antonio—is he visiting friends as we will be once we reach Santa Fe, or is he going there to settle?"

"I think a little of both. He apparently has some cousins or distant relatives that he will be staying with, and I think that, on advice given to him by his father, he intends to look into the possibility of settling in that area."

"I see," Beth answered vaguely, not particularly interested in Sebastian Savage. Yet, having dismissed him as one of the those charming, dilettante younger sons found so often in wealthy southern families, meeting him a few moments later, she was undeniably drawn to him.

Who wouldn't be? Sebastian Savage was an outrageously handsome and charming young scamp—such a delightful rake that few women could resist him. He stood over six feet tall and possessed the natural athlete's body. Having the greenest, thickest-lashed eyes imaginable, luxurious black curly hair, and the most engaging manners to be found on either side of the Mississippi River did little to lessen his impact upon the ladies. But most men found him an enjoyable companion too—always ready for any lark, a marvelous shot with the pistols, generous with his money, and a generally overpoweringly likable fellow. His detractors—and unfortunately there were a few, but only a *very* few—complained of his quick, hot temper and his cheerful, disgustingly eager willingness to settle the most trivial disagreement with a dawn duel fought "under the oaks" in New Orleans.

But Beth, knowing none of these things, was impressed favorably when she met him. And Sebastian... Well, poor Sebastian took one look at the exquisitely fair creature with the incredible violet eyes standing before him and fell rather precipitously and predictably in love—something his father, Jason Savage, claimed dryly Sebastian did with awkward regularity.

But Beth, much to Sebastian's chagrin, was completely oblivious of his obvious enslavement, seeing him only as a pleasant and entertaining companion. He was two years older than she, but as the days passed, she tended to think of him as a younger brother or a very old friend.

The lazy days as the ship steamed across the Gulf of Mexico toward Galveston gave them hours and hours, uncomplicated by the confines of normal society, to spend with each other and to learn more about the other, and also time for the easy relationship that soon existed between them to prosper. Nathan's habit of rising late and spending just about every waking hour below decks savoring tall, cool rum drinks as he played endless games of chance, contributed to Beth and Sebastian being left often in each other's company.

It was an innocent relationship on Beth's part. Sebastian was a charming rogue who made her smile and laugh and who instilled in her a gaiety she had never before experienced. He reminded her ever so much of a half-grown, forward puppy, certain of his welcome, playful and adorable, but not to be taken seriously. That more than one young lady on board the packet thought differently did not escape Beth, but she realized that while Sebastian might cause other hearts to beat a little faster hers never would. She enjoyed his company, she couldn't help but be flattered that a gentleman of his attributes found her company exhilarating. He completely ignored several languishing young ladies and gravitated with gratifying promptness in her direction whenever she appeared.

It was Sebastian who escorted Mrs. Ridgeway during her promenades along the deck; it was Sebastian who sat with her during the evenings in the main lounge and played harmless card games fit only for older ladies and young children; and it was Sebastian who amused her at the breakfast and luncheon table—while Nathan slept off a night spent gaming and drinking. Consequently it was no wonder Beth and Sebastian became such close friends.

The short journey to Galveston was nearing its end. The evening before they were to arrive in the port city, left alone as usual, Beth and Sebastian took a long stroll around the deck, stopping every now and then to stare out at the gently rolling waves and to talk of this and that.

Beth was looking especially lovely, her violet eyes bright with pleasure as they spoke of their arrival the next day in Galveston. The silvery-ash hair had been pulled up into a cluster of soft curls on the top of her head with a ruby velvet ribbon threaded throughout the thick hair, and, staring at the enchanting profile thus afforded him, Sebastian wondered again, as he had so frequently, how Nathan could prefer the pleasures of the gaming tables to the enjoyment of his very beautiful young wife.

A frown creasing his wide forehead, Sebastian couldn't help himself from asking, "Beth, does Nathan lose a great deal of money?" Seeing the slight reserve that flashed across her face, he cursed himself for asking such a personal question. "I apologize," he said abruptly. "I did not mean to pry."

Beth smiled faintly, not really blaming him for asking the question—Nathan's preoccupation with the gaming tables had been flagrant these past few days and it was only natural that someone as kind as Sebastian would be concerned. But she wasn't about to discuss her husband with this young man, and so gently she said, "Don't apologize. Let's just pretend that you never asked that question, shall we? The night is too lovely to be spoiled by quarreling."

"I certainly cannot take exception to that idea," Sebastian agreed easily enough, his mouth curving wryly. But still the thought lingered that the Ridgeways must have an extremely odd marriage—especially when he recalled the beautiful young man who seemed always to be at Nathan's side since the two had met three days before. He was a silly young fop by the name of Reginald Percy. Sebastian discerned a distasteful air of intimacy between the two. It was a damned odd situation. God knew, *he* wouldn't allow his wife to be so friendly with an out-and-out rake like himself and certainly he wouldn't leave her alone for hours on end while he clung happily to the arm of a willow-slim young man and gambled the night away. If Beth were his wife, he wouldn't be able to let her out of his sight... or his bed, he decided with a wicked, fleeting grin. Again his gaze traveled lightly over Beth's slender body and he sighed.

She was so lovely and so *damned* unaware of him as a man, he thought, half amused, half angry.

Completely oblivious of Sebastian's frustration, Beth murmured lightly, "I shall be sorry to say good-bye to you tomorrow. I have so enjoyed your company on the packet—it will seem strange not to see you every day."

"Ah, but you will! As we both are going to San Antonio, I have decided that instead of remaining in Galveston, I shall travel directly to San Antonio with your party. I've already mentioned it to your husband, and he seemed to have no objections. It will definitely be a much safer journey for all of us if I and my four servants join up with your party." And you, my icy little darling, Sebastian thought in exasperation as a smiling Beth turned to look up at him, have no idea that you are the only reason I've changed my plans.

The violet eyes twinkling gaily up at him, she said delightedly, "Oh, truly! You are not teasing me?"

Sebastian put on an affronted expression, but the green eyes glinted with mockery and the full, mobile mouth slanted teasingly. "Now, Beth, when have I ever teased you?"

Beth laughed at him. "All the time, my friend, *all* the time! You have done nothing but tease me since we met that first morning. And don't you try to deny it either!" Her face suddenly serious, impetuously she reached over and touched his strong, lean hand with her slim fingers. "And Sebastian, I have enjoyed it so much. I cannot begin to tell you how much you have lightened my days. You are truly a good friend to me—one I hope I shall have for a long time."

Almost somberly he said, "Don't worry, Beth, I have no intention of disappearing from your life too soon."

They conversed lightly a few minutes more and then Sebastian suggested that perhaps it was time for Beth to retire for the night. Shortly thereafter they were standing before her cabin door saying good night. And it was then that Sebastian found her simply too alluring, too temptingly desirable to resist.

Looking at the lovely, innocent features lifted to his, he was powerless to defy the urge to drop a brief, warm kiss on her unprepared lips. Startled, Beth instinctively stepped away, and Sebastian, realizing what he had done, rushed into hasty speech. "Beth, forgive me! I do not know what came over me. I do apologize." Giving her a lopsided, attractive grin, he finished outrageously, "It is just that I feel that you are like one of my sisters, even on this short acquaintance—and I *always* kiss my sisters good night!"

Beth was torn between the desire to box his ears and an unseemly urge to giggle. The giggle won out. "Sebastian, you are a scamp!" she scolded with a smile. "I don't think my husband would approve of such... such... warm sentiments being bestowed upon his wife by a young man so recently met."

His tall, broad-shouldered body blocking out the moonlight behind them, he put on an aggrieved air and mocked, "But Beth, I feel as if we have known each other forever. Surely we were soulmates in another life!"

Beth gave him a playful rap on his knuckles. "Enough of this nonsense—even if it is very enjoyable, it must stop! Behave yourself or I shall have to take stern measures against you, young man," she threatened, her eyes teasing him.

Unrepentantly Sebastian asked, "Am I forgiven, Beth?"

Unable to resist the laughter in his face, she replied honestly, "Yes, you are, but you shouldn't be! Now I must go. It is late and I don't want anyone to think that I am entertaining impudent young men in my cabin at night!"

A grin on his wide mouth, for several seconds Sebastian stood staring at the door that closed so precipitously in his face when Beth had swept tantalizingly into her cabin. Then, whistling softly to himself, he walked away, feeling inordinately pleased.

Despite the ease with which she had dismissed the incident to Sebastian, it troubled Beth. She recognized the fact that there could never be more than friendship between them, and she was too tenderhearted to encourage his hopes of a more serious relationship when she had no intention of allowing their association to take on any deeper meaning. No, Sebastian was not for her—he might be handsome, he might be charming, but her heart was untouched except in a sisterly way. Firmly Beth reminded herself that his kiss tonight had been just as he intimated—a brotherly salutation. She *knew* what it was like to be kissed with passion, and for just a moment Rafael Santana's dark face swam in her mind. With a decidedly breathless start she realized that part of Sebastian's charm was that in some strange way he made her remember another darker, wildly passionate personality, and the unpleasant idea occurred to her that perhaps part of Sebastian's appeal to her was simply because he *did* remind her of Rafael. Ruthlessly she banished that thought, forcing herself to think only of tonight. Sebastian's kiss had been just what he claimed, but she wondered if, perhaps, Sebastian's friendship with her was something more, and she bit her lip in vexation. She did so enjoy his company, and his bright, lively friendship meant much to her. He made her feel young and merry—and not staid and sedate and sensible, all those things she had been so long. She hadn't thought once of Briarwood or of the oddity of her marriage, nor longed for her future to have been different since meeting him. And not willingly would she slip back into possessing all those virtues she had come to dislike. She would be gay, and young, and happy...and...carefree! She *would!* And Sebastian would help her, she thought defiantly, she was *not* going to turn into a bitter, unfulfilled woman!

Sebastian would have been perfectly delighted to help Beth become a fulfilled woman, and recalling again how close he had come to betraying himself as they stood near her cabin door, he felt his chest tighten uncomfortably. For a moment he was dejected, but then he brightened. She hadn't been overly *dis*pleased and she had accepted his shameless excuse without a murmur. And as he savored his second brandy in a very few minutes, he proceeded to convince himself that she had only been shy and that his persistence was beginning to be rewarded.

Sebastian was not the only man savoring the progression of a seduction that night. Nathan had discovered that the young and daintily made Mr. Percy was of the same persuasion as himself, and he at last managed to find himself lost in a hungry embrace. Without one thought of his wife and with none of the impotence that marked his attempts to consummate his marriage, Nathan very successfully and expertly showed Mr. Percy what a rather skillful lover he was... with men. Somewhat recklessly, they spent the night together in Mr. Percy's cabin, which unfortunately happened to be next door to Sebastian's.

Worse, Sebastian had inadvertently ended up with Mr. Percy's snuffbox and, rising early that morning, he tapped on the door to leave it off. Hearing no answer, he tried the knob and, finding it unlocked, stuck his head around the door. The sight of Nathan and Mr. Percy in bed together was a shock of the first magnitude even to one as sophisticated as Sebastian. That the two sleeping men had been intimate was more than apparent from the way Mr. Percy nestled into Nathan's white shoulder and the way Nathan's arm was clasped around the younger man. Thoroughly revolted and horrified, Sebastian beat a hasty retreat, understanding instantly *exactly* why Nathan seemed to have no concern about leaving his wife in the company of another man.

But there Sebastian misjudged Nathan. Nathan was perfectly capable of turning a blind eye to a number of things another man would not have ignored. But he was also essentially a selfish man, and while he might think it very nice for Beth to have the companionship of a handsome young man like Sebastian and while he might normally be discreet about his little excursions, he was always on the alert for any threat to his own happiness. On that particular morning, after he had said a fond good-bye to Mr. Percy, for the packet would be docking at Galveston in a matter of hours, Nathan decided, after listening to Beth's happy conversation that was mainly about Sebastian, that perhaps it hadn't been so wise to have introduced that young man to his wife. Sebastian was a little *too* attractive, and Nathan didn't want Beth to get any silly ideas. Perhaps she would decide their rather odd marriage wasn't as satisfactory as it could be and that another man might make her happier.

Seeing the easy friendship that existed between Beth

and Sebastian, Nathan began to look with real disfavor upon the notion that Sebastian and his party would travel with them to San Antonio. But there was nothing he could do about it, he thought with regret, wishing with growing uneasiness that he had never consented to this wild whim of Beth's.

Most of the day was taken up with the landing at Galveston and finding rooms they would need for the few days they would be in Galveston before starting the overland journey to San Antonio. It proved fortunate that they were not remaining long in Galveston, because Nathan, after taking one incredulous glance at what was the most important port city of the Republic of Texas, was not impressed. His muttered complaints robbed Beth of much of her pleasure in the city. But Nathan's complaints weren't the only thing that distressed her as they wandered about the city—she had seen a tall, black-haired man disappear between two buildings as they approached, and for one terrifying moment she had been certain it was Rafael Santana.

It wasn't the sight of the dark-haired stranger that upset her so much as her own reaction to it. Her heart had leaped within her breast and her throat had gone dry at the violent thrill of anticipation and hope that had exploded through her slender body. But she quickly gained control of herself, frantically tamping down those emotions. What is the matter with me? she wondered furiously—it was only a man. *But a man that made you think of Rafael Santana,* her mind whispered slyly, and Beth was furious, furious with the knowledge that she couldn't subdue the yearnings of her stubborn, wayward heart for just the sight of one particular tall, dark man. Paying only half a mind to Nathan's sharp remarks, Beth kept her eyes on the spot where the stranger had disappeared. She could not help wondering why, if she was so content, so satisfied with her relationship with Nathan, she should react so strongly to a fleeting glance of a man who might not even have been the one her heart wanted him to be. And for the first time since she had made her decision to remain Nathan's wife, despite his impotency and his discreet affairs with the members of his own sex, she questioned whether she hadn't been foolish beyond belief. Perhaps I did us both an injustice, she decided miserably, and because she felt so very guilty for even having such a thought, she forced herself to pay particular attention to Nathan's comments about the city.

"Rustic" was the kindest word that Nathan applied to the growing, haphazard mass of wharves, warehouses, docks, and wooden houses that were scattered along the few dusty streets that led to the bay. Beth soothed his affronted sensibilities with promises that San Antonio, once they reached it, would be much more to his liking.

Beth hid her own dismay at the city, and for the first time the full magnitude of the journey she had undertaken so lightheartedly hit her. They were leaving behind the comfort and elegance they had known all their lives. They were going to the frontier, the frontier where people did live in a certain amount of style and comfort but where Briarwood's cool, green gardens, marble mantels, elegant curving staircases, and luxurious appointments were as foreign to them as was this sprawling, bustling, rough-looking city to her.

If Beth noticed that Nathan seemed to be rather cool to Sebastian and that there was the faintest hint of contempt in Sebastian's manner toward Nathan during their few days in Galveston, she gave no indication, her thoughts determinedly on how much she was enjoying herself. She *was* enjoying herself, but Nathan's continued scathing comments on their accommodations and his opinion of Galveston left her feeling vaguely depressed and effectively destroyed the pleasure she would have taken in exploring the robust, oddly appealing little city. She had known the country they were going to be traveling through would be primitive, and she had thought, unwisely it appeared, that Nathan had been aware of it too. Apparently all her explanations to him had been either forgotten or misunderstood, and she sighed unhappily as she realized that half of her time was going to be spent in soothing Nathan's discomforts and in convincing him that he was actually enjoying the trip. A difficult task, if not impossible, she decided dolefully the afternoon before they were to leave.

Nathan had been particularly venomous in his remarks earlier about the town, the people and even the countryside. Beth had fled to her tiny room at the hotel in order to keep from bursting out with some *very* unladylike comments of her own concerning *his* behavior.

Her unhappiness had been noted by both of the gentlemen, and each had his own interpretation of it. Nathan's was the most correct; he realized a bit belatedly that his undeniable dislike of the situation was ruining Beth's enjoyment of the journey. Feeling a little twinge of guilt over his brief liaison with Reginald Percy, he knocked on her door full of contrition.

At first Beth was not inclined to see Nathan, but then she made up her mind to have a frank discussion and she bade him enter.

Nathan gave her no chance to speak. Crossing the room with quick strides, he grasped her hand and kissed it lightly. "My dear," he said in a remorseful voice, the gray eyes pleading for forgiveness, "I have been an utter brute! I know how much this journey means to you and I know you would have preferred to come without me... and what must I do but find fault with everything about it! I should not ask it of you, but please, my darling, forgive me. I shall try very hard to be more agreeable and to keep my thoughts and comments to myself." Ruefully he added, "The entire reason that I even accompanied you was to see that everything went smoothly for you, and here I have been the one to cause you the most distress. Believe me, I did not mean to, and believe also that I shall try my utmost, from this moment on, to make this a journey that we shall remember with joy and fondness."

Beth's spirits lifted instantly. It was true that Nathan's inability to accept the conditions that were an integral part of any journey into the untamed portions of the continent had been destroying any pleasure she would have received. But it was also true that one of the things that made her marriage bearable was his willingness to please her once he knew that something meant a great deal to her. And he had the endearing quality of truly meaning what he said. He *would* see to it that there were no more unpleasant scenes, and even if it nearly killed him he would smile and manfully convince himself that he was having a marvelous time. There would be no further reproaches, no more of his petty complaints, and most of all, she would have his encouragement and would be able to confess some of her own dismay or disappointments about the trip, knowing he would comfort her and, as he often did, show her the amusing side of it.

Beth gave a faint chuckle. "Nathan, you have been a beast! But how thankful I am that you and I shall not be at daggers drawn any longer."

His face still contrite, he muttered, "You pamper me, Beth. You should have taken me to task before now and not have let me spoil your own enjoyment. Please, in the future, do not allow me to do so."

Beth smiled mistily up at him and reached up and gently kissed his cheek. "Very well, then, be warned that when I snap at you, you have given me permission. I'm afraid that I am developing a shocking temper!" she teased.

"You?" Nathan said with mock surprise. "Not my Beth! It was your sweetness of temper that first drew me to you—don't disillusion me now!"

When they met for dinner, Sebastian immediately noticed the air of warm intimacy between them and drew his own jealous conclusions. As they continued to exchange affectionate glances throughout the meal, his heart sank.

The fact that Nathan refrained from commenting on the quality of the food and the service and the fact that he actually expressed enjoyment of the huge, sizzling steak that he was served, did not escape Sebastian's notice either. His green eyes narrowing, he watched the way Beth smiled at Nathan and the way Nathan directed his conversation to his wife, attempting to make her laugh. The meal was an ordeal for Sebastian, and he spent most of it torturing himself by imagining how Beth had charmed Nathan into this excessively amiable frame of mind.

Consequently he excused himself somewhat abruptly from their table and declined to join them for a short after-dinner stroll. His lean face expressionless, he said quietly, "You'll forgive me if I don't accompany you? I have already made plans for the evening."

It was a lie, but he departed immediately, uncertain whether to challenge Nathan to a duel or strangle Beth for her coquettish behavior. His quick temper one flick away from exploding, he left the hotel and wandered into a small tavern not too far away and grimly ordered a stiff whiskey.

The tavern was not particularly pretentious, but it showed signs of attempting to raise itself above some of the others in the area. The wooden floor was polished and clean, the walls were white, and a scarlet, blue, and yellow Mexican blanket had been hung for decoration. The small tables and chairs were of oak and the long bar against the far end was of mahogany. A crystal chandelier looked strangely out of place dangling from the open-beam ceiling.

Sebastian drank in silence for some minutes; the tavern seemed at first glance to be empty except for himself and the bartender. Then he stiffened slightly as he discovered the presence of a third man.

The man was a dark outline in the shadows, sitting just beyond the light cast by the chandelier. His dusty black boots and long legs were clearly visible; a thin stream of smoke curled near his head and the red tip of a cigarillo glowed in the shadows. Sebastian had the unnerving impression that the other man was staring at him.

His emotions still lacerated by the sight of Beth and Nathan together, Sebastian was spoiling for a fight and decided that he didn't like the stranger's stare. His jaw set somewhat aggressively, he started to walk over to the man, only to be halted when the stranger in the shadows murmured mockingly, "Still as hot-tempered as always, young man? It is perhaps good that a pistol is no stranger to you."

At the sound of that slightly accented voice and the sight of those dark, lean features, the smoke-gray eyes glittering with cynical enjoyment, Sebastian's face broke into an incredulous smile. "*Rafael!*" he cried excitedly. "What in the name of God are you doing here? I hadn't expected to see you until I reached the hacienda."

CHAPTER EIGHT

A lazy smile curving the full mouth, Rafael Santana regarded the eager young man across from him and put out the thin cigarillo he had been smoking. "I do not, *amigo,* stay in the environs of San Antonio when Don Felipe is in residence at the rancho. Even you should have remembered that!"

Sebastian's face lost a little of its pleasure and he cursed himself for not remembering, not only that Rafael and his grandfather were as companionable as two vipers, but also that his father had told him that Don Felipe was making one of his infrequent visits to the family rancho near San Antonio. Lamely he muttered, "I'd forgotten your grandfather was there." An uncomfortable thought assailed him, and, after swallowing nervously, he asked, "He isn't *staying,* is he?"

Rafael laughed, the gray eyes filled with cold amusement. "No. If you take your time traveling to San Antonio, you should miss him by several days. He is leaving, I believe, this Monday for Mexico City."

His mercurial spirits restored by the news that he wouldn't have to undergo the ordeal of a meeting with the vitriolic Don Felipe, Sebastian grinned at Rafael. In a voice totally lacking in regret he murmured, "What a pity."

Rafael laughed and said dryly, "I can see that you are greatly disappointed in not seeing my esteemed grandfather."

They conversed for several moments longer, pleasantly exchanging family news. It was only when Rafael suggested that Sebastian might like to travel with him for a brief visit to Houston, and then together they could travel on down to San Antonio and the Santana hacienda, that the conversation took an uncomfortable turn.

Sebastian reluctantly refused, and when Rafael asked why, he shot him a wry look. "Well, if you must know, it is a woman. I met her on the packet coming from New Orleans, and as she is leaving tomorrow for San Antonio, I intend to be with her." Despite the anger with which he had stalked away from Beth, infatuation got the better of him and almost reverently he breathed, "She is an angel, Rafael, the most beautiful, the sweetest, the—"

"Spare me!" Rafael interrupted ruthlessly. "There are no women who are angels, *amigo. None!"* he ended in a hard voice.

His face taking on a stubborn expression, Sebastian replied doggedly, "Well, she is! And I intend to marry her!"

"Do not expect me to wish you well," Rafael returned disgustedly. "I will not wish you ill either, but I cannot bring myself to view the state of matrimony as anything other than a particularly vile hell that the devil created for the unwary."

There was such venom in Rafael's words that Sebastian was slightly taken aback, but then, remembering Consuela, he decided that perhaps there was good reason for Rafael's statement. And Rafael, thinking that he had been rather harsh on Sebastian, said more calmly, "When do you plan to wed—at San Antonio? Or will you be going back to New Orleans for the event?"

Sebastian squirmed uncomfortably in his chair, and as he hesitated, Rafael's suddenly suspicious eyes narrowed to silver slits, and he drawled, "Could it be that the *lady* is not free? That she is the type of woman who doesn't relieve herself of one husband before finding another?"

The green eyes angry, Sebastian snarled softly, "Do not go any further, Rafael! I will not allow even *you* to slander her."

Rafael's thick black eyebrows flew up and a considering glitter entered the gray eyes. "She means a great deal to you, this woman."

Stiffly Sebastian answered, "Yes, she does. She *is* married, but I do not think it is a happy marriage, and if at all possible I intend to do something about it."

Rafael's dark face revealed nothing as he sank back into the shadows and absently lit another of the black cigarillos he preferred, his mind busy with what Sebastian had just revealed. He didn't like it at all, and he was doubly certain that Jason wouldn't want his youngest son embroiled with this kind of woman—an older married woman who preyed upon wealthy young men. Idly he considered demanding an introduction to Sebastian's "angel," but he dismissed the thought almost at once. At the moment he didn't have the time to destroy Sebastian's unfortunate attachment. But if the creature proved too clinging or if by the time Sebastian reached San Antonio he had not come to his senses and recognized the woman for what she was... then something would have to be done. The gray eyes hardened unpleasantly and Rafael smiled thinly—it might be amusing, he decided grimly, to teach Sebastian's "angel" the dangers of casting her lures so unwisely.

An awkward silence had fallen after Sebastian's almost defiant words, and for several seconds neither man spoke as they sat sipping their whiskey. Anyone glancing at them would have guessed at once that they were related as they both possessed the long, steel-muscled bodies of men used to action, the same panther-black hair, and the same strong, devastatingly masculine features. And yet there was a great deal of contrast: Rafael's face was harder, leaner, perhaps crueler; his skin was burned Comanche bronze by the hot Texas sun, tiny lines radiating out from his startling light eyes. Sebastian was everything that was bright and gay; his eyes were eager and full of life; Rafael's were icy and inscrutable. Even in their smiles there was a difference—both had full, beautifully molded mouths, but while Sebastian's curved easily into laughter, Rafael's often had a caustic slant and his laughter usually had a derisive note.

Eventually the silence became too much for Sebastian and, looking over at Rafael's remote face, he said,

"This is hardly the way I expected our first meeting in two years to be."

Rafael shrugged, and then suddenly he grinned, his face appearing much younger, much more approachable. "Me either. I guess we are both a little too hotheaded for our own good. Why don't we just forget this conversation took place and meet as good friends at the hacienda, hmmm? By then, you will either have stolen your lady love or have decided she is not the angel you first thought, and we can meet as friends and not as enemies."

Sebastian agreed eagerly, his hero worship of his older relative making him more than ready to grasp the hand of friendship so quickly extended. The air of tension evaporated and almost immediately they fell into the rapport they had shared since Sebastian had first attached himself to his tall cousin some ten years before.

Staring unobtrusively across at Rafael as he lounged in his chair, Sebastian noted the changes the past two years had wrought. Deep grooves furrowed down the lean cheeks and enhanced the air of violence that was so much a part of him. In the sweat-stained calico shirt, the tight-fitting *calzoneras,* and the black boots with the roweled spurs, Sebastian thought, Rafael did indeed look the renegade that he had been called so often in his youth. The black hair was unfashionably long, the leather belt that rode low on his lean hips carried a holster with one of Samuel Colt's new revolvers in it. Sebastian knew from past experience that his cousin was a deadly shot with any pistol—and with something like the new Colt repeating pistol he would be doubly lethal.

Taking another sip of his whiskey, Sebastian asked, "What are you doing here? You never did say."

Rafael grimaced. "Remember Lorenzo Mendoza, Consuela's cousin?" At Sebastian's nod, he continued, "Well, Lorenzo has been acting as an agent for Mexico—at least I'm fairly certain he has, and so are several other people. He travels much of the time amongst the Comanches, attempting to convince them to join with Mexico and help drive the rest of us out of Texas.

I generally end up following right behind him and undoing whatever he accomplishes." Rafael gave a twisted grin and added, "Which is why a lot of people still think I am dealing with the Comanches myself and up to no good in the process! But, getting back to Lorenzo, he's finally become aware of my actions, and this time he took great pains that I did not find out where he went, so I haven't any idea how many bands of Indians he saw or what promises they gave him in return. I picked up his trail some days back and as it led here instead of San Antonio I grew more than just a little curious and decided to find out what brings him to Galveston."

"Did you find out?"

"Yeah," Rafael replied inelegantly. "I know he met with a fellow who supplies weapons to the Indians—which is why I'm heading out tomorrow for Houston. Sam Houston has quite a few of his own agents spread out over the Republic, and I think he could use the information. Certainly he can see that steps are taken to make the climate unhealthy for our friend here in Galveston. Lorenzo won't have it as easy the next time he wants to make a deal."

"Why the hell don't you just expose him? Or kill him?" Sebastian demanded.

"Because, *amigo,* it is better to know where the snake is. I could connect him with the man here in Galveston, but I'm certain they would have a clever tale to cover themselves. As for the dealings with the Comanches—we have no proof... precisely. Can you see my dragging in a Comanche and having him explain that Lorenzo promised him great wealth if he would help drive out the *tejanos?* Lorenzo has firmly entrenched himself with my father, and there are a lot of respectable people who think highly of him—some of them think *I'm* the disreputable one! Lorenzo would deny everything with adroit words and the Comanche would probably end up being hanged or shot for daring to speak against a white man."

Sebastian grunted in agreement, seeing the difficulty. But more than that he understood the great concern behind Rafael's careless words. If the Indian tribes united with Mexico it could spell doom to the Republic.

While most people in Texas dismissed such a possibility, it was something that several prominent people, including Sam Houston, the ex-President, feared might come true.

It was a damned shame, Sebastian thought idly, that the United States had refused to accept Texas into the Union four years ago and had forced the Republic into its present situation—an independent nation fighting for its life. The Republic needed the protection and stability of the Union, but the free states of the North had not wanted to admit another slave state. The fervent hope of the majority of Texas had been shattered when the news had finally arrived that Texas could not take her proud place as a member of the United States. It had been a bitter, bitter blow, but somehow Texas had managed to survive—barely.

Aloud Sebastian inquired, "How real is the threat from Mexico right now?"

The gray eyes bleak, Rafael answered, "Too real. The Republic has survived only because Mexico has been busy with her own internal troubles. We can only continue to survive if we can stop her from inflaming the Indians against us." Inhaling deeply on the black cigarillo, Rafael blew out a cloud of smoke and said quietly, "Since as early as '37 Mexico has been sending agents to meet with the Indians, first with the Cherokees in the eastern part of the Republic and, since that failed, now with the Comanches." Echoing Sebastian's thoughts earlier, Rafael said, "If Mexico can unite the various Comanche tribes, we will face our greatest danger as an independent nation so far. With the Indians attacking us from the north and the Mexican Army from the south, Texas would be hard-pressed to survive." Rafael leaned forward, the dark face intent. "The Antelopes, the northern Comanches, seem to be remaining, as they usually do, aloof, and are refusing to listen to the Mexican agents." Rafael smiled briefly. "One arrived there last year when I was passing through, and while polite, it was obvious that the Antelopes feel they have no need to join Mexico. Pray God they continue to think so. But the southern Comanches are different. Have you heard of the meeting that is to be held in San Antonio in March?"

Sebastian shook his head. Stubbing out his cigarillo, Rafael explained, "It will be a historic meeting if all goes well—for the first time ever the Comanches themselves asked for the meeting and Colonel Karnes agreed to it, provided the Comanches brought in all their white captives. And *that,*" Rafael said grimly, "is where the problem will arise."

"How? It seems straightforward to me."

Rafael pulled a face. "It would be if you weren't dealing with Comanches. The southern Comanches, the Pehnahterkuh, are by far the largest of all the Comanche tribes, and I fear that what they expect from the Texans is not what they will get. Nor do I think that the people of San Antonio are going to swallow the typical Comanche arrogance the way the Spaniards and the Mexicans did. The Comanches will demand gifts as they always have with the Spaniards and the Mexicans, and every captive they exchange will be paid for dearly. I don't think they're going to bring in all the captives as stipulated either—they'll bring them in one at a time and drive the best bargain for each one."

Sebastian whistled under his breath, seeing the problem with uncomfortable clarity—the angry Texans demanding that their people be released and the Comanches, thinking they were dealing with the same sort of fear and abasement that had characterized their relations with the Spaniards and Mexicans would treat the Texans like a conquered nation. Trouble there would undoubtedly be... unless there were some very cool heads amongst the Texans.

Rafael was thinking much the same thing, and almost frustratedly he said, "That proposed meeting could be a disaster—for everyone. And if it doesn't work, it's going to drive the Comanches straight into the arms of the Mexicans. Then we really will have trouble!" With a lightning change of mood, Rafael grinned and asked, "Are you so certain that you wish to settle in the Republic, after all?"

Sebastian returned the grin. "And miss a good fight? Of course I want to settle here!"

The conversation drifted then, and they talked until the early morning hours of Sebastian's plans and of the lands Rafael would show him. It was after Sebastian left for his hotel room and Rafael made his way slowly toward the livery stables that the Comanche question returned to haunt him. The meeting in San Antonio could bring about so much good if successful, but if not...

If only Sam Houston were still President, he thought savagely as he saddled his horse. Houston cared about the Indians, but Lamar, the current President, believed firmly that the only good Indian was a dead Indian. Rafael very much feared he intended to rid the Republic of Indians—*all* Indians, and under any ruse that would accomplish that aim. Tiredly Rafael rubbed a hand across his forehead, almost giving into the desire to sleep a few hours in Galveston before riding toward Houston and a meeting with Samuel Houston. But he denied it, knowing his mind was too full of Comanches and the conversation with Sebastian to gain any real rest.

The proposed meeting between the Comanches and the Texans in San Antonio preyed heavily upon Rafael's mind as he rode slowly away from Galveston in those pre-dawn hours. He only hoped that somehow, if there was any trouble, it wouldn't erupt into an orgy of bloodshed and fire along the entire frontier. Too many people will perish, he thought bleakly, Comanche and Texan alike.

With a sort of angry helplessness he remembered the massacre at Parker's Fort less than five years ago and the countless other encounters between Texans and Comanches that were only a foretaste of what could come to pass if the Comanches were mistreated or insulted at the peace talks in San Antonio. Rafael stirred restlessly in the saddle, recalling too vividly the treatment meted out to the captives of the Comanches and knowing that if the frontier blazed into war the wailing of captives would be heard unceasingly on the prairies.

Unable to find any solution, he let the thought of the Comanches fade from his mind and instead turned to speculation about Sebastian's latest folly.

Sebastian's involvement with a married woman annoyed and worried Rafael more than he would admit. That young man was definitely old enough to take care of himself—but Sebastian was also inclined to let his heart rule his head, and Rafael would have wagered an enormous sum of money that the woman who held Sebastian enthralled had little or no love for him. Women were such deceptive little bitches, he thought viciously as he kicked his horse into a gallop. They had faces like angels and bodies to drive men wild, and yet they lied, they cheated, and they would merrily rip a man's heart from his body for the sheer joy of watching him writhe.

But for just a moment his face softened and he recalled the sweet affection he shared with his little half-sister Arabela—pray God she did not change and grow into the kind of creature it seemed his fate to meet.

His lips thinned as he thought of the other women in his own life, and for the first time since he had given in to the incessant longing to see her once more and had traveled to Natchez before realizing just how ridiculously he was behaving, Rafael deliberately thought of Elizabeth Ridgeway. Thought of her and cursed under his breath at the sudden sweep of remembered pain.

CHAPTER NINE

San Antonio at last, thought Beth. The journey had not been arduous, and she was grateful to see the squat adobe buildings of San Antonio come into sight near the end of the second week of March. The trek from Galveston to San Antonio had been a revelation to her, and she had discovered that she could do without many of the trappings she had taken for granted all her young life. Some of them she had missed intensely. Most of all she disliked not having her bath, but she had gratefully made do with a pan of warmed water and a hasty wash behind one of the wagons.

Nathan kept his word and did not once open his mouth to complain. True, his lips had sometimes thinned in pained dislike and he could be forgiven for expressing himself somewhat forcibly the morning he discovered a rattlesnake curled near his blanket. And no one was particularly blithe the day a motley band of Kiowas followed them along the Camino Real for several hours. Stealing nervous, wary glances at the short, bronzed-skinned half-naked figures with their lances and bows and arrows, Beth was inordinately thankful that Sebastian and his party had joined theirs.

Sebastian had been a welcome addition to their party. Beth was happy to have his company, and somewhat grudgingly Nathan decided to make use of Sebastian's handiness with the dueling pistols and had, to pass the time in the evenings, asked that Sebastian show him how to fire the pistol. After that, most evenings were spent with Nathan assiduously firing at targets that he never seemed to hit. Beth, surprising herself and the gentlemen too, demanded that she be taught, and to her delight she became astonishingly proficient at hitting those same targets that eluded Nathan.

Traveling through the timbered wilderness that lay between Galveston and San Antonio had been a novel interlude for Beth. She found herself with literally nothing to do but to sit in the coach and stare dreamily at the towering pines, their pungent scent sharp in her nostrils. Day after day her thoughts drifted aimlessly, idle thoughts that were soon forgotten as their cavalcade moved steadily toward their destination.

At night, cozy in her bed in the back of a wagon, she gazed at the diamond-bright stars in the black sky and marveled at how very different this was from the almost smothering comfort of the silk-draped, softly luxurious beds she had known all her life. Lying in the darkness listening to the night sounds of the woods, the faraway hoot of a hunting owl, the occasional howl of a distant coyote, or the frightening scream of a cougar, she frequently wondered about the wisdom of this journey to Santa Fe. They had been advised to wait and join a merchant caravan that would start out in late March or early April from Independence, Missouri, traveling from there to the great rendezvous point of Council Grove in Indian territory. There would be dragoons guarding those wagons, and they would have been far safer. But Beth, driven by some inner compulsion, had not wanted to wait and join the annual caravan to Santa Fe. Deaf to all of Nathan's arguments at Briarwood, she had been determined to take the southern route, to travel to San Antonio and from there to Durango, deep into Mexico, to skirt the Great Plains and follow the trail the Spanish had used for years to Santa Fe. Even she had no idea why she was so obstinate about this, she only knew that the trip had taken on a monumental importance, that for once in her life she was satisfying her own dreams.

They were to stay in San Antonio only three days, just long enough to replenish supplies and to give everyone a rest from the journey. It was here in San Antonio that Sebastian was to leave them, taking his servants and traveling on to his relative's home; he had been dreading it with every mile they traveled. At least I have tonight, he thought glumly as the three of them parted momentarily to seek the comfort of their hotel rooms.

Nathan was looking forward to Sebastian's departure. He didn't really fear that Beth was enamored of the young man, but... Suddenly in need of reassurance as he and Beth were walking toward their rooms, Nathan couldn't help murmuring, "You care a great deal for Sebastian, don't you?"

"Oh, yes, I do, Nathan! He has been such a good friend to us, and I have so enjoyed his company. I will miss him when he leaves us tomorrow morning," Beth replied honestly, a faint shadow in her eyes.

Nathan, distressed as always when she was even slightly unhappy, patted her hand. "Come, now, my dear, it will not be the last you will see of him. Haven't we invited him to visit us at Natchez?"

Beth smiled at him. "So we have. I am sorry for seeming so gloomy, it is just that I have grown very fond of him in such a short time. I suppose it is because he is so exactly the sort of brother every girl would like to have."

Sebastian would have groaned out loud to hear those words, but they dispelled all Nathan's nebulous fears. Cheerfully he said, "Well, now, don't brood on his departure... we will see him again, I have no doubt. For the present, we have made it safely to San Antonio, and I must confess that after my initial reservations, I have, in a way, enjoyed the journey. If the trip from here to Santa Fe is as without incident as our travels have been so far, I will be most happy. And truly I will be quite insufferable once we return to Natchez, with my tales of having survived in this unknown and savage country."

Beth couldn't help the gurgle of laughter that escaped her at his words because they were so true. She could just imagine him languidly drinking his mint julep at Mansion House in Natchez and lording it over his various acquaintances. While they had gone tamely to London or Paris to visit, *he* had been exploring the vast untamed lands of the Republic of Texas and the province of Nuevo Méjico. She was still smiling when she entered the rooms that Nathan had found for them, and the sight of a steaming tin tub of hot water made her smile even wider.

Turning to Nathan, who stood just behind her, she exclaimed happily, "Oh, Nathan! How did you arrange it? And how did you know it was what I longed for most?"

Somewhat dryly, her husband answered, "Because it is exactly what *I* want most!"

Beth laughed. "Well, I certainly hope they have one waiting for you in your rooms, because I have no intention of postponing my bath or of sharing!"

Shaking his head in mock despair, Nathan left her. "You are suddenly a selfish little devil, Beth. But fortunately, I did have the foresight to order *two!*"

The bath was heavenly, and having her hair washed almost equaled the pleasure of feeling the warm water caress her skin. Tingling and feeling really clean for the first time in weeks, a short while later Beth celebrated the occasion by wearing one of the better gowns that had been packed to wear once they had reached Santa Fe. Since Galveston she had been wearing simple, striped gingham and calico gowns that had been ordered especially for traveling, and while the gowns were nice in their way, she was eager to slip into the sort of gown she normally wore. Charity had anticipated her desire and held up a charming gown of rose crepe with a white satin underskirt.

The hotel was pleasant. It was new and brash and very American, but Beth liked it even if it had none of the amenities to which she was accustomed. It was clean, it was reasonably comfortable, and the food was hot and plentiful. Beth thought it was sheer bliss, after weeks of campfire cooking to be served hot, spicy *chile guisado* and flat, warmed tortillas with which to take away the bite of the hot peppers used in the chile. There were also the usual staples of any Texan meal: succulent, thick beefsteaks, flaky biscuits, and steaming cups of rich, dark coffee.

The thick adobe walls allowed hardly any sound to seep inside, and as San Antonio was little more than a sleepy village on the edge of the expanding Texas frontier, there were few noises to be heard in the plaza—only the occasional hoofbeats of a horse across the open square, or the jingle of a spur or the sound of a barking dog—and briefly Beth thought she had heard a burst of laughter that must have come from one of the saloons.

Sebastian had been unusually silent during the meal, knowing that this was his last night with Beth for many months, maybe longer, and he was rather subdued in the face of the parting. And it was only when they were lingering over a final cup of coffee before retiring for the night that an idea occurred to him that would give him at least a few more days with Beth. His green eyes glittering with suppressed excitement, he leaned across the table and said eagerly, "I just realized that on your way to Durango you will pass not too many miles from the Hacienda del Cielo. Cielo is located about sixty miles south of here, and it would make a pleasant place for you to stop for a night or two. I know that my cousin, Don Miguel, would be more than pleased to offer you his hospitality—visitors are very welcome to those who live far away from their nearest neighbors." Very casually he added, "If you decide to do so, there is no reason why I should leave in the morning—I can delay my own departure a few days and travel with you. I know that you will enjoy visiting the hacienda—do say that you will!"

Beth found the idea extremely appealing, but she was not willing to impose upon strangers, and there was Nathan to consider. How did he feel about the invitation?

Despite the reassuring conversation with Beth earlier, Nathan was taking no chances—Sebastian was simply too devastatingly handsome to have dangling after one's wife! Suspecting that Beth's innate politeness would prompt her to refuse automatically, Nathan felt perfectly confident in declining the invitation. "We appreciate the offer, Sebastian, but I fear we must refuse. Perhaps on our return from Santa Fe?"

Sebastian didn't like it, but there was nothing more he could do—at least Nathan had held out the promise of a visit when they returned home. It was the best he could achieve at the moment, and so, with a resigned shrug of his broad shoulders, he said, "Very well. But I must confess that I am vastly disappointed. You, Beth, especially with your interest in the early Spanish explorers, would have found it most enjoyable. It is a very old rancho, one of the first ever settled in this area. Don Miguel says that there are family stories that one of Cabeza de Vaca's men is an ancestor." Sebastian knew it was underhanded to bait the hook so temptingly, but he was desperate.

Nathan knew exactly what Sebastian was up to, and not liking the way Beth had listened with such interest to Sebastian's words, he retorted testily, "Well, who the devil was this de Vaca fellow? I've never heard of him."

Her eyes round with astonishment, Beth exclaimed, "Nathan! Don't tell you haven't *ever* heard of Cabeza de Vaca, Alvar Núñez? Why, he was one of the first men to ever cross Texas. He and his men were lost nearly eight years and they were some of the first to mention Cibola, the seven cities of gold. How could you *not* have heard of him?"

"Oh, *that* de Vaca!" Nathan returned loftily, pretending very convincingly that he had known all along.

"Yes, that de Vaca!" Sebastian repeated with a mocking glint in the green eyes. "He and three others were shipwrecked on the Texas coast, some think at Galveston Island, in 1528, and after escaping slavery from the Indians, they made their way to Culiacán in Mexico."

Beth asked eagerly, "And which one of his companions was Don Miguel's ancestor?"

Sebastian's mouth curved wryly. "There you have me, Beth. It's only a family tale, and I'm not even sure it's true. But if it is, I'm afraid the ancestor is only identified as 'Estevanico,' who some people claim was an Arab or a Moor."

"But how thrilling!" Beth breathed, her romantic nature aroused by the possibilities of the story. Turning to Nathan, she asked impetuously, "Oh, Nathan, why don't we stop as Sebastian suggests? I would so like to meet Sebastian's cousin and see the hacienda. I'm certain that we would enjoy ourselves immensely."

There was very little that Nathan could ever deny

Beth, especially when she looked at him as she was now, the violet eyes large and full of excitement. Deciding a few more days of Sebastian's company couldn't hurt anything, he reluctantly capitulated. "Well, if you truly want to, my dear, I have no objections."

Beth reached over and gave her husband a quick rare kiss on his cheek. "Oh, thank you, Nathan! I know you will enjoy yourself too!"

Sebastian had been elated at the turnabout, but the sight of Beth kissing her husband, no matter how innocuous, annoyed him. The green eyes decidedly unfriendly as they rested on Nathan, he said with false heartiness, "Well, then, we can take it as planned that we all leave here together Friday morning." Glancing at Beth, he added, "I'm certain that you will find my cousin and his family such charming hosts that you may decide to stay even longer than just a night or two."

Smiling at him, Beth asked interestedly, "What is your cousin like? He is older or younger than you?"

Sebastian laughed. "Don Miguel? Much older. Why, even his son has a ten-year advantage over me."

Beth looked puzzled. "But how is this? If he is your cousin..."

"It's rather complicated, which is why in the family we have simply settled on 'cousin.' You see, my great-grandmother was Spanish, and she and Don Felipe, Don Miguel's father, were brother and sister."

"Quite a bit of difference in their ages, wasn't there?" Nathan asked in a bored tone.

"Oh, yes, that there was! My great-grandmother was already married and had borne my grandmother by the time Don Felipe was born. My great-grandmother was the eldest child and Don Felipe the youngest, with several brothers and sisters born in between. As I am the youngest in *my* family, it creates an even greater distance in ages."

For no apparent reason Beth felt a chill, wondering why this simple conversation should disturb her, why it seemed to strike some chord of memory. Slightly on edge, she excused herself a few minutes later and made her way to her room.

The bed was everything she could have asked for, soft and welcoming, the linen sheets crisply clean and smelling of hot Texas sunlight. After nights of sleeping on the hard boards of the wagon bottom, snuggled down in the first comfortable bed since they had left Galveston, Beth should have fallen asleep instantly, but sleep was oddly elusive. She tossed and turned for several hours, aware she was uneasy and yet unable to discover the source of her restlessness. Eventually, though, she did drift off to sleep, but it was not a peaceful sleep because, for the first time in years, she dreamed the old dream, her black-haired demon-lover coming to her again, his lips hard and urgent on hers and his hands frightening her with their intimate, demanding exploration of her body. And the terror was back too, the stark fear of impending doom so strong that she woke up trembling, with tears on her cheeks. Lying there in her bed, she gradually calmed herself, telling herself over and over again it was only a *dream*, no ominous portent of the future. When she finally fell asleep again it was to sleep deeply, no dreams disturbing her slumber.

When she awoke in the morning, the strange mood seemed to have passed, or at least she was determined to banish it from her mind. With a forced eagerness she threw aside her covers and walked across the wooden-planked floor to gaze out across the plaza.

Their hotel was situated on the main plaza of San Antonio, and idly she watched as a cart filled with straw and drawn by a pair of oxen slowly made its way toward one of the streets that radiated out from the plaza. A woman in a full scarlet skirt and a low-cut white blouse, a pottery jug on her dark head, caught her interest, and she smiled as she noticed a young Mexican boy running and laughing along the edge of the square, two nondescript mongrels at his heels.

There was a sleepy air about the town despite the movement in the plaza. The buildings of thick adobe with their flat red-tiled roofs seemed to drowse in the golden sunlight. There were few trees, but occasionally the branches of a giant cypress or the spreading shade of a cottonwood tree could be seen contrasting greenly against the pale sienna walls of the buildings. The shallow San Antonio River and the low-banked San Pedro Creek slowly wound along either side of the town and a vast grassland of gently rolling prairie, dotted with wooded springs, surrounded the area. It was a peaceful scene but Beth felt the night's uneasiness returning, and she was painfully conscious that she no longer had any taste for this journey, that she was filled with a queer premonition of danger. And it was then, inexplicably, that she felt Rafael Santana's forceful presence, could almost see him walking across the plaza with his long-legged stride.

He had been banished from her mind for so long, she had denied within herself his existence, and now, now without warning, he had boldly and blatantly invaded her thoughts; and Beth was furious... and terrified, as she suddenly realized that her dream devil-lover and Rafael were the *same* person!

It was something, she suspected sickly, she had known all along but hadn't wanted to acknowledge, and she felt slightly hysterical at the idea that even before she had met him she had dreamed of his kisses and his lean body against hers. Beth drew in a shaken breath. She was being foolish, of course. The man in her dreams had been faceless and she was acting like a silly, highly strung child to even think that she could sense Rafael Santana's presence—he was probably nowhere within a hundred miles of San Antonio. It soothed her somewhat to follow that line of reasoning, and grimly she fought down the almost overpowering urge to leave this place—to return to Briarwood with all possible speed.

If Nathan and Sebastian noticed that Beth's smile was strained or that there were deep circles under eyes, neither made mention of it. Instead, Nathan, displaying an irritating inclination to attach himself firmly to his wife's side, drove Sebastian almost to the brink of violence. Beth didn't help his temper any by appearing to be touchingly grateful for Nathan's presence, clinging to him with such warmth that Sebastian finally had to excuse himself for a while to keep from openly showing his jealousy. He was discovering that capturing Beth's heart wasn't going to be as easy as he had first thought.

And so, while Sebastian nursed what he was certain was a broken heart, Nathan and Beth leisurely explored the old Spanish town. Naturally they were directed with pride to the old Mission of San Antonio de Valero located on the little San Antonio River just across from the town. The mission had through the years been called simply "The Alamo," for a grove of alamo, or cottonwood, trees that grew nearby, and it was here less than five years ago that General Santa Anna had deliberately annihilated the brave Texan defenders who had been determined to wrest Texas from the oppressive Mexican rule. Staring at the ruined mission church that had collapsed long before the terrible battle, Beth was saddened. The last bloody fight had taken barely ninety minutes, but during that time one hundred and eighty-three heroic men with a dream had died, and such grand men, Beth thought with awe—Davy Crockett, Jim Bowie, Colonel William Travis, and many more—*all* heroes forever in Texas!

On Thursday, after a night of dreamless sleep, Beth was finally able to shake her queer mood and truly begin to enjoy their brief visit to San Antonio. The inhabitants were friendly, and, though they knew no one in the town, Beth and Nathan were greeted almost eagerly as they walked about. Most of the people were Texans but there was still a large Mexican population, and both races seemed to welcome them unstintingly, the women smiling and the men doffing either their huge sombreros or the similar wide-brimmed hats worn by the Texans.

That they were strangers was obvious from their fashionable dress. Beth's mauve silk gown with its slim-fitting bodice that ended in a point at her slender waist, the very full skirts and the long fitted sleeves gave evidence of this. Nathan was attired as stylishly as his wife, perhaps more so: his fair hair gleamed from under a gray chimney-pot hat; his double-breasted, tight-fitting tailcoat of dove-gray superfine was certainly more suitable for Natchez than the frontier town of San Antonio. His walking stick and his dazzling white gloves definitely indicated he was not from the local environs, and not unnaturally he attracted a few stares. Oblivious of that fact, Nathan continued his stroll with Beth, occasionally raising the monocle he had lately affected to make a closer inspection of some peculiar object that caught his eye.

Once he raised his monocle to gaze at a pair of those Spanish pantaloonlike garments, *calzoneras*. The outer part of the leg of the *calzoneras* was open from hip to ankle, the borders set with twinkling filigree buttons, and the whole fantastically trimmed with tinsel lace. The particular pair that aroused Nathan's obvious envy was worn proudly by a young Mexican *caballero* who stared haughtily back at Nathan. Beth had to smother a laugh, certain that Nathan would soon own a similar pair.

It was approaching noon and Beth was about to suggest that they return to their hotel for lunch, when an aristocratic-appearing gentleman and his young wife accosted them. They were both well dressed, the woman in a flattering brown silk gown and the gentleman in a well-fitting buff broadcloth coat and embroidered silk waistcoat.

Instead of passing them, the couple stopped and the gentleman said in a friendly voice, "We couldn't help noticing that you seem to be strangers, and we wondered if we could do anything to make you feel at home. I'm Sam Maverick, a rancher in these parts as well as a lawyer, and this is my wife, Mary. Are you new settlers to the area or are you, perhaps, visiting with relatives?" The man was courtesy itself, and Beth liked him on sight. Mary, her plain face welcoming, sent Beth a quiet, pleasant smile, and almost shyly Beth returned it. There were a few moments of polite conversation as the Ridgeways introduced themselves and Nathan explained that they were only stopping for a short rest in San Antonio before traveling eventually to Santa Fe, where they would be staying with his wife's friend, Stella Rodriguez. At the mention of Stella's name the conversation suddenly became more vivacious, as it turned out that the Mavericks had known Stella and her family for some time. In a very few minutes they were talking as if they'd known one another all their lives. At least Beth was, and Nathan, having met Stella only the one time in New Orleans, added little conversation but was content to see Beth enjoying herself and talking so animatedly.

They all might have stood there talking indefinitely if Mary Maverick hadn't suddenly said, "This is ridiculous, standing on a street corner gossiping! *Do* come to our house. It is just over there on the corner of the square. You see that giant cypress? Well, that is our house it is shading. Please say that you will come . . . and stay for lunch, too?"

Nathan and Beth gave the usual polite refusals that most people give at such an impromptu invitation, but Mary and Sam Maverick were warmly insistent. And as Beth was eager to continue the conversation and was finding the Mavericks so very friendly and Nathan was perfectly agreeable, shortly she found herself sitting comfortably on a chintz-covered sofa in the three-room stone house.

The unexpected visit with the Mavericks proved as pleasant and enjoyable as Beth had thought it would. Nathan, too, his natural curiosity aroused, became quite involved in a lively discussion about the rewards and pleasures to be found in settling in the Republic of Texas. Beth had reservations, and, remembering the band of Kiowas they had seen and Stella's tales of raiding Comanches, she blurted out, "But what about Indians? I understand that many lives are lost regularly because of them."

Sam Maverick frowned and admitted reluctantly, "What you say is perfectly true, I cannot deny it. Indians, especially the Comanches, are our greatest threat—besides the ever-present one of an invasion from Mexico." He paused, but, seeing he had the riveted attention of his two guests, he continued seriously, "At first the Comanches did not attack us, but in the past few years their raids have taken a terrible toll. Why, in '38 the slaughter became so great that Bastrop County was nearly denuded of settlers. It was shocking and dreadful, the killings that took place. Entire families wiped out. Dreadful." His expression lightening, he added encouragingly, "But we hope we have seen the last of those vicious raids—soon, if all goes well, the frontier will be secured and safe for all Texans."

Her face revealing her doubt, Beth questioned, "How will you accomplish that? Apparently you haven't been able to appease them in the past—what makes you think that the future will be any different?"

It was Mary who answered. Bending forward in her rocking chair, she said earnestly, "I would normally agree with you, Mrs. Ridgeway, but you see, a group of Comanches rode through here not long ago, and *they* expressed a wish for peace with us. Our gallant Texas Rangers have been able to strike back at those wicked creatures, often in their own territory, and we believe that they have begun to realize that we Texans will not allow them to intimidate us the way they did the Spanish and the Mexicans. A meeting has been arranged by Colonel Karnes, he is the Commander of the Southern Frontier, and everyone is hopeful that a lasting peace can be achieved. The fact that the Comanches themselves requested the peace meeting is what gives all of us renewed hope." Her face suddenly doubtful, she added, "The only problem will be whether or not the Comanches are willing to return all of their white captives. If they do not, there will be no peace."

"Captives?" Nathan spoke up in astonishment. "What the devil do they want with captives? Besides, I would think that any men captured by them would easily escape from simple savages."

Mrs. Maverick looked uncomfortable and then said in a low voice, "They never take men captive, only women of childbearing age and small children." Her expression embarrassed, she continued with difficulty. "They take the women to use as slaves and for an even fouler purpose—to force those poor wretched creatures to bear them half-breed children! The captured white children are usually adopted into the tribe and grow up thinking they are Comanches."

Beth was horrified and she moved uneasily upon the sofa, filled with a sudden, fierce terror, imagining herself in the clutches of some brutal savage and the humiliation she would suffer. Ghastly! Unbearable to consider! But the subject held a horrid fascination for her, and, unable to help herself, she inquired softly, "But do they survive?"

Both of the Mavericks looked grim, Sam Maverick saying harshly, "Some do, some don't. Some of them we never do know for certain *what* their fate is. The Parker children, taken during the Parker's Fort massacre in '36, are a good example . . . little Cynthia Anne was only nine, her brother John just six. There are rumors that she has been seen with the Comanches in the north, but no one knows for certain if she is still alive or what has happened to her brother. Those of their family that survived the slaughter pray that every little white girl sighted is their Cynthia Anne."

"Those poor, poor children," Beth breathed in horror.

"It is something that every Texan has lived with these past few years," Maverick said heavily. "Despite our attempts to make treaties with them, they continue their depredations upon us. The Rangers do their best, but they are too few men against the savage hordes that kill and slaughter at will. It simply *must* stop! The Comanches must be made to realize that we Texans are here to stay, and more importantly, we will not be intimidated as the Spanish and Mexicans were. We will not buy peace by giving them gifts and bribing them to leave us alone!" Angrily Maverick finished, "This is *our* land and we will not be driven from it!"

Perhaps both Mavericks felt that they had given their visitors a particularly gloomy and terrifying picture of life in Texas. Changing the subject almost abruptly, for the next several moments they stressed all the advantages: the huge tracts of land that were being given away—twelve hundred and eighty acres of *free* land to each family, six hundred and forty acres to each unmarried man; the climate and soils that made it so incredibly effortless to grow a handsome living. If crops didn't appeal to one, why there were literally *thousands* of longhorn cattle that had been left by the Spanish settlers when many had fled back to Mexico in 1835. Texas, as far as the Mavericks were concerned, was a veritable paradise.

By the time the Ridgeways had left the Maverick

home, the subject of Comanches and Parker's Fort had long been dismissed from everybody's mind. Except that Beth dreamed again that night, a terrifying nightmare in which she was naked and defenseless surrounded by a group of leering Comanches, the lust in their eyes almost tangible, causing her to shrink away in the utter fright. The firelight flickered on their savage faces as they closed in on her and then suddenly they were gone, and there was only one Comanche remaining, a tall, lean Comanche with a bloodied knife and gray eyes . . . a Comanche with the face of Rafael Santana!

CHAPTER TEN

The Hacienda del Cielo was situated in some of the most beautiful country that Beth had ever seen. Almost sixty miles southwest of San Antonio, it was set in a rugged area of live-oak-covered hills with picturesque green valleys and inviting blue streams which were edged by towering cypress trees. As they drew near the hacienda, they saw great herds of cattle, their enormous curving long horns identifying them as animals unique to the Republic of Texas.

They had left San Antonio at first light the previous day, and the ride to the hacienda had been without incident. Beth had been more than thankful, in view of her recent nightmares, that Sebastian and his four servants were still with them. It lulled her into a sense of security, and she preferred to forget the possibility of the danger that existed—danger from raiding Indians or the added peril that a roving band of Mexican *bandidos* who still ravaged the countryside might discover them; these *bandidos* pillaged, raped, and killed, apparently with the blessing, if not outright encouragement, of Mexico City.

Nathan brought up the subject of Indians, though, and as they discussed what the Mavericks had told them, Beth admitted to Nathan, "I think, perhaps, you were right, Nathan, about this trip. It *is* dangerous. Would you think me very foolish if I confessed that I have lost my taste for it?"

He didn't think that she was foolish, but he was amply surprised, and *very* relieved. Not even wanting to know what had brought about this devoutly longed-for reversal, Nathan asked eagerly, "Does that mean we do not have to go any farther? We can go back to Natchez?"

Beth thought about it for a long moment, remembering her deep desire to see Stella and the baby Elizabeth. She did want to see Stella almost desperately but she was frightened, and the journey that had started out with so many hopes and dreams now gave her an unshakable feeling of impending danger. Taking a deep breath, she said slowly, "Yes. We can stay with Sebastian's relatives for a night or two, then go back to San Antonio and return home the way we came."

Nathan was delighted, overjoyed in fact, and he made no attempt to disguise it. When they stopped to rest the horses and oxen, he couldn't contain himself. Happily, he burbled out the news to Sebastian, who had chosen to ride his horse rather than suffer the confines of the coach—even if it meant denying himself Beth's company and giving her husband a decided advantage. Astonishment written across his lean, attractive features, Sebastian said blankly, "Go back? You mean all the way to Natchez? You're not going on to Santa Fe?"

"No," Nathan replied with a wealth of satisfaction. "Beth has decided that she does not want to go any farther. We will still accept your kind invitation to stay at the hacienda, but when we leave, we will go back to San Antonio and from there to Natchez."

Sebastian looked hard at Beth, trying to discover a reason for this sudden and unexpected change of heart. Beth met his look steadily, but the expression in the violet eyes was embarrassed. She was being such a fool and she knew it, but if there had been an overpowering desire to embark upon this journey in the first place, it had been replaced with an equally overpowering desire to leave as soon as possible and to seek the safety of Briarwood. With difficulty she murmured to Sebastian, "I know you must think me the flightiest creature imaginable, but I find that I simply do not want to go any farther. I'll write my friend from San Antonio and explain everything to her."

Sebastian asked helplessly, "Are you certain it's what you want to do?"

"I'm positive," Beth stated firmly. "*Very* positive."

There was nothing more to be said, although it was obvious that Sebastian would have liked to discuss it further. But he let the moment pass, aware that whether Beth went on to Santa Fe or back to Natchez, she was still leaving his life within the next few days...unless he could convince her that she belonged with him. She must know of her husband's philandering with young men, he decided thoughtfully, must know that Nathan was not the ardent husband he should be. And with that in mind, wouldn't she be more inclined to accept an offer of marriage with a *real* man? A man who would never seek solace from another pair of arms—feminine or masculine? Sebastian's lip curled. Certainly *never* masculine! His mind made up, he resolved that before the Ridgeways began their long journey back to Natchez he would find some way to declare himself to Beth. That she seemed singularly unaware or uninterested in his suit he stubbornly refused to recognize.

Beth was slightly subdued for the remainder of the journey, but catching her first sight of the hacienda as they rounded a hill and entered a wide, verdant valley, she was strangely glad that they had accepted Sebastian's invitation. At the far end of the green, grassy valley the hacienda sat like a gleaming white-walled fortress, portions of the red-tiled roof of the *casa grande* visible above the thick adobe walls and the trees that surrounded the living compound. A wide, blue, sandy-bottomed stream lined with cypress and sweet gum trees ran through the valley, and the dusty, tawny road that led to the hacienda was edged with sprawling sycamores.

The outer walls soared some twelve to fifteen feet in the air; the top ledges were studded with tall iron spikes. Beth felt as if she were entering a medieval stronghold as the wide beaten-iron gates at the entrance clanged shut behind their party. It gave her an unsettled feeling as she realized that those walls were the only barrier between herself and the frightening savagery that the people here could and did face daily. Everywhere she looked, no matter how well-kept, no matter what signs of prosperity or wealth existed, there was some reminder that provisions had been made for protection from rampaging Indians; she was suddenly aware of how very lucky they had been to have gone so far unscathed and how *very* grateful she would be if they were able to reach Natchez without ever seeing another Indian. Those grim spikes reminded her that outside those walls, death rode a painted pony and struck without warning or mercy.

There were actually two sets of walls. The outer walls provided a stout barrier of protection for the adobes of the peasants and *vaqueros* that lived and worked on the ranch. The area encompassed was several acres; it was here that the granary was located, as were the storehouses, the community well, and the stables. The inner walls, though high and wide and amply defendable against attack, were simply to guarantee privacy for the *casa grande*.

When the coach reached the gates of the second wall, it halted. Sebastian quickly dismounted and, flinging open the coach door with a flourish, he helped Beth to alight. Bowing with lithe grace he said teasingly, "Madame, the Hacienda del Cielo awaits your lightest command."

Descending in his usual languid manner, Nathan murmured dryly, "Isn't that for your cousin to say . . . or have I mistaken the situation?"

Sebastian flushed angrily and said tightly, "There is no mistake, and the situation has not changed—not in the least. Now, if you will excuse me for a moment, I shall apprise my cousin of our arrival."

Sebastian stalked off and Beth turned to look at Nathan with puzzlement obvious in her expression. "What in the world was the meaning of all that?"

With an unruffled composure Nathan replied, "Nothing, my dear, just young Sebastian displaying a bit of childish temperament."

Beth had her own reservations about that, but she chose to say nothing, glancing interestedly about her, as she and Nathan strolled toward an archway through which Sebastian had disappeared. On the other side of the arch was another world, and Beth gave a gasp of pleasure. It was a world of elegance and grace, of flowering scarlet and purple bougainvillaea, orange and yellow climbing trumpet vines, sparkling fountains, flagstone courtyards, and tubs of leafy green trees that cast welcoming shade against the walls of the hacienda. The walls of the house itself glistened so white that it actually hurt Beth's eyes to look at them in the bright sunlight. Moorish arches and lacy ironwork balconies were evidence of the hacienda's past history, and Beth wondered excitedly if it were at all possible that indeed one of de Vaca's men, the one known only as "the Moor," might have seen to the construction of this magnificent house. Through another arch set in the side of the hacienda there was a tantalizing glimpse of a cool, sheltered inner courtyard, a three-tiered fountain of water tinkling merrily in the center of it.

They were crossing the outer courtyard, walking toward the three shallow steps that led to the interior of the hacienda, when Sebastian, accompanied by a slim, handsome man of about fifty, stepped out onto the portico. A plump, matronly lady, her dark hair covered with a black lace mantilla held in place with a high jeweled comb, joined them.

The dark-haired, olive-skinned man could be none other than Don Miguel—there was a proud assurance to the set of his shoulders, and his clothing spoke of wealth and position. His short cloth jacket was richly embroidered with braid and fancy barrel buttons; the red sash tied about his waist was of silk. The woman was dressed no less grandly—her ruby silk gown was of European style with long-fitted sleeves; the waist ended in a point, and the full skirts nearly brushed the ground. Several gold chains fell from her neck and rested on the plump bosom.

The gentleman's face broke into a broad welcoming smile and he cried out gaily, "So, you are Sebastian's friends, *sí!* Come, come inside and refresh yourself. The hacienda is at your disposal—we are most happy that you allowed our disreputable young relative to convince you to stop and stay awhile. Visitors are always welcome at the Hacienda del Cielo, but Sebastian's friends even more so."

There followed the usual polite exchanges of conversation, and it was only when they were all laughing over some remark made by Nathan that Sebastian said easily, "I think we have forgotten introductions, and before I forget my manners entirely, Doña Madelina and Don Miguel, I would like you to meet my friends, Mrs. Elizabeth Ridgeway and her husband, Mr. Nathan Ridgeway. Beth and Nathan, may I present my cousin's delightful wife, Doña Madelina Perez de la Santana and my cousin, Don Miguel López de la Santana y Higuera."

Sebastian grinned and added, "I think it would be easier if the names were reduced to simply Beth and Nathan and Miguel and Madelina."

It was Madelina who answered. Her great, liquid dark eyes beaming with pleasure, she murmured, "*Sí, joven*, such formality would certainly be a poor way to thank your friends for their kindness to you in your travels."

Beth's face had gone white at the Santana name, and almost frantically she sought to recover her composure. Striving to act normal, she said in what she hoped was an unruffled tone of voice, "But it was Sebastian who was kind to us! He even went so far as to rearrange his own trip to accompany us on ours. It is Sebastian who has been exceedingly kind to us, not the other way around."

Sebastian looked uncomfortable, and Miguel smiled knowingly as he glanced at his much younger cousin. "Perhaps Sebastian took it as a very great kindness that you accepted his sometimes outrageous company, hmmm?"

There was a slight ripple of laughter at his words, but Beth's was forced, her thoughts spinning in icy apprehension. Was it just one of those startling coincidences? Or had she blindly and unwittingly blundered into the tiger's lair?

Swallowing with difficulty, she couldn't help a quick, almost fearful glance around her, as if she expected to find Rafael watching her. But there was no one concealed in the shadows, just bright, warm sunlight and the gracious welcome that was being extended by Sebastian's cousins. Yet in spite of the warmth of the day, Beth shivered, wondering uneasily what she would do if it did turn out that these kind people were indeed related to Rafael Santana.

But there was little she could do except smile and accept the tall, cool glass of *sangría* that was pressed upon her once they had entered the house. They were seated in a large, elegant room that opened out onto a shaded patio where sprawling ferns and potted trees made leafy green umbrellas. The room was soothing, the white walls reflecting back the bright sunlight that poured in through tall, arched windows, the dark, heavy Spanish furniture contrasting attractively against the vibrant colors of the fine Brussels carpet.

Beth tried to relax, tried to join in the conversation that was taking place, but her jumbled thoughts would give her no rest. Until she knew for certain there was no relationship between these Santanas and Rafael, it would be impossible for her to do anything but sit there filled with dismay and anxiety. Nervously she twisted her untouched glass and smiled blankly at some comment that was made, wondering how she could discover if her worst fears were about to be realized.

Sebastian innocently did it for her. After the first flurry of exchanges had died down he asked Miguel, "Has Rafael arrived? I saw him at Galveston on our way through there, and he said he would meet me here."

Don Miguel smiled. "My son is like the wind—one never knows precisely where or *when* he will appear. Rest assured, though, that if he said he would be here, in time he will be."

The delicate crystal glass in Beth's hand slipped from her nerveless fingers and the only thing that saved it from shattering was the soft cushion of the carpet. The *sangría* spilled over her yellow muslin gown and almost dazedly she stared at the spreading pinkish stain, her thoughts whirling in wild confusion. Yet one thought remained like a spear in her chaotic mind—*Don Miguel is Rafael's father!* Unaware of it, a slight moan of sheer dismay escaped her pale lips, but in the rush that everyone made to alleviate the damage to her gown it went unnoticed.

Madelina, expertly bustling aside the gentlemen, said quickly, "Leave it, please! Come, Señora Ridgeway, I shall show you to the rooms where you will stay. We will have a servant cleanse it for you immediately." Turning to her husband, she added briskly, "Miguel, *amado,* have Pedro or Jesús bring Señora Ridgeway's trunks to the gold rooms so that she may change."

"Our servants can see to that, Doña Madelina," Nathan said politely.

"That will not be necessary—let them rest for a while, we have servants enough." Turning to Beth, Madelina urged, "Come now, señora, if you will follow me, I shall see to it that all is set right. Come, *mi cara,* come!"

Like a beautiful sleepwalker Beth followed the short, plump figure down the shady arcade that was created by the extended eaves of the hacienda and supported by graceful rounded arches that faced the central courtyard. It seemed like a long walk to Beth, but she was so shaken by the news that Rafael Santana was her host's son that she was not in full control of her senses. Even when they entered a spacious set of rooms decorated in white and gold, her thoughts were numb and incoherent. But she had to say something, she realized dully as Madelina gazed at her in some concern. She forced a smile and offered lamely, "I think that the trip from San Antonio must have tired me more than I thought."

Madelina's look of concern lessened. "*Sí,* it is a long and often uncomfortable journey," she commiserated instantly. "Would you like to lie down and rest until dinner? I can have a tray of refreshments sent to you. Would you like that?"

Eagerly Beth said, "Oh, señora, I would like it above all things!"

Smiling kindly, the older woman said, "Fine! I will leave you now, and in just a few moments one of our servants will see to your needs. Your own servants can assume their normal duties in the morning, if that meets with your approval."

Beth nodded her head, and seeing it, Madelina finished efficiently, "I believe that settles everything for the moment. Don't worry about anything, just rest and I shall see you later."

With the departure of Madelina, Beth's composure

fled. With trembling legs she stumbled to a chair and sat down. I must not be a fool, she told herself sternly, her hands clasping and unclasping agitatedly in her lap. There is nothing to be frightened of—he is only a man, he can't hurt me—he might not even remember me!

And suddenly, with a wild lurch in the region of her stomach, she realized that she would also be meeting Consuela, and at that thought her hands began to shake so badly that only by clasping them tightly together could she control them. Oh, God! Beth thought with anguish, I simply could not face Consuela, not greet her politely . . . and all the while have those flat black eyes watching me slyly, knowing of my degradation! And Consuela's cousin Lorenzo, what of him? Will he be present also?

Beth had no time to ponder her dilemma, for there was a slight tap on the door. An instant later, the heavy door was pushed open and, just as she had on that terrible afternoon in New Orleans, Consuela's servant Manuela entered the room bearing an ornate silver tray. Beth froze, her face paling in shocked dismay.

Manuela halted just inside the room, her calm dark eyes staring enigmatically at Beth's frozen face. She remained silent for a taut second and then said quietly, "You have nothing to fear from me, señora. I only obeyed my mistress that day, and I would not harm you now. Nor, except between the two of us, will I ever speak of it." When Beth made no move, when she stayed like a lovely frozen statue, Manuela sent her a long, assessing look and then set the tray down on a marble-topped table that was against one wall. She approached Beth slowly, taking her time, watching as one does when in the presence of a wild and easily startled animal. Manuela stopped a few paces in front of Beth and, her voice soft and filled with sincerity, she repeated, "You have nothing to fear from me, señora. Señora Consuela is dead, and with her died many things. Trust me, *niña,* I will not harm you. She is dead and the past is behind us."

Beth heard little beyond Manuela's words that Consuela was dead. Her eyes clinging to the lined, sallow features, she whispered disbelievingly, "*Dead?* How can that be? She was a young woman."

Her face impassive, Manuela answered steadily, "Comanches. She was leaving here—but on her way to the coast, where she hoped to board a ship that would take her to Spain, she and two female servants as well as the eight men who escorted her were killed. She suffered, *niña,* before she died. *Por Dios,* she suffered! I bathed and prepared her body for burial here in the family cemetery, and I saw the tortures that had been inflicted upon her. She suffered a thousand times more than you, señora. That does not excuse her, but perhaps you can find pity in your heart for the horrible way that she died."

Beth's heart skipped a beat and she heard again Consuela saying viciously, "I wonder why you have not hired some of your filthy, estupido savages before now to rid you of a wife like myself!" and Rafael's cruel reply, "I'm surprised I hadn't thought of it before now!" And in the serene, elegant room, Beth shivered.

It didn't bear thinking about, she told herself, trying to quell the ugly suspicions that were going through her mind. Her voice thick and rusty, she asked, "How was it that she was leaving? And why wasn't *he* with her?"

Manuela shrugged and then turned and walked over to the tray. Her thin hands moved quickly as she poured a tall glass of *sangría* and offered it to Beth. Numbly Beth took the glass from her and, staring at the cool, ruby-colored drink, she remembered inanely the wine stain on her gown.

She glanced down at it and muttered foolishly, "My gown. It is stained."

As if the other conversation had never been, Manuela said easily, "Yes, I see that it is. If you will permit me, I will help you out of it and see that one of the other maids has it soaked immediately."

Helplessly Beth agreed, unwilling to dwell on their conversation, unwilling to think that Rafael Santana had deliberately sent his wife to her death at the hands of the Comanches.

Manuela did nothing to break the fragile hold that

Beth had on herself, as she deftly stripped off the soiled gown. Leaving Beth momentarily in her lace-trimmed chemise and ruffled petticoats, Manuela disappeared into one of the rooms that comprised the suite. She returned almost instantly with a peignoir of French cambric trimmed down the front with a deep ruffle of Valenciennes lace. Beth recognized it as her own and rightly assumed that her baggage had been unpacked in the adjoining dressing room.

Manuela helped her into the peignoir and gently coaxed Beth to drink the *sangría*. Still in a state of blessed numbness, Beth did so.

The *sangría* warmed her and sent a tingle along her veins. It was pleasant, and almost absently she took the glass that Manuela had promptly refilled. At least, Beth thought half hysterically, if I drink enough, I won't feel anything. I won't feel anything and, most of all, I won't be able to think...to think the terrible thoughts that are waiting for me if I *dare* let them begin!

Manuela smoothly ushered her into the bedroom, urging her to sit in a comfortable chair of white-and-gold brocade. Moving quietly about the room, Manuela turned back the gold satin coverlet of the bed and opened twin doors that revealed a small patio off the room. She glanced at Beth and, seeing that some of the whiteness had left her face, she said practically, "I have given your gown to Maria and she will see to it. Doña Madelina asked me to assist you since, up until Señora Consuela's death, I had been a lady's maid....If you wish, you may request that someone else serve you."

Beth ran a hand wearily through her hair. "No," she finally said. "No, that won't be necessary. It would only raise speculation, and by tomorrow morning my own servant will take over from you." Beth was too aware of the raised eyebrows that would result from her refusal of Manuela's services and had decided it was best to let sleeping dogs lie...and yet, she wanted almost intolerably to know the facts of Consuela's death. She simply *had* to know. Tightly gripping the crystal glass, she pleaded, "Manuela, tell me of Consuela's death. Why was she leaving?"

Manuela hesitated and then said simply, "Señor Rafael was determined to divorce her. He gave her the choice of returning to Spain and seeking the divorce herself, or of remaining here and being humiliated while *he* sought the divorce." Manuela's face took on an expression of distaste. "How she raged and shrieked at him! She was like a madwoman—so incensed by his ultimatum that she did not even wait for her personal belongings to be packed. She had Lorenzo hire the men to escort her to the coast, and within three days she was gone, with two of the younger maids. I was to follow with all her trunks and baggage. I often thank the good God that she did not insist that I accompany her—she trusted me to see that all of her possessions were accounted for, and so I was spared." Flatly she ended, "The Comanches killed them all within two days of their departure."

"I see," Beth said in a shaky voice, wondering with revulsion if Rafael had met those same Comanches and had suggested to them precisely where they might find his wife. A quiver went through her at the ugly thought, not wanting to believe him capable of such vicious action and yet fearful that he was. There was just one more question she had to ask, "And Señor Mendoza, what of him?"

"He has his own rancho not far from here," Manuela answered. A pitying look on her face, she added, "I should warn you that Don Miguel still considers him a member of the family . . . and he will be *here* tonight for dinner!"

CHAPTER ELEVEN

Manuela proved to be an excellent lady's maid, for she had a fine eye for fabric and color; she was helpful without being obsequious. It was Manuela who decided that Beth would wear a rich silk gown of deep purple, and that the burnished, silvery curls would be arranged high on the small head, one long ringlet coaxed to lie curled against the white neck and slim shoulders revealed by the gown's low-cut bodice.

The two women did not discuss Consuela or what happened further, but it was never far from Beth's mind. And just as she was about to leave the room, she turned to Manuela and asked abruptly, "Does Rafael know the truth about me?"

Manuela bit her lip and would not meet Beth's eyes. "No, señora, he does not. Doña Consuela threatened me with physical harm if I ever spoke of it—and after her death the subject did not arise." Giving Beth an unhappy look, she added, "It would do little good to tell him now—he would not believe it and there is no proof." She glanced away and said in a low tone, "I would not want to reveal my part in it, señora. I am very much afraid that he would have me dismissed. I am not young, señora—I have no place to go, no place to live, and most of all I would have no work."

"But if you explained that it was because of Consuela's plotting that you did it—that she made you do it?" Beth persisted vehemently, wanting intensely for Rafael to know the truth, even now after all these years.

Manuela slowly shook her head. "I would like to do this thing for you, señora, truly I would, but I am afraid—please, do not ask it of me!"

Beth opened her mouth to reassure the other woman

that there was nothing to fear—she would take care of her—and it was then that she realized with frustration it would be useless to have Manuela speak now. Rafael was not likely to believe Consuela's ex-servant in any event—why should he? But more importantly, there was an extremely good probability that he would think that Beth had bribed her. It was dreadful enough that he already thought she was an adulterous little slut, Beth decided bitterly, without adding bribery to her list of crimes. Knowing she was defeated at the moment, she firmly shut her mouth. What did it matter anyway, she wondered rebelliously, and besides she and Nathan would have left the Hacienda del Cielo far behind them before Rafael Santana appeared on the scene.

A tap on the inner door of the sitting room ended the conversation. "Shall I answer it, señora?" Manuela asked quietly. "It is probably your husband. He has been given the suite which adjoins yours."

Beth nodded, and a moment later Nathan strolled into the room looking very elegant in a plum-colored coat with a black velvet collar and slim black pantaloons. He glanced appreciatively at his wife and murmured, "Ah, my dear, how lovely you are! I take it you have recovered from your earlier indisposition? It would be utterly frightful if you were to become ill just as we are about to return home." An unpleasant thought occurred to him, and he said with a delicate shudder, "Why, if you were ill, we might even have to delay our departure!"

Beth smiled with tolerant amusement, guessing that his anxiety to return to Natchez far outweighed his usual concern for her. "I'm feeling much better, Nathan," she answered gently. "I think it was merely that the journey from San Antonio proved more strenuous than I expected."

Nathan seemed satisfied with her explanation, but as they walked toward the *sala,* he glanced at her keenly and asked slowly, "It *was* just the journey, Beth? I saw your face, you know, and you looked as though you had experienced a terrible shock."

Her mouth dry, Beth stared wordlessly back at him. If Nathan guessed in whose house they were, if he realized who Rafael was, it could prove fatal. A duel would be inevitable, and remembering Nathan's ineptness with a pistol, she felt a quiver of fear. At all costs she had to allay Nathan's suspicions. Somehow she summoned a bright, carefree smile and said lightly, "Did I? Well I'm not surprised at all! I felt perfectly horrid! So giddy and nauseous from the ride that I was very much afraid I might faint at your feet—and *that* would have been shocking!"

He remained silent for a moment, his gray eyes searching her face intently. "Yes, I suppose it would have been," he said finally. Flicking an imaginary bit of fluff from his jacket sleeve, he added sedately, "Well, then, now that we have that behind us, shall we join our hosts and Sebastian?"

Hiding her unease, Beth agreed. Had she convinced him? Or increased his suspicions? She greatly feared it was the latter, but there was nothing she could do about it now—they had reached their destination.

Walking calmly into the main room that night, knowing that Lorenzo Mendoza would be there, that her husband was watching her closely, and that Rafael Santana could arrive at any moment, was one of the most difficult things Beth had ever done in her life. Fortunately she was, in her own unassuming manner, a woman with a great deal of inner strength, and so, even though she dreaded the coming evening, she entered the room with outward serenity. And no one seeing her lovely composed features would have guessed that inwardly she was an apprehensive mass of seething, churning emotions.

She saw Lorenzo almost as soon as she entered the room, and her heart sank when she glimpsed the flash of recognition that glittered in his eyes. Recognition—and something else that made her thankful they were meeting in a room full of people.

Lorenzo smiled caressingly at her when they were introduced, his eyes lingering on her mouth, and she knew he was remembering. But instead of being frightened, Beth found herself shaken with rage. How dare he smile at her so! Her eyes sparkling with a temper seldom aroused, Beth stared back defiantly, almost daring him to speak of that despicable afternoon.

Lorenzo had no intention of mentioning what had occurred in New Orleans four years ago. He was no fool and he was well aware that his position was at best precarious. All Beth had to do was open her entrancing mouth and he would find himself looking down the business end of a pistol. Almost as bad, he would lose his patron, Don Miguel, for there was little doubt that the other man would continue to lend his benefaction to someone accused of the crime that Beth could expose. It was absolutely imperative that Beth keep her mouth shut—he had no intention of allowing her to ruin his position. Bending over her hand he muttered, "I must talk to you alone, señora."

Don Miguel, who performed the introductions, had turned away to answer some question his wife asked, and under the cover of his answer to Dona Madelina, Beth hissed, "Are you insane? I have nothing to say to you, and if you are wise you will forget that you ever met me!"

The black eyes cold and calculating, he murmured, "My sentiments exactly!"

Don Miguel turned back just then, and there was no further opportunity for them to speak of an event uppermost in both of their minds.

Overwhelmingly relieved that Lorenzo had no more desire to speak of past history than she did, Beth relaxed slightly. But only slightly, too conscious of the fact that Rafael could appear at any moment, and whatever breathing room she had gained could disappear in an instant.

Dinner was superb, the spicy Spanish and Mexican food pleasantly hot and biting on Beth's tongue, the conversation light and lively, Sebastian and, surprisingly, Nathan both outdoing themselves in being clever and witty. Don Miguel was a charming host, effortlessly putting his guests at ease and conversing on a variety of subjects, which proved that though he and his family lived miles from any sophisticated center he was a man of culture and refinement. Doña Madelina had little to say, but it was obvious she adored her husband and that she was a warm and caring person; her glance was kind and friendly as she surveyed her guests, and an infectious smile was seen frequently on her lips throughout the meal.

Of Lorenzo Beth preferred not to think. She avoided his direction the entire time they sat at a long, elegant table eating dinner. But she could not make him vanish any more than she could banish Rafael from her mind. Staring at the debonair Don Miguel at the head of the table, she found herself unconsciously searching for some resemblance to Rafael, but she could find none, except for the black hair and the thick black eyebrows with their almost wicked slant. Don Miguel's face was kinder, softer, perhaps even weaker than his son's; his dark eyes were inclined to twinkle with amusement, and his chiseled lips quirked easily into a smile; his body was slimmer and shorter than his son's. And yet, when Lorenzo made some comment that annoyed him, he looked very much like Rafael, as his mouth tightened ominously and the black eyes hardened and lost their merry twinkle.

Beth and Doña Madelina left the gentlemen to their cigars and brandy as soon as dinner was finished, and they wandered out to the inner courtyard to enjoy the mild night air. Near the three-tiered fountain they seated themselves in sturdy iron chairs made extremely comfortable by fluffy scarlet cushions, and Doña Madelina reopened the conversation concerning Stella Rodriguez that had started during dinner.

"Imagine your being a friend of Estella's!" Madelina had exclaimed. "I remember how unhappy she was at being sent to school in England, and I couldn't really blame her. Her mother is English, you know, and she was most insistent that Estella attend her old school. So it was off to England for our darling Estella. And to think that now one of her friends from there is traveling to see her! How wonderful!"

Sebastian had obviously not told them of the change in plans, and Beth had hesitated to correct the impression that they were continuing on their journey, but Nathan had shown no such reticence. Blandly he had murmured, "Yes, it was a wonderful idea, but one we find with regret that we shall have to forget. When we leave here, we will be returning home to Natchez—Beth has found the journey simply too, too arduous, and I cannot allow her to damage her fragile health. Of course *I* would much prefer to press on, but you understand the situation."

Beth had nearly choked on her wine and had sent Nathan a speaking glance torn between amusement and annoyance. Nathan had smiled at her sheepishly and somewhat hastily changed the subject. Beyond the expressions of disappointment, the topic was dropped.

But now that she had Beth all to herself, Doña Madelina began, "What a pity that you are not continuing on your journey. After all, you have come a great way to turn back."

Beth made some tactful reply and asked, "Didn't Stella live near here before she and Juan moved to Santa Fe?"

It was the surest way to turn Doña Madelina's thoughts away from the canceled trip. "Oh, yes," she answered instantly. "The Hacienda del Torillo is not more than twenty miles away. Estella was often here at our home as a child—she and my second daughter, María, were great companions. Did you know that Estella is related to us?" Doña Madelina asked curiously, then added deprecatingly, "Of course, it is only distantly, you understand—María married Juan's eldest brother, and they live at the Rodriguez rancho, not more than a day's ride from here." Struck by a sudden thought, Doña Madelina said excitedly, "But of course! I shall send a rider over there tomorrow morning and invite María and Esteban to meet you! I am certain that you will enjoy María's company, and you two will no doubt find it amusing to exchange tales of Estella's escapades—she was always a lively thing."

Hastily Beth said, "Oh, no, Doña Madelina! We do not intend to stay more than a few days. We would not wish to put you to any trouble."

Disappointed, Doña Madelina murmured, "It wouldn't be a bit of trouble, but if you would rather not..."

"It isn't that I wouldn't want to meet your daughter,

it is just that, having made up our minds to return to Natchez, we would like to do it as soon as possible. You do understand?"

Doña Madelina smiled kindly at her. "Yes, my dear, I do. I simply wish that you and your husband were staying longer—we seldom have visitors, and when we do, it is like a holiday. Selfishly we would like it to last as long as possible."

Beth said nothing, wishing passionately that she dared take advantage of the warm hospitality offered. How much she would have enjoyed meeting a friend of Stella's! But it was imperative that they not linger, and so regretfully she changed the subject. "Do you have only the two daughters? Or are there more?"

"There are five," Doña Madelina replied proudly, always delighted to talk of her children. "The older ones are married, with families of their own—two of them in Spain." Her face saddened for a moment. "I miss them dreadfully, but Miguel has promised me that next year we will go to Spain for a long visit. Oh, how I shall enjoy it!"

"And the youngest? Is she not here with you?"

Doña Madelina's lips tightened. "No. Don Felipe, my husband's father, decided that Arabela needed to acquire some sophistication, and so when he departed for Mexico some weeks ago, he insisted she go with him. I did not like it, I can tell you that, but Don Felipe is rather hard to dissuade from any given idea—and my husband will not defy him."

"Perhaps she will like Mexico City," Beth offered gently. "Many young girls would, and I'm certain that she will be a comfort to her grandfather."

"Now, that I rather doubt!" Doña Madelina retorted tartly. Her expression a mixture of pride and uneasiness, she added, "Arabela is a constant joy to us, you understand, but she is so spirited! She does not take kindly to authority, and I am very much afraid Don Felipe will be too strict and she will defy him. My father-in-law has already suggested a match for her, and even though she is just fifteen she has *very* decided views about her future—and she flatly refused to consider it. She is very independent." Doña Madelina sighed. "She reminds me too frequently of her half-brother, Rafael. You may meet him before you leave, and you will see what I mean. He is extremely iron-willed—*nothing* stops him from doing precisely as he pleases! Rafael frightens me a little, but Arabela says that I am just silly."

Beth sent her a strained little smile, thinking that Arabela was the one who was silly. The conversation would have returned to the married daughters at that point had the gentlemen not joined the ladies just then.

At the sight of Lorenzo's swarthy face above his white shirt and gold brocade jacket, Beth's slightly relaxed mood vanished. She avoided his eyes as he attempted to catch her attention and threw herself into a gay, mild flirtation with the delighted Sebastian. But when Sebastian was unwillingly drawn into a conversation with Don Miguel and Nathan, Lorenzo neatly trapped Beth near one end of the courtyard where she had walked to inspect a particularly lovely potted palm tree. Sauntering up to her, he said harshly, "I *must* talk to you."

Her jaw set in a surprisingly hard line, Beth regarded him with open contempt. "And I told you I have nothing to say to you!"

Something ugly entered his eyes, and instinctively Beth stepped away from him, but he captured her wrist and threatened, "Don't scream—just listen to me!"

"I haven't much choice, have I?" she returned tightly. "Unless I wish to cause a scene we both might regret."

Forcing himself to speak calmly, he said softly, "I don't mean you any harm, please believe that. And I have no intention of admitting to anyone that we have met before or of even hinting at the circumstances—can I trust you to do the same?"

Bitterly Beth replied, "I am hardly likely to bring up the subject! But I think you have forgotten that Rafael is expected, and I doubt that *he* will keep his mouth shut."

Lorenzo bit his lip. "I know," he admitted with a slight air of nervousness. "I intend to be gone before he arrives—he and I do not make for agreeable company together." Shooting a glance at Beth from under his lids, he murmured, "He still doesn't know that my dearly departed cousin arranged that little tableau for him—

and somehow, I don't think he is going to inform his father that he caught you and me in an intimate situation. So shall we strike a bargain, you and I? I will forget that we ever met, if you will do the same."

Her flesh crawling with revulsion just talking to him, Beth stared mutinously up at Lorenzo's unnervingly intent features for a long minute, wishing there were some way to expose him to Don Miguel. And wretchedly she realized that it was impossible to do so... without telling the entire sordid tale of that afternoon in New Orleans. It had been hard enough to tell her husband, and even to him she had not revealed names, but to speak of it to a total stranger was beyond her—especially when that stranger was connected to the perpetrators by marriage... and blood. But, disliking it emphatically, she had no choice and so reluctantly she agreed. "Very well. We have never met... and, Lorenzo, I pray God we never meet *again!*"

The black eyes glowed dangerously and his hand tightened painfully around her wrist. "You no more than I, señora," he muttered.

Beth watched him walk away from her with frustrated relief... and unease. There had been something in his tone of voice when he had spoken of his "dearly departed cousin" that left her worried and just a little disquieted. Their bargain galled her; she longed to see him unmasked for the blackguard that he was.

Nathan strolled over to her and, scanning the wrist she was unconsciously rubbing with her other hand, he asked mildly, "Is everything all right with you, my dear? I couldn't help but notice the somewhat intense conversation you were having with that Mendoza fellow. Was he bothering you?"

"Why no, of course not!" Beth replied quickly, hating the lies that were beginning to fall so freely from her lips. "He was just being polite and making small talk—you know how it is."

"Certainly, but it appeared to me to be more than just... small talk."

Desperate to change the subject, Beth retorted with unusual sharpness, "Well, it wasn't! We were only *talking,* Nathan—not making an assignation!"

If Beth had hit him, her husband couldn't have been more surprised. His blond eyebrows soaring in astonishment, he regarded her angry face. There was a painful silence and then Beth murmured miserably, "Forgive me, Nathan. I don't know what has come over me."

"I rather think that you do, my dear," Nathan said slowly a second later. But as Beth opened her mouth to protest, he placed a restraining finger against her lips and stated tranquilly, "Hush, Beth. Something has obviously upset you, I am not blind, you know. But if you don't wish to tell me, fine—forced confidences have never been to my liking." The finger that had been on her lips gently traced her delicate jawline, and, his voice not quite steady, Nathan added, "You know that I care for you as deeply as it is possible for me to care for any woman. Keep your secrets, but remember that I am always at hand."

Beth knew her eyes were damp with tears and unhappily she stammered, "Oh, Nathan, I-I-I..."

Her husband put an end to her dilemma by bending over and softly kissing her lips. Smiling gently, he said, "Good night, Beth. I'll see you in the morning."

Her throat tight and raw with pain, she stared blindly at the flagstones of the courtyard as he walked away from her. If only she dared tell him! How much easier it would make things—but how much *deadlier* might the outcome be. The prospect of Nathan fighting a duel terrified her and there was little likelihood there would *not* be a duel if he knew the truth.

Beth wasted little time in seeking her own bed. She was exhausted emotionally as well as physically, and she yearned for nothing more than the oblivion that came with sleep. Quickly crossing the courtyard, she said good night to Don Miguel and Doña Madelina and absently declined Sebastian's strangely impassioned plea that they take a short walk around the grounds of the hacienda before she retired.

Angrily unhappy, Sebastian was inclined to press the issue, but he was very much aware that Beth was oddly inattentive and so, frustration boiling in his veins, he accepted her negative answer without further argument. Moodily his gaze rested on her face, wondering bleakly why she was now so remote when earlier she had been flirting so enchantingly. He had been elated with the turn of events, certain that he would be able to arrange a secluded meeting where he could reveal his heart's yearnings. The evening had been progressing nicely—until Lorenzo had spoken to her at the end of the courtyard. The green eyes narrowed, and speculatively Sebastian looked at Lorenzo.

Lorenzo was bending over Beth's hand as she said a stilted good night to him, and Sebastian heard his, "It was a pleasure to meet you, Señora Ridgeway. I am just sorry that I may not see you again before you leave."

Don Miguel entered the conversation at that point. "But why not, my friend? Surely you can remain a few days with us?"

Lorenzo looked at him meaningfully. "Have you forgotten that your son is due to arrive?"

Don Miguel gave a cluck of annoyance. "You two hotheaded fools! Why you cannot settle whatever differences you have between you and become friends I do not understand. You are part of our family, and this nonsense must stop!" he said with some heat.

Dryly Lorenzo replied, "Tell that to Rafael!"

Don Miguel pulled a face. "Oh, do whatever you like—you both will anyway," he retorted irritably, washing his hands of the situation.

Beth did not linger after that, and it was a relief to know that at least she need not fear that Lorenzo would reveal their earlier meeting. But if Beth had known what was in Lorenzo's mind as he rode away from the hacienda that night, she would not have gone to bed so encouraged.

It was a dark night, the moon not even half full, but Lorenzo pushed his horse hard—he had many miles to travel before too much time elapsed. Particularly if he was to arrange an explicitly *final* end to the Ridgeways' journey back to Natchez.

If Beth had been dismayed at Lorenzo's presence, *he* had been both dumbstruck and furious. A cold, deadly fury raged in his blood as he thought of how easily she could destroy his standing with Don Miguel—with *all* of the aristocratic families that now looked upon him as an agreeable gentleman. A gentleman who had amassed a sizeable fortune in just a few years and who came from a good family and who might be an acceptable son-in-law. Lorenzo had paid flattering attention to every rich Spanish family with a marriageable daughter too assiduously, too determinedly over the years to have Beth Ridgeway destroy all his plans. His final choice for a worthy bride had fallen on Arabela de la Santana—with Rafael dead, in time he would see himself as Don Miguel's heir. As for the other members of the family, he smiled cruelly. If they proved obstructive he could take care of them—the Comanches left no witnesses.

After Consuela's death only three people knew what really happened that afternoon in New Orleans. Lorenzo had dismissed Manuela as a danger long ago. She was only a servant, and who would believe her word over his? Besides, she was too frightened of what might happen to herself if she ever revealed the truth, and so he had taken no steps to still her tongue. But Beth Ridgeway was something else again, and he was taking no chances. If she had shown up once unexpectedly in Texas she could do so again, or their paths could cross somewhere else in the future when he least expected it, and he wasn't willing to run the risk. Somewhere between San Antonio and the Texas coast, the Ridgeway party would meet with disaster. Disaster in the shape of a Comanche raiding party....

Beth did not know of Lorenzo's deadly plans for her, but sleep proved just as elusive as it would have if she had been privy to them. She lay wearily in the handsome bed for what seemed an eternity, her thoughts scrambling wildly through her brain as she tried uselessly to sleep. Eventually, when she knew dawn could not be far, she slipped from her bed, pulled on her peignoir, and wandered out into the deserted inner courtyard seeking its peacefulness.

CHAPTER TWELVE

The courtyard was a beautiful place, she thought appreciatively, seating herself on the edge of the stone fountain and trailing one hand in the cool water. It was rectangular, completely enclosed by the four walls of the *casa grande*. The front of the *casa grande* was two-storied; Beth could look up and see the black filigreed-iron balconies garlanded with clinging bougainvillaea vines. The other three wings of the house were single-storied, appearing much wider than they actually were because the roofs had been extended to create the cool, wide arcades that served as hallways throughout the entire house. The extended red-tiled roofs were supported by graceful arches that bespoke the Moorish influence so prevalent in Spanish buildings, and from where Beth sat the arches resembled huge, curved windows draped in purple velvet.

It was silent in the courtyard except for the soothing sound of the water in the fountain. Silent and peaceful, the shapes and shadows of the tubs of plants, the iron chairs and round filigree tables muted softly in grays and mauves as the moon slowly disappeared before the sun took its place in the heavens. The stars had vanished and there was that slight chill in the air that precedes dawn. No one, not even the servants, was stirring yet. Once, though, Beth was certain that she heard the crow of a cock from one of the adobe houses near the hacienda.

Afterward she was never quite certain what caused her to glance over her shoulder. Had he made some sound when he entered the courtyard and saw her sitting there? Or had premonition compelled her to look in that direction? Whatever the reason, when she turned she saw Rafael Santana standing there in the dim, pre-dawn moments staring at her.

He stood in the shadows, more a disturbing presence than an actual form, but Beth recognized him instantly. It was not his height or the breadth of his shoulders that identified him, but the menacing stillness of a lethal predator that he so effortlessly projected. Not a word was said as they regarded each other across the long flagstone patio. Beth's heart was lodged somewhere in the back of her throat, and it was beating with such frantic painful strokes that she thought she would faint.

Rafael remained in the shadows, making no effort to ease the tension that suddenly charged the silence, making no effort to lessen the air of animal awareness that seemed to flow from him into the courtyard. Unable to move, unable to utter a sound, Beth sat frozen, her eyes straining to pierce the shadows around him to see if in fact it was the man that every instinct cried out it must be.

From her position at the edge of the fountain, she could just discern his shape, the tall, virile strength of him, and the faint scent of tobacco that drifted across the courtyard to assail her nostrils. Every nerve, every muscle, every fiber in her body was aware of him there in the shadows; every instinct, every emotion screamed that she should escape, and yet she was helpless to do so, her body seeming rooted to the fountain. How long, she wondered frantically, how long will he allow this dreadful moment to last?

Not long, it appeared. The tip of his cigarillo flamed brightly red and it made a fiery streak in the mauve shadows of dawn as he tossed it carelessly away. Deliberately he stepped from under the arch that had obscured him and stood revealed in the faint light.

Beth's first impression was that he hadn't changed a great deal in four years; the gray eyes were just as empty, although she thought she detected a hint of furious astonishment in them; the lean face was just as dangerously attractive; and the slim-hipped, long-legged figure was just as devastatingly male as it had been the night of the Costa soiree in New Orleans. But there was a definite change in him—if possible a deadlier emptiness to the eyes, a more cynical slant to the arrogant mouth, and there was definitely a difference in apparel.

Both times she had seen him—and it came as a stunning surprise to realize that she had only seen him twice in her life for the impact he had made upon it—he had been dressed in the clothes befitting a man of wealth and breeding, the trappings of a rich aristocrat. But such was not the case at the moment. Now he truly resembled the "renegade" of his name: the faint shadow of a day or two's beard darkening his jawline, the well-worn black *calzoneras,* showing their age and wear while clinging smoothly to his muscled thighs; the blue calico shirt of the kind a common *vaquero* would wear. A short black *chaqueta,* despite its dusty appearance, fitted his broad shoulders expertly, and the wide leather belt with its holster and jutting revolver increased his likeness to a desperado. Almost absently she noticed the large sombrero which hung carelessly from one hand, and the faint ruffle of the thick, unkempt blue-black hair as it was caressed lightly by a little breeze that suddenly swooped down into the courtyard.

He began to walk without haste toward her and, staring mutely into the cold, expressionless features, some of Beth's paralysis vanished and she rose slowly to her feet. And as he continued his unswerving approach, she was almost glad that the waiting was over, the uncertainties finished—whatever tenuous bond there was between them could finally and forever be broken.

Rafael's advance was indolent, his movements arrogantly graceful, almost insulting in the measured, unhurried steps he took. He halted abruptly barely a foot from her, his eyes brazenly assessing her, taking in the delicate peignoir, the agitated rise and fall of her small breasts, the gold-tipped lashes which framed wide eyes that were nearly purple with apprehension—and defiance.

He took his time with the blatant appraisal, still making no effort to banish the almost physical presence of tension that surrounded them. The gray eyes moved with insolent slowness over her face, lingering for a long agonizing moment on her mouth before slipping to her white throat, where the rapid beat of her pulse was very apparent, and then flicked suddenly and insultingly down her entire body before his gaze returned to her face.

"English," he said slowly, rolling the syllables off his tongue as if until that moment he had not been quite certain of her identity.

Beth swallowed painfully, wanting rashly to make some sound, some rejoinder, to say something that would give her the opportunity to lessen the tautness between them. But her tongue as well as her brain seemed frozen, and she could only stand there, nearly trembling with the force of the conflicting, turbulent emotions that coursed wildly through her blood. The wariness and nervousness she expected, but she wasn't prepared for the queer excitement that vibrated in her blood or the quick rush of fierce joy at seeing those dark, arrogant features again.

Rafael waited almost patiently for her to make some reply, but when several minutes had passed and Beth remained silent, her eyes locked hypnotically on his, he murmured, "Nothing to say? Perhaps it is just as well, for I do believe I did warn you to stay away from me, didn't I?"

She found her voice at that and stammered, "B-b-but I . . . it isn't . . . I didn't . . ." Stopping in sheer nervousness, she took a deep breath and said honestly, "I had no idea that *you* would be here! You must believe me! If Sebastian had mentioned your name just once we would never have—"

Her words were broken off sharply as Rafael moved with the swiftness of a striking panther, one steel-fingered hand closing with painful strength around her upper arm. The thick, arching black eyebrows snapping together in a frown and the gray eyes narrowing with sudden suspicion, Rafael snapped, "Sebastian? What does Sebastian have to do with you?" Comprehension dawning in that instant and his grip bruising the soft flesh, he said accusingly, "It was *you* he met on the ship! Of course, it has to be—his 'angel' is none other than the whoring little slut I met in New Orleans four years ago! What an unfortunate coincidence for you, English."

Beth's lips parted to protest, but Rafael gave her no chance. Jerking her up against his hard body, he threatened softly, "Leave Sebastian Savage alone, English! Work your wiles on someone who understands your kind of woman, but leave that boy alone! Do you understand me?"

"But I haven't—" Beth started to contradict, but she was never able to finish the sentence, for Rafael shook her ungently and snarled, "Quiet! I have neither the inclination nor the patience to listen to the lies that I am sure will fall sweetly from your lips. I don't know what you are up to, but one thing is for damn sure—you're leaving here!"

Some of the shock at seeing him so unexpectedly had faded, and Beth found that she was becoming angry, *very* angry at his confident assumption that he could just order her away. The violet eyes sparkling with temper, she furiously attempted to shake herself free of Rafael's increasingly brutal grasp, but his grip only tightened, the fingers biting bruisingly into her arm. "Let me go, you arrogant beast!" she said in a low, incensed tone of voice. Then, the sudden temper pushing her beyond her usual constraint, she spat, "How dare you speak to me in this fashion! Sebastian invited my husband and me to visit. Your parents, unlike you, have been most kind to us, and I refuse to insult their hospitality simply because you demand it!" Her breath coming in hard, angry gasps, she rushed on, "Do you think that for one moment I would have accepted Sebastian's invitation if I'd the slightest inkling that *you* were related to him?" She gave an odd choke of bitter laughter, "You are the last person I wished to meet! I detest you, Rafael Santana—you are a conceited overbearing devil!"

A derisive twist to his mouth, Rafael murmured, "How well you do it, English. All this, this outrage is so very sincere that if I didn't know better I would be tempted to believe you." He shook her roughly, adding, "You forget, *querida*, that I know you for what you are."

"You don't know me at all!" Beth snapped, her eyes flashing. "And from the way you have acted the few times I have met you, *I* have no desire to further my acquaintance with *you!* Now either release me or I shall be forced to cause an extremely embarrassing scene for both of us."

"Embarrassed? Me? English, I think you must have forgotten what little you may have learned about me four years ago. I don't," he said with deceptive gentleness, "*ever* embarrass. If you would like to scream and wake the hacienda, by all means do so. Besides, I am rather curious to meet this husband of yours—he appears to be a singularly complacent gentleman."

Beth nibbled her lip indecisively, wanting passionately to cause a scene of such epic proportions that Rafael *would* be shaken from his infuriating self-assurance and yet terrified of the ensuing commotion. But more than that she was unwilling to risk a confrontation between this man and Nathan. If Rafael was as cold-blooded and indifferent as he gave every indication of being, creating an ugly furor would accomplish nothing and would precipitate the one thing she feared most—a duel between Rafael and Nathan. Yet she was *so* enraged with his arrogant behavior that she longed to do something totally out of character for her, longed with increasing ferocity to strike and claw at his mocking face and jolt him from his scornful stance. Caution won out... this time, but her voice was shaking with suppressed anger as she stuttered, "L-l-leave m-m-my husband out of this! You have no right to assume anything about him! He is *not* complacent! He is a very nice man, a gentleman—something you could never be."

The gray eyes never left her face and his expression never changed except for one of those thick, black eyebrows, which rose in jeering disbelief. "Such a spirited defense! If I were not wise to your chicanery, English, I might find your words somewhat admirable, but as it is, I only find them a pathetic ruse."

Genuinely bewildered, Beth repeated stupidly, "Ruse? I'm afraid I don't understand what you mean."

Rafael smiled icily. "Sebastian is the one person I

am concerned about at the moment, *not* your husband, so do not attempt to change the subject."

"But you," Beth burst out heatedly, "you were the one who brought Nathan into this, not me!"

"Perhaps, but it matters little. What matters to me is your relationship with my cousin—if your husband is willing to allow you to parade your latest lover under his nose, that is his business! But when that newest conquest is Sebastian, then it becomes my business!"

Unable to help herself, Beth taunted, "Is Sebastian so weak that he cannot defend himself... against a mere woman?"

Rafael's face tightened, and if it were possible his grip on her arm grew more painful. "Do not," he said from between clenched teeth, "push me too far, English. I have ridden many miles to reach here, and I am tired and in no mood to exchange impudent remarks with you."

"Then don't!" Beth retorted instantly, wondering distressfully how he had so easily aroused a sleeping tigress that seemed to lurk deep within her and changed her into a volatile creature she did not recognize. Or was the roused tigress the real Beth, set free from all the suffocating precepts she had practiced all her life? It was an uncomfortable idea at any time and she certainly didn't need to explore it now, she thought angrily, hastily pushing it from her mind. No, now she needed all her wits about her, especially as she became more and more aware that a new disturbing element had entered the conflict between them. Incredibly, insidiously, she was becoming conscious of the sensual attraction of his lean, hard body so close to hers, remembering against her will what it felt like to have his hands on her breasts, how that recklessly slanted mouth plundered her lips.

Rafael was instantly aware of the unexpected change in the atmosphere, the gray eyes compulsively dropping again and again to the soft mouth just below his, his body very conscious of the fact that the lacy peignoir hid the silken curves and warm flesh that had given him countless nights of restless sleep before he had been able to tear it from his mind. That she had once had the power to trouble his thoughts enraged him, that she had dared to intrude upon his life again infuriated him. That she was the woman, the "angel" of Sebastian's outpourings, woke a violent feeling he had never before experienced in his life, but he recognized it with a dull sort of rage as jealousy. Furious and perhaps just a little staggered by that knowledge, he deliberately twisted her arm behind her back and, crushing her slim body up against his, he snarled harshly, "Stop arguing with me, you little slut, and listen to what I say! I don't care what kind of excuse you use, I don't give a damn how rude it may appear, but you goddamn *will* get yourself and your accommodating husband out of here today!"

Physically aware of her as he was, bringing her soft body next to his probably wasn't the wisest thing he could have done. With her breasts thrusting tantalizingly against his chest, the slender legs pressing intimately against his thighs, and her sweet lavender scent in his nostrils, Rafael was not immune to the fierce onslaught of desire that shook his body. He could feel himself stir and harden with a devastating hunger to feel this supple silken body beneath his and to taste the sweet mouth that had haunted him. The gray eyes darkening with passion, his cruel grasp unconsciously slackened and rhythmically his thumb began to caress the shapely arm he held. It was madness, he thought savagely, knowing he should fling her from him and yet unable to do so. With a muffled curse he threw restraint to the winds and brought his mouth down hard on hers.

Beth sensed the moment his mood changed and, fighting against herself as much as Rafael, she contrarily attempted to avoid his kiss, but he had her too firmly entrapped, the sombrero fluttering to the flagstones as he brought his other hand up to capture her opposite shoulder. Caught in his strong arms, Beth was helpless against the hungrily seeking mouth which thoroughly explored hers, his tongue forcing its way between her teeth, probing and darting, exciting, inflaming even as it enraged. What little control she had on her suddenly unruly temper evaporated and like a small, snared wildcat, she began to fight, twisting and turning, her fists beating furiously against him in her violent struggles to escape. Rafael only tightened his embrace, his mouth roaming freely across her face, leaving burning kisses that seared her temple and cheeks.

"English, English," he murmured into her neck, his tongue gently tracing a faint blue vein whose frantic pounding betrayed her susceptibility to his lovemaking. "I did warn you in New Orleans, didn't I? I seem to recall that I cautioned you to stay out of my territory . . . and that if you intruded into my life I would treat you as you deserved. You didn't heed me, did you?"

Beth stiffened in his arms, her furious fight to free herself ceasing abruptly. "If you will just listen to me!" she cried indignantly. "I didn't follow you out here and I had no idea that Sebastian was related to you! Do you honestly think that I would have intentionally sought you out after four years!" The violet eyes disdainful, she asked hotly, "What kind of a conceited fool do you take me for? I am not, nor have I ever been the type of creature that you think. Your wife *arranged* for you to find Lorenzo and me! And if you would just stop being so eager to believe ill of me, I could explain exactly what happened that afternoon."

At first Rafael seemed to be listening intently to her, his eyes fastened piercingly upon hers, and Beth had taken hope that at last the vicious misconception could be clarified. But as soon as she mentioned that ghastly afternoon, his face closed up and a sardonic expression crept into his eyes. His lips slanting with a mirthless smile, he slowly shook his head. "No, English. Don't. That subject is as dead as Consuela, and I do not want to discuss it—ever!"

Beth drew a shaky breath as a dreadful feeling of defeat spread through her. He was so implacable, so determined *not* to believe her, that she knew with a sickening lurch of her heart that it was useless to persist—Manuela had been right, he would *never* accept the truth. Fighting back an inexplicable urge to cry, she said quietly, "Very well. If you will not listen, if you have your mind so stubbornly set against me, then we do indeed have nothing to discuss. As that appears to be the case, I would appreciate it if you would allow me to return to my rooms."

"Certainly. I was about to suggest that we adjourn to either your room or mine so we can finish what we just started in comfort and privacy." A crooked smile lifting one corner of his mouth, he added, "There is little that I may do that would shock my family, but awakening and finding me making love to one of their guests in the middle of the courtyard might discompose them a little."

Unable to believe that she had heard him correctly, but very much afraid that she had, Beth stared at him with growing uneasiness. "You don't mean—! I don't want you to—!" Gathering her scattered wits, she finally got out: "Señor, if you think I have any intention of allowing you the liberties you took in New Orleans, you very much mistake the matter! I intend to return to my rooms—alone! I do not want or need or even desire *your* company!"

Rafael only smiled, a smile that was not reflected in the gray eyes. "No, madame, *you* mistake the matter! I have been a long while without a woman and, considering how free you are with your favors—what is one more man?"

Whatever leash Beth had placed on her temper vanished, and before she had time to consider the repercussions, her open palm connected with gratifying satisfaction against Rafael's lean cheek. "You animal!" she spat furiously, the violet eyes blazing with outrage and fury.

She was incredibly lovely as she stood slim and straight before him, the fair hair falling around her shoulders, the long gold-tipped lashes intensifying the amethyst blue of her eyes, and the small bosom heaving with resentment. For just a moment Rafael felt something tighten and coil agonizingly in his gut, and because of that, because he was perhaps caught off guard by his own emotions, he didn't strike her back as he would have done normally. Instead, with a smothered oath he swung her up in his arms. "I think this conversation has gone on long enough," he snarled. "And

I hope to God Doña Madelina has placed you in the gold rooms where she does most guests, because, sweetheart that's where we're going! Pray, English, that your husband does not share your bed this night, because if he does I am positive we are all in for an enlightening scene." And with that his mouth trapped hers, effectively stopping the scream that was rising in her throat. Beth strained frantically to escape him, but she was helplessly caught up in his arms. Ignoring her muffled cries, oblivious of her furious thrashing, Rafael sauntered almost leisurely to the gold rooms. Neither of them was aware of an astonished and disbelieving Sebastian who stood transfixed in the doorway of his rooms.

Sebastian hadn't been certain what woke him. With an inbred curiosity he had gotten out of bed and pulled on a pair of trousers, then opened the door to his suite of rooms. Glancing out into the courtyard, he saw that Rafael had arrived; he hadn't really even noticed Beth's presence before Rafael had swooped her up in his arms and carried her like a piece of booty out of sight. His mouth falling open in dumbstruck amazement, he stood there for several seconds not quite believing what he had seen.

Completely unaware of Sebastian's view of them, upon reaching the door of the rooms he wanted, hardly halting in his stride, almost carelessly Rafael kicked open the door and once inside slammed it shut with a powerful thrust of his shoulder.

Leaning comfortably against the door, Rafael slowly released Beth, letting her slender body slide down the length of his hard muscles. Imperceptibly the pressure of his mouth slackened and, no longer hurting her, the firm lips began to explore her mouth, his tongue once again forcing its way into the inner sweetness.

"Mmm, English, I think I have missed you," he said finally, raising his head slightly, the gray eyes nearly black with passion.

Beth drew a long shuddering breath, her emotions in such a turmoil that she couldn't begin to think coherently. To her burning mortification, she discovered that Rafael still exercised an unfair power over her body. She hungered for the feel of his body next to hers, and his deliberately arousing kisses went to her head like fine wine. She knew she should fight against him, knew that even now she should scream and alert the house, but in her hidden heart she didn't want to—she wanted him, and at the moment nothing else mattered very much but that Rafael was here and she was in his arms.

But she did make one last attempt. Her voice hardly above a whisper, she said, "Rafael, please don't do this to me. Please leave these rooms and allow me to keep my pride—it-it isn't asking a great deal of you."

His eyebrow rose mockingly. "Since when have whores had pride?" he sneered, very clearly remembering her in Lorenzo's arms. "No, English, I will not leave nor will I be deterred from having that lovely little body of yours." His eyes hardening, he added, "If you find me too repugnant after all your other lovers, close your eyes and imagine I am your husband."

Beth's gasp of outrage was lost as Rafael's mouth urgently sought hers and angrily she fought against the treacherous leap of her pulse as his warm lips moved with growing hunger on hers. She wanted to resist him, wanted, not so surprisingly, to slap his arrogant face again, but she had no defenses against the potent magic he wreaked upon her awakening senses—her body betraying her—and with a small moan of defeat her arms closed around his hard body and she returned his kisses ardently, reveling in the feel of his muscled chest against her breasts.

His lips never leaving hers, Rafael swept her up in his arms once again and carried her into the bedchamber. With a strange gentleness he laid her on the wide bed, his own body resting lightly on hers. Then, pushing himself away, swiftly, yet with controlled deft movements, he began to strip off his clothes, his eyes always on Beth's enchantingly flushed features.

Wanting to look away but driven by some inner need, Beth watched him. She had never really seen a naked man before, and now she found herself intensely curious about the male body—especially *this* male body!

Rafael, with his Comanche blood and upbringing, was indifferent to nakedness and there was, as in most of his actions, almost an arrogant pride in revealing himself to the woman who lay on the bed, her gaze oddly shy as it rested on him. He removed his boots first, the spurs jingling slightly as he tossed them aside, and with an emotion bordering on hysteria Beth was almost surprised that he didn't have the cloven hooves of Satan, so easily had he destroyed her desire to resist him. But from then on she had no time for such thoughts—instead she was caught and entrapped by the sheer magnificence of the tall masculine body before her.

Rafael's shoulders were broad, the arms revealing their well-honed muscles with every movement he made as first the black *chaqueta* and then the calico shirt were shrugged off and his chest with its smooth, almost hairless width was bared, the bronzed skin hardly a shade different from the dark face above it. Her eyes widened with astonishment when a moment later he laid a wide, wicked-looking knife that had been concealed under his clothes on top of the shirt. Then, the muscles of his powerful upper torso bunching and rippling, with an abrupt, almost violent tug he undid the leather gun belt, and after a quick all-encompassing glance around the room he placed the gun on a nearby chair—far enough away from Beth, yet close enough should he need it in a hurry. Nearly mesmerized, Beth stared back at him, noting the lean stomach and the first beginnings of the line of black hair that disappeared tantalizingly beneath the worn *calzoneras*. There was no disguising his arousal underneath the snug fabric, yet when at last the *calzoneras* were discarded, Beth drew in her breath sharply at the sight of his rigid maleness jutting fiercely from the tangle of thick black curly hair. Suffering a sudden attack of agonizing embarrassment, she swiftly dropped her eyes, staring blindly at the long well-shaped legs.

Time had seemed suspended as he had undressed, but when he joined her on the bed, Beth was instantly galvanized into frenzied action and she made one more frantic bid to escape him. As his arms reached hungrily for her, she suddenly twisted away, determined that if she could just reach the door that led to the courtyard, her own embarrassment aside, she would scream the hacienda down. For one tiny second she thought she had succeeded in her attempt to elude him, her wild unexpected movement catching Rafael off guard, and he delayed a heartbeat before springing upon her like a tiger on a fawn. Their bodies entwined, they rolled, twisted, and battled their way across the bed, the sheets and blankets tangling and coiling about them. Beth fought with a feverish intensity, her clenched fists striking Rafael on the face and shoulders, her body jerking and writhing in a furious effort to throw him off, to escape the steel fingers and arms that were inexorably winning the war between them. She bit his ear in desperation and with a certain amount of guilty satisfaction she heard the muffled curse he gave before he freed himself from her small white teeth.

They were breathing heavily, their breath intermingling even as their bodies did, until at last Rafael's much greater strength subdued Beth. His body trapping her against the bed, both her hands held tightly above her head in one of his, his other hand captured her chin and forced her wildly thrashing head still. For a moment they were both motionless, the black-lashed gray eyes staring intently into the wide rebellious violet ones.

For a timeless second Rafael's gaze searched her face, appreciating her disheveled beauty—the incredibly fair ash-blond curls tumbling in wild disorder across the pillows, the startling violet eyes with their long lashes, the faint pink flush of her cheeks, and the almost irresistible lure of the soft rosy mouth. His eyes seemed to be riveted there for a long time, but then they dropped to the small firm breasts that had become exposed during the struggle. The cambric peignoir as well as her thin nightgown was twisted up around her hips. The front of the peignoir had been ripped open during their ensuing fight, and half of the tiny bows that held her nightgown closed had become loosened, causing that garment to give little protection from Rafael's roaming eyes. With tormenting slowness he lowered his head and gently, deliberately nuzzled the smooth skin between her breasts, breathing in the scent of her and tasting the honey of her flesh before his mouth unerringly sought and found one breast. In spite of her determination to deny him, Beth's entire body jumped with shocked pleasure at the touch of that warm seeking mouth on her breast, her nipples hardening into tight, aching rosebuds that unashamedly begged him to continue as his tongue flicked and teased first one and then the other.

"Oh, please, please, stop!" she whispered in an anguished tone of voice, knowing that at any moment she was going to lose complete control of herself and give in to the mortifying swirling ache of desire that had attacked her body at Rafael's first searing kiss.

Rafael raised his head and sent her a cool, oddly assessing look. A half-mocking, half-rueful smile suddenly curving his full mouth, he shook his head and then, the smile fading, he trapped her lips with his.

He took his time kissing her, savoring the softness and warmth of her mouth. It was a strangely gentle kiss, unhurried and yet seeking and demanding at the same time, his tongue like a dart of fire thoroughly exploring and probing the inner sweetness. He captured her hands above her head while his other hand blatantly traveled over her slender body, methodically and determinedly undoing the rest of the peignoir and gown until the entire length of her was naked under him.

His kiss was nearly Beth's undoing, the touch of his mouth inflaming her further, arousing expertly all the sleeping passions that she had held in check for so long. Yet she fought against it, trying desperately to ignore the hot, hungry emotions that suddenly clawed their way through her body. Liquid fire flowed in her veins and her body no longer paid any heed to the frantic signals that her brain was sending, her breasts aching to feel Rafael's mouth again and her hips unconsciously seeking him, her lips brazenly allowing him to ravage her mouth.

She fought the silent battle within herself for as long as she could, but Rafael was no stumbling lover, no Nathan fumbling in the dark. He was an experienced man, a man who, when he wanted, knew how to please a woman; he was aware that Beth was fighting to remain indifferent and he deliberately broke down her fragile barriers, one by one. His lips were warm and firm and they cajoled, caressed and demanded that she surrender as they traveled from her softly bruised mouth across her jawline to nip half painfully, half caressingly at her earlobe, the tip of his tongue warmly searching out the shape and texture of her ear before returning with renewed hunger to her mouth. The one hand that had so expertly undone her clothing now began a featherlight exploration of her body, first gently cupping one swollen breast, his thumb rhythmically brushing the nipple, and then slowly, tormentingly, his hand slid down her body, caressing her silken skin as it went. Giving a small, strangled sound of defeat deep in her throat, Beth abandoned the unfair fight, her body melting into his, wanting now only to be possessed by him, to learn truly what it meant to be a woman.

She had been half drugged with belladonna the first time he had taken her and the emotions and sensations she was experiencing now were in a sense all new, all frightening and intoxicating, and her body was both eager and apprehensive—wanting and yet fearful. And so when Rafael's hand continued its exploration, brushing lightly and tantalizingly across her flat stomach, seeking the softness of her inner thighs, Beth was totally unprepared for the jolt of raw desire that hit her. Uncontrollably her body arched and twisted under his touch and his mouth lowered to her breasts, his teeth grazing the throbbing nipples, his free hand gently sliding along the inside of her thighs, willfully increasing the tight ache of anticipation that was spreading like wildfire through her blood.

When at last he did touch her there between her thighs, his fingers almost tenderly parting the silken flesh, probing and exploring, Beth gave a soft, shaken moan of pleasure. No longer wishing to fight him, wanting now only to caress and explore the long, lean body that was creating such sweet havoc with hers, her hands moved restlessly, unceasingly in the tight hold that he still retained.

Rafael had no intention of freeing her this time, the savage Comanche hunter that was so much a part of him enjoying the sensual brush of her naked, thrashing body against his as she struggled to free herself. Another time, another place and he would revel in her caresses, but at this moment he wanted to conquer her—to make her want him as she had wanted no other man, to drive her as mad with passion as she had him and to punish and yet pleasure her at the same time.

For Beth it was an exquisite agony, his lips and roaming hand exciting and arousing her in a manner she had never dreamed, and yet she was held helpless in his iron grip, able only to experience, to feel, to yield and not able to touch him, not able to discover his body as she hungrily longed to do. Nor was she able to prevent him from doing exactly what he pleased with her slender body, his mouth like a flick of fire running hot and passionate over her heated skin, tasting and nuzzling her shoulders, her neck, her breasts, and even, to her astonished pleasure, her flat, trembling stomach, while the fingers of his free hand penetrated gently between her thighs as he deliberately brought her to a shuddering, begging peak of desire.

But Beth was not the only one receiving pleasure from this half-rape, half-seduction; Rafael, too, was aroused to a point he had never felt possible, and yet, strangely enough, with his body tight and raging with desire, he forced himself to hold back, to prolong the aching pleasure of anticipation. She was so incredibly beautiful, with her flawless features and moonbeam hair, the small, slender body so perfectly formed, the skin so warm and silken to his touch, that he was like a starving man finding sustenance, his mouth almost devouring hers in his hunger, his free hand urgently, compulsively preparing the way for the deeply passionate mating of his body with hers.

Her body trembling with the force of the sensual emotions so violently unleashed by Rafael's half-savage, half-tender lovemaking, Beth was drowing in a sea of such exquisite pleasure that helplessly a soft muted plea broke from her, "Oh, please, *please*..."—only, to her intense shame, it was for him to continue, *not* to stop!

Rafael heard her involuntary words and with a low, satisfied growl deep in his throat, he swiftly covered her body with his. Using both of his hands to hold her arms on either side of her head, his knees nudged her thighs apart and the swollen rigid length of him plunged fiercely into the excited warmth of her.

In almost stunned acceptance, Beth felt her body fill with him, the delicate softness forced to accommodate the warm, hard, invading shaft of living flesh. He lay lightly on her for a long moment, his breath coming in gasping, hurtful breaths as if he were fighting to control himself, and Beth was overwhelmingly conscious of so many things about him—of the almost aphrodisiac scent of the aroused male; of the faint hint of horses and tobacco that clung to him; of his lean chest, smooth and disturbingly hot against her breasts; of his long body, joined so intimately with hers—and a muffled moan of pleasure escaped her, wanting him to continue this unashamedly sensual assault on her body. Unaware that she did it, her mouth sought his longingly, and Rafael instantly pressed his lips almost savagely against hers, his tongue feverishly exploring her mouth.

With a slow, tormenting pleasure he began to move on her, and instinctively Beth's hips rose to meet him, and as his movements quickened so did hers, until their bodies were meeting each other with a growing, flaming, driving urgency. Her head spinning madly, her body in the grip of such erotic abandonment that she became like a wild creature, her slender form writhed and twisted beneath the thrusting hunger of his, small animallike sounds of gratification coming from her throat. Suddenly, when she thought she could not bear the almost painful ache of pleasure that was coiling in her loins one moment longer, there was a wash of pleasure so intense, so achingly blissful that her entire body stiffened from it, her eyes flying open in a dazed breathless wonderment. Wave after wave of the most intense physical sensations she had ever experienced swept over her, her body feeling as if it had shattered into a thousand pieces of trembling, throbbing pleasure. She knew she groaned deep in her throat, but she couldn't control it any more than she could control the shudder Rafael's body gave when he, too, at last reached that pinnacle of pleasure and spilled himself inside her.

CHAPTER THIRTEEN

Still half-stunned by what she had just experienced, Beth remained motionless when Rafael released her arms and slid off her body, flinging himself face down beside her in the bed. Almost instantly, though, he reached up and captured the slender wrist nearest to him in an iron grip, as if even then he feared she would try to escape him. But at the moment Beth was too bewildered by her body's responses to his lovemaking to do more than make a token attempt to free herself from him, an attempt that was easily and insultingly, effortlessly foiled.

It was silent in the room except for their soft, muted breathing, and almost blindly Beth stared up at the white ceiling above, wondering at the ease with which her previously well-ordered life was falling in shambles about her. She had lied to her husband for the first time in their marriage just this past evening, and now, merely hours later, she had betrayed him physically. That she had also learned what was really meant by "making love" she pushed to the back of her mind, willing herself to think only of Nathan and their rapidly deteriorating relationship. Of Rafael, lying naked and disturbingly vital at her side, she refused to think; she would not speculate on the power this man seemed to wield over her usually calm and unruffled temperament.

If only she had never decided to embark upon this undeniably mad journey none of this would have happened, she thought wretchedly. She and Nathan would have lived out their lives in platonic tranquillity, he following his way of life and she, if not happy, at least satisfied with her lot in life. Nathan's kindly, concerned face suddenly swam in her vision and she felt a knot of tears clog the back of her throat as she remembered many of the truly happy times they had spent together.

"What are you thinking about?" Rafael asked abruptly, startling her into awareness that he still lay by her side.

She had been so lost in her own miserable thoughts that she hadn't noticed when he had changed positions, and she discovered that now he was propped up on one elbow staring intently down into her sad little face.

She swallowed with difficulty before saying honestly, "My husband."

The dark features froze, and Beth had the curious conviction that while her words had infuriated him, they had also given him a shock. His wide mouth curling sneeringly at the corners, he snarled softly, "Afraid he might enter and find us together? Or were you comparing our sexual prowess?"

Flooded with a sudden giddying burst of anger, Beth met his gray-eyed stare and retorted swiftly, "There is no comparison! In any contest that I could think of, Nathan Ridgeway would outstrip you with little or no effort. Now get out of my bed—and I shall do my utmost to be gone from here within the hour!"

"No." He said the word flatly, unemotionally, the expression in the black-lashed eyes hidden and inscrutable.

Bewilderment flashing across her expressive features, Beth blurted out, "But you said—you said that we must leave immediately! You demanded it!"

His gaze fixed on her soft mouth, he murmured huskily, "I've changed my mind."

"You can't change your mind!" she insisted angrily. "You can't!"

A thick black eyebrow soaring mockingly, Rafael contradicted her calmly. "I not only can, English, I have."

"Why?" she demanded instantly, the violet eyes fixed warily upon him.

"Let's just say that I would rather keep you in sight until I'm certain Sebastian has gotten over his unfortunate attachment."

Her jaw taking on a surprisingly mulish slant, Beth said mutinously, "Sebastian has nothing to do with this!

And you can't stop me from leaving either! You dare not hold my husband and me against our will."

"No, perhaps not," he said slowly, and something in the way he looked at her caused a shiver of apprehension to slide down her spine. Furious with herself for allowing him to even for one moment intimidate her, Beth began to struggle violently to free her wrist he still held captive, clawing recklessly at the hand that held her trapped, wanting nothing more than to be free of him in all ways. For several seconds Rafael dispassionately watched her frantic movements and then almost contemptuously he tossed her wrist away.

Instantly Beth scrambled away, crouching on the opposite side of the bed like a violet-eyed, silver-pelted spitting kitten. The unfastened peignoir and gown barely hid her body, the smooth alabaster skin and the taut, rose-tipped breasts tantalizingly exhibited to Rafael's narrowed-eyed gaze. My God, but she was lovely, he thought with a sharp intake of breath, feeling himself harden with a raging desire to feel that soft white body under his again. But with an effort he stilled the impulse to drag her into his arms and to lose himself in the beguilingly corrupt flesh, and instead of following his body's dictates he rolled away from her and rose lithely to his feet.

Silently he began to dress, and after watching him in uneasy surprise for a moment, Beth asked cautiously, "What are you going to do?"

Glancing over his shoulder as he pushed the calico shirt down into the *calzoneras,* he said dryly, "Clothe myself. What does it look like I'm doing—taking a bath?"

Beth flushed angrily. "I mean, what are you going to do about—me?"

"I haven't decided," he returned noncommittally, as he sat down on a nearby chair and deftly pulled on his boots.

The urge to fly across the room and claw his mocking face warred with prudence, and hating herself for being so spineless where he was concerned, she stuttered, "M-m-may Nathan and I leave? Y-y-you said you wanted us gone."

"I also told you that I'd changed my mind," he said in a hard voice. "I think it would be wisest, English, if you remained here for a few days before departing. I'll let you know when I think the time has come for you to leave the hospitality of my father's roof."

A swift urgent gust of fury shook her, her chin raised defiantly and, the violet eyes flashing like amethysts, she spat, "You arrogant devil! Do you think that for one moment I shall remain under the same roof with you? How dare you dictate to me! You can't prevent us from leaving any time we choose!"

An odd smile on the lean face, his sparse beard darkening the granite jawline, he walked with that catlike grace over to the bed. Instinctively, and furious with herself for doing so, Beth retreated as far away from him as she could. Rafael stared at her for a long moment and then reached over and captured her chin in one hand. He said just one word, "No?"

Wise for once in her dealings with him, she remained silent, knowing he could win any argument between them at the moment.

"I think we understand each other," he murmured at last, when it was apparent that, though rebellious, Beth had nothing to say. He turned away and, after strapping on his gun belt, he swung around and gave her a mockingly formal bow and said coolly, "*Adiós,* English. And unless you want the entire hacienda to know what just occurred here, I would suggest that when we next meet you pretend that it's for the first time...at least the first time today."

The insolent words were almost more than Beth could stomach; her small hands clenched into fists and she glared at him, the violet eyes hating him.

For a second longer Rafael regarded her from across the room, then, a crooked smile twitching at the corners of his mouth as if he knew how much she would like to claw his eyes and found it amusing, he walked over to her and kissed her hard on the lips. His voice unexpectedly husky, he muttered under his breath, "I *did* miss you, English." Before she had time to recover from her shocked surprise he spun on his heels and walked from the room. He wasted little time in Beth's rooms, slipping quietly out the door that he had carried her through earlier. Silently and unobserved, he made his way to his own suite of rooms, which were situated at the end of the wing which contained Beth and Nathan's apartments.

Rafael was seldom at the hacienda, seldom in the area except for the few times during the year the ranch or his father demanded his attention. And usually when he did return to the family estate, he stayed in a small cabin he had built himself some years ago, which was situated a few miles from the hacienda—near enough to suit his needs, yet far enough away from the stifling formality of the hacienda upon the occasions of Don Felipe's now-infrequent visits. But Don Miguel disliked the humble cabin intensely, feeling, perhaps rightly, that Rafael kept it as a barrier between himself and the remainder of the family, as if to point out the very differences that his father with patience and love had tried so desperately to eradicate. And in his fashion Don Miguel was as stubborn as his son, and so, despite being aware that they would be used only once or twice in a year, he had insisted that a set of rooms be maintained for Rafael's pleasure. To Don Miguel's surprise and gratification, he discovered that as long as Don Felipe was not in residence, and when Rafael's stay would be brief, his renegade son occupied the suite of rooms with every evidence of, if not enjoyment, at least acknowledgment of his father's attempts to lessen the distance between them.

If it were not for Sebastian's presence, Rafael would not have been in the area; he was too preoccupied with the Comanche problem to waste precious time dancing attendance on a family that could, he felt, do very well without him—as they had for some fifteen years while he had been a captive of the Comanches. But this time, Rafael had known that Sebastian would be waiting to see him, and so, in spite of the late hour, he had intended to slip into bed, snatch a few hours of greatly needed sleep, and be here in the morning when Sebastian awoke.

A wry twist to the mobile mouth, he admitted that Beth's presence had certainly put an end to any thought of sleep! He was still smiling when he entered the rather austere quarters set aside for his personal use. But the smile faded abruptly when Rafael discovered Sebastian, apparently comfortably seated in a squat, wooden chair, his booted feet propped negligently on a leather-bound chest, and one of Samuel Colt's new and extremely deadly revolvers pointed directly at the doorway where he stood!

His face expressionless, Rafael halted and, half-hidden by the shadows, with the habitual wariness and stealth of an animal scenting danger, he slid the bowie knife into his hand. He didn't *think* Sebastian meant to shoot him in cold blood, but just in case...

Sebastian had obviously been waiting for him, and as Rafael lingered in the shadows, his deep voice heavy with open aggression, he drawled, "*Entrez, mon ami.* And you are wise to hesitate—my feelings for you at the moment are definitely not friendly." He paused, examining his emotions, and added, "Hostile comes nearest to describing them—that or murderous!"

Eyeing the Colt revolver circumspectly, Rafael slowly eased into the room, taking his time, his brain coolly and methodically seeking a method to defuse the potentially deadly situation. If it had been any other man than Sebastian Savage pointing that pistol at him, there was no question what he would have done—one of them would be dead by now, and it wouldn't have been Rafael Santana!

There was only one reason that made any sense for Sebastian's belligerent attitude, and with deceptive mildness Rafael questioned, "The woman? You saw us earlier?"

Sebastian's full mouth thinned, and the green eyes glinting dangerously, he spat, "How very clever of you to guess! Did you also guess who she was? Is that why you seduced her? To make me think ill of her? I would like to hear your explanation before I send you to hell on a bullet!"

Rafael's temper was uncertain at the best of times, and just now he was in no mood to indulge Sebastian's hurt, angry pride. He was, in fact, deathly tired after several exhausting days of hard riding to reach the hacienda; the interlude with Beth had not been exactly restful, nor had it improved his frame of mind. Finding one of the few people in the world that he cared for holding him at gunpoint did nothing to improve an already frayed temper, and Sebastian's demand for an explanation was the final straw. Ignoring the pistol aimed steadily at his heart, he snarled, "I don't give explanations, Sebastian. Not to you or anybody else! So if you're so hell-bent on trying to kill me—go ahead! But rest assured, you young fool, that I'll take you with me!"

Slightly taken aback at the vehemence in Rafael's voice, Sebastian, his earlier aggression fading rapidly, blinked at him. "You really mean it, don't you?" he got out at last, never quite having found himself in this position before.

"I never bluff, Sebastian. *Never!*" Rafael returned in a hard voice. "So shoot me or put it away!"

Sebastian moved uneasily on the wooden chair, wishing he had thought a bit deeper before plunging headlong into a confrontation with his much-admired cousin. Wounded, furious, and feeling betrayed by what he had seen, after dragging on his clothes he had stormed down to Rafael's quarters intending to do God knows what when Rafael would eventually enter them. An often uncomfortably romantic young man, Sebastian was determined to uphold his lady's honor and avenge the insult done to her by Rafael. But now, face to face with an obviously angry and implacable Rafael, he was very definitely caught in a precarious position—he certainly didn't intend to kill his cousin, but neither could he placidly back down—besides, Rafael *did* owe him some explanation. His face a study of conflicting emotions, Sebastian finally lowered the pistol and muttered doggedly, "I don't want to kill you, but I think you should at least tell me how it comes about that I find you and Beth in the situation I just saw not too long ago."

Rafael relaxed slightly, the knife disappearing into his waistband. Absently he reached for a thin cigarillo from the pocket of his jacket, and when he finished lighting it from one of the whale-oil lamps that Sebastian had lit earlier, Rafael looked at the younger man. After inhaling deeply and expelling a cloud of smoke, Rafael countered smoothly, "Why don't you ask the lady? I'm sure she could explain it to your satisfaction."

Sebastian was outraged. "Why, you bastard! I wouldn't dare discuss such a thing with her!"

Rafael suddenly looked amused. "Why not? You might find it extremely illuminating." The amusement vanishing as quickly as it had appeared, he said thoughtfully, "I am not used to explaining myself to anyone, but considering the fact that Señora Ridgeway does have some special meaning to you, I will make an exception." He paused, not quite certain how much to tell, or how much he *wanted* to tell, and finally he said slowly, "I suppose you could say that there is a previous—ah—bond between us—one that not only supersedes your regrettable attachment, but which makes your suit highly unlikely to prosper." The moment the words left his lips he was aware he had been uncommonly clumsy; he cursed silently under his breath. All he had accomplished, he could see from Sebastian's stiffening form, was to make Sebastian even more determined to prove him wrong. It had been like waving a scarlet cape in front of a young and spirited bull. Seeking to turn the situation to his advantage, picking his words with great care, Rafael said quietly, "We met four years ago in New Orleans, when I came to talk to Jason about the possibility of the annexation of the Republic to the United States. You remember the time, don't you?"

"Are you trying to tell me that you and Beth have a long-standing liaison—one that started when she was barely seventeen and had been married only a matter of weeks?" Sebastian asked incredulously, making no attempts to hide his disbelief.

Sebastian wasn't to know it, but his words gave Rafael a shock—he had known Beth had been young when he had met her, but not *that* young, nor that her marriage had been as recent as Sebastian stated. Unconsciously he frowned, aware suddenly that there was something about what had happened that afternoon in New Orleans that he should have questioned. But he dismissed it instantly. This was not the time to examine something that had happened four years ago, and moreover it changed nothing—no matter how young she had been or how newly married, she *had* been Lorenzo's mistress and he'd seen it with his own eyes, heard her cries of encouragement to the other man before he had broken them apart. Memory of her with Lorenzo made it easier for him to give Sebastian an entirely erroneous view of his relationship with Beth Ridgeway, that and the strong desire, for Sebastian's own good of course, to make his cousin realize how very foolish this attachment with a married woman was. Coolly he queried, "What difference does that make? Since when has a young age or a new husband kept lovers apart?"

Sebastian swallowed tightly, feeling as if the ground was opening up under his feet, revealing a huge, awesome black pit. He could have sworn that Beth was not the type of woman to be any man's mistress, yet he *had* seen her in Rafael's arms, had seen Rafael carry her off into her rooms, and even more damning, Rafael himself had just admitted that they were lovers, had been lovers for quite some time. Chagrined and just a little sick at heart, Sebastian glared back at Rafael, wanting to call him a liar, but suddenly afraid that Rafael might be telling the truth—just because Beth had resisted his rather cautious overtures didn't necessarily mean that she was not open to the lures of other men. But he simply did not or would not believe it of her, and stubbornly he said, "I don't give a damn what you say, she is not that type of woman! I may be young and I may not have your experience, but I can spot a soiled dove as well as the next man—and *that* is one thing that Beth Ridgeway is not!"

Regarding the tip of his cigarillo with interest, Rafael asked casually, "Then how would you explain what you saw tonight?"

Sebastian's fists clenched and for one moment he almost threw himself at the other man. There was no other explanation for what he had seen, at least none that made any sense at the moment. But even if Beth had been Rafael's mistress for a number of years, it changed nothing in his heart, she had come to mean too much to him for Sebastian to easily dismiss the tenderness and affection he had for her.

Knowing that he had dealt Sebastian a bitter blow and not wishing for an unreconcilable estrangement between them, Rafael walked slowly over to where Sebastian sat and, putting a friendly hand on the other's shoulder, he said gently, "Whether she is my mistress or not makes little difference, *amigo*—she is not for you. Would you be satisfied to have her only as a mistress? And do you really want a woman that you had to steal from her husband?" His dark face intent, his voice deepening with emotion, he asked, "If you could steal her from him, what would stop another from doing the same to you? Could you live with that for the rest of your life, never knowing when she could be tempted away from you? Somehow, I think not."

Everything that Rafael said was true, but Sebastian fought against it, not willing to renounce his claim to Beth's affection. It was a fact that some of his reluctance to relinquish whatever claims he felt he had on Beth had to do with pride, but his heart was also deeply involved, perhaps more deeply involved than anyone realized, including Sebastian; and at the moment he was only aware of a throbbing sort of pain and disillusionment. He had enough confidence in his physical attributes to know that if he ever did capture Beth's affections that he would never fear another man taking her away from him—but that was before he had known that there was another man involved. Nathan he had always discounted, but Rafael was another story, and if Beth loved him, which she must in the face of Rafael's startling revelations, then he was indeed fighting a losing battle. Painfully he said, "Perhaps you are right, but don't ask me to stop loving her simply because you say she is your mistress." The green eyes full of anguish, he glanced away and said in a muffled tone, "She is one of the loveliest women I have ever seen, and I find it hard to believe that she has been having an adulterous liaison behind her husband's back for years."

Rafael's features were purposely blank in the face of Sebastian's unhappiness, but if he'd had Beth's slender neck in his hands, he would have broken it. He detested the role he was forced to play, nor did he like lying to Sebastian, but feeling as he did, thinking that he was protecting the other from a promiscuous little bitch, it was a grim necessity. Attempting for a light comment he murmured, "At the risk of finding myself challenged, I think, *amigo,* that your conception of the undoubtedly beautiful Beth is distorted. She is not, my young friend, the angel you perceive... believe me, *I know!*"

Flashing him a look of dislike, Sebastian replied heatedly, "And I think you are the one who has the distorted image! Consuela filled you with such hatred for all of her sex that you would not recognize a *good* woman even if she walked up and slapped your arrogant face for you!"

A strangely bitter smile curving his mouth, Rafael admitted, "Perhaps. And before we come to blows over her, I think it would be wise to drop the subject, *sí?*"

Unwillingly Sebastian agreed, dejectedly aware that nothing could be gained by discussing the topic further. Manfully he gathered himself together, determined not to reveal, any more than he had already, how devastating Rafael's disclosures had been. Rising to his feet, the pistol still clasped in his hand, he said quietly, "There seems to be nothing more to be said between us, so I shall bid you good morning." The young face stiff and almost unbearably proud, Sebastian added, "I trust you have no intention of seeking satisfaction for my attempts to purloin your property?"

Suddenly angry and showing it, Rafael snapped, "Don't try those dandified airs with me, *joven!* You know damn rightly I have no intention of doing such a thing!"

Some of his own anger boiling to the surface, Sebastian snarled back, "It might be better if you did!"

His eyes narrowing, the handsome nose flaring at the nostrils, Rafael asked softly, too softly, "And what the hell do you mean by that?"

His mouth sulky, Sebastian muttered, "You know very well what I mean. I find you with the woman I love in your arms, the woman I told you I planned to marry, and you tell me she is your mistress! Has been for four years. And then like some lapdog you expect me to just shrug it off and continue as we were." His voice thickening, he spat, "Well, it won't wash, cousin! You may have the woman, but I don't have to like it...or *you!*"

"Now goddammit, listen to me, Sebastian—" Rafael began, only to have his words stop abruptly as Sebastian stalked out of the room, slamming the door with unnecessary force as he went.

Fury and dismay tangled in Rafael's throat as he stared at the shut door, realizing with a fierce sorrow that the deep affection he and Sebastian shared for one another might very well have been shattered irreparably. He considered storming after Sebastian and telling him...*what,* for God's sake? That Beth Ridgeway was the "angel" Sebastian thought? And that he had taken base advantage of her virtue and innocence? Hardly! Not when he had seen her with his own eyes in Lorenzo's arms and not when she had offered herself to him immediately after Lorenzo's taking of her. What kind of a friend would he be if he allowed Sebastian to become entangled with a woman like that?

His eyes bleak, he stared blindly around the room. Far better to have Sebastian hate the very sight of him, he decided grimly, than just to stand by and watch Beth work her wiles on the younger man. But that didn't lessen the pain he felt as he remembered Sebastian's final words to him. Jesus! How in the hell did I get myself into this? he wondered angrily.

More weary than he could ever recall being, Rafael walked into his bedchamber and, sitting on a huge bed with soaring decorative iron posts, he moodily removed his boots, letting them drop where they may. He flung himself back on the bed and stared for a long moment at the open-beamed ceiling above before reaching over and almost viciously pulling on the bell rope that would summon one of the servants from their quarters. God knows what time it was, but if they aren't up, they should be, he thought irrationally.

Not too many minutes later there was a soft tap on the outer door of the rooms and not moving from the bed he barked irritably, *"Entre!"*

A Mexican of an undeterminable age appeared momentarily in his bedroom. The fat brown face broke into a wide grin at the sight of the dark, lean figure on the bed and the man said happily, "Señor Rafael! You are here at last! I could not believe my ears when I heard your bell ring."

Rafael smiled slightly, "*Buenos días,* Luis. I know the hour is unreasonable, but could you arrange a bath for me? I feel I have half the dirt of the Republic on me."

"*Sí, señor.* Of course, for you anything is possible." The dark eyes sly, he asked, "Shall I rouse Juanita to serve you? She has been most persistent in wanting to know of your return."

His mouth pulling wryly, Rafael shook his head. "Luis, I need a bath, *not* a woman."

In a remarkably brief time he was sitting in a brass tub filled with hot soapy water, having Luis deftly shave off the grubby beard that had grown over the past several days. The beard gone, Rafael scrubbed his entire body hard with the long-handled bristle brush that Luis passed to him, and, after washing the dark, unruly hair he rose in naked splendor from the water. A thick white towel was presented instantly by the hovering Luis and, drying himself swiftly, Rafael said, "Wake me at one, if you will, Luis. In the meantime, let Don Miguel know that I am here and that I don't want to be disturbed until then." He paused and then said slowly, "Ask the cook to pack enough food for two men for an overnight trip, and see that two horses are saddled and ready when I awake."

His face full of dismay, Luis asked, "You are leaving again? So soon? You have just arrived, señor!"

"Just overnight, Luis. There is something I have to take care of, and it won't wait. Now, off with you! Oh, and Luis, keep my request a secret from the family, will you?"

Puzzled, the little man shrugged. "*Sí, señor,* if you wish."

Rafael smiled. "I do. Two last things, though, that I would like done—deliver the note I am about to write to Sebastian as soon as possible. The message for my father I want delayed until the evening."

The notes were quickly written and dispatched, and not more than five minutes later Rafael was sprawled beneath the covers of his bed. Somehow he had to mend the breach between him and Sebastian, and suggesting that they ride out this afternoon and view the unclaimed land that adjoined the rancho's eastern boundary had been the only thing that he could think of to allow the two of them some privacy and time to begin healing the rift. It was flimsy and weak, he admitted to himself, but it seemed the only course open to him. Certainly it would be impossible to do anything at the hacienda, not with Sebastian acting frigid and polite in front of the others, but if they were away and on their own...Now, if only his rightfully affronted, hot-tempered cousin didn't simply rip the note in shreds and toss it in his face.

Beth Ridgeway he ruthlessly shoved to the back of his mind. First, Sebastian, then English....

Sebastian didn't rip Rafael's note to shreds, although that was his first reaction. But, staring at the thick black strokes on the heavy paper, he hesitated and finally decided to accept the invitation. He had held his older cousin in too high a regard to be able to put their affection for each other aside without a struggle. His heart did ache, though, as much from the estrangement with Rafael as the knowledge that his love for Beth was fruitless, but he, like Rafael, did not want the breach between them to be impassable. And so, even if he did not have quite the enthusiasm or spirit for a short sojourn with Rafael that he might have had only hours before, he was willing to accept his cousin's offering of the olive branch.

Of Beth Ridgeway and her connection with Rafael, he found himself curiously numb after the first ugly shock had worn off. Numb and just a little disillusioned with Beth, and yet deep in his heart he fought against that disillusionment, feeling vehemently that there was something about Rafael's tale that didn't quite ring true. Something that, if he could just put his finger on it, would give him the answer—and he was positive it wouldn't be the answer Rafael had given him. For one long moment he considered doing just what Rafael had suggested—asking Beth for her version of what had happened. But, while Sebastian was a brash young man, he couldn't quite bring himself to demand an explanation from her. Because he feared her answer? Even he wasn't certain why.

Tiredly he banished the subject from his mind. He couldn't change things, and somehow he didn't think hearing Beth's answer was going to make him feel any better.

If Beth had known that Sebastian had been a witness to that shameful meeting with Rafael, or of the half-truths Rafael had spun out for Sebastian's edification, she would have been divided between a strong desire to faint with mortification and as equally strong a desire to part Rafael's thick black hair with a bullet. As it was, she was filled with guilt and fury as she lay in her bed torturing herself by remembering how easily Rafael had overcome her protests. Writhing with angry remorse, she stared blankly around her room, almost unable to bring herself to face the day...and Nathan...and worse, to look into the icy gray eyes of Rafael Santana.

But pride would not allow her to hide away either, and common sense told her that she would have to leave the sanctuary of her rooms eventually. Her self-pitying mood lasted almost through the china pot of steaming hot coffee that a bright-eyed, beaming Charity had served about nine o'clock that morning. But by the time Beth finished the last cup and had dressed and Charity had arranged her hair, her shattered spirit was beginning to rouse itself and to search for a way to defeat Rafael on his own ground.

A finger on her lips, her mind busy on finding a way out of her dilemma, she sat quietly in one of the chairs of her sitting room. Outright defiance of his order not to leave hadn't occurred to her yet. At the moment she was more determined to make certain that there was no repeat of last night, and the only way she could be assured of that was to have someone else with her. Sleep in Nathan's rooms? No! That would involve too many explanations, explanations she didn't dare give, if she wanted her husband alive and not dead on the dueling field.

Thoughtfully Beth watched through the doorway into her bedroom as Manuela, acting as Charity's assistant, helped the younger woman hang a few of Beth's gowns in a massive mahogany wardrobe. Her gaze sharpened, and when Manuela prepared to leave the room a few minutes later, Beth called to her.

Manuela's face was wary as she approached, and it became even more so when an instant later Beth requested Charity to go to the kitchen and ask for another pot of coffee. Once Charity had left them alone, Beth looked directly into Manuela's eyes and stated baldly, "Rafael returned last night. From now and until we leave, I am going to have my servant sleep here in the rooms with me. Will you see that another bed is procured?"

Instantly aware of the reasons behind Beth's actions, Manuela nodded without hesitation. "It will be done. Occasionally guests prefer for a servant to sleep nearby. No one will wonder at it, no one need even know of it."

Beth let her breath out in a jagged sigh. "That's the problem, and that's where I need your help—I *want* everyone to know that Charity is sleeping in my rooms."

"I see," Manuela said slowly. "Very well, I shall make certain that the señora's fear of sleeping in a strange house without her maid nearby is well known. I will make especially certain that Luis, Señor Rafael's servant, knows of it."

Beth flashed her a warm, grateful smile. "Oh, Manuela! *Thank you!*"

CHAPTER FOURTEEN

Charity's presence in her bedroom at night was a frail barrier against Rafael's dark charm, but it was the only thing Beth could think of to give herself some protection. Of course she could have told her husband, but for obvious reasons she chose not to do so.

Facing Nathan when they met just before the midday meal was easier than Beth had imagined it would be. Smiling guilelessly into Nathan's pleasant features, Beth felt her heart squeeze painfully, hating herself for the role she was playing. Perhaps, she thought viciously, I am just naturally a liar, an adulterous woman of easy virtue. It was a totally unfair assessment of her character, but she was too involved with her struggle between anger, shame and guilt to think rationally. The guilt clogged her throat whenever she thought of Nathan, and shame washed over her at how easily Rafael had overcome her resistance. As for the anger, it flooded her body and made her want to lash out with helpless rage at the knowledge that she was apparently powerless to escape the dreadful coil in which she found herself. But I will find a way out of this maze, she vowed fiercely, I *will!*

The ordeal of meeting Rafael face to face was postponed; Don Miguel mentioned casually as they sat down to eat, that his son had arrived early that morning, but had taken Sebastian on a brief tour of some land that lay to the east of the ranch. "They should return in time for dinner tonight," he added, "but for the present, please accept my apologies for their absence."

Beth was more than willing to accept his apologies, and added silently the fervent wish that Rafael might break his arrogant neck during the tour, sparing her the necessity of continuing this distasteful charade. That his death might increase her present anguish she firmly refused to acknowledge.

Manuela, it appeared, had wasted little time in spreading the news of the Señora Ridgeway's apparent uneasiness about sleeping without her servant nearby, and Don Miguel spent several minutes as they were finishing the second course of the meal, a spicy green chile soup, earnestly explaining to Beth that she had nothing to fear while in the hacienda—the Comanches had never scaled the stout walls that surrounded them. She had listened with polite attention, longing to confess to her kindly host that it was not the enemy outside the walls that she feared, but the enemy *within!*

Nathan had made no comment while Don Miguel had been speaking to her, but Beth was very aware that he was looking at her closely. He remained silent, and it was only when they were alone, taking a short stroll through the lush and vibrant flower gardens that lay to the rear of the hacienda, that Nathan made mention of it. Idly examining a strikingly vivid display of scarlet poinsettias and dainty, white spider lilies, he asked quietly, "You afraid of something, Beth?"

"No! Of course not!" she said quickly, too quickly.

Nathan didn't say anything for a moment, his expression thoughtful. Finally he shrugged his shoulders and remarked, "Very well, my dear. I just wondered at Charity's presence. You have never struck me as being particularly skittish, and I found it somewhat strange that while sleeping in the back of a wagon far away from civilization, with wild Indians prowling about, never caused you to turn a hair—yet, now when we are safely behind two sets of stone walls and have all the protection one could wish for from the—er—savage elements of this country, you find it necessary to have a servant sleep by your bedside. Rather peculiar, wouldn't you say?"

Beth didn't meet his considering gaze, looking instead blindly in the direction of the hills that rose in the distance. Her voice slightly strangled, she said, "I know it is ridiculous, but it comforts me. It may be that I am not as brave as you think."

"Perhaps," he murmured, his gray eyes dwelling gravely on her averted face, positive that she was hiding something. But, as they were to leave within a few days and put this place behind them, he was not inclined to probe. Beth would tell him in her own good time, and he was not about to disrupt the harmony between them by forcing a confidence from her. Infusing a heartiness in his voice, he suggested, "Well, then, since we have exhausted that subject and have seen the gardens, shall we retire for a siesta? I believe it is customary at this time of the afternoon."

Beth readily agreed, needing the solace and quiet of her rooms to recover her shattered composure for the coming confrontation with Rafael this evening. But, restlessly pacing the confines of her sitting room, she found neither peace nor a solution. The most obvious solution was to tell Nathan, but if she did that...The picture of Nathan facing Rafael on the dueling field flashed across her brain again. No! She would *never* allow it!

By the time she left her rooms to join the others in the central courtyard, she was taut with anxiety and growing fury. But outwardly her face was serene, the violet eyes wide and limpid, the gently curved mouth soft and rosy, and her smile only slightly strained.

Everyone was already there except Sebastian and Rafael, and she sighed with relief. It would be so much easier for her to be already in the midst of the others when they met, rather than the other way around.

Doña Madelina was sitting in one of the iron chairs near the fountain, and Nathan, standing by her side, was listening courteously to something the Spanish woman was saying, while Don Miguel appeared to be conferring with one of the servants a short distance away. On a table nearby was a tempting array of refreshments, both to drink and eat. Beth's appetite had deserted her, and, after sitting herself next to Doña Madelina, she settled for a tall, cool glass of *sangría* that was quickly served by a servant in a loose-fitting white shirt and baggy trousers.

Don Miguel walked over to them, a frown of annoyance on his face. His displeasure obvious, he said, "It seems that I must again apologize for the absence of Rafael and Sebastian. I just received a note, which my son apparently arranged to have delivered at this late hour, saying that he and Sebastian will not return until tomorrow." His vexation growing, he grumbled, "I do not understand what Sebastian is thinking about, deserting his guests this way. I can only ask that you forgive him and put it down to Rafael's undue influence over him. Concerning my son, I cannot offer any excuse."

Sebastian's absence suited Nathan perfectly, and he murmured, "There is no need for you to apologize—I think, in the face of the charming and pleasant company of yourself and your lovely wife, Beth and I shall be well satisfied."

At the news that she would not be facing Rafael tonight, Beth was uncertain whether to laugh with relief or stamp her foot in rage. It didn't take a great deal of intelligence to understand why Rafael had waited until now to let his father know that he and Sebastian would be away for the night—if Beth had known earlier, there was a good chance that she not only could have but *would* have arranged an immediate departure. She would have been safe from any sort of reprisal until after Rafael returned and found her gone... by which time she would have several hours head start on him. Devil! she thought with unwonted violence, devil, *devil!*

Beth had surmised correctly Rafael's reasons for not wanting anyone to know of his intention to be away overnight and for the late delivery of his note. And that evening as he and Sebastian made camp, he thought with amusement for a brief moment of Beth's probable reaction, before he turned his mind to other things.

The afternoon had proved to be comparatively enjoyable once they had left the hacienda, and Sebastian's resentment and disillusionment had faded slightly. They had both been rather stiff with one another at first, but as the miles passed and they cautiously conversed with each other, gradually some of the old rapport returned. It was not as though everything was as it once had been, but there was a partial mending of the breach.

It helped enormously that both men wished to heal it and that both were doing their damnedest to do so. But it would take time for Sebastian's raw feeling of pain to disappear, for him to reconcile himself to the fact that the woman he had convinced himself he loved above all others was not the faultless goddess he had imagined, and for him to realize that her heart belonged to a man he held in the highest esteem. Bleakly he decided as they stopped for camp that if he had to lose Beth to another man that it probably hurt less that the man was Rafael—but not a whole lot less!

His heartburnings aside, Sebastian had been thoroughly pleased with the afternoon's excursion. They had left the hacienda shortly after one in the afternoon with the few supplies they would need for the brief trip snugly encased in saddlebags, Sebastian's heavy rawhide jacket tied across the back of his saddle and Rafael's brightly striped serape suffering the same treatment.

Although the pace had been steady as they rode toward the east, they had stopped now and then to water their horses from the clear, wide, sandy-banked rivers and streams or to stretch their own legs for a few minutes near a grove of sweet gums and maples. The weather was perfect, the sun shining brightly, the air warm and with more than just a hint of spring in it. As for the country through which they rode—magnificent, Sebastian thought dazedly, as he stared eagerly at the brush-covered hills and canyons; the myriad of trees, Spanish oak, sweet gum and pine, maple and cypress; the maidenhair-fern-lined creeks; the clear sweet springs that gushed over limestone bedrock; and the awe-inspiring outcroppings of massive granite. Without a doubt he intended to own a large section of it for himself.

About an hour before sunset Rafael had pulled up his horse and pointed to a rocky outcropping that topped a small rise. "We'll camp there for the night. It's off any trail and should offer a fairly defensible position in case there are some raiding Indians or Mexican *bandidos* in the area."

Sebastian had nodded, realizing uncomfortably that he hadn't thought of that sort of very real danger during the entire afternoon. He had been too busy wrestling with his injured feelings and drinking in the majestic untamed country through which they had ridden; not once had it occurred to him to worry over the possibility of attack by hostile savages or marauding bandits. Feeling slightly annoyed with himself, he asked, "Do you think we will be in danger from an attack?"

Rafael sent him a level look from underneath the black sombrero. "*Amigo,* if you would survive here in the Republic, you must *always* be prepared for an Indian raid—anywhere at any time."

On that rather chilling note they had turned their horses from the trail they had been following and rode briskly to the outcropping that Rafael had pointed out. The next half hour passed swiftly as camp was made and the horses tended.

By the time they had eaten, the sun had vanished completely and there was a distinct chill in the evening air. Rafael had made a small fire, and with their stomachs full of tortillas and spicy pemmican and the hot, strong coffee that had been brewed in a tin pot on the glowing coals, both men settled back against the boulders that embraced their camp and relaxed.

Sebastian sat nearest the remains of the fire, idly poking it with a long stick, his features gilded by the dying coals. The firelight intensified his rugged handsomeness and gave him a slightly ruthless air. He was wearing the heavy rawhide jacket to guard against the increasing coolness of the night air, and, not surprisingly, he had the Colt revolver, fitted snugly in a leather holster, hanging from a wide rawhide belt about his trim waist.

If Sebastian sat in the glow of the fire, Rafael lay in its shadows, his shape barely discernible in the gathering darkness. His long legs were stretched in front of him toward the warmth of the fire and his shoulders were propped negligently against one of the rounded boulders. He had not yet put on the brightly striped serape, and in the encroaching darkness of the night his black clothing blended into the shadows. The black sombrero, pulled low across his face, hid his expression, and the tip of a thin cigarillo that he was smoking gleamed redly in the darkness as he lay there staring at the fire.

There was a companionable silence between them, neither at the moment feeling the need for conversation. But the sudden unexpected scream of a cougar nearby caused Sebastian to start, and, seeing it, Rafael smiled faintly and murmured, "Nervous, *amigo?*"

Sebastian pulled a wry face. "Perhaps a little. You have to admit that all of this is very new to me, and I'm afraid I haven't as yet developed your indifference to the possibility of an Indian attack."

Rafael stirred impatiently. "Not indifference, Sebastian, never indifference. It's more taking precautions against being surprised—by anyone—and at the same time putting the thought out of your mind." He took a long deep drag of the cigarillo and tossed it carelessly on the dying fire. "I doubt that we have anything to fear tonight," he said calmly. "It is not yet fully into the raiding season, nor is the moon full—and we are camped in a place that is fairly defensible."

Sebastian assessingly glanced around him, noting the sheer, high rocky outcropping behind them and the mass of large, jumbled boulders that nearly encompassed their camp. The horses were tethered near a small spring not far from where they sat, and certainly no one could approach the animals without passing right through the middle of the two men. From their position near the top of the outcropping, in daylight there would be an excellent view of the relatively level plain a few hundred feet below them; during the dark hours it would be almost impossible to scale the rocky slope without rattling a few stones, which would alert them to danger.

Rafael watched Sebastian's appraisal and said, "It's one of the first rules of survival out here—unless you're traveling with a large contingent of heavily armed men, *never* camp in the open. Find something, even if it's no more than a dead snag at your back."

Somewhat ruefully Sebastian muttered, "With you, it is second nature to think of such things—I am, I'm afraid, much more comfortable and in my element while strolling the streets of New Orleans than I am out here."

A low sympathetic laugh came from Rafael. "And I, my young friend, am *very* ill-at-ease in New Orleans!" His face almost dreamy, he continued, "The hills, the vast prairies, and the unexplored territories, even with all the dangers that lurk there, are much more to my liking—believe me!"

Sebastian grinned at him. "Your actions never reveal it—as a matter of fact, I seem to recall that my father said something to the effect that you resembled a chameleon—throw you into any situation and you immediately blend into the surroundings, whether it be a ball at the governor's palace or a brawl on a riverboat!"

Rafael smiled briefly. "Your father is a very perceptive man. I have always thought, perhaps, *too* perceptive... especially if one had something to hide."

"Amen to that, cousin, amen," Sebastian said fervently, thinking of certain childhood pranks and their disconcerting discovery by his father. "There isn't a damned thing which happens that he doesn't know about!"

The conversation drifted for several moments onto Jason Savage, and soon the two men were eagerly exchanging stories of Jason's wild misspent youth, which they had both heard down through the years. Shaking his dark head in amused admiration, Sebastian said at last, "How he can dare lecture me on *my* lack of decorum is beyond me! At least I didn't kidnap an earl's daughter—even if he was deceived by the fact that mother was dancing at a Gypsy wedding!"

His face suddenly thoughtful, Rafael said slowly, "Perhaps there are things he has done that he regrets, and he does not want to see you make the same mistakes. You are very like him, you know."

Looking affronted, Sebastian burst out, "Not when it comes to women, I can assure you! Why, I would never—!"

"Where a woman is concerned, you can never be very adamant about what you will or will not do!" Rafael interrupted harshly.

Aware of the disruptive note in their conversation and thinking of Beth, Sebastian hesitated a moment. Picking his words with care, he asked finally, "If you think that Jason has regrets about the past—have you?"

"Some," Rafael bit out brusquely and in a tone that made Sebastian decide instantly not to pursue the subject further. The conversation naturally languished for several moments until, searching earnestly for a subject that would dispel the uncomfortable silence, Sebastian asked abruptly, "What did you mean about the full moon and the raiding season? I thought that the Indians attacked at any time."

"They do," Rafael returned quietly, just as determined as Sebastian to smooth over the momentary breach, "but like all hunting animals they prefer the full of the moon. The Spanish called it 'Comanche moon.' As for the season—in the spring when the grass grows thick and green, then through the summer until it is time for the fall buffalo hunts is when they do most of their raiding." An odd smile on his mobile mouth, Rafael murmured, "It is a way of life like no other. You cannot stop a Comanche from raiding and pillaging any more than you can forbid an eagle to soar."

Unnerved by that smile but not quite knowing why, Sebastian jabbed the stick into the glowing coals. Realizing exactly why he was so suddenly uncomfortable, he questioned tightly, "Did you ever—? I mean when you were...Did you take part in—?"

Rafael put an end to Sebastian's fumbling by saying simply, "Yes."

Sebastian took a deep shaken breath. "You mean you rode with those murdering devils and actually took part in attacking white people?" he demanded with angry indignation. "How could you bring yourself to do such a thing?"

Almost imperturbably, Rafael responded, "You forget, I think, that I was only two years old when my mother and I were captured by the Comanches. She died before I was three and with her died any memory of another life. The hacienda, my father, even Don Felipe—none of them existed in my memory. How could I have done any different?"

His mouth set, Sebastian said stubbornly, "Well, I think you should have known instinctively that you were attacking your own kind. Didn't you even once question what you were doing?" His voice thickening, he snarled, "I suppose next you'll tell me that you *enjoyed* it!"

Silence greeted his words. The silence, taut and heavy, lengthened as Rafael deliberately placed a cigarillo in his mouth and, leaning forward, lit it from the stick that Sebastian had just been using to prod the few lingering embers of the fire. When it was lit to his satisfaction he looked directly at Sebastian.

Rafael's lean, hard face was remote, the gray eyes very cool and distant as they stared steadily at the younger man. And Sebastian cursed his unruly tongue, aware that they were dangerously near to falling out again. Almost apologetically he began, "I shouldn't have said that. It is just that—"

"I was twelve years old the first time I went on a raid, and yes, I did enjoy it," Rafael interrupted coolly. "I was thirteen when I stole my first horse and scalped my first white man, and a year later I raped my first woman and took my first captive. By the time I was seventeen, I had been raiding with the warriors for over five years—I owned fifty horses, I had my own buffalo-skin teepee, three slaves of my own, and several scalps taken by my hand decorated my lance and favorite bridle." There was no hint of shame or regret in his voice and his gray eyes never wavered from Sebastian's. "I was a *Comanche!*" Rafael spat the words almost with pride. "One of the Nermernuh, 'the People,' and I lived by their ways." His voice had suddenly thickened with passion and for just a moment he had lost that cool aloofness that he cloaked himself with. Aware of it, Rafael stopped abruptly and took a long, jagged breath. In a quieter tone he continued, "I was a young warrior in a band of the Antelope Comanches, the Kwerharrehnuh, and my path to glory, my right to speak in council, my right to take a wife, my wealth, my very reasons for living were to raid, rape, rob, and kill. Sebastian, never doubt that I did all of those things, did them and reveled in doing them! I wasted not one opportunity to add prestige and honor to my name, to increase my standing within the tribe." His chiseled mouth curving with cynical amusement, he added, "I was very ambitious in those days, and I relished the raids upon the white man that dared to take land that was ours, and I yearned for the day that I would have earned enough glory to lead my own raid, to have the warriors follow my commands, knowing that I would bring them success. Oh, yes, I did all of those things, and I did them without regret. I took pride in counting coup, in returning triumphantly to the camp with my white captives—and, yes, with the scalps of those I had slain in honorable battle dangling from my lance and with the horses I had stolen plunging madly ahead of me."

In stunned awkward silence, Sebastian sat staring at him, uncertain whether he was appalled and outraged by what he had heard or strangely stirred and envious of the savage way that Rafael had lived. To his intense disgust he found he wanted unashamedly to know more, to learn even more of that time in his cousin's life that was never mentioned. In some dark, secret way it appealed to him, and he admitted unhappily to himself that perhaps he had inherited more from his father than just a physical appearance!

Rafael had looked away from Sebastian when he had stopped speaking, and, as the moments passed, he contented himself with smoking the slim black cigarillo. He felt drained; tonight had been the first time he had ever spoken to anyone about his life with the Comanches, and he discovered that it had brought back memories and primitive emotions—memories and emotions which he had thought he had conquered long ago. It wasn't pleasant to know that the blood lust still ran hotly in his veins. How easily I could revert, he thought grimly, remembering the wild, barbaric joys of that time. He glanced across at Sebastian, curious and yet oddly indifferent about the other's reaction.

Sebastian was still staring at him, but there wasn't the recoiling horror and furious condemnation that Rafael expected to see. Cocking an eyebrow at the younger man, he asked derisively, "No comment? You are usually so quick with words that I find your silence puzzling. Struggling to find just the right scathing observation, Sebastian?"

"No," Sebastian admitted honestly. "I was just realizing how very thin is our veneer of civilization. What you've just told me I find on one hand most revolting, but on the other..."

"On the other, you find that it calls to everything that is savage and untamed within you," Rafael finished dryly. "You're not alone—more than one returned captive has escaped his would-be-rescuer and eagerly hurried back to the Comanches."

"Why didn't you?"

Rafael laughed bitterly. "Because, my friend, my grandfather took every precaution to make damn certain I didn't!"

"But when you were in Spain, surely you were not watched the entire time?"

"Oh, no... there wasn't the need." At Sebastian's look of surprise, Rafael added wearily, "When Don Felipe undertook to... *re*capture me from the Comanches, luck was on his side—not only did he find me, but when I was captured, the two Comanches with me unfortunately happened to be the men I had thought of as my father and older brother. If I had known *who* had captured us, that damning bit of information wouldn't have come out. But none of us realized that we had been neatly surprised and trapped while out hunting by something more than merely a band of Mexican bandits who asked a hell of lot of questions. The fact that I had been singled out and deliberately captured didn't occur to any of us until too late. Catching Buffalo Horn, my adopted father, and Standing Horse, his son, was a piece of luck that Don Felipe hadn't counted on, but he took advantage of it damn quickly—in order to insure my cooperation, it was explained *very* carefully and in eloquent detail exactly what would happen to them if I didn't do precisely what Don Felipe wanted."

Sebastian whistled soundlessly under his breath, realizing the reasons behind a lot of the inexplicable things that Rafael had done—such as marrying Consuela! He moved uncomfortably, not certain what to say, yet not wanting to let the subject drop. Shooting a quick glance at Rafael's remote face, he wisely decided not to ask any questions concerning Don Felipe and instead murmured curiously, "Did you ever go back to the Comanches?"

"Certainly," Rafael replied promptly. "But by the time I did, I'm afraid Don Felipe and his priests and scholars had done their work too well, and I discovered that while the Comanches might welcome me back as a lost son, I could no longer live their way of life as I had once done. I knew too much of the world... I had, against my will, become the Spanish grandson that Don Felipe wanted—at any cost."

Sebastian wanted to question him further, but something in Rafael's face warned him that the other man had said just about all he was going to say on the subject. Sebastian was right, for a second later Rafael flipped the cigarillo on the coals and said quietly, "I think we've discussed my Indian past long enough, don't you? At any rate, I have no intention of talking about something that happened too long ago to make any difference now." As he finished speaking, almost angrily Rafael drew his saddle, which lay nearby, into a position that suited him, and then settled his dark head against it. The serape was roughly dragged over his body and, pulling the black sombrero down to where its brim rested on his nose, he said pointedly, "*Buenas noches.*"

Knowing that further questions would remain unanswered, Sebastian followed his lead. The leather saddle did not make a particularly comfortable pillow and, with his mind filled with thoughts of Comanches and Rafael's years with them, Sebastian found it hard indeed to fall asleep. But eventually he drowsed off and not too many minutes later he was deeply asleep, not once thinking of Beth and his aching heart.

For Rafael it was not quite as easy. The black sombrero, pulled low across his face, hid the fact that while he gave the impression of being asleep, he was wide awake. Too damned wide, he thought grimly, shifting slightly on the hard ground.

It had been extremely difficult to answer Sebastian's questions, to talk so casually of that time with the Comanches, not because of any painful memories—that period had been the happiest of his life. Then there had been no divided loyalties, no occasional black abyss of guilt to stumble into whenever he thought of the fact that he was allied with the white people, whose greed for land could very well be the death of the Comanche's proud and free way of life.

Rafael sighed heavily, thinking of the time with the Comanches. He had lived life as he found it, and in those days he had found it good indeed: the thrill of the buffalo hunt, the exultance of a successful coup, the almost frenzied excitement of knowing he had killed an enemy and that the enemy's woman lay beneath him in the dust as he had forced his will upon her. Rafael's mouth curved sardonically. Oh, yes, he *had* reveled in every aspect of the Comanche warrior's life—even the land itself called to him, those vast chaparraled savannas, brushlands, and butte-studded limestone plateaus in an awesome sea of grass that reached belly-high to a horse and extended as far as the eye could see and beyond. It was impossible to describe the Great Plains, to describe the effect of blinding blue sky and vague horizons, the endless expanses of waving grass that seemed to run on forever. And the winds, the wind that blew eternally, cutting through the silence with a sullen keening. He sighed again, suddenly longing for it unbearably.

Realizing that sleep was impossible, Rafael threw aside the serape and sat up. Stirring the lingering coals slightly, he managed to find enough flame to light another cigarillo. He was restless, his mind and thoughts dwelling too much on a part of his life he had always kept tightly locked away. Almost murderously, he glanced at Sebastian sleeping soundly. Damn him! If he hadn't asked those questions...

Taking a deep drag of the cigarillo, Rafael stared blindly at the faintly glowing remains of their fire. No, he admitted slowly, it wasn't the memories of the Comanche years that troubled him, it was the agonizing time that had followed his return to the life he had been born into—the life of the son of a noble Spanish family.

Even now, some fifteen years later, he could still

recall his frantic fury in those first days, days he had spent chained like an animal in a dirty underground prison of Don Felipe's making. There had been no warm sunlight upon his yearning, thirsting skin, no brilliantly blue sky to fill him with delight and pleasure, just darkness and humiliation. Around his right ankle he still bore the scars of that brutal incarceration—he had fought like a maddened, wild creature to escape the iron manacle that chained him in his small, suffocating prison, fought until his ankle was a bleeding mass of torn skin and flesh. And all the while, safely out of his reach, Don Felipe had watched, his black goatee and curving mustaches giving him the look of a devil, the cold black eyes expressionless.

Rafael's hand trembled slightly, and seeing it, he cursed virulently under his breath. Mother of God, how he despised his Spanish grandfather!

The Comanches were a cruel race, Rafael conceded, but theirs was not the calculated cruelty practiced by his grandfather. Don Felipe had enjoyed trying to break him, had enjoyed watching him, day by day, hour by hour, almost lose the struggle to maintain even a pitiful remnant of his youthful, bred-in-the-bone pride. Rafael smiled viciously, remembering the punishments, the degradations the older man had devised to break his spirit, to make him a weakling who obeyed without question. But somehow, someway, he had managed to remain defiant and untamed throughout it all—the deliberate lack of food that had left him gaunt and barely able to stand; the systematic beatings, the petty acts of outright cruelty and the vitriolic abuse hurled at him daily. But when all else had failed, Don Felipe crushed resistance by the simple expedient of dangling before Rafael the fate of the imprisoned Buffalo Horn and Standing Horse.

For the continuance of their lives, Rafael had learned the pure Castilian Spanish that Don Felipe demanded; for them he had studied diligently the books and syllabuses devised by his grandfather's priests; for them he had allowed himself to be groomed and taught the manners and ways of the heir to a proud and distinguished name. Had Don Felipe not threatened his Comanche family, Rafael would have starved to death and let the maggots feed on his rotting flesh before he would have obeyed even one command.

Don Felipe, determined to have no interference in his plans, had kept Rafael's father in complete ignorance of his actions. And it was only some ten months later—with Rafael, his glorious braids sheared off, his Spanish understandable, and very ill-at-ease in confining pantaloons and white linen shirt—that Don Miguel had looked upon the openly hostile face of the son he had never thought to see again.

Don Miguel had been overjoyed, and even to Rafael's distrustful gaze it had been obvious that the other man's emotions were genuine. Remembering the tears that had filled his father's eyes, he moved uneasily. He had never wanted Don Miguel's love, but he was, in his own way, grateful for it—certainly his father's presence had made the following two years bearable and at times almost pleasant.

But there had been a great deal of unpleasantness, too, for Rafael still fought against the prison walls that were minute by minute closing in on him. He yearned with every fiber of his being for the high country, for the freedom that had been his for as long as he could remember, for the life that he still thought of as the one worthy of a *man*. But after the desperate abortive attempt to free Buffalo Horn and Standing Horse from their wicked captivity, with a heart full of black fury he had put it behind him. Don Felipe's revenge had been swift and savage—he had calmly ordered that Buffalo Horn be blinded in one eye, stating indifferently that the next time the other eye would go, and of course then there was still Standing Horse.... Rafael had been forced to watch the blinding, and after that, there had been no more attempts to escape the limits set by his grandfather.

The cigarillo suddenly tasted vile, and, with a sharp, violent motion, Rafael tossed it from him. But Don Felipe had not won all of the battles, he thought harshly. No, not all of them. With pleasure he recalled the look on his grandfather's face when he had flatly refused to go to Spain...unless his adoptive relatives were freed.

The glossy black goatee had nearly quivered with rage, his pale olive skin had flushed with choler, and Don Felipe had almost suffered a fit of apoplexy when Rafael had coolly dictated his terms. At twenty Rafael was no longer a wild savage animal fighting frenziedly to escape an impossible trap. Tall and aloof, the gray eyes already cynical and icy, he had learned painfully to play by his grandfather's rules, and Don Felipe had not liked it at all. In the end the older man had offered a compromise, furiously aware that this time Rafael would remain implacable—no matter to whom or what punishment was inflicted. Bad temperedly Don Felipe had agreed that Buffalo Horn would go free if Rafael went to Spain, but under no circumstances would he release Standing Horse. It had been a stalemate, neither man gaining an outright victory.

Rafael had hated Spain, hated the priests in the sprawling gray-stoned monastery where he had been sent for further refinement, hated the bleakness of the monastery itself, hated the condescending attitude of the Spaniards he met, but most of all he had hated Spain because it had bred his grandfather... and Consuela.

The freedom of Standing Horse had been the price of Rafael's marriage to Consuela Valadez y Gutiérrez. Again Don Felipe had been enraged that his grandson had dared to bargain, enraged that for the first time in his life he had met another man with his own steel-edged determination. It made little difference to Don Felipe that now, at last, he had a grandson who appeared to be everything one could ever want in an heir—he could never quite forgive or forget the Comanche blood that ran in Rafael's veins.

The grand compliments paid Don Felipe by his powerful aristocratic friends in Spain on his grandson's grace and manners gave him no pleasure, knowing full well that it was all a veneer, a thin, brittle veneer that could shatter the instant Standing Horse galloped away from the hacienda, a free Comanche warrior once more. But he'd had no choice—that was more than apparent in the icy gleam of determination in Rafael's gray eyes. And so Standing Horse went free after his long captivity, and at twenty-four Rafael married a woman who despised him for the same reason that his grandfather did.

A mirthless chuckle escaped Rafael as he sat staring at the dead fire. Consuela and Don Felipe should have married—what a mating of vipers that would have been!

Perhaps if Consuela had managed to meet him even part of the way they might have made the ill-matched marriage work, for in those first days Rafael hadn't hated her. He had not liked her, but there might have been buried beneath the hard, unyielding exterior he projected, the faint hope that he could grow to care deeply for this woman he had been forced to marry. In the beginning he had pitied her, for Consuela had been given no choice in her marriage partner—the Gutiérrez family had been more than happy to see one of its daughters married into the powerful and *rich* Santana family, especially as it was the *heir* to the family fortune their daughter was marrying.

Thinking of her death at the hands of a Comanche raiding party, Rafael winced. Not even Consuela would he have condemned to that fate. But then he reminded himself that her own pigheadedness had brought it about. If she hadn't been in such an all-fired hurry to leave the hacienda, her path and that of the raiding party might never have crossed. And then again, who knew, fate had a way of catching up with one when least expected. Certainly her death had been a shock to him, and he had thought it one of life's grotesque ironies that she had died at the hands of the very people she despised most.

Aware of a slight cramp in his calf, Rafael stretched his long legs and glanced up at the black starless sky, feeling the night quiet steal over him, and with it came a certain amount of peace within himself. *¡Dios!* He must be mad to sit here brooding over events that had happened in what seemed another lifetime. It was all over now, so why did he let it haunt him this way?

Wryly he looked across at Sebastian's slumbering form, aware as he had never been before that affection and caring made one weak, that with fondness came a vulnerability he had never suspected, not even when he had bargained for the lives of Buffalo Horn and Standing Horse. Caring for someone, he decided bitterly, was a trap he would avoid in the future.

The chill of the night gradually seeped into his bones and, conscious now of a great tiredness, he lay back down again and pulled the serape around him for warmth. It was strange, he mused drowsily, how thinking of the past tonight had in some peculiar way made him at ease within himself—as if by finally facing the past, the memories had lost the power to hurt him. His hatred for Don Felipe was not diminished in any way, but the pain and torment he had kept locked inside of him was inexplicably gone. Maybe, he thought sleepily, Sebastian inadvertently did me a favor by asking those questions. A smile on his lips, he fell asleep.

CHAPTER FIFTEEN

The ride back to the hacienda was much more leisurely than the previous day's journey out; Rafael stopped more frequently to point out the various advantages of the land they traveled through. His eyes narrowed against the bright morning sun, he said knowledgeably, "It's good land, Sebastian. Abundant water, and grass enough to feed as much livestock as you would ever want. As for cropping, I think you'll find the soil more than just adequate."

Sebastian nodded in eager agreement, his mind already made up. The young face full of enthusiasm, he confessed, "I knew yesterday from what you'd shown me that I wanted it. It's an incredibly appealing country, Rafael; and I can hardly wait to write my father of my decision."

Rafael smiled easily, his glance openly fond as it rested on Sebastian's face. ¡"*Bueno!* It pleases me to know that Cielo will have a member of the Savage family as its nearest neighbor. Miguel, too, will be pleased." His face becoming serious, he said, "If you do intend to apply for the free land, I would suggest that you also buy up as much additional acreage as you can afford. At the moment land is the only thing that Texas seems to have in overabundance—except for Mexican interference and Indians! But it will not remain so."

Sebastian nodded in quick agreement. "I had already considered that—I plan to buy considerably more land than that which is free."

"Good! I suggest that we start back for the hacienda—Miguel is bound to be incensed already at the way I spirited you away from your guests, and to stay away another night would certainly bring down his wrath upon my head."

Rafael looked singularly unconcerned about that possibility, but some of Sebastian's good humor evaporated as the memory of Beth in Rafael's arms returned. Seeing Sebastian's mouth tighten and certain of the reason for it, Rafael cursed under his breath, very close to hating Beth Ridgeway.

Yet the brief trip away from the hacienda and the attendant entanglements had accomplished as much as Rafael could hope for in such a short time—Sebastian was much easier with him now, and the old bond between them seemed almost as strong as before. Time was Rafael's best ally; he would have to stand back and allow it to work its healing process.

Sebastian said nothing as they rode toward the hacienda, although his face did take on a grimmer aspect with every mile that brought them closer to a meeting with Beth. And something that had been bothering him since Rafael had first confessed that Beth was his mistress finally took shape. Twisting in his saddle to look at Rafael's impassive features, he said suspiciously, "It must have been a *very* long-distanced affair between the two of you. I mean with you here in Texas most of the time and Beth tidily tucked away on a plantation near Natchez, you must not have met very often."

Not even glancing at him, Rafael replied coolly, "We didn't... but it was often enough." His voice hardening unexpectedly, he said savagely, "Believe me, it was *more* than often enough!"

Startled by the violence in Rafael's voice, Sebastian stared at him, even more confused. Why the hell did Rafael sound like he hated his mistress?

Rafael was not a liar by nature, and it galled him to be forced to continue to lie, especially to Sebastian. Nor did he like being accountable to anyone for his actions, and he found himself in a most infuriating and uncomfortable position, caught up in a mass of lies and half-truths about English, even further complicated by his undeniable desire for her. He did hate her at the moment, as much for his belief in her entrapment of Sebastian as the urgent hunger to see her again that was clawing painfully through his body. But he fought against that hunger, unwilling to admit that he was eager, for once in his life, to see the red-tiled roof of the hacienda come into sight, and that the reason for his eagerness was a silver-haired, violet-eyed witch who was never far from his mind. He was not, he thought furiously, going to be taken in by that lovely, falsely innocent face again. Once was all he could bear!

It was late afternoon by the time they reached the hacienda. The companionable silence between them was slightly strained as they rode through the iron gates. Leaving their horses at the stables, they walked together toward the house, neither having a great deal to say to the other, and yet neither wishing to end what had been a fairly enjoyable time on this increasingly uncomfortable note. Just before they entered the courtyard from the rear, avoiding the main part of the house, Rafael halted, and facing Sebastian, he muttered angrily, "This is a damnable situation, *amigo!* If I could change things, I would."

It was the nearest Rafael would ever come to an apology, and Sebastian recognized it. He was also becoming more and more aware that Rafael's involvement with Beth was one of those hellishly unfortunate coincidences...for him. There was no way that Rafael could have known that he would lose his head over a woman the other man considered his own. It was, Sebastian decided hollowly, just damned bad luck on his part that the first woman he had ever considered marrying had to be this one. His voice faintly muffled, he said, "Forget it, Rafael! I can't deny that I did cherish certain notions about her that I can see now were absurd. And I must confess that I never received the least bit of encouragement from her." Painfully he admitted, "I've finally had to realize these past several hours that Beth only sees me as a friend—has always seen me as friend—so don't go thinking that she has played you false."

A tight smile on his mouth, the gray eyes inexplicably icy, Rafael retorted instantly, "I am relieved! I would hate to damage that delicate hide of hers by beating the hell out of her for playing the flirt with you."

Sebastian smiled feebly, his heartache easing slightly, and seeking for their old footing, he murmured, "I'm sure that I could think of something better to do with that delicate hide, as you call it, than give her a beating—even a deserved one."

Rafael laughed out loud at that. An amused glint in his eyes, he agreed, "So could I, *amigo,* so could I."

They parted a moment later, and each man felt pleased that they had managed to brush through a rather difficult situation with as little animosity and pain as possible.

It had been near the end of the siesta when the men had returned, and as she dressed for the evening, Beth was unaware that Rafael was once again at the hacienda. But she was prepared for him this time and half expected to meet him when she joined the others.

In a way it had been a tactical error on Rafael's part to leave her alone, for his absence had given Beth an opportunity to think and plan without his disruptive presence smashing her equanimity. Pulling a face at herself in the mirror as she watched Charity put the final touches on her hair arrangement, she admitted gloomily that there really wasn't much choice in a plan to escape the trap she was in. There was only one path open to her; she was going to have to defy his arrogant order that she remain at the hacienda. It was too dangerous to remain, and so whether Rafael was here tonight or not, Beth had every intention of announcing to her hosts that she and Nathan had decided to return to San Antonio—immediately.

Nathan had agreed readily enough when she had approached him about it. She had spent a restless night tossing and turning, searching madly for some solution, and flight seemed the answer. Leaving the hacienda and Rafael's disturbing presence was the only sensible thing to do. As she had been so *un*sensible about this entire disastrous journey so far, she was determined at least to do the sensible thing at its ignoble end.

Beth had dressed with meticulous care, telling herself repeatedly it was only to bolster her confidence and had absolutely *nothing* to do with wanting Rafael Santana to look at her with masculine appreciation. The gown she had finally chosen to wear was a favorite of hers, a silver-blue silk with a bertha of Brussels lace that framed her white bosom and shoulders. Following the fashion of the day, the gown was very low cut, leaving her shoulders bare and giving a tantalizing view of the top of her breasts. The silk material clung to her body, coming to a point at her slender waist in the front before falling in a full, pleated skirt to the floor; a starched lace-trimmed crinoline caused it to flare gently whenever she moved. She wore little jewelry, just a delicate cameo brooch nestled in the bertha of lace near her shoulder and a gold bracelet on one wrist. The silver-gilt hair had been arranged in long shining ringlets that fell on either side of her cheeks and the silver-blue color of the silk gown made her eyes appear a vivid violet-blue, while her mouth with its innocently sultry curve was a rosy invitation that most men would find hard to refuse.

Certainly Nathan found himself unable to resist it when he met her as she left her rooms. Stopping almost abruptly at the sight of her, he reached out for one of her hands and, drawing her near to him, he dropped a gentle passionless kiss on her lips. "How lovely you are this evening, my dear. It must be that traveling agrees with you . . . or"—his eyes suddenly questioning—"is it the thought of our departure tomorrow that turns you into this fairy creature?"

She smiled at him demurely and, a teasing note in her voice, she said, "Perhaps it is because *you* are so overjoyed at our departure that you see me in such extravagant terms, sir!"

Nathan laughed, and in complete harmony they wandered out onto the courtyard. The evening air had only the faintest hint of a chill in it and the sweet smell of daphne and lemon blossoms drifted through the courtyard. As had been the case the previous evenings, Doña Madelina was already there, seated in her favorite chair, and Don Miguel stood near the fountain talking animatedly to her.

Beth chose a seat near the fountain and, sipping her

glass of *sangría,* she chatted pleasantly with her hosts. Under any other circumstances Beth would have enjoyed this stay with Don Miguel and Doña Madelina. They were both so charming and warmhearted that she longed passionately to be precisely what she appeared to be—a chance-met friend of Sebastian's, not the ugly creature that Rafael thought she was. Each hour was another battle to be won, another hour in which she must act gay and carefree, to appear as if she were enjoying herself immensely—and all the while conscious of the lie she lived, conscious of how easily Rafael could saunter in and explode the situation.

The easy hospitality, the cheerful affection bestowed so quickly and freely upon her by Don Miguel and Doña Madelina were the only things that made the situation bearable. And yet those same things made Beth feel despicable, aware, as the others were not, of the hidden shadowy reefs that could suddenly and without warning rip apart the tranquillity of the hacienda.

Don Miguel was especially kind to her, and a cordial friendship had sprung up between them. Having learned of her interest in the Spanish explorations the previous evening, he had regaled her with stories of the first explorers and Texan legends. A twinkle in his dark eyes, almost as if he understood the yearning, adventurous heart that beat beneath the soft white breast, he had patiently answered her impetuous questions.

And this evening proved to be more of the same. While Nathan and Doña Madelina pragmatically exchanged anecdotes concerning life on a plantation and life on a rancho, Beth and Don Miguel, to their mutual enjoyment, were soon immersed in stories of exploration. The fears and worries that were always with her these past few days were forgotten for the moment, and her lovely face was animated with lively interest as she listened to Don Miguel's favorite theory that it was Cabeza de Vaca's stories, much distorted, concerning the awe-inspiring pueblos of the Pueblo Indians that had lent credence to the existence of the golden cities.

"Oh, Don Miguel, do not say so! There are such wondrous tales told of the cities—surely they must exist!" she protested.

An indulgent smile curving his mouth, he replied teasingly, "Perhaps you do not wish to believe that they are so simply explained away, because in your heart you want them to be real. You are, I think, señora, an incredibly beautiful dreamer."

Remembering the foolish, romantic dreams she once had, an unmistakably sad expression flitted across the small face. Seeing it, Don Miguel leaned forward and, laying a warm hand over hers, he asked concernedly, "*Niña,* what is it? Why do you look so unhappy?"

"Unhappy? A guest of ours, *mi padre?* Surely there is some mistake," Rafael drawled from behind them, and Beth stiffened in her seat, her heart thumping madly under the bertha of lace.

"Ah, my son, how like you to appear at such an inopportune moment," Don Miguel replied calmly as he turned to glance at his son.

"Inopportune? Now somehow I rather doubt that, Miguel," Rafael retorted. Leisurely he sauntered around to stand in front of Beth, and, his eyes hard and cold on her face, he said sardonically, "I would think it a most opportune time... even I would be gallant enough, in the face of Señora Ridgeway's beauty, to do my utmost to make her stay at Cielo extremely—er—happy. Introduce us, please."

A giddying sense of *déjà vu* swept over Beth. He stood before her as he had at the Costa Soiree, handsome in a short black velvet *chaqueta* trimmed in silver, the white ruffled shirt heightening his bronzed skin and blue-black hair, and the black velvet *calzoneras* almost indecently displaying his long-limbed figure. With a flutter in her chest Beth met the challenging glitter in his gray eyes.

Her small chin lifted defiantly as she stared coolly back. Her voice determinedly composed and devoid of all expression except politeness, she replied, "How do you do, señor? Your father has spoken of you frequently since we have arrived." The words gagging in her throat, she forced herself to add, "I have looked forward to meeting you."

Rafael smiled, but it didn't quite reach his eyes. Bending over her hand, he deliberately pressed an intimate kiss to the inside of her wrist, the heat of his mouth shocking her. "Now, did you, señora?" he murmured softly. His eyes glinting with mockery, he finished with, "After such a pretty compliment I must be on my best behavior, yes?"

Beth snatched her hand away, and Don Miguel, who had not noticed the surreptitious kiss, looked at her in surprise. Hastily Beth muttered, "I fear I am not used to your Spanish gallantry."

Don Miguel's expression eased. Telling his son to look after their guest, he wandered toward Nathan and Doña Madelina. Beth watched him go with dismay, but her face gave no sign of her inner turmoil.

Dryly Rafael said, "You carried that off superbly, English. I see that with all your other talents you are also a somewhat clever actress. No one would ever suspect that we weren't meeting for the first time. But that isn't the case, is it?"

The violet eyes flashing with anger, she spat in an undertone, "Perhaps you would have preferred for me to mention the circumstances of our last meeting? I'm certain your father and my husband would have found it a titillating dinner subject!"

Lowering himself with indolent grace into the chair next to hers, he said amusedly, "Titillating is the mildest word I can think of to describe their emotions!"

Her voice tight with suppressed feeling Beth snapped, "You find this all very entertaining, don't you?"

His eyes traveling almost caressingly over her face and bosom, he murmured, "I must confess that there are parts of this charade that I find *very* entertaining."

With difficulty Beth fought off the desire to reach across and slap his mocking face. Her clenched fists were hidden in the folds of her skirt but there was no way she could hide her anger, it being so very obvious in the rigid curve of her soft mouth and the belligerent set of her small rounded chin. Fortunately no one seemed to be paying them any heed, and, aware of the dire need *not* to have anyone notice anything out of the ordinary, with an effort Beth made herself relax. A deceptively limpid smile on her lips, she said sweetly, "You are a swine, señor! I *despise* you, and I would advise you not to turn your back on me—I might be tempted to bury a dagger in it!"

To Beth's discomfort, Rafael only sent her a lazy smile. A sudden flick of passion in his eyes that was at odds with the lightness of his tone of voice, he returned carelessly, "And I, English, happen to *desire* you . . . too much for my own liking."

Beth felt a queer jolt of excitement shoot through her at his words, and, swiftly averting her eyes from the blaze of desire in his, she asked tartly, "Have you considered denying yourself? I can assure you that I would be most delighted if you found some other—er—source of relieving yourself of this unwanted desire you claim to have."

Rafael gave a harsh bark of laughter. "Don't start *that* sort of argument in public," he threatened softly, "because if you do, I'll make damn sure we finish it in private!"

Beth was incensed enough to ignore his warning, but her heated reply was lost when Rafael, with a curt nod in the direction of the others, asked in an oddly taut voice, "The simpering dandy over by my stepmother, is he your husband? The one who is all the things that I am not?"

It was a strange way to phrase it, and yet she was instantly and unhappily aware of how very true it was. Nathan was everything that Rafael was not—kind and gentle where Rafael would be fierce and hard; Rafael decisive and adamant against those who disagreed with him, Nathan more likely to give in; Nathan as blond and unassuming as Rafael was dark and aggressive; Rafael blatantly masculine against Nathan's almost effeminate posturings; Nathan weak where Rafael was strong. It horrified Beth to discover the train of her thoughts, and she was angry all over again at Rafael for opening her mind to such disloyal musings. Rafael might be a strong, devastatingly masculine man, but who cared? Nathan was good to her, and now she was guilty of betraying him in mind, as well as her body. That very same feeling of guilt made her long to defend Nathan against Rafael's criticism, but there had been a note in his voice that made her tread cautiously. Picking her words with care she said with surprising mildness, "He is not simpering. But if someone who pays an inordinate amount of attention to his attire is called a dandy, then I would have to agree that Nathan is a dandy." Her eyes were on Nathan as she spoke, and he happened to look up just then and smile in her direction. Unaware of the way Rafael's eyes narrowed when her face immediately softened or of the warmth in the enchanting smile that she sent back to her husband, she added quietly, "A gentle, dear dandy at that."

There was an explosive expletive from Rafael; his sudden violent surge to his feet caused Beth to stare at him in bewilderment. "Is something wrong?" she asked innocently.

His heavy black eyebrows meeting in a scowling frown above the arrogantly jutting nose, Rafael snarled acidly, "No! Why should there be?"

Not waiting for her answer, his hand closed around her slender wrist and, almost jerking her upright, he snapped, "Walk over there with me—I want very much to meet this paragon of virtue."

But there was no need, for Nathan was already making his way toward them. Beth had just enough time to twist herself free from Rafael's grasp and step a little away from him before Nathan strolled up to them. A polite smile on his mouth, Nathan said, "You must be Rafael, Don Miguel's son. We have not met, but I am Madame Ridgeway's husband, Nathan."

The three of them presented a striking tableau—Beth, a bright slender figure with her shining ash-fair ringlets and silver-blue gown, standing stiffly between the two taller, darker-clothed men. She was trapped in the middle—Nathan standing in front of her, Rafael looming almost possessively by her side—and trapped was exactly how Beth felt as she stared from one man to the other. Terrified lest Nathan suspect that something was wrong, she said with a rush, "We were just on the point of joining you. Señor Santana had just said that he wanted to meet you."

It was lame, but Nathan seemed to sense nothing out of the ordinary. "Oh," he said, looking at Rafael. "Was there some particular reason?"

Beth's heart seemed to stop as she waited tensely for Rafael's answer, fearful and angry at the same time. If Nathan chanced to guess who this tall, intimidating man was... Unaware that she did it, her eyes clung to Rafael's dark face, a plea shimmering in the violet depths.

The second Nathan approached them, Rafael had brought under rigid control the fierce emotions that had erupted when Beth had smiled warmly at her husband and spoken of him with such odd tenderness. The furious inner battle was not apparent to the others, but Rafael was more than aware of it, infuriatingly conscious that instead of smiling politely and greeting Nathan with sophisticated charm, he wanted intensely to slit the man's throat—and abduct his wife! Illogically enraged with Beth for being the cause of this ugly conflict, he fleetingly considered being as disagreeable as possible. But the silent appeal of her lovely eyes stopped him and, not even thinking about it, reacting instinctively to the entreaty in her gaze, he found himself saying blandly, "Yes, as a matter of fact there was a particular reason—your tailor, I *must* have his name! I was just telling your"—he stumbled over the word—"er—wife, how much I admire the cut of your coat."

Nothing could have been more calculated to please Nathan, and, a gratified smile spreading over his face, he said with pleasure, "Oh, well, thank you very much! I firmly believe that a really good tailor is essential, and I would be most happy to give you the fellow's name. He is very clever, I must say." An anxious expression suddenly appearing on his face he added, "You do realize that he is in Natchez? I'm very much afraid that you would have to go to him, rather than the other way around."

Rafael smiled lazily. "Of course. How could it be any other way? As soon as I saw your coat, I knew it had to have been made east of the Mississippi River."

In stunned amazement, Beth stood between the two men, her pretty mouth nearly falling open in shock as Rafael continued to speak about the latest in men's fashion as if it were the overriding passion in his life, much to Nathan's evident enjoyment. Fortunately neither of them expected her to add to their conversation, and her astonished silence went unnoticed by Nathan, if not Rafael. As Nathan happily displayed the lilac satin lining of his frock coat, Rafael sent Beth a sharp look from under his heavy lids, the gray eyes taking in with quick amusement the staggered expression on her face.

Sebastian's arrival a second later seemed to shake Beth from her trancelike state and she breathed a cautious sigh of relief. It was highly unlikely that Rafael would say anything too awkward in front of Sebastian... at least she desperately hoped that he wouldn't.

If Beth had been astonished by Rafael's seemingly insatiable interest in the intricacies of masculine grooming, Sebastian was clearly astounded. When he discovered that the subject of the earnest discussion between the two men was the superiority of boot blacking mixed with champagne over more mundane concoctions, he could hardly contain himself. Nathan's burning absorption in clothing was no surprise—but *Rafael?*

Sebastian liked a certain style and elegance as well as the next man, but there were limits, and as the discussion shifted to the question of whether a primrose-figured silk was perhaps "just a trifle busy" for the lining of a formal black velvet jacket, he found Rafael's apparent interest in the topic ridiculous. His cousin dressed impeccably when in company, but he had never before realized that someone he had thought of as the *last* person to harbor the yearnings of a dandy, had a deep and fervent interest in the tiniest detail of presenting one's self as properly and stylishly attired.

Guessing the trend of Sebastian's disdainful thoughts, Rafael groaned inwardly. He must be every kind of a fool imaginable to prate this foolish bit of flummery simply for a plea in a pair of deceitful violet eyes. But it served the purpose, he decided reluctantly. Nathan was completely disarmed, and it had given him the chance to take his measure of the man. Rafael's assessment of Nathan was not flattering, but, having actually met English's husband at last, he began, he thought, to understand her predilection for the arms of other men. Nathan was a weak, foppish creature, more inclined to worry over the welfare of his wardrobe than his wife, and Rafael startled himself by feeling faintly sorry for English. Perhaps she was not as black as he had first presumed, he mused. Suddenly inordinately curious about their life together and not certain why, Rafael started casually questioning Nathan about Briarwood and Natchez. And Nathan, enjoying himself hugely, much to Beth's dismay was very happy to babble on about the plantation and Beth's exemplary management.

Naturally uneasy with Rafael and Nathan together, Beth attempted at least half a dozen times during the next twenty minutes to change the subject or pry Nathan loose, but nothing would deter him. He was, it seemed to Beth, determined to reveal, except for the most intimate details, every facet of their life in Natchez, from her experiments in crop rotation to his gambling and jaunts "under the hill." She was equally determined that Rafael find out as little as possible about them, but Nathan innocently defeated her at every turn, and Rafael displayed, she thought angrily, an almost indecent engrossment in events that were none of his affair. As they all joined Doña Madelina and Don Miguel in walking into the hacienda for dinner, Beth was sickly aware that there was little of her life that Rafael didn't know about.

Seated in the spacious dining room, she shot Rafael a wary glance, wondering what he thought of Nathan's revelations and why he had acted as he had—so easily could he have betrayed her or made Nathan suspicious about their relationship, but he hadn't. Instead, deliberately, she was positive, he had charmed and disarmed her husband, and that knowledge did little to lessen the tight knot of apprehension that clenched painfully in her chest. Rafael's lean face gave her no clue, but she surprised a lazily assessing gleam in his eyes that made her uneasiness increase. *What* was he up to now?

CHAPTER SIXTEEN

Rafael's thoughts would have astonished Beth had she been privy to them. For the first time in his entire life he found himself nonplussed, but his state of mind had little to do with what he had learned from Nathan. Rather it was his reaction to Nathan that perplexed him and disturbed him. He had never before hated a man on sight, not even Don Felipe, nor had he ever seriously considered stealing another man's wife. Yet this evening, behind a cool, polite face, he was doing both, and it made him edgy and angry.

Women had never meant a great deal to Rafael, partly due to his Comanche upbringing and partly due to the lack of any stable relationship with a woman. He had never known a mother's love, and his marriage had certainly not engendered any affection for women within him. As far as he was concerned women served two purposes: They gave a man physical pleasure and they bore children. Beyond that they had little value to him. He had never kept a mistress for more than a few weeks, nor had he ever pursued a woman; too many of them displayed an eagerness for his bed that he had found distasteful. There had been several married women amongst those who had known the devastation of his desire, but their husbands had never aroused any emotion in him but contempt... until now. Until he had met the husband of the woman who had haunted his thoughts more than he would have cared to admit.

His violent reaction to Nathan Ridgeway unsettled him, that and the fact that whenever English was referred to as Nathan's wife he longed to rip out the speaker's tongue. He could not even think of her as Beth—Beth was Nathan's wife, but English was *his!* And the thought of her lying in Nathan's arms filled him with such rage and pain that his mind went icily blank, unable to accept the idea that another man had a right to that slender white body, that another man had claim to her love.

What made her different? he asked himself angrily, staring obliquely across the table at her blond loveliness. He'd known women as lovely before—perhaps not *quite* as lovely, he amended slowly, admitting to himself that there had never been one with hair like hers or eyes of that incredible shade of violet, nor possessing a body that was so exquisitely perfect from the top of the small fair head to the soles of the slim arched feet. But the other women in his life had been lovely too, lush, lovely, passionate creatures who had clung to him and ardently returned his caresses until he had grown weary of them and their demands upon his time. But not English. She had resisted him from the beginning. Rafael remembered without humor how she had refused to look at him when he first strode up to Stella intent upon learning the name of the entrancing creature at her side. An ethereal creature with eyes like sparkling amethysts and sun-kissed moonbeam hair who had made his heart, until then a most reliable organ, suddenly leap painfully in his breast the moment he had caught sight of her across the shifting expanse of the Costa ballroom. And what had she done? Almost wrathfully he recalled that she had ignored him and smiled at some hovering gallant, arousing within him a savage desire to lift the young man's scalp.

But it wasn't her resistance to his physical attractions that had given rise to the queer emotions that swirled and twined through his veins, nor, he confessed reluctantly, was it the memory of that silken body writhing under his. Passion and resistance had nothing to do with a violent urge to protect and cherish. ...Rafael, who had never experienced those feelings, had done so the night of the Costa soiree and was doing so now, and it bewildered him as much as it infuriated him. Why *her* of all women, for God's sake! he wondered furiously. She was a slut—he knew that for a certainty; she betrayed her husband at every turn and ensnared unwary, romantic young men like Sebastian at the first opportunity. And yet—his long-lipped mouth twisted bitterly—and yet, dear God, he wanted her as he had never wanted anything in his life. Angrily he took a deep drink of the potent red wine that was served with dinner and stared with resentment at Beth's averted head as she turned to speak with Sebastian. How dared she disturb him this way! Deliberately he fed his anger and fury, reminding himself cynically over and over again of the incidents that proved his opinion of her wicked character. By the time the meal had ended, Rafael had managed to convince himself that he actually hated the sight of Beth Ridgeway and that his only interest in her was the fact that she had a beautiful body. Reducing his emotions to simple lust didn't allow him to banish her completely from his thoughts, but it at least let him think that he had overcome a momentary weakening. No woman was ever going to find her way into *his* heart!

Rafael's introspection had gone practically unnoticed during the meal, although Sebastian had glanced at him once or twice, curious about his sudden silence. Sebastian himself was not quite in his normal high spirits, his conversation with Beth slightly stilted upon occasion, especially whenever he chanced to find Rafael's speculating gaze upon them.

Sebastian had dreaded his next meeting with Beth, but despite his heartache and disillusionment he found it not the painful ordeal he had thought it would be. It helped enormously that Beth was completely unaware of his newfound knowledge, and after the first few uncomfortable moments Sebastian discovered to his surprise and delight that not a great deal had changed between them. Beth treated him as she always had, teasing him gently and smiling charmingly at his light banter, and if she appeared a bit distracted at times he put it down to the strain of maintaining an unruffled calm when one's husband and lover were seated side by side at the same dining table. But in spite of the ease with which he had quickly reestablished their association, he was more than happy to see the meal end, needing more time to come to grips with Beth's involvement with Rafael.

Nathan, Don Miguel, and Doña Madelina were the only ones that truly enjoyed the evening, and they were the only ones unaware of the tension in the air that increased as the evening drew near its end. Nathan should have been aware of it; more than that, his instincts that had served him so well in connection with Sebastian seemed to have deserted him when confronted with the first real threat to his future happiness.

Nathan had recognized Sebastian's infatuation almost immediately, but while he considered Rafael Santana to possess an urbane charm, he found him not at all to his liking once the first burst of pleasure at find ing someone who shared his passion for dandyism had passed. Rafael was too dark and vital for his taste, those startling and enigmatic gray eyes made him uneasy. His instincts did not let him down on one point though: Nathan sensed the power underneath Rafael's air of sophistication, and the streak of ruthlessness that lurked not too far from the elegant surface of the other man. And because he found Rafael's aggressive maleness faintly intimidating, because he didn't think the lean, powerful face particularly handsome, he made the mistake of assuming that a woman would feel the same. It never entered his head that he had just dined with the man he had feared most would one day appear in Beth's life. A man who could steal her heart away before she even realized what had happened.

Beth herself hadn't realized it either, but as the time approached to make the announcement that she and Nathan were departing in the morning, she was conscious of a strong reluctance to do so. Her reluctance had nothing to do with outfacing Rafael, but it did have everything to do with the knowledge that she was leaving him and might never see him again. She could chastise herself endlessly for being a weak-willed spineless creature where Rafael was concerned, she could remind herself over and over again of her marriage vows, but nothing seemed to help lessen the pain engendered by the thought of never seeing him again. She was torn by her duty and vows to Nathan on one hand and what she feared was her only chance for love on the other. That she even considered the possibility of love in connection with Rafael Santana, she knew was foolish, but she couldn't pretend that there was not a tenuous thread of emotion between them, a thread she would have given much to be able to spin into something stronger and more enduring. But she dared not. Nor, she admitted with anguish, could she close her heart to her marriage and Nathan.

Beth had hoped that Nathan would introduce the subject of their departure, but he appeared to be waiting for her to do so. And as the hour grew late and still she had not mentioned it, she was aware of the question in his eyes whenever they chanced to meet hers. Finally, knowing she could put it off no longer, knowing that leaving Rafael behind was the only sane path left open to her, as they were sipping a last glass of wine before retiring, she forced herself to say brightly, "Oh, what a marvelous visit this has been! Nathan and I shall be very sorry to say good-bye to you when we leave in the morning. You have been so very kind to us that we shall think of you a great deal on our journey back to Natchez."

There was a moment of silence, silence that to Beth seemed fraught with danger, and then there was the sudden babble as Don Miguel and Doña Madelina both expressed their regret and the wish that the Ridgeways would stay longer. Resolutely Beth resisted their entreaties, Nathan coming to her rescue by stating blandly that they simply had to leave in the morning.

Sebastian remained silent at first, uncertain whether he would be happy or miserable to see Beth leave. He decided after a second's thought that it was probably for the best. Compelling himself to smile naturally, Sebastian said with forced cheerfulness, "I'm sorry that you cannot avail yourself longer of my cousin's hospitality, but do not be at all surprised if later this year you see me in Natchez. After I have seen to all the legal documents pertaining to my ownership of the lands Rafael and I inspected, I will be returning to New Orleans to buy various supplies. Perhaps while there I will travel up the river and pay you a visit. That is, if the invitation is still open?"

Nathan halfheartedly assured him that it was, and with more warmth in his voice informed the Santanas that if they were ever east of the Mississippi they must make Briarwood Plantation one of the places that they visited. It was all done very politely, everyone voicing the polite things one does when a departure looms near—everyone, that is, except Rafael.

His body had stiffened when Beth had made her announcement and a hard glitter had entered the smoky gray eyes. He waited until most of the regrets and invitations were through and then, slowly putting down his snifter of brandy, he murmured, "How very convenient!" His narrowed eyes on Beth's face, he continued, "I too have reason to be riding into San Antonio tomorrow morning, and with your permission will accompany you."

Beth's tongue froze to the roof of her mouth and her heart began to thump. She had known she ran a risk in defying him and that he might take retaliatory action, but not even in her wildest imagination had she thought that he would insist on going with them to San Antonio. She realized now that it would have been far safer to remain at the hacienda with the others about than to put herself in the position in which she now found herself. Once the hacienda was out of sight, except for their servants, she and Nathan would be alone with him, and for one fleeting, chilling moment, she remembered Consuela's death. Had he arranged that? And did he hate her so much that he was arranging for history to repeat itself? She couldn't or wouldn't believe it of him, but she certainly did not want him escorting her and her husband back to San Antonio.

Nathan, however, had no such qualms and blithely accepted Rafael's invitation. "Oh, that would be splendid! It is always pleasant to have someone who knows the country traveling along."

Rafael bowed and said smoothly, "Good. And being as how I presume you will be staying a few days in San Antonio, I hope you will do me the honor of accepting the hospitality of a house I have there."

Beth would have rushed in with a refusal, but Sebastian's surprised comment cut her off. "You have a house in San Antonio?"

It was Don Miguel who answered. A testy note in his voice, he said, "His Grandfather Hawkins left him a sizable estate when he died a few years ago, and included in it was the house of which he speaks." Turning to Nathan, he added, "I had thought to suggest that you might like to stay in a small house we have on the outskirts of San Antonio, but my son has forestalled me. You will like his house just as well, though—it is a very nice house, señor, I think you would find it much more comfortable than a hotel."

"Well, that settles it, then!" Nathan said genially. "Of course we will accept your invitation, sir."

It was all arranged so quickly that Beth never had a chance to refute the plans, and, undressing for bed a short while later, she was filled with frustration and tears. She should have been more alert for Rafael to make some sort of move to thwart her, but she hadn't really thought that he would care one way or another. It was true he had warned her to remain at the hacienda, but upon deeper reflection she had decided he had been merely... Well, she didn't know what might have been in his mind at that moment, but she had felt fairly confident that if she forced the issue he wouldn't make any effort to stop her. After all, having the opinion of her that he had, surely he would be happy to see the last of her. Wouldn't he?

The fact that he wasn't willing to do so alarmed her and yet it also, she admitted shamefully, gave her a queer flutter of excitement. Which was the *last* emotion she should be feeling, she rounded on herself angrily. What sort of an empty-headed fool was she? Rafael Santana was dangerous—too dangerous for her peace of mind—and for a brief second she recalled reading of Lady Caroline Lamb's comment made decades ago concerning that dashing Lord Byron: "Mad, bad, and dangerous to know!" *That* certainly fitted Rafael Santana!

Sleep proved elusive, her thoughts tumbling and churning. She couldn't help but remember Manuela's recital of the facts leading to Consuela's death, and for a long time she lay in her bed wondering if Rafael really *had* arranged it. Her spirit rebelled against such an unworthy idea. Rafael might be dangerous, he might also be "mad and bad," but somehow she couldn't imagine him doing something that despicable. Beth was quite certain that he was capable of murder, but she was positive he would have been far more likely to strangle Consuela with his bare hands in a fit of fury than to cold-bloodedly set a pack of Comanche killers on her trail. That thought didn't make her feel any better, but at least it resolved one particular fear. If she'd had the slightest lingering doubt that Rafael was indeed capable of doing such a dastardly act, *nothing* would have compelled her to set foot outside of the hacienda.

Another fear was set partially to rest too that long sleepless night—Rafael hadn't betrayed their bitterly regretted association to Nathan, and, restlessly mulling it over, she came to the conclusion that for whatever devious reasons, he wasn't going to do so. That such a secret existed and that she was a party to it made her writhe with self-abomination. If only she had ignored Consuela's invitation that day in New Orleans....

Morning came at last and finally, after what seemed like days to Beth, the hour for their departure approached. There had been quite a bustle as their trunks and valises were packed and loaded, but Nathan gave Beth a nasty scare when he murmured mildly, "It is a shame that we have to leave in this hurly-burly manner. There really was no pressing reason for us not to stay for several more days, was there?"

Beth shot him an almost frightened look, but there was nothing in his face to alarm her and she said quickly, "No, there wasn't. But having made up our minds, I just naturally assumed that you would want to start back as soon as possible."

Nathan regarded her for a long moment, his gray eyes taking in the purple shadows under her eyes and the hint of strain that seemed to tighten her soft mouth. Despite discounting Rafael Santana's charms with the opposite sex, Nathan was very aware of the fact that his wife had been acting singularly strange ever since they had arrived at the hacienda, especially since Don

Miguel's son had appeared. He knew Beth rather well, and he'd have been a dunce not to have suspected that something was bothering her. He had tried a few times to get her to tell him but she had always shied away—just as she was doing now.

When the actual moment came to say good-bye, Beth found it oddly emotional. She hated bidding Sebastian farewell, he had come to mean a great deal to her, and Don Miguel and Doña Madelina had been so kind and hospitable that she felt a perfect wretch for leaving so swiftly. Doña Madelina's eyes were suspiciously misty when she said good-bye to Beth, and the surprising strength of the unexpected embrace she bestowed stayed with Beth for a long time. Don Miguel had kissed her gently on the forehead and whispered, "I shall hold the memory of your visit dear to me, *niña.*" Smiling warmly he added, "One would think that already having five lovely daughters I would object to a sixth—but if she were like you, I would thank God."

It was a generous compliment and Beth fought back tears. The hacienda was only a shimmering, blurring outline to her gaze, and the cries of "*¡Vaya con Dios!*" rang in her ears as the coach slowly moved away.

Don Miguel had insisted upon sending ten men to increase the size and protection of their party for the journey to San Antonio, and so it was a well-armed group that left the hacienda. Rafael, riding his big dapple-gray stallion like a centaur, his expression hidden under the brim of his large black sombrero, rode past the coach as they cleared the gates, his dynamic presence reminding Beth that she had not yet escaped from the peril he represented. The sight of the ever-present Colt pistol strapped to his thigh and the long black muzzle-loading rifles of the *vaqueros* brought home again to Beth the very real dangers of the journey she had undertaken so lightly. Suddenly she longed passionately for the quiet jasmine-lined streets of Natchez.

Nathan had been perfectly amenable to Beth's desire for the sudden departure, feeling more lighthearted than he had in ages. With the same languid grace with which he had descended from the coach three days previously he had ascended it that morning, and while he wouldn't have minded visiting with the Santanas for a more extended period, he watched the hacienda grow smaller in the distance with pleasure.

Beth's distress at leaving the hacienda had been obvious, and Nathan was certain there was more to it than just the sadness of bidding friends farewell. Perhaps she had discovered that she cared more deeply for Sebastian than she had realized? He frowned. No, of course not! So what was troubling her? It was not Nathan's nature to pry, nor was he likely to take offense at her desire to keep her thoughts to herself, but he decided he would make one last attempt to discover the cause of Beth's odd tenseness and unhappiness. He said nothing for several miles, deliberately giving Beth time to recover her composure. Finally, though, somewhat carefully regarding his expertly polished boots, he asked quietly, "Would you care to enlighten me as to the *real* reason we left the hacienda so abruptly?"

Beth kept her eyes on her gloved hands that were lying loosely in her lap, suddenly weary of the lies and half-truths. "Do you honestly want to know, Nathan?" she asked at last.

Now that she was on the point of telling him, Nathan wasn't so certain it was such a wise idea. He thought about it for quite some time and he said calmly, "No, I don't think I do, my dear."

She looked at him then and smiled faintly. "Have I ever told you, *dear* Nathan, that I care very deeply for you?"

An extremely gratified expression crossed his face. "Why, no, I don't believe you ever have," he said lightly. And, with an odd air of needing reassurance, he asked, "Do you?"

"Very much, Nathan, *very* much." Beth answered with a tremulous smile, her conscience pricking her at the deceit she had so unwillingly practiced on him.

There was little conversation between them after that, both of them lost in their own thoughts, Nathan congratulating himself on the wisdom of giving Beth her head, and of not allowing his unworthy suspicions and jealousy of Sebastian to burst its bounds.

As for Beth, she had not been merely saying words

to hear herself speak when she told her husband that she cared deeply for him. She did. And while she knew he would never arouse the wildly giddying passions that Rafael evoked so effortlessly, she was suddenly determined to work even harder at making their marriage stronger and more meaningful. At home she would be able to forget Rafael Santana and the dark pull he had on her heart.

Yet Beth was stubbornly positive that she did not *love* Rafael. Love did not come so quickly, so unwillingly, she thought desperately. Love was what she and Nathan shared, the pleasurable learning of one another slowly and leisurely, of day by day growing closer and closer as they had, *not* something that was like a thunderbolt out of a cloudless sky. Not something that caused her heart to beat erratically every time she saw Rafael's tall, powerful male figure, nor the queer fearful excitement that surged through her body at the thought of being in his arms and having his hard mouth plunder hers. No, *that* wasn't love—that was just silly infatuation, she told herself firmly. Silly, *foolish* infatuation! She would not consider it to be anything else. Somehow she was going to get through the next few miserable days and then at last she and Nathan would be on their way home to Briarwood, leaving Rafael and everything associated with him far behind.

But it was easier to make that vow than to keep it, as she found out that night when they finally stopped to make camp. They had made camp fairly early in a secluded spot near a small waterfall that formed a clear pool of water at its base; under other circumstances Beth would have found it charming. But there were two very good reasons why she didn't. The first was the deplorable fact that Nathan, inclined to celebrate their return to civilization a bit more exuberantly than necessary or seemly, had partaken far too freely of the brandy that he had carried with him from Natchez, and within a very short time he was snoring away in one of the wagons as drunk as Beth had ever seen him. It came as a shock, because while she had always known that Nathan drank, and heavily at that—what gentleman didn't?—he had never before done so in front of her, and she found it distressing. And of course, the other reason for her lack of enjoyment of the starry sky and cool evening breeze that rustled the leaves of the sycamore trees near the waterfall was Rafael's dark intrusive presence.

He had been frigidly polite all day long, and she had been able to avoid him simply because he chose to ride his horse rather than accept the comfort of the coach. Rafael's actions toward her were so stiffly correct that she wondered if she had mistaken his reason for accompanying them. She tried not to think of him, tried not to think of his purpose for traveling with them, but she failed dismally.

The reasons for Rafael's cool correctness were simple: He was so icily furious with Beth that he didn't dare trust himself to treat her with anything but punctilious civility. Not only had she caught him off guard by her defiance, but more than that, instead of letting her go out of his life as he would have any other woman, he discovered that he hadn't been able to do so. And what must I do, he thought viciously, but tag along behind her like a lovesick, callow fool!

It was true that he did have business in San Antonio, and it was true that he had planned to leave this morning for that city. But it was equally true that if it hadn't been for Beth he would have left Cielo at first light and could have beaten the slower-traveling Ridgeways there by as much as a half a day. It didn't improve his temper to know precisely why he hadn't done exactly that—English! Damn her beautiful hide!

Rafael had been drinking himself, but Nathan's steady assault on the bottle of brandy disturbed him, and once he had even thought to suggest that Nathan restrain his desire for the bottle until they were in more appropriate surroundings, but then he shrugged and turned away. Ridgeway was a grown man.

The evening meal, eaten by the light of the flickering campfire, had been decidedly uncomfortable. Nathan was by then already far too drunk to be an agreeable companion; though he said nothing particularly offensive, it was embarrassing to watch his less-than-adept handling of the utensils, and his rambling conversation left much to be desired. Between Beth and Rafael there was an unfriendly, tense silence.

With relief Beth at last sought the privacy of the wagon where she slept at night. But after tossing for some time and finding herself wakeful and restive after a day spent in the close confines of the coach, she slipped on the pale green robe of printed satin that Charity had left lying on the foot of the makeshift bed and climbed down gracefully from the wagon.

The camp was quiet except for the faint crackle of the dying fire and soft noises of the horses and oxen as they moved restlessly about. Everyone seemed to be asleep except for two men sitting near the remains of the fire, and Beth could make out the outline of a third as he stood guard near the coach. Rafael was nowhere in sight. Mindful of the fact that it wouldn't be wise to wander far, Beth hesitated and then couldn't resist a short walk to the waterfall just out of sight of the camp.

The moon was barely half full, but there was enough light to guide her. She reached the waterfall and, standing by it, listening to the soft splash the water made as it tumbled over the rocks before falling into the pool near her feet, she was filled with a sense of peace and tranquillity.

It didn't last. She had just reached out and cupped a handful of the sweet water to taste when Rafael's voice made her whirl about.

He was leaning negligently against a tree, his sombrero brim hiding the expression in the gray eyes, but the moonlight clearly revealed the mocking slant to his mouth.

"You didn't really think I was going to let you escape me this easily, did you, English?"

Beth hesitated, not certain of his mood. He didn't appear angry, and yet there was a note in his voice that she distrusted. But, exhausted by the struggle within herself, she had nothing left to fight him with and merely shrugged her shoulders, saying quietly, "No...but I hoped you would see the folly in our continued association. Nothing good can come from it, surely you can see that?"

He smiled a dangerously attractive smile and pushed

himself away from the tree in one, lithe, easy movement. Tipping back the rim of his sombrero with a finger, his eyes traveled over her body with a blatant sensuality. "Oh, I wouldn't say that, sweetheart, I can think of a lot of *good* things that could happen between us... have happened between us."

The innuendo was not lost on Beth, and her soft mouth hardened. It was difficult to remain cool, difficult to control the sudden blinding urge to throw caution to the winds and release all her inner guilty frustration and turmoil by flinging herself at him, scratching and clawing. Oh, what satisfaction it would give her to knock that mocking smile from his face, she thought fiercely, and unconsciously one of her hands curved into a small, determined fist.

Rafael saw the involuntary movement and his smile widened provokingly. Walking nearer to her, he said softly, "I wouldn't if I were you, English. Touch me and we both know what will happen."

Beth swallowed, wishing he weren't so close to her, wishing she weren't so shamefully aware of the attraction of that long, warm body. She stepped back nervously and felt the cool edge of rock behind her. Trapped, rock to her back and Rafael in front of her, she held her chin up belligerently and, striving for a calmness she didn't feel, murmured, "I don't think we have anything further to discuss. So if you will just step aside, I'll return to my bed."

"Alone?" he taunted.

It was then that she smelled the faint hint of whiskey on his breath, and, ignoring his question, she asked tightly, "Are you drunk too?"

He shook his head. "Hardly! Unlike your husband, I know how to hold my liquor. But I will confess that in the absence of more animated company, I have consoled myself with a very adequate liquid stimulus."

Beth flushed at the reference to Nathan. Heatedly she retorted, "You *are* drunk!"

"No. Your *husband* is drunk," Rafael returned coolly, a glitter of amusement in the gray eyes. "I have possibly imbibed more than I should have before calling upon a lady, but no, I am not drunk."

Rafael spoke the truth. He would never do anything so foolish as to get drunk on the trail. But it was true that he had consumed more whiskey than was perhaps wise under their present conditions. But even drunk he would still be more in command and control of himself than Nathan, and the condition he was in now only made him more reckless than usual, less cautious, infinitely more dangerous.... His earlier anger had evaporated, leaving in its place a strange vulnerability that he would have destroyed if the liquor hadn't blunted the iron command he kept on himself. But Beth was more potent than any liquor could ever be for him and, not even conscious that he did it, Rafael reached out and lightly traced the side of her face with the fingers of one hand. "You are very beautiful, English. So beautiful that I..." He stopped abruptly, the gray eyes searching hers intently as if he sought an answer to some dilemma within their violet depths.

The gentle touch of his hand on her cheek was a sweet agony, and her body trembled with the force of the emotions he evoked. Beth knew she should break the growing intimacy between them, knew she should slap his hand away, but she was caught in the spell of his powerful masculinity. Weakly she began, "Rafael, please..." But his mouth was already descending and the words died in her throat.

He had never kissed her quite this way before, and it was as if the whiskey had banished the hard, sarcastic man she knew so well and unknowingly revealed the gentle lover he kept so deeply submerged. There was a wealth of tenderness in his kiss as his mouth gently moved on hers, and helplessly Beth felt all her opposition vanish, her body seeking his comfort and warmth, her slim arms locking hungrily around his neck.

They were lost to the world around them, Rafael drinking deeply of the sweetness that Beth was giving freely, Beth accepting the ecstasy of being in his arms once more. His mouth was a soft flame as his lips clung to hers, his hands pulling her closer to him until she could feel the hard, insistent urgency of the growing desire within him.

Her body shuddered against his, the painful ache for

fulfillment that he had aroused and could assuage so effortlessly coiling in her loins, her breasts suddenly feeling full and yearning for the touch of his mouth. As if knowing instinctively what she wanted, Rafael unhurriedly pushed aside the silk robe and freed one white breast, his lips closing gently around the upthrusting coral nipple. Beth gave a small moan of pleasure, her head falling back against the rocks as she arched her body up nearer to his, wanting him and what he was doing against her will.

The sudden snort of one of the horses, not too far from where they stood, brought Rafael instantly back to reality. Breathing heavily, his body tight and pulsating with the burning passion to know again the exquisite sorcery of Beth's slender body, he lifted his head, listening intently, suddenly aware of the danger in what they were doing. Now was not the time, nor this the place for what he wanted from her, and with a dull sort of fury he acknowledged that the *right* time and place for him and the woman in his arms might never come to pass... unless he made it happen.

Beth felt his withdrawal, and she was filled with mortification at the wave of disappointment that hit her. Mentally she might try to resist him, but her body showed no such niceties, the yearning ache in the pit of her stomach very real, the throb of her swollen nipples almost painful.

After a tense moment Rafael was certain that the snort of the horse heralded nothing sinister. He looked down at Beth with a rueful smile. "As much as I want you, I'm not going to risk a lost scalp or the sight of your lovely hair hanging from a Comanche lance for the joy of it. Sorry, sweetheart, I think the best place for you right now is your wagon. Alone."

Humiliated by her reaction to his nearness as well as the easy way that he could dismiss what had just happened, Beth stiffened in his arms. Through clenched teeth she got out, "Will you please let me go, then?"

Rafael cursed under his breath, realizing how clumsy his words had been. Gripping her shoulders between his strong hands, he muttered, "I didn't mean that as lightly as it sounded." He slanted her a wry grin and murmured, "When I am with you I seem able only to concentrate on you . . . and out here that could be deadly. I am not used to explaining myself, English, but I didn't mean to belittle what just happened. It would be much safer for you if you returned to your wagon, and instead of kissing you I should have given you a blistering tongue-lashing for wandering about in the dark."

Tipping her head back to look up at his harsh features, and longing for an argument, Beth challenged, "Then why didn't you?"

But Rafael was not to be drawn. He pulled her closer to him, and, his breath warm against her cheek, he said softly, "You know as well as I do why I didn't." And, unable to withstand the lure of the rosy mouth inches from his own, he dropped his dark head and kissed her again, a long, lingering kiss that left Beth feeling weak and yearning for more.

Rafael, too, seemed oddly reluctant to end their intimacy, his arms holding her firmly to him, and his lips gently caressing her jawline. He was in such a strange mood that Beth found herself responding to his warm embrace as she never had before. There was almost a teasing quality about him, none of his usual coldness. It must be the whiskey, Beth thought half hysterically. There could be no other reason.

But Beth was only partially right. It was true that the whiskey had temporarily vanquished his fury and anger, but it was her allure that drew him, and he was unable, tonight, to fight against her or the unacknowledged longing of his own heart. Pleasantly tired himself after a long day in the saddle, the whiskey had been his undoing, that and Beth in his arms. He couldn't seem to let her go, and even though he knew it was madness, he wanted her next to him and in his arms at any price. Tomorrow he might be just as icily angry as he had been today, but for the moment, nothing mattered but that English was sweetly yielding under his caresses. She befuddled his brain like a fine wine and he found himself saying things he never would have. His lips nuzzling her ear, he suddenly asked huskily, "Did you know that I went to Natchez to find you?"

His mouth twisted and he added harshly, "But I heard how happily married you were, so I left."

Beth's eyes widened and she pushed him away, exclaiming, "It *was* you!"

He raised his head and glanced down at her, obviously puzzled. "What do you mean?"

Not meeting his gaze, she admitted, "About a year after . . . after we met, someone told me that a tall, dark stranger was asking about me."

He cocked an eyebrow at her and murmured sardonically, "And you just assumed it was me? It could have been Lorenzo, you know."

"Lorenzo is not tall!" she flushed, then bit her lip in vexation, for that had not been what she had meant to say at all. Recovering herself somewhat, she said coldly, "Lorenzo would not come looking for me! There is nothing between us, despite what you choose to believe."

Rafael shrugged noncommittally and replied flatly, "I don't wish to discuss Lorenzo." His eyes wandering over her moon-washed features, he added lightly, "I would much rather discuss us."

"There *is* no us!" Beth returned stoutly, knowing she wasn't telling the exact truth.

"You're lying, sweetheart. You might be married to that poor excuse for a man, but you're mine whether you want to admit it or not," he drawled, the gray eyes suddenly hard and intent.

Incensed and frightened that he might just be right, Beth struggled free of his grasp and, facing him with a heaving bosom, she spat, "I don't *belong* to anyone! Not you, not Nathan, not anyone!"

Rafael only grinned infuriatingly and murmured, "Time will tell, won't it?"

Smothering an angry retort, she shot him a furious glance and then, disdaining further arguments, she turned on her heels and marched smartly to her wagon. Arrogant beast!

The house that Rafael had inherited in San Antonio from his maternal grandfather was set at the edge of town near the shallow San Antonio Creek. And while Abe Hawkins had lived all of his adult life in Texas, when he had finally built his home in town, his early roots in Virginia were apparent in its construction. It was two-storied, a rarity in a town built mostly of single-storied adobes, and it had tall, graceful white columns across the front that instantly reminded one of the plantation houses of the cooler, greener state where Abe had been born.

It was not a huge house, but a comfortable one, the rooms large and surprisingly sumptuously furnished; fine Brussels carpets flowed tastefully throughout the rooms, crimson worsted curtains adorned the windows, and the furniture was all upholstered in rich fabrics. It was all obviously well cared for, the mahogany and walnut tables polished and gleaming; the pleasant smell of beeswax permeated the air. A bustling little Mexican woman in a loose white blouse and bright full skirt showed Beth and Nathan to their rooms upstairs.

It had been apparent from the excitement and hubbub occasioned by their arrival that Rafael was not often in residence. The servants greeted him with what appeared to be effusive affection and seemed to fall over themselves to carry out his casual commands. Beth was left with the distinct feeling that they held him in very high esteem.

Beth's room overlooked the rambling blue creek. Its appointments were as elegant as those in the rest of the house. A cream-and-pale-rose carpet lay on the floor, gauzy green curtains draped the wide windows, and a sofa with rolled arms covered in a tapestry print fabric and two Queen Anne chairs were set at one end near a pair of doors that opened onto a small balcony. A bed of delicately carved rosewood was placed at the opposite end of the room with a small lamp table next to it. There was a massive mahogany wardrobe against one wall, a dressing table with a tall gilt mirror, and a marble-topped washstand. If she hadn't known better, Beth would have thought she was in an elegant house in Natchez.

The room pleased her, perhaps because it did remind her of Natchez and made her forget for a brief moment that she was in Rafael Santana's house and that she still had to get through several more difficult and dangerous days. Her pleasure evaporated, though, when she discovered that she and Nathan were in totally separated rooms—there was no adjoining door. She and Nathan had not shared a room for a number of years, but Rafael didn't know that, and it was decidedly odd for a host to put a man and wife in sleeping quarters where there was not some connection between the two rooms.

Nathan seemed to think nothing of it when, after knocking on her door, he entered a moment later. As a matter of fact he looked slightly surprised that she should even comment on it.

His gray eyes puzzled, he said, "But it makes no difference, my dear, it is not as if we shared the normal intimacies of marriage."

Forgetting the need to be cautious, Beth snapped, "But *he* doesn't know that—no one does except ourselves!"

"Well, that may be, but I see nothing to complain about simply because our rooms do not connect—I am just down the hall from you."

Realizing that to persist would catapult her into the sort of situation she wished to avoid, she pushed aside her uneasiness and said with a forced carelessness, "You're absolutely correct—I am just being absurd." Shaking her head as if in amazement with her own actions, she added, "My fussing over such a trivial matter only shows you how much I have allowed this trip to unsettle me. Do not pay me any heed, Nathan."

The subject was put behind them, and in outward harmony they descended the broad sweeping staircase. But the niggling concern over the separate rooms would not leave Beth, and she caught her breath in sudden anger and dismay when the thought occurred to her that Rafael meant to take base advantage of the situation.

In that presumption Beth did Rafael an injustice. It was true that he was perfectly capable of coolly seducing another man's wife, but some sort of twisted honor prevented him from doing so when the man and his wife were guests under his own roof. Yet it was not an accident that Nathan was placed across and down the hall from Beth; Rafael might not attempt to make love to Beth, but he was *damned* if he would make it easy for Nathan to seek the bed and charms that were denied him!

Dinner that evening was not particularly lively. Beth concentrated on ignoring Rafael's dark magnetic presence at the head of the long table, and Rafael was too conscious of the sweetly desirable picture Beth made in a lavender silk to do more than abstractedly reply to Nathan's light prattle. Nathan, completely oblivious of the tingling, vibrating air of tautness between the other two people at the table, was busy relaxing and enjoying his comfortable surroundings. The fact that Beth was politely aloof from her host had not escaped him, but instead of being suspicious, he felt it only confirmed his earlier opinion—Santana's intimidating presence and forceful features were not appealing to most women, and his wife was only displaying her own good taste in finding their host not to her liking.

Realizing that it wasn't very gracious of him to harbor such unkind thoughts of the man who had opened his home to them, Nathan was at his most charming, and the meal progressed without incident. But by the time they had finished, Nathan was heartily bored and finding it rather rough going.

As soon as he and Rafael had exhausted the subject of wearing apparel, something they did very rapidly, as Rafael's apparent incipient dandyism had been entirely feigned the night they met, there was little common ground. Nathan had absolutely no interest in the more serious topics that interested Rafael and even less in the myriad problems that beset the Republic; Rafael, while possessing more than his share of sophistication and easy address, cared little for the frivolous pursuits that appealed to Nathan. Besides, he plain disliked the man, viewing Nathan's dainty posturings with growing distaste. Consequently by the end of the meal conversation had languished and Nathan, facing a dull evening with someone he was quickly deciding was a bore, was searching for some way to amuse himself.

If there had been only Beth and himself he would have bidden her a fond good night assuming she would find some womanly way of passing her time and would have gone off to enjoy himself at the various taverns and saloons, spending his evening much in the way he would have in Natchez. But while he had so unwisely discounted Rafael's charms on the opposite sex, he was reluctant to leave Beth alone in Santana's house. He certainly didn't fear that Rafael would be guilty of some ungentlemanly action, but while he wouldn't have given it a second thought if Sebastian had been their host, for some odd reason he felt a strong urge to remain at his wife's side. At any rate, after mulling over possible entertainments for the evening ahead, he finally hit upon the pleasant notion of attempting to renew their acquaintance with Sam and Mary Maverick.

His suggestion was met with gratifying appreciation. Rafael even went so far as to propose that a message be sent immediately inviting the Mavericks to join them for coffee, which could be served on the large patio at the rear of the house. Beth could have kissed her husband with sheer relief—she would enjoy meeting the Mavericks again and their company would help dispel the dangerous intimacy. But curiosity made her ask Rafael, "Do you know them?"

Rafael's mouth curved in a sardonic smile. "Yes, I count Sam and Mary among my few friends in San Antonio. The fact that my grandfather, whom they also knew, chose to align himself with a Comanche half-breed never made any difference to them. They were kind to my grandfather and they have been kind to me also."

Feeling as if she had somehow been guilty of a grave social solecism, Beth looked quickly away from the cynical gleam in his eyes and said in a small voice, "Oh."

This was the first time that Nathan had ever heard of the part-Comanche grandmother and he decided instantly that it was the Indian blood that accounted for his growing uneasiness around their host. A slight frown marring his forehead, he nervously twisted his wine glass. *Knew there was something odd about the fellow the moment I laid eyes on him,* he told himself, and regretfully he came to the conclusion that they would have to leave the luxuries offered them at the earliest possible moment. *Can't have Beth exposed to a damned Comanche—why there's no telling what he might take into his head to do!*

Fortunately Rafael's servant found the Mavericks at home and they were delighted to accept his impromptu invitation. An hour later they were seated on the patio enjoying the midnight air.

The conversation flowed smoothly right from the beginning, the Mavericks expressing their pleasure at seeing the Ridgeways again and also their regret that they were not continuing their journey on to Santa Fe.

"Stella will be so disappointed!" Mary had cried when it was explained how they came to be in San Antonio again, and Beth had felt a perfect fool.

Rafael let Beth flounder for a few minutes with lame excuses and then, almost as if taking pity on her, he had introduced a new topic of conversation. Putting down his snifter of brandy that he had chosen instead of the milky coffee that the ladies and Nathan were drinking, he looked at Sam Maverick and asked, "Is the meeting with the Pehnahterkuh chiefs still set for tomorrow?"

Sam nodded quickly and, his dark eyes full of speculation, he inquired, "Is that why you're here? To attend the meeting?"

Rafael lit a thin black cheroot and glanced at Beth a brief moment before admitting, "Yes. I met with Houston some days ago and he thought it would be a good idea if I were here. He wants me to 'observe' the meeting."

Beth felt her face grow hot with embarrassment and she was suddenly glad of the encroaching darkness. What a silly fool I was to think he came to San Antonio because of me! she thought with humiliation. And she was torn between chagrin and relief, one part of her overjoyed that Rafael's trip had nothing to do with her and another part of her...

Rafael and Sam Maverick talked of the Comanches for a while, the two ladies and Nathan listening with undisguised interest. There was a break in the conversation for a moment and Nathan, determined to see one of these dreaded raiders up close, asked Rafael easily,

"Would it be at all possible for me to attend the meeting with you tomorrow? I would most like to see a Comanche before I leave Texas."

Nathan spoke as did many a white man, as if a Comanche were some peculiar creature from another world, and Rafael was conscious of a quick sweep of rage. He might have snarled something he would have regretted, but Sam Maverick said with a laugh, "Well, if anyone can get you inside the council building tomorrow, it will be Rafael Santana—he comes with Sam Houston's approval!" Looking across at Rafael, Sam coaxed, "Why don't you take him with you? After all, it isn't every day you can see a Comanche and live to tell the tale. And if you're thinking that it is not a place for spectators, let me tell you that half the people there tomorrow are going to be spectators! Why we've got judges who have traveled here just to see the Comanches. Take him with you."

Reluctantly Rafael agreed. Nathan was the last person he wanted with him tomorrow, but he saw no way to refuse.

Mary turned to Beth and said quietly, "I am one of the women who will be taking care of the returned captives tomorrow. We don't know how many there will be or in what condition, but we could certainly use an extra pair of hands if you would be willing to help."

"Why certainly," Beth returned warmly, pleased that Mary felt that she could be of some use.

There was some more discussion of when and where they would meet. After taking a swallow of his own brandy, Maverick asked Rafael, "Do you think that there'll be any trouble? I know that Colonel Fisher is here with three companies of troops."

Rafael shrugged. "It depends on the terms that are offered and how those terms are presented. You have to remember that the Comanches are a proud people—they held this land, first against the might of Spain and then the Mexicans, and they are used to being treated, if not with awe, with at least something closely resembling it."

Sam's face darkened. "Rafael, if you think that we are going to bend our necks to a bunch of dirty, thieving—" He broke off suddenly, remembering that some of that "dirty, thieving" blood ran in Rafael's veins, but as Rafael said nothing, merely regarded the tip of his cheroot, Sam said in a calmer tone of voice, "Colonel Fisher has made it plain and he has reemphasized Colonel Karnes' earlier requirement—there will be no treaty unless every Texan captive is released to us tomorrow."

Rafael took a deep breath, his face expressionless in the faint light from the lanterns that hung nearby. Slowly he said, "Then in that case, you may have trouble, because I don't think they're going to bring in *every* captive. One, two, maybe is all I think you'll see at a time. You'll get them all eventually, but not all at once. Knowing Comanches, I can tell you that they intend most likely to bargain for every woman and child individually, and they will expect to be paid dearly for them."

In a voice filled with hostility and belligerence, Maverick replied hotly, "And we Texans do not intend to pay them one piece of tribute! We will not ransom people who should not have been taken captive in the first place."

Rafael smoked his cheroot in silence for a long moment. Flatly he said, "Then, *amigo,* you may very well have trouble!"

PART THREE

THE FATEFUL SEASON

Spring 1840

Defer not till tomorrow to be wise,
Tomorrow's sun to thee may never rise.

—WILLIAM CONGREVE
"Letter to Cobham"

CHAPTER SEVENTEEN

Thursday, the 19th of March, 1840, dawned bright and clear, the sky an endless azure lake, the sun a golden ball of fire in its center. Beth woke early feeling thankful that she had managed to get through the previous evening without putting her foot wrong. The arrival of Sam and Mary Maverick had helped enormously, and by the time they had finally departed for their home, the hour was late and Beth could safely bid Nathan good night, certain he would be seeking his own bed almost immediately and that he would have no private conversation with their host. As for Rafael, she didn't waste time speculating on his movements, and all she knew or cared, she told herself firmly, was that he hadn't sought her out in the intimacy of her bedroom.

Charity entered just then, bringing in a large silver tray laden with a coffeepot, a fine china cup, a small pitcher of cream, and a dish which contained a Mexican sweet bread known as *pan dulce.* Leaning comfortably back against lace-trimmed pillows, Beth enjoyed the rich, dark coffee; nibbling thoughtfully on the *pan dulce,* she considered the plans for the day ahead.

Nathan's arrangement to accompany Rafael to the meeting with the Comanches was not to her liking, and it made her decidedly uneasy every time she thought of it. But then, *any* instance that left her husband alone with Rafael made her uneasy!

At least they would be in the middle of a crowd, she reminded herself stoutly, and it was highly unlikely that the type of conversation she feared might spring up between them would take place under those circumstances. If only she knew what Rafael was thinking, or what he intended to do. He hadn't betrayed her . . . yet. Perhaps, like a cat with a mouse, he was merely torturing her? A feeling of helpless anger swept over her, and, disliking herself and Rafael very much at the moment, she threw back the covers with more violence than was necessary and slid out of bed.

Fortunately she would be busy helping Mary and the other women, and *that,* she decided firmly, should keep her mind off Nathan and Rafael! They should all manage to get through another day without any treacherous pitfalls suddenly opening up. Fervently she prayed it would be so. Her face brightened as it occurred to her that if the Comanches took up most of this day, there would be just one more dangerous day before they could politely bid their host *"Vaya con Dios,"* and begin the journey home. Just forty-eight hours, she thought with joy, completely numbing her mind to the anguish she would feel when she faced Rafael for the last time.

Not quite certain what would be expected of her when she met Mary and the other women, she selected a practical gown of pink gingham and had Charity arrange her hair into a neat cornet of silvery braids on top of her head. Thinking she appeared rather matronly, Beth was completely oblivious of the way the crown of silken braids gave her a regal air, revealing the lovely fragile bones of her face; the simple gown accented her graceful slender body rather than minimizing its attractiveness.

Rafael, watching her through narrowed eyes as she descended the staircase, decided he had never seen her look lovelier and he was bitterly aware that his heart had tightened painfully at the sight of her. It made him angry, as did any emotion that he couldn't control, and his unwelcome obsession for Beth Ridgeway definitely was against his will.

Unlike Beth, who, despite her understandable anxieties, had slept soundly, Rafael had not. He had lain awake, tossing and turning, determined to think only of the meeting tomorrow with the Comanches and yet finding that his very thoughts betrayed him as they strayed inexorably down the hall to where Beth was sleeping. He could picture her vividly in the rosewood bed, her glorious bright hair spread out across the pillows and her slim alabaster body curved gently in sleep. With an angry groan he admitted to himself that it would take very little persuasion for him to join her—her husband be damned! Cursing himself as well as Beth, he had given up all pretense of sleep and had spent the remainder of the night hours pacing like a caged black panther in the confines of his room, despising and wanting Beth at the same time.

No woman had ever come between him and his emotions before, but now it seemed, no matter how hard he tried to banish her from his thoughts, no matter how determinedly he concentrated on the importance of the meeting in the morning, no matter how grimly he considered the consequences of any overt act by the Texans against the Comanches, Beth's violet eyes and provocative mouth crept into his midnight musings, driving him half mad with longing. By the time the sun rose he was filled with icy rage that a woman could so insidiously invade his mind to the point where coherent thought vanished.

Beth wasn't aware of his presence at the bottom of the stairs until she was more than halfway down the wide steps. Suddenly catching sight of his tall, dark figure in the center of the spacious hallway, her step faltered and she came to an abrupt halt, wishing vehemently that her heart hadn't instantly plunged to her feet when her eyes met his. She hesitated a moment, gathering her erratic emotions, and then forced herself to smile and say politely, "Good morning, Señor Santana."

Rafael regarded her in silence. A crooked smile curved his full mouth as he said dryly, "I hardly think such formality is necessary, English—you know my given name and I would suggest that you use it!"

Beth stiffened with quick anger and came down the remainder of the steps with a rush. A decidedly militant sparkle in the violet eyes, she snapped, "I wish to Heaven that your name was the *only* thing I knew about you!"

The crooked smile left his face instantly, and bleakly he surveyed her flushed, lovely features, wanting with an intensity that was a physical pain to sweep her into his arms and kiss her so fiercely, so passionately that she would be aware of nothing but the hot, dark hunger that raged within him. He didn't, though, as much because he needed to prove to himself that he *did* have control over his emotions where she was concerned as the disagreeable awareness that this was neither the place nor the time to precipitate such a scene. Instead, seeking to treat her in the same manner she had him, he replied insultingly, "You no more than I, dear lady!"

Anger making her reckless, she retorted heatedly, "Fine! I think we understand each other... and I can see no reason to continue this distasteful conversation. *Anything* I have to say to you can be said in the company of others!"

An unpleasant smile lifting up one corner of his mouth, Rafael taunted, "Even your husband?"

Outraged that he would stoop so low, heedless of their surroundings, she spat, "You dare! You would deliberately wound a man for no other reason than to gain spiteful revenge?" Scornfully she added, "But what else could I expect from a creature like you!"

Strangely enough her words did not enrage him as might have been anticipated, although a muscle bunched in his cheek and the gray eyes grew hard as flint. Tightly he said, "I am not in the habit of telling tales—especially not sordid tales to another man about his wife's dalliances!" His hard gaze flicking contemptuously over her slender body, he drawled, "Your husband speaks highly of you, obviously he thinks you are without a blemish. And if everything he told me the other night is true, it would appear he had much to be proud of—a wife with all the virtues a man could desire." His voice taking on the crack of a whiplash, he snarled, "All the virtues except one—fidelity!"

Before she had time to think, before there was time to consider the repercussion of her actions, Beth struck him across the face, her open palm connecting very gratifyingly with his lean cheek. The sound of the blow seemed to echo in the hallway, and, appalled at her impulsive action, with horror Beth stared at the print of her small hand against his dark face. The sudden anger draining out of her and shaken by her own lack of control, she took an instinctive step backward.

His mouth a thin, white, angry line, Rafael said coolly, too coolly, "You are wise to move away from me, English. At the moment I could wring your neck!"

Risking a glance at his dark, furious face, Beth rather thought he might indeed wring her neck, but she wasn't about to retreat. He had insulted her grievously and he amply deserved precisely what she had given him! Her stance unusually belligerent, she glowered up at him as if daring him to carry out his threat.

Any other woman would have been reeling from the force of his retaliatory slap, but with Beth, all his normal reactions seemed to have been weakened. He found himself thinking that perhaps there was some justification for her action—after all, no one appreciates hearing certain home truths. Besides, hurting Beth was the farthest thought from his mind—he desperately wanted her warm and eager in his arms, instead of facing him like a wide-eyed, spitting, golden kitten. With an oddly vulnerable movement he rubbed one hand almost tiredly against the back of his neck and surprised her by saying, "I won't apologize, but I will admit that I shouldn't have said what I did. As for telling your husband"—his eyes met hers and Beth felt her throat go tight—"as for your husband," he repeated somberly, "rest easy on that count—I don't think what transpired between us was particularly admirable any way you view it. Shall we leave it in the past and start over again?"

Feeling the prick of tears behind her lids, she nodded, knowing that no matter how wrong it had been she would never forget those forbidden moments. In a small voice she said, "There isn't any reason to start over again—Nathan and I will be leaving for Natchez just as soon as possible. Perhaps even tomorrow."

Something that could have been pain crossed his face, but it was gone so swiftly Beth couldn't be sure. There was no hint of it in his voice though when he said gently, "Well, at least there need not be any animosity between us before you leave."

Beth gave him a tiny, wavering smile, wishing sadly

it was that simple, wishing with increasing despair that his dark compelling attraction didn't tug against her heartstrings every time she saw him. Her voice not quite steady, she murmured, "We seemed to have said everything there is to say." And, holding back the scalding tears that she knew were going to spill down her cheeks any second, she frantically sought to end the conversation as quickly as possible. Not looking at him and agitatedly smoothing her pink gingham gown, she stuttered, "Y-y-you m-m-must excuse me, I-I must finish getting ready to join M-M-Mary and the others."

She turned blindly away, not even certain where she was going, but Rafael's hand on her upper arm stopped her.

"It isn't necessary for you to help," he said slowly, a frown creasing his forehead. "As a matter of fact, I—" He broke off as one of the servants walked into the hall, and as if suddenly realizing where they were, he muttered something violent under his breath and almost dragged Beth into a nearby room, shutting the door firmly behind him.

It had not been to seek some intimate tête-à-tête with Beth that had prompted Rafael to bring her into the small library where they now stood, but to escape the interruptions that were sure to occur if they continued talking in the middle of the central hallway. And yet the instant he shut the door behind him, a new and disturbing atmosphere instantly enveloped both of them.

Staring mutely up into his bronzed powerful face, the high cheekbones and the smoky gray eyes beneath the winged black brows, Beth felt her heart contract as she realized how incredibly dear those features had become to her—how they would haunt her dreams for the rest of her life! This is how I will always remember him, she thought with anguish, her eyes hungrily noting the way the crisp blue-black hair brushed his temples, the way his long lashes hid the expression in the gray eyes, and the way his mouth curved when he smiled as he did now.

The smile was strained, only she didn't know that, she was too busy shoring up memories to last her a lifetime. Beth knew she would always picture him as he was now. He was dressed in Spanish attire—and as usual the colors of his clothes were black except for the white of his shirt and the crimson bandana knotted carelessly about the strong, brown throat... Suddenly she had an insane desire to press her lips against that warm brown throat where it joined his shoulder.

Frightened at her wild response to his nearness, she presented her charming back to him and said in a low voice, "Wh-what were you saying?"

Rafael was not immune to Beth's presence any more than she was to his, and his smile, which was meant to be only polite, had slipped just a little. It took every ounce of willpower he possessed not to take her into his arms and kiss her half senseless, and he was almost grateful that she had turned away from him. If he had continued to stare down into that lovely, enchanting face he wouldn't have been responsible for his actions. Recovering himself somewhat, he said lightly, "It wasn't anything important, merely that I would appreciate it if you didn't help Mary with the returned prisoners."

Her eyes wide and questioning, Beth swung around to face him. "Why?" she asked simply.

He stared at her fragile blond loveliness for a moment, and, thinking of the refined, *safe,* ordered life she lived in Natchez, he said bluntly, "Because I don't think you're strong enough! Mary will have enough on her hands without the possibility of you fainting at her feet."

Hurt and angry that he thought her so weak and useless, Beth drew in a gasp of outrage. "Well! Thank you very much, Señor Santana! But let me assure you, I am much stronger than I appear, and I wouldn't be so stupid as to faint at a critical point!"

Crossing the room to where she stood with quick impatient strides and grasping her shoulders in both of his hands, he shook her gently, saying exasperatedly, "Calm down, you little spitfire! I didn't mean that you aren't perfectly capable under circumstances that you are familiar with! But seeing someone who has been tortured and brutalized by the Comanches is not a pleasant sight—especially to someone like you!"

If he meant to pacify her he was failing dismally.

Her jaw set tightly, Beth gritted, "And what exactly do you mean by that?"

Rafael let out an irritated sigh. "English, I was raised as a Comanche and I know what they do to prisoners. I don't want you upset and revolted by the things you may see. It's that simple. Mary Maverick and the other women are better prepared than you—and some of them probably won't hold up too well either. Mary will understand when I tell her you won't be coming. If it will make you feel better, I'll send a couple of my own servants along to help."

It was unfortunate that Rafael was being so tactless, and if he hadn't just spent a sleepless night pacing the floor thinking of Beth and if he weren't so conscious of her slender body barely touching his, he might have chosen his words more carefully and Beth might have taken his advice. But he was being too arrogantly decisive for her to meekly accept his dictates, and, feeling that she had to prove something to him as well as herself, she said stubbornly, "I told Mary I would help and I intend to do so."

"You obstinate little fool!" he burst out angrily. "Damn it, I don't want you there! There could be trouble and I want to know that you're safe."

Her eyes suddenly anxious she whispered, "Nathan? He won't be in any danger?"

It was the spark that lit all of Rafael's smoldering frustrations and thoughtlessly he snarled, "Blast Nathan! He could be skewered by a Comanche lance for all I care!"

Her own temper rising mercurially, Beth twisted furiously in his hold. "Oh! How dare you say such a thing! He is good and kind, and and—" But the heated words she would have flung at him died in her throat at the tormented expression on his face.

There was sudden silence in the room as they gazed at one another, the violet eyes mesmerized by the blazing emotion that flickered briefly in the gray ones. It was a waiting silence which lasted for only a moment before Rafael muttered tautly, "*¡Por Dios! Why* must you always fight me?" And then, unable to deny himself any longer, his hard mouth swooped down hungrily on hers, his hands jerking her slender form against his.

It was a strangely bittersweet kiss between them, Rafael's mouth taking her lips with a tender urgency that was Beth's undoing. If his kiss had been brutal she might have found the will to resist him, but it wasn't. It was warm and compelling, irresistibly coaxing an instinctive response from her. Instead of fighting him, as she knew she should, instead of trying to escape, she clung to him ardently, her senses spinning and swirling wildly out of control. Helplessly her lips parted and his kiss deepened, one large hand coming up to cradle her head, keeping her a willing, eager captive as his mouth sweetly ravaged hers. Heedless of anything but the tall, muscled body pressed so passionately against hers, Beth reached up to tangle her fingers in his dark hair, and her body arched against his, her breasts aching to feel his touch, her body filled with a hungry longing to have him take her again. His lips trailed a fiery path down her throat and she gave a little moan of excitement when one of his hands cupped her buttocks and crushed her even closer to the rigid, throbbing length of him. Dizzy with desire, Beth would have denied him nothing if the sudden thought of her marriage and Nathan hadn't exploded in her brain. With a small ashamed sob she tore herself out of Rafael's arms and stepped away from him, one arm outstretched as if to ward him off.

They were both breathing heavily, Rafael's arousal very evident in the figure-hugging *calzoneras,* his hair slightly tousled from Beth's caressing fingers. In a tautly controlled voice he asked, "Would you mind telling me what the hell happened?"

The violet eyes met his steadily, despite her inner turmoil, and Beth said dully, "I think you know very well what happened. I remembered, if you did not, that I have a husband. A husband who loves me very much."

"Oh, I see," he said in a sneering tone. "You seem to have a very convenient memory! One minute you're in my arms and the next you *remember* your husband!" Almost accusingly he hurled at her, "You were able to forget him easily enough with Lorenzo!"

"That's not true! If you would only listen to me, I

could explain everything, and you would realize that you've had the most appalling misconception about me right from the beginning," Beth replied hotly, wishing... *Oh, God,* she didn't know what she wished!

Bleakly Rafael surveyed her, wanting her with an intolerable ache that drove him nearly crazy and yet wondering at the same time how he could be such a fool to do so. Furious at his own conflicting emotions, he inquired sarcastically, "Now, what could you tell me that I don't already know? That Lorenzo seduced you? He might have. But he must have had some damned obvious encouragement in the first place! And you forget, it wasn't enough that you had him as a lover—after you lay with him, you let me take you!" His voice suddenly thick with remembered rage and pain, he spat, "Do you think I'd forgotten *that?*"

Beth blanched at the naked loathing in his voice and, feeling as if she were shriveling inside, she forced herself to look at him unemotionally and say coolly, "I hardly see why you condemn me—certainly you didn't waste any time taking Lorenzo's place."

For one awful moment Beth thought he was going to strike her, but even though his fists clenched so tightly the knuckles showed white, he made no move to touch her. Stricken at the ugly things they had flung at each other, she said gently, "Nathan and I will leave tomorrow. Until then, I think it best if you and I avoid being alone with each other."

Rafael said nothing, only stared unwaveringly at her over the few feet that divided them. Then, his countenance icily remote, he bowed with a stilted courteous grace and replied expressionlessly, "Very wise. I will not apologize, for I am not sorry for anything that has passed between us. My only regret, if you can say I have one, is that I was foolish enough to let a moment's madness rule me—something no man should ever do." She thought he would leave then, but he surprised her by reaching out a curiously gentle hand, and lightly caressed her cheek. A hint of sadness in his deep voice, he murmured, "It is a pity, little angel face, that we did not meet long ago, in a different time and a different place. Perhaps then *both* our lives would be very different."

Unbearably moved, a shimmer of tears in her eyes, Beth nodded. The lump that was growing in her throat prevented a reply. Rafael stared at her intently for another moment and then, spinning on his heels, he stalked out of the room. Blindly Beth stared at the door, wondering if one really did die of a broken heart for surely hers had just shattered into a thousand pieces.

She sank down onto a nearby chair and looked blankly around her. What was there about him that he had the power to hurt and fill her with pleasure at the same time? The very sight of him caused her heart to behave most erratically, and yet they said such wicked things to one another—he believed such ugly, sordid things about her. I should despise him, she told herself with a mixture of anger and sorrow, if for no other reason than he thinks me so depraved a creature that I would change beds as readily as I change my clothes. It was no use sitting here thinking about it, she finally decided with painful determination, and, putting forth a deceptively serene face, she left the room.

Despite the tight ball of misery lodged firmly in her chest, Beth managed to act normal when she met Nathan a few minutes later in the dining room for breakfast. Beth merely picked at her food, the *pan dulce* and coffee she'd had a few hours earlier being sufficient, and the scene with Rafael effectively destroying what appetite she might have had.

Rafael joined them when they were about halfway through the meal, coolly apologizing for being late, but offering no reason for it. Never once glancing in Beth's direction, he drank two cups of coffee as he talked politely with Nathan. Yet Beth knew he was aware of her, simply because of the studious way he avoided either looking at or speaking to her.

Nathan didn't seem to notice anything out of the ordinary, and for that Beth was thankful. At least *he* seemed to be enjoying himself, she thought with a sudden spurt of crossness.

Nathan *was* enjoying himself. His sleep had been deep and untroubled, and upon awaking to the lovely spring morning, he was full of anticipation and excitement about seeing a real Indian face to face. Selecting a buff-colored coat and skin-tight fawn trousers to wear for what he viewed as a pleasurable excursion, he languidly had allowed his servant to dress him. Taking one last look at his decidedly natty reflection in the cheval glass, he decided he was appropriately dressed for the coming event, his expertly tailored clothes neither too somber nor especially flashy. Putting his monocle in his right eye, he took up a casual stance in front of the mirror, imagining himself regaling his cronies in Natchez with the marvelous tales of this unorthodox trip. Why, I shall be able to dine out for months on this story alone of seeing Comanches at close quarters, he thought complacently.

Feeling very satisfied with himself and the world in general, he happily toddled off in search of Beth and breakfast. The fact that his wife was not in her normal sweet spirits did not escape him, but he put it down to female megrims; dismissing it from his mind, he gustily attacked his breakfast. When Rafael eventually joined them, he eagerly plied him with endless and tactless questions about the meeting with the Indians.

By the time the meal was finished Rafael was wondering savagely how he was going to spend several hours in Nathan's company without throttling the fool. As for Beth, he had coldly and methodically shut her out of his thoughts, locking whatever emotions she may have aroused so deeply in his brain that even he wasn't positive that they had ever existed.

Rising from the table and throwing down his napkin, he looked over at Beth and said with bland politeness, "Nathan and I will escort you to the Maverick household whenever you are ready to leave. I would suggest that you not tarry—the Comanches have been sighted and you might like to see them arrive."

Beth risked a glance at his face and then wished she hadn't. His eyes were so icy, so empty, and so remote that in spite of the day's warmth she shivered. Keeping her face purposely unruffled, she replied casually, "If you will allow me to fetch my shawl, I shall be ready almost immediately."

Rafael nodded curtly, his mouth tightening slightly, and she knew that he was still angry with her decision to join Mary and the other women. Not waiting for any reply, she whisked herself out of the room and quickly found her shawl.

The three of them departed, walking leisurely in the direction of the Maverick house. They were not the only ones abroad, as the news of the meeting with the Comanches had been bruited about and more than a few settlers from the outlying areas had ridden into San Antonio to watch what was certain to be a historic meeting. Everyone, it appeared, wanted to see the barbaric and dreaded Comanches.

Rafael and the Ridgeways had just reached the Maverick house and had exchanged greetings with them when Mary, staring out at the broad San Antonio plain, said in a voice of excitement, "Look! The Comanches are coming."

Like everyone else in the group, Beth turned to look. Her first sight of a Comanche was not as thrilling as it might have been simply because the Comanches were still some distance from the town, and at first all she saw was a great cloud of dust. The figures of the Indians and their horses were barely discernible through the ocher haze.

"Why are there so many of them?" Nathan asked with puzzlement and just a little uneasiness. "I thought that there would only be a half dozen or so—not an entire tribe! After all, how many does it take to make a treaty?"

Rafael sent him a derisive look. "Every warrior in the tribe has to agree to it. And those who do not are not bound by it—they can continue to loot and raid. As for their number, councils are sacred to Comanches—they also usually last a lengthy time—and the chiefs and warriors who are attending this council have brought their wives and families. They will set up their lodges and stay for some time." His voice hardening as he glanced toward the troops that lounged around the main square of the town, he added, "They also do not expect treachery. They expect to bargain... and if they cannot reach an agreement, they expect to be allowed to leave—peaceably."

Sam Maverick moved restlessly, his dark eyes troubled. "But I don't think that the commissioners are going to let them leave if they don't bring in all the captives."

His face grim, Rafael squinted against the bright sunlight, his gaze never straying from the approaching Indians. "I'm aware of that. Before this morning's meeting, I'm seeing Colonel Fisher. If I can convince him that he will be endangering the lives of all the captives by making any forceful move against the Comanches that have come to council, perhaps disaster can be averted."

By now the Indians were close enough to be seen clearly and Nathan's astonished "My word!" expressed the opinion of most of those watching.

The Comanches were a magnificent sight. The warriors with their terrifying buffalo-horn headresses and painted faces sat tall and arrogant as they effortlessly controlled the snorting and cavorting horses. The men wore only breechclouts and moccasins that were actually a footcovering and a legging combined. This practical garment was in some cases painted blue and embellished with bright beads and silver. All the warriors had thick, coarse braids which often fell below their waists, and as their hair was one of their vanities, the braids were decorated with feathers and whatever took their fancy—silver ornaments, colored cloth, and beads. The horses, too, were no less grand, necks and haunches painted vermilion and eagle feathers woven into the manes and tails.

Without exception, the Comanches presented a proud appearance, their shoulders and backs ramrod straight, the expression on the painted faces haughty and imperious as they surveyed the crowd. Staring at them, Beth knew why they referred to themselves with simple pride as "the People" and why they have been called the lords of the high plains—they were indeed regal.

The women were little different, and although they were fully clothed, in beaded and fringed buckskin shirts and long full skirts, they were just as arrogant and rode their horses with the same ease and grace. But their hair was shorn, or rather hacked off short, and the face painting that the squaws practiced was a sight to behold. Their ears were reddened; their cheeks were orange with rouge; some of the faces were painted in a melange of colors that defied description.

Beth glanced at Rafael, recognizing that some of his arrogance must have been inherited from his Comanche ancestors. Looking at the thick black hair that just brushed the collar of his shirt, she wondered idly if his hair had once been worn in long braids and decorated with feathers and beads.

He felt her eyes on him and he looked at her, one eyebrow rising quizzically. When she flushed and dropped her gaze from his hair, he grinned and said, "Yes." Then, turning to Sam Maverick, he murmured, "I think it's time for my meeting with Colonel Fisher, so if you will excuse me, I'll be on my way." He took a few steps but then, as if remembering something with resignation, he turned around and glanced at Nathan. "I'll return in plenty of time to see that you get inside the courthouse," he told him. "In the meantime I would suggest that you wait here."

Beth watched his long, lean figure disappear with mixed emotions. She was relieved not to have his powerful presence interfering with her thoughts and yet she was also oddly bereft that he was no longer nearby. Determined not to dwell on him, she forced herself to think of the Comanches and to admire the bright sunlit day.

It *was* a bright sunlit day, a lovely spring day that held no portent of the brutal and violent events that would take place within a few hours. By the time the sun would set on this day, there would *never* again be a true peace between the whites and the People of the plains!

CHAPTER EIGHTEEN

The meeting with Colonel Fisher and the other two Commissioners, Colonel Cooke, the Acting Secretary of War, and Colonel MacLeod, the Texas Adjutant General, was not precisely friendly, nor was it particularly successful as far as Rafael was concerned. The three men were all military and had been appointed by President Lamar on Texas Secretary of War Johnston's advice. The three men reflected the Lamar-Johnston attitude toward the Comanches: *All* Indians were vicious savages and wild beasts and should be exterminated.

Rafael was slightly acquainted with Colonel Fisher—he had been Secretary of War in 1838 during Houston's term as President of the Republic—and it was to him that Rafael addressed most of his remarks. Fisher, however much he might admire Sam Houston, was in complete agreement with the Lamar-Johnston plan for handling Indians: Show the Indians force and make it plain that the Texans were not about to submit to the barbaric tyranny the Comanches had practiced upon the Spanish and Mexicans.

Rafael's meeting with the three Indian Commissioners was being held in the courthouse where the Council with the Comanches would take place; standing in front of the three men while they sat behind a rough oak table, Rafael felt as if he were on trial. All three men tough, hard-bitten military men, and, staring at their implacable features as they regarded him with ill-disguised hostility, his fear for the outcome of the meeting with the Comanches increased. If they take this attitude with the chiefs... That he hadn't lost his own temper surprised him, for it was difficult to remain civil when it was obvious they had made up their minds. At least he could tell himself that he had tried, he thought dismally.

Eloquently did Rafael plead that they honor the truce, that they attempt to understand the Comanche way, and that there be no show of force on what was supposedly neutral ground, but he could tell from their expressions that his words were falling on unreceptive ears. Finally, his temper rising, he snapped, "I cannot warn you strongly enough of the danger of not treating those Comanches out there with the same courtesy and respect you would accord a delegation from a foreign country. They *are* a foreign nation and they have come in good will to talk peace."

Colonel MacLeod, a headstrong man of average height and build, snorted disbelievingly, "Foreign nation! They're nothing but a bunch of savages—trespassers at will on our sovereign territory. They are no more a *nation* than a herd of buffalo!"

Rafael's eyes narrowed and he forgot himself long enough to snarl, "And you, sir, I hope do not live to regret those words!" He instantly recovered himself and, ignoring MacLeod, who had turned purple, he spoke directly to Fisher, "Sir, if you make any move against the chiefs who have come here today, you will destroy the sacredness of the council. More than that, you will endanger the lives of the captives and you will have destroyed forever any hope of making peace with the Comanches!"

Fisher, aware of MacLeod's animosity, attempted to put things on a less tense plane and murmured lightly, "What do you think I intend to do—murder them as they sleep in their teepees? Come now, man, be reasonable."

"No," Rafael admitted slowly. "But I think you might be foolish enough to try to keep them prisoner until they bring in all the captives."

The three military men exchanged glances. Fisher fiddled with some papers that lay on the table in front of him and, not meeting Rafael's eyes, he said dismissively, "Well, thank you very much for letting us know your feelings. We're aware that you are very familiar with their ways and we appreciate your comments but this is a military matter and we already have our orders from the President." A note of finality in his voice, he said, "We shall handle it as we think best."

Briefly Rafael considered arguing further but, fearing it was futile, he bowed stiffly and walked swiftly from the courthouse. The bright sunlight hurt his eyes as he stepped outside the courthouse, and he stood for a few seconds adjusting to the light. Abstractedly he lit a thin black cheroot and, after taking a few draws, began to walk across the square in the direction of the Maverick house. He was in a damnable quandary—should he tell the Comanche chiefs that he suspected the Texans were not playing by the same rules as were the Comanches? Or should he hold his peace and pray to God he was wrong?

Today was such an important day in the history of Texas, one that could change the course of events for the future. Never before had any major group of Comanches agreed to hold peace talks with the Texans, even though Houston had tried unceasingly to arrange such talks all through 1837. Both the Texans and the Comanches had excellent and urgent reasons for seeking a truce, if not an everlasting peace. Perhaps the Texans, occupied with the continuous fight with Mexico, would gain more from it than the Comanches—certainly it would give Texas the much-needed opportunity to consolidate her frontier communities without Comanche interference.

As for the Comanches, they had only to agree to halt raiding into Texas and give up some two hundred white captives, and accept a fictitious Texan sovereignty which would be, as far as they were concerned, no more effective than had been the Spanish sovereignty. The advantage to them would be that Jack Hays and his Rangers would no longer harass them in canyons where they liked to camp. Also, peace would open up trading between the Texans and the Comanches, something that many on both sides were eager to see. Everything hinged on this meeting.

Tossing aside his cheroot, Rafael made one of the most difficult decisions of his life—he would say nothing to the Comanches. Since he didn't know for certain that Fisher was prepared to risk losing everything by forcing a showdown if the Comanches had not brought in all of the captives, he didn't dare go to the Comanches and, by telling them of his own suspicions, wreck any chance of a treaty.

Reaching the Maverick house once again, Rafael was not in the best of tempers. It had galled him to play the diplomat, even with prodding from Houston. He was a man of action, not words, he thought sourly, and perhaps if he had felt his mission had been successful he might have been in a better frame of mind. But, frowning blackly, he walked into the house without knocking and, finding only Beth and Mary waiting there, he barked sharply, "Where the hell is your husband? I thought I told him to wait here."

Mary's plain, round face showed her surprise, not only at the profanity but the familiarity it betrayed, and she shot Beth a curious look. By sheer willpower Beth managed to keep her features smooth and polite despite the strong urge to shout back at him. Smiling coolly, she said, "Mr. Maverick wanted to show Nathan a horse that he owns and thinks is especially suitable for breeding. I believe that they will return in just a moment."

He hadn't meant to snap at her like that, and certainly not in front of someone else. Recovering himself, he said in a quieter tone, "Forgive me! I am not, I fear, particularly amiable at this time and spoke without thought."

It was on the tip of Beth's tongue to reply smartly, "As usual!" but in front of Mary Maverick she held back the words, graciously bowing her blond-braided head in acknowledgment of his apology.

Mary spoke up almost immediately, banishing whatever silence might have fallen. Anxiously she asked, "Your meeting did not go well?"

"No. I think I just wasted my time and everybody else's. The only thing I can hope is that I am being unduly pessimistic."

Sam Maverick and Nathan returned just then and the conversation once again focused on Rafael's meeting with the Commissioners. Rafael gave the two men a brief accounting and ended by saying reluctantly, "If you're ready, Ridgeway, I suggest that we start toward the courthouse—there is bound to be a crowd, and if you want a good view we had better be there early. Are you coming, Sam?"

Sam Maverick shook his head. "No, I have other things to attend to. I expect Mary will fill my ears with all the points of interest."

Mary smiled at her husband and, after giving him a quick peck on the cheek, she said to Beth, "Well, my dear, I think we, too, should be off to join the other women."

Painfully conscious of Rafael standing stiffly by her husband, Beth crossed over to Nathan and, gently touching one of his hands, murmured, "You will be safe? If there is any trouble, as Señor Santana fears, you will leave at the first sign?"

Nathan looked fondly down at her. "But of course, my dear. I think you refine too much on any danger. Now run along with Mrs. Maverick, I'll see you later."

She sent him a strained smile and, suddenly moved by something she didn't understand, Beth leaned up and kissed him sweetly on the mouth. Not even glancing at Rafael, who had gone curiously still, she hurried away with Mary Maverick.

Meeting two other ladies who were also on their way to offer their services, Mary and Beth discovered that one of the houses near the courthouse had been settled upon as the place where the returned captives would be taken. It was on her way there that Beth noticed Lorenzo Mendoza standing near one of the buildings next to the courthouse. Her step faltered, but she swiftly quickened her step, and to Lorenzo's greeting of "*Buenos días,* Señora Ridgeway," she merely inclined her head and kept right on walking beside Mary.

Once they had passed him, Mary muttered, "I am glad he did not choose to acknowledge my presence! I know he is related by marriage to the Santanas, but I cannot like him. You were wise not to tarry in conversation with him—he does not have a pleasant reputation for all his grand airs and connections."

Not thinking, Beth blurted out, "But I thought it was Rafael who was held in low esteem. Isn't he called 'Renegade'?"

"Oh, yes, there are those who dislike him intensely and who view his Comanche blood and continued association with the Comanches with the deepest suspicion. My husband and I, however, are not among them, nor are many others in San Antonio. Texas has a good friend in Rafael Santana, and while not everyone feels that way, there are many of us who see, possibly more clearly into his character." Her face hardening just a little, Mary added, "Those who think Rafael a villain would do better to look at his grandfather, Don Felipe."

Beth remained silent, not wishing to become involved in any conversation about Rafael Santana. She knew all she needed to know about him!

There were at least a half a dozen other women at the house when Beth and Mary arrived. Conversation between them all was concerned and speculative, no one quite certain what they could expect—how many returned captives there would be, nor in what condition they would be.

As Rafael had surmised, the Pehnahterkuh brought only two captives—a Mexican boy who meant nothing to Texans and a sixteen-year-old girl, Matilda Lockhart, who had been captured with her three-year-old sister in 1838. The Comanches had chosen unwisely in Matilda Lockhart; it would have been far better if they had brought in *no* captives.

Beth's first sight of the girl almost made her scream in horror, for the child had been savagely and hideously abused. Swallowing her revulsion, she forced a friendly smile for the girl and gently helped Mary and some of the other women bathe and dress her.

Matilda's appearance was, as Rafael had tried to warn her, enough to make even the stoutest stomach quail, and two of the women present had to leave the room. Beth wasn't one of them. As she helped wash away years of filth and dirt from the thin, scarred body, her tender heart bled for the plight of the poor girl, and she experienced a deep and bitter fury against the creatures that had done this to a mere child.

Matilda's head, arms and face were horribly scarred and full of bruises and ugly sores. Her nose had been burnt off to the bone, both nostrils being wide open and completely denuded of flesh. Matilda Lockhart was a fitting example of the horror of Indian captivity, and there wasn't a woman there that didn't thank God that she had been spared... for the moment.

The girl was aware of the revolting sight she must present and she begged piteously to be hidden away from curious eyes. Mary, Beth, and a few of the other ladies attempted vainly to soothe her, but looking at them through tear-drenched eyes, Matilda cried emotionally, "You do not understand! You can never understand! Yes, they held torches to my face to make me scream—look at me, my whole body bears scars from fire! But there is more—I am utterly degraded! The warriors shared me as if I were no better than a whore." Sobbing now almost uncontrollably, she turned her ruined face away, "I shall never be able to hold my head up again—my shame is complete."

Beth felt frozen inside, wondering how the girl had even managed to survive as she told of the further horrors she had been forced to endure, how the squaws had beaten her and how they would awaken her from sleep by sticking a chunk of fire to her flesh, especially her nose, and how they would laugh and shout when she screamed and writhed in agony. She could not bring herself to speak further of her sexual humiliations, and by the time she was fully dressed, every woman there was torn between pity and outrage.

Unfortunately for the Comanches, Matilda Lockhart was an extremely intelligent girl, and during her years of captivity she had learned the Comanche tongue. She actually overheard some of the warriors discussing their strategy for the release of the other captives. Mary instantly sent for Colonel Fisher, and with obviously growing fury he listened intently to Mary's account of the tortures the girl had suffered before he spoke quietly with Matilda. From her he learned that there were at least fifteen other white captives she knew of, and that the Comanches intended to strike expensive bargains for them. His face set and grim, Colonel Fisher thanked Matilda for her information and praised her for being a brave girl. Then, pivoting smartly on his heel, he marched out of the house. Watching him go, Beth suddenly wished that Nathan hadn't wanted to attend this wretched meeting. If the colonel's expression was anything to go by, violence was in the wind.

The council opened in the one-story limestone building adjacent to the San Antonio jail on the main plaza. It was a small building—and the courtroom itself had a packed earth floor, certainly it was not a pretentious place—but a building that from this day forth would always be known as the "Council House."

Rafael and Nathan were standing near the door when the twelve war chiefs, led by the bald, old head man, Mook-war-ruh, the Spirit Talker, filed arrogantly past them in their finest attire, the copper faces painted brightly and garishly in honor of the ceremonial occasion, and Nathan stared goggle-eyed. As the door shut behind the last Indian, Rafael stirred restlessly—Comanches did not like closed-in places, and it was a feeling he understood.

The chiefs squatted on the dirt floor and exchanged greetings with the Texan officials through an interpreter. Outside the courthouse all was apparently calm and relaxed—the Comanche women sat patiently by the building, the warriors staring aloofly into the distance, the young boys playing war games in the dusty streets. The onlookers, a mixed crowd of Texans and native San Antonio Mexicans, gathered to watch the proceedings. Beth and Mary, their help no longer needed with Matilda, were among them. Some of the men tossed coins in the air for the Comanche boys to use as marks for their miniature arrows, everyone expressing admiration at the boys' skill.

Curiosity seemed to be the mood of those outside, everyone wanting to see the peculiar and greatly feared Comanches. But Beth was not as curious as she once might have been; the sight of poor Matilda Lockhart's face and body would stay with her for a long time, and she was still incensed at what, perhaps, even some of these Indian women sitting in the hot sun in front of the courthouse had done to her. As for the sexual humiliations inflicted by the warriors, she was almost physically ill thinking of what the young girl had been made to suffer. And, remembering the fierce, terrifying faces of the warriors, thinking of their short, squat bodies violating hers, Beth shuddered.

Inside the Council House, Colonel Fisher had quickly shared with the other two commissioners what the Lockhart girl had told him. He had spared no detail of her conditions and mistreatment at the hands of the Comanches, and as word spread, the temperament inside the room was one of seething wrath and outrage. Most Texans were from the southern states, and while they had all fought Indians at one time or another, most had never encountered the brutality and cruelty of the Comanches. The "semicivilized" tribes of the east and south, while capable of their own brand of savagery, had never in the past hundred years deliberately abducted, raped, and killed white women, and the Texans were aroused to an almost hysterical fury by these acts.

The Comanches themselves were completely unaware of the reactions of the Texans in the room—the treatment of the Lockhart girl had been no worse than that of any other captive. Every woman captured by the Comanches was automatically raped by the entire raiding party once they had made camp for the night—it was a ritual they had found effective in bringing about utter and total obedience. As for passing her from man to man, they shared their wives with their brothers, so why shouldn't they also share a captive woman?

By the time the Indians were finally settled and all the customary greetings were exchanged, Colonel Fisher wasted little time in further formality. Standing in front of the impassive Comanches as they sat before him, some of them unconsciously caressing their favorite weapon, he demanded through the interpreter, "Why were there only two captives returned? We know of at least fifteen other captives—where are they?"

Spirit Talker, the old civil chief, his black eyes unblinkingly on Fisher, said through the interpreter, "It is true that there are many other captives—but these are in other camps of the Nermernuh, over which we have no control." He spoke a partial truth, although none of the Texans believed him. The white man had always had trouble understanding the autonomous nature of the Comanches—each band was a law unto itself.

Spirit Talker spoke eloquently for some minutes, the interpreter, a Mexican youth who was a former Comanche captive, quickly translating the guttural language into English. Much of what Spirit Talker had to say was of no interest to the Texans in the room, but finally he said something that everyone had been waiting for. Glancing around the packed room, certain he had the full attention of all who were there, he said slowly, "But I believe that all the captives can be ransomed for a great price—for many goods and ammunition, for blankets and much vermilion."

The Comanches had thought out their strategy well, but they had made a grave mistake in thinking the Texans, like the Mexicans, were willing to have peace with them, and their captives returned, at any price. Unfortunately too, the Comanches viewed the captives as simply the spoils of war, and it was incomprehensible to them that the Texans assumed any inherent right to the captives.

Certain the Texans would see the logic of their demands, Spirit Talker regarded the crowd confidently and ended his oration by questioning calmly, "How do you like that answer?"

There was a mutter of anger at the sheer arrogance of his reply, and Rafael tensed. Unobtrusively he judged the distance to the door, and somewhat ruthlessly began to maneuver Nathan toward it. Nathan, however, proved difficult and, attempting to shake his arm free of Rafael's guiding hand, he demanded in an angry undertone, "What the devil are you doing? I don't want to miss any of this, and I can't concentrate with you pushing and pulling at me."

Rafael gritted his teeth and, barely controlling his temper, he snapped in a low tone, "I'm trying to save your life! In this crowd, in the temper they're in, anything could happen, and you're leaving now whether you like it or not!"

But the delay had cost precious seconds. Colonel

Fisher's face stiffened at the blatant insolence and grimly he showed how he liked the answer by curtly ordering a file of Texan soldiers into the Council House. Quickly and efficiently the soldiers took up positions along the walls, one now guarding the door Rafael had been making for. Rafael's mouth tightened and, despite the crush and the crowd, inexorably he steered a resisting and contrary Nathan in that direction. They had just about reached the door and Rafael was on the point of breathing a sigh of relief when Nathan surprised both of them by deftly twitching his arm free and saying smugly, "*I* am not leaving! You may do so, if you wish." And with that he turned back to watch the proceedings.

Momentarily, Rafael seriously considered deserting Nathan, but remembering the anxious look in a pair of lovely violet eyes, he cursed under his breath and stood resignedly behind the other man, the expression on his face murderous. There was going to be trouble, he could smell it, and any faint hope he had cherished that the meeting would be a success had died the instant Colonel Fisher had ordered the troops into the already packed room. The hatred and violence that each people felt for the other was almost tangible, and instinctively Rafael eased his Colt pistol from the holster strapped to his thigh.

As soon as the soldiers had marched into the room, the Comanche chiefs began to move restively, one or two even rising to their feet, others clasping their knives and bows and arrows more aggressively than before. Colonel Fisher, seeing that his men were in place, said tersely, "I do not like your answer at all! You were told not to come here for council unless you brought in *all* captives. Your women and children may depart in peace and your warriors may go so that they may tell your people to bring in the other captives. When all the captives are returned, *then* we will speak of presents and *then* you and the other chiefs here today can go free. Until *then* you are our prisoners!"

The interpreter went white, his fright very obvious, and bluntly he refused to deliver such a message. His brown eyes dilating with fear, he said agitatedly, "The chiefs will fight to the death before they will allow themselves to be taken captive! You cannot capture them without a fight—a bloody fight!"

Colonel Cooke, who was the senior officer, came over to stand near Colonel Fisher and, his face darkening with anger, he demanded furiously, "Do you dare to tell us how to conduct this affair? Repeat the message as stated, you insolent dog, and do it *now!*"

Rafael's blood ran cold and, forgetting Nathan, he surged violently through the crowd, determined to make one last attempt to avoid bloodshed, but he was too late. Even as Rafael fought his way toward the front of the room, the interpreter shrugged his shoulders fatalistically and hastily translated Colonel Fisher's reply. Then, before anyone could stop him, he bolted from the room, his sudden and unexpected rush catching the guard in front of the door by surprise as he pushed him aside and ran out into the street.

The interpreter's words momentarily stunned the chiefs, but then, as their import sank in, almost as one they leaped to their feet, terrifying Comanche war whoops vibrating in the air. Thinking to follow the path of the interpreter, one chief lunged for the door and, meeting the soldier who guarded it more zealously this time, he plunged his knife into the guard, but the man, though badly wounded, fought back, his revolver effectively dispatching the Comanche.

Someone yelled for the troops to fire and the courtroom was instantly filled with gunsmoke and the shrieks and cries of the wounded. In the confined space there was no escaping for anyone, and both Comanches and Texans were hit by the fusillade. The room was in chaos, shouts and screams and the sound of musket fire shattering the air, the smell of smoke and hot blood quickly permeating every corner of the room.

It was a deadly melee and Rafael was caught in the middle, unable to fire on the Comanches and equally unwilling to shoot at the Texans. He fought a defensive action, using the butt end of his pistol to clear his way toward Nathan and the door. Like several others, Nathan was unarmed and totally unprepared, his gray eyes nearly starting from his head in fright as he stood frozen where Rafael had left him.

Ranger Matthew Caldwell, also unarmed and only an onlooker, who was standing near Nathan, took a bullet in the leg, but with deadly promptness, he grabbed a musket from one of the chiefs and blew off the Indian's head with it. At the sight of all the blood Nathan nearly swooned, but there were more horrors happening right in front of his eyes and, like a rabbit staring into the hypnotic gaze of a rattlesnake, he couldn't look away.

Mook-war-ruh, shrieking his outrage and disdain, his knife glittering in the gloom of the room, tangled with a Ranger captain. In the vicious struggle the captain was stabbed in the side. His military sword proved ineffective in such close quarters, and, nearly fainting from the loss of blood, he captured Mook-war-ruh by the hand and shouted to one of the soldiers to fire at the Comanche. A second later the old civil chief lay dead upon the dirt floor.

Bystanders and soldiers alike fought for their lives. Judge John Hemphill, the District Judge, efficiently disemboweled with a bowie knife one of the chiefs as they grappled in a mortal fight. The Council House rang with shots and the screams of the wounded and dying; the powder smoke was heavy in the confined space.

Rafael had managed to avoid killing anyone, although there were several men who were going to wonder who the hell had tapped them with less than gentle force on the head as he had struggled to Nathan. Reaching Nathan's side at last, he savagely shoved Nathan up against the wall and, positioning his body in front of the smaller man, he snarled over his shoulder, "Stay there! If you so much as move an eyelash, I'll gut you myself!"

Nathan stayed, hardly daring to move a muscle, staring with bulging eyes at the wide back, more frightened of Rafael than of any Comanche in the room. But the sight of a painted savage figure, suddenly appearing out of the smoke and shifting crowd, that leaped for Rafael caused him to moan with terror and shrink closer to the limestone wall.

Rafael met the Comanche's charge easily, one steel-fingered hand capturing the upraised arm that held a bloodstained knife. Nathan heard him say something harshly in the guttural tongue of the Comanche, and, peering nervously over Rafael's broad shoulder, he saw the Indian's black eyes open wide in startled recognition.

"Stalking Spirit!" the Comanche cried almost joyously, and then without warning there was deafening reverberation and the man's face changed as he crumpled to the floor, shot in the back by one of the soldiers. His face blank, Rafael stared across at the young soldier still holding the smoking musket and then at the body on the floor. He didn't say anything; he couldn't. His own inadvertent role in the tragedy had strangled speech.

The chiefs fought a bloody valiant battle, but they were outnumbered. One by one they were struck down mercilessly, the last few finally breaking through the door and spilling out into the streets of San Antonio. As they emerged, their shrieks and screams alerted the Comanches outside to a frenzy.

The white onlookers outside did not understand what was happening, and for the first few moments stood in a daze, as the squaws and children joined the remaining warriors in fighting for their lives. Seizing any weapon available, their hideous cries of rage splitting the hot sunlit day, the Indians turned on the hapless citizens of San Antonio. An Indian child shot a toy arrow into the heart of a visiting circuit judge, killing him instantly, just a second before the reserve soldiers, who had been kept in the background, opened fire. In the confusion, in the milling and mingling of both Indian and white, both sides suffered losses as the soldiers opened fire.

Somehow, Beth and Mary were separated. As shots and screams filled the air, Beth was trapped in the midst of the crowd. Desperately she tried to escape, but the surging, shifting mass carried her helplessly along.

The Comanches were intent only on escaping this place of betrayal. Always fearful of closed spaces, they were terrified, running and killing indiscriminately as they went. Most ran for the river. A few frantically tried to commandeer horses, others tried to hide in nearby houses, but at that point nearly every inhabitant of San Antonio had joined the fray—and, as they usually went armed, the fight became a slaughter, the Comanches heavily outnumbered.

Rafael, Nathan dragged along with him, was one of the first from the Council House to reach the street, and instinctively he glanced around for Beth, praying fiercely that she was safe at the Maverick house. Intently he scanned the fleeing throng, desperately hoping not to see Beth among them. He had almost started to relax, had almost begun to shift his thoughts to getting Nathan to a place of safety, when he caught sight of Beth's fair head in the shifting mass. The silvery braids were a magnetic beacon to him, and, seeing her abortive, frantic struggles to fight her way free from the melee, hearing the shots in the air, seeing the arrows and lances flying on their paths, for the first time in his life Rafael experienced the dry taste of fear in his mouth. Everything was forgotten—Nathan, the whine of the deadly missiles, the leaping copper bodies with their knives flashing in the sunlight, the men of San Antonio with their smoking guns, everything disappeared for him except the small bright figure being swept along with the scattering mob.

One second Rafael was next to Nathan in front of the Council House and the next he was flying down the street, the Colt pistol cocked and a hair trigger away from discharging. Oblivious of anything but Beth, he zigzagged down the street, instinctively keeping himself from becoming an easy target for either Comanche or white marksman.

More frightened than she had ever been in her life, Beth saw an opening in the crowd and nimbly dashed for it, her one thought being to escape from the line of fire. Gasping for breath, her heart pounding like it would burst from her throat, she clung to the adobe wall of the building, barely aware of the brush of the others as they plunged passed her.

Hands outstretched against the warm adobe, one cheek pressed tightly to the wall, she had her back to the street, the pink gown a vivid splash of color against the sienna walls. The cornet of braids had come unpinned during the scramble, one thick braid resting on her breast, the other, half undone, waving down her back. She could not know that the shining fair hair was a dangerous enticement for the Comanche who thought to have its owner as his captive . . . or the scalp to swing from his lodgepole!

Beth wasn't even aware of the copper figure that swerved toward her, his scalping knife already whetted with blood. Her first inkling of his deadly presence was the grasp of cruel hands on shoulders as he whipped her around. Eyes wide with terror, she stared at a face that nightmares are made of, the broad stripes of scarlet and yellow paint distorting further the Comanche's savage features. But only for a moment did she stare, and whether the Comanche meant to take her captive or merely lift her scalp was never decided, because Beth, reacting with a courage and speed born of fear, attacked the Indian like a golden wildcat. The knife was her first objective and, instantly catching his forearm in both of her hands, with surprising ferociousness she sank her teeth deeply into his wrist. The taste of blood in her mouth nearly made her gag, but grimly she held on as the infuriated Comanche, twisting and dancing about in the dusty street, attempted to shake her off. His free hand tangled in the fair hair, and Beth's eyes filled with tears of pain as he viciously tried to yank her head from his wrist.

Like a dog with a bone she refused to release her grip as they fought, knowing that if she did, the bloody knife would be the end of her. In their desperate struggle they crashed into the wall of the adobe, and with dismay and horror Beth felt her hold weakening. Frantically she tried to hang onto his arm, but the Indian was too swift for her and with a grunt of triumph he tore himself loose from her.

Her back against the wall, the fair hair half braided and half undone, tumbling wildly about her shoulders, she faced him defiantly, her breast heaving. Strangely, she wasn't frightened anymore, just plain angry, and with eyes that shot violet flames, stared furiously back at the Comanche, almost daring him to continue their unfair fight.

Warily now, the warrior watched her, uncertain

whether the gilt hair was worth the struggle, especially under the circumstances. Certainly he no longer wanted her as a captive, if that had been his original plan. But that extraordinary silvery-blond hair...

He crouched into an attacking stance and one thought hammered painfully through Beth's head—the knife, the knife, don't let him use *the knife!*

Tightening his hold on that particular weapon, the Comanche leaped toward her, and suddenly like a bolt out of the sky Beth found herself flying through the air as a hard hand unceremoniously shoved her out of the way. She plunged full length in the street, the breath knocked out of her, her ears ringing from the terrifying blast of a pistol that had exploded nearby only seconds before she had hit the dirt. Her face toward the street, with wide disbelieving eyes she stared as the Comanche fell to the ground near her, a bloody gaping wound in his chest, his body writhing and twisting in a grotesque dance of death.

Beth had barely time to assimilate the scene before hands as powerful and cruel as the Comanche's jerked her upright, and she felt herself crushed to a warm, hard chest and heard Rafael's voice breathe shakily in her ear, "Sweet Jesus! I thought I was going to be too late!"

His arms held her with a fierce protectiveness, their strength filling her with a lovely, warm sense of sanity in a world gone mad. He was breathing heavily, she could feel the rapid, labored rise and fall of his chest and hear the thundering beat of his heart against her cheek, and unconsciously her slender arms tightened around him. Dimly she became aware of the light ardent kisses that were being rained upon her head and temples and the soft Spanish words that were being whispered passionately in her ear. She didn't understand what he was saying, but it satisfied something within her and made her long recklessly for this exquisitely sweet embrace never to end.

Eventually, though, his arms loosened fractionally and he moved her slightly away from him. The dark face intent, the gray eyes moving swiftly over her face, he demanded in a husky tone of voice, "You're not hurt? He didn't manage to strike you anywhere, did he?"

Some of the horror of the day was beginning to fade and her eyes misty with emotion, she looked up at him and said softly, "You saved my life."

Rafael gave her a twisted, bitter smile and shook his head. Dryly he replied, "My own, I think."

She frowned at that, not understanding his meaning but too shattered by the violent event to puzzle it out. Reality was intruding, and almost self-consciously she stepped away from his embrace, and, avoiding his eyes, she began to concentrate with an odd intensity on brushing off the dust and dirt from her skirts. Unwillingly she remembered precisely their positions and stiffly she said, "I thank you very much, Señor Santana, for your more than timely intervention. You saved my life, and for that I can never repay you. Please accept my profound gratitude."

Rafael's face tightened and his eyes narrowed dangerously. Under his breath, he said harshly, "Don't start that type of mawkish behavior with me—*not now!*"

The violet eyes sparkling with sudden temper and pain, she looked at him and asked sharply, "*What* do you mean by that?"

His expression inscrutable, he regarded her. Almost as if the words were torn from him, he said savagely, "Simply that I think it's time we have the conversation we should have had four years ago!"

CHAPTER NINETEEN

Caught totally by surprise, Beth stared up at him. Hesitantly she began, "I don't think I under—" when Nathan's voice interrupted them.

"Beth! What are you doing out here?" he cried plaintively, thoroughly and completely disenchanted with everything about Texas, Comanches in particular. And not, if the truth be known, exactly enamored of his host any longer.

There had been so much violent activity, so much vivid action happening right under his very nose that it had taken him several minutes to discover where Rafael had disappeared to. Seeing the man he'd begun to think of as a savage, unpredictable beast standing with his wife didn't please him overmuch either. A peevish expression marring his blond fairness he approached them.

By this time most of the worst fighting had ceased, although there were still sporadic sounds of gunfire and an occasional shriek or yell heard in the distance. Several people were cautiously beginning to peek out of their various hiding places and a few of the braver souls were stepping warily into the plaza and beginning to walk toward the wounded or dead that lay scattered about. Everyone was on edge, alert for any sign of stray Indians still in the vicinity. Determined to get Beth safely away, Rafael looked down at her and said abruptly, "This is no place for you." And his eyes suddenly kindling with anger that hid his earlier fear and relief, he snapped, "What the hell were you doing out here by yourself in the first place? You could have been killed, you little fool!"

Nathan, who had reached them by now, not unnaturally took umbrage at not only the familiar tone of voice but also the high-handed way Rafael was speaking to Beth. Drawing himself up stiffly, he said testily, "I think you forget yourself, Santana! Beth is, after all, *my wife,* and I do not take kindly to others speaking so to her!"

Rafael went rigid, his face dark with barely leashed fury, and for one terrifying moment Beth feared that he would strike Nathan. His eyes mere slits of icy silver, he snarled dangerously, "And where the hell were you when she was fighting for her life? Hiding somewhere out of the line of fire?"

The three of them were standing almost in the middle of the street, Rafael and Beth facing Nathan. At Rafael's words, Nathan's fair skin turned a bright and unbecoming scarlet. His muttonchop whiskers bristling with outrage, and stuttering with choler, he got out, "H-h-how d-d-dare you s-s-speak to m-me like th-that!"

Contemptuously Rafael raked him with his gaze, but before he could reply, a slight movement where there should have been no movement on the top of one of the adobe houses just beyond Nathan's shoulder caught his attention. Not waiting to discover what caused it, Rafael was already drawing his pistol and throwing Beth to the ground when a Comanche warrior, his face hideously distorted by rage, a deadly lance in his hand, rose up from the roof of the house. Two things happened simultaneously, the warrior hurled the lance on its lethal journey and Rafael's gun spat lead. Both found a human target. The Comanche, clutching his throat, the death rattle carrying with unpleasant clarity in the warm air, pitched sideways off the roof, and Nathan, his face the picture of incredulity, stared down at the vivid patch of blood on his vest, the iron tip of the lance protruding from his stomach.

"Why, I've been wounded," he said in a voice of wonderment before he fell face down in the dusty street, the long Comanche lance swaying gently from where it had lodged in his back.

Her eyes wide with horror, Beth had stared at her husband's still form and a silent scream echoed through her brain. *No! He couldn't be dead!* Not this way, not slain so uselessly by a creature that should only inhabit nightmares. It was all a horridly bad dream.

Nothing had truly seemed real to her from the moment Rafael had shoved her into the street a second time, not the exploding sound of his gun, nor the sight of Nathan lying spread-eagle in the dusty street, a Comanche lance sticking grotesquely out of his back. Numbly she continued to look at Nathan. Watching the spreading stain of blood defacing his buff coat, she thought foolishly, *Oh, dear, his jacket will be ruined. He won't like that.* Her brain simply blocked out any emotion except the most mundane and prosaic.

Rafael knelt beside Nathan and after a moment he said in a quiet tone, "English, he's still alive! He's not dead!"

Beth felt a wave of thankfulness suffuse her body—He's alive! Thank God! But the shock and terror of the day was too much for her, and, beyond comprehending that Nathan was still alive, nothing else made sense. Even when Rafael helped her gently to her feet and Nathan was carried to Rafael's house and the doctor arrived, nothing touched her except in a hazy, dreamlike way.

It had seemed like hours that the doctor had worked over Nathan, and when he had at last entered the room where Beth sat so white-faced and still, his words were not overly optimistic. "He is badly wounded, Mrs. Ridgeway. I have done all that I can. With rest and care it is possible that he will recover, but..." His voice had trailed off. It had been an ugly wound and the little German doctor had worked desperately to remove the weapon without inflicting further damage. At the moment Nathan was resting comfortably under a heavy dose of opium, but only the following days would tell if he would survive the wound. Gently the doctor said, "There is hope, my dear. His case is not hopeless."

Beth clung to his words in the days that followed as to a lifeline, and over and over she repeated them—there is hope, *there is hope!* But the rest of the world receded from her—she ate when she was told, slept when she was told, and wore whatever was laid out for her. The remainder of the time she sat in Nathan's room, holding his hand and staring blindly into space until Nathan would moan in pain, and then she would tenderly smooth his brow and whisper soft, comforting words. Beth didn't know what she said during those days, mostly she just crooned meaningless little endearments that seemed to calm him temporarily.

As soon as Nathan had been carried to the house and the doctor had arrived, Rafael had spared a few minutes to send a rider posthaste to Cielo with the news of what had transpired. With Beth's husband incapacitated, it was imperative, in order to avoid any talk, that he find some respectable woman to stay in the house. He chafed against the insanity of it, but to avoid the inevitable raised eyebrows and wagging tongues he must have another woman in the house to protect Beth's reputation. For his own he didn't give a damn, but for her sake he dredged up some obscure Spanish relative, a widow of about sixty years of age who lived in San Antonio, and within the hour had her installed in the house.

There had been several other casualties besides Nathan, and during the long night that followed, what Mary Maverick would call in her diary "the day of horrors," the immigrant German doctor, San Antonio's only surgeon, had labored unceasingly through the night to save those that he could.

The Comanche loss was by far the worst. Of the sixty-five Indians who had come to council, thirty-three chiefs, warriors, women, and children had died in the massacre. The remaining thirty-two, all women and children, many of them wounded, had been captured and thrown into jail. Only seven whites had been killed, including the sheriff of San Antonio.

It had been a bloodbath in the end, the last stages of the fight becoming a hunt as the whites had scoured the town killing every frightened Comanche who did not immediately surrender. None of the Comanches managed to escape the town and were either killed on the spot or thrown into jail.

After Rafael had Beth safely back at the house and he had done what he could about Nathan's condition, he turned his mind to the repercussions of the day's happening. It was not a pleasant contemplation. And, rousing himself from the vision of burned-out homesteads and the mutilated bodies of settlers' families, as well as the knowledge that the Comanche camps would suffer too, he sent another rider thundering off into the night. This one rode toward Austin and Sam Houston.

His note to Houston was brief, merely a recital of the facts and the information that he would be staying in San Antonio indefinitely. If Houston needed him, he knew where to find him. Only at the end of the note did his frustration and rage show through. "You know," he wrote in thick black strokes, "if Fisher and the others had deliberately planned to drive the Comanches straight into the arms of the Mexicans, they couldn't have chosen a better way! God help us all!"

He had nothing to discuss with any of the military men involved—the time for talking was past—but he still took a keen interest in their plans. Early the next morning, while Beth slept dreamlessly under the influence of the prescribed laudanum and San Antonio still buzzed with shock and rumor, Rafael was at the jail when the Commissioners, their faces unyielding and rock-hard, took one of the Indian women, the wife of one of the greatest dead chiefs, and put her on a horse. In hostile silence they gave her food and water, and then she was told bluntly, "Go to the camps of your people and tell them that the survivors of the Council House fight will be put to death unless all of the captives spoken of by Matilda Lockhart are returned. You have twelve days from where the sun stands now to deliver our message and return with the captives." The Indian woman listened impassively, her features never betraying her grief and rage. Nothing else was said, and, watching her ride out of town, Rafael knew with a sickening sense of futility that though she would deliver the ultimatum, the helpless captives would scream their lives away under the torturing knives of the wailing squaws in the camps, condemned to death by the treachery of the very men who sought to free them.

He turned furiously on his heel and strode angrily away, unable to look at these men, who had with such righteous arrogance brought about the end of hope for any peace between the Comanches and the whites, without taking some reckless and violent action against them. Rafael had a hot temper, but he also had an iron control over his volatile emotions. This was obviously not the right time or the place to express his fury and disgust.

He had done all that he could, and if his conscience pricked him with painful regularity because he had not warned the Comanches of his fears and suspicions, he could console himself with the knowledge that hind-sight is *always* infallible. He had tried his best to convince the Indian Commissioners of the importance of this particuliar meeting. It was cold comfort to him, especially when he enumerated all the powerful men of the Pehnahterkuh who had died, leaving the largest group of Comanches virtually leaderless. As he figured it, there was only one chief who had escaped the Council House Massacre, and that would be the great war chief Buffalo Hump. At least they have *him,* he decided bitterly.

Rafael had done something the day of the Council House fight that he had never thought himself capable of—he had killed not one but two Comanches. Granted they had not been members of the Kwerhar-rehnuh, who had raised him, but they had been Comanches nonetheless and he had killed them deliberately. He had killed men before—Apaches, whites, and Mexicans—but never a Comanche, and it made him realize now how firmly he was allied with the white man. And how intensely Beth Ridgeway affected his emotions.

He hadn't forgotten the snake of terror that had slithered down his spine when he saw her fighting so valiantly with the Comanche warrior, nor had he forgotten the burst of scarlet rage that had exploded through his body when Nathan had taken him to task and said the words *my wife.*

And if he hadn't forgotten the terror or the rage that came so effortlessly to him, he also had not forgotten his own angry words to Beth only hours before Nathan's wounding. They echoed around his brain like enraged hornets, the sentence "He could be skewered by a Comanche lance for all I care!" buzzing round and round in his brain until he felt nearly demented. What damnable luck that he should prove to be such an excellent prophet of doom!

Now Nathan might die, and Rafael was grimly aware that in death he might prove to be a greater barrier than in life. One thing Rafael knew for damn sure—Beth was not going too far away from San Antonio until they had settled whatever was between them. He was *not* going to go through the remainder of his life tortured by visions of a violet-eyed slut with the face of an angel! They were going to come to some understanding and she was going to stay put until they did!

It was arrogant—even he was aware of that—but he would have had to have been a blind man not to know that there was a bond between them. Perhaps only a physical one; with one part of him he hoped viciously it would turn out to be just that—that once they established an easy intimacy between them, the fierce emotions she aroused would disappear and after a few weeks he could pack her off to Natchez and out of his life. It was what he wanted, he told himself vehemently, his jaw clenching with anger. And *yet*...

Where Beth was concerned Rafael was a tangle of conflicting, seething emotions—jealousy, rage, uncertainty, and passion all fighting for dominance—one moment jealousy the driving force, passion the next, and in between a curiously painful tenderness that disturbed him far more than all of the other emotions combined. Rage he could deal with, jealousy he could ignore, uncertainty he could put behind him, and passion he could slake, but tenderness...?

He was not a tender man, had never been a tender man except perhaps with his young half sister Arabela. Consequently, the emotion confused him and made him especially wary of the person who aroused it—wary and angry that she could make him feel anything except contempt. Walking toward the house, he thought with cold rage, What the hell do I care what happens to her—it would have been easier to let that damned Comanche take her with him, or scalp her, whichever he preferred.

It wasn't that simple and he knew it. But he chose to avoid her at the house for several reasons—her husband was gravely wounded, perhaps mortally, and now was not the time for the conversation or anything else that he wanted between them. There was also the fact that he couldn't bear to watch her croon over Nathan. Even if the man *was* badly injured, Rafael didn't like his being the object of Beth's attentions, especially when the thought occurred to him that if it had been left up to her husband to rescue her, Beth would be dead or a Comanche's captive. And finally there was one more reason he avoided her, and he acknowledged it reluctantly: Beth might not want to see him—after all, he *had* in a moment of hot fury wished her husband dead! Consequently Rafael stayed in the background, seeing that everything that could be done was done and that Beth had everything that she could possibly want, not only for herself but Nathan as well. I owe him that much, Rafael admitted harshly.

Don Miguel, Doña Madelina, and Sebastian, as well as various servants and *vaqueros* from Cielo, arrived in San Antonio the fourth evening after the massacre. Beth hadn't known of their arrival until Rafael's relative, Señora López, had forced her from Nathan's bedside, insisting in a mixture of Spanish and broken English that she eat something.

Finding the newcomers already seated at the table for dinner, Beth stopped in surprise and almost dazedly she murmured, "Oh, I didn't expect to see all of you here. When did you arrive?"

The men rose instantly, and both Don Miguel and Sebastian swiftly approached her with concerned faces and a warm sympathy that made her eyes well up with sudden tears of gratitude for their continued kindness. She quickly recovered herself, though, and, seated next to Doña Madelina, who held her hand tightly and coaxed her to eat a bite of this and that, she managed to get through the meal with tolerable composure. Everyone was most considerate of her, and beyond mentioning Nathan's name once or twice the others kept up a light, soothing flow of conversation, no one inclined toward levity.

Rafael had made no move from his place at the head of the long, linen-draped table when Beth had entered the room, other than rising politely to his feet. Neither he nor she directed any observations toward the other except for the most commonplace remarks, and they had exchanged no conversation of any note since the moment Nathan had been struck down. But he watched her critically, the hard gray eyes not liking the pallor of her face nor the haunted, other-world expression in the violet eyes. Seeing how little she ate and noticing angrily the growing fragility of her fine-boned face and delicate wrists, his mouth tightened and he experienced a jabbing sense of frustration. There was nothing *he* could do that he hadn't done already, and he was thoroughly aware that any move he might make to settle things between them would more than likely precipitate an emotional crisis that she could well do without under the circumstances.

Beth was alone with Nathan when he finally roused himself and recognized her. The doctor had kept him heavily sedated with an opium mixture to ease the pain, but about eleven o'clock that night, just as Beth was thinking of seeking her own bed, Nathan regained a certain amount of consciousness. His eyes were still cloudy from the drug but he appeared to be remarkably clear-headed and, seeing Beth sitting by his bedside, he smiled, a sweet gentle smile that tore at Beth's heartstrings. "My dear," he whispered, "what are you doing here?"

Her throat aching with unshed tears, she returned his smile and said softly, "I was just keeping you company for a little while."

His eyes closed briefly and he murmured lightly, "I am so tired, but it is most pleasant to wake and find your lovely face nearby."

It was a mundane conversation to be having with him. But at the time that didn't occur to Beth and all she could think of was that Nathan was awake—and for the moment she was content.

He became aware of the bandages about his middle and a feeling of pain. Looking up at her with anxious gray eyes, he asked worriedly, "I'm all right, aren't I?"

Her face shining with growing confidence, she answered instantly, "Of course you are, love! You have been gravely wounded, though, and you must rest for now."

He relaxed and, clumsily capturing one of her hands in his, he brought it to his lips. "What a sorry state this is! Just as soon as I am well, we shall go home—and Beth, if you don't mind, I would just as soon not go traveling in the wilds again."

Her smile wobbled only slightly. "I couldn't agree with you more, my dear." Sorrowfully she admitted, "I should have listened to you in the first place, Nathan."

"Oh, come now, such humility! It doesn't become you, Beth. You have always been a bit of a minx, and I shouldn't want you to change now," he teased her gently. He looked very young as he lay against the white pillows, his fair hair curling near his temples, and Beth's heart tightened painfully in her breast.

He moved as if in pain and Beth asked quickly, "Is something the matter?"

Nathan shook his head and tenderly kissed her fingers. Their clasped hands lying on his chest, he said, "I think I shall rest awhile, if you don't mind, my dear," and drifted off to sleep.

He spoke only once more to her that night. Seeming to fight his way to consciousness again about half an hour later, he looked directly at Beth and said clearly, "I do love you, you know, in my way."

Softly Beth replied, "I know you do, my dear," and kissed him on the forehead.

He gave a small sigh, as if satisfied with her answer, and lapsed back into unconsciousness, his hand still holding hers. How long Beth sat there she didn't know... or even exactly when Nathan had left her. One minute both of them were in the room together and the next she was alone with her husband's body.

The others were still up enjoying a last bit of refreshment before retiring, the gentlemen sipping their whiskey, the ladies drinking coffee laced with brandy, when Beth entered the room. The inconsequential chatter ceased abruptly and every eye swung to her. Standing wraithlike in the doorway, she surveyed them dazedly and said numbly, "My husband is dead."

There was a concerted murmur of sympathy from

everyone, but Rafael, who turned away, was fighting an overpowering urge to crush her protectively in his arms and to croon into the bright hair the same sort of gentle nonsense that she had to Nathan. At the moment he would have even willed Nathan to live, if it would erase the pain she must be feeling.

Both the ladies embraced her, murmuring words of condolences and comfort. Doña Madelina kept her arm around her and urged her to a long, green sofa. "Come, my child, come, you must sit down," she said gently, absently patting Beth's arm as she did so.

To Señora López, Doña Madelina murmured, "Ring for a servant and have some milk warmed and mixed with the laudanum the doctor left."

Dutifully Beth sat on the sofa as she was told, and like an obedient child she drank the milk and laudanum when it was presented to her. She didn't speak again nor did she cry, she simply sat stunned on the sofa, her thoughts far away from the present. It was as if everything were frozen inside of her, so deeply frozen that she could feel no emotion, only a great emptiness.

There were not many people at Nathan's funeral the next afternoon, just Rafael, the other Santanas, the Mavericks, Sebastian, and the German doctor who had tried to save him. There were one or two others but Beth, wrapped in her numbing emptiness, didn't recognize them. She was a beautiful zombie, her gaze blank, her movements slow and dreamlike, her voice mute. And, staring at her as she watched the first shovelful of dirt cascade down on Nathan's wooden coffin, Rafael would have liked to shake her furiously and slap her half silly, do anything to make her express some emotion even if it were nothing more than rage and fury at his apparent insensitivity—*anything* would be better than the frozen, silent creature who now inhabited Beth's body!

She made a lovely widow. The black silk gown, easily procured in a former Spanish city like San Antonio, where the women frequently wore black, intensified her air of fragility and contrasted with an almost sensual vividness against the alabaster skin and masses of ash-blond hair. The only bright color about her was the pale rose of her mouth and the purple hue of her eyes, everything else either light or dark.

It was only when they were preparing to leave the small cemetery that she did something on her own. Blindly turning back toward the half-filled grave, she walked to its edge and, standing there, she looked a long time at the gold band on her finger, and then with infinite slowness removed her wedding ring and dropped it into the grave.

Time passed as it always does, but nothing seemed to shake Beth from her dreamlike state. She slept for hours and hours each day and night, hating to awake from the blessed blankness of the laudanum that she took with frightening regularity. The laudanum helped to make everything hazy and keep at bay the ugly, unwelcome reality that awaited her if she allowed its stupor to wear off.

Most people were highly sympathetic to her grief, believing erroneously that she and Nathan had been so madly in love that she was unable to cope in a world without him any longer. And of course, there was a great deal of pity for so young and beautiful a widow, a lovely creature with no family or friends of long standing to share her sorrow with. Naturally the Santanas were doing all that was right and proper, but they were, after all, only chance-met acquaintances, and somehow that wasn't the same as family, no matter how kind and considerate they were.

As for Rafael, for the time being he was, if not content, at least willing to leave the consoling to the women in his family. Let Doña Madelina and Señora López hover over her and coddle her—it was probably what she needed most.

Rafael didn't for one second believe that she had been so deeply in love with Nathan that she couldn't bear the thought of the future without him. He quite vehemently refused to credit such a reason for her listless, shocked state. Instead he chose to lay the blame on something nearer the truth—that Beth's condition came as much from the horror of seeing Matilda Lockhart and the eruption of violence that followed, as well as her own brush with death, as it did from her husband's tragic demise. He didn't doubt that she grieved for Nathan, but he couldn't accept the idea that it was *only* his death that had turned Beth into a lovely zombie.

Rafael was nearer the mark than he realized. But what he discounted was something he had no way of knowing—that Beth was suffering under a crushing load of the strongest guilt imaginable. And it was to escape from facing it that she kept herself half drugged with laudanum and kept any emotions from disturbing the soothing emptiness she felt inside.

It had been *her* idea to visit Stella. It had been *her* desire to travel the southern route instead of joining up with the spring caravan to Santa Fe. It had been *she* who had wanted to visit Rancho del Cielo. *She* who had decided to terminate the journey and return to Santa Fe. And in death she imparted to Nathan all sorts of virtues he hadn't possessed. There was also her admitted fascination for Rafael Santana, and that tormented her far more than anything else. Nathan's death, she thought dully one night before the laudanum completely clouded her brain, was God's punishment on her for her lustful preoccupation with Rafael, that and her capricious and willful disregard of her husband's very reasonable wishes.

In her orgy of guilt and condemnation, Beth chose to forget that Nathan hadn't been forced to come with her—too, that *he* had been the one who insisted upon attending the fateful meeting with Rafael! She also refused to remember his selfish reason for marrying her, his philanderings, and his gambling and drinking excesses. She remembered only the good—his kindness to her and his concern for her happiness—and she made him into a saintly being who was totally unrecognizable as Nathan Ridgeway. Eventually her own good common sense would exert itself, but for the present she wandered in an unhappy haze through the days that followed, the effects of laudanum never completely out of her system.

While Beth drifted in her self-induced haze, Rafael had not been idle. The day after the funeral, to his surprise he received a note requesting his presence at the Mission San José, where Colonel Fisher and his troops had withdrawn with the Indian prisoners. Reading Colonel Fisher's curt missive, he had half a mind to ignore the summons, but curiosity got the better of him. What could Colonel Fisher possibly have to say to him?

The Mission San José was on the outskirts of the town, and it took Rafael but a short time to saddle his horse and ride there. Shown into the colonel's quarters by a grim-faced young soldier, he was slightly disconcerted to discover that Colonel Fisher was seriously ill. But when he would have excused himself and murmured that he would call again when the colonel was in better health, Fisher snapped, "My health is no concern of yours! I wanted to see you and I wanted to see you now!"

It was not, perhaps, the most conciliatory opening for their conversation. But then, Colonel Fisher was not in a very conciliatory mood. He was quite ill, so ill in fact that the young Captain Redd was in command of the garrison, and he was uncomfortably conscious of the fact that the meeting with the Comanches could have been handled with more tact. Not wasting any time in polite banter, he came right to the point.

"You are very familiar with the Comanche ways. Do you think they are going to bring in the captives when the twelve days we gave them are past?" he demanded from his bed.

Rafael, who had refused the proffered chair, stood with unconscious arrogance in the center of the room, his thumbs hooked casually on either side of the large silver buckle of the wide leather belt he wore, his black sombrero half-hiding the expression in the hard gray eyes. Bluntly he replied, "No. Why should they? You murdered their chiefs who came under a peace truce to talk of a treaty, and as far as they are concerned, the survivors you hold captive are as good as dead. What inducement do you offer them *to* bring in their captives?"

Fisher's normally tanned face was pale from illness, and there was a lackluster sheen in the dark eyes. Distractedly his fingers plucked at the edge of the sheets of his bed as he said doggedly, "We will not be held to ransom! They had no right to abduct our women and children in the first place—and we *will not* be intimidated!"

Rafael shrugged. "Then there's nothing to discuss, is there? If you will excuse me, I have other things to do." He spun on his heel and had started to walk toward the door when Fisher's voice stopped him.

"Wait!"

Looking back at the colonel, his face set in uncompromising lines, Rafael asked, "Yes?"

Fisher rested back weakly against his pillows. Tiredly he admitted, "We had our orders and we followed them. Certainly none of us believed that a massacre would result."

"Oh? You expected the Comanche chiefs to meekly allow themselves to be taken captive?" Rafael taunted.

"Damn it, they were only Indians! All we wanted was our captives. They'd been told not to come to council *unless* they brought them all in—your precious Comanches were as much at fault as we were." Hastily he clarified, "Not that there was any fault on our side—the Comanches started the fight, after all."

His gray eyes full of scorn, Rafael said harshly, "I don't see much point in this conversation. So, if you will excuse me . . . ?"

"Santana, don't go!" Reluctantly Fisher added, "I need your help. Texas needs your help. We need to know information that you can give us. You know about Comanches better probably than any man in Texas. What can we expect now?"

There was a time, and not too distant in the past either, when Rafael would have refused to answer such a question. He would have felt a traitor. But his own killing of the two Comanches, for whatever reasons, had made him irrevocably aware that his lot was with the white man. Still, the words came hard, and he almost spat them out. "First of all, I would advise you to give up any hope of seeing the captives alive!" he snapped. "Any of the white women and children that haven't already been formally adopted into a Comanche family are probably dead by now. As soon as the Indian woman you sent to the Comanche camp arrived, their fates were sealed. The only ones who *might* escape death by torture are the adopted captives, but I wouldn't hold out much hope even for them." His eyes bleak and unforgiving he snarled, "When you broke the sacredness of the council, didn't it ever occur to you, even fleetingly, that you could be sacrificing innocent women and children?"

Fisher wouldn't meet his eyes, and Rafael snorted with disgust. With an effort he controlled his rising temper, and, pulling up the chair he had refused earlier, he turned it around and straddled it easily, his crossed arms resting lightly on the wooden back. Honesty made him say, "I can't tell you exactly what will happen, but I can tell you what I think they will do." Frowning, he sent a hard look across at the other man. "I suspect that sooner or later you're going to have one wrathful war party appear on the horizon screaming for the blood of every Texan. As for the twelve-day truce you so generously offered, I wouldn't hang any hope on it. The Comanches are going to be outraged and furious, feeling, I think, justifiably betrayed. On the other hand, they are going to be confused and uncertain, something that may work to our advantage... at first." Unemotionally Rafael said, "You've killed all their great leaders, and I doubt that there are very many warriors of sufficient prestige within the tribe who can weld them into a concerted force. In time, yes, but at the present, no. That won't stop them from seeking revenge, though." His face becoming increasingly grim, he continued, "You can also expect to have raiding and killing on the frontier the like of which you have never dreamed... not even in nightmares! They have no reason to hold back *now*. You have given them a just cause to hate us with all the ferocity and unforgivingness of their nature." His voice as unyielding as granite and the gray eyes like flecks of obsidian, Rafael ended stingingly, "And I'm sure you realize why they will not be willing to sit down to any peace talks you might want to offer them. The Council House Massacre will be viewed by them as the vilest treachery possible—they will *never* forget or forgive it. Worse, you, Lamar, Johnston, and all the others have given them a common cause that could—

I don't say will—but *could* lead to the unification of *all* the Comanche tribes. In short, sir, you can expect a war with the Comanches that will not end until either the Texans are driven from the Republic or the last Comanche has been killed."

CHAPTER TWENTY

Rafael left the Mission San José full of rage and frustration. He had almost enjoyed flinging those last words at Colonel Fisher, and yet deep inside he was sick. Everything that he and all the others had sought to avoid would happen and all because of one senseless outbreak of violence.

His mood was surly for the rest of the day, and he avoided the house, being in no mood for polite conversation. Instead he rode the big dapple-gray stallion out toward the limestone hills and spent the afternoon gaining peace from the clear blue sky and wide vista.

It was late when he arrived back at the house. The ladies had retired some time ago and even his father had gone to bed, leaving Sebastian the only one still awake except for a stray servant or two.

Rafael wasn't deliberately searching for companionship, but when he discovered Sebastian, nursing a brandy in the small study at the rear of the house, he was almost pleased.

Sebastian looked up when he entered and asked, "Where did you disappear to? Everyone was quite concerned when you were not at dinner."

Rafael grimaced. "I keep forgetting to tell someone where I'm going. Blame it on a life spent in solitude on the plains."

Sebastian smiled in commiseration. They drank in companionable silence for a few minutes, Rafael lounging carelessly in a worn Spanish leather overstuffed chair, his long legs stretched in front of him, his booted feet crossed at the ankles. After a while they began to talk of Sebastian's plans for the future, more specifically of the land he was going to apply for the next day.

Sebastian's young face was eager, the emerald eyes flashing with enthusiasm. Leaning forward in his chair, he confessed, "When Father first mentioned Texas, I had my reservations. I could have gone to England and taken over some of Mother's estates, or Father even thought I might like to try my hand at running the plantation in Virginia, but neither appealed to me." He gave a rueful laugh. "It seemed so *tame.* When I said as much to Father, it was then that he suggested that possibly I might find it more to my liking if I created my own lands in the manner I saw fit. He said, in that rather dry way he has, that Texas was as good a place as any for a young man of my talents." Sebastian grinned, his wide mouth curving attractively. "He wasn't wrong, either! I can't begin to tell you how eager I am to start carving out my own estate. It gives me, I think, much the same feeling father must have had at the prospect of taming Terre du Coeur." After taking a sip of his brandy, he finished with "I guess that I am feeling the same urge that he did to take raw land and subdue it and form it into one's liking . . . or dreams, if you care to call it such."

At first, listening with indulgent affection, Rafael was unmoved by Sebastian's words, but the thought of taking untamed, wild land and making it into the stuff that dreams are made of woke an emotion that had been slumbering deep inside of him. Staring with great interest at the tip of his booted foot, he was aware of a spark of something that resembled envy at Sebastian's future. No, envy wasn't the right word—Rafael envied no man—but he was suddenly conscious of the fact that he wanted intensely to do exactly as Sebastian was going to do. To take untamed land and form it into dreams . . .

Rafael had always been conscious that part of his indifference to Cielo had its roots in the fact that there was no challenge connected with the rancho, unless one counted Indians and Mexican *bandidos.* Cielo was beautiful, that was undeniable; but the land had been tamed long ago, and he took no pride in the gracious hacienda with its sumptuous furnishings, nor in the million or so acres that teemed with herds of cattle and horses, as much because of his hatred of Don Felipe as due to his Comanche upbringing.

But the Comanche days were past, and Rafael discovered that he no longer truly yearned for them. He had made his own modest fortune over the years, trapping and trading as had his American grandfather, as well as capturing wild horses to sell for more than just a tidy profit. It was a fortune he could call his own, a fortune that owed nothing to Cielo and Don Felipe. The lands and money he had inherited from his maternal grandfather, Abe Hawkins, had increased in size to commendable proportions, making Rafael a man of substance without even touching the Santana wealth. As he and Sebastian sat talking, Rafael was thinking of the land he owned some miles north of Houston in the eastern part of the Republic, land he had grudgingly purchased after Texas had gained her independence and simply because Abe had thought it would round out his own smaller holding nicely.

It was part of an old Spanish rancho that had failed. Some thirty-five years previously, Abe had staked out about a hundred and fifty thousand acres for himself, including the crumbling, abandoned hacienda, and when the adjacent land came up for sale some thirty years later, Abe had been most insistent that Rafael purchase them. At the time Rafael hadn't known why it was so important he buy the additional two hundred thousand acres of woodlands and meadows, but now he did. Abe had known there would come a time when he would want his *own* land—not land inherited, but land he had bought with money earned by his own sweat and blood. And perhaps the time had come, Rafael reflected moodily.

Thinking of it, thinking of the pine forests and lakes, of the dogwood that bloomed in the spring, of the hardwood and palmetto forests, he knew with stunning certainty that it was there he wanted to be—not at Cielo with its painful memories, nor on the plains with the memory of what could never be, but at Enchantress, the name his grandfather had given the lands some thirty-odd years before when Black Fawn, his wife, had been alive.

Almost self-consciously Rafael mentioned the land, telling Sebastian how he had come to own it and how his grandfather had named it Enchantress after his Indian wife. They talked about its possibilities for several minutes before Sebastian asked idly, "What do you intend to do with it? Sell it? Or have you considered working it?"

Rafael stared moodily down into his glass of whiskey. "I don't know. It depends on..." He stopped, realizing how very far he had come in his thoughts. Frowning he said slowly, "I think I might ride up there some time in the next few weeks and see what condition the old hacienda is in, and possibly hire a few men to start clearing the land. It's good land for either cattle or crops, but first it has to be cleared." Smiling wryly, he said, "It will take months of backbreaking labor before anything can be done with it. But in time..." There was an odd note in Rafael's voice that caused Sebastian to glance at him sharply.

"Are you considering this seriously?" he demanded in surprise. "If I didn't know it was impossible, I would think you were considering settling down... and at Enchantress at that!"

The gray eyes hooded and a bland smile on his mouth, Rafael said lightly, "All things are possible, *amigo*. Sometimes it just takes a man a while to discover what he really wants out of life. Enchantress seems as good as any place to find out if a life of respectability appeals to me."

There was more news concerning the Comanches in the morning, but it told the Texans little more than they had known already. A Mrs. Webster, having been captured with her son and infant daughter the year before when her husband and the party they had been traveling with had been ambushed and killed at Brushy Creek, near Georgetown, had managed a daring escape from the Comanches. She had stolen a horse and, with her small daughter clinging desperately to her back, had ridden with all haste and fear to San Antonio, arriving on March 26. She was a pitiful sight, famished, her clothes in rags and her eyes full of remembered terror. She'd had to leave her son behind, and that, more than anything, distressed her. Having disregarded Rafael's advice once, Colonel Fisher now seemed determined to have his counsel on everything. Consequently Rafael was there when Mrs. Webster was interviewed by the military. The information she imparted that her son, Booker, had been adopted by a Comanche family gave Rafael hope that at least some of the white captives would escape death, but beyond saying that there were many captives among the Comanches and that the Comanches had been grief-stricken at the news of the massacre at the Council House, she could tell them nothing more.

Rafael was filled with a sort of helpless fury as he fought the battle within himself—the Comanche days of his past urging him to throw his lot with the Indians, to offer them his knowledge of the white man's ways, and yet every instinct reminding him that his place now was with the white man—and for the present he could do nothing but wait, like the rest of the inhabitants of San Antonio, for the Comanches to make the first move.

Two days after Mrs. Webster's return, the Comanches came. But, devoid of leadership as Rafael had said, they were helpless, and instead of wreaking the violence and death that they could have, they simply swarmed the hills northwest of the city, full of rage and uncertainty. There were close to three hundred of them, each screaming his defiance and hatred, and yet without their chiefs, with their councils divided, there was no one to lead an attack.

One minor chief, Isimanca, braver—or perhaps more foolhardy—than the others, galloped daringly into the middle of the public square and for several moments he and a companion rode around the plaza, shouting challenges to the astonished onlookers. Stopping in front of Bluck's Saloon on the northeast corner of the square, his black paint grotesquely distorting his proud features, his naked chest heaving with emotion, he stood up in his stirrups and, shaking a clenched fist at the bystanders, he raved and shouted at them, determined to fight with someone. Fortunately, everyone seemed more bemused than afraid, and after a bit, an interpreter informed the Comanche that if he wanted a fight he should go to the Mission San José and that Colonel Fisher and the soldiers would be glad to oblige him. Glaring at them, the black eyes flashing with fury, he nodded curtly, and with a shrieking whoop he and his fellow Comanche rode out of town at breakneck speed.

Captain Redd and his men were surprised when shortly thereafter some three hundred screaming and threatening Comanches thundered up to the limestone walls of the mission. The troops were eager to start firing, but Captain Redd, conscious of the fact that the truce had officially three more days to run, ordered his men to hold their fire. There was a great deal of grumbling but the soldiers did as ordered, as the Comanches galloped madly about hurling insults and challenges, their lances upraised in aggressive positions, some even notching their arrows to their bows. But despite all their hostile actions, the Comanches were not quite daring enough to start a battle with the men safely ensconced behind the high walls of the mission, and eventually they rode off in frustration.

The men of the First Texas Regiment were incensed at the orders not to fire, and Captain Lysander Wells went so far as to accuse Captain Redd of cowardice. Heated words were hurled, and with two hot-tempered Southern gentlemen, a duel was the only way to solve the not so thinly disguised insults. Grim-faced, they stepped out the twenty paces and wounded each other fatally. The Comanches would have been pleased.

Beth was oblivious of most things, but by the time Nathan had been buried a week, her own common sense told her that she was accomplishing nothing by remaining in a half-drugged state. Her guilt had not lessened, and while she resolutely stopped taking the laudanum during the daylight hours, she simply couldn't face the night without it. She was aware that she should do something, make some effort to pick up the pieces of her life, but she seemed momentarily helpless to do anything but accept the sympathy and kindness of the Santanas. That it was Rafael's hospitality she accepted she preferred not to acknowledge, and with Sebastian and the older Santanas in the house it was very easy to pretend it was *their* unstinting hospitality that she so very willingly accepted.

No one appeared in any hurry to break up the small gathering in San Antonio. Sebastian was busy seeing about his land patents and overseeing the buying of various implements to start carving out his estate near Cielo; Doña Madelina always enjoyed being in town and she was constantly visiting her acquaintances. Don Miguel frequently accompanied her and he was apparently as eager as she to postpone their return trip to Cielo. Señora López was more than happy to continue her not very arduous duties of companion to Beth rather than return to the loneliness of her quiet little house, and perhaps she secretly hoped that Rafael would allow her to stay indefinitely.

Rafael had his own reason for being, if not content, at least satisfied to have his family filling the empty rooms of the house in San Antonio. It gave him an odd sense of belonging for the first time in his entire life and he found it a good feeling, one he did not necessarily wish to disrupt. He and his father had exchanged more conversation in the past week than they had in all the years that had gone before, and even Doña Madelina, confronted by a man who was a gracious and considerate host, seemed to have lost her fear of her tall intimidating stepson and acted more relaxed and vivacious in his presence.

As for Beth, the possibility that she should return to Natchez never crossed anyone's mind except her own. Somehow, during the days that had followed Nathan's death, it had been assumed that she would be remaining in San Antonio indefinitely. She was being, whether she was aware of it or not, gently but relentlessly absorbed into the Santana family.

Sebastian had the most logical reason for believing that Beth would never return to Natchez. Rafael's tale of their long-time association made him naturally assume that with her husband dead Rafael would see to her future—and what better place for her to be than San Antonio? He still experienced a shaft of pain every time he thought of their liaison, but time *was* healing his bruised heart and he had very determinedly put Beth Ridgeway out of his plans for the future.

If Sebastian had a logical reason for assuming that Beth would be staying in San Antonio, Don Miguel had an entirely irrational one. He wanted Beth to marry his son. Not only did he find her an enchanting young creature but she was also a wealthy widow and her father was an English lord, so why shouldn't this lovely, eminently suitable woman become a member of the Santana family? He had just about given up hope of his son ever marrying again, but every action Rafael had taken since Beth had come into his life filled Don Miguel with the optimistic idea that this woman had captured his son's stubborn, savage heart. The very fact that Beth and Nathan had been invited to stay at Rafael's house gave a strong indication that his son was more than just a little interested. Don Miguel could remember at no time in the past had Rafael ever had *anyone* stay at the house, even other members of the family. But the note requesting that his family come to San Antonio when Nathan had been wounded was the most significant clue—Rafael's actions were clearly those of a man determined to lessen and soothe the pain of a woman dear to him. It was true that Rafael gave no overt sign of his feelings—in many ways he seemed to ignore Beth's presence—but Don Miguel had noticed the way his son's gaze often strayed in her direction. Doña Madelina had noticed it too. At night as they lay in bed like two conspirators, exchanging the bits and pieces of events that they hoped would result in a marriage, Don Miguel dared to scheme and pray just a little that out of tragedy would spring bliss.

It was true Beth had been widowed barely a week, but in a land where death was a way of life, so was the forging of new life. As Don Miguel and Doña Madelina had discussed only the previous night, a few months' time would be a respectable interval between the death of one husband and the taking of another. This was not Spain, with its rigid, interminable, black-robed obeisance to death—this was Texas, where every moment of every day was to be lived!

Rafael hadn't gotten quite that far in his thoughts,

and in actuality, marriage was the farthest thing from his mind. But he did begin to make immediate plans to go to Enchantress. There were men to be hired, supplies, wagons, livestock such as chickens, pigs, and milk cows to be bought, as well as myriad other things to be seen to.

Don Miguel had been most displeased when he finally heard of the scheme, but, beyond pursing his lips in vexation, there was nothing he could do. His voice very dry, he asked, "Isn't Cielo enough for you?"

Rafael had glanced at him from under heavy, black brows and answered bluntly, "No, and it never will be. Cielo belongs to the Santanas, but Enchantress will be *mine!*"

Looking at Rafael's set face a few minutes later as they walked over to Bluck's Saloon for a bit of entertainment and whiskey, Sebastian inquired, "Enchantress has come to mean a lot to you, hasn't it?"

Rafael pulled a wry face. "I don't know whether it's that, or simply that it has come to represent my freedom *from* Cielo."

Sebastian could understand what Rafael meant. Hadn't he come west to escape from the almost overpowering influence of his own father?

Together they walked into the saloon and made their way to the bar. A few men here and there called out a greeting to Rafael, but Sebastian noticed there were one or two who threw his cousin a nervous look, as if they suddenly expected him to turn into a bloodthirsty Comanche before their very eyes.

They drank in companionable silence. Rafael lounging with his elbows and back resting against the wooden bar and lazily surveying the room. Sebastian assumed the same position and, glancing around, he became aware of someone who looked vaguely familiar sitting off at a table in the shadows. Turning to Rafael, he asked, "Is that Lorenzo sitting over there next to the blond fellow in the red shirt near the side door?"

Rafael's eyes moved casually around the room. Finding the man Sebastian referred to, he returned, "Probably. Lorenzo's like a snake, always slithering into view when you least expect him."

Sebastian whistled under his breath. "There really is enmity between you two, isn't there? I thought Lorenzo was just exaggerating, that night at Cielo when he said he must leave before you arrived. He wasn't, was he?"

Rafael's gaze sharpened and he asked, "What night at Cielo?"

"Why, the night that I arrived with the Ridgeways," Sebastian said with some surprise. "Is it important?"

The smoky gray eyes suddenly bleak, Rafael shrugged. "No, but I find it interesting." And driven by some inner need to know, he asked baldly, "Did you happen to notice if Lorenzo paid any particular attention to the fair Mrs. Ridgeway."

Sebastian didn't like his tone of voice. There was something dangerous in it. Feeling as if he were stumbling through a field pitted with traps, he said slowly, "Not that I observed." Frowning as he tried to remember that evening, he added, "If anything, Beth seemed to dislike him. It wasn't anything you could put your finger on, just that she seemed to avoid his company and did not seem to have a great deal to say to him."

Rafael smiled grimly. "No, perhaps not."

His young face troubled, Sebastian probed, "I don't mean to pry, but it seems that there is something you know about Lorenzo and Beth that I don't. Should I?"

Rafael snorted. "No! Let's just say that in my advanced years, I am growing suspicious of every man who approaches my—er—mistress."

It was possible, Sebastian conceded thoughtfully. Rafael would be a jealous lover, one who would brook no other man making advances to a woman he considered his own. And yet . . . and yet there was something about the entire situation that left him feeling he had missed the first act of a play.

Referring back to Rafael's hostility toward Lorenzo, Sebastian said, "It must be rather difficult for the family if you and Lorenzo are such enemies. Have you always been so?"

"Probably—Lorenzo has been involved in unscrupulous deals ever since I first met him, but I am in no mood to discuss precisely when I decided that the world would be a better place if Lorenzo were removed from it."

"No wonder Lorenzo disappears whenever you're expected!"

Rafael smiled, not a nice smile, and, nodding his head in the direction where Lorenzo had been seated, he said, "Naturally. And you'll note that he has already disappeared this time."

It was true. Sebastian looked over to where Lorenzo had been seated and only an empty chair remained. Clearing his throat, he asked uneasily, "If you two hate each other so much—why hasn't the situation been resolved before now?"

Taking a long drink of his whiskey, Rafael savored it a moment, considering Sebastian's question. "I suppose," he said finally, "because he hasn't quite made me angry enough . . . *yet!*"

Sebastian departed the next day, riding out at dawn with his men and equipment. With Don Miguel's blessing he planned to make Cielo his temporary headquarters until some sort of dwelling could be erected on his own property. His going left a void; even Beth, still submerged in her misery, missed him, for he had been a lively spirit about the house.

Not only did Sebastian's leaving create a void, but Rafael was seldom home these days either, leaving his guests to fend for themselves, which was no arduous task considering the well-trained servants at their call.

Rising at dawn each morning, Rafael was up and about his business long before the others found their way downstairs, and many nights the house was dark and silent when he returned. His long hours were amply rewarded, though, for he was able to push thoughts of Beth and the future aside, and by the first of April he had assembled everything he might need for the initial trip to Enchantress. He made plans to leave San Antonio the following Wednesday, taking about ten men with him and ordering that the remaining fifteen or so men would follow with the slower, heavily laden wagons and the livestock.

There had been little activity as far as the Comanches were concerned until very early April. Then, much to everyone's surprise, a lesser chief known to the Texans as Piava came into San Antonio with a woman. There had been some earlier dealings with Piava, and the Texans had no reason to trust him—he was known to be crafty and treacherous. At any rate, he said that the Pehnahterkuh had many white captives and they were willing to exchange them for the Comanche prisoners held by the Texans.

It was an unfriendly meeting, and, watching keenly from the sidelines, Rafael wondered if Piava was telling the truth, if indeed there were any captives left alive at all.

Crossing quickly to Colonel Fisher when Piava and the woman had left, Rafael said, "If I were you, I'd send out some of the best Rangers you have available and have them scout out the Comanche encampment. For myself, I wouldn't believe one word of what he said."

Fisher took Rafael's advice and some of the more daring Rangers did indeed scout out the Comanche camp, returning to report that they saw few, if any, whites. Looking at Colonel Fisher pityingly, Rafael said bluntly, "I warned you—give up any hope of captives, they are all long since dead."

It seemed Rafael was wrong, though, at least at first, because on Saturday, April the fourth, Piava brought in a Mexican captive and an adopted five-year-old girl by the name of Putnam. The white child had been as hideously abused as poor Matilda Lockhart, her face horribly marked by scars. She could speak no English and cried piteously for her Comanche "mother."

Looking hard at Piava, the soldiers with their rifles cocked and ready behind him, Fisher demanded, "And the others? You said you had many."

Piava and the braves who had accompanied him stared back with arrogance and hatred. Several of the warriors had their bowstrings notched as they sat on their ponies, ready to attack at the first sign of aggression by the Texans.

Piava would not answer Fisher's questions. Instead he just gazed impassively at the white men. Angry and beginning to show it, Fisher probed repeatedly for more information about the captives, but to no avail. Piava flatly refused to discuss the other captives, but admitted finally that he did have one more white child for exchange.

The Comanches were allowed to take two of the Indians held by the Texans, and in defeat Fisher angrily agreed that if they brought in the white child, they could have their choice of a Comanche prisoner.

It was when Piava returned with another Mexican captive and a white boy, Booker Webster, that the Texans eventually learned the fate of the remaining captives. Once Piava had chosen his exchange prisoner and ridden off in great haste, the Texans began to question the boy, and it was then they heard of the final gruesome fate of the helpless white captives.

Booker was about ten years old. His eyes haunted with remembered horror, his voice breaking as he choked back tears, he told the tale. "They tortured them, every one, to death!" he cried, his throat working with the emotion that ran deep inside him.

Rafael, along with the others, listened to that high, frightened voice, and he felt his stomach muscles crawl. He had known what would happen, but it was far more chilling to hear it from a mere child, a child who had been spared only because he had been adopted by a Comanche family.

Booker glanced around the room at the rigid faces and said with a gulp and a stammer, "Th-they t-t-tore their clothes o-o-off and m-m-made them—made them n-n-naked. They was...was staked out spread-eagle and...and th-th-then the squaws skinned them!" His bottom lip trembled but, as if driven to speak of it, he blurted out, "They s-s-skinned them alive...cut, cut them in stripes and...and..." He stopped, unable to continue. There was silence and then, not looking at anyone, his eyes on his bare feet, he said in an ashamed voice, "I couldn't do nothing! I could hear them all hollering and screaming and yelling and...and hollering and hollering, but there wasn't nothing I could do." He broke down and sobbed then, his anguish and shame at being unable to help the others obvious. Someone patted him kindly on the shoulder and there was a murmur of comforting words and one man passed him a glass of water.

Recovering himself somewhat, Booker said in a firmer voice, "The squaws was set on making them all suffer for what happened to the warriors, and...and...they w-w-worked all day and night on th-them." He shuddered, remembering what he had seen and heard. "Me and that little girl that was exchanged was the only ones that didn't get killed. All the rest, no matter what...b-b-baby or w-w-woman...they tortured them all. Th-th-they kept them alive just so they could burn th-th-them to death at the end."

Rafael heard the tale without comment, then, looking at Fisher's shocked face, he couldn't help himself from saying bitterly, "And it could have ended so very differently. I trust you are satisfied with the results." He spun on his heels and walked away, too angry and frustrated to remain in the vicinity of the men who had so virtuously and righteously destroyed any hope for peace with the Comanches.

CHAPTER TWENTY-ONE

Rafael returned to a quiet house. Don Miguel and his wife had left early that morning for an overnight visit with some of Doña Madelina's distant relatives, who lived several miles from San Antonio. Rafael had been dubious of the scheme for a number of reasons, the main one being the possibility of attack by the Comanches. But Don Miguel was insistent, and when he pointed out that they would be traveling with a well-armed escort, Rafael was forced to drop his objections. And of course the other reason was Beth Ridgeway.

It was true that Señora López had stayed behind to keep proprieties, but Rafael still didn't like it. There would only be the two women in the house besides the servants until Don Miguel and Doña Madelina returned, once he himself left in the morning. But if Rafael had qualms about leaving Beth alone without a male protector, he was just as adamant that he would be leaving in the morning rather than postpone his trip another day or two until Don Miguel came back. Consequently he had already said his farewell to his father when Don Miguel had departed for the short visit.

"You're certain, you won't wait until we return?" Don Miguel had asked almost plaintively.

Rather suspecting that the entire purpose of the visit in the first place was to delay his departure, Rafael had replied coolly, "Positive! You knew I was leaving on Wednesday before you planned this sudden trip. I'm sorry, *mi padre,* but everything is ready, and we pull out tomorrow at dawn for Enchantress."

His handsome face disgruntled, Don Miguel snorted, "Enchantress! What a fanciful name! I'd like to know what Abel Hawkins was about when he chose that name for it!"

The gray eyes steady on his father's face, Rafael had said, "Perhaps he had his wife in mind—she was an Enchantress, wasn't she? Just as her daughter was?"

Don Miguel's features softened, an odd light in his dark eyes. "Yes," he had admitted in a low, husky voice. "Yes, your mother was indeed an Enchantress."

At loose ends, with everything settled for the departure the next day, Rafael found that time dragged interminably. After a solitary early-afternoon meal in the dining room, Beth and Señora López having ordered trays, Rafael busied himself in going over all his arrangements, but that took little time, and to his intense annoyance he discovered that his thoughts had a decided tendency to stray to the forbidden subject of English.

He had purposely not said anything to her directly about his trip to Enchantress, but he was certain she knew that he would be leaving in the morning—she couldn't help but know, considering how Don Miguel had grumbled about nothing else since he had learned of the plan. And while he had said his good-byes to everyone, including Señora López, when night fell he had still said nothing to Beth.

He had seen little of her, taken up with the preparations for departure, and she still spent an excessive amount of time in her room. Rafael didn't like it, but for once in his life, uncertain, he made no attempt to shake her from her lethargy, feeling that possibly she needed more time than most to come to grips with the tragedy that had widowed her so suddenly and unexpectedly. But his patience was growing thin. Nathan had been dead now for over two weeks, and he thought it time that Beth stopped hiding herself away from people and that she at least attempt to pick up the broken threads of her life. Precisely what those threads would be, he wasn't positive—he wasn't even certain that he wanted Beth making *any* decisions at this time—but he damn well wanted the pale little ghost with the sad eyes gone from Beth's body. He wanted her back again, back from the haunted world that she had retreated to, even if it meant she was once again spitting abuse at him and fighting with him.

That night, long after the last whale-oil lamp had been extinguished and the last servant had sought out his quarters, as he lay sleepless in his bed, Rafael knew that he couldn't leave without having a private word with Beth. There were things that needed to be said between them, and this was as good a time as any. They were alone in the house except for Señora López, and she was a heavy sleeper and half deaf in the bargain, so it was unlikely that any argument he and Beth had would be overheard.

Slipping naked from his bed, he shrugged on a wine-red silk robe and knotted the tasseled belt loosely about his lean waist. He considered dressing completely, but dismissed it. What he had to say to Beth wouldn't take long.

Beth too had found sleep elusive, and she was fighting against the tempting oblivion that the laudanum would give her. The past few nights she had managed to sleep without its soothing properties and she had hoped she was no longer dependent upon it. Not so, she decided gloomily when she finally gave up and had vacated her tangled bed, the rumpled sheets and blankets proof of her twistings and turnings.

It was a pleasant night, the air cool but not chilly, and, crossing to the double doors that led to the little balcony which overlooked the creek, Beth stepped out onto the balcony, drinking in the calming silence of the night. She was wearing a soft, diaphanous nightgown in the palest pink imaginable, and the full moon shining overhead outlined the slender whiteness of her body, the rosy nipples of her small breasts obvious through the sheerness of the delicate material, the slim hips and the lovely legs—all silhouetted by the moonlight. The moon turned the fair hair that tumbled down her back into pure silver and kissed the shadowy V where her breasts nestled. The gown was sleeveless, and her bare arms and fine features took on a silvery hue from the moonlight as she stood on the balcony staring blindly into space.

Rafael tapped softly on her door, but Beth, lost in

her own unhappy thoughts, didn't hear his knock. Standing in the hallway, Rafael frowned and briefly considered returning to his own rooms. But something stronger than convention was riding him, and so, giving in to a nameless urge to see her once again, he opened the door and walked into the moonlit room.

The sound of the door shutting behind him was the first inkling that Beth had that Rafael was in her room. Startled that anyone would enter her rooms unannounced and at this hour of the night, she whirled around, her heart thumping madly in her breast when she recognized the tall, dark figure striding toward her.

The moonlight behind her gave Rafael an unobstructed view of her slender loveliness, hiding nothing of her lovely limbs and body, and the sudden fierce desire that shot through his body drove every thought but one from his mind. A man of deep primitive passions, he had neither the inclination nor the willpower to stop his body from throbbing and hardening with instant sexual arousal.

Beth watched his approach with wide, half-wary eyes, the moonlight making them deep, velvety pools of purple. She wanted to run, she wanted to scream, and yet she also wanted, with an intensity that frightened her, to stand exactly where she was and let the passion so clearly defined on Rafael's dark face envelop them both.

He halted a few feet from her, his face a contrast of silver and black—the haughty, soaring eyebrows were black as always, the arrogant nose silver, the wide reckless mouth with its frankly sensual curve silver too, in the light of the moon. The wine-red robe was dark, so dark in the moonlight that its color was barely guessed at. The V which formed where it met almost at his waist reflected back gleaming silvery skin, but no light penetrated the blue-black hair, and it remained dark, dark as midnight.

They stared wordlessly at one another, and, knowing that if she didn't break the silence she would be lost, Beth demanded with a sudden spurt of temper, "What do you mean by entering my room at this hour of the night? Have you gone mad?"

Rafael smiled, merely a twist of his lips with no

humor in it. "Probably. But I wanted to speak with you before I left in the morning, and as you don't rise at dawn, this seemed as good a time as any." His face sardonic, he added, "You *do* know that I'm leaving for several weeks in the morning?"

Beth nodded, suddenly filled with an anguish she had no business feeling. And the guilt and remorse that Nathan's death had caused flooded through her body, inflaming her to the point of near-madness, as she reminded herself furiously that Rafael Santana's movements had nothing to do with her, and that if she'd never met him none of this would have happened—Nathan would be alive, not dead and buried, killed by a Comanche lance in the back. It was all *his* fault, she thought with the twisted logic of someone half insane with grief and guilt, and, venting all her anger within herself, all the guilt that ate like a canker in her breast, she spat, "Yes! And for all I care you can go to hell!"

Those were shocking words for her to utter, but her thoughts were so jumbled, so incoherent, that the words sprang from her lips before she could stop them. Rafael's presence in her room was like a spark to all the smoldering guilt and remorse that had lain in her breast these past weeks, and uncaringly, actually hating him at the moment, she said recklessly, "Have you come to gloat, señor? Now that my husband is dead, do you think that I am helpless against the likes of you?" Her voice rising with increasing hysteria, she cried, "Well, think again, you black-hearted devil! I have nothing to say to you, not now, not at any time! And if you're not out of my room in the next instant, I'll . . . I'll . . ." She stopped, her mind going blank as she searched for the vilest thing she could do to him.

"You'll do what?" Rafael inquired softly. "Shoot me? Stab me?" His eyes on her soft mouth, he whispered, "Or love me to death?" as he swept her into his arms.

His mouth was hungry on hers, and the feel of that barely clad body against the thin barrier of his robe was nearly more than Rafael could bear. Urgently his lips parted hers and his tongue filled her mouth, demanding a response as deep and driving as the one that coursed through his body.

For one mad, wild moment Beth gave into it, drowning in the sensuous thrusting of his tongue and the pleasurable pain of being crushed once again in those strong arms. She could feel his arousal, it was there hard against her stomach, almost with a life of its own as the heat and size of it nudged her eagerly. But with a small cry of fury she broke from his arms and, with her eyes spitting sparks of violet fire, she said hotly, "How can you dare? My husband not dead but two weeks and, and . . . !" Her breasts heaving with emotion, she suddenly voiced the thought that she had never admitted to. "You wanted him dead!" she accused. "You did! You did! You even said so that dreadful day!" Losing her temper completely she flew at him, her small fists striking his face and chest, the tears that had never surfaced before beginning to flood her eyes. "You wanted him dead!" she cried over and over again. *"You did!"*

Rafael was considerably bigger and far stronger than Beth, but her fury gave her strength that surprised them both, and she managed to land several painful and bruising blows on his face and neck before he was able to subdue her. Finally, though, both of them breathing heavily, he held her in front of him, both her wrists captured in his hands.

She glared up at him rebelliously, the sheen of tears not yet shed giving her eyes a luminous glow. Staring down into the lovely flushed features, Rafael admitted harshly, "I wanted him out of your life! Not necessarily dead!"

"Why?" she flashed. "So that you could make me your mistress? Did you really think I would be such an easy conquest?" Like quicksilver she suddenly slipped from his grasp and, looking up at him, she said in a voice shaking with outrage, "Never! Never, never, *never!* Do you hear me? I *hate* you! I hate you and I'd die before I'd let your dirty Comanche hands touch me!" It was the worst thing she could have said to him, but she was driven by devils that Rafael couldn't even guess at and she was hurting herself as much as she was hurting him, one part of her standing back and staring, appalled, at the creature before him.

His expression remained unchanged and, suddenly

goaded beyond reason, Beth swung at him, the open palm of her hand striking him sharply across the mouth and cheek. Rafael regarded her for one moment longer, and then with deliberate intention he struck her. Not as hard as he could have, but hard enough so that Beth's head snapped back on her neck, the sound of the slap ringing out like a pistol shot in the room.

The imprint of his hand was a stinging red scar on her pale cheek, and with a small, broken whimper Beth ran from him and flung herself face down on the bed—the sobs, the tears, the crying that had not fallen when Nathan died or when he was buried suddenly unleashing like a broken dam. She cried for a long time, and Rafael, his passion gone, his face empty, watched her until he could stand it no longer.

Not a gentle man or a tender one, he was all of those things when, at last unable to bear the sight of her distress, he sank down on the bed beside her and gathered her sobbing, shaking form into his arms. For timeless seconds they clung to each other, Beth crying all the bitter, guilty tears that had been locked inside of her and Rafael gently and tenderly holding her in his arms, his mouth brushing the bright hair that tickled his chin, his hands lightly and tenderly caressing her arms and shoulders, and all the while murmuring soft words of comfort, perhaps even unknowingly words of love.

Gradually the tears were spent and Beth was left weak and exhausted, her tear-damp cheek leaning against the warm wall of Rafael's bare chest. She was empty inside, all the anguish she had kept tamped down finally having been expelled, leaving her with nothing but an aimless, lonely future. And as coherent thought came creeping back into her brain, she suddenly became conscious of the intimacy between her and Rafael.

They were lying together on her bed, his arms holding her loosely, her face pressed to his chest where his robe parted, and one of his hands was lightly (and at the moment impersonally) caressing her hip and thigh, just a light touch but one that, now that she was aware of it, seemed to burn like a flame through the thinness of her scanty nightgown. His other hand was gently moving over her head and shoulders, pushing back the tumbled heavy swathe of thick, silvery hair, his mouth pressing soft, comforting kisses on her temple and forehead. She lay very still, wanting to treasure this moment and keep it forever—she was in his arms and he was showing her all the tenderness and gentleness, all the care and comfort any woman could ever wish for.

Just when he stopped comforting her, just when the touch became more than impersonal, Beth would always remember. She looked up into his face, intending to apologize for her loss of control, but the expression in the gray eyes staring intently into hers took her breath away and made her heart begin to beat with thick, almost paralyzing strokes. Mesmerized, she stared back up at his dark, lean face, loving the way his heavy black eyebrows curved sardonically over those gray eyes and the crease that appeared in each cheek when he smiled.

Rafael wasn't smiling now, though—he was memorizing the lovely delicate features before him. Beth was one of those fortunate women whose beauty was enhanced by tears rather than diminished. Her eyes were a clear, luminous violet; the golden-brown lashes, spiky from the tears, made her look like a wide-eyed kitten; her cheeks were tinted a soft rosy hue; and her mouth was a temptation that no man could resist, the ruby lips slightly swollen and even more inviting. With an effort Rafael tore his gaze from them, but his eyes slipped lower to where the V of her gown met the small valley between her breasts, her pink-tipped nipples thrusting proudly against the nearly transparent material—and he knew he wouldn't be able to put her from him.

He did try, but it seemed everything was against him. She was soft and warm in his arms, and when he reluctantly eased away from her, more of her charms were revealed by the not-so-modest nightgown—the lovely line of her hips and the slender shapeliness of her thighs were clearly seen through the misty material. Like a beggar in a countinghouse, he stared at the slim body so tantalizingly displayed, his eyes stopping for an endless moment at the junction of those white thighs as he stared fixedly at the barely discernible triangle of golden hair that grew there. With a groan he gathered her back against him, his mouth compulsively seeking hers, his touch not the least bit impersonal any longer.

The other times that Rafael had made love to her there had been an element of violence about it, but not tonight. Tonight he was the exciting dream lover that every woman yearns for, his touch an exquisite caress like nothing else in the world.

Despite the urgency of his own body, Rafael took his time, his hands slowly but determinedly removing the flimsy scrap of nightwear that clouded all the beauties of Beth's body from his hungry eyes. And Beth, almost hypnotized by the naked desire in the gray eyes, made no move to stop him, her body arching up, begging for the touch of his dark hand against her pale skin.

But he didn't touch her immediately. Instead, lifting his head, he stared at the small fragile body before him, the small breasts swollen with passion, the enticing curve of the slim waist, the white, white skin of her flat stomach and the slender thighs. She was incredibly desirable to him, her body an alabaster-and-pink altar that he paid homage to, his own body hardening and tightening with delicious hunger to feel himself lost again in the hot, satiny sheath of her.

He bent his head, his warm mouth finding a pink begging nipple, his tongue curling caressingly around it, his teeth gently nipping and tasting it while his hand gently cupped the other breast, his thumb rhythmically sliding across it, causing Beth to gasp with sudden shocking pleasure. With a little cry of encouragement she reached for him, but her fingers only met the springy darkness of his head. That seemed to satisfy her for the moment, her fingers reveling in the feel of that thick blue-black hair. But it wasn't enough as Rafael's mouth swung back up to hers, his tongue sweetly ravaging her mouth, his lips pressing urgently against hers, and her hands slipped to his shoulders, pushing away the silken robe that covered him.

Not taking his lips from hers, Rafael shrugged out of the robe, but his hands were too busy to bother with the knotted belt, and against her mouth he breathed, "Untie it, I want nothing between us."

Beth hesitated, then, driven by the same hunger that ate at Rafael, her fingers sought the knot and deftly undid it and the robe fell to the bed, leaving him naked and warm next to her. But she didn't stop there. Emboldened with a sensual courage that overcame her usual inhibitions, she slid her hand across his taut stomach, shivering with pleasure when he groaned and lightly bit her neck.

Rafael's hands were exploring her body intimately, his long fingers slipping down her back, his hands curving possessively about her firm buttocks, pulling her closer. His mouth seemed everywhere, on her lips, her shoulders, her breasts, and Beth was nearly trembling with the force of the passion he evoked, wanting his hard body on hers with a fierce intensity.

Brashly she began her own exploration, wanting to discover what made this man the one man who could make her lose control of herself and turn her into a wanton creature who only wanted his body to possess hers. Brazenly her hands traveled down the smooth, muscled chest, delighted with the heavy satin feel of it, but not content with that, one hand slid lower until at last her trembling fingers closed around him. The size and heat of him brought a surprised little moan of excitement from her lips, and almost convulsively her hand tightened around him, giving Rafael such a jolt of pleasure that for one agonizing second he was afraid it was all over for him.

In a shaken voice he murmured, "Sweet Jesus, English! Don't touch me yet! I am too full of wanting you."

But Beth was in the grip of sensual discovery and she wanted desperately to continue discovering what made a man's body so very different from a woman's, and gently, her fingers caressed the throbbing pulsating length of him, excited that she could touch him this way and that her untutored movements gave him as much pleasure as his experienced hand did her.

It was too much for Rafael to endure, and with a muffled groan he jerked himself away from her, gazing down into her wondering face with eyes that were nearly black with emotion. "Don't!" he said thickly, "unless you want me to spill myself on you instead of *in* you!"

The words gave her a feeling of triumph, and she was aroused even further to know that she could make him lose complete control of himself, that with her hands she could drive him as wild as he did her. A small satisfied smile curving her mouth, she arched her body up against him, her nipples like twin peaks of fire burning against his chest, and deliberately, her eyes locked on his, she reached for him again.

His body jumped when she touched him, and whatever restraint he had placed on himself vanished, his mouth closing with a punishing demand on hers, its very urgency and hunger making Beth forget this new tantalizing game she had discovered. Like a famished creature he fed on her mouth, bruising the soft lips, but Beth returned the kiss just as passionately, her newfound sensuality leading her on to new territories as hesitantly she thrust her tongue into his mouth.

Her tongue was like a small, darting flame and, finding that Rafael was making no attempt to reverse things, she continued her eager, excited exploration of his mouth, inflaming herself as much as she did Rafael. Enchanted with this new aspect of lovemaking, she closed both of her hands around his face, her small hands resting gently against his cheeks as she kissed him even more deeply.

There was no way that Beth could tell him what intriguing, fascinating things she was discovering this night. He would never believe that she had never kissed a man this way, never explored a man's body like this and had never felt the soft-skinned hardness of a man's member. It was intoxicating to her, and, almost heady with the discoveries she had made, she let the hot tide of passion sweep over her, holding nothing back, ready to go wherever Rafael's caresses would lead her.

Rafael had made love to many women, but none had ever inflamed or enslaved him as did English—she was like a powerful narcotic in his blood as he caressed and explored her slender body. Every other woman he had ever known vanished from his mind and there was only room for English in his brain... and possibly his heart?

No longer content to merely caress the smooth flesh so near his own, compulsively Rafael's hands sought the small V at the joining of her thighs, and gently, his hand between her legs, he began to thrust his finger within her, making Beth moan and twist with mounting desire. Her breasts ached for his mouth, and as if sensing it, Rafael left her lips and once again his tongue and teeth teased her nipples, sending exploding sparks of pleasure through Beth's entire body.

His mouth traveled from breast to breast, and then suddenly his lips began a slow sensual descent down her diaphragm and across her flat stomach until his mouth was buried in the soft golden curls at the top of her thighs. Beth stiffened and, feeling her uncertainty, he stopped and looked up at her with fever-bright eyes. "Let me," he muttered roughly. "You are as beautiful there as anywhere, and I want the taste of you on my mouth, the scent of you in my nostrils. Let me!"

If mere words themselves can be aphrodisiacs, Rafael's certainly were to Beth. Already aroused to a fever pitch, Beth could not resist him and imperceptibly she relaxed, her body quivering with anticipation.

Gently Rafael pushed her legs apart, his mouth moving with agonizing slowness down across the golden curls, and Beth thought her heart would choke her, it was beating so fast. His tongue when it touched her there was exquisite torture, and as it penetrated her, jabbing like a flick of flame, Beth's entire body went rigid with stunning passion. A sobbing moan of pleasure escaped her and almost convulsively she reached for Rafael, uncertain whether she wanted him to stop or continue. She had no choice in the matter. Having found what he sought, Rafael drew in the exciting perfume of her body, his breath warm and arousing as it seemed to caress her there too. His tongue explored her thoroughly, seeking the inner softness and gently exploring all the hidden delights of that golden triangle.

One hand slipped under her hips, bringing her body even closer, if that were possible, and Rafael held her tightly to his lips as his mouth and tongue drove her mad with ecstasy. She was crying out—she knew she was but for what she couldn't guess—and she wanted to touch Rafael, to give him the same wild pleasure that he was giving her, yet all she could do was twist frenziedly on the bed, her mind stunned by the shattering pleasure Rafael's probing tongue evoked.

Panting, every nerve of her body seemingly centered there where his mouth tasted and touched and searched out with such sensual enjoyment, Beth thrashed frantically under his lips, pushing her body hard against his mouth with something akin to frantic desire. And then it happened. Wave after wave of the most incredible pleasure imaginable swept over her body and, unable to help herself, she cried out her gratification, her body jumping and quivering with the force of emotions unleashed by Rafael's tender assault on her.

Feeling her response and knowing what she had experienced, Rafael gave a small sigh of satisfaction, his body further excited and inflamed by her involuntary movements and cries. His mouth slowly left its former place, tasting and nibbling as it went, and he finally found her lips with his own, his tongue seeking out the wine-sweetness of her mouth.

The smell and taste of herself on him was strange at first, but when his hands set about fondling her breasts and caressing her hips and thighs, Beth's thoughts scattered before the onslaught of his hungry lovemaking. His fingers found her again and to her astonishment she felt the tight knot of desire kindle again, her body wanting him with an intensity that was overwhelming.

Rafael shifted slightly, and then she felt her thighs nudged apart, and with a moan of sheer ecstasy she was filled with his warm hard shaft. Gently he moved on her, his movements unhurried as if he were taking great pleasure in the feel and heat of her body, but Beth was hungry for more, wanting him to hurry and give her more of the pleasure that only he seemed capable of giving.

Her hands moved over his broad back and cupped his buttocks, her fingers loving the feel of the tensing, taut muscles as his body increased its rhythm. "Oh, yes," she breathed against his mouth. *"Oh yes!"*

Unable to bear the exquisite denial any longer, Rafael groaned and his body slammed into hers hard and fast, giving them both the pleasure they sought until with a low, incoherent moan Rafael's body fulfilled its purpose. Beth felt his body jump with the power of his release, and the knowledge that *she* had given him "the little death" that comes from total satisfaction sent such an explosion of flaming pleasure through her whole body that she was left damp and shaking from it.

They lay together, their limbs entwined, neither having the wish to disturb the warm intimacy between them. Rafael's mouth was unbearably tender as he kissed her face, lingering on her eyelids and nose before kissing her mouth with such gentleness that Beth felt tears start to her eyes. Both of them, exhausted and spent by the passion that had existed between them, seemed unable to move, their limbs heavy and lethargic with the aftermath of passion.

Rafael spent the night with her, unable to bring himself to leave her, and twice more before the sun shed its red-gold light at the break of dawn Beth knew the devastation of his possession—the last time a quick, urgent taking that left her breathless by its very, frantic fierceness. She slipped back to sleep, her head resting contentedly on his strong arm, his lips at her temple, but when she woke, the sun was high in the sky and she was alone—the indentation on the snowy-white pillow being the only indication that she had been in his arms.

CHAPTER TWENTY-TWO

Rafael rode hard to reach Enchantress, pushing his men as much as he dared. He hadn't wanted to leave Beth, not then, not with the words unspoken between them that needed desperately to be said. But, rising reluctantly from beside her warm body in the cold light of dawn, he had decided to continue with his original plan. Perhaps it was best that he did leave her alone for a while, giving her a chance to come to grips with Nathan's death and himself time to learn the full extent of his commitment to her.

Marriage wasn't on his mind even then, but, staring at the ruined wreck of Enchantress, he knew he would make it beautiful again and make it beautiful for his own enchantress. And so, with his thoughts still unclear on their eventual relationship, he sent his men about their tasks, clearing away the verdant growth that crowded the old hacienda and hid its former beauty. It was back-breaking work, some thirty-odd years of tangled wood and vine that nearly encompassed the house and needed to be removed before anything else could be done.

Enchantress *had* been beautiful. A small, gemlike Spanish-style house set in a pine forest that sheltered the leafy cinnamon fern and the coral honeysuckle, which twined itself hungrily about the tall, towering pines themselves. The forest around it teemed with life of all kinds—lovely, fragile wild azaleas, yellow-fringed orchids, and the peculiar-appearing pitcher plants; deer, wood ducks, razorback hogs, cougars, and bobcats, as well as the dangerous rattlesnakes and deadly coral snakes.

The house had been built almost a hundred years

before, and when the creepers and vines were eventually cleared away it had mellow beauty. Two-storied, with delicate filigreed balconies across the second story and deep-set curved windows, the house pleased Rafael. It had the typically Spanish red-tiled roof, and although badly in need of repair, the faded tiles gave it a charm all of its own. It was maybe half the size of the *casa grande* at Cielo, but, walking gingerly through the debris-scattered rooms, Rafael was well satisfied. The rooms were large and spacious, and the arrangement comfortable. Refurbished, the windows cleaned, the walls scrubbed, then tinted and papered, the flooring repaired and covered with carpets, it would be a home that any man would be proud of . . . and any woman glad to live in?

There were several things to be seen to, the first obviously being to clear the house and make it habitable—not an easy task, Rafael conceded as he viewed the second day's hard work. They'd killed a coral snake on the balcony and a rattler in what would be the main salon, as well as disturbed hundreds of spiders that had made it their home.

Once the house was livable he intended that his men should sleep there until such time as the wagons and other supplies should arrive and suitable cabins could be erected for them. With the man he had designated his lieutenant, Renaldo Sánchez, he had walked and explored the forest near the house, deciding where to build the new barn, the corrals, the cabins for the men and which sections of land to clear for the home garden and the like.

He drove himself hard, not wanting to remain here a minute longer than necessary. Beth and their undecided future were uppermost in his mind. Five days after his arrival he was ready to return to San Antonio. Leaving Renaldo with all the necessary instructions, like a man following the irresistible song of a siren, he rode eagerly toward Beth.

When Beth had awakened and found him gone, her first thought had been that she had dreamed their encounter, but, staring at the indentation where his head had rested and later, when she dressed and saw the bruising marks of his passion on her white body, she knew it had been no dream. Rafael *had* spent the night in her arms, and she had given herself to him with unstinting ardor.

The memory of her actions the night before made her face burn red; she wondered what had come over her to cause her to behave in such an uncharacteristically wanton manner. Thinking of the things she had done to him and precisely what he had done to her, she felt her skin grow hot and her body go weak with a wave of desire.

Ashamed of herself for such wicked reactions to a night that should have filled her with repugnance, Beth left the seclusion of her bedroom, not certain what she would say to Rafael when next they met. She was stunned when she heard the news of his departure from Señora López. She hadn't known what to expect, she wasn't even clear in her own mind what bearing last night had on her own future, but she was stricken that he had ridden away without any word to her, no message to give her some inkling of his thoughts.

Suddenly feeling used and dirty, she turned away from the kind black eyes of Señora López and walked to the small garden at the rear of the house. Wandering blindly along the small stream that ran there, she thought bitterly, *It didn't mean a thing to him! He merely wanted a body and mine was available.* Nearly writhing in shame, she remembered her easy capitulation and this time it brought no wave of desire.

She realized now that she had been foolish in the extreme to think that his exquisitely tender lovemaking had meant anything more to him than a slaking of desire. How stupid of her not to have guessed that!

Grimly she made up her mind that it was time to leave San Antonio. Her life must go on, even if her heart was breaking.

When Don Miguel and Doña Madelina returned that next day from their visit, they were met by an extremely agitated Señora López. "She is leaving!" she wailed. "This morning she informed me of it! She has been giving her servants orders to ready their wagons and animals so that they might leave on Saturday for Natchez!"

Appalled and seeing the end to all their hopes for a marriage disappearing, both the Santanas rushed to the small salon where Beth was busily perusing her list of things that should be done before she and her servants could leave. She looked up in surprise when they entered the room in such distress. Instantly concerned for them, she stood up and hurried over to them.

"What is wrong?" she asked apprehensively, terrified that they might be bringing bad news of Rafael.

Don Miguel recovered himself first; his face taking on a stern air, he said gravely, "What is wrong? This unseemly scheme of yours to return to Natchez unescorted is what is wrong! You cannot think to travel all that great distance without a *man* to lend you his assistance."

Looking very fragile and lovely in her black silk gown, the silvery hair looped in braids over her ears, she smiled at him slightly. "Now that my husband is dead, señor, I have no other choice. I must return home. I cannot remain here forever abusing your—" She hesitated and continued: "—and your son's hospitality. I cannot thank you enough for your many kindnesses, but it is time now for me to pick up the reins of my life and begin anew."

"But you cannot!" cried Doña Madelina. "We have such hopes that you and . . ." Her voice trailed off at the warning glance her husband shot her. Recovering herself, Doña Madelina said more calmly, "There is no need for you to bustle off this way. Wait until my stepson returns, and *he* can escort you to your home."

Pleased at his wife's suggestion, Don Miguel beamed at her and said eagerly, "Yes! It would be unwise for you, a mere woman alone, to undertake such a journey with only your servants. It is unthinkable! Wait until Rafael returns—he will only be gone a matter of weeks, and then he, I am sure, will be more than willing to accompany you on your journey home."

That was the *last* thing Beth wanted. Her violet eyes surprisingly hard, she said quietly, "No, I'm sorry, I cannot delay any longer. I know it is not proper for a young woman like myself to travel without the protection of a male relative or family friend, but I have no choice."

There was no swaying her; Beth was adamant in her determination to leave on Saturday. Everyone was distressed at the thought of her departure, including Beth herself. Deliberately turning her back on Rafael was causing her untold heartache, but it had to be done. Even with Nathan dead there still were barriers between them, she thought miserably as she lay in bed that night. How could she have even begun to think otherwise? He still thought her a slut capable of cuckolding her husband at every turn, and the way he so arrogantly used her body whenever he felt like it should have warned her that he had absolutely no feeling for her, that what was to her a matter of earth-shaking importance was nothing to him. Nothing at all, she decided bleakly.

In spite of the heavy pressure put on her by the Santanas, in spite of the intervention of the Mavericks, Beth held steadfast. And she would indeed have left on Saturday, except for the fact that Friday evening she came down with one of those mysterious fevers so prevalent in the area and which struck without warning.

At first it was just a listlessness and a nagging headache that she put down to depression, but by the time she woke Saturday morning, she had a raging fever and could not leave her bed. It was a particularly violent attack, and for several days there was the very real threat that she might join her husband in his lonely grave.

She spent the next several weeks in bed so weakened by the virulent fever which racked her body that she was barely able to lift her head to sip barley water offered her by Señora López and Doña Madelina. The attack left her so drained and helpless that it was well into the first week of May before she finally left her bed for the first time since she had been taken ill.

Sebastian returned, looking tanned and rugged, the second day after she had risen from her bed, and he was shocked by her appearance. In her black widow's garb, she appeared so tiny and fragile that he feared a puff of wind would blow her away. The nearly translucent, pale skin, the very obvious blue veins at her temples and throat, and the purple shadows under the violet eyes, were clear signs that she had been dangerously ill.

Everyone treated her as if she were made of a particularly priceless porcelain, and while she chafed at it, Beth was inordinately grateful for their care and concern. The weeks that Doña Madelina and Señora López had so tenderly nursed her had made the three women very close, and Beth, never having experienced the warmth and comfort that comes from being part of a family, dreaded the journey to Natchez. It would be a wrenching experience, not only because of Rafael but because of the deep and abiding affection she now held for Rafael's relatives.

As the days passed she gained her health rapidly, as much from her own determination to do so as from the solicitous care and nourishing viands pressed on her. The first few days out of bed she spent mostly resting in the garden under the shade of a huge cottonwood tree, rebuilding her badly depleted strength, and then, as she began to grow stronger, when the purple shadows had faded to mere enchantment of the violet eyes and some of the weight she had lost had been replaced, Sebastian took her for pleasant rides in an open gig around the environs of San Antonio—never too far from town these days for fear of Comanches.

It was spring in the hill country, and the acres of bluebonnets that covered the meadows, the saucy black-eyed Susans, the purple gay-feather with its spidery plumes, and the bright golden color of the goldenrods brought an exclamation of pleasure to her lips. Even the cacti—the prickly pear with its orange and yellow bloom, and the delicate magenta shade of the rainbow cactus flower—astonished her.

The open rides were good for her. The sun painted a hint of gold on her pale cheeks and the exercise and fresh air revitalized her enormously, and the violet eyes again became clear and bright. Pleased with her recovery, Beth began once again to think of leaving for Natchez, aware that Rafael could return any day now.

Riding in the gig one afternoon with Sebastian, her face protected from the strong rays of the sun by a delightful leghorn bonnet trimmed with a black velvet ribbon and by the most frivolous black silk parasol imaginable, she said casually, "I shall miss these rides with you immensely once I am back in Natchez—the rides, the marvelous and varied countryside, and of course dear Señora López and Don Miguel and Doña Madelina."

Keeping his eyes on the shining haunches of the little chestnut mare that pulled the gig, Sebastian asked in a deliberately bland tone of voice, "Oh? Are you thinking of leaving us?"

Her lovely face troubled, she answered truthfully, "I must. I have written Nathan's parents of his death, and my own father also, but there are things that will need to be done and I must do them. I cannot remain here in San Antonio forever. My home is in Natchez, and it is there that I must go... and soon."

Sebastian frowned. He had finally gotten over his infatuation with Beth, but unfortunately, in doing so he had become unusually cynical. That she could have fooled him so completely stung his pride and made him begin to wonder if most women weren't cheats and flirts behind their gentle airs. With his newfound cynicism his pain had lessened, and as the cynic in him took over, so had he abandoned all of his previous arguments in her defense. He truly believed that she was Rafael's mistress and he wouldn't be taken in by her apparent innocence again!

And what was she up to now? Surely Rafael wanted her to remain in San Antonio? Had they quarreled before his cousin had left for Enchantress, and was she planning on punishing Rafael by leaving?

He glanced at her then, not quite able to believe her guilty of that kind of spiteful coquetry. And yet, *why* not?—it would be the action typical of the kind of creature he now knew her to be!

Feeling he should make some push to prevent her leaving, he said carefully, "Is that wise, do you think? What does Rafael say about it?"

Unconsciously Beth's black-gloved hand tightened

about the carved ebony handle of her parasol. Was the dark fascination that Rafael held for her so very obvious? she thought painfully. Her eyes shadowed, she replied calmly enough, "I hardly think Señor Santana is concerned with my plans." And, curious that Sebastian would make such a statement in the first place, she asked with apparent airiness, "Besides, what difference would it make to him?"

Sebastian's lips thinned at her mendaciousness. How could she sit there and act as if nothing existed between her and Rafael? What a little Jezebel she was behind those fine eyes and sweet features!

Thinking it high time that he acquaint her with what he knew of her true character, he said grimly, "You can quit playing off your innocent airs on me!" Staring at her with unfriendly emerald eyes, he added almost accusingly, "Rafael told me about you, you know."

Beth stiffened, and with eyes just as unfriendly as his, she demanded, "What do you mean by that? What could he possibly tell you about me?"

Not bothering to hide his feelings, Sebastian gave an ugly laugh and retorted angrily, "A damn sight more than I would have suspected, I can tell you that!" Seeing the shocked expression on her face, he said bitterly, "Oh, for God's sake, you can act naturally around *me!* Even knowing what you are, I am not about to tell anyone else, so don't worry I'll betray you to the gentle ladies of San Antonio."

Her voice dangerously controlled, Beth asked, "And *what* exactly is it that Rafael told you? What is this dark forbidden secret?"

Sebastian shot her a quick look, for the first time in weeks beginning to wonder about what Rafael had told him. But he instantly dismissed the notion as a weakening of his resolve not to trust a pair of beautiful eyes. Tiredly he finally said, "I saw you that night at Cielo when you and Rafael exchanged that rather revealing embrace in the courtyard, and I later taxed him with it. Considering I had seen how it was between you, he had no choice but to confess that you were his mistress, that you two had a long-standing liaison." Almost a sneering note in his voice, he finished, "You've been his mistress for years, so why pretend the need to go back to Natchez? Now that your husband is dead, I'm certain you won't have to be put to the usual shifts in meeting one another."

Beth was so taken aback at Sebastian's revelations that for one moment she was literally struck dumb, and then, as the full import sunk in, she was so angry that she feared if he said just one more word to her she would explode in a shower of sparks like a Fourth of July sparkler. A furious and hurt glitter in the violet eyes, she snapped, "What gossips men are! So I have been his mistress, have I? Well, thank you for letting me know about it! And you can rest assured that when I next see your abominable cousin, I shall express my appreciation for his assassination of my character." Her eyes full of contempt, the soft upper lip curling with scorn, she spat, "And you, you fool, you believed him! I thought you were my friend!"

Nettled, Sebastian replied heatedly, "I *am* your friend! Your being Rafael's mistress makes little difference to me. I just wanted you to be aware that I knew of your relationship so you could drop this pretense that Rafael is almost a stranger to you. I dislike hypocrisy above all things, and I would not have thought it of you, Beth."

So full of rage at the unjust remarks made about her, Beth was nearly in danger of losing her temper. How *could* he? she thought furiously. How could he dare to tell Sebastian an outright lie like that? She'd kill him, she thought half-hysterically. It wasn't enough that he overcame her scruples, that he took advantage of her weakness for him, but to claim that she was a creature of loose morals—his mistress—and to speak of it to someone else! What a dastardly act! And Sebastian had believed him! Dismayed, hurt almost unbearably, and blazingly angry at the same time, Beth stared stonily ahead, thinking that she would like to whack her parasol over Sebastian's head and then find Rafael and...and...She was so outraged she couldn't even think of a retaliation wicked enough to pay him back. But she would, she thought grimly, she would.

There was a frigid silence between them as they rode toward the house in San Antonio. Although Sebastian, aware he had handled the affair badly, made several attempts to redeem himself in Beth's graces, his friendly overtures were met with an icy look of disdain, and by the time they reached the house Sebastian was in a quandary.

My God, he mused furiously, what difference does it make that I know? I wouldn't betray her, and surely she must know that it changed little between us—which wasn't precisely true, and he knew it. He would never quite feel the same way about another woman, and at the moment, instead of feeling justified at his remarks, he had the uncomfortable suspicion that he had somehow given Beth a grievous insult—one she would not forgive easily.

It was not to be a pleasant day for Beth. She returned to the house, out of sorts with Sebastian and deeply wounded that he could believe Rafael's lies about her and in a flaming temper with Rafael himself. She had been barely helped down from the gig and had just entered the front hallway when she was met by Doña Madelina with the news that Charity had run away with a Mexican youth this very morning. Dispirited as much by her maid's needless defection as the knowledge that she would miss Charity's merry face, Beth took off her bonnet and murmured tiredly, "Now, why did she have to go to that extreme? Surely she knew that I would set her free to go away with a husband that was not one of my own slaves? Am I such an inhuman monster that my own servants are afraid to approach me?"

Her dark eyes full of sympathy, Doña Madelina shook her head. "No, *niña,* I think it was merely that she knew you would object to what she meant to do. You see, Jesús already has a wife and child in Mexico and Charity knew it. She also was aware of what she was doing when she rode away with him this morning. Do you wish to put out a reward for her return?"

Beth shook her head. "No. I have always had my doubts about the system of slavery, and to force her to return when she obviously has made her choice will do no good—she would only run away again, and would resent and hate me."

There was more unpleasant news, but she didn't find

out about it until after the heavy afternoon meal. Anticipating that as her health improved she would once again think of returning to Natchez, Don Miguel, determined to nip such thoughts in the bud at least until his son returned, had somewhat underhandedly sent all her servants to Cielo that very morning while she had been receiving Sebastian's insulting disclosures. His eyes guileless, he said mildly, "I hope you don't mind, *mi cara,* but a messenger arrived from Cielo while you were out and there has been a slight crisis at the rancho. As your servants were idle here in San Antonio, I'm afraid I took it upon myself to make use of them. They shouldn't be gone more than a few weeks." Innocently he asked, "You had no immediate need of them, had you?"

Beth gritted her teeth in vexation, suspecting his motives. It was uncharacteristically high-handed of Don Miguel to do such a thing without consulting her, but, knowing how adamant he was about her leaving without a male escort, his son in particular, she could be forgiven for being suspicious of his actions. It was rather odd, too, that the crisis was of such a magnitude that it required the instant help of ten strong men, and yet Don Miguel was in no rush to hurry back himself.

Feeling considerably ill-used and put upon, Beth felt her temper rise. It was almost as if Don Miguel had foreseen that she would return to the house with every intention of immediately making plans to go home, and to find that she had been neatly scotched was the final straw to an already beastly day. Her head beginning to ache, her feelings scraped raw, and her temper soaring mercurially, she rose from the table and, in a decidedly unfriendly voice, she said, "Why, of course not! Why should I? You have been so kind to me that it is only natural that I help you in your hour of need. And if having my servants whisked away with neither my permission nor my knowledge is how I have to repay you, then it will have to suffice."

It was, perhaps, not very gracious of her, and under any other circumstances Beth would never have spoken to someone in that manner, especially not someone she had a great deal of affection for and who had been so very kind to her during these past trying weeks. An uncomfortable silence greeted her words, and Don Miguel moved a little guiltily in his seat, but Beth, not in the mood to be polite, excused herself coolly and swept from the room, leaving the others to stare at one an other with startled, dismayed eyes. Somewhat ruefully Don Miguel admitted, "I suppose I wasn't too tactful."

"You were not, my husband!" Doña Madelina agreed with unflattering promptness. "Surely you could have spoken with her first before you sent away all her servants—she is a good woman and would not have denied them to you." And, to the mystification of both Sebastian and Señora López, she added, "I understand what you are about, but there was probably a better way to accomplish it."

What Doña Madelina said was true. All Don Miguel would have had to do was ask and Beth would have given him anything she possessed, but to steal her servants so meanly when her back was turned went against the grain, and Beth was more than a little annoyed. She spent most of the remainder of the day secluded in her room, more from the pain that had rapidly developed into a devastating sick headache than because she was sulking or at odds with Don Miguel and Sebastian.

When the nausea in her stomach and the almost unbearably painful pounding in her temple had ceased, it was well into evening, and while her disappointment and anger with Sebastian had not abated one whit, she was beginning to feel slightly ashamed at her outburst in the dining room. She was the most wretched creature alive to have spoken so pettily to a man who had shown her nothing but generous hospitality and overwhelming consideration.

Rising from her bed, she rang for Charity, only to remember with depression that Charity would serve her no longer. I hope she's truly happy with her lover, Beth thought sadly, thinking of the difficulties ahead for the laughing little black girl.

She would have to start training Judith, the other Negress she had brought along, more as a companion to Charity than any other reason, she decided without enthusiasm. And, thinking it would be Judith who answered her ring, she was considerably surprised when Manuela knocked and entered the room.

They stared at one another, these two women with their unwillingly shared ugly secret, and Beth finally said with resignation, "Don't tell me—Doña Madelina has assigned you to serve me in view of Charity's desertion."

Manuela smiled faintly and nodded. "*Si, señora.* As soon as it was discovered what had happened, Doña Madelina informed me that I would act as your personal maid until other arrangements could be made. Do you object?"

Beth shook her head slowly and smiled wryly. "It seems that you and I are destined to remain together. I suppose I should stop fighting against it and let fate take its course."

Manuela gave a fatalistic shrug. "It would seem so, señora." And, looking uncertainly at Beth, she asked anxiously, "Do you mind?"

"No. At least not anymore," Beth answered truthfully, discovering with surprise that it was true. So much had happened to her during these past months that New Orleans and the events that had taken place there four years ago seemed as if they had occurred to another person. She would never forget it, but it no longer had the power to hurt her—she had new wounds now that were far more painful.

Competently, as if she had been Beth's personal servant for years, Manuela set about preparing her mistress for the evening. A hip bath was provided, and after Beth had bathed and powered herself, she reluctantly approved the gown Manuela had selected.

It was a beautiful gown of black satin with touches of black lace at the throat and wrists, but already, with Nathan dead barely six weeks, Beth was beginning to hate the sight of black. How she was going to endure the months ahead always in widow's color, she didn't know.

The gown became her, it was undoubtedly true, her high bosom neatly enhanced by the perfect fit and her narrow waist emphasized by the figure-hugging cut of the gown before it fell in full, voluminous skirts to the tops of her little heelless slippers. She had no need of a corset of any type—Nathan's death and her own illness had left her reed-slender—and with her silvery hair piled on top of her head in curls and her alabaster skin gleaming above the black satin, she was very lovely.

She descended the stairs intent upon making her apologies to Don Miguel. Finding him in the main salon, she did so, very prettily and sincerely. He accepted them in the spirit with which they had been conveyed, and in a matter of moments the entire affair was put behind them and things were very much as they had been... except for her stiffness with Sebastian. It would be a long time before she forgave him for believing Rafael's lies!

Everyone was gathered in the salon, the ladies sipping *sangría,* the two gentlemen enjoying a particularly fine brandy, when Lorenzo Mendoza was announced. Unconsciously Beth went rigid, wondering at his purpose, for certainly he knew Rafael would not tolerate his presence in his house.

But Don Miguel would and did, much to Beth's dismay. It seemed that during the days that she had been ill, Lorenzo, knowing Rafael was absent, had been a frequent visitor. With his serpent's grace he had renewed his insinuation into Don Miguel's favor, and from the bits and pieces of their conversation she overheard, apparently Don Miguel was determined to put an end to the estrangement between his son and a man he clearly regarded as a member of the family.

"This is a ridiculous state of affairs!" Don Miguel stated firmly. "You only able to show your face when my hotheaded son is not around. I admire your unwillingness to precipitate an ugly scene, but surely you see that you two *must* put aside your differences. The day will come when I am no longer alive and you will be invaluable to my son in helping him with the running of the rancho."

Lorenzo smiled modestly, but the man's fawning mannerisms grated on Sebastian's nerves and under his breath he muttered, "Unwillingness or cowardice?"

Fortunately no one but Beth heard his low-voiced

comment—at least she thought she had been the only one until she happened to glance over at Lorenzo and saw the malevolent look he shot Sebastian, who then smiled at him sweetly and raised his glass as if to emphasize that he had indeed said the words. Lorenzo's black eyes went opaque but he made no attempt to challenge the insult.

It had been a most frustrating time for Lorenzo since Beth had arrived in San Antonio. His hopes had been bolstered, only to be dashed as Beth seemed to escape from a tragic death time after time. He had bitterly regretted that the Comanche lance that had killed her husband had not buried itself in her soft bosom. Then, when she had come down with the fever, he had been delighted, especially when she hovered near death's door, but much to his fury she had recovered—and her eventual death had become almost an obsession with Lorenzo!

He feared her, knowing that with one sentence she could destroy all that he had worked for over the years, and because he feared her, he hated her intensely. He wanted her *dead,* but he wanted no wind of blame to travel his way. He dare not hire it done, and he was aware that Beth would never allow herself to be lured away in his company so that he might do the deed himself. And so, like a deadly reptile coiled and waiting for his prey, he watched and lurked.

As long as she remained under the Santana protection she was safe, and yet every day she spent with Don Miguel and Doña Madelina terrified Lorenzo, frightened that with their growing intimacy Beth might speak of his part in Consuela's scheme. He wanted to avoid the house, feeling that the less Beth saw of him the less likely it was she would speak, and at the same time he found himself unable to stay away, calling frequently to discover whether he was still in favor or if the killing blow had fallen.

When Beth had been ill there had been no danger, but as she increased in health so had Lorenzo's fear and fury. *She must be silenced!* He would not live the rest of his days knowing that when he least expected it she could reappear, as she had done this time, and upset all his carefully erected plans.

But if Beth had been saved from him thus far, her time was running out. Sooner or later she would leave San Antonio, and once she was away from the safety it and the Santanas afforded... Who knew what would happen then?

PART FOUR

DUELS, DEVILS, AND LOVERS

The time and my intents are savage-wild,
More fierce and more inexorable far
Than empty tigers or the roaring sea.

WILLIAM SHAKESPEARE,
Romeo and Juliet, Act V, Scene III

CHAPTER TWENTY-THREE

While Beth had lain so ill, the Comanches, filled with a hitherto unknown bitterness and deadly zeal, had been viciously harrying the frontier with lethal lightning raids. They struck everywhere from north of Austin, the new capital, to the Mexican border, attacking without warning and with a particularly terrifying vindictiveness. The Texas Rangers, their numbers never very great, were helpless to stop or contain the widespread raiding and looting.

Smoking, burned-out homesteads, charred and mutilated bodies became a common occurrence, and in desperation, knowing his rangers were not enough, Jack Hays organized a posse of men from San Antonio to help strengthen his own hard-pressed forces. These "Minute Men," as the volunteers became known, were in service constantly, their horses, arms, and provisions kept for instant use. The signals that sent them running for their mounts were the raising of a flag over the courthouse and the mournful ringing of the San Fernando church bell. As the weeks passed everyone began to dread the sight of that flag and the pealing of the bell.

Other communities suffering the same losses and bloody attacks formed their own companies of Minute Men, but there was no stopping or halting the Comanche war. It had become the nightmare Rafael had predicted.

The Minute Men, though seeing service almost daily, were of little use against the Comanches. They dared not follow the Indians too far into *Comanchería,* and as they were never called into service until *after* an attack, more often than not the most they accomplished was the burial of the dead left in the wake of the Comanche depredations.

The Republic's regular army was almost useless when fighting Indians. Against other infantry the army was awesome, and when ensconced behind stone walls the soldiers were very nearly unbeatable, but against the highly mobile and widely ranging Comanches they were as ineffectual as had been the Spanish troops before them. Wisely, the Comanches refused to battle with the grouped infantry, and it was impossible for the foot soldiers to follow and attack the well-mounted enemy. Nothing seemed to stop the relentless, deadly raids.

Only Jack Hays's rangers, riding and tracking like the Indians themselves, were able to strike back but they were too small a force against the concentrated efforts of the Pehnahterkuh. The Comanches mauled the frontier until it was a blackened, bleeding mass of destroyed homes, hopes, and lives.

Some of this Beth learned in the days that had followed her recovery, but in most cases people did not talk of it in front of her, considering how Nathan had died.

If the unrelenting war with the Comanches was not trouble enough, in May rumor spread like wildfire that there was an impending invasion from Mexico. Worse, it was said that the Indians would be acting as the allies of the Mexicans.

Hearing the rumors the nearer he rode toward San Antonio, Rafael's face grew grimmer and grimmer. It was as he had feared. God*damn* those stupid, sanctimonious bastards who had thought to hold the Comanche chiefs captive!

The raids and rumors were what finally dissipated the little gathering at Rafael's house in San Antonio. Sebastian had already left, the day after his unfortunate conversation with Beth, feeling his place was with his own men in case of trouble and thinking that he needed to put a little distance between himself and the *very* icy Mrs. Ridgeway. Don Miguel, after much reluctance, not at all liking the idea of leaving Beth in a house with no male protector, finally decided that he and Doña Madelina must return to Cielo. Beth would be safe in town, and there was always Lorenzo or the Mavericks to aid her in case of real trouble. Besides, he thought slyly, Rafael's courting would progress at a faster rate if there were not relatives constantly in the house.

Consequently, in a bewilderingly short space of time the house was deserted except for Beth, Señora López, and the various servants. Manuela had stayed behind at Doña Madelina's suggestion and Beth found herself growing more and more at ease with her. Manuela had her own reasons for being more than willing to remain behind in San Antonio—she found the Señora Ridgeway a most pleasant mistress and she enjoyed her position of being the personal maid of the woman everyone suspected would become the bride of Señor Rafael.

In the small, tight-knit household little escaped the eyes of the servants, and Don Miguel had made his hopes obvious in more ways than one. Excited eager gossip had flown from kitchen to stables, from the lowest housemaid to the highest servant, and Beth had begun to wonder if it were her imagination or if the servants did seem to pay her more attention than was necessary.

Determined to put no impediment in the way of the courtship, before leaving Doña Madelina had taken Señora López to one side and suggested gently that she not pursue her duties as duena *too* assiduously. With a knowing, dreamy smile she had murmured, "After all, Señora Beth is not an innocent maid who has never known a man...and Señor Rafael is *very* much a man, *sí?*" Señora López had smiled in agreement, thinking the match eminently suitable.

Unfortunately there was one who did not think so, and even more unfortunately, in his enthusiasm for the match Don Miguel had made two rather disastrous miscalculations. The first was his letter to his father, written almost immediately following Nathan's death, in which he expressed his hopes of the marriage, and the second his indiscreet sharing of the scheme with Lorenzo Mendoza.

How Lorenzo managed to hide his fury from Don Miguel when he heard of the plans spinning so merrily in the older man's head he never knew. But, his heart full of hatred and bitterness, he had forced himself to smile and nod as if the news gave him great pleasure. More than anyone involved he knew these hopes and schemes could become reality. Too well he remembered Consuela's certainty that the little English girl held more than a passing interest for Rafael, and even more vividly he remembered Rafael's face when he had found them together. If he had ever considered allowing Beth to return unharmed to Natchez, this new possibility made her death absolutely necessary. Rafael *must* not marry and sire heirs, if his plans were to come to fruition! And until his own position was secured he dared not kill him. Not yet, not until he had made certain of marriage to Arabela . . . something he knew Rafael would object to violently. But once he had Don Felipe's permission to pay court to his youngest granddaughter, *then* would be time enough to arrange for Rafael's tragic demise.

Beth was oblivious of all the plotting going on around her, except for the sudden, almost embarrassing deference and interest displayed by the servants. She had been depressed when Don Miguel and Doña Madelina had left, for she had grown extremely fond of them both, and if they seemed to treat this parting as only temporary, she knew in her heart that just as soon as Don Miguel felt it was safe to send her servants back to San Antonio she would be leaving for Natchez. Watching their cavalcade—the heavily armed *vaqueros* and the coach that carried the Santanas—move down the dusty streets of San Antonio, her eyes filled with tears. The remainder of the day passed interminably for her as she wandered listlessly through the unbearably quiet house.

His thoughts always on Beth, Rafael also found the hours interminable, despite the changing countryside and the feel of the horse beneath him. It had never occurred to him to consider the possibility that she would think of leaving for Natchez. Like his father, he found it inconceivable that she travel alone across the Republic with only her servants—especially now in these dangerous, uncertain times. Thinking of the horrors of the Comanche attacks along the frontier, he wished violently that Enchantress was ready for her. She'd be safe and well protected there. Nestled as it was in the pine forests of the eastern part of the Republic, Enchantress was far away from the raiding paths of the Comanches, who kept to the wide flat plains they knew so well.

Beth's image was with him always—a slim, silvery-haired wraith who never seemed to leave his mind for a moment. At Enchantress she had been everywhere he looked, his imagination seeing her walking gracefully under the towering, pungent-scented pines, or stepping lightly down the wide, curving staircase in the house, or seated quietly in the main salon. At night she filled his dreams, her mouth flaming sweetly on his, her arms entwined passionately around his neck, her body arching itself against him and begging for his possession. And now as he rode so unceasingly toward her, with little sleep, few stops, changing horses, from the string of four he had brought with him, in mid-gallop like the Comanches, she rode with him, her small, lovely face and bright hair a blazing beacon at the end of a long, dark, lonely trail.

Never having loved before, except for the deep fondness he had for his little half-sister Arabela, he didn't recognize the emotions that surged and thudded through his body—he only knew that Beth was *his* and *nothing* this side of Heaven, or Hell for that matter, was going to keep them apart! But if he did not recognize love, he did acknowledge the bond which had existed between them since he had looked across the ballroom floor at the Costa soiree and had seen her standing shyly next to Stella, and he cursed the wasted years. I should have taken her with me when she asked, he thought, divided between fury and ruefulness, for try as he might he had never been quite able to forget her. Sometimes months had passed without her image invading his mind, and then something, a fair head, a small, neatly turned figure, or the curve of a pale cheek, would remind him, and then he would remember her and curse his own foolishness for remembering.

She had betrayed her husband, and there was little

doubt in his mind that if he hadn't put an end to it she would have become Sebastian's lover too. She won't do that to *me*, he thought grimly. I'll keep her so damned busy that she won't have time for even a thought of anyone else—and if I *ever* find her with another man...!

It suddenly occurred to him that half of his rage, that day he had found her and Lorenzo in bed together, had not been just to discover that she was a woman of easy morals, but that the man she had chosen to cuckold her husband with was someone other than himself! God knows, he'd been willing enough. He smiled mirthlessly to himself as he realized how ridiculous his thoughts were.

But she wasn't going to have the chance to put a pair of horns on him, he decided firmly. He'd exhaust that slender, bewitching body with his lovemaking and keep her filled with child in the bargain. The idea of Beth swollen with his child was a new, unexpected thought, a startling thought, and with it came a rush of such fierce tenderness and possession that Rafael's entire body seemed to suddenly go weak from it. I might just have to marry her after all, he conceded with angry despair.

The idea of marriage was repugnant to him—life with Consuela had assured that! And because he found himself even considering it, he grew furious not only with himself but with Beth as well. He had no intention of falling into that particular trap again, no matter how desperately he wanted the woman, yet all his actions of the past weeks had been those of a man contemplating marriage, and he knew it. His lips thinned as he admitted it, and the gray eyes grew strangely bleak and full of rage at the same time.

The conflict within him was not something to be easily overcome. He wanted Beth, wanted her as he had wanted no other woman, and with that wanting came the desire to bind her to him in every way that he could—his protection, his possessions, his body, his children, and...marriage. And yet he fought against it as a man would against a deadly, emasculating fate, determined not to fall into the pit of pain and disillusionment that Beth represented. She's a little whore, he muttered furiously under his breath, reminding himself over and over again of her sins. But it did little good. He couldn't control the anguished longing, the hungry yearning to hold her once more in his arms, to taste the honey of her mouth and to see those lovely features animated and smiling at him.

His emotions shredded raw by the violent battle that raged so frenziedly within him, Rafael reached San Antonio by mid-May, in a black uncertain temper. His mood wavered between the sweet anticipation of seeing Beth again and an almost savage antagonism that simmered just under the surface of his apparent coolness. It did his temper little good to discover that his quarry was not there, the servants informing him of the changes in the household and of the fact that Señora Ridgeway and Señora López were visitors at the Maverick household and would be back later.

He took the news of the departure of the others indifferently, but his eyes had narrowed and his mouth had curved unpleasantly when Santiago, his personal servant in San Antonio, mentioned that Señor Mendoza had been a frequent visitor during the time he had been gone. Very earnestly Santiago had finished, "And when Don Miguel left, he was most grateful for Señor Mendoza's offer to see after the ladies until you returned." Rafael said something ugly under his breath and ordered a bath and a change of clothes.

It turned out that the visit to the Mavericks was rather protracted, for Rafael had time not only to bathe but to dress as well, in a pair of tight-fitting black *calzoneras* trimmed with silver lace and silver buttons, and a fine, white silky shirt with long, full sleeves that billowed gracefully near his lean wrists where the soft material was sewn into the narrow cuffs. He wore the shirt half open, exposing a V of smooth brown skin that nearly met the scarlet sash wound around his waist, and with his face burned even darker by the days in the sun, his blue-black hair crisp and clean from the bath, and the smoky-gray eyes bright between the thick, black lashes, he looked so magnificently vital and dynamically handsome that the very air around him seemed suddenly to crackle with the force of his powerful presence.

Beth and Señora López still had not returned when he descended the stairs in long, swift strides. Hungry, for he had eaten little but handfuls of dried corn and strips of venison jerky during his grueling race to San Antonio, he requested that some food be prepared for him. It was only after he had eaten a hastily served meal of *tortillas rellenas* and the ever-present *frijoles de olla* along with several glasses of tequila that Beth and Señora López arrived back at the house.

Rafael was lounging in the front salon when he first heard their voices out in the main hall. He had been drinking, not heavily but steadily, and he had been thinking—not very nice thoughts either. The news that just as soon as his back was turned Lorenzo and Beth seemed to seek each other out left him with a decidedly nasty taste in his mouth, and the half-formed dreams that had hovered so tantalizingly on his horizon these past weeks seemed to have evaporated and turned into something ugly and tawdry. I am, he thought viciously, a fool! To think that I nearly let that lovely face blind me. And unfortunately, only adding to the rage that was now seething through his body, who should be escorting the ladies home but Lorenzo.

If Don Miguel had made a drastic miscalculation by informing Lorenzo of his hopes of a marriage between the widow and his son, Lorenzo had also greatly miscalculated Rafael's return to San Antonio. When he heard of the plans concerning Enchantress from Don Miguel, he had dismissed it as merely dust thrown in the eyes of everyone just to hide Rafael's true destination—the high plains and a meeting with the Comanches to attempt to dissuade them from joining with the Mexicans. And because he had assumed Rafael would be occupied far away in the Palo Duro Canyon area, he hadn't expected him back for several days yet. To find him sitting comfortably in the salon was a somewhat unpleasant shock.

Lorenzo and the two ladies had entered the salon, unaware of Rafael's return, and Señora López was politely pressing Lorenzo to remain for some light refreshment when Rafael slowly and unhurriedly uncoiled his tall frame from its relaxed position. Lorenzo saw him first. He stiffened, aware that there was no Don Miguel to intercede for him and that he was in his enemy's own house.

Beth and Señora López noticed him only a second after Lorenzo did, and Señora López's excited greetings gave both Lorenzo and Beth a moment to gather their wits. For Lorenzo it was easy—all he had to do was beat a rather hasty retreat, which he promptly did, disappearing so quickly and abruptly that Señora López stared after him in some surprise and disapproval at his lack of manners. For Beth it wasn't as easy, the unexpected sight of Rafael causing her heart to behave in a most incomprehensible fashion, as it seemed first to plunge to her toes and then leap to her throat. There was a wild, giddy feeling in the pit of her stomach, and she knew an almost uncontrollable urge to fling herself into his arms and press her lips fervently against his. For one tiny second she was full of joy at his return, feeling more alive than she had in weeks, but that feeling was gone so swiftly it might never have existed, as she remembered that last disgraceful night they had spent together as well as the deliberate lies he had told Sebastian.

For Rafael there was no one else in the room but Beth. His eyes, their expression shadowed, traveled up and down with a sort of hidden, hungry assessment of her slender body. She was, as usual, dressed in black, a high-necked gown with tight-fitting long sleeves made of taffeta and trimmed with a black ruching of lace at the throat, wrists and down the front to her waist. Her fair hair was braided and arranged in a coronet, much as she had worn it the day Nathan had been wounded, and there was a faint charming flush to her cheeks. To Rafael, the violet eyes, which met his so icily across the space that divided them, seemed like two bright amethyst jewels between the gold-tipped lashes. She was, he discovered warily and with a little puzzlement, angry—and the anger seemed to be directed at him! *Now, why?* he wondered with a sudden frown. *Surely, I am the one to be angry, you wanton, lovely, little slut!*

Beth *was* angry. The first foolish rush of emotion at seeing him again had been conquered, and she was left with only the hurt and fury that had been her constant companion since Sebastian had told her that Rafael had named her his mistress. At night as she had lain sleepless in her bed, she had been tormented equally by the memory of Rafael's lovemaking in that very bed and the pain and anguish Sebastian's words had given her. She had known that Rafael did not hold her in high esteem—his every act was evidence of that! But she found it a bitter draught to swallow that he had deliberately vilified her to Sebastian. And to how many more, she wondered dismally. Now that she was face to face with her accuser, she felt an anger the like of which she had never known sweep through her body, until only by exercising the greatest self-control was she able to keep from flying across the room to scratch and claw at Rafael's coldly smiling face.

They greeted one another with frigid politeness, Señora López thinking with disappointment that, perchance, everyone had misjudged the affair, but then she caught a brief flicker of something in Rafael's eyes that made her smile. So, he *isn't* indifferent, she thought happily to herself.

Señora López, at sixty-two years of age, was still a romanticist. She had been a widow for over twenty years but she could still remember clearly her own courting days—the storms, the misunderstandings, and the tempestuous reconciliations. Discreetly, remembering Doña Madelina's advice, she withdrew from the room, mentioning some minor errand that the remaining two never heard, their engrossment with one another too keen, too intent to be disrupted by softly spoken words.

The moment Señora López left the room, though, Rafael turned away and, pouring himself another glass of tequila, he said sneeringly over his shoulder, "I see that you and Lorenzo have managed to renew your acquaintance. Tell me, is he as satisfactory a lover as I? Or are you still making comparisons?"

His eyes damning her and his mouth curving dangerously, he flung himself down on the sofa he had so recently vacated and stared at Beth contemptuously.

When she remained icily silent, the increased brightness of her eyes being the only sign that she had heard his words, he demanded in an ugly tone, "Well? Haven't you any answer? Or is your silence meant to be an answer?"

Like an alabaster-and-ebony statue Beth faced him, the sheer fury that was scalding through her veins making her earlier rush of anger seem like tepid milkwater. His unfair taunts were the final insult. Deep inside of her a flame of rebellion flickered, and then suddenly, like an explosive prairie fire, it burst into a fiery conflagration that swept through her entire body. Something happened to Beth in those few fleeting seconds as she stared across at her dark-faced tormentor, changing her from the woman she had been to the vibrant, scintillatingly beautiful creature who now faced Rafael with wrathful fury. The white-hot rage that consumed her woke the sleeping tigress that had always lain within her breast, and gone forever was the shy, apprehensive girl who had married to escape an indifferent father and cold stepmother, the gentle compassionate girl who had placated and soothed a selfish, impotent husband, and the gullible girl who had gone to make peace with Consuela only to be so cruelly used. Even the reserved, outwardly composed young woman Rafael had discovered at the Rancho del Cielo had vanished, leaving this defiant, passionate woman who stood in front of him now. Beth wasn't aware of the change within herself, at least not at the moment. At the moment all her energies were directed at Rafael's arrogantly lounging figure, and through a red mist of fury she regarded him balefully. Words fought in her throat for utterance, but they were too hot, too angry to make any sense, and with the newly aroused spirit and rebellion driving her, she searched for some physical means of giving him the answer he deserved.

Without thinking, moved by some inward turbulent force, Beth crossed swiftly to where Rafael had put down the crystal decanter and with a strangled snort of fury she snatched it up and spun around to face him. The crystal felt cool under her fingers, the tequila sloshing about and giving it a satisfactory weight as she held it in her hand. The violet eyes nearly incandescent with wrath, she flew across the few feet that separated them to stand with a heaving bosom in front of Rafael. In a voice shaking with temper she spat, "You insufferable beast! You dare to condemn me with no knowledge of the truth, and yet you tell blatant lies about me that are even more vile than anything I could ever do!"

He cast a watchful eye toward the crystal decanter that she held so threateningly, but demanded just as angrily as she, "What the hell do you mean by that?" His eyebrows met in a black scowl above his nose and the aura of explosive anger that radiated from him was almost tangible. Tightly he added, "I don't tell lies about anyone—not even you!"

"Liar!" Beth returned hotly, the violet eyes flashing. "You lied to Sebastian when you told him I was your mistress and had been for a number of years!"

A mirthless sort of smile crossed the lean features, and infuriatingly he murmured, "Oh, that."

Beth nearly choked on her rage and a gasp of outrage escaped her before she could prevent it. But then, taking a deep, steadying breath, she suddenly smiled—rather sweetly too, which should have warned him, but unfortunately he was enjoying this new Beth, this enchanting spitfire, and his guard was down. "Yes, *that!*" she said dulcetly and, with all her strength behind it, brought the crystal decanter unerringly down on his dark head.

The sound of the decanter connecting with Rafael's head gave a gratifying thud in the quiet room before the fragile crystal shattered and shards of glass and splatters of tequila went flying in all directions. With more satisfaction than she had felt in a long time, she surveyed Rafael's astonished features. Pieces of broken crystal sparkled in the thick blue-black hair, the hair itself was wetly plastered against his scalp, and his white silk shirt clung damply to his shoulders as he sat there staring up with narrowing eyes at her unashamedly pleased expression.

But only for a second. Then like an enraged black panther he erupted from his seat, swearing and shaking his head violently, drops of tequila and even tiny splinters of glass hitting Beth. "Why, you damned little hell-cat! I ought to throttle you and be done with it!" he snarled, the gray eyes hard and threatening.

But Beth wasn't about to be intimidated by him this time, and even when he loomed up so darkly dangerous in front of her, she didn't back down. Almost enjoying their confrontation, a feeling of throbbing excitement flooding her body, with arms akimbo she faced him and said belligerently, "Just you try it! Lay one hand on me and I'll scratch your eyes out!"

From under heavy black brows he glared at her, knowing that strangling her was the *last* thing he wanted to do. Sweet Jesus, but she was beautiful, he thought foolishly as his gaze wandered from the shining coronet of silvery braids to the soft, coral mouth. Some of his earlier anger was fading and he was very much afraid that no matter what she ever did, no matter how many lovers she had, either in the past or the future, she would always have the power to touch him, to shatter the cold, defensive shell he kept around himself. The thought terrified him, to think that one slender woman could destroy a lifetime of carefully erected protections against...love. Instantly he shied away from that idea, unwilling to admit such folly, and angry again that she could make him, even for one brief second, consider such a thought.

For a long moment their eyes clashed and fought across the small space that divided them, neither willing to make the first move, neither exactly certain what the next move was. The ridiculousness of the situation struck Rafael, and a glint of laughter flickered in the gray eyes as the minutes spun out and they continued to stand staring at one another like two arched-backed cats.

Not so with Beth, however. She was too angry and had too much justification to find anything remotely amusing in the current confrontation. Seeing the laughter in his eyes, she exploded again. With a cry of rage she launched herself at him, her fists striking at his chest. "Don't you dare laugh at me!" Nearly crying with frustration, she got out furiously, "You've used me from the moment we first met, and *now* you're *laughing* about it! You lied to Sebastian about me and he thinks I am a creature without redemption, and *you* laugh! I am not your mistress!" Her fists pounding and hitting wherever they could against Rafael's seemingly unfeeling body, it was almost like an incantation as she cried, "I am not your mistress! I am not! I am *not!*"

With humiliating ease he captured her flailing fists and jerked her roughly next to him, the dampness of his shirt staining the taffeta gown where it touched. An odd expression on his arrogant face, he looked down into her stormy features and said with a queer note in his voice. "But aren't you? Aren't you the mistress of my heart?"

The words were said so low that in her anger Beth nearly missed what he had said, but then she had no time to ponder it, because Rafael's mouth swooped down hard on hers in a hungry, urgent kiss that blotted out everything but the dark magic he could arouse so effortlessly. She fought against it—and might have won if he had merely kissed her with passion, but as his warm lips deepened their pressure against hers, some indefinable element entered into the kiss, and Beth responded to it blindly. There was passion in the kiss, but there was also tenderness and a hungry yearning that, as the minutes passed, drained away her anger until she didn't even remember the reason for it—she knew only that she was in Rafael's arms and it was where she wanted to be more than anywhere else in the world!

His hand came up and cupped her face, holding her still as his mouth moved across her cheeks and brows before it came back and settled urgently on her lips once more, and, with a small moan of defeat, Beth leaned weakly into his hard, warm body, unable to fight against her own inclinations or the wishes of her heart any longer. At her surrender the kiss changed imperceptibly, his leashed desire struggling to snap the control Rafael had on it, and demandingly his lips explored hers, taking now where before they had only tasted.

Lost in the sensuous web Rafael was weaving, Beth made no demurrer when he swept her up in his arms and carried her over to a wide velvet sofa. As if she were made of delicate china he gently laid her down on it, his mouth never leaving hers. Kneeling beside the sofa, his dark head bent to hers, his hands now persuasively touching and caressing her small breasts, Beth felt her nipples go tight with longing and giddily she felt desire stir deep within her.

Rafael knew desire too, his entire body filled with a gnawing hunger to feel her soft white body beneath his, and with a strange, trembling eagerness his fingers sought the fastenings of her gown. It was the touch of his hand undoing the back of her gown that suddenly brought Beth back to reality and made her realize with a sickening lurch of her stomach how easy it was for him to make her act the part of a wanton.

With a little cry of anguish and fury she pushed him violently away and leaped to her feet. "Don't!" she half commanded, half implored, torn between the urgings of her heart and the commonsense dictates of her brain. Her eyes shimmering behind a veil of tears, she said thickly, "Don't do this to me! Don't berate me one minute for my supposed failings, and then in the next, take advantage of the very thing you condemn me for! Stop *using* me!"

His eyes bleak and barren, the expression on the dark lean face remote, Rafael gracefully stood up in front of her. Startling her, he said simply, "I'm sorry. Where you are concerned, I seem to act contrary to my own principles."

Beth gave a bitter little laugh. "Do you have any principles? I sometimes wonder. Certainly I've never seen you exercise any of them."

His voice dangerously quiet, he said, "Haven't you? I thought leaving you in New Orleans was rather high-principled of me—I didn't want to, you know. But amongst other things, it went against the grain to let you in for the kind of life I could have given you then—a runaway wife kept by a married man with a not-so-savory reputation—so I denied my own desires and left you." Beth's face went white, but Rafael went on expressionlessly, giving her no chance to speak, "Your husband didn't die by my hand, but he could have so easily. I told you I wanted him out of your life, and it would have been the simplest thing in the world to challenge him to a duel at any time I felt like it." His eyes boring into hers, he added coldly, "I would have killed him, too, had we met on the dueling ground. But when he died, I don't remember that I immediately forced myself on you, which I would have done if I had listened to just my own wants." The gray eyes suddenly icy, he snarled softly, "You don't know how damned lucky you are, English—I could have ruined you any number of times since we first met, but I didn't. Oh, I wanted you, believe me! I wanted you badly enough to steal you from your husband, and the scandal be *damned!*—and I could have made you the talk of New Orleans and even the Republic of Texas, simply by reaching out and taking you." Unkindly he continued, "Can you imagine the talk, the whispers, the scandal there would have been if I had done as I wished, and kidnapped you out from under your husband's very nose? I can if you can't, so the next time you think of me as completely unprincipled, just remember I could have destroyed your reputation anytime I chose. But for whatever reasons—and I'm not even certain of them myself—I didn't."

Looking into those cool gray eyes and seeing the reckless slant of his mouth, Beth realized with a queer, shameful thud of excitement that he meant exactly what he said, and she swallowed, painfully aware now of how many times she had hovered on the brink of disaster. But then she was disgusted with herself. So what if he wanted her—she already knew *that!* And it was disgraceful of her to feel anything but revulsion to his admission, yet while she felt a great many conflicting emotions, strangely enough none of them was revulsion.

Eyeing him uncertainly, she clutched at the one thing she knew for a fact. "You *lied* to Sebastian!—you said I was your mistress when you *knew* it was a lie!"

Rafael shrugged his broad shoulders. He had handled her gently for the last time, his patience, never very great, was exhausted, and he wanted this fencing between them over with. English was *his* and it was time she learned it—learned it and realized that where she was concerned he could be very unprincipled indeed. Legs slightly spread, his arms folded across his chest, he stared at her for an unnerving second and then said sardonically, "I never precisely called you my mistress—I merely said we had a long-standing liaison—which is true." His eyes slid over her with an inscrutable expression in their depths and harshly he said, "You're *mine,* English, you have been since the moment I laid eyes on you, and you know it!—if you're honest within yourself." He smiled cynically, adding, "Something most women, I have discovered, are not! I can and will claim you by whatever name I choose, and whether it be mistress or woman, *you belong to me!"*

CHAPTER TWENTY-FOUR

With something between a cry of fury and the spitting sound of a thwarted kitten, Beth fled the room, certain that if she stayed one second longer she would do something more drastic than merely break a decanter of tequila over his head. *How dare he!* she thought wrathfully as she sped up the stairs to the sanctuary of her room. *I belong to him! Ha! We'll just see about that, you arrogant devil. Call me your mistress, will you?*

Reaching her room, she spent several minutes pacing the floor, her thoughts furiously concentrated on finding a way of defying Rafael, of making him choke on his words. Even possibly of humiliating or embarrassing him. He had said he never embarrassed; well we'll just see about that, Beth decided spiritedly. He had practically thrown down a challenge to her, and it was up to her to meet it. And by Heaven she would, she vowed stormily. And it was only when Manuela came in to see about her bath and to prepare whichever gown she wished to wear that evening that an idea came to her.

Manuela was busy seeing that the bath was set up and the hot water procured, when Beth said suddenly, "Manuela, I want you to get me a gown."

"Why, of course, señora, which one would you like to wear this evening? The black silk or perhaps the new black muslin?" Manuela asked sedately.

A hard sheen in the usually soft, violet eyes, Beth said succinctly, "None of those. I want a harlot's gown."

"A har—! You mean a whore's gown?" Manuela squeaked with astonishment, her large brown eyes nearly starting from her head.

Beth smiled a grim little smile and nodded her head. "And I want it tonight. Can you get one?"

Manuela spread her hands helplessly, her lined face the picture of disapproval and bewilderment. "I don't know. I-I-I'll have to ask around." Looking a bit affronted, she added stiffly, "I am not in the habit of consorting with such women!"

"Neither am I!" Beth retorted sharply, feeling very sensitive on the subject. But then, ashamed of herself, she said with a note of pleading, "Please, Manuela, it's important to me! Very important, and I need it this evening—I don't care what it costs, just get me one." Tightly she finished, "And the more outrageous the better!"

Deciding the American señora must still be suffering from a touch of the fever, Manuela agreed, not knowing what else to do. Having been a servant since childhood, it never occurred to her to do anything different from what her mistress had asked. And so with great reluctance she sought out one of the young men who worked in the stables, and from him was able to get the necessary information she needed. Discreet from the years as Consuela's servant, she undertook to carry out the task herself, telling no one why she needed to run a sudden errand across town.

The bordello was a shock to Manuela, but nothing compared to the amazement of the madam when she discovered what this very proper and respectable servant wanted. The sight of gold, though, made her shrug her fleshy shoulders above the indecently low-cut scarlet gown she wore, and she and Manuela after inspecting several garments, each more outrageous and vulgar than the last, finally struck a bargain.

The gown cost more than Manuela had wanted to pay, her thrifty soul revolting at being charged an exorbitant price for the cheaply made gown, but with Beth's words ringing in her ears she reluctantly paid the sum. Hurrying back to the house, she consoled herself with the knowledge that at least the gown was new, and so possibly it was well worth the price she'd had to pay. There were others she might have chosen, but she simply could not bring herself to buy for her lady a perspiration-stained, tobacco-smelling gown which had been worn by another woman, and a whore at that—no matter what Señora Beth had said!

Beth had already bathed and was restlessly lying on her bed in a soft, silky lavender peignoir when Manuela returned with an obviously hastily wrapped package. At Manuela's entrance into the room, she jerked upright and asked with a determined eagerness, "Were you successful?"

Manuela nodded her head and grimaced disapprovingly. "*Sí, señora,* I was able to buy one, but..."

"Don't scold me," Beth interrupted her pleadingly. "I know you think this is all very scandalous, and it is, but don't desert me now, Manuela."

"Very well, señora, but I think you are playing a dangerous game. Señor Rafael," she said repressively, "will not like what I think you are planning."

If Manuela had wanted to insure that Beth continue with her madcap plan, she could not have chosen more inflaming words. Beth's wavering resolve hardened in that instant. Slipping from bed, she said with a hint of defiance in her voice, "Let me see it."

A gasp of shock and admiration burst from her when at last Manuela unveiled the gown. "Oh, Manuela...!" she breathed with reverence, undecided whether to giggle with nervousness at the thought of actually wearing it or to order Manuela to destroy it instantly! It was truly a strumpet's gown, and the half-hysterical thought occurred to her that at least it was black. But not entirely black....

Looking at the gown and thinking about appearing before him in it gave her pause, and for several minutes she almost put the scheme aside. It was going to make him angry, of that she was certain, and did she have the courage to flaunt herself in that shocking garment?

Her chin lifted rebelliously. Of course she had the courage! And why should she worry of his reaction?—it was to shake him, to throw his words back in his teeth, that she had embarked upon this preposterous path, wasn't it?

Shortly, wearing the gown and standing in front of the mirror, she stared with widening eyes at herself, wondering if she truly did have the nerve to appear in public in such a gown. The dress had not fit perfectly to begin with, but with a few expert tucks and stitches here and there Manuela had managed to rectify the problem, the black satin gown, what there was of it, now clinging like a second skin to Beth's slender curves.

A strumpet's gown indeed, Beth thought with a tiny choke of uneasy laughter. There was hardly any back at all, she decided with awe as she twirled in front of the mirror and glanced over her shoulder at the expanse of smooth magnolia flesh that met her eye. She was literally naked from the small puff sleeves at the soft shoulders to her waist, the black satin molding lovingly to her rounded buttocks before falling in a series of long ruffles to the floor. But the front—! A deep V, which started from underneath her breasts and ran to well below her navel, was made of a transparent scarlet gauze, and it contrasted vividly with the black satin of the remainder of the gown. The gown was definitely outrageous, the black satin cut so low as to leave her entire bosom bare except for the sheer scarlet gauze that was draped rather provocatively across her small breasts, the thrust of her nipples very apparent through the flimsy material. Her alabaster skin took on a rosy tone through the gauzy covering, which offered little in the way of protection, giving enticing glimpses of her midrift, navel, and flat stomach before it ended in a point just above decency.

Manuela clucked disapprovingly about her, and even Beth almost thought better of the idea, but then she remembered the exchange with Rafael and her jaw took on a mulish slant. A mistress, was she? Then it was certainly time she acted and looked the part!

She had even had Manuela apply cosmetics to her face, and her mouth was a pouting, bright scarlet blossom, the violet eyes seeming more mysterious and deeper in color between the darkened lashes, and the small black beauty-patch near the corner of her mouth just begged to be kissed. The silvery hair had been arranged in a graceful tangle of curls that cascaded from the top of her head to below her shoulders, and a small fringe of curls lay across her brow. Jewelry was the only thing that presented any trouble, as she longed for a pair of vulgar, glittering earrings, but having forgotten to ask Manuela to buy some of those also, she had to do without. All in all, she was well pleased with her scarlet-and-black gown and painted mouth—if a little nervous of Rafael's reaction.

Manuela was not at all pleased with Beth's appearance. Nearly wringing her hands in distress, she asked despairingly, "You are not going downstairs to dine looking like that, are you, señora?"

A strained smile on her mouth and a determined glint in the violet eyes that hid her own trepidations, Beth said with false calmness, "Of course! Why else did I have you buy the gown?" But, seeing the other woman was truly concerned, Beth said more gently, "Don't worry, Manuela, no blame can come to you—after all, I *ordered* you to buy the gown."

It was all very well to tell Manuela not to worry, Beth thought with disquietude a few minutes later as she somewhat gingerly descended the staircase on her way to the dining room, but it was something entirely different when she was on the point of meeting Rafael face to face. For a second she remembered with regret and a bit of cowardice the black, lacy shawl Manuela had nearly begged her to wear just as she had left the room. Now she wished she had, as she glanced down at the front of her dress. It really *was* indecent, she reflected with growing uneasiness. Perhaps she shouldn't have chosen this particular way to fling Rafael's words back in his face, and she seriously considered returning to her room and changing before it was too late. But the decision, whatever it might have been, was taken out of her hands when the door to the dining room opened and Rafael stepped out into the hall and saw her standing there on the steps.

He had come specifically for her. Waiting with Señora López in the main salon before dinner, Rafael had not thought too much about it; but as the first course was about to be served and she still had not put in an appearance, and also thinking of their earlier quarrel, he had decided cynically that she might be sulking in her room. He was on the point of finding her and removing her forcibly from its safety if that proved to be the case.

The first thing he noticed was the black velvet patch near the corner of her scarlet mouth, but then, as he crossed to stand at the foot of the stairs and looked up at her just a few steps above him, the full impact of the gown hit him. "Holy Mother of God!" he sighed irreverently as his eyes slid down the scarlet V, appreciating the alluring view it afforded. Immediately guessing what she was about, he found himself both furious and amused at the same time. *Little minx!* he thought with angry enjoyment of the spectacle she presented.

Her chin set at an antagonistic angle, she glared down at him, waiting with a fast-beating heart for his next move. When it appeared that he was leaving all the moves up to her, she asked with bravado, "Do you like it? I thought the gown rather appropriate for your opinion of me."

His amusement gone, he slanted a sardonic eyebrow upward and inquired in a harsh voice, "And you intended to announce to the world our relationship with this display? Is that what you had in mind?"

"Yes! And the word is *intend,* not intend*ed!"*

"Oh, but I beg to differ with you, *mi cara,"* he drawled insolently, his eyes flickering with the hard shine of desire as they roamed over her. "You're not going anywhere in that gown, except where it belongs... a bordello or a bedroom. Certainly I'm not going to have you offend Señora López by appearing in it, nor am I going to allow my servants to look upon what I consider my own."

"You can't stop me!" she hissed furiously, wary of the look on his face and the way his mouth had taken on a sensuous curve.

Rafael took two steps nearer to her, their faces level with each other, and, with his breath warm on her lips, he muttered, "Can't I? Shall we just—?" He stopped as his *mayordomo,* Paco, walked out into the hall.

Beth's body was blocked from his view and, not sensing the undercurrents that flowed between the other two, he announced apologetically, "The *aperitivo* is served, señor, señora."

Not looking at him, his eyes locked on Beth's, Rafael said carelessly, "Tell Señora López we will not be dining with her this evening. Give her our apologies."

"No!" Beth burst out, reading the hungry desire that flamed in Rafael's gray eyes.

Rafael suddenly grinned, "Oh, yes, *querida*. Oh, *yes!*" he said huskily, reaching out for her. "It's what you bought the gown for, after all."

"That's not true!" she cried indignantly, wondering bleakly if maybe she hadn't meant to provoke this sort of reprisal. But, unwilling to admit it even to herself, she started fighting back the instant Rafael's hands closed around her shoulders, struggling to escape his hold.

Rafael only laughed. And in front of Paco's amused, admiring eyes he swung her over his shoulder, ignoring the furious fists that pounded on his back and the wildly kicking legs and feet that pummeled the front of him, and then, turning to Paco, he said lightly, "The señora is not feeling well and I must put her to bed. You understand, *sí?*"

A wide smile on his brown face and a knowing gleam in the dark eyes, Paco nodded and said approvingly, "*Sí, señor, sí!*"

A muffled scream of pure rage was heard from Beth as, without another word, Rafael swung around and began climbing the stairs with her still slung over his shoulder like a piece of booty. Reaching the landing at the top of the stairs, instead of going in the direction of her room he went the opposite way, and Beth knew with a sinking heart and a deplorable quiver of desire in the pit of her stomach that he was taking her to his own room.

Determined to resist, even if it went against her own yearnings, she spat, "Put me down, you bastard!" and landed a particularly vicious blow somewhere near his ear as she wiggled and fought to gain her footing.

"What language for a lady, and from England at that! I am appalled by your lack of manners, English," Rafael teased, his amusement very obvious.

Stopping in front of a door some distance down the wide hall from her room, he opened it and walked inside. Crossing swiftly through what must have been a sitting room, Beth getting an upside-down view of a lush ruby carpet and the legs of chairs and a desk as he went through, he then pushed open a set of double doors that led to his bedchamber. With quick strides he approached a big bed with old-fashioned hangings of rich blue velvet and unceremoniously dumped Beth on it.

Grinning down at her, an odd light in his eyes, he murmured, "I've dreamed of you lying there often enough, but I find the reality far more agreeable than mere dreams."

"You'll regret this!" Beth promised recklessly, her silvery curls having come undone and tumbling in artless disarray around her lovely face.

Shrugging out of his *chaqueta* and tossing aside his white linen shirt, he said bluntly, "I doubt it! There is little if anything that I regret in my life, and *this* certainly won't trouble me, except..." He added wickedly, "if I didn't do it."

Fighting down the rising excitement that swirled betrayingly through her body, Beth looked around desperately for some way of escape. It was a huge, elegant room in which she found herself, a very masculine room, from the dark, heavy furniture and gold silk-hung walls to the rich jeweled tones of the Brussels carpet that covered the entire floor. There were three sets of double doors: One glass pair obviously led to a balcony like her own; another pair must lead to a connecting bedchamber, she decided thoughtfully; and the final set was the pair that they had just entered through. The sets of doors were made of carved mahogany, and from the appointments of the room and the size, Beth guessed that these must be the rooms that the master and mistress of the house would usually share. Rafael's almost naked body, his *calzoneras* the only piece of clothing still on him, blocked escape through the sitting room, and the balcony doors would do her little good. Eyeing the distance to the third set of doors, she edged cautiously toward the side of the bed. When Rafael undid the *calzoneras* and started to step out of them, she leaped from the bed and raced frantically toward what she prayed was escape.

Breathing hard, her heart thumping madly in her breast, she reached the doors and feverishly tugged on the crystal doorknobs—to no avail. From behind her Rafael said derisively, "They're locked, English."

She whirled about to face him, the wood cool against her back, her eyes wide and angry. He was entirely naked. Watching his arrogant approach mesmerized, she wondered distractedly why she had ever thought to get the better of him.

Rafael stopped directly in front of her, and with one hand he gently tipped her face up. His mouth touched hers lightly and he said against her lips, "It is such a lovely gown, I hate to ruin it—but the body it clothes is far more enticing." And before she had a chance to understand what he meant, a hand just above each breast, with one violent tug he ripped the gown right down the center, the remains falling silently to the floor, leaving Beth standing naked in front of him, the scarlet and black material a soft heap around her ankles.

For a long moment they stared wordlessly at each other, then with a low groan of desire Rafael swept her up into his arms and began carrying her toward the bed once again. The touch of his arms made her tremble with desire, but, unwilling to be defeated so easily, she suddenly exploded into a clawing, scratching little cat.

Unaware that her struggles inflamed rather than cooled his passion, Beth twisted and squirmed in the strong arms, her hands pushing and clawing futilely against his shoulders. She hadn't wanted this to happen—she had only wanted to defy him, to make him angry, and to exert herself in some way, to prove to him that she was not the docile, willing silly creature he thought. And yet her body was beginning to respond to the warm nearness of his, and she almost wept from the unfairness of it all.

Oblivious of anything but the soft, silken, thrashing body in his arms, blindly Rafael's mouth sought hers and found it. Hungrily he kissed her, the weeks he had been denied even the sight of her making his desire more urgent, more demanding, and now that she was in his arms he went a little mad with the exquisite feeling of her naked body next to him.

Even though her body betrayed her and in spite of the hot waves of yearning that were sweeping her, Beth still fought against him. With increasing languor she still sought to escape from his dark dominance, her hands pushing him away, her body accepting the caresses pressed upon it but never returning any, her mouth allowing him the intimacy he demanded but never giving.

Rafael wasn't so lost in his own pleasure that he wasn't aware of her resistance, useless though it might be. As the minutes passed and she continued to hold back from him, to deny him the eager willing submission that he wanted, he kissed her more fiercely, as if he would impart to her the same driving passion that flamed through his blood.

Once he would have taken her without compunction, caring only for his own satisfaction. But his relationship with Beth had come far since those days and, having known the joy of her surrender, the memory of their last night together vivid and dear in his mind, he hesitated. Suddenly tasting the salt of tears on his mouth, he raised his head and looked down at her.

Beth wasn't even conscious that she was crying. She only knew that it was agony to have him this near, to have his mouth and hands arousing emotions she had no control over, and yet know that he felt nothing but contempt for her. Her body might be on fire to know the black sorcery of his possession, but her mind and brain were writhing in anguish and torment.

His dark face looming above her, the gray eyes nearly black with passion, Rafael asked indistinctly, "English? Why do you weep? Have I hurt you?"

Her body looked very white against the deep blue of the coverlet, the fair hair like strands of spun silver splayed out across the velvet material, and with eyes that were pleading and stormy at the same time, Beth said thickly, "You hurt me every time you take me, thinking that I am a whore. Every time you touch me, thinking that I have lain with Lorenzo, that I would lay with Sebastian at any time, you hurt me."

His face tensed, and between them she could feel his passion dying. The full mouth thinned in quick blazing anger, Rafael retorted harshly, "And what else am I *to* think? It isn't as if I merely imagined you in Lorenzo's arms, is it? That particular affair I know for a fact!" Almost reluctantly he added, "With Sebastian I'll acquit you—even he admits that the relationship between the two of you was innocuous, and not from his want of trying to make it something else. But don't ask me to deny the proof of my own eyes."

Her throat aching with suppressed anger, the violet eyes darkening with emotion, Beth demanded hotly, "Am I supposed to be grateful that because Sebastian says I am innocent, you believe him? No, thank you!"

Catching him by surprise, she pushed him furiously away, and when he landed on his back on the bed beside her, she swiftly moved so that her body was half lying on his, her slender weight momentarily pinning him to the bed. The long, silvery hair brushing his chest and the taut breasts pushing distractingly against him, Beth asked mockingly, "What if I say Sebastian lies? Which one of us will you now believe?"

He frowned, the thick black eyebrows meeting in an uncertain scowl over his aquiline nose. Sebastian hadn't lied, of that he was certain, but not certain why. Fencing for time and suddenly very wary, he inquired, "Did he?"

Beth gave a little moan of frustration and her clenched fist beat unconsciously on Rafael's shoulder. "That's not the point! Don't your own instincts tell you anything? Didn't that day you found me with Lorenzo shock you? I know we had only met the one time, but didn't you find it strange that after refusing to meet you secretly—that such a short while later you should find me naked in the arms of another man? Didn't you ever wonder how Consuela knew exactly where to find us?" Sobbing quietly, the tears sliding unheeded down her pale cheeks, Beth's fist beating against him in a tatoo of pain and desperation, she cried half-hysterically, "Consuela planned it, you great bloody fool! She sent me a message, and like the green girl I was, hoping to avert a scandal and maybe set her mind at ease, I met her where she had said. She drugged me, Rafael!" Crying in earnest now, her breath coming in hiccuping little jerks, she said miserably, "It was in the tea—and she *paid* Lorenzo to be there! Between the two of them they planned it—she—she thought you were too interested in me at the Costa soiree, and she said that she wanted to make certain that you forgot about me, that I wouldn't be a threat to your marriage."

Rafael had stiffened when she first started speaking. When his face remained remote as she finished the sordid story, she looked at him with growing despair. "You don't believe me, do you?" she asked dully, defeat washing over her like a black, relentless tide.

Making no move to comfort her, although he had to fight bitterly against the urge to do so, he said flatly, "It's rather an improbable tale, isn't it? There was nothing in our marriage to save, and Consuela knew it, so I hardly see her going to the lengths that you claim she did. What would she gain from such a scheme? We had practically lived apart for years, and she knew how I felt about her."

Desperately taking another tack, she pleaded earnestly, "All right, forget that part of the story for now and tell me instead what you thought when you saw me that first time at the Costa soiree. Did I look like the kind of woman to betray her husband? When we danced, what did you think?"

As if the words were torn from him, he muttered, "I thought you were the loveliest creature I had ever seen—and you damn well know it! Why else did I follow you to the cloakroom, and why else did I try to get you to meet me somewhere private?" His eyes darkening like thunderclouds, he snarled, "But you had other plans, *querida,* didn't you? Plans that included an assignation, to be sure, but with Lorenzo!"

Anger suddenly rising like a flame through her body, she snapped furiously, "Of course, the fact that *you* were married didn't make any difference, did it? I am to be condemned for supposedly breaking my marriage vows, while for you it doesn't hold true? What sort of hypocrite are you, Rafael?"

An arrested expression flickering in the gray eyes, he admitted dryly, "The worst kind, it appears." And at Beth's look of open-mouthed astonishment, he grinned. "It's true," he said easily. "I'd already come to the conclusion that it wasn't so much the fact of your infidelity as it was the fact that you chose Lorenzo over me—I'd never liked him before, but seeing you two together made me literally *hate* him!"

"But I *didn't* choose Lorenzo!" Beth cried with real exasperation. "You just won't believe me, will you?" Through gritted teeth she said tightly, "Consuela *drugged* me! She *paid* Lorenzo to be there! And she *made certain* you knew where we were!" And, seeing the jeering disbelief creeping across his face, she said insistently, "Manuela was there. She'll tell you the truth. Go ask *her!*"

His mouth curved cynically. "Of course she will—she's your maid now, and I'm quite certain she would say whatever you told her to."

Beth drew in a gasp of fury. "You think I would involve my own servant in a lie?"

Rafael shrugged. "Why not? If you're lying yourself, making Manuela part of the lie is the most logical step."

"If I'm lying myself . . . !" Beth broke off, so infuriated she couldn't even speak. The violet eyes blazing with wrath and the soft red mouth taking on a grim line, she started to twist away from him, but Rafael swiftly clamped his arms around her and held her prisoner next to him.

"Be still!" he commanded as Beth began to thrash and fight to free herself. "I've listened to you—now you listen to me!" His eyes meeting hers steadily, he said tautly, "I only know what I saw that day—you and Lorenzo making love together. You claim Consuela drugged you and paid him to be there, and I'll concede that it could have happened that way, but I find it damned difficult to believe."

Her body stiff and unyielding near his, she shot out, "Why? Because Consuela was such a paragon of virtue? Or because you think I am a whoring little slut?"

Rafael bit off a curse under his breath and, throwing Beth down on the bed, he reversed their positions, his hands holding her arms prisoner one on either side of her head. "Neither!" he said sharply. "English, it is such an unlikely tale that I find it impossible to believe—especially knowing Consuela as I did. She was vicious—yes, I'll grant you that—but setting up the sort of trap you claim she did, I simply cannot accept. Consuela only did things if they benefited her, and no matter from which angle I view it I can see nothing that she could have gained from doing as you say."

Defeatedly, Beth looked away from the gray eyes and said in a low little voice, "Never mind. It doesn't matter anymore." Her eyes swung back to his and she smiled bitterly. "I am now also a liar, it seems."

That appeared to sting him for some reason, because his face darkened and the lean jawline went taut, a muscle bunching in his cheek. Roughly he murmured, "I don't know whether you are or not, I only know that when I have you in my arms, nothing else seems to matter, not your liaison with Lorenzo, not the possibility that you lie, nothing... except *this!*" And his mouth closed over hers, his lips warm and bruising as they searched hers.

With a muffled moan of despair and pleasure Beth fought him, but it was no use—she had lost every battle between them so far, and tonight was no exception. Despite her anger and crushing disappointment at the outcome of her confession of what had really happened that day in New Orleans, despite all that had gone before, she discovered with a stunning surprise that she loved him—perhaps loved even the very traits that made it impossible for him to believe her. And loving him, even knowing he didn't believe her, she wanted him as passionately as it appeared he wanted her. The weeks he had been gone, her body had yearned for his touch, and now with him pressing intimately against her naked skin, his hands traveling over her body with sweet torment, she couldn't deny him. She was in Rafael's arms and his hands and mouth were envoking a response she couldn't control any longer. Almost with a will of their own, her arms slipped around his strong neck, one small hand caressing and cradling his dark head as it moved over her body, his mouth like a burning brand of desire wherever it touched. A bittersweet craving for his body curled languidly through her until Rafael's half-savage, half-tender lovemaking ignited a blazing need that matched his own.

He gave her no chance to think, no chance to escape him, his mouth taking hers and forcing an instinctive response from deep within her—she loved him and she could no more deny him or the wants of her own body than she could stop breathing. Having lost the battle with herself, she was generous in defeat, her mouth, her body, her arms, every fiber of her being reacting eagerly and excitingly to the sensuous assault Rafael made upon her.

At Beth's capitulation, what little control he had over himself vanished, and with a low sigh of unabashed pleasure Rafael slid between her thighs and lost himself in the enveloping, welcoming satin warmth. Passionately his mouth searched hers as slowly his body moved on hers, his hands cupping her buttocks, pulling her even closer to him if that were possible.

Nearly delirious with desire, Beth ardently accepted the warm invasion of Rafael's body, her own reveling in the feeling of him buried deep within her. And when he began to move gently against her, his tormentingly slow and tantalizing languid thrusts in direct contrast to the molten passion that she knew intuitively was scalding through his veins, she arched eagerly to meet the rise and fall of his hips, wanting the overwhelming release that only he could give her.

Trembling with the force of the tangled emotions that coursed through his body, Rafael could hardly bear the exciting torture of Beth's movements beneath him. Feeling his hot seed rising within him, urgently he increased the tempo of their bodies. The parting and meeting of their flesh became almost frenzied as they both sought to prolong the sweetness of their joining, yet each wanted the shattering pleasure that heralded complete fulfillment. Desperately Rafael fought down the almost overpowering urge to release himself within the velvet softness of her, holding himself back by sheer willpower until he knew that she too would be satisfied. Feeling the throbbing jump her body gave a second later and hearing the soft moan of pleasure she couldn't control, his own body reacted instantly, and with an animallike growl deep in his throat, he too experienced the exquisite, exploding pleasure that was bursting through her body.

CHAPTER TWENTY-FIVE

The room was silent except for their labored breathing, and as their bodies gradually assumed a more normal state, even that ceased to be heard. Rafael did not immediately withdraw. Instead, his body still pressing against hers, he propped himself up on one elbow and, with something that could have been tenderness, he stared down at Beth's flushed features.

Embarrassed, even now, even after all they had shared together, Beth looked away from his steady gaze, wondering bleakly how she could love him and yet almost hate him at the same time. Having gotten over the first shock of acknowledging her love for him, she accepted it as she had so many things in her life. But, unlike other events, this one she treasured despite the pain she knew it would bring. For whatever reasons, no matter how mad and insane it might be, *she loved Rafael Santana!*

I always have, she thought with a start, ever since I saw him at the Costa ball. No, that isn't true, the more practical side of her nature countered—been attracted to, dreamed about, and hungered after, but not loved...not until now.

The touch of Rafael's fingers on her chin startled her and, wide-eyed, her gaze instantly swung back to his dark face above her. A crooked smile curved his mouth and he murmured, "Come back. You had gone far away from me."

Unable to help herself, she inquired with sudden bitterness, "How can you say so, when your body holds mine prisoner?"

His eyes hardened, but he said quietly, "Yes, I have

your body, but I want your mind too. You were very far away from me—what were you thinking of?"

Some of the bitterness seeping away, she replied honestly, "The Costa ball and the first time we saw each other."

"It started there, didn't it," he stated rather than questioned. "This thing between us, this thing that neither of us wanted or wants, and yet it exists and has since that moment."

Astonished that he would admit such a thing, Beth stared up at him open-mouthed. In a small uncertain voice she asked, "You feel it too?"

His face taking on a sardonic expression, he shifted his body slightly so that now he lay next to her, and said, "Why not? If I didn't feel something for you I wouldn't have reacted the way I did when I found you with Lorenzo, nor would I have been so furious and delighted at the same time when I saw you again at Cielo."

It was as much as he was willing to admit to at the moment, but his words gave Beth a shivery feeling of anticipation. She swallowed with difficulty and, her heart beating with thick painful strokes, she got out, "And what do we do about it?"

His fingers tightening fractionally on her chin and his eyes on her mouth, he admitted softly, "I don't know. Shall we just take each day as it comes and see what happens?"

"I-I-I don't know," Beth answered truthfully. A troubled expression on her face, she added, "I wouldn't like being your mistress. Don't you think it will be rather futile for us to continue as we are—you thinking me a liar and an adulteress and me—" Beth stopped abruptly, realizing how very nearly she had come to confessing that she loved him.

"And you what?" Rafael questioned, the gray eyes now looking at her with a considering glint deep in their depths.

Beth bit her lip and glanced away. "Nothing." Almost with anguish she blurted out, "I should go back to Natchez."

Mention of her possible departure from his life staggered him, and with eyes gone suddenly dark with some undefinable emotion, as if the words were torn from him, he said in a low voice, "Stay, English. Stay and let us pretend that the past never existed and that we have only the future to look forward to." His eyes left her face and, gazing on some point far away, he added, "I won't force you to come to me, at least," he admitted slowly, "not right away. But give us time to find out what this thing is that exists between us, and give *me* time to reconcile what you have told me with what I have seen and heard."

Beth took a deep breath, wanting to give him the time that he asked for and yet terrified that the longer they were together the more deeply in love with him she would fall, and the more likely it was that he would find out that she had been foolish enough to fall in love with him. What power over her that would give him!

Seeing the indecision in her face, he suddenly pulled her to him and kissed her deeply, tenderly, hungrily, and Beth, unable to help herself, melted into him. "Stay," he murmured against her mouth. "Stay and let the future take care of itself. Will you?"

Dumbly Beth nodded her head, incapable of denying him anything. He kissed her again, a kiss that was meant to be light and gentle but that flared instantly into passion, and together they were swept up in the sensual world of physical desire.

It was very late, not too many hours before dawn, when Rafael dressed and, wrapping Beth in an enveloping robe of his, swiftly carried her down the darkened hallway to her own room. Setting her down gently at the doorway, he kissed her again lingeringly, and said half teasingly, half seriously, "I'll try not to compromise you further until we come to some decision. Tonight will have to last me...for a while."

Bemusedly Beth watched him disappear in the darkness. Exhausted from his lovemaking as well as her own turbulent feelings, she entered her room and gratefully sank down on her own bed. Sleep came quickly, and tonight for the first time in months she slept soundlessly, no dreams, no guilt, no nightmares haunting her.

For Rafael, though, there was no sleep. Lying in the emptiness of his bed, longing for the warmth of Beth's small shape next to him, he stared blindly into space. He had taken the first steps down the road to a commitment he still fought against. And yet when it would have been so simple to deny the attraction that existed between them he had admitted it. Worse, he had even begun to wonder if perhaps she hadn't told the truth about what had happened that afternoon in New Orleans. And if she had told the truth . . . With a curse he sat up in bed and, flicking the light covering aside, he left the bed and prowled about the room naked as the day he was born.

Standing at the glass doors that led out onto the small balcony, he gazed unseeingly at the vivid rays of daylight streaking across the horizon. A cold man, not so much by nature as due to the events that had formed him, he found it inconceivable that one woman could smash down all the icy barriers he had erected to protect himself against pain and disillusionment. With those crumbling with every passing hour, he found himself feeling as vulnerable as a foolish love-stricken youth of sixteen. With others he would always be cool and aloof, but with English he was helpless, wanting her, needing her . . . loving her?

He balked at that. No. I will not *love* her, his mind coldly dictated, but his heart rebelled, wanting to let the sweetness and warmth that Beth represented to come flooding through his body and to drive out the iciness that was with him always.

The battle raged unceasingly within him—had she told the truth or hadn't she? Did it matter? Would she betray him in the future? Had there been other lovers? Did it matter?

Confused, his emotions battered raw by the battle raging within him, he finally sought his bed, nothing clear in his mind except that he wanted Beth to stay. Let time show him the way . . . and the truth.

As the days passed Beth wondered if he had come to believe her. Certainly his actions toward her were quite different. If she had been older or wiser, or if she had been allowed to have her season in London instead of being rushed into marriage with the first eligible young man who appeared on the scene, she would have realized that she was being courted.

It was there in everything that Rafael did, whether either of them realized it or not, from the agreeable excursions he planned especially for her enjoyment to the small and thoughtful gifts that were so often and unexpectedly dropped in her lap—an expensive bar of delicately perfumed soap, a beautifully shaped and carved comb for her hair, a box of sweetmeats, a pair of gloves.

Except for the odd fact that she was living in his house with only his distant cousin for chaperon, Rafael did everything that a courting man would do, his manner to her unfailingly polite and courteous. Not once did he put her in an embarrassing situation or take undue liberties. Except that he couldn't control his eyes, and it happened frequently that Beth's gaze would meet his and she would see the hungry desire that burned steadily in their gray depths and her heart would begin to race.

That he denied himself made her love him even more, for so easily he could have forced her, so easily he could have discreetly continued to visit her rooms, or have made private assignations where she would have been unable to refuse. But he didn't, although the desire to do so was very apparent in his eyes and the way his glance lingered on her mouth or soft shoulders.

For Beth it was one of the happiest times of her life. The man she loved was always near and attentive and the future had begun to look very bright indeed. The thought of returning to Natchez receded and she had even begun to believe that Rafael might seriously be thinking of marriage.

She and Rafael had been cautious with one another at first, each treading very carefully, each not wanting to be the one to destroy the growing relationship between them, each conscious of the past and the pitfalls that it represented. And as the days had gone by, sunny, warm, and beautiful, so had their association ripened, their conversation more easy, more relaxed, their knowledge of the other growing and widening.

Rafael was for the first and only time in his life held enthralled by a woman. The bitter edge that had been heard so often in his voice was missing, and he found that there were other ways to enjoy a woman—the pleasure of seeing Beth's enchanting smile flit across her face, or the ways her eyes glistened with delight when he did something that particularly pleased her, the sound of her laughter or the way she walked, all added to his enslavement. And yet he hesitated to make that final commitment, frightened that the English who smiled at him so captivatingly and who filled his heart with delight was a mirage, that one day she would betray him. Grimly he refused to think of that afternoon in New Orleans, wanting to believe Beth and willing for the present relentlessly to submerge the cold cynic in him who disbelieved *anything* a woman said. It wasn't an easy task for him to put aside years of distrust and contempt for the female sex, but gradually, as the weeks passed, almost imperceptibly he did, Beth's warm and gentle influence softening and mellowing the hardness, the icy indifference that was so much a part of him.

The taming of Renegade Santana was watched with awe by half of San Antonio, and by the middle of June everyone was expecting the announcement of their marriage. The side of him the population had seen these past weeks had caused more than one to revise their opinion of him and to remind themselves that the name "Renegade" had been given to him in his wild youth. Certainly he seemed a changed man—still an unpredictable, dangerous man to be sure, still that aura of coolness and savagery about him, but changed, less forbidding, more approachable.

Old Abel Hawkins's house in San Antonio rang with the laughter of guests these days, as the Mavericks, Juan Seguín, a Mexican aristocrat who had sided with the Texans in their war for independence, and his family, José Antonio Navarro, another Mexican who had done the same, as well as the slim, steely-eyed Jack Hays and other prominent members of San Antonio came to call and visit. There were meals held *al fresco* on the spacious grounds at the rear of the house and riding parties to fill the days, the ladies taking Beth to their hearts, the gentlemen finding Rafael a man with a great deal of charisma when he chose to display it.

Beth bloomed like a slender, white rosebud opening eagerly to the warm sunlight. Slanting her an appreciative glance as they returned one day from an early morning ride, Rafael decided he had never seen her in such looks. The violet eyes sparkled with pleasure, the alabaster skin glowed with vitality, and even her slender shape seemed to have blossomed, her breasts seeming fuller, her hips more alluringly rounded in the slim-fitting riding habit she wore. His eyes stopped their interested appraisal as he felt himself harden with desire and, looking at her lovely face to keep his mind off the delectable body that haunted his nights, he noticed a slight frown marring her forehead, a frown he had noticed more than once the past three days or so. Frowning himself, he asked abruptly, "Is anything wrong? Has the heat been too much for you?"

Beth sent him a strained little smile. "No. It is just that I am not feeling too well this morning and I should probably have remained in bed instead of coming on this ride."

Señora López, who was of course chaperoning them, examined Beth with concern. "You are not sickening with another attack of the fever, are you?" she asked worriedly.

"No, I'm certain of that. It must be just a little upset stomach from all those deliciously spicy dishes I have been eating lately," Beth replied easily, and eager to change the subject, she said quickly, "Oh, look at those lovely pink flowers over there on the hill! What are they?"

Easily diverted, Señora López looked in the direction of Beth's pointing finger and said, "Those clumps there? That's mountain pink, they're quite common in this area."

The conversation went on from there, and for the rest of the day Beth was careful to keep her expression carefree and to act as if she hadn't a worry in the world. But unfortunately it was all a clever performance, because she very definitely *did* have a worry.

Alone in her room that night, she sat on her bed

biting her lower lip and tried to remember the exact date of something that shouldn't have slipped her mind. Not since Nathan's death, in March, she thought with a queer little flutter in the region of her heart. She'd had too much to concern her these past months to keep track of such a simple natural thing as her body's womanly functions, but now, thinking of the queasiness that had attacked her the last five mornings in a row, she was forced to think about it. Not since March, she thought again, torn between a rising thrill of excitement and sheer terror.

Slipping from her bed and lighting a small whale-oil lamp, she walked over to stand in front of the cheval glass mirror. With trembling hands she lifted the fine lawn nightgown she wore and, laying it aside with wondering eyes, she examined her slender body. No doubt about it, her breasts *were* fuller, and she had noticed already that some of her gowns were too tight in the waist. There were no other outward signs to prove or disprove her growing suspicions, her stomach as flat as ever...but weren't her hips just the tiniest bit wider, almost as if already they were accommodating the growth of...

Unable to complete the thought, with shaking fingers she slipped her gown back on, put out the light, and scrambled back in bed. She was just being foolish! Just because April, May, and part of June had passed without— She cut her mind away to something else, fighting the obvious conclusion and yet aware of a warm feeling of wonder.

The next morning she was embarrassingly and thoroughly ill and could not deny the evidence of her own eyes and mind. She was going to have Rafael's child!

With a mixture of joy and horror, like someone in a daze, Beth allowed Manuela to dress her. The thought of having a child of her own was a rapturous one until reality intruded and shattered her growing exhilaration and pleasure.

What in Heaven's name was she to do? Tell Rafael immediately? Nervously pacing her room that afternoon, she decided the answer to that question was *no*, and for two very good reasons. They had come so far these past weeks in their relationship with one another that she wanted *nothing* to disrupt it. No matter what eventually happened, she was determined the outcome would be based on their feelings for one another, *not* the advent of a child. If she told him and he instantly offered marriage, she would never be quite certain whether it was because of the child or because he had at last fallen in love with her. There would always be a nagging doubt about his motivations. And if she told him and he didn't offer marriage...

Strangely enough, the disgrace and social disapproval she would face never gave Beth a qualm. All her worries and fears centered around the father of her unborn child. What would he think? And God in Heaven, when or how was she to tell him?

It was a long tension-fraught day for Beth. At least a half a dozen times she almost threw caution to the winds and requested a word alone with Rafael and told him. But, wanting desperately to be loved and married for herself alone, if he even offered marriage, she held back. *I'll wait another week,* she decided anxiously as she lay in bed that night. *Then if nothing is changed between us I'll...what? Tell him and take my chances or slink away like a beaten dog to lick my wounds?* She found no answer in her fevered twistings and turnings, and the next morning there were purple smudges under the violet eyes and a shadow in their depths.

Despite the signs of a restless night showing in her eyes, Beth looked lovely as she entered the dining room wearing a becoming gown of black dimity with bell sleeves. Staring at her as she greeted Señora López and then turned to smile good morning to him, Rafael felt pulses leap and his entire body respond just to the sight of her. It was such exquisite torture to have her so near him, to have her smiling and laughing with him, to have learned so much about her and yet be denied the one thing that was missing from their relationship with each other. *A platonic man I am not,* he thought sardonically as his eyes unconsciously caressed her lips and breasts, and he knew that no matter what he had promised he wasn't going to be able to keep his hands off her very much longer.

As a matter of fact, not more than several hours longer, as it turned out. He hadn't deliberately planned it, but it happened that he and Beth were alone that evening as they walked in the moonlight near the creek at the rear of the house, Señora López busy with her needlework in the front salon.

Rafael had noticed the faint air of strain about Beth and, remembering the frowns of the past few days as they walked companionably in the silver light of the moon, the creek gurgling pleasantly near their feet, he asked abruptly, "Are you happy here, English?"

Beth looked up at him in surprise, her thoughts on their unborn child and the knowledge that she must tell him sooner or later. Honesty compelled her to answer, "I am not *un*happy here, but—" Her eyes darkening with pain, she finished, "I have to admit that San Antonio will always hold unpleasant memories for me. Nor can I forget that my... that Nathan was killed here."

Rafael muttered something violent under his breath. Nathan was one subject that they avoided, partly because Beth could not bring herself to explain her odd marriage and partly because Rafael still couldn't control the fierce jealousy that surged through his body whenever he thought of the years that Nathan had known her sweetness and the many nights of tender passion the other man must have experienced in her arms. But her answer disturbed him on a more immediate plane and frowning he inquired, "Don't you like the Republic?"

Glad to have the subject changed slightly, she replied easily, "Some of it. Especially the pine forests. When we traveled through them I thought they were so cool and inviting."

Her answer pleased him and, an odd glitter in the smoky-gray eyes, he asked, almost demanding, "Could you make your home there?"

It was for Rafael very thin ice, and if Beth hadn't been so distracted by the certainty that she was carrying his child, she might have realized it and pressed her advantage; but as it was, the significance of his question passed her by. Abstractedly she said, "Oh, I suppose so. Anywhere can be home if one wants it to be."

They had stopped their perambulations near a tangled mass of greenery that hid them from the house, and both stood staring silently for some seconds at the silver sparkle of the water in the moonlight. Each was lost in thought, each vacillating on the edge of decision, and almost simultaneously they both turned to the other, intending to speak.

Taking her courage in both hands Beth looked up at the dark lean face above hers, the moonlight hiding the expression in the gray eyes and intensifying the harshness of his features. "Rafael...I'm—" She stopped, unable to make such an announcement without any warning. Swallowing with difficulty, she sought anxiously for some beginning that would allow her to lead up to the subject of the baby gradually, something that would give him an inkling of what was coming.

She was very beautiful in the moonlight, her eyes appearing purple and mysterious, the fair hair picking up the rays of moonlight that spilled over them and the words that he had been going to speak died in his throat at her sheer loveliness. His eyes locked compulsively on the soft mouth just below his and, not thinking, like a man in a daze, he pulled her into his arms and his mouth unerringly found hers.

It had been madness to kiss her, and he knew it the moment his lips touched hers, for the passion that had been so rigidly suppressed these past weeks suddenly exploded through his body and he was blind to anything but the soft, yielding shape in his arms. His arms tightened around her, crushing her breasts against his chest and forcing her hips hard against him as his mouth urgently explored hers, his tongue hungrily tasting and devouring the sweetness to be found between her lips.

Beth gave herself gladly to his almost brutal embrace, relishing the nearly painful pleasure of having his arms crush her to him, the ache of desire that swirled through her body as his mouth continued its almost savage attack against hers. Savage and yet not savage as his lips moved from her mouth to her eyes to her mouth again and then dropped lower to teasingly kiss the tops of her breasts showing above the low-cut gown she had changed into for the evening.

If Rafael had longed to have her in his arms again, so had she longed to be there once more, again to know the sweet torment of his possession, again to feel that tall, hard body take hers and give her again the wild passionate release that only he could. He had taught her body the joy of passion, and she as much as he had yearned for the intoxicating kisses and the hungry joining of their bodies that they had shared in the past.

On her own accord her arms clasped ardently around his strong brown neck, her body arching up against him as they strained nearer to one another, desire flicking through their veins, each as lost to their surroundings as the other. Even when his searching hand freed one breast and began to caress it, Beth was blind to everything but the fact that his mouth was on hers and that his body was pressed sensuously next to hers. Through their clothing she could feel him hard and throbbing with desire, and with something like frustration she unconsciously curved her body even closer, driving Rafael nearly insane with the need to lose himself in her silken flesh.

Señora López's voice calling them from the house was like a dash of icy water, and Rafael was uncertain whether to thank the woman or march over to her and strangle her on the spot.

Lifting his mouth from Beth's, he shouted back, "We'll be right there. Señora Ridgeway was just admiring the creek in the moonlight."

Feeling she had done her duty, Señora López turned away and, with a smile, went back to her needlework. Ah, to be young and in love, she thought dreamily.

Silently Rafael straightened Beth's dress, his fingers lingering on the soft breast as he pulled the gown over it. Glancing down at her flushed features, he said thickly, "It's just as well she called, because if she hadn't, in another minute I would have tumbled you on the ground and proven to myself that I am not the eunuch I have played these last weeks."

Her body still on fire for his, Beth could only nod weakly, wishing rather shamefully that Señora López had waited several minutes longer before interrupting them. Sighing as much for the lost opportunity to tell him of the child as for the abrupt and unsatisfactory end to their lovemaking, Beth walked with him to the house.

Several of the men from Enchantress, along with a lengthy report from Renaldo, arrived the next morning just as they were finishing the morning meal. Rafael excused himself, explaining that he would probably be busy for the entire day—could the ladies amuse themselves? Beth welcomed the respite, glad of the unexpected chance to have several hours to herself in which to collect her increasingly jumbled thoughts.

Rafael was both pleased and displeased by the arrival of the men from Enchantress—pleased about the progress Renaldo wrote of and displeased that it interrupted his time with Beth. It proved, as he had suspected, to be a busy day for him. He had to order supplies, implements, and miscellaneous items that Renaldo had requested. There was even more to be sent out this time than the first because now, with the men's quarters completed, their familes would be joining them. It proved to be a long, exhausting day for him, and it was almost dusk before he returned to the house.

The day had stretched endlessly before Beth once Rafael had left the house, and for a few minutes she wandered uncertainly from room to room before deciding to enjoy the warmth of the morning sun before the day grew too hot. Leaving Señora López to her seemingly endless needlework, Beth walked outside and sat down in a comfortable chair at the edge of the rear courtyard, her body half-shaded by a huge, old cottonwood tree. Blankly she stared down at the creek where she and Rafael had walked the previous night, her thoughts very much on the child and the need to make some final decision. I'm such a coward, she mused angrily. Just tell him! When he comes home this afternoon, ask to see him in the study alone and tell him. It would be so easy. It was what she *should* do, she knew, and yet her heart wanted the reassurance of his love—first! Not afterward, if it came at all. Even now, in spite of the growing bond between them, she wasn't certain of the depth of his feelings, and she dreaded the possibility that her confession would bring back the snarling, sardonic man who had greeted her that dawn at Cielo. He might love her—her heart believed that he did—but then again, he might just want her body. It was a depressing thought, one that she instantly dismissed.

She sat there for quite some time. The day was becoming hot and, deciding to seek the coolness of the house, Beth had just risen to her feet when she heard the sound of many horses at the front of the house and the sound of several voices. Paco's she recognized, but not the harsh autocratic bark of the other, and then she thought she heard Don Miguel's voice as if he were soothing and attempting to placate someone. Apparently it did no good, because the harsh voice broke out in an impassioned denunciation in rapid Spanish that Beth couldn't follow, only the tone. Señora López's voice was heard briefly too, but she was drowned out by the curt commands thrown out by the hard voice.

Curious, she made her way to the house and wasn't at all surprised to be met by Señora López, an expression of vexation and anxiety on her face.

"Ah, Señora Beth, come quickly to the front veranda!" the Spanish woman cried distractedly when she saw Beth.

Wary and just a little uneasy, Beth followed the other woman, not hurrying and yet not exactly dragging her feet either. Entering the main hall, she became aware of the bustle that seemed to have overtaken the house as two maidservants with harassed expressions scurried up the stairs, four menservants quickly following them with what looked suspiciously like her trunks. She stared up after them in amazement for a second and then turned her gaze toward the front of the house.

The white double front doors were open to their fullest extent, with Paco, a sullen expression on his usually smiling face, standing somewhat helplessly near the entrance. Looking out across the wide veranda Beth was startled to see a veritable cavalcade of mounted Spaniards.

As her bewildered gaze traveled over the dozen or

so men, she recognized only Don Miguel, appearing embarrassed and uncomfortable, and Lorenzo, a pleased expression on his dark face. The others were all strangers, all well-armed *vaqueros*...except one—the slim, aquiline-nosed old man in the center of the group.

Astride a magnificent black stallion, the saddle and bridle artfully worked with silver that glittered and sparkled in the hot sunlight, he sat on the restive, spirited animal with all the arrogance and pride of a conquistador. His black sombrero was heavily embellished with silver embroidery work, as well as the ruby cloth *chaqueta* and the black *calzoneras* he wore. Wicked-looking silver spurs jutted out from fine leather boots, and the hands that held the reins of the big stallion so effortlessly were covered in black leather gloves.

Self-importance and superciliousness fairly radiated from him, and haughtily he stared back at Beth, making no move to dismount, to greet her, or even to politely doff his sombrero in acknowledgment of her presence. The lined and seamed face still bore evidence of the strikingly handsome man he must have been once, but it also showed cruelty and selfishness in the curve of the thin mouth beneath a slim drooping mustache and the set of the arrogant chin. His eyes were black, black as ebony, and showed as much emotion as a reptile's as they moved insolently over Beth's slender shape. In a heavily accented voice he demanded in English, "You are the Señora Ridgeway?"

Beth stiffened, liking neither the tone nor the way his eyes traveled over her, assessing her as if she were an animal to be bought. Nor did she like being questioned by rude strangers. From Paco's sullenness to Don Miguel's uncomfortable expression and the fact that no move was being made to dismount, it was also apparent that this overbearing creature had refused to enter the house. Treating him with the same contempt he did her, she nodded curtly and asked crisply, "And you—who might you be?"

One thin, arrogantly arched eyebrow rose. "I?" he said in surprise as if it were incomprehensible that she didn't know him. "I am Don Felipe."

CHAPTER TWENTY-SIX

So this was the terrifying and autocratic Don Felipe! thought Beth as she regarded him through hastily lowered lashes. What a cold, imperious face he has, she mused silently; even his mustache seems to curl with contempt for his fellow man.

It was not only his face that showed his imperiousness but his manner as well. The reptilian black eyes never leaving her face, he informed her harshly, "The servants have been ordered to pack your things. It is not proper, I think, for you to reside in my grandson's house with only Señora López as chaperon. And as I and the other members of my family will not dirty our feet by stepping inside the house of Abel Hawkins, you will come with us this afternoon." As Beth stared at him with stunned fury, he added condescendingly, "Doña Madelina is waiting for you at the hacienda the family uses whenever there is need to remain overnight in San Antonio."

Swallowing the hot retort that sprang to her lips, Beth opened her eyes very wide and queried sweetly, "Even your grandson, Rafael?"

Don Felipe's thin lips tightened. "No! He prefers to flaunt his plebeian blood and stay in the house of a *gringo* trapper!" He snarled and, throwing his son a speaking glance, he added, "I was greatly offended to discover that there are others in my family who think differently—but rest assured it shall not happen again!" He finished loftily, "But that has nothing to do with you—you will come with us. A coach is behind us, and you will have just enough time to prepare yourself for departure before it arrives." When Beth started to protest angrily, he glared at her and thundered, "And I will have no argument out of you—I do not have the time to waste exchanging comments with a woman."

Beth took a deep breath, fighting furiously to control her blazing temper. Her chin held at a defiant angle, she met Don Felipe's black-eyed stare and said coolly, "Thank you very much for your kind offer, but I prefer to stay where I am. If *I* decide it is not proper for me to remain here, then I shall remove myself to a hotel." Scornfully she finished, "You may intimidate the other members of your family, but you don't particularly impress me!"

The black eyes narrowed and a mirthless smile cracked across the old face. "She has spirit," he said approvingly, as if Beth were not standing there. "A certain amount of spirit is a good thing in a woman—she should breed spirited sons worthy of the Santana name." Almost as an afterthought he tacked on, "A pity, however, that she is a *gringo,* but she should do well enough. At least her father is a lord, although I could have wished for a duke."

Beth's gasp of outrage and astonishment was lost as one of her trunks and a small valise was carried past her by Rafael's servants. The servants looked uncomfortable and uncertain, and it was apparent that while they resented and objected to being ordered about by this arrogant old man, they were too frightened not to obey him. Not so Beth. The violet eyes glittering with rage, Beth burst out angrily, "Now wait just one damn minute!—put those things down!—I am not going anywhere!" With quick, furious strides she crossed the veranda and stood on the second step, glaring at Don Felipe. "You have no right, first of all, to order about servants not your own!" she raged. "And secondly and most importantly, you have absolutely *no* authority over me! So you can just forget any idea you might have had of removing me from this house!"

Don Felipe, thinking it was as well that he had made plans for her foolish stubbornness, looked her up and down. Obviously she was not going to accept his orders meekly and climb sedately into the coach when it arrived, so it would have to be the other way—and with an expression of boredom on his proud face he flicked a couple of fingers, and before Beth had any idea of what was happening, she found herself swept off the steps and held prisoner in front of Lorenzo. His horse shied a little at the unexpected addition of her weight, and the high saddlehorn bit into her hip as furiously she wiggled about, struggling to escape Lorenzo's brutal hold.

Don Miguel, who had remained a silent, slightly sullen observer as his father dominated the scene, suddenly spoke up, objecting angrily at the unanticipated event, but a sharp rejoinder in rapid Spanish from his father caused him to subside in embarrassed silence. He threw Beth a look of commiseration and apology, but made no effort to stop what was virtually an abduction, and Beth realized in that instant that Don Miguel would always give in to a stronger man.

Don Felipe, ignoring Beth's muttered animadversions and her obvious attempts to free herself from Lorenzo, snapped something to Paco and Señora López, which Beth later learned was a message to Rafael as to her whereabouts and instructions for the removal of the remainder of her possessions. Then, with a signal to his men, he turned his horse away and the entire group immediately followed, leaving Paco and Señora López dazed as they stood on the veranda watching Beth's bright head disappear in the cloud of dust made by the horses' hooves.

Barely a second later Paco sent a servant hurrying around town trying to locate Señor Rafael and relate to him what had happened, while Señora López and Manuela began the necessary preparations for the removal to the hacienda where Beth had been taken. Don Felipe had graciously informed them that when the coach arrived they were to accompany Beth's various trunks, as well as their own, to the hacienda.

It never occurred to Señora López to do otherwise, although she may have thought Don Felipe rather high-handed in his actions. As for Manuela, she was only a servant and had even less to say about matters than Señora López, and so with a troubled expression she began to pack Señora Beth's belongings, wondering uneasily what the outcome of this day would be.

Knowing it was useless, as well as undignified, to keep fighting, Beth eventually stopped her struggles and subsided into a tight-lipped furious silence as the town disappeared behind them. The sun beat down on her uncovered head, and they hadn't gone a mile before she had the beginnings of a severe headache—a headache brought on as much by indignant temper as the blazing sun.

Don Miguel maneuvered his horse near Lorenzo's and apologetically he murmured to Beth, "I am so sorry this had to happen, *cara*, but my father is a stubborn old man. He is not always polite or conventional, and unfortunately he has lived all his life doing as he pleases."

Unencouragingly Beth retorted, "And I suppose it never occurred to anyone to defy him? Why didn't you do anything to stop him back there? You could have, you know."

Don Miguel wouldn't meet her eyes. Instead he cleared his throat uncomfortably and said in a low voice, "The habits of a lifetime are difficult to break, señora. I obey him because I have been trained to do so. He does not tolerate defiance of his dictates—I have found life much easier when I do what he wants rather than rebel. I may disagree with him, but I cannot bring myself to go against his wishes."

"I see," Beth murmured slowly, strongly aware again of the weakness that his charm had hidden from her. Don Miguel *was* a charming man, but, unlike his father and his son, he would always defer to a more powerful personality. Looking at him with new eyes, she said suddenly, "I wonder that you dared to marry Rafael's mother."

He flushed and replied stiffly, "That has nothing to do with this."

Accepting the snub, Beth stared ahead at the ears of Lorenzo's horse, very conscious of Lorenzo's hard chest at her side, and the wiry-muscled arms that encompassed her. She could feel his breath on her neck and she knew he was holding her tighter than strictly necessary. Beth glanced up at him, intending to rebuke him for the sly intimacies he was taking, but, meeting those black eyes and seeing the hot flame of desire that burned in their depths, she looked quickly away.

As they traveled farther away from San Antonio, Don Miguel kept his horse by their side, while Don Felipe rode at the head of the cavalcade like a returning king at the head of his army. Since signaling for her capture, Don Felipe had neither looked at Beth nor addressed any talk her way. He was not one to waste words—especially on a woman.

But Don Miguel, essentially a gentle man and a kind one, was greatly troubled by what had occurred and, looking at Beth's set face, he said softly, "Señora Beth, try not to think too harshly of me. My father is right about one thing—it really was not exactly proper for you to remain in San Antonio with only Señora López to protect your good name. Doña Madelina and I were very remiss in thinking otherwise—as my father somewhat scathingly pointed out. We should have taken you with us when we returned to Cielo, or remained in San Antonio until . . ." He stopped abruptly, unwilling to say more.

A dangerous sparkle in her eyes, Beth prompted, "Until what?" And when Don Miguel seemed disinclined to tread on shaky ground, she demanded, "Where did your father get the ridiculous idea that I am to 'breed Santana sons'? And I would like very much to know by what right he inquired into my family background."

Don Miguel looked even more uncomfortable and embarrassed. "It is my fault," he finally confessed. Staring earnestly into Beth's decidedly unfriendly features, he said sincerely, "It was presumptuous of me, I know, but I wrote to my father telling him about you and of my hopes that you and my son would make a match of it. It was a mistake, I can see that now—I never expected my father to interfere in this manner." His eyes almost begging for forgiveness, he continued in a nearly inaudible tone, "You are so sweet and lovely, and it seemed that Rafael was not immune to your charms. It would have solved so many things—you would not return to Natchez a widow, and my son perhaps at last would have found happiness." Don Miguel sighed.

"When I wrote to my father, I had forgotten how very ruthless he can be when he has set his mind on something. He has long wanted Rafael to remarry, and when I wrote him about you, he instantly seized upon it—especially when, through a friend at the British consul in Mexico City, he was able to confirm your background."

Beth maintained a stony silence, but her earlier anger at Don Miguel was fading. He could not help being a weak man and he and his wife had been very kind to her, she reminded herself honestly. It was Don Felipe who was her enemy—Don Felipe who, with his high-handed arrogance, might have destroyed any chance she and Rafael had to discover the true depth of their feelings.

It was obvious that he intended to force a marriage between them. Obvious that by whatever means, fair or foul, Rafael was going to be compelled to make a decision he might not be ready for. As for herself, there was no doubt in her mind that she loved and wanted to marry Rafael, but *only* if he loved and wanted to marry her!—certainly not at the command of an overbearing tyrant like Don Felipe!

She and Rafael had been so close, so near, possibly, to declaring what was in their hearts, and now this wicked old man may have ruined everything. The violet eyes suddenly hard, she glared daggers at Don Felipe's ramrod-straight back several riders in front of her. *Damn him!*

If Beth was furious with Don Felipe, Lorenzo was delighted. When Don Felipe's message had reached him yesterday afternoon to meet with him at the hacienda, he had nearly crowed with excitement when he heard what was planned. It didn't matter that the marriage he feared between Beth and Rafael was one step nearer. What *had* mattered was the fact that Don Felipe was intent upon removing Beth from San Antonio—away from the protection of the town, away from safety!

Lorenzo had wasted little time once he had left the meeting with the head of the Santana family. Riding to the limestone hills to the west, he had broken off the green leaves and twigs that he needed for a smoky fire, and within minutes billows of gray and white smoke had drifted up against the bright blue of the sky. His serape proved an effective blanket, and soon puffs of white smoke were seen rising at regular intervals as Lorenzo covered and uncovered the fire with his serape. The smoke could be seen for miles, and he smiled a wolfish smile of satisfaction when shortly he saw the answer to his signal in the distance. Good! The Comanche raiding party was not more than one day's journey from him.

Beth's slender body next to his brought Lorenzo's thoughts back to the present, and, feeling himself harden with desire, he knew that before he left her with the Comanches to die he would possess her. The urge to have that white, silken skin against him was the only thing that would keep Beth alive one moment longer than necessary. Perhaps it was even the real reason he proposed to dispose of her as he did. First he would have his pleasure, and then he would watch as the Comanches had theirs, before...

The Santana house was situated about six miles from San Antonio in a small valley near a branch of the San Antonio River, and, despite the fact that it was seldom used, it was always staffed and kept in readiness for any member of the family in the vicinity. It was nowhere near the size of Cielo but was certainly as luxurious in its furnishings and accommodations, Beth thought to herself as she was shown to her room.

Her room was as large as the one at Cielo, and although she did not have a separate sitting room, there were several chairs upholstered in crimson velvet and a long, low sofa covered in a rich shade of blue brocade at one end that would serve the purpose. Her bed, as was common in Spanish houses, was made of black iron with delicate, intricate filigree work in the high headboard and low footboard. A crimson quilt of satin squares lay across the plump mattress and a gray marble stand with an oil lamp of fine crystal stood nearby. The slate floor was covered by a lovely carpet in jewel tones of crimson and blue, and at her windows, which looked out on a small garden, hung curtains of sapphire-blue velvet.

But while the room was delightful, it was a prison, and watching impassively as a Mexican woman in a brightly striped skirt and white blouse hung up the clothes that had come in a trunk which had been brought with them, Beth wondered what would happen next. Apparently, even though she was literally a prisoner, Don Felipe did not mean to mistreat her—as long, Beth thought cynically, as she did nothing to annoy the family despot.

Doña Madelina had greeted her with open affection when she had been deposited none too gently in the inner courtyard only minutes before, and Beth, in spite of her resentment and anger, could not bring herself to act coldly toward the warmth and kindness that radiated from Doña Madelina. Doña Madelina had clucked and scolded when she had seen Beth's heat-flushed face and had instantly seen that she was shown to the room she now occupied to rest and recover herself from the unplanned journey.

It appeared, Beth decided slowly, that while Don Miguel and Doña Madelina might disagree with Don Felipe's handling of the situation, neither of them had any real objections to the eventual outcome. It was becoming shockingly clear that the Santana family had determined that she and Rafael should marry, and that at least in Don Felipe's case they would allow nothing to interfere with that plan.

Thankful that no one except herself knew of the child she carried, Beth washed her face and hands in a bowl of cool water. Shaking out the dust from her black muslin gown and straightening her hair in the gilt-edged mirror above a mahogany lowboy, she considered her situation. Obviously, demanding to be taken back to San Antonio was out of the question. Planning an escape was also foolish—she knew no one to bribe for a horse and she wasn't exactly enthralled with the idea of making her way alone through a countryside known to have suffered recently from raiding Comanches. So, for the present, it appeared she would simply have to make the best of things.

An opportunity to make her displeasure and position evident came immediately. There was a tap on the door, and when the Mexican woman answered it, it was to receive a message that Don Felipe demanded Beth's instant presence in the library. Beth's hands formed into fists and, fighting back the urge to reply that Don Felipe could go to hell, she followed the white-garbed male servant down the cool, arched walkway to the room he indicated.

Entering it, she found Don Felipe pouring a glass of fine wine from a crystal decanter and then, looking over his shoulder at her, he asked punctiliously, "Would you care for a glass of sherry? I had a bottle brought up from the cellar for you."

Beth stood stiffly in the center of the room, one part of her noting the leather-bound books that lined the walls and the Moroccan leather couch and heavy walnut sideboy where a tray of refreshments had been set out. Meeting Don Felipe's black-eyed look, she said levelly, "No, thank you. I do not take refreshments with my jailer."

He smiled, but the expression in the black eyes didn't change. Seen off his horse, Beth discovered that he wasn't such a tall man, actually not more than three inches taller than herself, but for all his slender height he exuded pride and power in great abundance. He had changed his clothes, but these he wore now were as richly embellished as his earlier ones, the gold velvet *chaqueta* lavishly embroidered with sparkling metallic black thread and the black *calzoneras* trimmed with gold braid. There was no doubt that he was an arresting figure of a man even for his age, which Beth guessed to be somewhere in his seventies, despite the head of surprisingly thick, black hair that held no thread of gray. Regarding her over the rim of his glass, he said finally, "Spirit in a woman is to be admired, but belligerence is something that I abhor. I hope, señora, you will not make the mistake of overstepping that narrow line."

It was a not so thinly veiled threat, and Beth reacted to it instantly. Not bothering to hide her contempt and dislike, she spat, "It is a long time, señor, since I left my governess and the rules of the schoolroom behind me! Certainly I do not intend to be either intimidated or dictated to by you! I trust you understand me?"

He nodded, the black eyes hooded. Looking at Beth as she stood angrily before him, he wondered at the fairness of the bright hair and considered idly the possibility that if she proved too intractable perhaps he would take her to Mexico City as his mistress. At seventy-four he still desired women, and when he tired of her, with that fair skin and ash-blond hair he would have no trouble selling her—and for a great price. But then he dismissed the idea—it was more important that his grandson marry and breed heirs for Cielo than to satisfy a momentary hunger of the flesh. Don Felipe always kept his priorities in order.

Meeting Beth's angry gaze, he murmured, "Very well, we understand each other. And as you appear to be a forthright young woman, I shall waste little time in polite words." He waved an arm in the direction of the couch. "Would you care to sit down while we discuss the situation?"

"No," Beth bit out, her eyes flashing and a becoming spot of angry color burning in each cheek.

"So. Then if you don't mind, I shall do so," he replied calmly, and proceeded to sit down. His eyes traveled over her once again, appreciating the high, full bosom and slender hips hinted at under the full skirts of her gown. Taking a sip of his sherry, he began easily, "What we have here is a very simple situation. You are a young and very beautiful widow of wealth and breeding. I have a handsome and virile grandson whom I would like very much to see married and fathering children... particularly male children. It is very simple, *sí?* You marry my grandson and your widowhood is at an end—no longer are you alone without a man to guide and protect you. And I am happy because at last my only male heir is married and will, in due time, present me with great-grandsons."

Beth was torn between an outrageous urge to laugh at his cool effrontery and a burst of fury. How dare he think to arrange her life this way!

Hands on her hips, the captivating face vibrant with barely controlled anger, Beth snapped, "I have *no* desire to enter into such a cold-blooded arrangement. My first marriage was arranged for me, and if I ever remarry, it will be for *love*—definitely not for expediency's sake!"

Don Felipe shrugged. "How very noble... but childish. After you have given me a great-grandson, it would make little difference if you had lovers. Surely marriage with my grandson cannot be that distasteful to you. After all, you have spent many weeks in his household and have not found his company too burdensome."

"Why me?" Beth asked in a hard little voice. "If it is so important for Rafael to marry, why not present him with a suitable bride of your choice?"

Negligently setting aside his glass, Don Felipe pulled at his lip. "I had contemplated such a scheme," he admitted surprisingly. "But wealthy young brides are not that easily found, and his reputation with women is such that doting fathers are somewhat reluctant to give their daughters in marriage to a man with his past. Besides, it is true that I could force him into a marriage again, but if he did not *desire* the woman, it would do me little good. You understand me? Without a consummated marriage I would gain no heirs for Cielo, and from what my son has told me, Rafael does apparently have some feeling for you, *sí?*"

Beth choked back a hysterical giggle, wondering what this arrogant old man would do if he knew that even now she carried Rafael's child. Chilled by his words, but curious too, she asked helplessly, "Even if I agreed to such a cold-blooded arrangement, tell me, what could you possibly do to make Rafael agree?"

Don Felipe smiled and Beth shivered. Rising from his seat he walked over to a velvet bellrope and gave it one sharp pull. Almost instantly, as if the servant had been waiting outside the door, there was a knock and Don Felipe called, *"Entre."*

To the servant who appeared in the doorway he said, "Bring the Señorita Arabela to us."

Alone again, he looked at Beth and remarked, "Arabela is the baby of the family. I had taken her to Mexico City with me, but she proved most troublesome, so when I received Miguel's letter I brought her back with me." Picking up his glass again, he took another sip and continued, "You will find her quite a delightful child, and by some strange chemistry, of all his half sisters, she is the only one that Rafael has ever shown any affection for. But wait until you see her, you will see what I mean."

Beth did. Not five minutes later, the door burst open and a young girl of not more than fifteen danced into the room. Arabela was indeed delightful, if a shock. Used to the darkness so common amongst the Mexicans and Spaniards, Beth was astonished by the flaming red of Arabela's hair and the brilliance of the sapphire-blue eyes.

Don Felipe noticed Beth's expression and said lightly, "A red-haired Spaniard is unusual but not unheard of."

Arabela paid no attention to her grandfather, and instead ran up with fleet graceful steps to Beth. "Oh, how lovely you are! *Madre* said you were, but I didn't believe her," she exclaimed with open candor, the blue eyes bright with warmth and laughter as they twinkled merrily up at Beth. Dressed in a simple gown of white muslin with small puffed sleeves and a gaily embroidered hem, Arabela herself was very enchanting.

At fifteen there were already the signs of the strikingly beautiful woman she would be one day. The fiery hair was arranged in two demure little clusters near each ear with a few rebellious curls escaping at her temples; her lashes and brows were dark and the sapphire-blue eyes had an enchanting tilt at the corners; her mouth was full and sweetly curved, almost as if Arabela were always smiling. She was small for her age, but already her little breasts and slender waist were apparent.

Unable to help herself, Beth found that she was responding immediately to Arabela's gay charm. "Why, thank you," she replied and added gently, "You are very pretty too."

Arabela gave an infectious gurgle of laughter. "Now I know I shall like you!" Impetuously, for Arabela was impetuous, she caught Beth by surprise and hugged her. "I am so glad that Rafael is going to marry you! Consuela was a witch, and I did not like her at all! She was wicked to him, but you would be kind to him."

Beth stiffened and Arabela looked at her with puzzlement. Before she could say more, though, Don Felipe scolded icily, "Your manners are deplorable, Arabela! Surely your mother taught you better!"

Some of the gaiety and light died out of the little animated face, and, turning to her grandfather, she gave a stilted curtsy and in a colorless voice murmured, "Forgive me, Grandfather. I forgot myself." It was an astonishing change from the vital creature of a second ago, but Beth was pleased to note the imp of defiance that peeked from the blue eyes as Arabela cast her a sideways glance. So Arabela was not *quite* in awe of her grandfather like everyone else.

In the same colorless little voice Arabela asked, "Was there something you wanted, Grandfather?"

"I merely wished Señora Beth to meet you, and now that she has, you may leave. And possibly learn some manners before I see you the next time."

Don Felipe turned away, and only Beth saw the quick, impudent tongue that Arabela stuck out and the encouraging wink she gave before she skipped out of the room.

Her own voice devoid of any emotion, Beth said, "A charming child. But what does she have to do with our conversation?"

Don Felipe walked over to the sideboard and poured himself another glass of sherry. "Everything, *cara*, everything." His glass refilled, he walked toward Beth. Taking a sip of the sherry, he smiled and murmured, "You see, Arabela is the one vulnerable spot in Rafael's armor. He would do just about anything to see her happy. It is really very simple, as I told you earlier. Either Rafael marries you, or I shall see to it that Arabela is married off to the oldest, ugliest old rakehell that I can find." The black eyes full of malicious satisfaction, he asked, "Do you think he would allow that—especially when all he has to do to save her is marry a woman he already finds attractive?"

Beth blanched and felt her throat go tight. No, Rafael wouldn't allow that. No one would. Arabela was too bright, too gay to deserve such a fate. Swallowing with difficulty, she said, "You're foul!—a black, ugly beast with no heart!"

Don Felipe shrugged carelessly. "Perhaps. Names matter little to me. It is winning that matters. And I think, at last, I have won."

Through stiff lips, Beth snapped, "Not quite! You may be able to coerce your grandson, but tell me, how do you intend to insure that I agree to marry him?"

"Oh, that! Piffle! I don't have to do a thing," he replied smugly. "Rafael will do it, you see. Do you think he would let your refusal stand in his way if it meant Arabela's marriage to a doddering old *roué?*" Don Felipe laughed.

Sickened, Beth didn't even remember walking back to her room. Everything Don Felipe said was true, and her heart felt heavy in her breast. Rafael could be as ruthless as his grandfather, of that she was certain, and if Don Felipe gave him the choice of marriage to herself or seeing Arabela married off to a disgusting old man, Beth knew what his choice would be. *And me, what about me?* her heart cried. *Could I bear being married to him knowing that he had been compelled to say his vows?*

Somehow she got through the evening that followed, smiling politely and giving the correct responses to any conversation that was directed her way. And, watching Arabela's lively countenance and hearing her gay, tinkling laughter, her spirits sank even lower. Could *she* allow that enchanting little creature to be married off so cruelly? More importantly, how was Rafael going to react to this state of affairs?

Rafael was furious! Arriving home, eager to see Beth after a long, busy day away from her, with growing rage he listened in tight-lipped silence to Paco's understandably nervous recital of the facts. Even the news that a servant had been sent to find him, but always seemed to be one step behind where Rafael had been, did nothing to lighten the darkening fury on Rafael's face.

"I see," he said at last in a frightening, quiet voice. "And Señora López, she has gone too? And the maid, Manuela?"

"*Sí. No,*" Paco muttered uneasily, not liking the set of his master's jaw nor the expression in the gray eyes. "Señora López left in the coach your grandfather sent, but the woman Manuela is still here. She had not finished packing Señora Beth's things, and it was decided that she would ride out with you in the morning."

Manuela's not being ready to leave when the coach arrived had been deliberate. She had moved with irritating slowness in the packing of Beth's clothing, and finally in exasperation Señora López had suggested that Manuela accompany Rafael in the morning, as there was no doubt in anyone's mind that he would be riding fast and furiously to the hacienda where Beth was. Smiling to herself, Manuela agreed. Knowing Señor Rafael, somehow she didn't think that Señora Beth would remain long under his grandfather's roof.

Rafael took the stairs two at a time and a moment later burst into the room Beth had occupied, startling Manuela who was halfheartedly pretending she was still packing Beth's remaining clothes. Rafael took one look at the trunk and snarled, "Put those things back! Señora Beth will be returning."

A small smile curving her lips, Manuela watched him slam from the room and almost happily she began unpacking the clothes. Unless she was very much mistaken, Señora Beth would sleep tomorrow night in this bed... and possibly not alone either!

Leaving the room, Rafael was halfway down the stairs when Paco answered a knock on the front door and opened it to admit a travel-stained Sebastian. Rafael stopped his rapid descent and demanded ungraciously, "What the hell brings you here?"

Sebastian grimaced and retorted sharply, "Certainly not your charming company!" But then, aware that now was not the time to start an argument with his cousin, he added in a more normal tone, "I just learned yesterday morning that your grandfather had been at Cielo, and I rode in as fast as I could to warn you that he will probably be paying you a call—soon."

Rafael pulled a face and came slowly down the remainder of the stairs. "I thank you for the news and I'm sorry that I snapped at you. Unfortunately, for all your haste you are several hours too late—he was here this morning and took Beth with him." His lips quirking sarcastically, he finished, "Apparently he didn't feel Señora López was an adequate chaperon."

Despite the gravity of the situation, Sebastian grinned and asked, "Was she?"

Rafael's lips twitched and, remembering the night of the harlot's gown, he said softly, "No, indeed not!" But then, frowning, he said, "I was just on my way out to the hacienda where the family is staying. I must see Beth alone before my grandfather has had a chance to fill her head with preposterous ideas."

"Well, what are we waiting for?" Sebastian demanded with a quick smile.

CHAPTER TWENTY-SEVEN

It took only a few minutes to saddle Diablo and procure a fresh horse for Sebastian. In silence the two men rode out into the night, Rafael too busy with his own thoughts to make conversation, and Sebastian, after the hard two-day ride into San Antonio, simply too tired.

Rafael had sensed that Beth was no longer in the house the instant he had stepped into the main hallway. There had been a sudden feeling of loss, an emptiness that had assailed him, and he had known that something was terribly wrong even before Paco had begun his nervous explanation.

To know that she was gone, to know that through his own indecision he may have lost her, terrified and enraged him. He knew his grandfather too well, knew the man's ruthless, heavy-handed way of gaining his own ends, and Rafael very much feared that when he did finally see Beth she would no longer be the sweet, yielding creature of these past weeks. No, once his grandfather started arranging things, Beth was far more likely to greet him with anger and hostility than with open arms and honeyed kisses. It would take him months to undo the damage, months he didn't want to waste.

It didn't take much intelligence on Rafael's part to guess what had been his grandfather's motive, or to guess how Don Felipe had learned of Beth in the first place. Almost as if he had been an unseen observer, he guessed what his grandfather was up to and the cold-blooded, arrogant way he would go about it. What he didn't know was what threat his grandfather would use against Beth or precisely how he hoped to bring about the marriage. He did know for certain that Beth would be furious, and he couldn't say that he blamed her.

Rafael broke the silence when he and Sebastian were about a half a mile from their destination. The lights of the hacienda could be seen clearly. Pulling up his horse, Rafael said, "I'm not going in with you. I want you to arrive just as if you've come to join the family. You will, of course, inform my grandfather that you have spoken to me, and that I have more or less told you and him to go to the devil."

Sebastian looked surprised, as well he might. "If you're not going in with me, *what* are you going to be doing?"

Rafael smiled, his teeth flashing in the darkness. "Seeing Beth, what else?"

"How?" Sebastian asked resignedly.

"Under the cover of your arrival, I'll slip into the hacienda. It shouldn't take me long to find which of the rooms Beth has been put in." Leaning forward in the saddle, he added, "If by chance she is still with the others, find a way to let her know I'll be waiting in her room."

Sebastian made a face. "You make it sound so easy! As if Don Felipe won't be the least bit suspicious."

"Probably he will be. But while he will suspect your motives, he won't guess what *I'm* up to, and that's all that matters." Earnestly, Rafael continued, "Sebastian, I *have* to see Beth alone." He added grimly, "And before I have any conversation with my grandfather!"

"Very well. Do I see you again tonight?"

"Yes, I think we had better meet before I return to San Antonio. It's late enough now, so your request to retire for the night shouldn't be a surprise. A half an hour after you've been shown to your room, go to the stables. I'll meet you there."

Beth was indeed still with the others. She greeted Sebastian courteously, but coolly, for she still hadn't forgotten how they had last parted. But finally his odd grimaces, raised eyebrows, rolling eyes, and weird twitches whenever no one was looking at them convinced Beth that he was trying to tell her something, and, with a heart pounding like a war drum in her breast, she managed for them to be alone for a moment.

Out of the corner of his mouth Sebastian muttered hastily, "Go to your room—Rafael is there!"

Hoping her face didn't betray her, she smiled charmingly at Sebastian. A few minutes later she excused herself for the night. The blood singing in her veins, she hurried to her room.

She had barely shut the door when Rafael's dark shape emerged from the shadows, and a moment later she was locked in his arms. They kissed hungrily, joyously, each one for the moment content merely to have the other near. But then sanity prevailed and they slowly separated.

"Are you unharmed?" Rafael asked harshly, suddenly intent upon destroying the hacienda and everyone in it if one hair on her head had been touched.

Beth shook her head. "Yes. A little frightened at first, perhaps, and *very* angry!"

There was a tap on the door and with wide, scared eyes Beth motioned Rafael away from her. Running to the door, she opened it and nearly sagged with relief when she discovered the Mexican woman who had been acting as her maid standing there. The woman had come to help Beth undress, but somewhat hurriedly Beth told her that there was no need, and she could retire for the night.

Alone again, Beth was inexplicably shy and Rafael strangely wary. It was almost as if they knew that the time for subterfuge was past and what was in their hearts had to be spoken. Uncertainly Rafael eyed Beth in the dimness of the room, the only light coming from the oil lamp near Beth's bed. Now that Rafael was with Beth he found himself oddly tongue-tied and ill at ease.

For all his success with women, there had never been one that mattered to him, nor had he ever told a woman he loved her. Seduction and soft words had never been his way, he had always simply reached out and taken, but with Beth he was uncertain and hesitant.

For Beth, watching him as she leaned back against the door, tonight was the culmination of every meeting, every exchange they had ever had. Every minute they had ever shared had been suddenly telescoped to this moment. Looking at him as he stood in the center of the room, legs slightly apart, his thumbs hooked in the wide leather belt around his lean waist, she thought her heart would burst with love for him. He was so dear, so loved, and yet, if Don Felipe had his way, an uncrossable chasm yawned at their feet. And the memory of that meeting with Don Felipe this afternoon prompted her to ask huskily, "Have you talked with your grandfather?"

Rafael gave an ugly laugh. "No, *amada*, and I have no intention of talking to him!"

With a painful intensity her eyes searched his face, wanting to believe him and yet fearful that at some time in the afternoon while she had been closeted in her room Don Felipe had seen and talked with Rafael. This rendezvous could have been arranged to lull her suspicions, to make her believe that Rafael came on his own and not at the bidding of his grandfather.

Beth wasn't aware how her thoughts betrayed her, but to Rafael, it was obvious that his grandfather had already put some poisonous idea in her mind. His eyes narrowed, and in a dangerous voice he demanded, "Don't you believe me?"

Frightened by the violence she sensed in him, she stammered honestly, "I-I-I don't know!"

That was all it took to ignite the smoldering fury that raged in his breast, and with a curse he crossed the short space that divided them, his hands closing cruelly around Beth's shoulders. Like a dog with a rat he shook her, the soft, fair hair tumbling down from the loose chignon she had worn. "When have I ever lied to you?" he snarled softly. "Why would I start now, now when everything I have done these past weeks has been to teach you to trust me. Has everything I've done been for nothing? Do you think so little of me that my grandfather can destroy, in one afternoon, something that has been growing between us since the night of the Costa ball?"

The violet eyes looked on the smoky-gray ones so near her own. Beth slowly shook her head. "No, I believe you," she said in a low voice. Then, as if trying to explain, she said quickly, "Don Felipe is a ruthless man and he frightened me." Her eyes full of pleading, she added almost in a whisper, "He plans to force you to marry me."

Rafael's hold on her lessened, and in a weary voice he said, "I had figured that much out by myself."

Her heart freezing in her breast, she asked fearfully, "You wouldn't allow him to do it?"

Rafael gave her a queer smile. "Would marriage to me be so very terrible?"

A new emotion seemed to have entered the room, and his hands were lightly caressing now as they rested on her shoulders, and the ugly violence she had sensed earlier had vanished. Unaccountably shy, Beth fixed her eyes on the strong, brown throat, unable to meet his piercing gaze. "It would depend," she got out in a barely audible tone.

Gently he pulled her closer to him and, with his lips brushing the curls at her temple, he asked thickly, "On what?"

One hand nervously toying with the barrel button of his black *chaqueta* and regarding it intently, she said softly, "On why you wanted to marry me."

It was a delectable moment, a duel of words between them, both prolonging it, yet each one, hardly able to stand the suspense, wanted the words said, wanted to know what was in the other's heart. They stood close—Beth's black gown melting into the blackness of Rafael's clothes, her fair head almost resting on his chest, his black head bent next to hers—and both of them were unbearably aware of the vital importance of this tantalizing, elusive moment.

She felt so soft and warm in his arms that he never wanted to let her go, and, finally admitting to himself the knowledge he had denied for weeks, months, as the words burst from him he said explosively, "Oh, sweet Jesus, English, *I'm in love with you!* Isn't *that* reason enough to marry me and put me out of my misery?"

It wasn't the way he had meant to tell her, and he swore at his own clumsiness. But for Beth it was everything she had ever wanted to hear from him, *everything* and the *only thing* that mattered—*he loved her!*

Her eyes blazing with the love she had kept hidden for so long, Beth gazed up at him and Rafael caught his breath at what her expression revealed. As his hands tightened around her slender shoulders, he felt an emotion far stronger, far more enduring than anything he had ever experienced. Almost hesitantly, as if he were afraid to believe what was transparently obvious, he began tentatively, "English, do you...?"

Beth nodded vigorously, and impulsively she threw her arms about his neck and said softly, "I've *loved* you for *so long*, even"—with misty eyes—"when you didn't deserve to be loved."

She felt his body tremble, and then she was swept up in an embrace so fierce, so hungrily demanding, so sweetly painful that the present receded and they were alone in a new, hazy dream world. Beth gave herself up gladly to his arms and lips, her own arms locked tightly about his neck, her mouth yielding tenderly, knowing this was the moment she had lived all her life for, and now at last the dream lover, the dark renegade who had haunted her dreams, was hers and she was his... as she *always* had been!

But unfortunately there were pitfalls in front of them, and eventually Rafael eased his mouth away from hers to say unsteadily, "We have to talk. I don't want to, there are things I would far rather do, but my grandfather has placed us in a peculiar position." His gray eyes bleak and hard, he said harshly, "English, I will *not* allow him to dictate to me the where and the when and the how of my marriage. I love you and I want to marry you—and I want it done without his interference! I have waited all my life for love, and I will *not* have him sully the feeling between us—you understand me?

Beth nodded, understanding very well exactly what he meant. Don Felipe's cold-blooded scheme for their marriage would destroy the joy and happiness the event should bring, and she, like Rafael, did not want his grandfather to have *any* say in the vows that would join them together. "What do we do?" she asked quietly.

He frowned and absently dropped a kiss on her forehead, as his brain raced for a solution. "Would you very much mind being married very quickly and very quietly by a priest? I can see one first thing in the morning in

San Antonio and procure a license. This time tomorrow evening we can be married." He looked at her keenly. "Will you dislike the fact that it will not be a grand affair? No lace and orange blossoms and hundreds of guests?"

Beth sent him a tremulous smile. "I had that once, and it brought me little happiness." She reached up and gently kissed his warm mouth. "Rafael, it is not the trappings that I care for, but the man," she reassured him gravely.

He gave a small groan and gathered her close in his arms again, his mouth seeking hers with an almost frantic urgency. In a voice deep with suppressed passion he muttered, "I, too, once had a wedding that was all glitter and pomp, and it brought me nothing but bitterness and hatred. When I marry you, I want no reminders of either of our marriages." His eyes very hard he said, "You're *mine!* I love you and I will not share you—not even with memories, especially not memories of another man!"

"Shhh," Beth said against his lips. "Someday I shall tell you of Nathan. But not now, not tonight, tonight is ours, and I do not want to hear any more of what went before—we have each other and *we* start from here."

A twisted smile crossed his face. "You are suddenly very wise, my dove. There is so much in our past to forget, isn't there? And yet there is so much that I *cannot* forget."

Suddenly unsure and an icy coldness stealing into her heart, she asked, "What do you mean?"

His face incredibly tender, he said softly, "The way you looked at the Costa ball—how can I ever forget that? Or the sweetness of your mouth when I kissed you that first time. Do you want me to forget that—I swear I could not—not even if I lived to be a hundred." The gray eyes darkening with remembrance, he added, "Or even the sight of your naked white body against the ruby of that quilt in the house on the ramparts—that, too, I cannot forget—it has driven me half crazy for years."

Beth bent her head into his chest and in a low, trembling voice said, "Perhaps some of the past we can never forget—nor, as you say, want to. But there is much of it..." She stopped and glanced up at him, wondering if in spite of his avowal of love, he still believed that she had gone willingly to Lorenzo's arms. It was instantly very important to know, and baldly she asked, "Do you believe what I told you about that day?"

It was the one question that Rafael had dreaded she would ask, his own thoughts still unclear, but, staring down into the fragile features, the honest violet eyes that met his so steadily, and the generous, sweetly curved mouth, he knew the answer. "Yes," he said simply. "What Consuela hoped to gain by it, I still cannot conceive—but I know you, and when I put aside my own jealous demons, I know that you could never have arranged to meet Lorenzo." His voice suddenly fervent and impassioned, he added, "I have to believe you—if I didn't I should go mad with the evil thoughts that would fill my mind. I would not be able to bear to have you even look at another man for fear you would take him for a lover. So I must believe you, for my own sanity as well as the truth and honesty that I see in your eyes."

One tiny tear slid down Beth's cheek that she wasn't even aware of, so desperately intent had she been on his words. But Rafael noticed it, and in a gentle voice he teased, "What's this, tears? Is this the way you greet a passionate declaration of trust and love? Tears?"

Beth gave a watery smile. "No, it is just that it means so much to me to know that you believe me. I have so longed for you to know the truth, and I feared that even now..."

He shook his black head. "How could I continue to believe that and yet say I love you? Don't you know it was your sweetness and warmth that first drew me to you? If I hadn't been out of my head with jealousy, I would never have fallen so easily into Consuela's trap. Forget it, English, and just remember that in spite of believing evil of you, I carried the picture of you in my heart until I saw you again at Cielo. Then I'm afraid I fell hopelessly and helplessly in love with you all over again." He flashed her a crooked smile. "I've fought against it ever since I saw you standing by that blasted fountain—why do you think I've begun work on Enchantress?" At Beth's look of surprise he gave her a gentle shake. "Yes. As a matter of fact I came back from Enchantress, a proposal hovering on my lips, and what must you do but walk in with Lorenzo?"

"But I didn't want him there!" Beth protested earnestly. "I hated it when he was around, but I could do nothing about it."

Rafael's mouth thinned. "Don't worry about Lorenzo—one of the first things I may do as your husband is kill him!"

In a small voice Beth said, "If you don't mind, I would really rather you didn't. We have just found each other—I wouldn't want to lose you too soon. Lorenzo is treacherous, and while I'm certain you could kill him in a fair fight, I very much fear he would not know the meaning of fair."

"Are you so very sure that I do?"

"Probably not!" Beth answered with unflattering promptness. "But I don't think I would like his corpse for a wedding present!"

He laughed under his breath and kissed her soundly. "Enough of this! Sebastian is waiting at the stables for me, and you and I still have things to plan. But first—no more shadows? No unholy secrets you would like to confess while I am in such an amiable mood?"

Rafael said it in a teasing manner, but for Beth it was the opening she had longed for. Toying again with one of his buttons on the black *chaqueta,* she murmured, "There is just one thing."

"Oh?" he asked, an eyebrow rising quizzically, thinking that she had some minor transgression to confess.

All in a rush and giving herself no chance to have second thoughts, she blurted, *"I'm going to have our baby!"*

Thunderstruck, Rafael stared down at her, and incredulously he regarded her slightly apprehensive face. Then to her surprise, he laughed, a low, delighted laugh that melted her fears. "Truly?" he asked, an incredibly tender light blazing in the smoky-gray eyes.

Beth nodded, her lips curved with burgeoning happiness. "Truly," she echoed, and wondered why she had feared to tell him. Perchance love does work miracles, she thought hazily, for certainly this tall man with the gentle hands and tender eyes bore little resemblance to the cold, icy stranger who had met her that first night at Cielo.

For Rafael this night was more miraculous than Beth could ever begin to guess. Raised with the savage Comanches, then nearly beaten into submission by his cold-blooded calculating grandfather, married to a woman who hated and despised him—he had been denied love and gentleness all his life. And now, now he was like a bewildered man who had suddenly stumbled in from a cold and barren life into a place of warmth and light. The gentleness and love had always been there within him, perhaps even laughter and gaiety, but it had been fiercely hidden away. But now, now with his golden English in his arms, her eyes shining with love for him, he could feel the last vestiges of his icy, protective shell melting in the warmth of her love. Gently he pulled her closer to him, his mouth sliding softly across her cheek and lips. His lips found hers and clung as he kissed her warmly, sweetly—no passion, no desire, just love and tenderness in his caress.

Moving his lips to her ear, he whispered with a hint of laughter in his voice, "It is, perhaps, a good thing that we marry tomorrow night—I would want our child to have some semblance of respectability." His hand rested on her stomach and there was both protectiveness and possession in his touch. But he frowned and asked with an odd urgency, "The night at Cielo or before I left for Enchantress?" When Beth hesitated, he said in surprise, "Surely not the night of the harlot's gown?"

Beth blushed at the memory of that night and said quickly, "Before you left for Enchantress."

He sighed. "I'm glad. The night at Cielo I wanted to hurt you, and I would not like to think that our child would be born from that time." A glitter in the gray eyes, he added, "Ah, but the night before Enchantress..."

It was a delightful time for both of them, but all too soon Rafael had to tear himself away from her and make plans for the immediate future. Putting her from him, he muttered, "I have to go. Sebastian is waiting and there are things I must do. And in order to keep my grandfather from trying to abduct you again and making us dance to his tune, I must leave you here tonight and tomorrow—can you face it?"

She touched his face lightly with one hand, her own face glowing with an inner happiness. "I can manage—provided you do not leave me too long with Don Felipe. I fear my joy will be hard to hide from him, but for one day I think I can conceal it." Her eyes suddenly brimming with amusement, she teased, "But one day only. Longer and I shall reveal that you have compromised me dreadfully."

A fleeting grin lit his dark face. "Threats already? I can see that I shall have to be a stern husband." Then the grin vanished and he said seriously, "Plead an illness tomorrow night and retire early. Just as soon as it is dark I'll come for you. Be ready." Wryly he finished, "Hopefully no one will check on you until the morning, and by then it will be too late for my grandfather to do anything but offer us congratulations... before we leave for Enchantress. I want our child born there."

To Beth it sounded like heaven. The thought that this time tomorrow night she would be his wife was something she could cling to throughout the long night and day that stretched before her. Their parting a few minutes later was bittersweet, and it was all Rafael could do to force himself not to take her with him. But knowing Don Felipe would be after her immediately upon discovering her disappearance and knowing there wouldn't have been enough time to arrange a hasty marriage, reluctantly he put her from him and disappeared out her window.

Sebastian was impatiently waiting for him at the stables. "What took so long?" he demanded in an angry undertone. "I'm going to have a hell of a lot of explaining to do if one of the guards finds me loitering about at this time of night, especially since I told your not-so-believing grandfather that I was exhausted and needed my sleep. I don't think he believed one word of what I've said all evening, and I didn't like the way he watched Beth when she left. You did see her?"

Rafael nodded and, still bemused by the knowledge that Beth loved him and that there was to be a child, he said softly, "Wish me well, Sebastian, for English and I marry tomorrow night."

For just a moment, Sebastian was assailed with a pang of envy. But then, happy for his cousin, he said gruffly, "I do indeed wish you well! And Beth too! But tell me, how does this come about—particularly as I'm quite certain Don Felipe has no quick wedding in mind."

Rafael's face tightened and succinctly he explained what had been decided. "Will you come with us? I would like you there."

Rafael's invitation was sincere and he had no thought of causing Sebastian pain, almost having forgotten Sebastian's involvement with Beth. Surprising even himself, Sebastian agreed, discovering he was not so heartbroken at the idea of this marriage as he would have thought. Possibly I am becoming a cynic, he thought dryly.

They shook hands and Sebastian said truthfully, "I'm glad for both of you, and at least this time Beth will have a *man* for her husband—of that I have little doubt."

Curious, Rafael glanced at him and asked, "Meaning?"

Sebastian raised an eyebrow. "She didn't tell you?" And at Rafael's negative gesture, he told of seeing Nathan in Mr. Percy's bed.

Rafael said something vicious under his breath, and Sebastian thought it was a good thing that Nathan had already passed from this earth.

After they parted, Rafael wasted little time in useless speculation about what Sebastian had told him—in time Beth would tell him all he needed to know about Nathan. The warmth and happiness that she had instilled in him was still there, flooding his body with joy, and as San Antonio drew nearer, his thoughts were on his love and the wonderful life that lay before them.

Lorenzo was also about this night, only within him there was no love or thought of life, merely hatred and death. The day that had started out so brightly had faded dismally, and when he rode to his meeting with the Comanche raiders he was brooding on the cruel words Don Felipe had flung at him not more than an hour before.

Despite Lorenzo's fawning and servile manner, Don Felipe had never treated him with anything but polite contempt. Yesterday when he had received Don Felipe's message, Lorenzo had been elated; it seemed that his calculated attempts to gain favor with Don Felipe had finally borne fruit. Hadn't he been included in the private session between the father and son when it had been decided that Beth should be brought to the family house? And hadn't Don Felipe chosen him to carry out his commands? Hadn't *he* been the favored one to be taken aside after Don Miguel had left the room? Had he not been told exactly what the old man wanted if the señora proved intractable?

All these things were true, and Lorenzo had been well pleased, thinking that Don Felipe had come to appreciate his worth and that this might be the time to mention his wish for a closer tie with the Santana family. All during the day he had been buoyed up with a feeling of gleeful anticipation. Soon all his schemes would come to fruition—Beth would die within a matter of days, killed by Comanches, thereby stilling her tongue and stopping any marriage with Rafael; and if Don Felipe was indeed looking with favor upon him, his suit for the hand of Arabela would prosper. Once Arabela's hand was actually his, there would then remain only *one* person in his way, *Rafael*... and Rafael *could* so easily go the way of the *poor* Señora Beth!

Unfortunately his designs had suffered a rude jolt when, after everyone had retired, he had sought an interview with Don Felipe, who was in the library savoring one last glass of sherry. Lorenzo was not sleeping at the house, and Don Felipe was slightly surprised to find him still about the house, having thought he had already departed.

But, feeling rather benign, certain that he could force a marriage between his recalcitrant grandson and the eminently suitable Señora Beth, Don Felipe bade him enter the room and even went so far as to offer him a glass of sherry. Encouraged by this further sign of the great man's unbending toward him, after a few minutes of desultory conversation Lorenzo had made the mistake of slyly hinting in which directions his ambitions ran.

Don Felipe had stiffened and the cold, black eyes had rested on Lorenzo's face. In a contemptuous voice Don Felipe had inquired, "Correct me if I am wrong, but wasn't your mother so foolish and headstrong that she ran away with her dancing master? And after she had disgraced her family and caused an embarrassing scandal, didn't she have the temerity to return begging her father to take her, along with her bastard child, back?"

At Lorenzo's unpleasant start, Don Felipe had smiled pityingly. "Did you think I didn't know your background? Did you think I never questioned why a supposed cousin of Consuela's should be so poor and treated so disdainfully by her family? And did you think that even for one minute I would consider aligning my family with the bastard of a dancing master?"

Don Felipe had laughed. "Lorenzo, you are a good servant. I can make use of you—but only as long as you keep your place and *know* your place! Now leave me, I am weary and there are things I must plan."

Dismissed so summarily, there had been nothing for Lorenzo to do *but* leave. And he left, but he left with an undying hatred for Don Felipe, and as he rode toward the meeting with the Comanche renegades, he plotted not only Beth's sudden demise but Don Felipe's as well. Tomorrow, he thought viciously, tomorrow I'll see them both dead!

Unaware of this treachery, Beth woke early the next morning and stretched luxuriously, a delicious sense of well-being curling through her slim body. Tonight she would be Rafael's wife! How strange to think that only yesterday she had been so uncertain and unhappy.

A dreamy, faraway expression on her delicate features, Beth docilely allowed herself to be bathed by the servant, María, and she came back to the present only when María diffidently inquired which gown the señora wished to wear today. Making a face, Beth forced herself to choose one. I *hate* black! she thought rebelliously as she examined the black gowns hanging in the wardrobe. Longingly she gazed at some of her other gowns, hanging at the far end of the big wardrobe. The soft hues, the pale pinks, the delicate lavenders, and the sunny yellows all held far more appeal than the widow's garb convention dictated she wear.

Reluctantly she chose a simple gown of black muslin with a wide bertha of lace that gave the somber garb an almost frivolous air. I will *not,* she decided mutinously, be married in black! And covertly she eyed a beautiful gown of mauve satin. Hidden under a full, black cloak...

Smiling to herself, she turned away and watched idly as María arranged her hair in a large round chignon on top of her head. Wide ivory combs held the fair hair in place, and while the woman did not have Manuela's skill, Beth was more than satisfied with the effect of the cool, unruffled elegance the arrangement effected.

Standing up and twitching her gown into place, Beth was ready to face the world, particularly Don Felipe! Taking one last look at herself in the mirror and disliking anew the color of black, she grimaced. But then her conscience smote her. What a dreadful creature she was! Nathan dead barely three months and already she was carrying another man's child and looking forward to marrying a man she loved. *Disgraceful!*

Feeling wretched about her happiness when Nathan lay in his grave, the light died in her eyes and her expression was suitably subdued when she joined the others. Don Felipe put it down to acceptance of the fate he had planned for her and would have been astonished to know her pensive demeanor was caused by guilt. Life was offering her so much, and yet Nathan was dead, and dead because of her. She didn't *deserve* to be happy! she thought mournfully. Oh, but she was, God forgive her, she *was* happy!

CHAPTER TWENTY-EIGHT

For Rafael the time sped by and yet moved on leaden feet. The procuring of the license took but a minute, and then he stopped by the Maverick house, explaining what had transpired, and somewhat offhandedly inquired if Mary and Sam would care to witness his marriage. Hiding their delight, the Mavericks accepted instantly.

Relaxed and cheerful, he returned home and drove the servants mad with his demands. The suite next to his must be aired and cleaned—tonight his bride would sleep there. And there must be flowers—flowers in her rooms, flowers throughout the house. And food and wine, there must be both suitable for the occasion. And... his wants seemed endless, and all for Beth.

For Beth the day passed almost pleasantly. Left alone most of the time with Doña Madelina, Señora López, and Arabela, she actually enjoyed herself, although it was very hard to keep her joy from spilling out and giving away her secret. The siesta hours were very hard for her, for she could do nothing but lie in her bed and think of Rafael.

About four o'clock the family met for some light refreshment in the small open courtyard, and it was then that Don Felipe suggested that perhaps the younger two ladies would like to accompany him on his afternoon ride. At first Beth demurred, but relented when Arabela begged her prettily and Sebastian, who had spent a harrowing day with Don Felipe, added his plea.

From his outpost in the hills near the house, Lorenzo watched the party leave the protection of the high walls—Don Felipe, Don Miguel, Beth, Sebastian, Arabela, and about a half dozen armed riders. He frowned.

Unless there was some way of separating Arabela and Don Miguel from the others, he dared not have the Comanches attack.

But fate played into his hands, for the party had not gone a half mile when a young rabbit suddenly jumped up under Arabela's horse, causing it to rear. And as Arabela had been in a spirited argument with Sebastian she hadn't been paying any attention to her horse and was promptly thrown. She was only shaken, and Don Miguel, who hadn't particularly wanted to come along in the first place, proposed that he and Arabela return to the house. Regally Don Felipe gave them permission to leave the party. Wanting the pleasure of a beautiful woman all to himself, he also decided that Sebastian would be best employed amusing his cousin. After all, it was *his* fault she hadn't been paying attention to her riding.

Grudgingly Sebastian accepted Don Felipe's order, and Beth could have boxed his ears for leaving her alone with the autocratic old devil. And he knew it too, from the audacious look he sent her way before he kicked his horse into a canter and headed back.

Lorenzo smiled as he observed the proceedings. Clambering down from the huge, flat rock, he hurried down the hillside to an impatient group of about fifteen Comanche warriors. This was not the first time Lorenzo had worked with the Comanches, and their dealings in the past had proved mutually profitable. This, though, was the first time that Lorenzo had organized a raid simply for his own gain, except for Consuela's death, and then there had been many horses and trunks of clothing and trinkets for all.

Lorenzo and the Comanches carefully chose their spot for ambush. Like a wolf on the trail of a wounded deer, one Comanche had followed the little party for a short distance to discover which of the many trails Don Felipe was taking. Signaled by a series of animal and bird calls, the Comanches positioned themselves for the attack.

The trail led through a short, narrow arroyo; the sides of the arroyo sloped down to a trail. For the Comanches it was simple to station warriors at either end while the others hid just out of sight on either side of the brush-covered arroyo. When Don Felipe and his party rode by the concealed Comanches at the entrance, the trap would be sprung.

Beth was not enjoying her ride. Don Felipe had been asking her very personal questions and slyly flirting. She wished she had been brave enough to defy him and return with the others. Eager to return, she asked, "Are we to go much farther?" And, falling back on female megrims, she said plaintively, "I am growing tired and I fear I have a headache coming on."

Don Felipe slewed around in his saddle and had just opened his mouth to speak, when the Comanches attacked from all sides. It was a slaughter. Caught by surprise, completely surrounded, and badly outnumbered, the men had absolutely no chance to protect themselves. The Comanche arrows and lances felled the guards before they could even draw their clumsy muzzle-loading weapons.

With horror Beth heard the terrifying Comanche war cry and watched almost paralyzed with terror as they came hurtling from all directions. The rider by her side gave an odd little gurgle and before Beth's fearful stare he died, an arrow in the throat. To her right, another man took a lance in the back—all around her were the screams of dying men and frightened horses. It was a wild melee of rearing, bolting horses and falling bodies. Galvanized by stark, unreasoning panic, she tried to fight her way clear of the action, but she was caught helplessly in the middle and only by sheer luck escaped with nothing more serious than a grazed cheek.

A sudden ghastly silence fell, and with icy dread Beth realized that of the little riding party she was the only one still mounted...and alive. Dry-mouthed with fear, her heart thudding painfully, she stared around her at the ring of savage Indians who surrounded her. Everything that Matilda Lockhart had spoken of, that day in San Antonio, came rushing back, and for one awful moment Beth thought she would faint with terror. But then spirit and pride came to her rescue, and, hiding her fear, she defiantly met the black-eyed stares of the Comanches.

They were terrifying, the broad-nosed, dark-skinned faces cruel and fierce under their black stripes of war paint. Some wore the buffalo-horn headress that gave them the look of a nightmare, others only a few feathers. All were naked except for a loincloth, and all had long hair, some having braids, others merely long, lank black hair that hung around their shoulders. A slight breeze ruffled the feathers on their lances and the ornaments of the round buffalo-hide war shields, but otherwise all was still, silent as if waiting... and waiting... and...

An agonized groan from one of the men lying on the ground broke the tension-filled quiet, and to Beth's horror she watched one of the Comanches lift his lance, intent upon dealing the death blow—it was Don Felipe who had made the sound—and the Comanche was already moving his horse in that direction when a voice stopped him.

"No," Lorenzo said with relish, having also recognized the lone man who still lived. "Save him for the women. I shall enjoy watching him scream out his life under the knives of the squaws."

Revulsion showing on her face, Beth spat, "*You!* Are you so beneath human feeling that you will join with these creatures against your own kind?"

Lorenzo smiled, moving his horse between the Comanches that ringed her. "Why, of course. You should know that for money I will do just about anything." His face grew ugly. "Even kill my own kind."

And the suspicion that had formed in her mind the instant she had seen him with the Comanches suddenly hardened into belief. "It was you!" she burst out. "*You* who killed Consuela!"

Lorenzo actually preened himself. "Of course! It was so childishly easy. Consuela was a stupid woman. Did you know that she refused to pay me for my part in our little scene in New Orleans?" Not waiting for her reply, nor really expecting any, he went on casually, "I never let her know she had made me angry, and she was so arrogant that she thought I would let her trample me however she chose. Ha! I showed her the error of her ways in the end. I took a great pleasure in watching what the Comanches did to her. Of course, the warriors are not as proficient with the knives and the tortures as the squaws, but they did well enough."

Unable to control it, Beth shivered at the note of enjoyment in his voice, and, seeing the movement, Lorenzo looked at her full in the face and smiled. Then he said something to one of the Comanches, and a moment later Don Felipe's bloody form was tossed over one of the horses and another warrior roughly jerked the reins from Beth's hands. A brief second was taken to strip the bodies of weapons and any plunder that caught the eyes of the victorious Comanches, and then, driving the riderless horses before them, Beth and Don Felipe being brought along at the rear, the Indians departed at breakneck speed. Beth could only hang on to her saddlehorn and wonder at what fate had in store for her.

Nothing pleasant, as she was to learn painfully, bitterly through the long terrifying night that followed and the even more humiliating, punishing day that followed. The Comanches rode swiftly all night. They stopped for nothing, and for that Beth was thankful—knowing that when camp was made she would face the inevitable rape by each one of the warriors. Matilda Lockhart's burned and scarred face seemed to dance in front of her eyes. Would *she* soon resemble that poor creature?

They struck an isolated ranch just before dawn, and it, too, was an easy victory, as Lorenzo had told them it would be; the men were slaughtered as they woke and reached for their weapons, the three women raped, then lanced and left for dead. Lorenzo had remained with Beth and the barely alive Don Felipe, and, watching the horror on her face, he taunted softly, "Tonight it will be your turn. Do you think the Comanches will prove to be kind lovers?" He laughed at her shudder.

And it was then that the real terror began. After the two easy victories the arrogant Comanches were in high spirits. Whooping and cavorting about, they emptied the ranch of all livestock, killing some of the cattle for sport but herding the horses and mules to join the other horses they had captured.

Their real objective obtained, their eyes turned to Beth and Don Felipe. Don Felipe had been badly wounded by a lance in the side and an arrow in the shoulder. How he had survived the reckless journey through the night, Beth didn't know. She herself was exhausted, as much from fear as from a night without sleep, a night in which every terror she had ever imagined had begun to come true.

There was only one reason why she was still alive—before he left her to the Comanches, Lorenzo intended to taste fully what he had been denied that afternoon in New Orleans. Briefly he had considered the possibility of taking her immediately and then leaving to appear at the Santana house as if he had never been away from San Antonio. But no, he waited, enjoying her terror and the hot thrill of anticipation that ran through his blood. Yet he didn't really care what happened to either Beth or Don Felipe, and when one of the Comanche warriors yanked Beth from her horse and began to ruthlessly strip her clothes from her, he said nothing, merely watched and took pleasure in the lovely body that was being bared.

Thinking she was to be raped, Beth fought viciously, kicking, biting, scratching and clawing, but to no avail. She was cuffed and slapped savagely as the Comanche's knife did its work, cutting away every vestige of clothing she wore. The long, silvery hair had lost its neat chignon hours ago, but now in her struggles the last ivory comb slid from it and the glorious hair came spilling and tumbling down around her naked body.

Almost with wonder the Comanche touched it, but Beth flew at him, determined to fight to the very last. Effortlessly the Comanche caught her hands, and, holding her struggling body captive, he cruelly pinched one breast and laughed when she screamed as much from pain as rage. Then with a careless flick of his wrist he tossed her from himself and turned to Don Felipe.

Don Felipe was meted out the same rough treatment, only there was no fight left in the old man. From where she had landed on the hard ground Beth felt something like pity for him as the Comanche stripped him too and just as carelessly threw him to the ground.

Lorenzo was looking at Beth, lust flaming in his eyes. She was irresistibly beautiful, he thought as he viewed the white, slender body through the veil of silvery hair. The pink-tipped breasts seemed to jut proudly through the half-concealing hair, and nothing hid the slender waist or the beauty of the slim, beautifully formed legs.

Lorenzo's were not the only eyes that held lust, and with a feeling that she was suffocating Beth saw that same look reflected in all the faces that stared down at her. But again she was spared the final humiliation, for it was imperative they put a great distance between themselves and this latest scene of depredations.

Only now Beth began to suffer the true fate of a Comanche captive—no horse, no clothes, no shoes, only a rope around her neck that tightened painfully if she stumbled or slackened the punishing pace the Comanches set. All day in the hot, blistering sun she ran, her breath coming in painful, gasping breaths, the sun burning the delicate skin, the rocky, rough ground tearing the soft soles of her feet—but she ran, and ran . . . and ran!

Perspiration poured from her and her body ached and screamed with silent pain as the sun rose higher and higher and then at last began slowly to descend. Once during the afternoon Lorenzo, fearful possibly that she might die before he took his revenge and pleasure, stopped his horse and offered his hand, intending to take her up in front of him for a while. The violet eyes glittering with hatred and contempt, with what little strength she had Beth flung his hand away and spat on the ground near his horse. Her actions brought a murmur of approval from the warriors, for above all else they admired courage. But Lorenzo was enraged and, his face twisting into a snarl, he lashed out with his booted foot, catching Beth fully on the chest and stomach, knocking the breath out of her and causing her to fall heavily to the ground. For a long, agonizing time Beth lay there, almost ready to give in to defeat and simply lie down and die under the hot sun on the wide expanse of prairie. But painfully, slowly, agonizingly, she staggered to her feet, the will to live stronger than the desire for relief from the pains that were tearing through her battered, bruised body.

When the Comanches stopped to water their horses, Don Felipe lay down next to Beth and through swollen lips he muttered, "That was foolish, señora, brave but foolish. If you wish to live, next time take his hand."

Not looking at him, she asked savagely, "Would you?"

Dying and knowing it, Don Felipe slowly shook his head. "No."

When they had finished watering their horses and the terrible journey was to begin anew, there was no movement from Don Felipe's ruined body, and Beth could find it in her heart to feel compassion for him. One of the Comanches viewed him for a moment and then indifferently stuck a lance through him before turning his horse aside.

Rafael found his grandfather's body an hour later. Like the stalking spirit the Comanches had named him, he followed the trail, the expression in the gray eyes frightening to see.

The previous evening, when dusk had barely begun to fall, Rafael, impatient to see Beth and hardly able to contain himself until it would be time to steal away with his bride, had ridden out of San Antonio toward his grandfather's house. He intended to wait in the nearby hills until it was time to breach the walls of the house. But he hadn't ridden more than a mile when he was met by a grim-faced Sebastian. The instant he recognized Sebastian and saw the look on his face, Rafael's body went rigid with a queer premonition. His body braced, his voice rough with emotion, he demanded, "What is it? Is Beth safe?"

Sebastian had thought himself a brave man, but when he stared into Rafael's dark face and knew what he must tell him, he almost balked. And Rafael, demons already flying in his brain, reached out with the speed of a striking snake and grasped Sebastian's wrist in a viselike hold and snarled, "Tell me, damn you! Tell me!"

Sebastian did. As briefly and unemotionally as he could, he told how it came about that Don Felipe and Beth were the only ones except for the guards to continue on the ride, how as the hour had grown late they had grown concerned, how Don Miguel had gone out with a search party and what they found. Sebastian's voice had broken at the end and the fear and impotent fury that raged in his veins were evident. "The Comanches have her, Rafael! My God, what are we to do?"

The green eyes fastened beseechingly on Rafael's face and then slid away, unable to bear the naked pain that the hard features revealed. Rafael's face was a terrible thing to see, the look of stark anguish at frightening variance with the fierce, lethal glitter in the gray eyes. For one long, tortuous moment there was silence as Rafael stared off at the hills where Beth had disappeared. Then with something like the scream of a wounded animal, his spurs dug into Diablo's side and like a madman he rode toward the Santana house, Sebastian hard on his heels.

An air of tragedy hung over the house, but Rafael jerking the snorting, blowing Diablo to a rearing halt just inside the gates was oblivious to it. The blanket-draped bodies of the six men killed in the unexpected attack lay just inside the walls, and the faint sounds of a woman wailing could be heard from one of the small houses within the compound. The gray eyes deliberately impassive, he looked in Don Miguel's direction, the pain and anguish that Sebastian had glimpsed for those few fleeting seconds now a thing of the past, hidden deeply within him where no one could see it.

His face was cold and hard, emotionless, and if Sebastian hadn't seen with his own eyes the grief in the other's face, he would have thought him entirely indifferent and unmoved by what had happened. Inside, Rafael was a mass of ripped and bleeding pain, his heart feeling as if wolves and vultures fed on it even as it beat within his breast, but outwardly there was only an icy violence, a savage implacability that caused more than one Mexican who saw him that night to nervously make the sign of the cross to protect themselves from the force of the fierce desire for vengeance that radiated from him.

Don Miguel stepped up next to the restless stallion and laid a comforting hand on the lean fingers that clenched the reins. "My son," he began gently, but Rafael's voice cut him off.

Harshly, flatly he demanded, "I want four horses and a pack mule. I'll need blankets, food, and soft cloths for binding wounds—as well as clothing."

Don Miguel risked a glance at the rigidly controlled features and gave the order. "How many men do you wish to accompany you?"

It was then that Rafael looked directly at him, the gray eyes blazing with fury. Savagely he rapped out, "Do you know what they'll do to her if they're attacked? She'll be shot so full of arrows her corpse couldn't be loaded onto a horse for return for decent burial!" Realizing his father had meant well, Rafael said in a more normal tone, "I go alone, and when I find them I enter camp as a Comanche." He gave an ugly shout of laughter. "For once I am grateful for my dual heritage! A Comanche is always a Comanche to them, and they will accept me as such. When it is made clear that she is my woman, *if* she's still alive, I should be able to get her without too much argument. It may cost me a horse or two, but they'll give her up."

In a low voice Don Miguel ventured, "My father?"

Rafael sent him a long, thoughtful look. His tones clipped, he said, "They will have no use for an old man. He'll be easier to redeem than Beth!"

Within minutes Rafael, after a short, harsh argument with Sebastian, rode out into the encroaching darkness alone, the string of horses and the mule behind him. Sebastian stared after him until he could see no more, and with Rafael's words ringing in his ears he wondered bleakly if he had seen his cousin for the last time. "I'll either bring her back alive or I won't return—for me there will be no life without her. So rest assured, *amigo,* that I will do everything within my power to find her . . . dead or alive!" Rafael had vowed.

Even by the light of the rising moon the trail wasn't difficult to follow, for Rafael was an expert tracker, taught by the Comanches themselves. He had the advantage of knowing their ways, knowing they would ride without stopping until they felt safe from pursuers. He also knew in which direction they would go; the tracks and signs of twenty-four horses weren't easy to hide, nor were the Comanches making any attempt to conceal their trail—they never did, confident no one would follow them too far into the *Comanchería*.

By his calculations they weren't much more than three hours ahead of him, and with a reckless disregard for life and limb he pushed himself and the horses remorselessly through the night. By daylight he was sickly aware that he had gained no more than an hour on them.

The smoking ruins of the ranch gave him renewed hope. They had lost time with that detour, and the fifty or so horses and mules stolen from the ranch made it even easier to follow the trail. For the first time since Sebastian had given him the news he felt a flicker of hope. The fact that he hadn't come across the body of either Beth or his grandfather fed his growing optimism that he might, by the grace of whatever gods blessed him, be successful.

Finding Beth's and Don Miguel's ripped and bloodied clothing had been a terrible, terrifying moment, and Rafael was visibly shaken when he left that spot. Deliberately he kept his mind blank of what Beth was going through, deliberately wiping his mind clear of what he knew Comanches did to captive women. All that mattered was that he find her . . . *alive!*

He came upon Don Felipe's naked body unexpectedly, and for one horrifying moment he had thought it was Beth, until his sanity reasserted itself and he realized it was his grandfather who lay there in the dust. He dismounted and approached the body. With an odd gentleness he turned over the slim, battered body and was amazed when one of Don Felipe's eyelids flickered. The black eyes were suddenly staring into his, and Don Felipe's lips twisted into a travesty of a smile. "I knew you would come," he croaked. "Not for me, but for the woman. She is alive and brave. Very brave, and as yet unharmed."

Rafael almost went limp with the rush of relief that surged through his body. He started to lay the old man down and go for his water bag, but Don Felipe, guessing his intentions, shook his head feebly. "It won't help me," he said. "I knew I was dying, and so I refused to move this last time, hoping they would think I was already dead." The words came slowly, painfully, but Don Felipe was determined to say them. "I wanted to stay alive, you see, alive long enough to see you and tell you." He coughed and there was blood at the corner of his mouth. The words came even more painfully and he gasped, "It was Lorenzo. Lorenzo did this." A clawlike hand gripping Rafael's arm, Don Felipe rasped, "Kill him, Rafael, *kill him!*"

It was the last thing Don Felipe said, and Rafael found it completely within his grandfather's character. The old devil had willed himself to stay alive, not for rescue, not even to help Beth, but to make certain that his killer suffered for what he had done.

Emotionlessly Rafael viewed his grandfather's body. He dare not take the time to bury him, nor could he ride into the Comanche encampment with the dead man strapped onto the back of a spare horse.

The vast prairie stretched before him. Beth was somewhere out there, and she was alive—Don Felipe was dead. His mind made up, he spared one minute longer to lay the body under the concealing, sparse shade of a mesquite bush, disturbing a rattlesnake in the process.

Galloping away, Rafael decided grimly that perhaps it was fitting that his grandfather lay at rest with a viper for companionship. He could feel regret for the manner of his grandfather's death, but nothing had changed in his heart.

The Comanches made camp just as dusk was falling. They chose a spot near a wide, clear stream that would provide water for the many horses they now had. Beth fell in an exhausted, painful heap near a spiky group of chaparral, knowing that the tearing cramps in her stomach were not going to go away and that she was losing her baby. For the first time, tears slid down her sun-ravaged cheeks and, unnoticed as the Comanches set up camp, she wept bitter, gulping tears. Not for herself, not for Don Felipe, but for the tiny life that would grow no more within her. Even as she lay there she felt the first warm trickle of blood seep down her thigh and her anguish was unbearable.

The Comanches were in a jovial mood. Their raid had been immensely successful and they were far away from any pursuit. And of course, there was the woman....

Lost in her own misery, Beth hadn't noticed the falling darkness, nor that having eaten and seen to their horses, the Comanches were beginning to cast eyes in her direction. Lorenzo, sitting near the fire, saw the glances sent her way and, smiling with anticipation, his manhood ripe and hard within his *calzoneras,* he made a crude jest that caused the Comanches to laugh loudly.

Through her bitter sorrow, Beth heard the laughter and she suddenly became aware that she was the object of every eye in the camp. Her tears dried and wildly she looked for some escape. Staggering to her feet, she started to run, but Lorenzo moved swiftly and caught her, dragging her twisting, struggling naked body up to his.

And it was then that Rafael rode slowly out of the darkness into the light of the campfire, the gray stallion Diablo looking ghostly in the firelight, Rafael's black form like a specter of death. There was a hushed superstitious silence, and then as one or two of the warriors recognized him, the whispered name "Stalking Spirit" was passed from mouth to mouth.

Lorenzo froze, and Beth closed her eyes in silent, weeping thankfulness. Leisurely Rafael dismounted, every move cool and calculated. With gentle menace he said, "Release her, Lorenzo." And then, turning to the Comanches, he greeted them in their tongue and told them with great eloquence of his pain and despair at the discovery of his woman's abduction, of his journey to find her, and of the personal vendetta between him and Lorenzo Mendoza.

Rafael chose his words with care, knowing that not only did he have to convince the Comanches that Beth belonged to him, but that Lorenzo was a wife-stealer and that there was a long-standing feud between them, a feud that could only be ended by the death of one of them. The Indians listened. Stalking Spirit, for all his living and dealings with the whites, had been one of them, while Lorenzo . . .

The Comanches might conspire with Lorenzo when convenient, but they had little respect for him. He had arranged many a profitable raid for this bunch, but he did not display himself well in battle; his cowardice had not gone unnoticed or unremarked. They needed no one to tell them which settlers to attack or which wagons to raid, but it had been agreeable to have this Spaniard give them information, and the careless partnership had worked very well. But if the warriors had to take sides between Stalking Spirit and Lorenzo . . . Even now, in the camps of the Comanches some of the elders still talked of the exploits of the young warrior Stalking Spirit, of his daring and his bravery in battle.

The shift in mood was imperceptible, but Lorenzo felt it and, his face twisted with rage and hatred, he flung Beth from him. The black eyes squinting with fury, he shrieked, "You'll die this night, Santana, and then I'll take your woman on your warm corpse before I slit her throat!"

"Will you?" Rafael asked with a deadly calm, the gray eyes having sought Beth's crumpled form and having noted with a cold, dangerous wrath the scrapes, the bruises, and the signs of her exhausted state. Tonight she was to have been his bride, and except for this creature before him, she would have been; and Don Felipe, for all his arrogant, cold-blooded ways, would still have been alive.

Slowly, his movements supple and unhurried, Rafael undid the wide leather belt at his waist and tossed it with the Colt revolver aside. The sombrero followed, then his *chaqueta* and shirt, and last his boots. Standing in the firelight, the Comanches forming an impassive audience, Rafael brought forth his wide-bladed bowie knife, the firelight glinting on the steel edge.

Lorenzo, too, began to strip down to his *calzoneras*, but his were the jerky, frantic movements of a man torn by fury and fear. He had no knife, and reluctantly one of the warriors tossed him a long Spanish dagger.

Warily the two men circled each other around the campfire, Lorenzo not eager to come in contact with the bowie knife. Rafael was smiling, a cool, mocking smile that did nothing for Lorenzo's confidence.

For Rafael time had rolled back and he was again a Comanche—the smells were the same—the sagebrush fire, the horses, even the smell of victory was there, and the woman waited for him just out of the light of the fire. The knife felt good in his hand, the coolness of the prairie night was a balm on his bare chest, and the ground was hard and packed beneath his feet. Even the bloodlust was there—he *wanted* to kill Lorenzo, he *yearned* to kill him—and he eagerly longed to plunge the knife into his enemy and to feel the warm blood of the dying man against his skin.

Rafael held the bowie knife lightly, expertly in his right hand, and with his left he motioned Lorenzo closer. "Come nearer, *amigo*. We cannot settle this if you are content merely to dance around the fire. Come closer," Rafael taunted.

Enraged, Lorenzo leaped for him, but like a cat Rafael spun away, his knife slashing a long, bloody gash in Lorenzo's arm as the other man came past him. Like a maddened, half-crazed animal, Lorenzo turned and lunged wildly again and again in Rafael's direction, but Rafael, his smile taking on a deadly curve, was always just out of reach, yet each time he managed to inflict another nick, another slash, another telling wound on his enemy.

There was a low murmur of enjoyment from the watching Indians, and as Comanches like to gamble, wagers were made as to the eventual winner. Few were willing to take Lorenzo.

Knowing he was losing blood and growing frightened for the first time, Lorenzo changed his tactics and caught Rafael off guard. He lunged for Rafael but then feinted and treacherously stuck his foot between Rafael's legs, tripping him.

Feeling himself fall, Rafael reacted with the agility of a wild animal, twisting his body around so that he landed on his back on the dirt and was ready for Lorenzo's attack. Lorenzo leaped onto Rafael's chest, his dagger held low and stabbing toward Rafael's stomach. With a superhuman effort Rafael warded him off, and received only a thin red scratch across his lean lower torso.

With horror, from her place of concealment in the shadows, Beth watched the two men, her heart in her mouth when she saw Rafael fall to the ground. Unable to help herself, she inched closer to the fight wanting to see, yet terrified of what she might see.

Lorenzo straddled Rafael's body, his knee holding down the knife arm as he brought up the dagger to strike at Rafael's throat, but Rafael countered by smashing his left fist into Lorenzo's face. As Lorenzo jerked back from the force of the blow, Rafael flung him from his body and almost in the same second leaped after him.

His mouth bleeding from the punishing strength of Rafael's fist, Lorenzo scrambled desperately away, gaining his feet after stumbling for a second, his clenched left hand full of dirt. Rafael was right behind him and he caught him right in front of where Beth watched the fight with wide, dilated eyes.

But Lorenzo, knowing he was no match for the stronger, more agile man, threw the dirt into Rafael's eyes, blinding him momentarily. There was a shocked gasp from the onlookers. Rafael reeled back, trying frantically to clear his eyes and protect himself at the same time from the shadowy killer that was Lorenzo.

Lorenzo smiled for the first time and moved in for the kill. But Beth, her sweet face fierce with determination, entered the fray herself, flinging her slender, naked body wildly on Lorenzo's back, clawing and biting, doing anything to divert Lorenzo from Rafael. With a snarl Lorenzo forgot Rafael and spun to meet this new attack.

Relishing the thought of her dying in front of Rafael, forgetting even his desire for her in the heat of the moment, he was able to dislodge her from his back and, his eyes gleaming with cruel pleasure, he advanced as she retreated in front of him on the ground where she had landed. It was a mistake, the last one he ever made.

Rafael's sudden shout behind Lorenzo broke his concentration, and, startled, he turned and met the knife Rafael hurled so unerringly through the air. The bowie knife sank into the middle of Lorenzo's chest and for one astonished second he stared at it before falling face down in the dirt.

Uncaring of what happened next, Beth flung herself into Rafael's welcoming arms, her warm flesh meeting the solid strength of his. Gently he cradled her to him, oblivious of the Comanches, some of whom were already arguing over Lorenzo's belongings. He crooned soothing, healing words of reassurance into her tangled hair and then swept her up into his arms and carried her to the waiting Diablo.

The Comanches made no move to stop him. They had enjoyed a good fight and Stalking Spirit had reclaimed his woman and his honor from the man who had stolen her. She was a worthy mate for him, this silver woman—she fought like a Comanche squaw for her man, and the warriors approved.

Beth and Rafael did not travel far, just a little over a mile upstream from the Comanches to where he had left the other horses and supplies. And it was there that he discovered the loss of their child. His face twisted in silent regret. And gently he bathed and cleaned Beth's battered body in the clear waters of the stream, speaking soft words that made no sense but seemed to comfort her. They slept wrapped together in a long cloak, Rafael's big body curved protectively next to hers.

Rafael woke at dawn, and for the moment he didn't know where he was. Then he noticed the warmth of Beth's small body and a shudder went through him. He had almost been too late. And if she hadn't launched herself at Lorenzo and given him those precious seconds...

She was safe and he would keep her so always, he promised himself fiercely, staring intently at her sleeping features. Her face was burned by the sun, the full lips cracked and blistered from her ordeal, her hair a tangled mass, but to him she was the most lovely thing in the world.

She needed rest and she needed care, all of which she would get at San Antonio, but he hesitated. It was a long, hard way back the way he had come, and the journey would take longer—he couldn't push her at the same pace he had come.

She'd lost their baby and she had lost blood and would lose more before it was over. He frowned. Far better to head east to the nearest settlement and from there to Enchantress. He wanted her far away from all the tragedy and horror she had suffered, and in the cool, pine-scented woods of Enchantress she would be safe—safe and cosseted, and oh, so dearly loved!

CHAPTER TWENTY-NINE

Enchantress dozed in the warm October sunshine, the new red-tiled roof gleaming brightly above the soft yellow walls of the hacienda. The fresh black paint on the balconies and filigreed ironwork contrasted pleasingly with the faded, mellow color of the building. There was an air of renewed vigor about the old Spanish house; the windows gleamed and sparkled, the grounds were meticulously and lovingly cultivated, and from within there was a bustle and the sound of voices and laughter.

The towering, pungent pine trees were scattered here and there near the house, but through their trunks could be seen the signs of new construction—the corrals, the fenceposts and railings, the light color of new lumber, the barn in the distance. It was only the small cluster of cottages, some distance beyond the barn, to which whitewash had been applied, and the whiteness of their walls was bright and clean in the fall sunshine.

At the rear of the hacienda was a charming courtyard, not large and yet most spacious. The courtyard was shaded by the wide-spreading branches of a sycamore tree, the leaves already beginning to change color and fall to the ground as the season changed. But there were still orange and yellow blossoms on the trumpet-flower vine that rioted across the back balcony, and the Virginia creeper that covered one wing of the hacienda was still a cooling green mass of five-fingered leaflets.

Two women sat in the courtyard enjoying the pleasant warmth of the late afternoon. One was Stella Rodriguez and the other was Beth Santana. They both appeared to be looking at the two men who stood just a short distance away, talking and smiling as they smoked thin black cigarillos.

Stella and her family had arrived at Enchantress two weeks ago and Beth could hardly contain herself as she had nearly tumbled out the front door of the house in her excitement to see her dear friend. Stella had been as bad, springing down from the coach before it had fully stopped. And then there were the children to see, the gurgling, happy baby, Elizabeth, and the sturdy little son, Pablo, at three the very picture of his father, Juan.

The past two weeks had flown, as Beth and Stella had gossiped and exchanged their news, Juan and Rafael inspecting the property and spending many hours discussing Rafael's plans for Enchantress. They talked of the horses Rafael was importing from Spain to improve the lines of his horses, of the cattle that were already roaming through the cleared areas of the forests, and of the crops he was considering planting in the spring—if enough land had been cleared and the stumps burned off.

If the past two weeks had flown for Beth, it was nothing compared to the speed at which the months had gone by since Rafael had rescued her from the Comanches. She remembered little of the journey to the tiny frontier settlement where Rafael had taken her and where they had stayed several days as Beth regained strength and health before they pushed on to Enchantress. Their marriage, at the end of July in Houston, she remembered very well.

It had been a very private affair, just Sebastian, Don Miguel, and Doña Madelina, as well as a wide-eyed interested Arabela, traveling over from San Antonio to witness the simple ceremony. Beth had worn the mauve gown, her fair hair shining through the white mantilla Doña Madelina had pressed on her, and Rafael had looked very handsome in a lavishly embroidered Spanish suit of purple so dark it was almost black.

Enchantress had only been partially readied for her, but Beth had thrown herself into the task of making it a home—her first *real* home. The hard work and the enjoyable satisfaction of seeing it take shape as the weeks passed, as well as the sweetly passionate nights spent in the arms of her husband, had done much to lessen the horrors and pain of the awful time she had spent as a Comanche captive. Nothing could ever compensate her for the loss of her baby, but this was the future and for Beth there was no looking back.

Manuela had accompanied the elder Santanas to Enchantress when they had come to the wedding in July and she had remained behind, very happy to be Beth's personal servant. Mary Eames and most of the servants from Briarwood were now in residence, as well as a few favored pieces of furniture and knickknacks she had written for them to bring when they came. Briarwood was to be sold, Rafael having his newly acquired man of business in New Orleans seeing to it.

The money to be gained from that sale had caused their first serious quarrel, Beth wanting to use the money at Enchantress and Rafael, his gray eyes darkening with anger, adamantly opposed to it. They had compromised—the money was hers to do with as she willed, and if there were certain things that she wanted for Enchantress, then he would quell his pride and allow her to buy them with her own money. The money in the trust her father had set up, they had both agreed, would be kept for their children, and both of them hoped fervently there would be several filling the many rooms of Enchantress.

Life had been very good to her lately, Beth thought as she sat next to Stella and dreamily watched her husband talking quietly with Juan.

"Beth, honey, the look on your face is positively indecent!" Stella suddenly teased, the dark eyes alight with affection and amusement.

Beth flushed and immediately stopped gazing at Rafael's tall, dark form. "I love him so much, Stella, I can't help it," Beth said honestly.

Stella patted her hand fondly, thinking that Beth was not the only one who was deeply in love. The change in Rafael had been startling, especially to someone who hadn't seen the gradual evolving of his personality.

The icy edges had almost virtually disappeared, although Stella suspected that in certain circumstances he would easily revert to the cold, hard man he had been. There was a soft light in the smoky-gray eyes whenever his gaze rested on Beth's enchanting features, and a certain note in his voice when he called her "English" that made Stella blush. Oh, yes, Renegade Santana was a man deeply, irrevocably in love!

That evening as Manuela dressed her for dinner, Beth thought of how very different this marriage was from her first. Nathan had always been kind, it was true, but he had never loved her, and now that she knew the difference, she wondered how she had endured those sterile, wasted years of her life and a little sigh escaped her.

The señora looked very beautiful, Manuela decided as she gave a last flick to the skirt of the pink, gossamer satin gown Beth had chosen. Her white, delicate shoulders rose proudly above the deep décolletage of the evening gown and her slender midriff was intensified by the sharp point that the bodice made at the waist before the voluminous skirts fell gracefully to the ground. Manuela was just congratulating herself on Beth's appearance when she heard the sigh.

"Something is wrong, señora? You do not like the way the skirt hangs?"

Beth smiled at Manuela. "No, I was just thinking some unpleasant thoughts—something I shouldn't do." And she glanced around the sumptuous dressing room, knowing she had so much to be grateful for. Through the half-opened doorway that led to their bedchamber, she could see Rafael pacing about as he waited restlessly for her to finish dressing before they would go down and join the Rodriguezes together, and she smiled. No, she should never think of the past—it was behind her.

But Manuela was troubled, and her conscience pricked her. Looking at Beth, she asked worriedly, "You do not still brood over what Consuela did, do you? He knows the truth, doesn't he?"

Gently Beth reassured her. "Yes, he knows."

Rafael, wondering what was keeping Beth, had just put his hand on the door to enter the dressing room when Manuela's words halted him in his tracks.

"He knows *everything?* Even that you were a virgin when he first took you that afternoon?"

Her eyes startled, Beth began, "How did you—?" And Manuela said reasonably, "You forget, señora, I washed you afterward, I saw the blood and the blood-stained sheets." Shrugging her shoulders, she finished, "It was obvious."

Beth shook her head slowly. "But not to Rafael, and it is such a tangled, improbable tale that I will probably never speak of it to him. It doesn't matter, Manuela. He loves me and it is time to let the past die. Even explaining about Nathan I find difficult to do, and I could not tell of one without the other. Let it be, we are happy and we need speak no more of what happened that day."

His face pale with shock, Rafael turned swiftly away from the door, needing a few moments to recover from the jolt the conversation had given him. Sweet Jesus! A virgin! And he remembered that brief, fleeting moment when that same thought had occurred to him.

He took a deep breath, the primitive, savage male in him full of joy and exultance, but the new, more tender Rafael filled with remorse for the ruthless way he had made her a woman that afternoon in New Orleans. Should he tell her he knew? She had said she didn't wish to speak of the past... In time, he decided slowly, in time they would talk of it.

That night when they lay in bed together, their naked bodies side by side, Beth thought blissfully that he had never been so gentle, so tender, so passionate in his lovemaking. There had been some new element in his touch, and she would have been unbearably moved to know that in his own way he had tried to make amends with his body for what he had done to her so long ago. Her head resting on his shoulder, she gave a sigh of contentment.

Hearing it, Rafael's arms tightened around her. Into the soft hair under his chin, he murmured thickly, "Happy? No more nightmares?"

Sleepily Beth shook her head. "Mmmm, none," and then half teasingly, half seriously, "except that I might awake and find that all this is a dream. Or that you no longer loved me."

"Never!" he said fiercely. With one hand he twisted

her face up to his mouth. "Never as long as I live," he breathed against her lips and then kissed her with an urgent tenderness. *"Never!"* His mouth hardened into passion, and, giving herself up to the magic of his desire, Beth thought hazily, Tomorrow I'll tell him. Tomorrow I'll tell him of the new child that grows within me.

EPILOGUE

ENCHANTRESS

True love's the gift which God has
 given
To man alone beneath the heaven;
It is not fantasy's hot fire,
 whose wishes, soon as granted, fly;
It liveth not in fierce desire,
 with dead desire it doth not die;
It is the secret sympathy,
The silver link, the silken tie,
Which heart to heart and mind to mind
In body and in soul can bind.

SIR WALTER SCOTT
The Lay of the Last Minstrel,
Canto V Stanza 13